DECOYS

DECOYS

A NOVEL OF MURDER
MYSTERY
LOVE
INDISCRETION
AND HUNTING

KENNETH TETZEL

SUNSTONE
PRESS

SANTA FE

Sunstone books may be purchased for educational, business, or sales promotional use.
For information please write: Special Markets Department, Sunstone Press,
P.O. Box 2321, Santa Fe, New Mexico 87504-2321.

Book and cover design › Vicki Ahl
Body typeface › Baskerville
Printed on acid-free paper
⊗
eBook 978-1-61139-484-9

Library of Congress Cataloging-in-Publication Data

Names: Tetzel, Kenneth, 1953- author.
Title: Decoys : a novel of murder, mystery, love, indiscretion and hunting /
by Kenneth Tetzel.
Description: Santa Fe : Sunstone Press, 2016.
Identifiers: LCCN 2016026533 (print) | LCCN 2016039879 (ebook) | ISBN
9781632931177 (softcover : alk. paper) | ISBN 9781611394849
Subjects: LCSH: Murder–Investigation–California–Central Valley–Fiction. |
Hunting–California–Central Valley–Fiction. | Cold cases (Criminal
investigation)–Fiction. | GSAFD: Suspense fiction.
Classification: LCC PS3620.E89 D43 2016 (print) | LCC PS3620.E89 (ebook) |
DDC 813/.6-dc23
LC record available at https://lccn.loc.gov/2016026533

SUNSTONE PRESS IS COMMITTED TO MINIMIZING OUR ENVIRONMENTAL IMPACT ON THE PLANET. THE PAPER USED IN THIS BOOK IS FROM
RESPONSIBLY MANAGED FORESTS. OUR PRINTER HAS RECEIVED CHAIN OF CUSTODY (COC) CERTIFICATION FROM: THE FOREST STEWARDSHIP
COUNCIL™ (FSC®), PROGRAMME FOR THE ENDORSEMENT OF FOREST CERTIFICATION™ (PEFC™), AND THE SUSTAINABLE FORESTRY INITIATIVE® (SFI®).
THE FSC® COUNCIL IS A NON-PROFIT ORGANIZATION, PROMOTING THE ENVIRONMENTALLY APPROPRIATE, SOCIALLY BENEFICIAL AND
ECONOMICALLY VIABLE MANAGEMENT OF THE WORLD'S FORESTS. FSC® CERTIFICATION IS RECOGNIZED INTERNATIONALLY AS A
RIGOROUS ENVIRONMENTAL AND SOCIAL STANDARD FOR RESPONSIBLE FOREST MANAGEMENT.

WWW.SUNSTONEPRESS.COM
SUNSTONE PRESS / POST OFFICE BOX 2321 / SANTA FE, NM 87504-2321 /USA
(505) 988-4418 / ORDERS ONLY (800) 243-5644 / FAX (505) 988-1025

Dedicated to Janet, Emily and Alex.
My Love, My Life, My Family.

Acknowledgments

I have to acknowledge those folks who manage and toil on the Public Lands of California. They maintain The Refuge Areas which keep waterfowl and wildlife habitat healthy and secure, thus allowing myself, birders and nature lovers access to our wonderful wetlands.

Preface

Sitting in a duck blind surrounded by balmy weather offers one ample time to think, fantasize and dream. As mild winters continue to infect California's Central Valley, thinking up new scenarios for a compelling mystery becomes nothing short of habit. As plot, characters, details and surprises firm up, dreams of best sellers with piles of sales receipts creep inside sleep deprived rational. At this point fantasies amount to noisy migrating flocks of unwary waterfowl. Wild scenes of wild ducks targeting my sparse decoy sets as shots ring out, feathers fly, ducks fall into splashy spray, easy hunting. Once in a great while my fantasies become reality but rarely in balmy weather. Dreams give way to linear thoughts. More time to think about my story at hand.

This is my way of developing a mystery novel. At least the setting is inviting. Nothing like sitting in tules, cattails, cold water and gooey mud to get a writer's juices flowing. I'm not sure how many would agree with this allegation and I sometimes get the feeling that sleep deficits add a little too much to acceptable creativity. Which ushers in the damn hard work of actually writing, editing, changing, editing and final editing. Writing sucks! Dreaming in a California duck blind is the fun part!

However, bringing pen to paper and fingers to keyboard is the only way to breathe life into Regina Gonzalez, Chris Davis, Mrs. Patterson, Tom Ellis, Douglas Sheets, Franny Braden and a canny pair of gorgeous gadwalls. All within the loveliness and the malevolence, of California's San Joaquin Valley. But carried along is an undertone of poor professional and personal judgment, leading toward two unsolved, but in some way, related murders.

I suppose this could be an effect the Central Valley has on people. Not that every Valley inhabitant is prone to poor judgment or repeated lapses, like my tale, which has more than a handful who do succumb to violence, deceptive lies as well as secret passions. After all, these are often the vey actions that keep my audience drawn in, keep us judging, keep us reading. Once caught by a good mystery it takes a stunning conclusion to achieve resolution. The ending always determines success or failure. Not unlike the hunter. Not unlike the hunted. Hunters take their prey then perhaps becoming hunted themselves. The prey run, hide, deceive and lie. But if they grow to be very smart, they learn to Decoy.

Part I

Los Banos State Wildlife Refuge

Gadwalls

Shooting ducks over decoys can become an addiction. Wings held stiff and balanced two gadwalls sailed lower, aiming center to a large open pond. Knowing all too well from past flights into new wintering grounds, dark figures and loud noises hid among dense patches of tules and cattails, choosing to do them harm. It would be dark soon and their flight south, from northern valley marshes, all but drained both birds of needed fat reserves. Their timing was good however, pointing to a routine finish, locating secure cover with food and water before getting some much needed rest. So far, quiet surrounded this rather large, exposed pond. No obvious movements were spotted and the occasional, distant loud noises seemed powerless to cause them harm. Feeling comfortable two agile ducks swerved into an arcing spiral widening their search. Gusty winds heaving across the pond caused a normally alert hen to become careless, drifting near dense vegetation outlining the pond's border. Twisting wings and shifting both feet, she caught herself launching a panic rise to gain altitude and safety. The drake bird, a few yards behind and a little left sensed danger much earlier as alarmed wings pushed air below. He veered for open water rising well beyond another dangerous perimeter. Liquid, dark brown eyes failed to spot any menacing movements and relieved no loud noises roared from thick stands of cover below.

Northwest winds gathered momentum as the day progressed, increasing sway among stands of tules, making it harder for the keenest of eyes to detect irregular shapes or movements. Western slopes of the distant Sierras, snowcapped and drowned in angled sunlight glowed with jagged peaks and ridges. Winter currents of air preceding an impending cold front released gusty winds. At times churning water into small waves and sweeping a blue sky free of clouds. Evening sunshine drenched the pond in brilliant light, reflecting off energetic running waves, shimmering like fire. At difficult angles, ducks attempting a safe landing would essentially become blind by harsh glare. Keeping the sun behind them as long as possible was critical to avoiding loud booms and possible death. Still, all seemed harmless, prompting a fast dive in unison close to water near the pond's center. Calm but not fully committed, two nervous gadwalls turned into the wind, rising fast, gaining altitude and security. Preferring to settle in close to the pond's edge where thick tules would fracture steady wind, offering more comfort for the cold night ahead.

Being a rather large pond, kidney shaped and uneven, laying on a slight northeast-southwest axis. Very much a small lake by western standards. Both ducks glimpsed flocks of coots scurrying about, like play, launching splashes and mini rooster tails over muddy water. Their jerk-bobbing heads and dark shapes were easily spotted while both birds flew in very high, beginning another pass to investigate water below. Coots are a poor indicator of safety however. Many younger ducks are killed by loud noises with ponds and lakes populated by the noisome birds, appearing safe. Always a mystery to the hen gadwall why the dark figures never harmed swimming coots. Maybe their loud noises just couldn't kill coots swimming on open water?

Both gadwalls swung low over the pond again. Eyeballing everything. This time the drake caught sight of white objects floating in a somewhat slender cove on the northwest side. They rose, almost in unison, as the male bird took lead on a direct route for the white specs while the hen began a higher but steady track. Obvious these were not coots. Closing upon the flock, white breasts and long tails were evident of whistling birds they both knew well. A small group but they seemed to be moving on developing waves like real ducks. Unlike those stiff birds encountered along the flyway, which mystified the hen gadwall also. She became very adept at recognizing fake birds. On calm days in particular, when the stiff mystery ducks would sit in one spot, never moving, splashing, or tipping up to feed. Terrible loud noises had erupted around the mysterious birds also, remembering many losses, all but eliminating the pair's original flock.

Closing on the resting ducks, their whistling chirps became audible. Nothing like the volume heard on northern breeding grounds where pintails congregate by the hundreds and chirping males create a crescendo of music. This was slow, methodic whistles from a few resting drakes but reassuring no less. Closer yet as fluttering wings from the whistling flock grew visible, common to preening birds exercising stiff muscles afloat and resting. A loud series of calls resonated across the pond, typically from large green-headed ducks, triggering a careful search below. No green! Instigating slight alarm to the hen's wings after failing to spot any green headed ducks among the flock. She opted for safety with a quick, short rise. Her mate chose an opposite tack, stiffening wings to begin a continuous but nervous descent toward the resting pintails below. Not a full commit with tail and legs lowered, tipping in confidence from side to side. This was more of a calculated drop to closer inspect an invitation to land. Tules waved back and forth as sunlight covered his frontal vision, banking toward the western horizon. Poor vision too often proved fatal and a nervous hen seemed to realize this risk was too great on first pass. She squealed a subtle quack nosing higher into the darkening sky. Horizons began changing color to reddish-yellow below a small band of violet, erasing the daytime blue above this Central Valley marsh. Loose V-formations of snow geese and widgeon were on the move to other ponds scattered about the refuge.

Still descending, the drake gadwall opted to continue but lost sight of his mate. She was neither left or right and soon realized his rash tactics might get him killed, commencing a sharp move into the wind to gain altitude. Better to plan a second pass for a more deliberate look. His height wasn't safe but this low pass offered much better vision into dense vegetation bordering the pond and his lengthy scan along waving foliage revealed no movements, dark shapes or loud noises. Quiet. The hen continued her higher flight spotting nothing but vacant tules and feeling good about security. Each bird climbed higher still, moving out to the pond's center and setting up for a low, fast pitch, into resting pintails. Their chirping whistles came in crystal clear again as well as a few low tone chuckles from unseen green headed ducks. Which continued to bother the female gadwall. She dropped a few feet behind the falling drake then shifted above, settling firm to the open water side, maintaining her low fast descent to an inviting shoreline. Both were reminded of hunger as tired wings grew heavier and muscles exhausted. They needed rest. All remained quiet as two gadwalls lowered their wings even more, permitting buoyant air to spill with a loud hiss on approach, Still a safe distance from the dangerous edge but still hugging open water.

Tom

"C'mon you two," the shooter whispered aloud. "That's it. Set your wings. Be relaxed." Hidden snug inside matted tules, Tom guessed the spinner decoy helped to draw each bird closer. Not in range yet but one more pass without spooking them, gave him confidence they'd commit. Squeezing himself as far as possible, deeper into weeds and water, trying to disappear.

Somewhat long sleek birds, gadwalls become shy as winter lengthens and hunting pressure tends to sharpen elder senses, while yearling birds alas, are shot away along their winter journey south. Two and three year old birds, much bigger, experienced, clever to noises and sudden movements make challenging prey for hunters needing to acquire kill shots. Male gadwalls exhibit splendid breast vermiculations and delicate maroon back feathers which grow bright and pronounced as they age. Soft gray, barred side pockets, with shiny black rumps and bills make for an elegant bird to more experienced shooters. Newcomers find them somewhat drab compared to a mallard's vibrant green head and bright orange feet. No match at all to flashy green-winged and cinnamon teal. These tiny ducks rival birds painted in the tropics with iridescent green, bronze and reddish brown hues.

Tom knelt extremely low in the tules. But more important needing to remain motionless, guessing the pair would cross inside killing range if he kept calm and limited any careless movement. Soft feeding chuckles played out on a mallard call. On the birds first pass, Tom leaned his body under a tent like clump of tules, constructed earlier in the morning, refusing an urge to look up. Fearing the ducks might see his face shining in reflected sunlight. Very still but switching to the sprig whistle releasing low tone chirps, shifting eyes up and side to side for a fast peak at his targets. Reaching his decoys, Tom noticed the hen take alarm, rising fast into evening air. For a moment he assumed they had him spotted but felt better once they leveled off and dropped again, appearing set for another pass. His thoughts kept returning to how significant one of these ducks could be. One more bird secured his seven bird limit. He must have one of these ducks.

Tom's location couldn't really be called a duck blind as he merely positioned himself a few yards inside dense tules then kneeled into cold, dirty water. His position relative to wind, light and preferred water was much more critical for good shooting. "Location and position," became his mantra. Even though cold winds were raiding his body of heat, he cherished the entire moment developing around him. Experienced quite a few times during many waterfowl seasons. One or two birds short of a limit against sunset, which marked the end of legal shooting time. Evening flights of waterfowl could be somewhat easier to decoy into killing range and this evening was getting better with cold wind and a sparse hunter turnout. The beauty of a Central Valley Refuge in late evening felt wonderfully serene, even though it involved the likely death of splendid birds. His past sensations of quick guilt following a kill and the moral debate over principles preceding a kill didn't surface much anymore. No need to justify actions to himself or to anyone else for that matter. Hunting waterfowl had become an enjoyed and normal behavior. In fact, Tom would be a lost spirit without his hunts, thriving on the contest. Sometimes win, sometimes lose. Never positive of the outcome for sure, but cherishing every decoy routine nonetheless.

More and more flights passed high overhead. Two groups of ducks broke away beginning to circle the pond in tight V-formations, watching weed lines and observing two gadwalls approaching danger below. An unusually large flock of widgeon were heard shrieking their distinctive high and low tone whistles, accompanied by a single drake mallard, tired but keeping pace on the extreme left wing. Tom couldn't spot the group but appreciated how widgeon often come in for a low pass, materializing from nowhere, straining to glimpse their position. In the distance, large flocks of black birds performed acrobatic flights.

Hundreds at a time rising in unity like insect clouds, falling earthward preparing to land then rising again, banking and flying off to who knows where? Three cinnamon teal winging a rigid triangle, flew by very low and very fast, but from directly behind catching Tom off guard. Hearing wings slice through cold air with wind behind them, Tom froze, having to pass on a quick shot. Too risky and not about to spoil the setup on the deceived pair of gadwalls working his decoys. Being well hidden made him feel more confident. The teal passed directly over, settling fast in the pond's center amongst squealing coots and three grebes diving for aquatic food. From the pond, both gadwalls moved off to his right, wings set and cutting a straight line toward swimming decoys.

The drake gadwall witnessed all three teal sail into a roiling pond, very low from the cove. With no loud noises blasted, his senses registered safe and sound near the long tail ducks. Deciding at once to cut across the pond, descend and quarter into stiff wind, then at the last moment lower his left wing, bank sharp and execute a very swift landing. This way, if danger emerged, adjusting to a fast rise on approach would be easier and perhaps life saving. In the distance loud noises fired. Four in succession were clearly heard. Muffled and too far off to do harm but reminding the female gadwall of potential danger lurking below. She plunged too, taking position off his right wing but not quite sold on the safety of the cove, growing determined to avoid at all cost being pinned against dense vegetation ahead. Due to her maneuver, another flock rushing toward her right flank went unseen with a lone bird equally steadfast in joining the pintails too. She knew what her partner had in mind, committed to a landing too but favoring open water just in case. Well over half way to reach the flock, starting their sharp bank, a vulnerable drake honed in on louder whistles from pintails bobbing ahead. He dropped one foot, wobbling him to the right side then letting go his other foot to settle out the glide. Quite the striking scene to witness ducks coming in for a water landing. Holding the wind in rigid wings, under firm control as his view ahead seemed absolute normal and quiet. But a skittish hen veered wild to her right soon after their final bank, rising as fast as she could, able to witness her bold companion from the corner of her eye.

She panicked because intense glare on the water blinded her scrutiny in front, never again trusting to blind landings. Scores of loud noises had killed companions from past flights, trying desperately to land blind. High above she watched the whole sport play out below. Observing a dark shape materialize from thick weeds near the long tailed ducks. A sharp jolt of adrenaline and fear rocked her, transporting the hen even higher. Clear views of her mate transpired, head and neck cocked upward, yellow feet hanging low, flight speculums shining white in bright sunshine but disappearing into brilliant glare. A solitary boom echoed from the dark figure. More adrenaline. Just one, somewhat subdued thump. Bright glare blinded her vision unaware of her companion's fate as well as the unseen intruder, flanking the drake at a right angle. She turned inside for a better view, glimpsing a bird with folded wings and limp body falling into blue water with a loud splash, emitting wild spray among the fake ducks. Her heart sank knowing he'd been downed, but hoping anyway to see the bold drake flying out to join up. No additional booms erupted.

•••

Tom was focused on shooting the completely fooled gadwall all along. "I love drake gadwalls," he said, grinning. His complete attention on nothing else, clicking the safety off of a bit worn Citori, still concentrating on the fast approaching gadwall. He tried moving his front foot and bent leg forward, making sure sticky mud wouldn't lock his boot in place and cause a stumble when he rose to shoot. Stiff muck held firm however, forcing a few wiggles to free his foot but still cautious to avoid spooking the gadwall. This delay kept him from rising to an easy target but allowed his ears to catch a new sound. Repeated soft quacks. Unmistakable sounds of a drake mallard. Wet reedy calls. Not the loud bellowing hails, hen mallards scream out.

Unlocked at last and free to move, a confused mallard appeared from his left over swimming decoys, between him and the incoming gadwall. Fluttering in place, stationary, not entirely fooled by bobbing decoys but in need of a safe place to land, soon. By his reckless approach, any place would do. This green-head completed an even longer flight south from northern refuge areas near the Oregon border. Tule Lake and Klamath Refuge Complex. A large agricultural area funneling birds headed west from the Rocky Mountain Flyway as well as Pacific Flyway migrants. It takes freezing cold snaps to move these migrating birds southbound, which would increase in the next few days. Even though the mallard had a strong tailwind, he still used the fat energy he owned, feeling very heavy in cold, evening air. Becoming separated from the large flock of widgeon and now alone was dangerous to say the least. His final approach wouldn't be fast, compounding risk in a blinding glare. Leveling out over shallow water and tempting decoys but way too close to the weed line, offering an almost fixed target. Tom wouldn't make the mistake of following the gadwall knowing this big greenhead offered an uncomplicated shot. Almost too easy. He didn't miss and continued to watch the blinded gadwall sail overhead very close, clearly making out where the white belly gave way to dark breast feathers and black rump. So close that light gray wings exposed individual flight feathers and detecting a sharp whistle, emitted from onrushing wings. Superb.

Top center in the steel pattern, this young mallard never felt pain as several shot ripped through his body. Seven pellets would strike vital organs. One penetrating a beating heart and both lungs pierced twice. Two would crush the liver as two more shot managed to cut through neck vertebrae severing the spinal cord. This alone would have killed him. The dead mallard slapped water hard and fast but darkness had already settled in, unable to feel cold water penetrating soft, loose feathers about his back and neck. Lying still in precise death.

···

Blinded by watery glare, the drake gadwall never realized another target was closing fast, intersecting his own landing zone. Never seeing the figure rise, swing his weapon on an unsuspecting mallard and pull the trigger. Unable to register the ear splitting explosion from a surprise gun blast. Too close! He did absorb much of the concussion however, sending the bird for a moment into shock. Fortunately, instincts took charge, adding speed, gaining altitude and wellbeing, as fast as possible, hurling straight over the figure, but never spotting him. Momentum carried a bolting gadwall out over high weeds blanketing the rear of the pond. Finally sensing enough altitude and his head clear, the drake gadwall traced a bee line toward the pond's center. Rejoining his relieved mate and breathing hard. They flew on until dark before landing soft in a small backwater channel, spending the cold night tucked very close to one another, scared but feeling very good to be together and alive.

···

Tom's mallard lay belly up in dirty water. Wings limp. Bright orange feet, soft gray belly feathers, chestnut brown breast, the iridescent green head drifting profile in bloody water bordered by an eminent white ring. A thin trail of dark red blood drifted from his bill and spilled lightly from the lower stomach. Looking more like blobs of oil near the yellow bill before dispersing and disappearing into pond water. His webbed feet still moved, twitching in alternating stop and go swimming motions, nerves firing after life had left him. Convulsing feet coupled with thick blood achieved the stark reminder a life had been taken. The twitching feet always effected Tom. Even with perfect shots the leg twitches were still present on dead birds, trying to craft their instinctive final swim to safety.

"How could this happen?" Tom seized the hefty bird about its neck, lifted into fading light, admiring impressive color and markings. Oozing blood swirled down over wet fingers mixing with refuge water. He didn't notice with drake mallards being prized birds. Bent over, grabbing two cords and slinging two pintail dekes over sore shoulders to gather gear in the fading light. Packed remaining shells, calls, jacket and other gear into the decoy bag. Dead birds filled his strap. Not a great limit but a fair mixed bag. Two drake mallards, two green-winged teal, one cinnamon teal, hen widgeon and the proverbial hen spoony. All handsome ducks to Tom, minus the spoony (Northern Shovelor). Under good hunting conditions Tom would likely pass on spoonies. Today he didn't have that luxury, taking every bird available and too early in the season to discriminate against the less desirable, proving to be the right strategy.

Darkness was winning as he crossed the pond, sliding boots in hard mud steadied by a wood staff. At his age the staff saved him from falling into icy water many times, reaching firm levee dirt and solid footing, making his hike easier. Shotgun, decoy bag and dead birds strained sore shoulders but somehow feeling strong on his walk back to Parking Lot Four.

Flocks of secure ducks glided overhead settling onto quiet and safe refuge ponds. Darkness became their ally now making Tom wonder how the birds knew this too. A few hours before, virtually impossible to call into shooting range, these same ducks became fearless as mallards fluttered down along edges of the smallest ponds echoing loud calls and whistling wings. Walking in, often a back breaking affair, hikers become distracted by a large night flight in progress. Forgetting their pains for a few welcomed minutes. Headlamps flashed in various directions revealing other hunters who opted to hunt late. In the direction of his lot bright headlights flared indicating a short grunt remained. A few more turns on the refuge road and a little sweat, would find Tom back at his truck in twenty minutes, followed by an interesting ride home.

■■■

High beams lead the way as his vibrating truck bounced over a gravel roadway, away from lot number four. Small birds flashed right and left, vanishing in the dark, spooked and drawn by intense light. Tom's thoughts focused to the waiting check station still a couple miles out, as the truck shuttered along, unnoticed. He worried about the check out person including all of his ducks and a documented report card. "Stupid ass," shaking himself from a mental fog. "Of course they'll record my take. You can't leave the refuge without turning in your report card." Currently, Los Banos Wildlife Area conducted random sampling from birds killed at the refuge. A student-intern from Humboldt State and future Fish & Wildlife biologist clipped wings from harvested ducks. Weighing and drawing blood samples to determine general health and possible infection. "I should look into the study to get more information," thinking to himself but knowing deep inside, it probably wouldn't happen. Still, taking part in the science and protection of his prized birds, would make him feel more involved in something worthy. It felt good.

Turning from Henry Miller Road into a paved parking lot, Ellis noticed a gal at the counter inside he didn't recognize. "It wouldn't matter," assuring himself. She seemed busy recording data and filing papers or report cards. Tom set the brake on his Nissan, retrieved a heavy strap of stiff ducks from the truck bed, and continued through the check station door. Excited.

Never looking up, a thirtyish lady yelled out, "how'd you do?" sounding put off at the late hour.

"Well, not too bad," Tom replied without bragging. Unable to view the young woman's face, growing curious but as always, turning tail and shy around attractive women. Still a no-show. "I managed a limit." Giving the woman cause to look up quite fast.

She paused, beaming him square in the eye. "You're kidding?" showing a crooked smile. It was kind of early in the season for Los Banos hunters to be shooting limits of ducks. The refuge had seen only one limit since opening weekend and even then, the jerk proudly displayed his birds which included two illegal hen pintails. He paid a high price for those birds and was prohibited from hunting Los Banos Refuge for the remainder of hunting season. "You have the ducks with ya?" she asked with less attitude, mixing in some charm.

Tom lifted the strap displaying seven ducks over the counter. In a calm mood now after getting a good look at the woman. First, she wasn't that young anymore and quite certain the poor lady never made it to the Miss Los Banos pageant in her younger days.

"Whoa, hold 'em back on your side of the counter please. I don't need any blood splatters on my paper work," she warned with amusement. Her attitude more genteel now. Taking a close look at Tom and realized he had the most exquisite blue eyes, for an older man. Even with faded and smeared camo paint lingering on cheeks and forehead. "Why are the good ones too old for me?" asking herself. Tom's birds threw her a little off too. A decent limit of ducks with two mallards, a few teal and actually drawn to the little hen spoony hanging between two greenheads.

"Got the final bird right at shoot time," Tom added.

"You were hunting out of parking lot four, weren't you?" Still admiring his eyes which were now admiring his ducks. Tom confirmed his location and started reciting common names and sexes of each bird. Jennifer couldn't help it, but she was staring at Tom, thinking, "this guy's kinda hot. Yikes!" Distracted and losing count as he itemized his individual kills.

"Two drake mallards. Two green wing teal, one drake, one hen. One drake cinnamon teal." Its reddish brown feathers looked fresh and shiny. "Hen widgeon and the proverbial hen spoony." Tom reported.

Jennifer Sweeny. Tom noted her name tag, while she checked off the dead birds on his report card. He peeked closer making sure all seven birds were recorded. Jennifer glanced up gaining eye contact again, smiled, blinked her eyes, leaned an elbow on the counter, chin resting in the palm of a nervous hand, twisting her head for effect. "Everything look okay?" hoping the attractive man recognized her flirt. But, in came the graduate student from the side door, interrupting her hunt, appreciating his ducks. Jennifer rolled both eyes and resumed her tallies.

"Nice job," the student said. "Mind if I take a few wing samples for my study?"

"Sure. Take all the wings you want," Tom permitted. "What's the study about, by the way?" he asked.

"Oh," then came a sudden pause which raised eyebrows for a moment. Tom wanted to let the kid know, in a nice way, he was no dumb ass and understood technical stuff! The grad student was instructed to keep his explanations short without detail. He decided to do just that with a cut off, "bird flu."

Tom sort of flinched at the answer. "Find any?" hoping he'd say no.

"Not yet," answering with a tight lip, grabbing Tom's dead birds and heading for a side door.

Tom had to follow, observing the future biologist at his sample station outside. Actually, a simple wood table holding technical collection materials. Knife, scissors, latex gloves and meat scale. Rough to say the least! "So, are all the wing samples recorded with report cards?" Tom asked, realizing he was being somewhat of a nuisance but persisted anyway.

"What's that?" the student asked, turning his head toward Tom and squinting, just as he was about to clip a teal wing with hefty wire cutters. "What's this guy's problem," he thought?

"Just wondering if you record wing samples with their report cards? Maybe I could get a toxicology report? You know, see if any of the ducks I shot were exposed to flu virus." Tom felt pleased for coming up with the toxicology report comment. Trying to come across like he knew what he talked about.

"Toxicology report?" sounding a little more bewildered. "Uh, I don't think any of these birds suffered from bird flu," a flustered student offered, wanting to clip the next set of wings then get this inquiring pest on his way. "You don't have anything to worry about." Stuffing wings into plastic specimen bags.

Tom continued to press. "I was told there would be a report posted online." He stepped a little closer to the table now and began inspecting peel off labels sticking to the bags. Noticing information included date, species, harvest site and hunting license number. "This is what I've been looking for," Tom thought to himself. "Maybe I can view results posted online, to make sure my birds are clean?" giving the impression of being very satisfied with Fish & Wildlife procedures, grabbing his strap of clipped birds and backed away toward the parking lot.

The student didn't know how to answer and gave Tom a long look. Frustration and redness started to fade. "You know, that's a pretty good idea," thinking he should mention the suggestion to his supervisor. "Here's the website. Send me an email and I'll try to confirm the results," the student suggested, pondering the hunter's idea then handing him a business card with his name on it. "Give it a week or two. It takes a while for our lab to get samples analyzed."

Tom took his card, read the name and confirmed a website address. "Hey thanks Ben. Ben Suzuki," pausing to check the card again. "You'll be hearing from me in a few days," he said, stuffing Ben's card into a shirt pocket. They shook hands. "My name's Tom. Tom Ellis." Ben nodded wishing him a good evening.

Tom Ellis walked to his truck looking back toward the check station. He saw Jennifer tracking him. She even waved with a cupped hand as he smiled and waved back. "Still got it, I guess!" Ellis joked to himself and chuckling at his embellishment, while setting a heavy strap of birds inside the camper shell.

Driving back to Gustine wouldn't take long but Tom had a full day's field work lined up for tomorrow. He avoided listening to news or talk shows on the way home, really wishing baseball was still in season. "I'd even take a football game for the ride back." Loading a Pink Floyd CD instead. Relaxed. Tomorrow would be for plucking and cleaning birds, looking forward to grilling one or two this weekend. A long day had ended.

Marcus and Beatrice
Tracy, California

Earlier that same morning a dark painted truck turned right onto Arlington Street. Slowing to a crawl, as two light beams cut through modest fog, collecting moisture laden mist drifting across a narrow roadway. Every so often dense fog would lay just above windshield level, imparting a clear view of paved street below, and high beams illuminating cloud cover above. Odd weather conditions like this, especially at high speeds, portray an image of driving through smoke filled tubes. Completing a second pass around this block an apprehensive driver aimed at a lengthy open space between two parked cars. Arlington Street curves and winds its way through an upscale neighborhood in eastern Tracy. Large, new houses lined a wide street with nurtured landscape and broad, stone pathways lead to well lit doorways. Conceived by a design architect obviously favoring wood double doors resting at almost every entrance.

Unfortunately many 'for sale' signs occupied those front lawns. Fallout from an economic meltdown and real estate market that went south faster than migrating waterfowl in December. Cutting orchards and grading vegetable fields to construct housing developments, which bloomed heavily in the eighties and nineties. Prodigious housing tracts colonized by working class families moving further east in search of affordable, large homes. Only to turn one hundred eighty degrees, commuting west every morning to Silicon Valley and many prosperous East Bay cities. Tracy, California lies at the extreme southern edge of the magnificent Sacramento-San Joaquin Delta. A huge triangular shaped network of waterways which collects springtime snow melt from a generous Sierra Nevada western slope. Water, from snow cascading west, into the Central Valley. Scenic cold water rivers such as the Sacramento, Pitt, Feather and Yuba in the north. American, Mokelumne and Stanislaus draining the center of California as the Tuolumne, Merced and Kings empty southern ranges.

Add another score of vibrant streams and you have California's torrent of critical blood, if permitted to pass through a maze of reservoirs, into lower reaches of the Sacramento and San Joaquin Rivers, creating the largest fresh water estuary on North America's west coast. The delta forms a key nursery for great runs of salmon, sturgeon and striped bass. Migrating waterfowl utilize open and abundant waterways as wintering grounds and rest stops. Summer weekends usually bring out hoards of water skiers and bass anglers from East Bay cities such as Fremont, Walnut Creek and Pleasanton. Their spraying hulls clogging sloughs and flooded islands with fast running boats and huge outboards. But beyond recreation, this water creates one of the world's great agricultural gardens. One that rivals the greater Ag centers of the Golden State's Central Valley lying to the north and south. A few farming families have been blessed with great wealth from this region, growing produce such as asparagus, tomatoes, cherries and almonds. The Crosby dynasty was one such family. Marcus Crosby was a third generation land holder in his late thirties. A self proclaimed farmer but most folks that got to know him long enough, knew he was anything but an accomplished farmer. In fact he didn't know the business end of a spade shovel and looked upon farming as something beneath his dignity. But like many other well-heeled producers in the Delta and Central Valley, an inheritor of great wealth due to hard working relatives before him.

Moving ever so slow along a shrouded curb without stopping, the truck changed direction hard left, swinging near a parked Ford pick-up. A driver obviously inspecting the street and sidewalk for anyone walking in chilly, early morning air. All seemed quiet which wasn't surprising at this hour. Inside the cab everything was silence but anxiety rose. An open area between two houses on the right side was unoccupied just as the driver suspected, after many trips scouting this scene from vehicle as well as on foot. Advancing further the truck settled just beyond the far side 'T' of a three way stop at Arlington Street and Anaheim Drive. Sloping steady uphill toward the intersection, presented the driver an elevated view down into Anaheim Drive. Looking left, "I've got a clear view through two front yards, one walkway," pausing to twist a little more, "and his entire driveway." Third house from the corner, 957 Anaheim Drive. The main event was beginning to move forward.

Just past 6:30 suggesting daylight was about to win over darkness, checking time constantly and estimating Marcus' morning appearance at about ten minutes. "What the fuck!" Decision made and door swinging open with a brief look in every direction, walking behind the truck, raising a rear tinted window, tailgate down and a prompt climb inside. With only soft clicks both window and gate went shut, but deep throaty breaths revealed a jumpy, nervous condition.

Listening close, everything seemed in place. Once inside and settled, the driver peered out from each side window. Nothing. Which did wonders to help reduce loud, deep breaths. The simple act of climbing into a pick-up's bed at this hour was most worrisome. Absolute failure if someone noticed.

Arlington and Anaheim remained calm and deserted. First, removing the rifle from its clothe case, reeking of oil. Second, crouching low into the passenger side bed corner. Third, reaching out for the opposite side, stretching cramped back muscles and sliding a narrow plastic window forward a few inches. Listening. Except for far off traffic noise, quiet dominated. Flimsy screening was still intact exhibiting a few small tears and punctures near the window frame. "One more won't matter," thinking out loud while bringing the weapon up, left hand cradling its wood forearm. Left elbow fixed atop a bent left knee, like a makeshift prop. Rifle stock pushed against the right shoulder, not too tight, squinting into a seven power scope. Plenty of light to perceive details throughout the shooting zone. Nevertheless, one concern developed as glare from a driveway light had to be avoided. Each time a scan crossed into bright light the shooter's vision went almost blind. "Keep your sights low," the driver whispered very soft. Line of sight would be clear and balanced across three driveways, over a parked BMW in the nearest and into much of the Crosby walkway. A large sycamore tree just behind new sidewalk helped divide two properties. Low ground lights edging Marcus' walkway and lawn helped brighten the shooting zone nicely. Three weeks of practice and two dry runs made the setup feel routine. One question remained. "Will I?"

"Okay, nothing new, let's be on time today," the driver murmured low while inserting ear plugs. "No point in going deaf this morning." Lifting a lethal muzzle and splitting the side window gap. "Not too close now. Don't wanna' wake the neighbors," mumbling with a nervous chuckle when headlights rudely lit the camper shell. Panic set in as the rifle came down with a thud. "Shit! That's not good?" hoping the scope's aim wasn't affected.

Approaching along Arlington Street, headlights steered a slow, suspicious and deliberate course. The shooter held perfectly still, like a frightened bird, then crouched low. Something was thrown from the driver's side!

"What the hell was that?" panting hard, uttered in a subtle undertone. Followed by another item launched from the other side to an opposite driveway. Shoulders drooped to calm. Realizing now, morning papers were being delivered! A sigh of relief followed. The delivery route turned left onto Anaheim Drive with newspapers tossed left and right, well up onto lawns and driveways but some vanished into thick shrubs too. "That guy's very good," measuring each toss to infield practice. Driving all the while too! Swinging the firearm back into position but watching red tail lights go smaller and dimmer. Another left turn and gone.

If nothing else, Marcus was punctual and lived according to a rigid schedules. His deceased wife had paid dearly many mornings, for causing Marcus to be just a few minutes late. Always leaving for his office or golf game or local skank at 6:40 sharp. Coffee and scone at Starbucks. "No room for cream today, Marcus!" The sniper whispered. Crosby's promptness and schedule proved the easiest of details to work out. On time, every time.

"A few more minutes," whispering with nervousness, but still a go. Gun and shooter lay secure sensing the target would be easy to strike. Two rounds loaded inside the flat shooting .222 caliber rifle with minimum recoil, perfect for this distance. Sound was the thing to worry most about. One prior test didn't seem to make much noise, but not being outside the shell, it was hard to tell how loud it might be. Lifting the bolt on a dull steel action then drawn back. Shiny, new brass cartridges bounced up, chambering a round while pushing the bolt forward. Loaded. Scanning a dim driveway again waiting for any sign of porch light glow, illuminating the shooting zone and Marcus Crosby's arrival. Maybe leaving this world too, for good!

Nothing yet. 6:35 and Marcus wasn't running early today. The shooters eyes adjusted even more to faint morning light as the scope presented clear driveway detail. No trouble spotting targets today. Driveway lights were losing effectiveness as morning evolved. Fog thinned.

It occurred with an abrupt blink. Just as two times previous, entry light glow, emanating beyond the garage corner which blocked the sniper's view of Marcus' doorway. Mr. Crosby was about to make his grand entrance. The shooter made ready to scope target and focus crosshairs. A shot of adrenaline rushed into both legs and for a moment, hesitation revisited. Slightly lowering the rifle.

...

Mrs. Patterson exited her garage door, entering a side yard bordered by a redwood fence, separating her property from the Crosby's. A neighbor's tan cat rushed by her feet, scampering to the backyard, scaring her, producing a jump and shout of a few expletives at the feline.

"Stay the fuck out of here Striper, you little bastard," her charming English accent thriving. She was approaching sixty eight short years, sporting a much younger figure due to plenty of walking and keeping bright silver hair swept offset with an attractive low curl. Quite the stunning blonde in her younger days with many older guys in town still chasing her around. She always dressed in a skirt or dress and this day was no exception. Even if it meant a hard workday ahead. Pants were just not ladylike.

She hadn't slept well. Deciding to rise early and get some needed work done, sprucing landscape, trimming back a few shrubs, raking fallen leaves from the nearby sycamore and cleaning all five beloved bird feeders. Beatrice

Patterson was rarely ever about and roaming her property early in the morning. Since retiring from Kaiser Medical as a surgical nurse she liked to linger in bed, then linger even longer over coffee and breakfast, reading the morning newspaper thoroughly. Late morning became time to start a days' work. Today was different for some reason. Hearing the paper slap hard on her concrete driveway a few minutes before, she went out to bring it inside.

Beatrice hated foggy mornings in Tracy, arriving in late fall and persisting through winter. A wet coldness who's nature it was to steal away the modest warmth from older people, like a careless thief. Beatrice was too old now to fight off this seeping chill. Choosing instead to simply wait it out most days.

"God damn fog," grumbling to herself, reaching for the latch and pushing open a wood gate. Just as Marcus closed his front door and locking it behind him. She didn't hear his door closing but soon noticed footsteps approaching the driveway. Hard leather heels clicking on smoothed concrete like delicate hooves over cobblestone. She knew who was coming and walked faster wanting to avoid eye contact with whom she considered the 'damn beast' next door! Her fence gate was offset a few feet back from the face of her house, completely hidden and blind to the unsuspecting, waiting beyond the street intersection. Hurrying through the gate Beatrice knew Marcus was just around the corner. "A bit faster old gal," urging herself on then hearing shrill beeps from his electronic key unlocking doors on a brass colored Lexus. Keeping her own direction steady toward the newspaper lying in the driveway, lifted the daily and peeled away rubber bands holding its fold. Beatrice pretended to read front page news giving Marcus enough time to enter his car. Acting as though he wasn't there, not wanting to be face to face rude but maintaining civility after all.

Mrs. Patterson, fixed on a front page photo, was staggered by a violent sound resonating from her right, causing a shuddering flinch and shallow stoop. Not a sharp bang, but a noise likened to something very large falling to a cement floor in confined space. Followed almost straight away by a low tone snap, similar to a tree branch splitting, from the direction of Marcus Crosby's car. She turned left on reflex to see what caused the sound. Beatrice couldn't make sense of a bewildering scene unfolding on the driver's side of Marcus' Lexus. She swore blood was present but didn't believe her eyes at first. "Marcus. Are you all right?" she shouted.

...

Marcus became visible at the corner of his house pushing buttons on his key lock. He always looked immaculate in golf shirt and slacks. Hair perfect, combed back, shiny gold watch gleaming on his left wrist contrasted well with his dark olive skin. He was a bit on the short side at just above five feet seven inches and fifteen pounds overweight.

Rounding the front of his car, Marcus noticed Beatrice in her driveway, almost saying good morning but declined. They disliked each other and both knew it too. It gave him pause to see his elderly neighbor up this early and stopped to look at her. Strange enough, Mrs. Patterson would be the last thing he'd ever see.

Shifting the gun barrel slightly left, acquiring rapid focus on target just emerging from behind the garage. Crosby's long strides made it tough keeping fine crosshairs aligned on his forehead. Still holding aim, Marcus paused for some reason and stood still. Black crosshairs rested dead center on his neck, held tight, trigger squeezed without moving the gun's position. Dazed by the contained explosion and a bright muzzle flash which illuminated the camper shell's interior like a flash bulb. Blinking both eyes to regain vision without lowering aim, the shooter stared into a dark scope trying to get a clear look. Somehow, it must be determined if the shot had completed the kill, as Mrs. Patterson walked down her driveway unseen.

The hollow point struck Marcus clean to the side and rear half of exposed neck, exploding into multiple fragments as it penetrated, shattering his second vertebrae. Bone fragments with metal shrapnel streamed into muscle tissue and blood vessels throughout his neck. The charge all but severing head from body. Blood gushed from an exposed carotid artery, spewing across the Lexus, running down his shiny, clean windshield. Small bits of flesh and hair splattered over the hood from the exploding projectile. Still upright, both legs refused to give way, keeping him bolstered against the car door. His gruesome looking head sliding and flopping along the top of the closed door. More blood shot from his open neck spraying the door again, soaking his yellow golf shirt and pooling on smooth concrete below. Eyes open but seeing blackness and feeling little pain except for a slight burning sensation around his shoulders. Marcus became a trembling figure now. His left hand somehow grasping at the windshield, trying to cheat death. A futile effort, at this point unconscious, Mr. Crosby passed away a few seconds later. In slow motion he began a slide along the car door leaving streaks of smeared blood contrasting with shiny metal. Legs finally dying, beginning to fold and give way. Falling in a hideous slump with distinctive sounds of flesh hitting pavement, like a rotten pumpkin hitting the kitchen floor. His head jarred at a right angle to his body. Both eyes open wide, mouth gaping as if to yell out the horror he'd become. Stillness settled in.

Beatrice moved toward her neighbor's driveway seeing it all now, as Marcus slid along the car door. She also blocked the killer's line of sight. Marcus Crosby's head dangled, almost free of his shoulders, sliding down his car door, taking a while, but the sound his corpse produced hitting the driveway made her recoil in fright. She fell to one knee, looking away, vomiting.

"What the fuck? Where did she come from?" an anxious shooter gasped out loud. "Piss poor luck again." As Beatrice fell, the shooter got a faint glimpse of Crosby's body sliding down along the Lexus, noticing how limp his head wobbled. Very bizarre. Was Marcus dead? "I have to get a clear look. To make sure," mumbling louder, dreading the move as adrenaline flowed through back and arm muscles. "Where'd the lady go?" Scoping a murder scene and breathing much harder. "Where the hell is she?" When Mrs. Patterson dropped she disappeared from view. Blocked in part by a neighbors white BMW. Flopping inside confined space and sliding close to the shell window, desperation set in to glimpse anything in the Crosby driveway. Without the scope, morning light was still too dim to view details at this distance.

"What the hell have I done? You shouldn't have done this. Christ! No one has the right to," the shooter screeched, wishing now the trigger hadn't been pulled, releasing this violent revenge. But straining to see anything outside.

"It's finished, so shut up, stay alert, think and get out of here," the sniper set the rifle down and rolled over to lift the rear window, unconcerned with noise. Climbing outside over a raised tailgate and slipping on a dew covered bumper, tripping to a sprawled flop onto cold, wet grass. "Shit, be careful," scolding too loud, rushing a beeline for the front door, hopping inside and turning the key. "I had to do it. I had to do it now," starting again what would become an endless mental debate. Looking back to both driveways but seeing nothing.

"My God," Beatrice gasped into her cupped hands. Somehow getting upright then stumbling back three or four steps coming to rest against the large sycamore, remaining hidden from view. Beatrice had witnessed many blood soaked episodes in the surgical ward. Emergency patients in particular. She could take blood and gore but it wasn't just medical experience helping to regain self control. By way of her most vivid British accent she looked upon the grotesque Crosby shape that was once her 'Monster Marcus' and scowled, "you bloody well deserved all this Marcus!" At first, Beatrice moved toward her walkway. Senses clear enough knowing she had to make a police call right away. Then noticing a vehicle coming down Anaheim, oddly enough, and instead moved toward it.

"Maybe she went inside her house?" hoping out loud while shifting gears. "This might give me enough time to check Marcus then get the hell out of here," the frenzied shooter began to regain composure. "Marcus you killed Sarah you lousy piece of shit!" Forcing a hard left u-turn around Arlington followed by an even sharper right, tortured but proceeding very slow along Anaheim Drive, headlights off. Rolling beyond two driveways, slowing more, the killer strained hard to view where Marcus fell. Finished. Seeing his jumbled body on cold cement with a vicious neck wound fully exposed, blood everywhere, realizing the round had finished its job. Nerves continued firing causing Marcus' left leg and foot to tremble and sway back and forth. The driver braked and fixated.

Full sun hadn't appeared yet and visibility wasn't perfect but being so close, with an early morning glow to the rear made the scene easy to survey. Mrs. Patterson materialized like an apparition from behind the sycamore tree, stumbling with her arm raised resembling a zombie. She managed a few timid steps toward the truck. Another complete surprise, dropping the killer's jaw with an audible gush! "What the hell, is she a ghost or what?" Beatrice and driver looked directly at each other yet neither quite knew what to do next. Beatrice even waived her arm as if appealing for the truck to stop and help.

Alarmed by dimmed headlights, Mrs. Patterson couldn't get a clear picture of the driver and it didn't take long to calculate the potential killer could be driving this truck. "My God Beatrice don't get yourself shot too," whimpering to herself. Watching. Scared to her petticoat. As the vehicle rolled by, rear lights illuminated, she tried reading the license plate. There was probably a six, shaking and somewhat vague, but able to clearly make out a number three followed by an N and I. The truck gained sped then disappeared down Anaheim like a menacing carnivore, leaving its kill behind. Killing for killing's sake. Beatrice repeated, "three, N and I," under her breath, over and over. Burning the set into memory and ran inside for a phone.

Speeding down Anaheim Drive the shooter sobbed openly. "You robbed me of the one good thing in my life, you prick. Now we're even." Tears of hatred and wild passion obscured direction as well as asphalt. It took time before emotional control was regained. Sunshine busted through at last and stiff north breezes were building, sweeping away what little fog remained, turning the sky deeper blue than usual. Becoming colder too. Somehow, by instinct, the driver morphed killer, made it to a busy freeway driving way too fast. Clearing skies and lifting fog seemed to reflect the killer's mood. In a short time rational thinking returned becoming more coherent. "It had to be done. I had to do it. Marcus couldn't be allowed to walk away from murder." Grasping to believe anything, justifying the action. A plan was hatched to dispose of the rifle outside of Tracy and needing some luck for another crucial job to be completed today. Relying on luck.

Chris

"Jesus Christ! Is his head blown off?" Detective Davis said aloud, peeling back a short towel covering what remained of Marcus' head and part of his shoulders.

Yellow crime scene tape was being strung to hold back neighbors interfering with police activity, just arriving on scene. Their job was to make sure no one else was hurt or in danger and to secure the site from inquisitive bystanders. Approaching eight in the morning, filtered sun drenched most of the killing zone with Marcus still resting in plain sight. One officer tried to keep the body blocked from view, especially since a few of the neighborhood kids, at present, were stealing peeks whenever an opportunity allowed.

"Hey Steve, get me a blanket over here, will ya," the newest arrival on scene bellowed to a uniformed patrolman, fixing yellow tape to a wood gatepost. Smirking with resentment, the officer galloped to a patrol car, opened the trunk and removed a thin, gray, cotton blanket wrapped in plastic. Its first use was to cover bodies, keeping someone warm, second. He brought the blanket over to Detective Christopher Davis, crouched beside the murder victim jabbing a pencil into pink muscle tissue, just beneath Marcus' chin. He tried skidding the bloody head just enough to better see the condition of splintered vertebrae.

"Thanks Steve," taking the blanket and covering Marcus' body.

"It's Mark," came a rather stern response from the patrolman.

"Come again?" Davis asked, standing to look at 'Steve' with a quizzed stare.

"My name. It's not Steve, for the third time. It's Mark. Mark Kennedy. Remember detective. I've been in the Advancement Program assisting you and your partner with crime scene duty for two months now." Knowing very well he could exhibit modest attitude with Detective Davis. Chris wasn't fixated on his own status to come down on patrol officers working to move up.

"Oh Christ. Sorry about that Mark. I'm awful with names. My memory sucks at this time of day," Davis apologized, slapping Kennedy on his shoulder trying to ease the young officer's angst. "Keep reminding me when I forget. I'll get it straight eventually." Feeling guilty. "The crime scene looks good by the way," handing Kennedy a compliment, further payment for his wrong name blunder. Davis hated when he messed up with uniforms. In particular, the patrolmen names, being there himself a long time ago.

Chris entered the Tracy Police Department riding motorcycle duty, finding Harley's irresistible at just twenty three, feeling more like a warrior in those days. Being black, Davis loved the surprised looks he'd get from redneck speeders he ran down. Making it a point to approach very slow, helmet on, knee high leather boots, gloves, wrapping a body still tight from glory days playing high school football, which continued on weekends with pick-up games. Chris thrived on competition. When the face shield came up and helmet removed, jaws would drop and eyes opened bright, impressive at six foot three and very dark, black skin. Often he'd pause, take the look eye to eye and state in a low tone, "license?" Reveling in the respect he commanded at his young age.

Detective Davis cashed in motorcycles after one too many close calls in the field. Riding high performance bikes was a thrill, but learned soon enough, how tough and dangerous it can be. High speed on crowded roads catches up, sooner or later. Forced to lay his bike down one beautiful spring morning on Grant Line Road, struggling to evade stopped cars while chasing a pick-up load of crazy punks. The good 'ole boys got away and by luck, Davis did too, with his body intact. He tested high for detective work, enrolling in classes for investigation training, earned a shield, assigned to homicide and loved his work for almost fifteen years. He only gained five pounds over those years, but a bitter divorce and one daughter whom he rarely saw anymore, induced the first thoughts of retirement to creep inside his head. Not for long however, as Chris Davis was the type to likely die on duty.

Davis still preferred eye to eye methods in his investigations. Looking into a suspect's face and reading eyes. He relied on hunches, feelings and innate abilities to know when a suspect was hiding something. In his judgment anyway, this was how police work was done. The Crosby case would test his abilities and beliefs like nothing else before.

"Please call me Chris. I don't go for that formality shit," Davis said, looking at Kennedy who appeared much more relaxed. Which seemed misleading to the patrolman as Detective Davis always dressed sharp with dark pants, gray jackets or sweaters. Most days included shirt and tie but never donning sport shirts. "Speaking of formality, have you seen my partner anywhere?"

"Not yet detect, I mean Chris. I'll tell Detective Gonzalez you're tired of waiting," flashing a crooked grin and walking away to check out a few onlookers gathering near the driveway.

"Hey Mark. You better string more tape further down the block," Chris offered. "When it gets out how the guy was killed, this neighborhood's going to become a circus!" Kennedy waved in confirmation, stopped and walked back to tell the detective a certain Mrs. Patterson was in her house waiting to answer questions.

"Ah yes, the eyewitness. I was told she's an older gal? I wonder if she can provide an ID?" asking himself as well as patrolman Kennedy.

"She's a sharp gal Chris, be ready," nodding for affect and leaving with tape in hand.

Davis strolled up the next door driveway then followed a curved brick path. Arriving at heavy, wood doors just swinging open, hearing an accent from Beatrice Patterson. "I suppose you want me to come downtown?" with emphasis on downtown, belaying her sarcasm for Tracy's 'downtown' police headquarters. "Can I ride in your patrol car Captain?" Sounding a little eccentric but seeming to take the murder event in stride. At least to Davis.

"No mame, nothing like that right now. My name's Chris Davis. I'm a homicide detective with the City of Tracy police. May I come inside?" asking with a polite tone but in reality, ordering. Beatrice swung each door open, welcoming Chris inside with a gentle nod. He was hit straight away, by the delightful aroma of coffee brewing. "Oh man, that smells great Mrs. Patterson," complimenting in a polite way but in reality begging! She dashed off to pour them both a cup.

"How do you take your coffee Colonel?" she asked Davis, yelling from the kitchen counter.

Chris responded with a loud, "black!" Mrs. Patterson noticed how professional the detective carried himself. He didn't beg outright but hinted with a polite manner, he'd welcome a cup of coffee. Beatrice liked this young man already.

Regina

As Chris was getting comfortable in a knick knack covered living room, someone knocked hard, shaking both front doors. He offered to address the visitor. Mrs. Patterson, looking down her kitchen hallway, responded, "please, if you don't mind." Knowing she could trust her guest to be civil.

Swinging wood doors wide open, Davis grinned wide and hissed, "you're late."

"Tough you know what," Gonzalez responded with fake attitude, giving her partner a gentle shove, moving him back from the entrance. Cold winds blew inside pushing one door open. Regina turned, closing the door behind with difficulty. "It's cold out there," she said, shaking chilly arms. Two cops entered Mrs. Patterson's living room just as Beatrice returned, carrying a tray with two cups of steaming French Roast. Davis made a slight move toward one hot cup but was promptly cut off. "Oh, fresh coffee. That is so nice of you. I really need this." Regina declared, snatching the nearest cup, pressing its brim to her red lips, inhaling vapors with both hands cupped around a warm mug. "Do you have any cream?" she asked Beatrice, innocent enough, leaving faint lipstick stains printed just below the rim.

Mrs. Patterson had to step back to compose herself. "Your coffee Colonel," she said, looking at Regina with a scowl but really thinking, 'bloody hell, who the fuck do you think you are, young lady!'

"Uh, yes I can bring you some cream, miss," Mrs. Patterson held a long pause, attempting to get a name from this perceived urchin.

"Oh, sorry mame. I'm Regina Gonzalez," speaking through rising vapors while extending a hand toward Beatrice for a cordial shake. "Me and Chris are partners," she declared, nodding her head as Davis was just permitted to acquire his cup.

Mrs. Patterson turned without shaking hands, heading back to her kitchen mumbling about poor grammar and lousy manners from the young Hispanic gal. Chris heard the woman's words. "It's Chris and I. Not me and Chris. Dumbass!" Marching down the long hallway. Regina made herself at home, removing a brown leather jacket, dropping it over a chair nearest her coffee.

Davis looked at the detective with one of his occasional harsh scowls and held it for a while. Enjoying another sip.

"What?" Regina replied.

"Watch your lousy manners Gonzalez." Chris whispered.

Regina was unaware what went wrong but whenever her partner used last names, she knew he was annoyed. Striving to release some bad air from the moment, Gonzalez lowered her gaze asking in a meek tone, smiling all the while, "so, when did you make colonel?" Davis couldn't help but grin, shaking his head while slurping another long drink. "I didn't know Tracy P.D. even had that rank!" Her dry wit and sharp glances dressed Regina Gonzalez in a cloak of charm and enjoyment. She looked away with soft giggles. Chris laughed again, but more than that, he cherished the innocent humor Regina brought to their partnership, keeping them both loose. Knowing well, this lady proved a determined and awfully sly, homicide investigator.

Regina was Hispanic. Her mother and father emigrating from Central America before she was born. Mama worked odd jobs by and large until she died, leaving Regina as a child. Retaining but a few snapshot memories of her mother's vibrant spirit. A beautiful woman. The detective was raised by her father, Enrique, becoming the most influential person in her life. Regina was a somewhat lanky woman with brown skin. Not too dark, but her long brown hair, almost black, was unfortunately her best part. Gonzalez wasn't a homely girl by any stretch but not Madonna blessed with classic Spanish beauty either. She did possess those interesting facial features however, which drove a select group of men wild. Entertaining a few boyfriends over the years, no problem there, but most didn't last long. Without a doubt the committal type but all that personality and confidence found many men perhaps, intimidated. At present, single, not looking too hard and not too concerned.

"Okay officers, what would you like to know?" Mrs. Patterson announced, returning to her living room with more coffee, cream and sugar just in case the young lady needed that too. "Your cream, Rachel," hitting back, using a wrong name in exchange for her poor etiquette. "How do you like your eggs, my dear?" in a dry, rude tone.

"It's Regina," reaching for cream and correcting her host's mistake. "No eggs for me, thanks. Waistline thing, you know." Gonzalez declined, sensing a tiny shortness from the lady now.

"I wouldn't know about that," Beatrice shot back. "I love eggs in the morning." Smiling.

Regina sneaked a peek at Chris, seeing a loose fist over his mouth containing a laugh. Recalling his own first name mistake earlier, with officer Kennedy.

"Please, sit down. Enjoy your coffee. It's been a hectic morning," Beatrice insisted showing off her appealing accent which Detective Davis envied. Seeming as if Beatrice had gained control of the meeting.

▪▪▪

Regina leaned forward across the coffee table anticipating Mrs. Patterson being hard of hearing. "It must be kinda' hard for you, having to deal with everything that went on today," groping for the right words. Wishing to bring their mini-battle to a truce. "If you like we could talk later. That would be fine," sounding way too much the patriarch.

Beatrice leaned back, her chair creaking, crossed a leg, pulled at a thick skirt and reached for coffee. Enjoying a long drink, tasting good and savoring every gulp. Slight pause before remarking, "oh no, it's fine dear. I don't mind talking at all," coming across relaxed and matter of fact! "It's sort of exciting really," taking both cops by surprise. In fact, Detective Gonzalez just realized how calm Mrs. Patterson acted at the moment. Unusual?

"Okay then, Beatrice. Why don't you," hesitating to ask a naïve question. "Do you mind if I call you Betty?" Gonzalez inquired, reaching for a notepad inside her rather large black purse. Davis sat up on hearing the query, guessing Mrs. Patterson wouldn't go for it. Regina looked back to 'Betty' in the midst of a pleasant smile.

"Betty? You have some nerve. Do I look like some Stockton floozy?" Beatrice scolded. Her accent becoming more pronounced. "I think not. My name is Beatrice. Do you mind if I call you Reggie?" holding a pursed frown, burning a line directly into the younger woman's face. Waiting. Uncomfortable silence followed.

"Uh, well okay. Beatrice it shall be." Reggie's face going bright red, looking at Chris a little perplexed. "Of course I meant no disrespect Mrs. Patterson," trying to dampen the spotlight on her, beaming from the older gal. "Whew, this lady is something," Regina thought to herself and stifled a chuckle to keep from getting slapped. "I was just trying," pausing and tripping over each word while fumbling with her note pad. Davis sort of enjoyed the tense moment however, looking forward to see how Regina might extricate herself from the situation. "I don't really care for Reggie either," Gonzalez added, forcing a fake laugh but appearing embarrassed.

Mrs. Patterson realized she overstepped the boundary line and lowered her stare. "Captain, would you like more coffee?" she asked, wanting to appear polite and signaling Regina, she was off the hook for now. Davis accepted and shot a quick smirk to his partner while Beatrice filled his cup. Regina looked back, shrugging her shoulders and held them in place. She grimaced a fake grin beginning to push back into her padded chair. An innocent look displayed on her face as if to say, "what've I done now?"

Chris, on the other hand, was fascinated by the whole exchange. Recalling his father's joke, albeit archaic, forewarning his young son about imminent danger with two women in a room together. Dad always said, "more often than not, war will break out."

"Mrs. Patterson, why don't you tell us what you witnessed this morning," Chris asked, hoping the elder woman would begin describing a murder and perhaps end hostilities. Regina kept silent prepping herself to take notes, head down with a broad smile. She couldn't help but feel good about Beatrice Patterson even if things started poor.

"Well," Mrs. Patterson commenced, "I'm convinced Marcus Crosby murdered his wife. Lord, I loved that poor girl as if she was my own blood," she disclosed with pity and anger scratched onto her face. Two detectives squinted puzzled eyes very hard at the women. Beatrice stared back. At Chris first, then to Regina. Beatrice realized they had no idea yet, whose head was blown off, lying in a bloody heap just beyond her door. She smirked and said nothing.

"Um, I was wondering what you may have witnessed," Davis interjected then stopped cold, in thought for a moment, asking a new question. "Just who are you talking about here?" Realizing much too slow, who THIS Crosby might be.

Regina's light bulb lit up simultaneous, pressing the palm of her hand against her forehead, asking Beatrice, "is this the same Crosby from the notorious 'Murdered Wife' case?" asking in an odd way.

"Bingo," the elegant lady answered, leaned back to take it all in as both cops looked at each other, unable to say a word.

■■■

One more stop. Forcing a slowdown, followed by a long edge of pavement glide and halting the dark truck to the near side of a narrow, risky roadway. Ahead, concrete and metal bridgework spanned a medium size channel. Bright glare blanketed the crossing as intense sunlight flooded through a stand of leafless willows bordering a steep stream bank. It was getting late. Intending to chuck the .222 into muddy water the shooter assumed would become its final and safe resting place. Expecting the rifle to settle fast into soft muck, never to be seen again. Originally planning to walk downstream a short way from the bridge, but heavier than anticipated traffic killed that idea. Appearing way too risky now, walking around in broad daylight armed with a rifle. "I'll have to pitch it from the bridge as far as I can heave it," thinking out loud, cracking the side door open, dying to get started. But the driver had to pause as a large red truck rumbled into view. Staying put inside a darkened cab, waiting much too long for the labor truck to clear.

Elderly farm workers riding inside paid no attention to a vehicle parked along this road as a sleepy driver held out his hand blocking intense glare. Besides, any truck parked along this road was all too common in Ag country.

"All clear." Looking fore and aft, the shooter hurried, grabbed a concealed murder weapon from a crowded truck bed and ran with all remaining energy. Needing as much momentum as possible to launch a long throw and shifting a thin barrel into both hands, the gun was hurled high into cold, windy air. Rotating horizontal, muzzle to butt. It went further than planned however, landing closer to one side of slow moving creek. Settling with a loud, gigantic splash, spraying water upstream twelve to fifteen feet from the northern bank. Not liking the weapon's final location but realizing nothing more could be done now. With any luck, the rifle's last resting place. "I'm done," speaking out loud. "It should be safe and if ever recovered, by some remote chance, the .222 was too old to be traced."

Hidden from sight however, sat a young Hispanic boy watching this entire, odd occurrence from the opposite bank. Estefan sat just below a tree lined bank hidden in bright glare.

···

Regina and Chris were embarrassed for failing to recognizing the victim. An hectic crime scene was about to explode and neither were ready for the mayhem. Davis knew time wasn't on their side, speaking up after seeing Regina writing with fury in her notebook. "Tell us what you saw in the driveway this morning Mrs. Patterson," Davis implored, all of a sudden much less congenial and more professional.

"There isn't that much to tell really," beginning to disclose events up to the presumed rifle blast. "The gun shot wasn't especially loud. More like a very strong thud," Mrs. Patterson explained, choosing her words with care. "Thinking about it now, the killer must have shot Marcus from inside a vehicle, I suppose. In fact, the sound of the bullet striking Marcus caught my attention. I'm not even positive what direction the shot came from," recalling this detail just now, which seemed odd? "When I first saw Marcus sliding along his car I didn't know what to think, with no comprehension of what was happening. But reaching the driveway, that appalling view of his neck and all the blood," Beatrice shook her head back and forth in disgust. "It made me stumble and step back. I lost it right there." Looking down to elude eye contact, frowning and wishing the awful image wouldn't remain too long.

"At this point a truck or car drove by. Correct?" Davis asked, knowing it was a truck but testing Mrs. Patterson to see if she'd confirm. "With the headlights off."

"Uhm, well, maybe a few minutes later. I'm not really sure of the exact moment," Beatrice responded with difficulty. "I was bent over on one knee trying to get control of myself. Initially wanting to hurry back inside to call the cops," she said playing the incident over again in her mind then looking to Regina. "I heard an engine running and looked back to see a truck, moving ever so slow." Beatrice and Regina made eye contact and smiled at one another.

"Could you tell what make or model?" Regina asked, hoping Betty wouldn't confront her again.

"Sorry, I'm terrible with cars these days. They all look alike." Realizing she couldn't even be positive about the color. "It was a smaller truck or SVU, I imagine," Betty responded, uncomfortable at the moment.

"You mean SUV don't you, Mrs. Patterson?" Reggie corrected in as gentle a tone as possible.

"What's that dear?" the older lady asked.

"Oh no, here she comes again," Gonzalez assumed, deciding not to press her point. "Sport Utility Vehicle," Regina amended. "We have to get everything perfectly clear for our investigation." Waiting for the boom to be lowered.

"Oh. Yes. Quite so," in her proper British accent. "As I said Regina, I'm just not into cars."

Regina felt better and relieved. "Addressed by my first name! We're making progress," positive thoughts for a change, then continued. "Did you notice a camper shell or was the body shape whole?" Gonzalez asked slow but knew the elder woman would be confused.

Mrs. Patterson squirmed in a high back chair smoothing out her skirt but only presented another, "I'm not sure." Regina couldn't help feeling sorry for the lady now, obvious Mrs. Patterson felt bad about her vague responses and the detective didn't posses the heart to push for specific answers.

Chris on the other hand was getting antsy so he grabbed the ball. "Can you remember the color mame?" asking with a firm voice.

Beatrice paused for time to think, shifting each leg and standing to get comfortable. "I knew you were going to ask me that Sergeant, but you must remember," appearing very nervous, well aware she wasn't helping much. "I was a little dazed to say the least. It didn't occur to me, at that moment, to start identifying color and truck models." Mrs. Patterson raised her voice in a defensive nature. "Christ, I didn't want to get shot myself!"

Both cops looked at each other as Chris raised his left eyebrow. Their signal between themselves for Regina to take over. "Mrs. Patterson, do you remember if the truck was white, black or some unusual color?" Gonzalez asked.

"No, it wasn't white. I'm sure," she answered confident for a change. "It was a dark color like brown, I think, but not black." Shaking her head in disgust with nothing but uncertainty. Beatrice returned to her chair rubbing a clammy forehead and stroking gray hair. She considered herself old right now. "I'm sorry Miss Gonzalez, I just can't say definitely," Beatrice uttered her regret, knowing she disappointed the officer. Extended silence filled the room as everyone grew a tad uncomfortable.

"Did you get a good look at the driver Mrs. Patterson?" Regina asked, gently again, but not expecting anything firm.

"Between the window glare and poor morning light obstructing my vision, I'm afraid I couldn't see the driver's face at all." Standing from her chair as if it helped to concentrate, thinking hard. "At that moment I just assumed a man would be driving," Beatrice whispered, inhaling a deep breath. Unsure about her next words. "This may sound strange but the person driving looked female to me. Quite small for a man, I recall," not one hundred percent certain about sex either. "One thing I do know, he or she wore a baseball hat. No doubt!" At last, decisive. "Sunlight glared from behind the vehicle right into my face. I could only see a silhouette," Mrs. Patterson explained in a low tone. "I'm not being much help am I?"

"You're doing fine Mrs. Patterson. Just relax and try to think," Gonzalez replied. "Did you see the license plate?"

Mrs. Patterson had more bad news, dropping her shoulders in frustration, troubled over this item too. "The truck's headlights came on after passing me in the driveway," she explained. "My eyes aren't near as young as yours my dear, nor as charming," Betty said smiling, handing Regina a compliment. "But I did get a brief look at the first three digits. I'm sure of a three followed by NI, with the number six, I believe, falling somewhere."

Davis turned his head thinking three digits are better than none. We might be able to work with that. "That third digit, Mrs. Patterson, was it the letter I or number one?" Chris asked knowing first hand this was a common error in number identification. Plate ID can be difficult. Chris recognized how 6 might be confused with G. Number 5 looks like S at a distance. Same with 3 and 8 also.

"I'm almost sure it was the letter I," returning unsure again as her voice tailed off at the end. "I mean, it had to be an I?" Questioning herself out loud. "Oh boy. I really feel like a dumb fu," Beatrice stopped in mid sentence. "Don't get in the gutter," she warned herself, taking a seat on the sofa. "The truck continued down Anaheim Drive and disappeared," following with a deep sigh, staring hard through a large window. Watching outside as oak and sycamore leaves vibrated on thin limbs, facing away from both detectives also. "May I get either of you more coffee," signaling an end to the information she held. Beatrice felt like being alone now but then added one more observation. "I did see a bumper sticker on the right side of the bumper. Couldn't tell you exactly what it was. Way too far away for me to read." But with an afterthought, "shaped like a badge come to think of it." In the middle of a sudden memory burst. "The bumper was chrome. If that's any help at all?" Mrs. Patterson added.

Regina entered the brief note thinking it wouldn't matter. "I'm fine with my coffee, thank you. I don't have any more questions at this time." She declined, looking at Beatrice, busy gathering cups and napkins. Gonzalez couldn't help but sense some good feelings surfacing with this lady. "Chris?"

"Uh no, nothing here." Reading his notes to make sure. Davis bit down on his lower lip in a tender way, deciding now to ask Beatrice for her opinion. Not sure why. "Maybe one last matter Mrs. Patterson," he began. "Do you believe, whoever it was driving that truck, to be the shooter?" The question caught Regina's attention and she wanted to see the older lady's reaction.

Beatrice stopped cleaning to consider the query. He's asking for my opinion she thought. "I have to assume that driver committed the murder," she stated emphatically. "Driving so slow with head lights dimmed followed by that long look at Marcus laying on his driveway. Not stopping to help. He or she was definitely the shooter detective." Addressing Davis by his correct rank. "Absolutely."

Anderson

Mrs. Patterson escorted both officers to the front door. Each cop expressed gratitude for her hospitality. An opened door was likened to raising the curtain on a melodrama in full production. Turning to survey their crime scene, each partner wished to turn right around and go back inside. The press had arrived and they expected answers. Especially a bosomy redhead who just slithered from a Channel Forty Newsroom van.

Beatrice looked out over her front yard watching all the commotion. "Goodness, here we go again. Just like the first murder," telling both officers. "I'm sure it'll be even bigger this time."

"Oh boy, there she is already," Regina groaned. "How does that woman look so good this early in the morning?"

Beatrice laughed out loud slapping one hand to her leg, "I think it may be my time to take a walk." She said.

"Can I join you?" Chris asked, joking and serious at the same time.

Yellow caution tape draped from both corner houses, blocking access to Anaheim Drive and continuing three or four doors past 860 Anaheim. The growing crime scene achieved an appearance similar to that of an angry protest. Onlookers from frightened neighbors asked every ridiculous question imaginable; uniformed police tried their best to keep their crime scene free of contamination; soccer moms stuffed kids into mini-vans for rides to school: working men and women weaved cars out of driveways: a fire truck manned by a few bored firefighters; crime scene investigators taking pictures, securing samples and drawing chalk outlines; more plainclothes detectives; videographers recording field reporters interviewing just about anybody with a uniform; with more yellow and blue flashing lights seen at an Oakland Coliseum rock concert. Remarkable, what the site of blood will do to people.

···

Near the corner of Mrs. Patterson's driveway, standing on the sidewalk just opposite the sycamore tree, stood a man in his early forties. His bulging stomach pouch indicated a lack of exercise. Pale skin tones contrasted against dark brown hair, he kept wet looking and combed straight back. Dressed in charcoal gray slacks, plane white shirt, and his signature maroon-yellow striped tie loose at the collar. Captain Anderson's uniform. He donned this same look, more or less, each day. Billy Anderson, third generation career police investigator. A family business.

Granddad, from his mother's side, became well known in the Fresno area for his high rate of success solving murders. Of course Grampa Chuck was blessed with ample practice, as Fresno morphed into a violent, medium size city in the late seventies. Increased farm labor demand attracted some unsightly characters from Central America and even more lethal corporate Ag growers, bent on increasing productive acreage in this part of the Central Valley's less prosperous. Time and again guns were employed to exact payment for unpaid farm wages. Distressed people resorting to reckless acts. Violent work, which encouraged Billy Anderson's father to study engineering. Dad ended up designing water canals for local Irrigation Districts. Safe work, which forced mom to carry on the police service tradition. She did. Doing it well, rising to lieutenant on the Fresno Police force.

Unfortunately Gene Anderson, the most pleasant cop one might ever encounter, just wasn't stimulated by police work. She never grew to adopt the 'us against them' attitude needed for tenacious crime investigation. Poor gal trusted everyone! Which lead to almost being killed during a botched armed robbery. Convinced she would get a drunken redneck to surrender his handgun, Gene Anderson took one too many steps toward the low life, resulting in a pulled trigger on his smallish .22 caliber weapon. Only because he was drunk and a dreadful shot, she took the bullet in her upper thigh, managing to nick the femoral artery however, which led to torrential bleeding. Gene's leg never managed to heal in full and early retirement was recommended. She left the police force running, with a permanent limp, never looking back. In no time, finished her teaching credential and lectured high school students concerning the beauty of English Literature. Her passion.

Next to Billy Anderson stood one uniformed officer. A woman in her mid thirties, appeared to be explaining how the murder took place. Pointing away toward the Arlington and Anaheim three way stop, then back to the Crosby house. A quick motion with one hand pantomimed Marcus' neck wound. Anderson fixed his attention on the street intersection when Chris and

Regina meandered through a maze of caution tape, meeting with their boss.

"Say Chris," Billy contested his staff before saying hello or good morning. "You need to cordon off that whole three way stop. Not just the far side of Arlington Street. Shots were taken from up there I'm told and the crime scene unit will be sweeping that entire intersection for possible evidence," not openly scolding his detective but updating him, with a show of urgency. "Hell, it looks like a few neighbors have already entered the crime scene," Anderson observed, straining to get a look at someone shuffling around the grass devil strip with her head down, carrying a coffee mug. Regina and Chris got caught up in the number of reporters entering the area. Glancing to Arlington Street took them by surprise.

"Hey partner, is that Mrs. Patterson over there?" Chris asked somewhat flabbergasted.

"What the hell," Regina wondered cupping both hands over her eyes to shade the glaring sunlight. "It's her all right, but why is she?" stopping abrupt and thinking, "Betty, you're a suspicious lady, aren't you?"

"Let's get Kennedy up there with more tape and check out what the hell Beatrice is doing." Chris directed Gonzalez to see to it her new friend is escorted from the shooting zone, right away.

"Who's Beatrice?" Anderson interrupted.

"She's our, somewhat partial, eyewitness to the murder," Davis noted, emphasizing somewhat, due to the scant information obtained from Mrs. Patterson. "She lives next door," pointing out her home. "We questioned her about ten minutes ago, getting a partial license plate number but not much more."

"Well, you better get that plate number over to Vehicle, so they can start a trace," Billy directed.

"I sent it to Max already," Davis added. Mad Max, as referred to, handled the department's license plate searches.

"I'll see what she's doing," Regina said, in motion toward the intersection, turning her head from side to side trying to locate officer Kennedy. She spotted him talking with a reporter. "Mark!" yelling loud enough to impress her urgency, getting his attention and ending the interview. Kennedy weaved through mounting press corps making his way to Gonzales. Mark always liked working with Regina who worked well with uniforms. She learned fast from Davis, keeping these patrolmen on her good side and they'd become invaluable helping to cover crime incidents. Kennedy also had an immense crush on her, but held back, preferring to keep their working relationship professional. Gonzalez was clueless.

"You have to expand the tape area," instructing Mark and noticing Mrs. Patterson in a full crouch, running her right hand over thick grass bordering the concrete curb. "Block off this whole intersection," Gonzalez instructed.

"Yes mame," Kennedy responded. Yelling out to block more press intrusion.

"Beatrice! Mrs. Patterson!" Detective Gonzalez shouted quickening her lope. "Mrs. Patterson you can't be in here now," yelling as she stepped off the curb in front of a large white corner house facing Anaheim Drive. She angled toward the lady, having to detour around the rear end of a large fire engine. Beatrice stood, twisting gradually to the left, cupping her right hand away from Regina. Raising her left hand in a mock wave, smiling cheerful, then deftly dropped an object from her right hand into a baggy sweater pocket. Unnoticed.

"Beatrice, we have to keep this area isolated," Regina instructed, nearing the gutter lip trying to avoid sounding belligerent. Taking hold of her right arm, the police woman led Mrs. Patterson further along Arlington Street. "This whole intersection has to be scanned for evidence. You didn't disturb anything I hope?" Regina asked polite and trusted she didn't.

"Oh, heavens no dear. I just wondered from my house for a short walk and ended up over here," Beatrice explained innocent enough, revealing a gentle smirk. "I thought the shooter's truck may have been parked further to this side of Anaheim." She raised a loose fist to her mouth, biting soft on the knuckle of her index finger. Visualizing a shooter in action, paused for a moment, then continued. "Look how much more driveway is visible," Mrs. Patterson explained, pointing toward the victim's residence.

Regina checked the view and nodded in agreement. "You're right Beatrice. That's why we need to increase the examination area." Kennedy and another patrolman strung additional tape lines from a few trees and fences, completing a substantial barricade across Arlington.

Gonzalez pondered the line of sight and wondered if Mrs. Patterson knew more than she let on during the interview. She considered it further, uncertain now if she and Chris had been asking the right questions? Mrs. Patterson seemed almost too intent on making her opinion known. Concerning Marcus Crosby in particular.

Back at the Crosby house, Billy informed Chris, he and Gonzalez would be lead investigators from here on in. "You two are the department's lead homicide team now. Work up a game plan and let me know who you need to assist. I'll be heading downtown to give Chief Yung a preliminary report." Using a department joke about Tracy's nonexistent downtown. "With what we have now, this murder will never be solved," Billy spoke with a sober voice. Looking around the crime scene feeling even more dire. "What's your read Chris?"

"I can't say for sure, right now," Chris admitted. "At first it appeared to be a professional hit. Gangs maybe? But a little stylish for that group." Captain Anderson shook his head in agreement and got the feeling Chris didn't believe it was gang related. "Blacks and Mexicans are at each other these days but after talking with our witness lady, my hunch says, classic revenge killing," Davis responded with a strong conviction in his voice. "Regina and I will question more of the neighbors. Maybe somebody will have something new to offer, but don't count on it." Remembering his partner went off to check on the older gal, glancing in that direction. He saw them both sitting together on a brick stairway leading to a well kept home opposite the shooter's assumed location. Chris' first impression appeared as though Mrs. Patterson was holding court. Gonzalez had her head down writing high-speed notes. Fallen sycamore leaves, dried in yellows and browns, were being windblown around them, on the lawn and sidewalk. Neither gal noticed.

Captain Anderson turned in the direction of his detective's stare, noticing two ladies perched on the steps too. "I hope Gonzalez is trying to get something new," sounding confused as to how Regina was working her witness. "They look to be planning a dinner party," as Billy exhibited a rare brand of sarcasm.

"Don't be concerned with Regina's technique Captain," Davis commented with subtle praise. "She's very good at keeping witnesses talking. She's a smart detective," fixing on Gonzalez and feeling lucky to have a partner like her.

...

"Tell me about the Crosby's," Gonzalez nudged in her comfortable tone looking directly at Beatrice.

Mrs. Patterson stared at the ground in front of her as a rapid gust of wind blew an inch or two of curled, gray hair about her cheek. Regina noticed a slight frown. She tugged her heavy sweater tighter about a narrow waist pulling the cloth belt firm. "It's getting much colder with this wind," Beatrice whispered like an older lady. She stepped back on the sidewalk and turned herself to face the sunlight, throwing a long shadow, reaching green grass beyond the sidewalk. Winter sunshine warmed her face and shoulders but increasing winds stirred lingering dry leaves through the top branches of nearby trees. Similar to the dark feelings beginning to stir deep within. Seizing Regina's arm this time, leading her back to the brick steps behind them. Mrs. Patterson began her story.

Sarah

Beatrice commenced. "Let's see. Where do I start?" Telling Regina of those early days when the Crosby's arrived in her neighborhood. Nothing unusual to tell at first. "They behaved like any normal married couple."

"When did they move in?" Regina asked.

"Mm, a little over three years ago. In mid October." Telling Regina how sociable Sarah behaved and they connected in a few short days. "She popped her head over my fence one morning, said hi and invited herself over," Beatrice recalled with a small grin envisioning her face right now. "Sarah brought over coffee and pastry. We ate too much and talked late into the afternoon." Which resulted in sharing wonderful backyard conversations over coffee and Sarah asking Beatrice to coach her in gardening. "We eventually competed with each other for best of show, beefsteak tomatoes," the heartbroken lady told Regina staring off in the distance. Gonzalez respected her silent reminiscence. Beatrice suffered her lonesome thoughts, surfacing now and again, leading to intense pain and hatred. "I'd start an outdoor fire on chilly mornings, especially in early fall. Sarah and I would sit together, gossiping about anything and everyone," Mrs. Patterson revealed, remembering their long talks bundled in sweaters and blankets.

"On occasion we even talked about Marcus. How great he seemed in the early days of their engagement. Sarah claimed his outbreaks of anger began when the family business started to suffer," Beatrice conveyed, but didn't buy that excuse. "Marcus' mean streak had boiled within for a long time. Like a wild predator waiting to ambush its victim," adding a cruel inflection.

"I'm by no means a spousal abuse expert, by any stretch. But that's very common when we respond to domestic violence calls," Regina commented. "Most women say they had no idea her husband or boyfriend was capable of such anger. I hate domestic violence calls. Child abuse is rock bottom, by far," declaring her contempt with passion. "I prefer the most grisly murders, any day." Gonzalez thought of all the crying women and children she's witnessed. Spending too many nights herself, lying in bed, crying, fantasizing revenge. Playing music as loud as she could. Contriving any means to drown her grief.

"It took a few months before I learned of the fighting," Mrs. Patterson described the first night she heard Marcus going off. "I couldn't believe how livid he became," she revealed to Regina and slowly shook her head in a disbelief. Always over the smallest matters. "Late with breakfast or dinner. Clothes not hung properly. The newspaper for God's sake. He beat that poor girl senseless because she didn't put the God damned newspaper back in order!" Choking air with sorrow for her young, make believe adopted daughter. "Soon after, I noticed bruises on her arms then around her neck."

"Did Sarah tell you about the beatings?" Regina asked the wounded woman while rubbing Mrs. Patterson's arm with a gentle palm. Hoping, in a small way, to help ease the pain.

Beatrice went on to tell Regina how the beatings increased. "Sarah stayed away from me. Obeying orders I assumed." Longer and longer periods without leaving the house. She knew Sarah was embarrassed allowing her bruises ample time to disappear, before visiting again.

"I should've gone to the police," Beatrice admitted. "Correction. I could've gone to the police, but didn't," snarling this time. "But no, I had to act such proper British I suppose." Looking at Regina with a twisted frown, feigning a snooty look on her face. "It's not civilized to pry into another's dirty laundry," sounding quite disappointed within herself. "I helped to kill my poor girl as if I stabbed her in the back myself." Believing the words deep into her soul, which would accompany her to the grave. Mrs. Patterson knew, beyond a shadow of doubt, she was obliged to report the violent abuse.

Gonzalez agreed. She should've reported the abuse but would never say as much. "Beatrice you can't blame this on," but was cut off straight away.

"I was a nurse for the love of God!" she exclaimed. "I was obligated, as part of my profession and as a simple decent person. One doesn't just ignore violence like that." Covering part of her mouth with a clenched fist, looking away from Regina, eyes swollen with tears. "But, I did." A small droplet trickled along a crow's feet wrinkle, slid down her cheek and splashed on the bottom step. Leaving a wet brown dot on red brick. Wind blew through her hair again, drying the splash mark. She felt winter cold seep into her aging bones again. "I was obligated to go."

Over a minute of silence passed before Mrs. Patterson composed herself. Regina didn't have the heart to speak. What could she say? This tormented woman craved to bury her guilt, somehow.

Gonzalez took in the event around them noticing a mass of blinking lights and police activity surrounding the area. She almost forgot how active and fresh this crime scene remained. But the detective stayed captivated by Betty's tale. Two women, sitting like old friends in a comfortable neighborhood setting, pouring their hearts out to each other. Not one police investigator nor any uniforms stringing extra yellow tape paid them interest. Two reporters walked by twice, each assuming they were the usual curious neighbors. Two girls, encapsulated in a sort of open air chrysalis. But Gonzalez cultivated a gut feeling, Mrs. Patterson could, just maybe, in some small way, expose something about Marcus or Sarah. "Which might help unlock this case too. Lucky for us, Beatrice was very close to Sarah Crosby," Regina thought to herself. "There could be some sort of deep secret waiting to be revealed. Maybe." Writing in another note.

"You okay Betty?" the brash detective was peeking at her new friend with a sly grin. It's all she could think of, wanting to break the silence. It worked. Beatrice looked back, cracking a colossal smile. She leaned forward and pressed her forehead against Regina's, becoming their defined moment of affection. A comic slight followed by a light touch. Friends.

"Sorry Reggie, I'm a little emotional right now. Forgive me," Beatrice offered an unnecessary apology.

"I forgive you," Regina whispered a modest snicker. They laughed again.

Mrs. Patterson continued telling Regina about Sarah. She had an ever so slight olive complexion and dark hair. But not like her father's brown hair.

Dark, dark brown and very thick. Her blue eyes were somewhat thin. Unlike her mother's eyes which are green and round. "I loved teasing her that maybe she was conceived with the mailman," she told Regina in a happier manner. "Not a dead ringer for her parents, that's for sure."

"Do you think she was?" the cop asked with wide open eyes waiting for a response.

"Oh, I don't think so Regina," Beatrice said. "Her mother doesn't seem the type to," pausing to keep it British, "you know what I mean."

"Can't always tell with sex, ya know." Sounding preachy. "We've come across a few incredible circumstances. From nuns to so called happy house-wives," Regina disclosed.

"I'm sure you have dear. When you meet Deborah Braden, you'll know what I mean," Beatrice explained. "A desperate sort of married woman," she added.

Regina didn't catch on to Mrs. Patterson's definition. 'Married and Des-perate' with bold letters, entered into a detailed notebook. She knew her and Chris would be questioning the Braden's very soon. "We'll see if I can find out what she means," Gonzalez instructed herself.

"It was last year just before Thanksgiving. That's when they had their last fight inside this house," unveiling more of her story once again. Beatrice recounted how this attack was over something trivial again. "Overcooked fish if I recall." Remembering a lot of shouting and screams. Followed by sudden silence. Mrs. Patterson was in her back yard relaxing and forced to hear it all, too well. "One of those grand Indian Summer days that make California such a desirable place. Late fall, calm and warm followed by a cool night. Perfect weather."

"Marcus left the house a few minutes later. Got into his car and drove off somewhere," Mrs. Patterson told Gonzalez. "This fight was different however. This time Sarah tried to fight back," telling Regina in a satisfied tone. Proud of the beaten girl for standing her ground. "I could hear my friend crying as she closed all the doors and windows of her house. Alone inside, Sarah wanted to keep her tears secret. It didn't work. I had to see my daugh," stopping cold, "my friend, and make her move away," Beatrice stated firm.

Sarah wouldn't open the door at first, asking Beatrice to go away. "I grabbed that damn handle and shook the door as hard as I could." Not the smartest thing to do the older lady admitted. "I must've sounded like Marcus at that point?" Sarah gave in. Granting Beatrice access and peered out, half hidden behind the wood door. "I will never forget the way she looked at me as long as I live. Sarah was so ashamed of herself," Beatrice told Regina in a low sorrowful voice. "Without saying a word I just walked in and hugged her," a brokenhearted older woman explained to the detective. She didn't know what else to do. "Sarah put both arms around me and we held one another tight." Mrs. Patterson had to stop. Her lips and mouth quivered choking back strong emotions. A quiet sob escaped, but soon recovered. "To think Sarah would be the one ashamed?"

"I never had children. Like spoiled idiots, my husband and I got so caught up in our glorious careers, we completely ignored the one important adventure in life," Betty scolded herself again. "But this embrace made me feel, for once, as though I was comforting my daughter. She just hugged me. It was exquisite at the time. However, it would be our farewell moment. She was saying goodbye to me." Regina could tell the older woman was on the verge of breaking down. "Holding another and helping them when they're in pain. Never once did I feel this same connect, in all my years as a nurse. That's odd isn't it?" Raising the question and standing. Beatrice realized at this moment she never linked with patients the way she did with Sarah. "I helped a load of people in my career. None of that aid ever gave me the same feeling?" Glaring at Regina with a perplexed look on her face. "I thought many times, and this must sound weird, if it wasn't for Marcus beating her, I wouldn't have grown so close to Sarah. Oh God I'm sorry," Beatrice whimpered, bowing her head, making a fast sign of the cross. Regina took notice. "That's a horrible thing to say to you. Please forgive me."

"I don't know what to say. I don't have children either." But flooding Regina's mind were fleeting images of her own mother. Long brown hair, gentle voice and a whirlwind in her kitchen. Short clips of mother-daughter affection. Teaching Regina how to bake, then fill and roll tortillas.

"Make sure you have one child my dear," Beatrice encouraged the young woman.

"You got it," Gonzalez tilted her head, nodding affirmative.

Beatrice continued. Telling the detective Sarah's face wasn't bruised but a very red mark glowed on her jaw. Blood ran from her left ear. "Seeing the blood I could only think, this poor girl is certain to be killed by Marcus." Explaining how she pleaded with her to move out. Now. "I offered to take her in myself but Sarah wouldn't take the step. She wouldn't leave Marcus. Hoping to eventually get professional help, as if her husband would agree to counseling. Right!" A dejected woman, head held low, as more leaves swirled in a tiny vortex at her feet. Beatrice clenched jaw muscles tight revealing her opinion. "It was complete folly for Sarah to hang onto an idea like that. Moving slow to be seated on the step once again. "That was the last time I saw my daughter," Mrs. Patterson said without flinching. Showing the detective a blank stare. "Forgive me, but I just had to say that. Just this once I need to believe she was my own blood," speaking now with much pain and much relief. "God, I love that girl. I miss her."

Hearing 'my daughter' sent a chill through Regina's shoulders and neck.

"Beatrice, I'm so sorry." reflecting how charming Mrs. Patterson sounded right now.

"I must be a little off my rocking chair, I'm afraid? Sorry about all this, Reggie." Having to calm herself and the moment.

"In fact, I'm kinda jealous," Gonzalez admitted, adoring her Reggie tag.

Around the Crosby house Davis still talked with Captain Anderson. Regina noticed the Channel Forty news woman, locating her cameraman just right, to record from her good side. She could see the lanky redhead grow frustrated with wind directions and the way cold air blew long scarlet curls around that television face. Regina chuckled and thought, "Big Red won't stand for hair blocking her face, on TV! How disappointing to loyal viewers." She took three stabs to get herself just right on camera, becoming frustrated with the crew and it showed. On one attempt she stopped a take, feinting a microphone slam to the pavement and screaming at her audio man, "what the fuck are you doing? You're blocking the camera!" Regina had little need to hear her words, coming across loud and clear reading the redhead's lips.

"What a piece of work," the detective thought to herself. Figuring she was desperate to prepare a lead in to the murder story airing on tonight's six o'clock news.

Miss Bailey's sudden commotion primed Regina to recall a story Davis told about the buxom reporter, during a past murder investigation. It seems that an intern was showing up in background shoots way too often. Patricia became frustrated and angry, threatening to fire the young student. He innocently responded by telling the newsgirl he couldn't be fired. "I'm not being paid!" It turned out the intern volunteered at no pay, working for experience. "Go fuck yourself bitch!" The young student yelled out, before being released. Her entire crew broke out laughing, recording the entire episode. They played the highlight on cell phones and after work at beer bars, joking about the poor guy with guts and working for nothing. Since that day staff members never took her serious. She became their Redheaded Dominatrix!

Getting back to Beatrice, Regina asked a question, "Did you testify in court?"

"I sure as fu," Beatrice bawled, catching herself again. "Sure as heck wanted to, but the DA in Tuolumne County said I may be too volatile in the courtroom," laughing under her breath. "What gave him that idea?"

"Gees, I can't imagine," Regina replied in a dry tone, two woman laughing as a gust of north wind chilled their red faces.

Mrs. Patterson told the detective about the Crosby's family cabin near Groveland, a small foothill town west of Yosemite National Park. Marcus and Sarah spent Thanksgiving holidays there, being Sarah's favorite time of year in Yosemite. "She would go on and on about warm afternoons and subtle foliage change from older willow trees, lining shallow banks along the Merced River. It revitalized her." Beatrice went on remembering Sarah talking about tree shadows. "Of all things?" The way they appeared in meadows during late afternoons. So much longer in the fall season due to low angled sunlight. Emitting yellow and red tints from the granite canyon walls. "Can you imagine. Murdering his wife near such hallowed ground as Yosemite?" Beatrice sounded like she was scolding Regina in a sickened tone.

"Where were we? Uh no. I kept waiting to be called to testify, but it never happened. The DA or his legal team in Tuolumne County must be the most incompetent lawyers in California," Mrs. Patterson said. Explaining, in her opinion, how the Crosby family had plenty of money and connections. Hiring the best defense attorneys to buy their brand of justice. "Sarah's justice hinged on a jury decision. Needing only one juror to descent. When they returned declaring a hung jury," triggering more anger, bringing her face to a deep red, dodged by the right words in frustration. "Just unbelievable." Beatrice detailed the DA, convinced he was an abysmal lawyer. "He had enough evidence to prove Marcus killed Sarah. That's a lawyer who just didn't do his job," maintaining a stern face as the older lady relived the momentous trial.

"His phony excuse about the break in was preposterous. No hard evidence surfaced indicating forced entry. No broken windows, no damaged doors, no jimmied locks. Unreal." Beatrice went on, recounting her impressions of a certain look on Marcus' face during the trial. "As if proclaiming, yeah I did it, so what!"

Wanting to hear actual testimony first hand Beatrice related her trial visit. After a few weeks the local onlookers lost interest and Mrs. Patterson made it into the courtroom. "I hated the way he looked," the elder woman hissed. Describing defense strategy, parading bought and paid for local politicians in front of the jury. "Each whore testifying what an asset the Crosby family had become to 'our' local economy. As if that means it's now acceptable to murder young girls. As long as your business is doing well!"

"I thought the Crosby farms were out around Oakdale and Lodi?" Regina asked.

"They are! Hell, I contribute to those economies too," Beatrice was almost shouting her dismissal of invented facts. Then going on at length, bringing Gonzalez up to speed about wine grapes the Crosby family grows. Mainly Zinfandel grapes originally planted in the foothills region during the seventies. Rocky soils proved suitable for growing bulk, low quality grapes thriving in the summer heat. Large volume wine making needs cheaper grapes. As the family acreage swelled, so did their income. Crosby Vineyards mushroomed, now supplying many large wineries in Livermore, Napa and Sonoma Valleys with bulk grapes for mass produced, low to mid quality blended reds. Regina was impressed with

Betty's knowledge of the Crosby family business, adding a note about future information.

"Kinda like the O.J. trial, I suppose. Justice being served most often by the clever and highly paid attorney laying doubt in one juror's mind," Mrs. Patterson spoke with a degree of empathy. It wasn't as if Beatrice didn't trust the legal system, knowing as well as anyone our system has it's pitfalls. "In this case Sarah didn't receive her due. The guilty went free. And now," stopping cold, looking back over her shoulder in the direction of Marcus' bloody remains.

"Now he lies upon cold concrete with a neck wound the size of a catcher's mitt," Regina completed Mrs. Patterson's statement, writing more notes in her log book.

Beatrice slowly looked back to the young girl and contemplated her somewhat crude remark. Thinking it didn't fit her personality. "I can't figure this bird out?" Mrs. Patterson said to herself, mulling it over but concluding how she liked the feathers of this bird too. Much colder now with blustery winds flowing steady. Small birds flocked together behind two ladies, chirping a racket. Gusts shoved them sideways as they flew from tree to tree, announcing an impending coldness due to settle in. Inserting cold hands into her sweater pocket reminded Beatrice about the object she found earlier. Twirling it along cold fingertips, Betty contemplated showing Reggie what she discovered. "I'll keep it to myself for now."

Patricia

Using the Crosby house as backdrop, Patricia Bailey raised her microphone, hesitated for a second making sure everything was set to begin her interview of Captain Anderson. Billy decided to run interference for Chris Davis. He'd take on a determined press freeing Davis to stay with his investigation.

"Captain Anderson," Ms. Bailey inquired, "we're told the victim is one Marcus Crosby, husband of murdered Sarah Crosby. Killed by an assassin's bullet, leaving for work, in his own driveway, just a few hours ago."

"That seems to be the case," Captain Anderson's words were well rehearsed. "Expressed very well Oprha, I might add," unable to resist taking the shot. It wasn't so much a dislike being around this particular newswoman. Hell, Billy would go pretty deep for a chance to know her better, physically. Instead he detested the way some reporters, Patricia included, over dramatized an event. Always the showgirl. He knew Bailey was a good reporter but she needed to cut down her 'over the top' drama. Anderson enjoyed working with most reporters and in no way, was he remotely anti media. Knowing full well how ranking cops did everything possible to dodge the press, believing this to be a serious flaw in law enforcement. Simply understanding reporters come with the job, for a particular rank. Believing police departments should be as transparent as possible and always available to the public. "We serve them first, not our departments. End of discussion," he said many times.

If actually trained as journalists, most reporters conducted themselves in a professional manner, when in Billy's company covering criminal cases. It was understood between police and press, murder and child abuse cases would be granted some leeway. Longing for as much limp rope as he could get for this case. Advancing a slow walk around the driveway, Anderson wished to scrape the girl away. No luck. Patricia maintained a stubborn pace.

"Mr. Crosby became renowned last year in his wife's mysterious murder near Yosemite." Bailey then added, "the well known Mountain Murder." Asking quick, "is that right Captain?"

"Uh yes. It appears the victim is Marcus Crosby. We'll verify identity later today as his wound is very extensive," Billy informed the reporter then wished to take those words back. He knew what was going to happen next. She would just love to get some gory details for the viewers. "Stay on your toes here," Anderson told himself.

"Marcus Crosby was shot in the neck, we're told," the reporter declared, looking at the officer with a formidable stare. As if to say, "you brought it up dumbo." Patricia continued her assault, "judging by the extent of blood visible around the victims car and driveway, one has to conclude a rather large caliber gun was used? A rifle maybe? What information can you give us?"

"Our ballistics department will examine the wound for bullet fragments. They'll determine what type of weapon was used." Billy answered, thinking it didn't have to be a large gun to cause such a massive wound. Not about to elaborate that point however, continuing his movement through the crime scene, with Patty dogging him like a German shorthair.

Billy remembered when Ms. Bailey first debuted, four or five years ago, to file crime scene reports. She looked to be the up and comer. Gorgeous woman and Captain Anderson would never relinquish his boyhood crush on the reporter.

Bailey got her feet wet with a brief stint as a field reporter then rushed off to a San Francisco network station as weekend anchor. A quick look to see how she'd perform in a major market. With great looks she should've been a lead pipe cinch for network broadcasts in no time. It turned out to be a very fast look. Patricia had one big problem. One must be capable to read cue cards or a teleprompter, if you're going to anchor the news. She just couldn't nail down that natural form of reading the prompter and talking to the camera. It intimidated her fiercely. Similar to many major league hitters who can't get that clutch knock with runners in scoring position. Patty was a choke. Unable to shake it, sounding like a schoolgirl learning to read. Channel Forty tried her out and then backed away also, for some serious training sessions. No luck. Poor, beautiful kid just didn't have it. Patricia was sent back to field reporting and has stayed there ever since. As long as she got the right questions, short and quick, Patty still commanded a little star power. "Good looks will help ya too," Anderson thought to himself. "Just think if I had those good looks?"

Bailey had an active love life into her late twenties, with no lack of men coming on to her. She accepted plenty advances too. Short lived boyfriends, love affairs, a tryst with a married television executive, even a one-night stand or two. They all crashed down around her in pathetic shallow romances. It was different now, with the inevitable growing need for a child, maybe a secure family life and wanting another chance to anchor big time news. Patricia wouldn't give up and agreed to accept help.

"Do you have any suspects yet, Captain Anderson?" Bailey inquired, realizing the ridiculous question was way too premature.

"Damn Patricia, we've only been on the scene an hour or so. Cut me a little slack." Rolling eyes but then smiling. Billy couldn't quit staring at her red hair blowing in the cold wind which painted her cheeks a deep red and a low cut blouse which fluttered in the slightest breeze, opening just the right amount of cleavage. "For now all we have is a partial license plate number from a suspicious looking truck passing by right after the killing," kinda wishing he hadn't said that too.

"That plate number came from one of the next door neighbors?" Bailey asked rather firm wanting confirmation of which house to approach next, scanning the neighborhood homes.

"We'll be giving more details later, at the press report," Billy stated and sped up again. "I don't really have much more at this time." Imparting a smart glance, nodding his head to inform her that's it. Reaching out to cover her mike with his left hand and bluffing the cameraman to stop filming. "Even if you slept with me this afternoon Patty, you wouldn't get zilch. It's all I have." Anderson declared with enthusiasm, but there just wasn't anything else. He thought again how tough this murder could be to unravel.

Patty was taken nicely by surprise with Anderson's off camera remark, blushed and flashed the cop a passing grin. Having interviewed Billy a few times before she still didn't know him well enough to flirt at ease. With soaring confidence now, she grabbed the Captain's arm, to keep him from getting away and asked, "in your professional opinion Captain Anderson, would you label this as a revenge killing?" Looking straight into the policeman's face and raising one well manicured eyebrow as the cameraman zoomed in close on her. Then panning to a close-up of Anderson's face. Waiting for his response.

Billy squinted his eyes and pressed his lips to one side, looking intense at the redhead's sexy features and responded, "it sure as hell looks like revenge to me, Ms. Bailey." Anderson was hoping for something more personal from the reporter. Wondering what a stupid question she just asked.

Patricia thought for a moment and welcomed the honest answer. Pretty cool, she thought. But missed the obvious fact by a mile. What other motive could there be? She kept her watch glued to Anderson, likewise her cameraman, as Billy walked slow to the Crosby driveway waiting for him to turn and look back. He did, giving away a quick, sexy wink. Patricia liked it. "I can work with that," she whispered.

...

Detective Davis moved his way toward the three way intersection, deciding to touch base with Regina and see what new discoveries, if any, she made. Captain Anderson saved him from the hungry reporters. One part of his job he didn't do well. Davis was of the type that didn't give away hard earned info too easy. His comments amounting to, "it's way too early to tell at this time." At present, he couldn't help but feel this case had already become arctic and was barely three hours old.

Chris didn't like interrupting his partner in the middle of her second going over with Mrs. Patterson. But he seemed at a loss for what to do next. No immediate witnesses to question. Not a single family member at the Crosby house. Not even a pet. No need to reexamine the murder scenes. Currently, the shooter's assumed location was being inspected for a second time. Zero, as usual turned up.

Walking across Arlington Street, he made eye contact with Mrs. Patterson.

"Hello again Captain Davis," Beatrice hailed, back to his incorrect rank. "How are things shaping up at the Crosby house?"

"I think it's getting squared away," Davis said. "The body will be taken to the morgue soon." Looking over his shoulder, one hand shading bright sunlight, checking if the ambulance had arrived.

"I've completed my follow-up here," Regina told Chris. "Who's next? The Crosby family? Mrs. Crosby will likely be a force. Don't you think?" asking her partner.

"To say the least. I recall a few news clips from the Mountain Murder," Chris declared. "She was brutal on that prosecutor if I remember right. Knew how to manipulate the press too." Then added, "maybe I'll give her to you?"

Regina laughed. "After talking to Beatrice, I can't wait to meet Sarah Crosby's parents too," telling Davis as a northern gust blew a cluster of leaves around all three. A stark reminder how cold it became in no time.

Much of the Crosby house commotion began diminishing. Emergency lights were dimming by now, except for a City of Tracy fire engine with lights still flashing appeared odd and out of place. Several police cars had departed. Press vehicles were being loaded with reporters having finished what little there was to a slim storyline. Outside of a grizzly neck wound, which will get plenty of play, not too much remained to hype. The fact of Marcus Crosby being the victim, accused and found innocent in his wife's murder, would generate most news copy over the next few days.

"Man oh man, we don't have much to go on partner, do we," asking Regina but not expecting a comment. Chris recognized this killer was very thorough, leaving nothing behind. "I hope the license plate will turn up something," Davis added. "Before heading back downtown, let's knock on a few doors in the neighborhood. Maybe, by some remote chance, somebody saw or heard something."

Looking to Beatrice, he asked what houses might be occupied. Mrs. Patterson confirmed several immediate neighbors and pointed out those homes. "The older folks will be available, I'm sure. What info you'll get, who knows?" Beatrice stated.

"Beatrice, thanks for your time. I get the impression I've discovered some clues to work on," Regina said, standing to give her new friend a short hug. "I may be back in a few days to talk again if that's all right?" she asked tucking away her notebook.

"Anytime you want, just drop by. My door's always open," the gray haired lady responded with a smirk. "Brrr, it's cold," she whimpered, serving a short goodbye to each officer before making her way home. Twirling the object in her pocket again and thinking to herself, "I'm glad I decided to keep this."

Regina looked at her partner. Shrugged. "Seems like an interesting case, I fear," addressing Chris in her sarcastic nature.

"It's too early to tell at this time. Another day in Tracy, another murder," Davis responded with a nod and a glance around Arlington Street. "You take the houses on the right and I'll ask the folks on the left."

"Sounds good." she agreed.

An interesting case to say the least. For both officers. A life changing event? Maybe? The scene was progressing fast around the neighborhood once again. In Crosby's driveway procedures were finally getting quiet. Yellow tape held lingering onlookers at bay. Two investigators managed access inside Marcus' home and appeared to enjoy themselves rummaging through the dead man's files and personal belongings. One female investigator launched his computer, searching Outlook for recent emails and various contacts, knowing she was stretching things, legally. Not much was discovered here either. No emails found in the 'trash bin' screaming, "you'll be dead by sunrise Marcus Crosby!" Signed so and so. The usual junk mail and a few notes to his office staff.

Searching deeper however, one techy investigator located a folder containing a number of racy notes to a lady in Modesto. Her email was noted and the department would be contacting her soon. One more lead at least.

Outside, a handful of curious diehards socialized and exchanged hunches over who murdered their neighbor. Other groups, already bored to tears, began informing one another of the most mundane parts of their lives, leading to even greater tedium. On Anaheim Drive this murder was old news by ten o'clock. Some folks became reacquainted with people they lived next to for years, with whom they rarely associated? First and last names had to be recited. Being California, many people living in the commuter driven subdivisions don't know families living next door, except to wave hello when leaving for work each day. So much precious time spent driving to and from well paying jobs in San Jose, parts of Silicon Valley or Walnut Creek. Marcus preferred to be left alone. No wonder a majority of adjacent households were clueless to his routine of battering Sarah. Two neighbors living a few houses down Anaheim Drive hadn't heard of Marcus Crosby and his well publicized Mountain Murder.

Mrs. Patterson was the exception however. She managed to keep in touch with all of her immediate neighbors. Almost to a fault, making a nuisance of herself at times. Not with gossipy gibberish, as she never said a word about Marcus abusing his wife. Beatrice was raised with a noble intention of assisting and watching out for those who lived nearby, hoping others would be willing to reciprocate. A concept all but lost in our modern housing tracts of which Tracy had quickly subdivided into. More time spent at work, driving to work, daycare centers, grotesque fast food dining, internet loneliness, all adding up to less time relating with people living just beyond the proverbial six foot redwood fence. If only, Beatrice continued to second guess her inaction. If only, she had taken one additional step and rallied to Sarah's aid. Maybe her dear friend would still be here, sitting together under a fall sun, sharing small talk. If only, like mother and daughter.

Bright sunshine obliquely illuminated the cold, late morning crime setting. Extended shadows ran across concrete driveways and trimmed grass lawns. Steady winds eclipsed the intense sunshine of its warmth and comfort. Small gray songbirds among shrubs and backyard feeders sang aloud to each other, like location rally cries. Their movements progressively slowed however, conserving fuel to generate heat their tiny bodies would need for a cold night ahead. Fires were lit in living rooms to stave off falling temperatures as well as an all new, too close to home violence, amongst them. Light gray smoke scattered from chimney tops by zealous winds, filling neighborhood senses with a pungent smell of burnt oak and cedar. Reminiscent of burning incense on Sunday morning church service. But indeed, no religious depiction could be attached to this horrible undertaking. Cruelty and revenge doesn't exist within the divinity. It exists on earth in men and women.

Three hundred yards east, riding the wind south, a low formation of Canada geese dashed over the neighborhood. A thin line of birds waved up and down ever so slight as each stroke of their forceful wings pulled them upward, then pushed them along. Bright white bibs under each chin shined against black neck feathers. Their honking calls went unnoticed by everyone on Anaheim Drive. Flying out to feeding and resting grounds which might hold bloodshed and some say brutality, which coexists in men and women.

■■■

Davis and Gonzalez scarcely spoke to one another during their ride 'downtown'. Both cops admitted to being unusually tired. More important, they needed time to pore through and analyze the whole gruesome murder, then attempt to piece together what little evidence they had to begin a logical pursuit. A jumble of obscure details ran through Regina's mind, which interfered with her failed concentration. Although she'd witnessed multiple bloody murder scenes, it was clear the wretched neck wound and blood soaked body lying in the driveway, spoiled her focus, paging inattentive through her notebook, rereading notes and adding new ones. Sometimes the brain and senses demand time, dealing with and sorting through emotional prerequisites after being intimate with an horrific event. Post reaction. Gonzalez leaned back into a warm seat fixing her elbow on the door's armrest and laying her head back attempting to clear her mind. Sunlight draped on her shoulders imparting warm comfort, almost forced to relax her heightened nerves. She fell into a blank stare permitting images beyond her window to roll past. Similar to the way one often views a music video. Strange enough, Regina's thoughts settled on Mrs. Patterson and the way she referred to Sarah as her daughter. She reflected on her mother, being childless and for some unknown reason, even to herself, Regina began to cry. Turning her head to face away from Chris she fought to regain self control, all the while someplace deep inside, a heavy sadness overwhelmed. Large tear drops formed under dark brown eyes then dribbled the length of her reddened cheeks. Biting knuckles and covering her mouth did little to stem the emotional surge. Thoughts of mother, father, brother and the senseless violence lying in a concrete driveway, captured her. Able to hold back the tender sobs at first, then forced to cover her grieving face with both hands, beginning a gloomy weep. Her hands trembled and Regina's chest heaved as painful memories became part of an uncontrolled release. Venting an equal mix of personal pain, and the normal anxieties associated with vicious murder.

Chris heard her first whimpers and steered right, entering a small commercial lot, killing the engine. Davis felt uneasy, almost embarrassed to be there. He thought about leaving the car so Regina could be alone, but waited silent for a moment, then gently slid next to his partner. Wrapping arms around her, saying nothing, holding on. Regina wrapped one arm around Chris' neck and cried intense, leaving small wet spots on his jacket shoulder. Her outbreak caused Davis to tear up also. His tears however, were more of pure pleasure.

Granting him a delightful reaction, being able to console his partner. Similar to comforting his absent daughter or even his ex wife, on occasion.

They were a team and these personal episodes anchored their trust even deeper. Regina had behaved this way twice before and Chris knew it would pass soon. No words would be exchanged. No offers of appreciation would be spoken. Nothing expected. Knowing someday he would probably need his partner's kindness too. Regina left the car needing a few minutes alone, breathing in cold fresh air and soon became well, as though nothing happened. In no time resuming their way 'downtown'.

Station 3009

Station 3009, a neutral stucco and glass building in central Tracy resembled commercial office space. An ordinary bland sign, City of Tracy Police, mounted below the front façade was overlooked by most people driving Tracy Boulevard. Chris and Regina made their way inside and up to the second floor Investigation Offices. They shared a sizeable cubicle having little more than a desk and computer for each detective. Typical, gray toned fabric partitions holding plastic windows, separated individuals from all the other fabric walled cubicles. Allowing minimal natural light and privacy, permitted the most subtle conversation to be shared loud and clear inside a bordering office. It's been done this way in rural areas for some time, lacking resources to provide more space and an upscale atmosphere. Becoming commonplace in larger cities too, for that matter. Police budgets in economic downturns don't allow for much comfort.

Reports would be submitted to Captain Anderson, used to arrange his brief to Chief Yung. Going out on a limb, Chris Davis would propose a personnel request. They, Gonzalez and himself, needed help. One part time detective as well as one uniformed officer to assist.

"Hey partner, who would you recommend as assistant investigator?" Davis asked. Then added, "and don't say Chavez, you know she's booked with the Jackson drive by case." Anna Chavez was a relatively new detective. Express promotions lifted her from uniformed duty bearing all the smarts of an experienced investigator. Gonzalez and Chavez hit it off great, working well together when given the chance. Both detectives being Hispanic didn't hurt, making for a good working relationship. Two minority girls forcing their way into Tracy's male dominated police force. However, nowhere near as comfortable working with Davis. Regina's latest poignant episode on the drive over, was proof enough.

"That sucks. Shoot. I already had Anna up and throwing, in the bullpen," Gonzalez said, a little glum. "You know who that leaves. Buck! He's the only one left," sounding concerned. "Both Moss and Devine are buried working their own cases and Pennington's on maternity leave," informing her partner.

"Oh, right. What did Pennington have anyway?" Davis asked in a crude way.

"Gees Chris, how considerate," sounding perturbed about the question. "I hope she's about to have her baby, any day now," Gonzalez delivered a strong accent on baby. "But hell, who knows, maybe she'll push out a litter of black labs instead."

"Don't go racial with me Gonzalez. You know what happens when people start up with that black shit," smiling and kinda proud with his comeback. "Sorry Gonzo, but you chicks are too sensitive," Chris spoke with sarcastic emphasis on chicks still not sounding apologetic. "I'd love to have Pennington assist. She's hot," covering his mouth like a school kid. Fearing the other cubicles heard his comment.

"Mmmm Guapasima!" Regina responded with a sexy tang and shook her head releasing the proverbial sigh.

"What's that?

"Never mind. How about Kennedy for the uniform? He helped us out today. Seems like a nice guy and wow, is he hot. Guapasimo!" Needling Davis, knowing he didn't understand a single word of Spanish.

"That's cute. I'll go with Kennedy," Davis agreed. "I keep forgetting his first name. He made me feel like an idiot today for botching his name. I owe him one," he said. "What's up with the Guasipo thing?" Chris asked, failing miserably to pronounce it right.

"Forget it. We have Buck and Kennedy in the bullpen," teasing her partner and smiling. Knowing Chris wasn't a fan of her baseball lingo. "Let's find out what Captain Anderson thinks of our Triple-A lineup."

"Baseball. Always the damn baseball," showing fake annoyance with Regina's continuing attention to favorite sport metaphors. He thought about her crying outburst, earlier in the car, hoping it was just a passing release. Davis would need Regina to be in control during this investigation, with a gut feeling this would be a grueling case for both detectives.

A minute later, Captain Anderson appeared in their cubicle, jerking Davis out of his deliberation. "Okay you two, if you're ready, let's meet in my office in about five minutes," Anderson announced to his team. They both understood, "if you're ready," meant now. Billy Anderson turned and hustled back to his lair. A closed door with glass partitions separated the Captain from his homicide staff. Regina and Chris climbed from their chairs, moving down a narrow hall between cubicles in route to the Captain's meeting. Regina made a hard right before reaching Billy's office, telling Davis she'd return in five minutes. "I need to use the bathroom," excusing herself.

"Yeah, right." Chris knew very well where Gonzo was going.

Gang of Four

Taking a left turn just before Tracy's Chief of Police, Regina sprinted toward the bathrooms but quickly detoured once again after spotting three compadres gathered in their meeting area. Seeing a grin on Maria's face, she hustled into the employee kitchen giving her usual giggle and, "what's up ladies?"

The Gang of Four assembled early mornings or lunch hours trading social minutes concerning personal as well as office gossip. Much of their time was occupied with who they were dating or whom they'd like to be sleeping with. Three singles and one married, for her second time. Denise, being the only gang member married at present, went to great lengths convincing the gang of her happiness. She worked hard on a regular basis, convincing herself of contented wedding bliss.

Regina wouldn't miss these treasured meetings for too long. Savoring to hear each new exploit and conquest, not believing how some members revealed their gory details. The more risqué the better the details! Gonzalez was no prude by any stretch, but as a gang member she came across, hands down, as most conservative. Relationship speaking.

"Gonzo, que pasa," Maria shouted her greeting over today's third diet coke. "We missed you sweetheart. Where the fricken hell you been?" The Foursome was made up of Pam, Maria, Denise and Regina. Meeting at least twice a month for the better part of three years. Growing to a five-some when the group accepted a young man named Jack, who lived openly gay and very proud of it. Jack was forced to move back east earlier this year, somewhere in upstate New York, when his lover accepted a job promotion. They hated to see him go, being by far, the most graphic in his tales. All four loved him too. For now at least, it remained the original four. Most meetings had been held in the office kitchen but as of late, more conferences were arranged for lunch or after work, usually to a nearby pub. Like most offices the very best gossip was garnered by a heads up clerical staff. They always seemed to be first in hearing those hidden, juicy bits and pieces that go around and under the typical office cubicle environment.

Denise loved kicking off their discussions bragging about her husband, Arthur. Painting a picture of wedded harmony, using a wide bristle brush, based in total on Arthur's devotion to cooking dinner for the family. Her first five minutes today was used on Arthur's willingness to help around the house. Boiled down, Arthur's help amounted to grilling hot dogs or brats. Denise admired his culinary skills as her husband had mastered, "grilling links and toasting buns at the same time! What talent," she implied. Unable to reign in her blind admiration. Gang members chalked it up to love and a straightforward menu, never questioning Denise's reverence.

If Arthur could just maintain a regular job. "What a catch he might be," Regina often joked to Maria.

"I'd give anything, almost anything, to find a guy who would cook for me. Just once," Maria admitted. "It's kind of a, you know, a bit of a turn on having a guy cook for me," starting to sound aroused. "Something good though. A real dinner, you know. One that takes some time to prep and then present it well," speaking the words with a comical, dream world look, working perfect with her delightfully thin accent. Maria was on the short side and just plain overweight. Fat! She dated on occasion but always kept a lookout for stray males. Even those needing a clean up, so to speak, were fine by her. The Gang of Four as well as the entire office staff, loved Maria. She wasn't shy by any stretch, and her blunt comments came gushing forth at the oddest moment, embarrassing at times but most often innocent. "Even an ugly guy could get me into bed pretty easy after a nice dinner, if you know what I mean?" speaking with a wistful pause, as gaudy laughter broke out. She smirked at each woman sitting around the table, guzzling a long chug of diet coke.

"I know of what you speak Maria. Many a night after dinner and I can't help myself. I'm all over Arthur," Denise, a rather tall, thin black woman, bragged in her typical matter of fact tone. Regina and Pam made quick eye contact, just managing to stifle laughs.

"You hang in there girl, you'll find him," Pam cajoled. "Extra time at the Happy Hours can be a good place to troll," Pam told Maria, locking onto her gaze, refusing to let go. "Remember, wear your hair just right, make sure the jeans go on tight and the boys'll be around all night."

"Jesus Christ where did you come up with that," Denise chimed in. "Don't encourage her to hang out in one of your dens," flashing Pam a quick half smile letting know she was just partly serious.

Pam was earning the role as 'our sexually permissive gal in the office', and the remaining members became captivated by it all. Nowhere near a fully fledged slut, but with a few more swings on her experimenting path, a full transition might be possible. She liked her men, that's for sure! In return, they stayed attracted to her auburn hair and tanned complexion. Combining good looks with her careless character, how could any boy resist? Most didn't! "I met a cute guy last night matter of fact," Pam announced proud. "I'm hoping to hook up with him tonight after work."

"Pam, that's the second one this week," Regina blurted out. "You gotta hold something back?"

"Oh I'm holding things, you can bank that," the loose gal replied in her distinctive provocative voice triggering another round of lewd laughs. She went on to reveal a few gory details from her latest encounters. Good stuff here, Regina and Maria thought to themselves. With a little sex in the car, the ladies room and finally in front of her two cats on the dining room floor. All in a couple hours on a work night! Efficiency.

"That's so romantic," Maria laughed out, which made Regina and Denise crack up too.

"What?" is all Pam could say.

"I gotta get out of here and back to Anderson's office," Regina said, still chuckling, leaving the impromptu gathering. "Pam, let me know how he works out tonight. Details."

"Oh, I will," she shot back. "Or, I do. Right Denise," Pam said mocking the only married women.

"What about you Gonzo," Maria asked awkwardly. "Hot date this weekend?"

"Nothing on the horizon. Some guy cooking me a mediocre dinner tonight sounds great," with obvious disappointment in her current love life, disappearing down the hall to Anderson's office. The Gang's humor did wonders for her right now.

•••

"Sorry. I got hung up," conveying a smart ass smirk at Chris, hurrying into a vacant seat, front and center of Anderson's desk.

"How's the Gang?" Anderson inquired, peeking above his reading glasses after lowering a fistful of paper. Titled: Preliminary Report. In bold print on the cover. Subtitled: Marcus Crosby Murder. "Wasn't that Maria I heard laughing, pretty loud, just a minute ago? Any gossip to report?"

"I have nothing to say," Regina told the detectives. Chris could care less if she had any slimy news or not. Couldn't be less interested.

"Hey, if your little group of smut peddlers hears anything on that Channel Forty reporter, Patty Bailey, let me know, will ya?" Anderson asked, trying his best to appear flippant. Failing stupid, wanting to hide his red face after blurting out that announcement. Instead, whirling in his chair, opening a cabinet drawer behind him, pretending some sort of file search.

Anderson's comment had Chris sitting up to take notice. Regina glimpsed her partner. They both shrugged to one another in mild surprise over the remark their boss just tossed out. Way out of character for Billy Anderson who's normally reserved, to say the least, about his personal life.

"Uhm, well we don't always, you know, dig up stuff on," Regina stammered then asked direct, "we're talking about that reporter on site today?" wishing she'd just said okay. Davis glared at Gonzalez, fake smiling and shaking his head back and forth in disbelief. All the while hoping she would drop it. Now!

"Yeah. That's her. Patricia Bailey," Billy answered much less embarrassed.

"Well sure, Captain. If I hear something, you'll be the first to know," Gonzalez replied, in obvious discomfort.

"So, Captain. About the murder today," Chris interrupted, to get things moving along. "First, we have requests for assistant help." Running fast through a short two man lineup to see how Billy would respond.

"Sounds fine to me," Anderson agreed with modification in his tone. "Your new assistants will be on part-time duty at best. I can't budget another uniform to work as a personal chauffer. You can have Kennedy and Buck for twenty hours per week, max." Then added fast, "you may get those hours cut back too, depending how long this case lasts before we find this damned shooter."

"That's okay with you partner," Chris expected a simple yes.

"If there's no budget, it has to be enough," Regina said. "I have no social life anyway. I'm available to work late. Pick up some slack." Looking at her partner expecting an offer of extra time as well.

"Kind of a spot starter, huh?" Davis stated looking at his disappointed partner, using his own baseball metaphor for a change .

"Oh, good one Chris. You don't even know what spot starter means," Regina shot back with her toothy grin and trademark dimple, displayed deep in her right cheek.

Upon hearing the combative words, Anderson leaned back, deep into his high back chair, raised both hands nestling the back of his head into locked palms. Billy often chose to observe while his detectives launched their verbal assaults on one another. Some exchanges proved quite amusing. Especially when the race cards were played. It never failed to amaze Anderson how many slurs and off color jabs Regina would cut loose on Chris. Davis seemed to enjoy, in a strange way, the put downs she heaved his way. Often laughing out loud at her racial stereotypes knowing she didn't mean it. Captain Anderson wondered however, if Chris would allow a white guy to get away with the same comments. He didn't think so. Not about to test his theory, sitting back, observing while the war raged on.

For now, it was about baseball and Captain Anderson knew from experience the exchange would be brief. Davis had no real attachments to the diamond or any other sports for that matter. Seeming odd he would breach the subject. Perhaps the murder or a building strain lay ahead. This case, not quite a day old, could already be testing both detectives. Captain Anderson observed in silence. To all three seasoned cops, weird crimes and brutality were the events homicide detectives signed on for. Paid well to deal with appalling horrors becoming far too routine among the immediate Central Valley culture. Marcus Crosby's head being blown off shouted foul and bizarre to say the least.

Billy still had tools in his workbox. More than anything else, Captain

Anderson understood his detectives and knew how well they worked together. He even presumed they loved one another. Not in a carnal way however, but closer to a brother-sister relationship. Complete confidence and committed to receive the very best from each other.

"A's suck, Gonzalez," Davis teased. His way of hoisting a white flag, concluding the skirmish ended.

"Thanks Chris," Regina said a bit annoyed, declaring a ceasefire. "When will DMV have our license plate ID's completed?" Regina asked Anderson.

"I take it you two have finished sparing," Anderson stated with a mock look of boredom. The list, he hoped, would be on his desk by tomorrow. "I want us all to review the roll of names together," expecting a long but useless roster. With only three numbers to go on, most registration names would be made up of old men and women, high school or college students and innocent folks with ironclad alibis. Over half would end up further than a hundred miles from the murder scene.

"If we get five solid suspects from DMV, I'll be happy," said Captain Anderson, coming across uneasy, lowering his voice. He contemplated what might happen if nothing firm develops. "What the hell happens then," thinking to himself. "I'll have zip to go on. This killer left nothing to draw on. Jesus, I hope that old woman got the plate numbers right."

"I would expect to get at least five suspects Captain. What do you think partner?" Regina asked, looking at Davis for some encouragement.

"I don't know," Chris exhaled in low expectations." Three numbers on a plate, out of order maybe. That can be a lot of cars partner and even more potential suspects per vehicle. All useless, except for one of course," he stated with irony. "We have to hit a lottery!" Three overwhelmed cops understood at this time it will take a few days sorting through the obviously innocent. "Over a hundred background checks to run!"

"That wasn't your upbeat response I longed for Chris," Regina replied.

"Look, this was an obvious execution. Agreed?" Chris stated.

"Agreed."

"Had to be retaliation for killing his wife, it would seem," Davis spoke emphasizing the word seem with a dry grin. "Or, a retaliation hit for a drug deal gone bad? Lousy business dealings? Maybe we have a possible serial killer just surfacing and shooting people at random with a high powered rifle." Davis sounded as though he was thinking out loud again. No one bought into a possible serial killer. "Serials tend to kill their victims up close and personal. They don't stand way off and shoot people. Their whole crime is about getting in close, able to touch their victims," Davis said. "As far as I know Captain, the department isn't investigating any possible serial murders, are they?"

"None that I know," Anderson said then mulled over serial murders in recollection. "I heard Stockton has some nut killing prostitutes again. But he employs a knife, to finish his deeds."

"Lovely," Regina mumbled.

Anderson thought about schedule and case load, scribbled a few notes into his notebook then directed both detectives to clear their dockets of old and cold cases. "Get 'em off your desks any way you can. If needed, we'll send them over to second division," instructing them both. "I want you two concentrated on this case. There's going to be way too much press coverage for our budget cutbacks to handle," he said with a sigh. But occurring to Billy, a good thing could result. It might bring Miss Bailey into town more often! "I'll be a full time press officer for a week at least," Billy mumbled to himself. Thinking how uneasy he became speaking to large groups on camera. Hating their way of pouncing on any erroneous statements. "So, the more tied up I get the more you should be free to investigate. How's that sound?"

"Sounds reasonable Captain," Gonzalez responded with Chris nodding affirmative.

Interrupted by a powerful gust of wind which shook a large plate glass window to the Captain's right. Creaking in its frame, compelling all three to notice the vibrating pane.

"It's howling out there," Davis commented, staring outside as leaves and branches scattered across deep green lawns surrounding police headquarters.

Regina noticed heavy tree limbs swaying back and forth at the mercy of blustery air streams. Leaves disappeared from sycamore and oak trees aligned in a row, like a natural picket fence protecting the building front, flooding Tracy's sidewalks and streets below with ghost like shadows.

•••

Late afternoon sunshine diminished as the first day of a small city murder came to conclusion. Air temperatures would drop noticeably after dark, feeling as though an early winter was squeezing away the Central Valley's last remaining heat. Developing tule fog would grow dense on each cold morning permitting thick blankets of low clouds to smother valley farms, orchards, wildlife areas and towns even deeper as the year moved further into winter. Located too far east from the Pacific's influences, California's interior valley registered a less stable climate compared to Bay Area cities. Coastal regions would enjoy some of their clearest weather during late fall and winter, with seasonal temperature ranges of the immediate San Francisco Bay cities, being much less erratic. Valley towns resembled dessert climates with extremely hot summers and cold, foggy winters. As dry high pressure systems invaded late in winter, the valley becomes cold and colder. Only when pacific rainstorms finally sweep through, does valley fog decrease allowing temperatures to rise. Farming activity comes to a standstill, to the casual viewer, almost as still as the air masses which control the great valley's weather. Surrounding Tracy, immense orchard groves of almonds, walnuts and pistachios lay dormant, having shed their crop in the previous weeks. Determined leaves lingered on in acre after acre of organized trees, all in aligned rows. To untrained eyes, an unknown crop somehow cultivated from the sleeping limbs. Similar to the empty clues surrounding Marcus Crosby's murder. A mangled body, an older lady's relationship with another murder victim and at best, a questionable series of numbers, was everything exposed so far. What clues would possibly blossom from these dormant branches? Offering little to nurture, nor much to grow.

Regina and Chris couldn't help but suffer the cold air and recoiled upon exit from police headquarters, making brief, courteous small talk. Chris offered to buy a drink.

She considered the invite, wanting to say yes. But declined. "I have some things to do at home." Telling Davis to have one on her but don't stay too late, "we have to be sharp tomorrow." She knew Chris' drinking was far too regular the last year or more. He seemed lost away from work and she wondered if a stable woman might help his social life right now.

Chris was being polite when he offered to buy his partner a round. Hoping and fully expecting Regina to decline. Davis anticipated a heated meeting tonight with his recent flame, Doris, from a local hangout. "Gonzo could really use a nice guy in her life," he thought to himself, sensing Regina had been living alone for too long and wondered if a hot romance might do her good? "Don't worry about me. I'll be ready tomorrow, and rested." Chris' inside humor defined what 'rested' meant to him. "See ya."

Saying goodnight and walking away to their after work lives of minor loneliness and modest boredom. Marcus Crosby's murder would remove some boredom but loneliness always proves harder to drag away. Complete darkness now but north winds continued to blow.

Mrs. Crosby

It's unusual seeing a Lexus Hybrid screech to a fast stop in front of Tracy Police headquarters. Two uniformed officers stopped cold as an anxious driver barely killed the ignition before exiting. The driver's side door didn't quite close all the way behind her. Abigail Crosby never looked back to check and stormed around the front of her Japanese import.

"Hey lady," the nearest patrolman shouted out, perturbed. "Your car door is open and you can't park there."

"Watch me you little prick," Abbey snorted aloud continuing toward the station stairway.

"Miss. You can't park there," Frank Kilbey yelled out, launching an intersecting angle toward Abbey with his overweight frame, walking quick to intercept the older lady. "You cannot park there and you're acting very rude also." He met Mrs. Crosby just as she reached the foot of the second step.

"Mame please, hold it a minute," Kilbey pleaded, forced to keep pace with Abbey as a wide grin developed on his face, somewhat amused now with the situation. A lady of her age was acting extremely bold to say the least. Frank reached out with his right hand attempting a gentle grasp of her lower arm. "Look lady," was all the officer got out. They reached the middle landing of a concrete staircase and Abigail pivoted to her left, bringing her face to face with trouble, as the officer's hand slipped from her suede jacket. Kilbey was taken by complete surprise as the senior lady swung both arms up, shoving the cop away with each hand pressed to his bulky chest. He had no choice but to give ground retreating one step back then heard fresh footsteps coming from behind. Kilbey sensed his momentum wouldn't allow a step down and away from her unexpected push. Shuffling his left foot back a half step or so, but beginning to lose balance, hoping a metal handrail would catch his fall to keep him upright.

"Touch me again and my lawyer will end your miserable career tomorrow," Abbey scolded, leaning toward the retreating patrolman. Catching Frank further off guard demanding one final step in reverse. This time his heel wedged firm against a raised curb edging the concrete staircase, shifting balance yet again, assuming the handrail should've caught him by now. Regrettable for the overweight officer, his saving handrail had a short gap at its drop point in the landing. Precisely where his heel had stopped, now fixed, due to his out of control weight shift. As gravity triumphed, Kilbey decided on reaching behind his back, taking a shot at catching the damn rail which still hadn't arrived. Stretching his left hand out toward Abigail to prevent her from walking away and preventing himself from falling off the staircase. His sight never strayed from the woman, which was a big mistake, prohibiting his balance from equalizing.

Mrs. Crosby slapped the cop's hand up and away with her left forearm. Kilby leaned further back as the handrail still wasn't acquired. Both arms outstretched and at this point flailing in circular twirls. A well dressed woman climbing the stairs with loud footsteps, oblivious to all the commotion going on above, finally looked up to see a man twisted above the stairs. She screamed, watching Kilby about to go over. A short streak of embarrassment ran through the officer, leaning even more.

"Leave me alone," Abbey reported over her shoulder continuing her interrupted climb up the next flight of stairs. Frank struggled to adjust his foot lodged against the raised impediment and realized at this moment, if he didn't abandon his stare on the older gal and shift his weight to free his heal, nothing would stop him from toppling over the staircase. Impossible to lift his foot, weight shifting beyond his center of gravity, arms whirling out of control, Kilby's only choice was to turn his face and body into the momentum, hoping his arms or hands might catch his fall. Odd, but this entire accident happened in a frame of ten to fifteen seconds. He was going to fall. The well dressed lady screamed again but never tried reaching out to offer help. Frozen with hands covering her face!

Kilby, fully twisted, lost his stare on Abigail hearing another officer yell out, "watch it Frank!"

But poor Frank was just too far gone. One hand glanced off the extreme end of the lower handrail section, "finally made contact," thinking to himself. The left foot rose upward as he bent over the raised curb. One remaining move was to lay his extended belly face down, upon the curb. A leg on each side looking like a uniformed fool, dry humping the concrete retaining wall! Interesting sight to say the least.

Raising his red face to peek back over his shoulder toward Abbey, yelling out, "get back here lady!" Just as Abigail Crosby vanished through a pair of glass doors, held open by a fellow patrolman, of course!

Chief Yung

Once inside it appeared as though the Booking Sergeant would be Abigail's next victim. But lingering at the wooden counter enjoying his morning Italian Roast stood Tracy's Chief of Police, Alex Yung, admiring his staff of patrolmen. Schmoozing with some of the officers prior to their morning briefings and departing for morning shifts. Alex knew any one of these uniforms, due to unfortunate chances, may not return this evening. Their daily risk. Yung envied routine field work of everyday patrolmen, realizing he was in his glory working a daily beat. Buzzing town in his patrol car, viewing himself as the ultimate good guy cop stopping criminals from taking control of his hometown. Now, the Chief's time was all politics, begging for money to keep his department staffed and equipped. Alex did a good job, the best he could, even though his heart was no longer as dedicated. It boiled down to a higher pay grade and counting the years to a cushy retirement. Promotions can suck sometimes, he told himself. One thing Alex Yung never lost was his connection to the uniformed officers and his detectives. Respect for the staff never waned.

As Abbey strolled through the glass doors, Yung was facing away from the entrance and she failed to recognize the Chief at first.

"Sergeant," Mrs. Crosby said in her demanding tone scanning his nameplate, "Forester." The display on her face made a rather large man behind the high counter snap to attention.

"Yes mame, how can I help you?" Forester offered beginning to clear away old paperwork cluttering his counter.

"I need to see Chief Yung and I need to see him now," staring into the flinching eye of the robust, booking cop. Seeing him thrown off balance by her sudden attack and fully prepared to go for the throat should he offer resistance. Forester belonged to Abbey now.

"Uh, well the Chief's right over," halting the thought to regain his own momentum. Fearing Chief Yung might see him acting like a rookie cop, fresh from Academy Training, being pushed around by an old lady. "Did you have an appointment to see the Chief?" Forester asked.

Interrupting their exchange at the counter came a loud greeting bellowed by her desire. "Well, well. If it isn't my old girlfriend." Yung chuckled, catching the attention of just about everyone in the entire staging area. Low tone murmurs were the only sounds heard now. The usual shuffle had come to a screeching stop with most cops savoring what might happen next.

"Under the circumstances, your remark is inappropriate right now." Abbey's bold comment even caught Yung off guard. Her son was gunned down, just yesterday morning, in his own driveway. She expected a degree of sympathy and consideration from Tracy's Chief. Beyond professional, they had known each other since high school.

"Sorry Abbey," Alex said with a gentle smirk setting his coffee on the counter. Everyone in the room went still, expecting to hear something exciting from one of the older combatants. "I've kinda been expecting," just as a loud yell of, "Chief," echoed from the doorway, combined with hurried commotion cutting Alex off in mid sentence.

Slipping and stumbling through double glass doors, officer Kilbey appeared and repeated, "Chief Yung. This woman," heavily emphasizing woman, "pushed me over the steps outside and left her car in the no parking zone out front." His chest heaving with moisture covering a pinkish red face, Frank stood, propped on the counter top by his left hand, facing his boss and breathing hard. After a two second pause he heard the room full of officers and civilian clerks break into a fit of laughter and snickers! Even Mrs. Crosby had to bite down hard on a red lower lip to contain her amusement. Kilbey's wet face turned from pink to bright red realizing how wimpy he appeared to a roomful of peers.

"Okay folks," Chief Yung yelled out trying to save the man's dignity by halting the laughs. "Let's get back to those jobs you're paid to do today," yelling above lingering giggles and gaffs. But his self-assured personality just couldn't resist a moment of spotlight, deciding to sacrifice officer Kilbey's pride. "Abigail Crosby, tell me you're not out beating up on my patrol staff." Alex maintained a straight look over his somewhat aging face. Rocking slow back and forth, one hand in his pants pocket and holding a retrieved coffee cup with his other hand. A subdued laugh resonated from the area again. "Tell me this fine officer has mistaken you for another," pausing for effect, "another typical, intimidating matriarch." Alex held a firm stare in place knowing he went an insult too far. Abigail appeared extremely upset at the moment. He could see she was either going to burst into tears or pounce on him, ripping both eyes from his sockets!

"Mr. Yung," Abigail announced, declaring in her way, the humiliating banter had concluded. Mrs. Crosby revived scenes from their laid-back high school days when Abbey ruled the roost like a resourceful feline. A maniacal judge, holding power, granting or depriving approval to other kids begging to be a member of her court. She was out of her courtroom now.

"Officer Kilbey," Yung addressed the fallen cop after draining what remained of his lukewarm coffee and tossed the empty cup into an overwhelmed trash can. "I think we can lend Mrs. Crosby some latitude as to her parking location, don't you?" Nothing but silence from an embarrassed police officer and yet another uneasy pause in the station room. The veteran cop played his cards to the fullest and nobody within earshot dared a word. "Do you intend pressing charges against Mrs. Crosby for her rough treatment?" Triggering his audience, hanging on every word now to choke off a few quiet laughs.

"I could let the officer move the car if it's that important, Alex," Abigail offered with all sincerity, reaching into her purse rummaging for keys.

Alex looked away shaking his head in mock ridicule. Abbey didn't notice. "We don't offer valet service in my station, Abbey." Speaking with a low voice, shifting attention to Mrs. Crosby for a response. Silence. "Your car will be fine for the time being."

Officer Kilbey shifted his focus from the Chief, looking straight away at Abigail for a few tense seconds. If looks could kill, Abbey would be hitting the floor soon. The policeman turned slow and away from Mrs. Crosby, deciding a hasty retreat to his patrol car would be sound strategy. Abbey never flinched nor acknowledged any truce, humiliating Frank Kilbey by the incident. Which Mrs. Crosby had a knack for doing to people at times.

"Abbey, why don't we withdraw to my office. We can talk in private." This time Alex came across with more sympathy and less attitude, thinking it might offer a chance to garner some additional information about the case. "Right this way," extending his arm to show the way.

Abby knew perfectly well she gave the impression of a contemptible diva, which in no way bothered her however. Always able to handle men in her life like young children and she wasn't about to change now. All her past victories merely encouraged the behavior. "I was hoping you would offer some confidential time to discuss this dreadful murder." No sooner had she finished her words, they walked down a long hallway away from the bustling booking room. Moving further from the noisy room, the pair said nothing as their heels rang loud in the building silence. Chief Yung felt an awkward quiet grow with each clanging step and couldn't reach his office door soon enough.

One last turn had Alex holding the door for Abigail, instructing a sleepy secretary to hold all calls. "No interruptions, short of an Al Qaida attack on police headquarters. Right this way Ms. Hernandez," he said with an ever so slight malicious smile, referring to Abbey's maiden name.

She looked at the Chief rolling eyes upward, recognizing the remark as none too innocent. "It's Mrs. Crosby to you, Alexander." Knowing he hated being addressed by his full, formal name, demanding Alex.

"So it is, Mrs. Crosby. How are you holding up Abigail? Considering all the trauma that's been chasing your family recently." Alex thought he should try being more compassionate at this time. Knowing he pressed the woman hard, for the river of water having passed under their bridges. "Please, sit and try to relax," in a courteous pause for the queen to be seated. Yung remembered their high school and college romance. Pledges made and promises broken. Dumped and dismantled a long time ago. The Chief still carried a tender heart. "What can I do for you, Abigail?"

"Cut the crap Alex, you and I both know who shot my Marcus," Abbey wished she wouldn't have used 'my Marcus.' It helped maintain an image of immaturity, pinned on her son his whole, short life.

"Well," Chief Yung said sliding into his padded leather chair, getting comfortable, never removing focused eyes away from the older woman. "Please enlighten me Abbey." Thinking how little Abbey had changed, going all the way back to high school, insistent on retaining command of every situation. But Alex knew her strongest suit was the way she commanded her own intelligence. Abigail was all too clever, with an innate ability to react, maneuver and out think the competition, on her feet. Rarely did she lose an argument, even if overmatched by proof. Her sheer will to win out would carry the day.

Alex thought how this dominance seemed to leave her during Marcus' murder trial last year. Too much latent grandstanding before the press. Too often resorting to name calling. Too many cruel comments. Becoming obvious, even she realized her son was probably guilty of killing his wife. She seized onto a concocted alibi that it had to be an intruder and held to it tight, like any mother would do for their only child. Unable to account for his history of abuse glossing over the seamy part of her son's habit, repeating over and over, "I never saw my boy lay a hand on his wife. Besides, Sarah had never mentioned any violence to me!" As if her daughter in law would ever confide in Abbey, concerning Marcus' behavior. Sarah learned, well before their marriage, very little happened inside the Crosby family without Abbey knowing. Asking Abbey for help would do as much good as Sarah's prayers did.

Mrs. Crosby's outbursts throughout the trial were acts of a desperate woman. Willing to save her son but striving even harder to rescue the family name. Alex believed the latter being her base motivation. "It must've worked, if only a little," he thought to himself. "Marcus was found not guilty." For some reason he knew what was coming next.

"Oh Christ Alex, c'mon! You know as well as I. It has to be Sarah's father," came Abigail's simple statement but with a slight whimper and glassy eyes. "He's always fooled around with those damn guns. Both Braden's are a couple of gun nuts and you know it. Shit, Franny Braden could be the shooter for that matter," standing, speaking out loud, mostly to herself, setting a back and forth pace, thinking what to say next. "She loves to shoot those guns. From what I hear Franny is damn good with a rifle. Wasn't my Marcus shot with a rifle?" Abigail was almost rambling by this time but Alex didn't make any moves to calm her. "Henry Braden has to be your number one suspect," she yelled with a cracked voice and heavy tears dripping from her nose. Chief Yung, becoming a bit uneasy at this point, didn't say a word. Abbey turned away from his desk, preferring to hide her emotions. Sensing her relentless control beginning to melt away.

Alex saw no need to respond. Of course, Henry Braden was an obvious suspect. Plenty of motive as a grief stricken father goes off, taking revenge into his hands and blowing away the man who, in all likely hood, murdered his daughter. Henry's motive was the most obvious, by far. "Hell," he thought to himself, "Franny Braden had to be a suspect too." Rumor had it, she could outshoot half of the Tracy police force! In his mind, Chief Yung conceived an image of Sarah's mother, Franny, pulling the trigger on Marcus Crosby in dead of night. A picture surfaced, in a sniper outfit complete with face paint, seemed all to bizarre even with his robust imagination. Holding his tongue allowing Abbey to squirm like a night crawler surrounded by hungry bluegills. Alex had bad feelings about this woman. Extremely jealous. Didn't trust her.

Abigail turned, moving to the center of his office. Coming to rest in a soft padded chair fronting Alex's desk, relaxing further into the chair and twisted her head away staring down at the floor, avoiding Alex's gaze. She needn't bother however, as the Chief avoided eye contact too. Unsure at the moment, thinking he might cave if he looked upon her now. Silence intensified the whole setting. Abbey propped her chin between thumb and index finger resting the full weight of her head on a bent elbow. Sustaining a blank stare to the right of Alex's desk. Stillness and the uncomfortable hush continued to flood the office a few more seconds.

"I've lost my whole family Alex," Abbey mumbled in low volume. "It just struck me," stopping her words, thinking, wanting to quit revealing her feelings. Abbey never disclosed real emotions to people, but for some reason now she kept talking. "I don't know what to do now. Another long drawn out trial. The second in two years." Raising her head to see Alex looking away, appearing neutral in his stare, but she continued. "I don't know if I'm up for another fight, having to face it alone this time." Abigail acted nothing like her familiar, I'm in command here character.

"Almost pathetic," Chief Yung said to himself. By this time, with any other grieving woman, Alex would be at the woman's side, hand in hand, comforting her distress. Pleading to stay strong and clear headed. Reassuring it was only a matter of time before the killer would be found and dragged into custody. Maybe holding her if necessary.

Not this time. Here was Abigail Crosby, the very one who captured Alex's younger days, possessed him hopeless and his love. Abbey didn't love him. Spurned him. Embarrassed him. Today he enjoyed her pain. Justice. Retribution. Revenge. These feelings never lasted long with Tracy's Police Chief, recognizing how foolish and unprofessional he acted, but never coming out from behind his desk. Not now. His wooden fortress separated them. Abigail couldn't hurt him now and it felt fuzzy, warm and safe, on his side.

"Well Abbey," breaking silence, removing a box of Kleenex from his desk's top left drawer, almost pitching them to Abbey's side of the desk. His rude act caused her to look at him firm with recognizable anger beaming from her face. She grabbed the box in a swipe, plucked two tissues and tossed the box back toward Chief Yung. Missing it's mark and tumbling on the floor as if to say, 'thanks for nothing jack-ass!' Mrs. Crosby dabbed the corners of her tear filled eyes, taking great care not to disturb the immaculate make-up on her cheeks.

For a very brief moment Alex had a profound desire to reach out to Abigail, but caught himself going weak, even though feeling somewhat sad. "It's not the eighties and Abbey doesn't deserve sympathy." Alex surprised himself how cold he'd become. Odd to say the least. Deciding now to switch the focus. "We've considered Henry and Franny Braden as possible suspects and plan on questioning them soon. But I'm not a hundred percent convinced either one of them could pull the trigger," Alex said, hesitating to see her reaction.

"What the hell does that mean? You and I saw the way they acted throughout the trial," Abbey stated.

Mrs. Crosby rose from her seat beginning a fleeting pace just beyond her chair. She broke into a litany of vague statements and quoted Henry Braden from the first days of the sensational trial. "Often being goaded along by that red-haired, Channel Forty newswoman."

"Taking revenge. Someone is going to pay. Justice will be served, I guarantee that much." Mrs. Crosby continued and realized just then, how she was portrayed on the nightly news also. Having plenty of air time tight in the faces of unsuspecting prosecutors as well as police. She kept talking, barely taking a breath, not allowing her old boyfriend a chance to throw that in her face. "You know as well as I, he killed Marcus," comprehending her strategy failed when Alex's interruption forced a stop and withdraw.

"I saw your mug on the damn TV more than anyone else, if I recall." Leaning into his high back leather chair with both hands behind his head, just dying to say, "don't tell me about using the press to get your two cents in, Mrs. Crosby." Chief Yung could only fantasize.

"Oh gimme' a break," was all Abbey mustered knowing she walked into one! Resuming cat like paces thinking what to say next.

Chief Yung could tell Abbey was planning strategy and he felt arrogant knowing how easy he grabbed her spotlight, fascinated by her movements. Like watching a movie, as the bad guy begins to squirm knowing his bold plans somehow went all wrong. Her own son murdered two days before and here she stood, in the police head quarters, trying to run the investigation. "Who the fuck do you think you are," thinking to himself, wanting to shout his words out loud.

She still didn't have a word to say. Working different ideas inside her head while pacing fast wasn't the way she reacted in her younger days. Even in college Abigail Crosby would've been bullying her attackers into submission. Maybe the fight inside was lacking in her mature years. Abbey, with all her family support dead and to be buried soon. Abbey would be on her own now.

"We talked to the neighbor lady," checking notes to get her name correct. "An older gal. Mrs. Patterson." Offering an olive branch as feelings of sympathy began to emerge, in a strange way. But no sooner had he softened, the wounded matriarch sprang from her lair, reared up and bit down hard on his offered hand.

"Oh Christ, Mrs. Patterson for heaven's sake. She's the nosiest damn woman I've ever had the misfortune to know. I hate her!" hissing the hate word with extra venom which even had Alex flinching.

"C'mon now Abbey," in a raised voice, Yung jumped from his padded chair.

She cut him off, "I assume you'll be sending out a few of your flunkies to make an arrest soon," knowing the statement sounded crude and rather desperate, but all she could muster. Mrs. Crosby realized this discussion wasn't going in her direction.

"Jesus!" Alex raised both arms then quickly dropped them in mock frustration. Turning away from Abigail.

"You know, before they try to flee or something?" Abbey pleaded.

"Holy shit Abbey. I don't have the authority to go out and handcuff the Braden's. Haul 'em back and toss them in a cell. Even you must realize that?" Alex responded, not expecting a reply but facing her direct nonetheless. She had no answer and turned herself around. Alex walked to the window in his office and peered outside. Chilly air had combined with dense valley fog outside. "Damn fog," speaking loud, then each returning silent for a minute. It seemed longer as both parties positioned themselves for additional verbal salvos.

"I have to talk to the D.A. and show some legitimate just cause before an arrest can be made. We still live in a civil country you know." Yung thought to himself how little "cause" he had at the moment to arrest anyone in this case. "It's way too early to talk of arrest Abbey."

"That D.A. is an idiot," Abbey bellowed while looking through the window herself. Raising a hand to her forehead, beginning to rub a palm across her brow. Her mind raced, admitting she was only reacting to every statement Alex made, disappointed how bad her performance was executed.

"Look, when we get our license plate matches, we'll begin to move faster," the Chief offered, realizing this discussion had run its course and Abbey wasn't about to offer any additional information toward solving this case. "If any numbers identified by Mrs. Patterson show up on a top suspect's plate, we'll be moving fast. The initial findings might be in tomorrow, with luck."

"Mrs. Patterson. Christ! I hope to hell your department isn't resting this case on what she's seen," Abbey yelled, sounding every bit ridiculous to the Chief and having about enough.

"That's it Abbey. We'll be in touch," Alex stated. He moved toward the door, opened it and stared directly into Abbeys face. Signaling the meeting just ended and she had to leave.

Mrs. Crosby gathered her coat, scurried to leave the office and strode to the door. "My lawyer will be in touch Alex," she muttered in a muffled tone, marching by but ignoring his extended hand held for a courteous handshake.

"I can't tell you how much I look forward to meeting him," Alex responded in a civil manner, intending sarcasm. "You can't scare me Abbey," thinking the words to himself but no guts to say them aloud.

Abigail sailed through the door. "Good hunting Alexander," she volleyed with coat tails flying in different directions and turning sharp to her right on a high heel. This caught Alex's attention, wanting to yell out, "you should be going the other way." He stopped on purpose, knowing she would reach a dead end hallway. The green exit sign above and across his office door shined bright, but ignored. Now her highness would have to turn around and pass his door again, coming across lame and a lot less regal! This was beginning to feel more like high school all the time.

Chief Yung decided to strike a pose visible through the office door. Removing his sport coat and standing fixed while leaning back against the front edge of his desk. Holding a stack of papers in hand for effect and for some reason, he wore a shoulder holster today. This was a rare occasion for the senior officer to be armed, forgetting he carried his sidearm today. The 9mm automatic hung loose along bony ribs, but evident, hearing Abbeys heels click in the hallway, approaching louder and louder. He'd look right at her when she passed.

Just as he thought, she peered inside his office as if to say, "you dickhead, letting me turn the wrong way!" But, caught sight of the handgun causing her head to recoil ever so slight, eyes bulging in surprise. Abbey's feet kept marching forward while staying true to the weapon. Alex had accomplished his task without uttering a word or moving a muscle, nodding ever so timid as she scurried by. "Gottcha!" Satisfied this time.

Station 3009

Friday morning had Regina arriving to work late, yet again. Even later than normal. Finding herself casually behind schedule for most of her life but habitually late to most colleagues. Getting those first few steps behind her and out of bed each morning, became the hardest steps of the day. For the last two or three years she seemed to linger in bed longer and longer. Continuous pressing of the snooze button, craving to get that extra ten minutes of slumber. She thought a more robust sex life might improve her sleep. After all, that's what Pam would tell her, in most of their Gang meetings!

"Morning guys," Regina greeted a dejected pair of officers. No response. "What's up?" followed again by silky silence. Both men were consumed by a number of computer printouts. "What-chya got there guys? Naked chicks again?" Tossing her hand at a little morning humor. But even a soft porn comment didn't break their fixes.

Her memory kicked in all at once. "Oh shit, are those the license plate matches?" Gonzalez asked with a trace of dread in her question. Still no response. "What's a-matter guys?" she yelled out! Snapping both men and their faces to her direction, catching Captain Anderson off guard by her arrival. He barely managed a greeting.

"Morning Gonzalez. You're late again." Billy remarked.

"Screw that, what have you got there?" she asked in a defiant manner.

"Ten pages of possible suspects," her partner shot back, quite dumbfounded, holding his printed stack of papers. "Over two hundred potential matches," Davis announced with a short chuckle followed by a long winded exhale. "We have a boat load of names to weed out Gonzalez."

"C'mon now. With all three of us sorting out the improbable, it shouldn't take that long to wade through two hundred names. I don't think?" Regina eyeballed Captain Anderson now, her brown eyes looking soft and in need. Giving it her all, to convey the, 'you'll help out too, won't ya, Captain?' Billy and Chris looked straight into her shining, naïve face. One cop sort of squinting, the other with teeth clenched firm and head tilted forward.

"That's only half." Chris revealed.

Captain Anderson raised the second list of names, with his childish expression and childlike screech, "this is your list of two hundred names." Holding a ridiculous pose, following up with a, "dig in!" Further exaggerating his smirk to the female officer, holding out another folder, fanning through the bound pages. Chris just smiled at Regina, both knew this wasn't Anderson's customary way to express himself.

"Oh sh..." catching herself and quickly changed, "oh shoot, this is going to be too much fun. You two keep at it for now and I'll check on the Coroner's Report." Using her best super professional voice, spinning on a sharp heel, taking a few quick steps to exit the room.

"You're not going anywhere Gonzo. Get your tight ass back in here and get some brain cells working." Davis barked. Regina stopped fast after the sexist remark, turning slow.

She was taken off guard by Chris's statement and stumped in the best way to respond. "It's too early in the morning," surrendering in silence, weighing her options, deciding to ignore it all. So she deftly tossed her purse on the nearby desk and like a grammar school girl, plopped into a chair, shoulders fallen, head down, muttering some Spanish which neither man decoded.

"Captain Anderson, I'll be filing a formal grievance of sexism against my partner," Regina announced, trying hard to sound annoyed and serious, "for his comment concerning the condition of my rear extremities. I plan on pressing full charges."

Billy walked to her desk as Gonzalez announced the complaint, handed her the Crosby file folder and replied, "I'll back you one hundred percent Gonzo, after you locate this killer."

Regina grabbed the folder, sliding it from Billy's grasp, holding it stationary while gazing at her boss. Waiting, then allowing it to fall to her desk top with a soft slap. Folding the cover over revealed page one of names and corresponding plate numbers. She fanned a few more pages scanning quickly through various names. Who knows, maybe she'd recognize a friend or family member? Regina's vision came to rest on one name. California plate number EN1365S, 941 West Avenue, Gustine, California. Occupation: Land Surveyor. Age forty eight. Driver's License current. For reasons unpublished, Regina locked onto the listing and stayed there. She paid no attention to his name, fixating instead on the small valley town she was vaguely familiar with. Opening a flood of childhood memories to the forefront of her mind. "Are you a cold blooded killer Mr. Ellis?" Regina whispered, rubbing her hands together, thinking of Gustine, imagining aspects of a killer.

"Too bad for us Mrs. Patterson only saw three numbers," Chris told Regina. "In no reliable order either! This unlocks the possibilities exponentially. Not to mention probable mistakes leading to misread numbers and letters and da-da! The wrong plates. Letters will resemble numbers at a given distance.

Even at the distance Beatrice read, in low morning light to boot." Davis reached a near preacher like state at this point, venting frustrations at his partner and the Captain too.

"Tell me something I don't already know Chris," Regina responded with attitude showing.

"Parts of a letter can be covered by a poorly made plate holder. The letter L can have its base obscured and look like number one. C will resemble a six in poor light. Q is often mistaken for the letter O or a zero." Chris stated knowing he was sounding a little too resolute. "And so it goes, sixes to S then M to N, and vice versa."

"I know. I know. Duh," his partner groaned.

"License plate ID is routinely flawed, Gonzalez. Kinda like your baseball. Remember that." Chris held a long grin, peering into Regina's face.

"Oh boy," she complained, holding her head down and rubbing dark brown eyes.

Chris toned it down, speaking in a normal manner to Captain Anderson. "Now, look here." He pointed out 3RN0614, Erubial Cassila. "Seventy three years young, listing his current address as Fall River Mills, California. Isn't that like, almost in Oregon? I have to guess Erubial will land in our unlikely pile for now."

Most matches would be discarded after profiles were briefly studied. Contacting sixty or seventy year old men and women would be a huge waste of time. "This old gal living in San Diego and that old guy living near Arcata won't be investigated by me," Davis exclaimed aloud then looked at Regina for some sort of response.

"Bingo," she called out examining her list highly animated, getting the attention of both cops. Captain Anderson even offered a step in her direction before recognizing the fraud. "One Miss Maria Shriver Schwarzenegger!" Still staring at the name, "listed as currently residing in Sacramento, California. I always had a hunch the ex-governor's ex-wife could be a psycho sniper!" Regina alleged in her sarcastic tone with one eye shut and faking a mock pose, aiming an imaginary rifle.

"Set her up for interrogation," the Captain spoke loud. "I've always wanted to tie up, gag and grill the hell out of our First Lady of California, under a bright light!" Billy stared right into Regina's wide eyes holding a fierce expression.

Anderson's words gave Chris and Regina a reason to pause and glance at one another. They both held a look of obvious disbelief. "The Captain just said that," they thought to themselves simultaneously. Regina lost her control emitting a delicate chuckle as she attempted to hold back a full belly laugh, lost a louder giggle but regained self control pretending to study her suspect list.

Shaking her head with Anderson's amazing disclosure. Chris remained neutral issuing a long deep sigh.

So it went for much of the weekend and continued into the following week. Two cops reading and rereading their long list of potential murderers. Cutting out what they perceived as a waste of resources and keeping those that could be, however remote, considered a possible murderer. Connections to the victim would have to be established. Somehow?

Sorting suspects into three distinct groups. Impossible; Unlikely; Maybe. The Maybe group was still very small amounting to suspects they wanted to question. Face to face. A few suspected murderers would be called in for questioning. Others would be met with unannounced visits. Regina and Chris favored the cold visit. A great deal will be learned about a person in a relatively short time, once a detective walks up and begins grilling his prey. As a team, Regina would often bust in with her Latin attitude. Just letting Mr. or Mrs. Criminal know, "I'm not intimidated by you in the least." All a bluff of course but still effective.

Chris was much more subtle. At first glance, almost bordering on a 'Columbo' routine. Let the suspect begin to feel altogether warm and fuzzy. Then yank the rug out from under him. Get a person off balance and as he liked to put it, "never let up. Bite down harder. Go for the kill!"

Beyond the catalog of maybe suspects each detective had one primary person fitting the bill as a sniper. Chris Davis elected to track down the Braden family. Parents of Sarah Crosby. Sarah Braden using her maiden name. No surprise that Henry Braden's name surfaced on the license plate list. He drives a truck. A dark midsized pick-up. After conferring with Regina, Chief Yung and Captain Anderson, Franny Braden was to be considered a possible suspect too.

Regina obtained, who else but deputy Douglas Sheets! Considered the second most plausible suspect in terms of motive. Batting leader of the license plate matches! Mr. Sheets happened to be the arresting officer in Sarah Crosby's murder case.

∎∎∎

"What the fuck? Are you crazy?" the voice shrieking into the payphone sounded stressed to say the least as hard breathing came across unhurried but clear, on the other end of the line. "I can't believe you just gunned him down. Right in his own driveway for Christ's sake." The caller lagged for a moment, waiting a reply, hoping it was all a mistake and the person on the other end would set things straight.

"Who is this?" came a very calm response. "If you're calling from your cell phone, we're both dead."

"I'm not that stupid, but I sure as fuck know you are! What the hell were you thinking, you dumb fuck. This will ruin both of us, goddamnit!" A frightened caller grew more frantic to the person on the other end.

"I have to go," connection broken, gone to dial tone after a sharp click.

The Braden's

Henry Braden and his younger wife Franny were certainly capable of executing the man who, without a doubt to all but one juror, abused and murdered their daughter. "In terms of pure motivation they're act of vengeance would be no surprise," Detective Davis contemplated, gunning the silver toned department vehicle onto eastbound Highway 205 from Tracy Boulevard's on ramp. Chris phoned his suspects two days earlier just before leaving work, making contact with Mrs. Braden after four or five tries. They talked a short time but she seemed apprehensive to say the least. Answering methodically, "I don't know, you'll have to talk with Henry," to just about every question. It didn't matter and didn't surprise him too much either. Davis wanted his face to face meeting. Talking at close range, judging if they possessed the killer instincts needed to carry out murder? "Motive is one part of crime," mumbling to himself as morning sunshine lit his roadway and the brash for sale banners lining block sound walls behind new developments east of town.

Henry possessed revenge as a motive, no doubt. He also owned marksmanship qualifications and more than enough weaponry to finish the job. His garage took on the look of a small armory at times. Rifles, reloading tools, gunpowder, primers and ammunition scattered about his gun room. All the tools necessary to commit murder. During his investigation career, Chris Davis chased many people having all the tools to commit murder but few contained the psychological make up to follow through with murder to its bitter end. It almost became his instinctive sense to reliably rule some people out. The tricky part is determining those to be undeniably capable. "Does Henry have balls mean enough to pull the trigger?" Davis kept thinking over and over. "Does he posses that twisted behavior necessary to carry out a deed as vicious as this murder? Probably," was all he could muster at this time. "We'll see in a short while if he's an executioner," Chris deliberated, realizing he might be going a bit overboard with the psycho-babble. Was his wife involved too? "Probably," concluding out loud with a slow nod of his head. "A team project. That's possible? More than possible. Expected! One shooter and one driver. Makes sense," he whispered. "Maybe, just maybe I'll get the information needed to make a quick arrest. Yeah, right. Don't count on it," admitting to himself.

Driving east to Oakdale, from Tracy will take thirty to forty five minutes. As always however, in California, depending on traffic. Leaving Interstate 5 north of Tracy to eastbound Highway 120 in Manteca, cuts a path through vast acreage of almond and walnut orchards. Miles of nut trees, irrigation canals, Hispanic farm labor, corporate farms and government bailouts. This section of California's Central Valley, known as the San Joaquin. Its name acquired from an impressive but bygone river of the same name, draining southern Sierra Nevada canyons. The San Joaquin River flows north to the Delta, suffering from severe overdraft but still supplying much needed irrigation water to the massive interior valley. Lying here is some of the country's, if not the world's, most precious and productive farmland. The variety of food crops growing in these productive valley soils is staggering. Countless fields of tomatoes, cucumbers, peppers, onions, beans, and the catalog goes on and on. Fruits prosper in the valley heat like no other area. Citrus groves of oranges, lemons, limes, grapefruits and nectarines are nothing short of famous. Apples and pears too. Grape vines thrive now in various regions of the valley from Fresno north to Lodi and east to the foothills. Many San Joaquin vineyards produce grapes for lower end, high volume bulk wine in cheaper vintages of Merlots, and red table wines. An exception being wine makers surrounding the city of Lodi, east of the delta, make nothing short of world class Zinfandel and Italian varietals. Barbera, Sangiovese, Primitivo do well in the drier climate. Further south, farms near Fresno and Visalia, yield grapes with no intention of delivering wine, but cultivate great eating table grapes or raisons. Four or five different varieties of large melons, cherries, kiwi to dainty blueberries with their sparse shrubs flourishing on a handful of acres. This section of the Central Valley doesn't include countless flooded fields of rice harvested each year, to the north, into the grand Sacramento Valley. More mundane crops include alfalfa, oat hay, cotton from the lower San Joaquin, herbs, sweet corn, delta asparagus, sunflowers, safflower, olives and pistachios. The list seems endless.

"First things first," talking aloud as Chris slowed, beginning to veer right on approach to his fruit stand. His palace of joy sitting at the corner of Highway 120 and Jack Tone Road, east of Manteca. Chris looked forward to any drive toward Manteca or Oakdale. Perfect for a quick stop to procure the toffee covered nuts, olives, dried fruit and maybe some good apples. Too bad it was so late in the fall. No more white nectarines.

"Shoot," Chris knew all too well the sweet fruits were way out of season.

The large, locally grown globes of succulent produce became a near obsession since his discovery at this fruit stand. Convinced he couldn't get nectarines as good as these from his local Safeway or Lucky grocery stores. Performing an obsessive investigation for some time! Beforehand, Davis wasn't a big fan of nectarines, until one hot, late summer weekend. Examining a heavy fruit, it seemed too hard and probably under ripe. However, his first bite into the reddish-gold gem found it firm but juicy sweet, as sugary nectar rolled down his cheek spotting his new sport shirt. This wonderful delicate crunch, straight away forever hooked. Often driving thirty minutes or more in commute traffic to his beloved stand on any given workday, in full surrender to his desires. Going overboard with each purchase, as ripening fruit grew soft and mushy before eating them all. Never once considering to share his treasure!

Munching away on toffee cashews, Chris noticed very little of the pastoral setting during his ride toward Oakdale. Still disappointed for missing out on his beloved addiction, yearning for the enticing combination of sweet citrus, toffee and crisp nuts. Davis often pulled his car over, devouring at least two sugary fruits at any given moment, rarely, if ever, taking in the subtle beauty laid out before him. Nature's vistas were just not a part of his make-up. Taste was most important. Fixed logic and mental contests with people ruled his mind, leaving little left over for everyday sights of simple loveliness.

Driving sixty and splitting orchards still possessed of bright yellow leaves clutching late harvest walnut trees. Dormant almond orchards were long bare by now revealing their immaculate rows of smooth packed dirt between trees. Good reason for sustained maintenance as almond harvests are highly mechanized. Tree shakers, sporting grips resembling large pincher bugs with elongated mandibles, shake rigid trunks, dislodging bounty from vibrating limbs for large powerful vacuums to sweep the plentiful nuts into shipping boxes. Harvest efficiency at its peak needing minor hand picking.

Between orchards lie dormant vegetable fields, picked clean with fertile soils turned to prevent windborne dust accumulating on dry winds. Lingering acres of seed corn drying brown beneath the fall sunshine is about all that remains in food production. Low angled sunlight, even now in late morning, cast long shadows across the roadway as Chris's route took an occasional slight bend northeast before returning due east. Cutting through calm San Joaquin Valley air now, typical in late fall, which usually follows high winds ushered in by cold air masses from the north. Fitting this murder investigation well. A calm before the storm lying ahead. In some years, Northern California's Indian Summer will linger through Thanksgiving and into December. Warm, calm afternoons set a peaceful, comfortable mood like nowhere else in the country.

Originally, most soils in the Central Valley weren't suitable for all types of agriculture. Hard pans and clay made up a big percentage of the original inland basin. Large landowners, tilling soils away from the river's more fertile alluvials, had to make the dirt work for them. Over many seasons, thru decades of fills and enhancement, valley soils finally achieved the preferred combination of chemistry, dirt, and moisture.

Available, but most critical, are reliable water supplies, which rules agriculture in the Central Valley. Water determines crop success or failure, in the hot interior valley. Unlike Midwestern and Southern farms, rainfall during the growing season isn't much of a factor for cultivating crops in California.

Significant rainfall almost never reaches the Central Valley beyond March or April! Irrigation plays the crucial theme. A political, monetary and bloodthirsty fist fight for the precious resource flowing right past many productive farms and eventually reaching the delta and San Francisco Bay. To the irrigators point of view, an obvious waste of resource, reminding us often, no water no food. To those more conservation sensitive, increased westerly flows are vital, if a healthy ecosystem will be maintained in the San Joaquin River and delta. Reminding us often enough, fish, waterfowl and people need clean water too. A never-ending fight for limited water supplies and which way it flows. West or south.

Precious water descends as snow, covering elevated peaks along western slopes of California's Sierra Nevada Mountains. Vital, priceless snowmelt, filling rugged cold water rivers, flowing west into long narrow river canyons to be met eventually, by the state's extensive network of reservoirs. To environmentalists, river adventurers such as kayakers and rafters, sport and commercial fisheries advocates, these reservoirs represent the 'Evil Empire'. Huge concrete and earthen dams, obstacles to a clear, cold liquid surge westward. By the same token, obstructing eastward runs of gallant pacific salmon and glimmering steelhead trout.

It's also hard to argue against the many blessings these dams provide the Golden State, beyond the water stored behind them. Central Valley agriculture in conjunction with the State Department of Water Resources controls, which many say in name only, state irrigation networks supplying water for thirsty crops in blistering summertime heat. Plus the high quality and reliable urban drinking water funneled west out of foothill reservoirs, to expanding coastal cities consumed by homeowners, commercial, industry as well as dedicated environmentalists. Many California natives and recent newcomers, have no idea, San Francisco's drinking water originates in Yosemite Valley. An engineered delivery system of river channels, flumes, pipes, canals and pumps from Hetch Hetchy, across the Central Valley, eventually cascading from Bay Area faucets and lawn sprinklers. Over one hundred miles of utility conveyance. Water held back in reservoirs provides flood control to valley cities. Most notably the state Capitol, Sacramento. Manmade lakes see to it that valley towns stay dry throughout rainy winter months as well as the spring runoff. The same water released from those large lakes roar through hydro electric turbines then back into river canyons, provide the lion's share of electricity used by everyone in the Golden State, including environmentalists. Arguably, a positive tradeoff for renting river flows in production of clean energy. In a novel way, withholding water sustains various forms of recreation too. Although somewhat artificial, a healthy cold water trout fishery thrives in many tail water sections below existing dams. White water enthusiasts have plenty of rapids to run during summer dry periods with stored supplies flooding wintering grounds throughout California's extensive Refuge Areas, for migrating birds.

On the opposite river bank rests the environmental community. Viewing California's intricate plumbing as nothing more than a grab for cheap irrigation water, subsidized by state taxpayers. Untold criminal damages caused by water overdrafts from the delta and river diversions by an array of Irrigation and Public Water Districts. Intersecting the State Department of Water Resources and demanding a fair share of dwindling resources, lie the conservation groups composed of commercial fishermen, recreational anglers, birders, boaters and waterfowl hunters. They see their government agencies looking the other way, refusing to shield the resource they're sworn to protect. How much water does California over allocate to various agencies in the Sacramento/San Joaquin River Delta? So much in fact, that allocation quantities exceed the total amount of water flowing into the delta during any average rainfall year. In other words, more is promised than able to supply!

It isn't a stretch, to say the least, California's Central Valley suffers from a lack of water even in normal rainfall years. Historically, the very opposite was standard. Far too much water plagued the lowland. Each spring, in above average rainfall years, melting snow filled rivers to their banks in high elevations as gravity pushed the deluge into foothill regions. Dams were absent to check stream flows. The onslaught continued west, as rushing torrents reached comparatively level ground, breaching river banks thus producing great flood waters. Transforming the valley into inland marsh. Standing water would broaden southward to Bakersfield and extended north to Willows. Some two hundred miles of inland sea brimming with fresh water! Filling vital needs of wildlife and filling vital aquifers, hundreds of feet below the valley surface. Cavernous wells, over five hundred feet deep, forming subterranean reservoirs of additional sources of water. Groundwater has been pumped up and onto thirsty fields of produce for the past few decades. An expensive resource, precious to farms but overtaxing supply once more. Aquifers are dewatered, soil clays shrink, ground sinks called subsidence. Some areas of the San Joaquin Valley has sunk fifty feet or more, as non-acting government bureaucracies create and leave, geotechnical problems to future generations. Waterfowl thrived in these enormous wetlands by the tens of millions. An unlimited fresh water haven to wintering ducks and geese. A paradise. Modern day hunters only imagine the historic mass migrations into California's wetlands taking place in the early nineteen hundreds. A majority of North America's pintail population converged on the valley flood each winter.

Chris Davis couldn't determine a pintail duck from a Canada goose. Didn't care either. The detective's idea of a duck was hot and Peking style from the nearest Chinese Restaurant. This he cared about. Lifting another handful of candied nuts, delivered to his waiting mouth, one at a time. Driving on, thinking strategy and questions to ask Mr. Braden, oblivious to dry irrigation ditches and transfer canals, intersecting Highway 120.

Pintail numbers help to illustrate a growing environmental decline and the subtle, continuing wane in Central Valley bounty. Other species such as summer and fall runs of king salmon and steelhead trout have suffered serious population declines. They receive much more press than pintails, as maybe they should, since numbers of returning spawners are in decline. All three suffer from the same ailment, lack of water. California's unique location on North America's west coast facilitates the distinct pattern of returning various species to wintering grounds or nursery sites. Waterfowl, salmon, striped bass, song birds, marine mammals and butterflies all claim the state as a sensitive location in their migratory and reproduction cycles.

The Northern Pintail, appearing as regal as a bird can be. California's quintessential duck. Referring to them as 'sprig' by waterfowl hunters. Drakes possess a distinctive blue-gray bill fronting an iridescent chocolate brown head. White breast feathers extending up behind long stylish necks, splitting into fine white 'sprigs' lining each side of the head. Gray and dun body feathers edged in black mingle with graceful wing scapulars draped across fluffed backs at rest. Vermiculations, contrasting black and white rumps setting off a bright green wing speculum, all terminating into two elongated, charcoal black tail feathers, balancing out the lines and grace of an extraordinary bird. As if their extraordinary appearance wasn't enough, they're graceful flyers too. Usually spotted in tight flocks when approaching decoys, drakes call out a soft chirping whistle while hens emit chattering quacks, often heard while surveying resting water from a safe altitude, out of gun range.

Sprig and other waterfowl species stream into valley lowlands through mountain passes, fleeing cold fronts from Oregon, Idaho and Northern Nevada. Their endless search for open water and sufficient aquatic vegetation to sustain them during wintering stops. In winter months, it's hard to fathom the momentous crescendo created by tens of thousands chirping sprig concentrated on any given valley wetland.

Decades of twenty five bird hunting limits at the start of the century, failed to put a dent into tremendous population numbers. Plenty of healthy birds would head north each spring to replenish and build numbers for the next season's return. In the fifties and sixties however, more dams were constructed by Federal and State Bureaucracies. Levees built along valley rivers helped to stem winter floods making more and more land reliably arable. Fewer floods, fewer wetlands, more dry land. Needless to say, agribusiness boomed.

Waterfowl numbers would begin to decline just as a few forward thinking hunters stepped forward from waterfowl conservation groups like Ducks Unlimited and California Waterfowl, demanding a ten bird daily bag limit. Which must have seemed like a colossal shift in the mindset of hunters. Looking back, ten ducks on a strap seems grotesque and out of place today. Pintail numbers were still huge by any measure. Private hunting clubs multiplied throughout the valley as hunters slaughtered, legally, thousands of birds on any given weekend during the season. Wealthy men and women, from the Bay Area would travel to hunting blinds around Colusa, Marysville, Stockton, Gustine and Los Banos. Only a short time later bird limits had to be reduced once again, to seven birds. Dam sites increased, people populated the Golden State as California exploded, agriculture grew but pintail numbers leveled off and then declined.

It wouldn't be fair to lay the entire blame on California for pintail declines, however. The lack of breeding habitat in the upper Midwest and Canadian prairies was the real culprit. Breeding grounds to the north in Canada fell to increased farming which required marshes and wetlands to be drained. Combined with a new criminal appearing in the form of consecutive drought years, causing severe water shortages across the Central Valley. Wintering grounds forced birds onto fewer congested ponds leading to avian flu and botulism outbreaks, wreaking heavy tolls on historic population numbers. Less wintering habitat and more prairie potholes were being filled and plowed for larger expanses of wheat and corn. Fewer birds, fewer hatches, fewer broods, fewer birds coming south. The eighties witnessed drastic pintail declines.

There was talk in the biological community of extinction, even though somewhat remote, if measures weren't taken immediately. Droughts in the west continued to linger causing fewer birds to complete their journeys back to breeding grounds. By the mid eighties pintail breeding pairs reached historic lows and daily bag limits were drastically cut to one bird. Only drakes could be harvested, attempting to send back as many females as possible to lay eggs. To think that bird numbers of a previously overwhelming population could drop so low in a span of thirty years, seems staggering. Hunting limits curtailed from twenty five to one bird, per day! Testimony to how rapid the pace of change, can infect the ecosystems of California's Central Valley. Land and water. Reduce or expand one or both, and just watch the curious changes to follow. A wonderful fluid landscape, to say the least.

Overhead and oblivious to Chris in his comfortable vehicle, a late migrating flight of fifteen to twenty sprig soared westward toward the delta in search of quiet resting water. An occasional low pitched chirp articulated now and then, for anyone who cared to listen, revealed a loose flock of streamlined migrating ducks. Waterfowl hunters would care enough to notice this flock.

This wasn't remotely, any part of Chris Davis' life. He didn't worry in the least about river flows, irrigation thresholds, habitat, orchards or farming techniques. As long as water fell from his faucet, air conditioning kept valley heat at bay and nectarines remained plentiful, life was just fine thank you. His world unfortunately, grew more narrow with each passing year. Crime and criminals. Could he find them? Could he outsmart them? Could he put them away? That's all that mattered. Most time away from being a cop was now spent drinking his beloved bourbons. Jack Daniels would become a bigger part of his life, helping to soften the self perceived shortcomings and a shallow love life.

"Just focus on the crimes," Davis whispered into his own ear.

Highway 120 continued its winding way through the flat landscape. Escalon appeared following the nectarine stop in Manteca. Typical small valley town, little more than a few gas stations and fast food stops for commuting campers and sight seers making their way to and from Yosemite. Escalon sported a highly touted high school football program, for a few seasons. Old growth sycamores still line the road through town, offering a brief glimpse of what the valley could look like. Grand old trees lining broad boulevards offering shade and comfort in sweltering summertime heat. Escalon and Manteca experienced sudden growth spurts beginning in the early 1990's and continued for fifteen or so years. Home buyers from East Bay cities like Fremont, Berkeley, Pleasanton and Concord headed east for their 'affordable' colossal home. Area Code 209 became one of the Golden State's fastest growing regions, populated with those obsessed by the California dream, to achieve that illusive two thousand square feet of living space. Size seems to matter very much to many Californians and to hell with how far one must drive to get it. Half occupied developments begging for buyers in the form of large red banners bellowing announcements to come by and look at these oversized houses. Commute schedules became more important now as home values continued their downward slide, before the Great Recession finally bottomed out. A tribute to free market economics craziness. Chris didn't care about the ailing economy. As far as he was concerned, the Valley always suffered from high unemployment rates. That's just how life is in the 209 area code. He retired to his two bedroom apartment every night. Maybe a cocktail or two or three, unconcerned about his drinking just yet. This was a whole new crime. A new challenge for Detective Davis to focus on. In a weird way, he felt glad about the shooting. Game on! What he did miss however, was the damn nectarines.

It's somewhat peculiar to contemplate the variety of transitory species moving through California's Central Valley? Salmon, striped bass, songbirds, waterfowl and people. Out of nowhere they seem to ramble into the area, use up available resources, then move on to more favorable locales. The entire Central Valley bedroom cultivation changed almost overnight. Property values dropped in 2008, jobs evaporated, mortgages went unpaid, houses lay empty, renters and owners moved on. Migratory? Farming remains intact however. Fruits, nuts and vegetables thrive in the valley heat. Land continues to be plowed if it hasn't been planted with strip malls, light commercial or subdivided with neighborhoods and future bankruptcy. Fighting for water remains as it migrates through, to meet its Pacific destination. Fog rolls in as waterfowl continue their commutes into valley wetlands each winter, only to vanish in March for migration north. Always moving through.

A few things do stay put in the Valley although most residents yearn for their migration too, in any direction. High unemployment, high crime rates, high drug use and supply linger on. Much too high by national and state standards. Also remaining high is a curious spirit among Valley residents. Those who've been able to succeed by adapting to changes the valley demands. Drought and flood; market booms and bankruptcy; heat and cold; movement and stubbornness; cultural change and tradition. Somehow, someway, a few manage to prosper.

Chris would be entering Oakdale in a few minutes. Passing what he considered to be a strange location for the Cheese Factory on his left, then over a bridge span crossing the main stem of the Stanislaus River. Davis, by no means noticed the flowing stream below, directing his focus instead on the Braden's. Conceiving mental images of question and answer routines in his head, losing road concentration and almost missing the Highway 120/108 hard left turn, in the middle of town. Reaching for cashews Davis barely managed a turn lane maneuver, after cutting off a mini-van closing fast on his left. He made the arrow, turning left onto Oakdale's main drag. Highway 108 in eastern Oakdale and he didn't like it. Too many fast food outlets and vacant storefronts. Another grim reminder of an ailing Central Valley.

Moving through town, reading from Google directions on the passenger seat. Not too difficult. Straight forward with a left turn onto Orange Blossom Road about a mile or so east of town.

"I wonder how these two will act?" Chris imagined the couple to himself. He didn't follow the Sarah Crosby murder trial too close and couldn't recall either of the Braden's faces. "In a way, I kinda hope they're fairly aggressive," Davis whispered, feeling a clash would put himself more at ease to grow bold and aggressive too. "It's damn hard, trying to rough up on friendly folks."

Passing an Arco station dividing North and South Maag Avenue and slowing to check out the metal sculptures of monsters, dinosaurs, geometric artwork and various animals displayed next to the Indian Artifacts Store. Across the road stood a small fruit stand selling cherries. A dollar a quart, the sign read. "That's a good deal," Chris thought, mentally scheduling a stop on the way out of town, forgetting cherries were out of season. Typical snapshots of valley life in the slow lane.

Climbing a short grade out of town offers a quick peak of steep foothills laying eastward. To the west in the detectives rear view, unnoticed, brings the prodigious Central Valley landscape painting with its multi-colored rectangular outlines. A patchwork of orchards, fields and pastures, showing off under a bright blue sky. At a low summit, Chris entered a left turn lane making his way onto Orange Blossom Road. Finding himself under overhanging trees and driving a riparian corridor formed by the lower Stanislaus River, navigating a slow right turn to the northeast. Song birds flew from low hanging limbs indicating a zone of ample cover, food and water. Google's estimate of four miles came up a little short as Chris arrived at 222 Orange Blossom Road. Bright red numbers glowing visible on their white mailbox, struck Chris with an eerie coincidence. The Coroner's Report indicated bullet fragments retrieved from Marcus' body, were probably those from a .222 or .223 caliber rifle.

The Braden household, complete with a convenient location on the right side of Orange Blossom Road with an asphalt driveway bordering a well maintained front yard. For some reason, Chris was expecting a rundown home. Davis stopped his car within the spacious drive, forced a scowl, climbed a small brick staircase and pushed the doorbell.

The 209

Regina departed Tracy police headquarters soon after Davis left for Oakdale. Forced to drive her own car, as two unmarked department vehicles were out of service, having trouble getting parts for scheduled maintenance. One patrol car was available and Gonzalez loved driving the bubbletops, enjoying in great fun playing mind games with vulnerable drivers. Zooming up behind unsuspecting motorists, seeing how long it took before noticing a cop on their tail. Often times a mile or more would pass, prior to brake light display. Regina relished the frightened looks on faces as she sped by, then observing her smiles at the wheel. No idea what the hell was going on.

Driving her own car, would help to arrive as subtle as possible, to another county's Sheriff's Department. "Let's not appear too brazen. We must respect our fellow peace officers," she told Captain Anderson the night before. Chris agreed with the tactics. It might be smart, in his opinion, to make the questioning appear routine. "Sheets knows police procedures all too well and he'll crawl into a black hole at the first sign of confrontation," as Regina continued pushing for a low key approach.

Her driving route veered east. Detective Douglas Sheets, head investigating officer in Sarah Crosby's murder case, worked in Sonora. A Tuolumne County Investigator. What little she gathered indicated a short tempered cop. Sheets' file included two reprimands for excessive force and one police brutality allegation which seemed to be conveniently dropped. "His personality type often leads to extreme danger in the field," reminding Gonzalez of past partners with short fuses. These reckless cops have a knack for turning dangerous situations, into deadly tragedies. On one hand, Sheets seemed highly motivated, and decorated for doing exemplary work. Maybe a little too perfect. On the downside, quick tempered lawmen were notorious for their tendency to draw guns way too fast. Dangerous. Too often pulling triggers at the worst possible moment. Another problem, covered in training classes, was a capacity to remember for too long. Some cases go smooth and some go bad. Some go well but the guilty manage to go free. It's part of the job and like Gonzalez' beloved baseball, you can't win 'em all. As the diamond often proves, your last strikeout must be forgotten in order to focus on the next at bat. "If you can't let it go, anger turns to rage. Combine that with a short temper and unrealistic expectations of perfection, it's inevitable to end up in violent explosions," Regina concluded her silent discourse. "Douglas Sheets you have to show me you're capable of walking away and moving on. I'll find out, soon enough."

Regina's venture reached the Highway 120 exit, bridging the San Joaquin River when her cell phone scared her out of deep thoughts. She jumped in her seat, transmitting steering control to her left hand, avoiding a sudden lane change. Caller ID indicated Captain Anderson was calling.

Gonzalez had the uneasy sense her trip was about to be canceled. "Ah crap, something must be up at the station. Damn it!" Presuming all her prep work was for naught. "Can't shine the boss," she told herself still wanting to skip the call. Moving her car far right she flipped the cover, breathing into the cell with her best, throaty sex. "Good morning Captain Anderson, I was hoping you might call."

"Good morning Gonzo and nice try. You need to work on the panting, but keep at it. Phone sex could be a rewarding second career choice after washing out on sexual harassment charges," Alex responded with his usual dead pan reply.

"Mmmm, what's up?" phone sex Regina continued whispering low moans back to Anderson amid all the hard breathing she could deliver without choking. Dead silence on the other end.

"Captain? You still there?" dropping her sex tone assuming his call had dropped.

"You finished Gonzo?"

"Uh, yes sir. Guess I went a little nutso there. Sorry." Gonzalez felt uncomfortable with Anderson's lukewarm reception, but surprised why he didn't welcome the attempted humor.

"That's okay. I can use a little comedy right now," her boss sounded somewhat gloomy.

Before he continued, Regina had to chime in. "Hey, it was a little provocative, wasn't it?" trying to stifle a short laugh.

"Mui, caliente," Billy shot back, ending the absurd discussion. "I just got off the phone with Sonora's H.R. Department.

"Uh oh."

"Afraid so," the Captain answered. "It seems our boy is conveniently out sick today, strange enough," demonstrating his usual sarcasm. "H.R. hinted Sheets may have changed his mind last night and decided he better have his lawyer present."

Regina had taken the Airport Way exit, finding an open parking lot on her right. "Sounds like our cop has started to run scared. Can you say sheriff's revenge?" Exhibiting a small amount of harsh conclusion. "His character has sure changed."

"Maybe Gonzo. Maybe. But I think I'd have a lawyer with me too. Anyway, the meeting's been rescheduled for Friday morning at ten." Billy confirmed her calendar will be open.

"Well, okay," the detective responded a little dejected. "I've already exited the highway Captain. I can turn around and head back downtown. I should be able," not expecting Anderson's cut-off.

Captain Anderson, keeping the investigation moving along, had set up another interview with Regina's secondary suspect. "No, you won't be coming back this way today. You, lucky lady, get to head south to picturesque Mendota."

"Where?" Regina shouted. Hearing her boss loud and clear but taken by full surprise.

"Mendota. Just south of Los Banos. You know where it is?" he asked his detective, a little baffled, knowing Regina grew up in that area of the Central Valley.

"I know exactly where it is," Gonzalez snapped back too strong. At the same time a weak feeling overwhelmed her stomach.

"Gees, sorry Regina," the Captain said with a 'my mistake' apology. "I thought we could still make some progress today and have you question one potential suspect."

"Sorry Captain. It's not you. I just," she stumbled for the right words, "I was prepared for something else." Not up for discussing her thoughts on Mendota right now. "I'm getting back onto Highway 120 and making for my old home town!" Regina confirmed.

"I just sent you a text with a name and address," reviewing his notes. "Your meeting site is at the intersection of Bass Avenue and Blanco Street. One o'clock sharp. Let me know if you need directions," Anderson relayed, trying to be as helpful as possible, as usual.

"Uh, hmm. No directions necessary. I know right where that is. It's a small town Captain," Regina confirmed but still upset over Billy's change in plans. "And who am I interviewing?"

"You know. Tom Ellis. His name came up on the plate search. Kinda close match if I recall," Billy responded.

"Yes, I remember him," the annoyed detective answered. "This seems sort of fast Captain, don't you think?"

"C'mon Gonzo, we're being pressed right now," urging her along. "Can you be there by one o'clock? You should have enough time?" asking firm.

"Yeah, I can make it by one," Regina told Anderson, thinking through the route she'll take but not looking forward to it.

"You have to check in at the Contractor's Trailer, before seeing our suspect." The Captain was aiming to sound routine, hoping his detective wouldn't be too upset.

Confirming his fears, instead. "Contractor? Captain, is this a fricken job site?" Regina demanded to know.

"Phone babe. Would I do that to my favorite team member?" chuckling into the phone, amused with himself. "You 'betchya', it is!" As Anderson continued guiding his detective with vague directions and information about a civil engineer on site. Billy struggled to avoid upsetting her anymore.

"Hey Captain," maneuvering her vehicle into a wide open fast lane then navigating a long slow curve to the left onto Highway 5 south, back over the San Joaquin River bridge. "I'm not prepared for this meeting you know." Eager for a reprieve.

"Handle it Gonzo. The Contractor's name is Mazzaro. Ted Mazzaro. Be sure to check in with him first, before getting permission to enter the job site. He'll set you up with Ellis." Anderson was guessing she had calmed down by now. "Besides, I think this Ellis guy is a real long shot, no pun intended, to be involved with any of this. Don't you?" her boss asked.

"Good one Captain and I agree. All right, I'll give it my best shot, no pun intended," a little more comfortable now. "I just hope this guy isn't some nut-so redneck," Gonzalez tried to convince herself, even a stupid hick doesn't want to mess with the cops. "I'll get ya' my details later today or tomorrow morning," she said.

"Perfect. Good luck Gonzo," Anderson conveyed, quickly hanging up. "She'll handle this all right," he thought to himself, with a slim but lingering sense of concern. Something he hadn't felt for a long time. Anderson seldom worried about Regina's capabilities or security. "She can handle herself," speaking out loud then reaching for his phone to call her back, but hung up, feeling rather foolish. "She'll be fine?"

Regina experienced a mild spell of anxiety right away. Realizing this suspect was taking her into the area she preferred to leave behind. Los Banos, Dos Palos, Firebaugh and decrepit Mendota. Mendota the land of poverty and meth-heads as far she was concerned. Those four small towns made up the biggest part of her heritage and helped to shape what she is today. Today, on her way back to the farmlands where she was raised, possessing memories of heartbreak for quite some time. Even now, it pained her to recall the loss. Grief and little happiness as a child growing up, when she needed her mother and father most, to delight in family joy. The love a child needs.

Her route would soon be changing southerly onto Interstate 5. A high use concrete conveyance skirting Tracy's eastern flank before entering the West Side Freeway, taking her south. Avoiding town, to connect with California's renowned I-5 corridor at the base of jagged foothills separating Tracy from the Livermore Valley, with its quaint vineyards and rustic wineries. Itself, growing steady in wine making and popularity attempting to rival the celebrated wine growing region of Napa and Sonoma. California's establishment wine country. A sliver of roadway, Highway 580, surmounting Altamont Pass, jammed each day with a clogged flow of employees heading west to careers, business deals and mundane jobs in Pleasanton, surrounding East Bay communities and further to Silicon Valley. Driving to work where most can't afford to live unfortunately.

Regina, pushing seventy five over well worn roadway shared her trip with semi-trailers transporting every sort of load imaginable, north and south. Late season vacationers rumbled in Winnebago's on hard pavement as sportsmen hauled bass boats and gun dogs. Waterfowl hunters, just starting to enjoy early winter chases and anglers finishing up on late season pursuits of trout and striped bass. Some, lucky enough to find both throughout the valley and foothills. Quite an expanse of recreation area to roam at this time of the year.

Running parallel to I-5 and rarely leaving clear sight, courses the notorious California Aqueduct. Built in the sixties, thirty five feet wide and twenty to thirty feet deep. Reminding those who care, of yet another concrete conveyance impacting California. However, this conveyance, in reality a concrete river, removes that familiar resource growing more precious all the time. Always water. Water reaching the delta from Sierra snow, gravity fed through river canyons, dodging canals and reservoirs. Finally reaching its ultimate destination and performing the epoch duty of keeping salty waters of San Francisco Bay in check. Securing fresh water for delta farms, food, fish, wildlife and human consumption. But now, delta water is collected once again and pumped into the California Aqueduct for shipment south. Irrigating a thirsty agribusiness in the Imperial Valley and then spreading itself out, with the help of the Metropolitan Water District, to water faucets in arid Los Angeles. Northern California residents have long viewed the structure like a concrete serpent and the main culprit providing for uncontrolled growth in the greater L.A. basin.

Regina was aware of the artificial inland waterway and sympathized with most 'no more water for desert development' groups, protesting another south state water grab. In the end she grew to understand but didn't appreciate the canal's existence as vital, eventually viewing the structure and its flowing plunder with deep emotional contempt, which gradually amplified to scorn. Coursing its way not much further east, yet another snake carried water south. Regina's dreaded Delta-Mendota Canal. This canal takes water from the delta, leaving some in a large lake, San Luis Reservoir west of Los Banos, only to be returned to the San Joaquin river. The balance is carried to the Mendota Pool, just outside of her home town. Too familiar with this structure since childhood, Gonzalez would cross the canal, her Rubicon, this day, with water headed for West Side irrigation, farms, farm workers and Mendota. Like her! She reached the Patterson exit. Another homogenous fast food and gas stop planted at regular intervals along the interstate.

The canal, the orchards, the cultivated fields, the machinery, the farm labor. This was her entrenched legacy. Defining the Gonzalez family heritage, rooted in her view by their entrapment in California agriculture. To this day she looked away from well kept orchards, fields of full-grown corn, drying grapes, ripening vegetables and low paid workers stooped in furrows of dirt. Their sweat and misery keeping the food of a prosperous nation affordable. Regina fully comprehended the aqueduct as a key component in keeping agribusiness and her heritage flourishing in the California. With never-ending flows, the aqueduct never stopped reminding her.

Chris Davis, no more than forty miles to her northeast, drove through an identical landscape. Yet each held a drastic contrast of opinion which, between Regina and her partner, couldn't be more dissimilar. Their working relationship was a tight bond, but each possessed their own individual way of looking at wealth reaped from valley soils. Davis wouldn't look twice at a tractor plowing a field. Nor feel remotely compassionate for Hispanic laborers toiling behind and under a searing sun. He viewed those working the fields as ordinary employees, doing their jobs, altogether realizing they worked for low pay. Not racism, nor labor being cheated, nothing dishonest. To Chris, this is how the market functioned in the Central Valley.

Whenever Regina neared home a wave of personal regret and wounded shame boiled up, spilling over with bitter childhood memories. The valley's most subtle of splendid views in mid fall reminded her. Full lovely smells and flavor of fresh picked produce reminded her. Cobalt blue evening skies adorned with a rising moon over glowing foothills reminded her. Croaking frogs and millions of earthbound crickets chirping at midnight reminded her. How an evening delta breeze combined with ice cold cerveza turned a miserable hot afternoon into splendid sanctuary reminded her. Low flying flocks of snow geese crying out melodious calls reminded her. Good or bad there was no escape. It always reminded her.

She thought of her incredible father, forcing endless hours of work onto himself. All but a few rare mornings, before waking for school, papa would already be working the orchards. Sunday morning Mass with mother and little brother walking off to Saint Anne's church. A quaint, farm workers wooden chapel, hidden behind an aged walnut grove, unnoticed to cars roaring the outskirts of Mendota as Papa attended trees, machinery or irrigation. Gonzalez recalled the Padre delivering his loud sermons, preaching a simple equation to a simple flock. Staying faithful to the will of God and nurturing a strong family bond equates to a full religious life. Which equals salvation. A bit loose on the spin but close enough, the middle aged priest thought, of Christ's plea to simply love God and love thy neighbor. This Padre knew the strain families of farm workers were under, as their abject poverty broke them apart much too often. His calling, he believed unconditionally, arrived direct from God. Father Pablo accepted his mission, giving all to see that hard working families stayed together. Helping at times, to pay their heavy dues in fields of harvest. Finding salvation, was all most of them would ever own.

"Maybe he was right," Regina wondered aloud cresting one of I-5's periodic small rises. An uneven grade at the base of steep slopes forced her sight from the roadway. Gazing east, the valley in its spacious magnitude came into full view. A patchwork vista where squares and rectangles stretched as far as she could see. The limits seemed to disappear off the horizon as if tacking a boat on the Pacific Ocean. Symmetrical shapes painted in two or three shades of green. Scattered bright yellow fills located harvested walnut groves. Charcoal gray and deep umber revealed dormant fields. Their produce, long ago picked clean and common at this time of year. Breaking up a tiled mosaic were small towns intersecting the valley's main roads. Clear and visible. Especially at night as small splashes of lights popped in a geometric fit. One color lacking from her elevated pulpit was blue. No water. No ponds or lakes dispersed around a haphazard natural setting. The San Joaquin River, hidden from sight, would be one of a few areas holding water. Fertile soils, sunlight and heat. But the lack of water failed to complete the Central Valley as a second biblical Garden of Eden. This missed blessing of plentiful water often turns the Eden into Battleground. Regina noticed the dryness too and as time passed, longed to be near water. Feeling, in some way, more at home in cold waters of Sierra streams and mountain lakes, likely a result of her background. Fields of dry dirt surrounded Mendota and every other farming town where dust devils formed in midday summertime heat, swirling over plowed fields like angry swarms of hornets. A fine flour like powder infiltrated every crevice and open window. Valley dust which never lost a battle to any amount of clean up. It reminded her.

"My family is all but gone and so is my faith," Regina declared out loud, squirming into her seat, repositioning a sore butt, struggling to get comfortable. "Maybe you're right Padre?" flooding her mind with those few wonderful memories of mother. "Mama you are so beautiful," Regina thought of mother's grace and classic Spanish looks. Her wonderful smile. How she maintained to smile under those conditions always amazed her. No money to speak of. Barely getting enough to eat many days. Patches on her jeans resembled the patchwork fields her husband labored in, dominating a meager wardrobe.

She passed away so young and Regina's snapshot memories, coupled with a precious few faded pictures, are all that remain. Papa, never quite himself after her funeral, focused on raising his children for a better life. The life he dreamed about for his family, but never reached. Regina noticed papa's change. Unable to explain why, as Enrique became so much more gentle with both children. His usual spankings stopped cold and taking more time teaching his young kids about life's important values like working hard, religion, family and education. Above all, education. Enrique knew too well, education was the only way for Regina and her brother to break their farm labor tradition. He understood they'd have to learn the hard way, with a fare share of luck thrown in.

Enrique

Regina's father, Enrique, or Henry as he would prefer, entered California's Central Valley in the early seventies with next to nothing. Similar to most migrant farm workers departing Mexico and various Central American countries, heading for a better life, north. He endured the long overland trip from Nicaragua, summoning a relative, whom he'd never met face to face. Together they contacted a shady, low key migrant smuggler going by the laughable name of 'American Express' and developed plans to be smuggled into the states. Here he was, at the ripe old age of twenty four, shoved into an overheated cab-over camper, over loaded onto an old but fair running Ford One Fifty pick-up. Enrique, typical of the illegal crossing industry, was crammed in with another dozen illegal's who also paid exorbitant fares to be smuggled across. Guards were bribed on both sides of the border. As long as American Express made it to the correct check stations, all should go as planned. If not, Enrique just lost all the money he paid in bribes and transport fees. It seems American Express caught on fast to itemizing payment charges too. Just like major corporations, fees had to be justified! After all, gas, truck upkeep, food and various small bribes were on the rise. 'Express' realized, like high paid guns of corporate America, a list of fees didn't look as expensive as a list of charges, for some reason! Enrique worried more about what might happen, in jail, if the crossing was botched. It cost what it cost and he was willing to pay. Would luck be his on this night? But even bad luck, sometimes, leads to unexpected change.

A couple hours before midnight, but summer heat wouldn't abate anytime soon. Even strong desert breezes stayed warm though the sun had set hours ago. Blacktop pavements remained warm and most people, those who had to be out of air-conditioned rooms, sweated freely. For Enrique, anything that could go wrong began to go that way, late this evening. First, inside the superheated camper, two migrants, a young married couple were well into a raucous argument. Enrique and another middle aged man were failing in a miserable attempt at calming the young wife. The poor girl was overcome with fear, due to claustrophobia and early pregnancy pleaded with her spouse to back out of the deal, right now! Screaming tears of fear about going to prison. Her husband, realizing their ride to prosperity was well beyond the fail safe point, begged his love to stop yelling. Tears streamed down his petrified face too, trying to convince her, it was way too late to back out now. She wasn't buying and became violent to anyone nearby. The ford pick-up was only a car or two short of the check station. Enrique's common sense told him this feeble operation was about to blow apart.

American Express hauled every bit of illegal cargo himself. Santiago was his real name, just shy of intoxicated after two o'clock each day except Sundays and a devout Dodger fan. Midsummer and his beloved Dodgers contended for the National League West pennant lead. Extra innings and a throwing error by Ron Cey had Santiago very upset. After all, it was Cey's second error of the game! Both throws following routine grounders to the third baseman. Santiago mumbled something about that fucking pato and his lousy play, interrupting his concentration. Three sips of tequila in the last few minutes wasn't helping to stay focused either. His Ford pick-up, somehow ended up in the wrong lane and like Cey's throw, Santiago was about to miss his bribed crossing guard! While his pick-up approached an honorable Federal, 'Express' finally realized his own error. He swerved hard to the left, without looking of course, but at no time losing audible touch with the play by play action going down at Chaves Ravine. A bold attempt to switch his rig into the correct lane, due to those four cervesas consumed, fed Santiago way too much self confidence. American Express heard a sickening screech of metal on metal as his door scraped the front right corner of a shiny, new Chevy one ton.

An obvious collision shudder was felt by everyone riding inside the camper. Arguments and crying stopped in an instant, as fear and silence consumed the hiding capsule. However, the married girl's eyeballs were ready to burst from their sockets. Enrique knew she was about to lose it. Everyone inside was about to lose also too. For some mysterious reason, Enrique felt utter calmness, understanding he was about to be exposed. Comparable to an ensnared impala, knowing the chase was lost, accepting its fate, soon to be killed and eaten by a hungry lioness. Unknown to Enrique, a dented Chevy truck was about to change his young life forever.

Two lanes out of three were at a dead standstill. Friday night, too hot and far too many gringos growing upset with unexpected delays. From inside the Chevy pick-up emerged a rather tall, skinny figure dressed in a pair of scuffed, black cowboy boots, white cotton shirt and matching white cowboy hat. Clay Blevins wasn't about to let some damn Ford driver ding his new Chevrolet.

"Hey pal, I don't want any trouble or anything," Clay stared firm at a red faced, Mexican driver eye to eye. The cowboy noticed how much bigger he was too. "I hope to hell you have insurance," realizing he sounded a bit on the pathetic side, forcing a sociable smile.

Santiago didn't say a word. Exiting the Ford, stumbling hard to his right and falling harder against the fender of a Dodge Charger stopped next to Clay's truck, then sprawled in an awkward mess onto the pavement.

"Ah Christ! You're drunk on your ass," Clay said to the inebriated Santiago, having a go at lifting himself off a rather warm roadway.

Behind a floundering smuggler and pissed off cowboy in white, traffic became even more snarled as cars continued flooding toward the border. Near the end of a row of check stations, a well dressed Federal materialized from a small brick building. Peering outside from behind a large, dirty plate glass window, the officer could see a possible confrontation developing. "I better get out there," he said leaving behind a group of fellow officers seated around two wobbly metal tables. It was break time after all.

As the Mexican officer reached his three quarter mark to Clays truck, all hell broke loose from Santiago's panic stricken camper. Loud shrieks tore through stalled cars catching everyone's attention. A woman in deep trouble no doubt. Right on cue, the camper's rear door swung open violently, separating from three weak hinges, bouncing off the rear bumper, toppling backward, crashing over the hood of a red BMW also stopped in line. Followed soon after by two Hispanic men locked in mortal combat, with a young pregnant woman swinging hard but missing at one falling contender. All landed with a loud thud heaped over a shiny hood and windshield of the unsuspecting BMW, helping to break their fall!

Neither woman inside the Beemer, two thirty something San Diego shoppers, could envisage a nightmare like this happening to them. Locking doors and laying on the horn was all that came to mind. Throw in a faulty car alarm screeching two rows over, and you have the sudden attention of additional drivers, check station guards and the entire break room of Federales!

From his position, Clay stood amazed by the steady stream of folks leaping clear of the camper's stern. "How many fucking people are in there, for Christ's sake?" the cowboy shouted out loud amid a gang of young Hispanics running in all directions. One laborer, slipping and sliding, looked around bewildered, as others cried in terror. A few even laughed hysterically. Guards gave chase as more horns blared, drowning out a Mexican lady broadcasting in broken

English over a loudspeaker, encouraging everyone to stay calm and remain inside their vehicles.

By this time, Clay realized he stood in the middle of a botched smuggling attempt of illegal farm workers. He chuckled to himself and began a visual scan for his drunken driver of the Ford truck. Blevins spotted Santiago opening his truck door and yelled out, "hey you drunken bastard, you're gunna' pay for this." Santiago turned to face his accuser wielding a large, red pipe wrench. This wrench, along with Santiago, began to approach his plaintiff. Clay, being a smart cowboy, retreated a few steps but stumbled over the last person leaving the camper, Enrique, scared as hell but with enough sense to locate a nearby escape route. Deciding left, to start his run for freedom. Rounding the Ford, he soon found himself between the club wielding driver, whom he'd paid good money for this failed crossing and a Gringo cowboy wearing a white hat. Enrique, by instinct and reflex, reached up to block the arm in command of the red wrench! Santiago, taken by complete surprise stumbled and hesitated, thus barely feeling Enrique's fist connect solid to his left temple. Enrique knew he just lost both fees paid to the whacked out drunken slob. However, that single punch putting Santiago on the ground, went a long way to compensate for his lost cash.

As American Express lay crumpled against his own truck, the well dressed Mexican Federal approached with a fast gate. Grabbing Enrique by his sleeve, he howled at him to remain still. "What's your name?" the officer screamed with a scowl, both fists clenched tight. He glimpsed the home run clout delivered by Enrique forcing him to stand ready, responding in kind if necessary.

Enrique, all the while, surveyed his next escape route while answering what seemed at the moment a ridiculous question. "Uhm, my name is Pedro," he lied. Swearing he heard the gringo cowboy say something just as another disturbance of more loud screams, transpired a few cars behind the Chevy.

"Hey Capitan, he's with me," triggering both men to look in Clays direction. Surprised and puzzled. "Pedro, get back in the truck." Clay was reacting by instinct too. He owed the young man something after all. Pedro may have just saved his life, let alone foiling a pounding wrench! "Sorry all this got so far out of hand. We'd just like to get the hell out'a here."

The Federal was taken by surprise again. "What about damages to your truck, senior? Will you be filing a claim against the drunk driver?" the officer asked.

"No sir. Too much red tape now. We'd like to forget the whole incident, if it's all the same with you." An agitated guard contemplated his offer but expected to obtain statements from all traffic accidents. Thinking longer, just as another scream went out followed by one more smuggled farm worker running for parts unknown, in clear view of the irritated officer and Clay. The cowboy just smiled.

"You two get back inside your truck and stay there," a sweating Fed responded and off he ran to corral yet another young lad, intent on advancing his career path, up north. Enrique didn't know what to do. He wanted to run away himself, momentarily. But Clay grabbed the frightened man's arm and led him toward his truck. Once inside, two complete strangers absorbed the view developing around them. They laughed hysterically!

"Do you speak English?" Clay asked, offering his new passenger a cold Pepsi. "I take it your name isn't Pedro?" Conceding he wouldn't have given his real name either.

"My English is not bad but not great," the young Hispanic answered with a fairly thick accent but easily understood. "My real name is Enrique." Everything changed so fast with fear and confusion set to overtake Enrique. "What am I doing here," asking himself? "Maybe I should make a run for it. When the Feds are gone?" Enrique accepted the cold soda, his dry mouth aching for a cold drink. He needed time to think.

"You saved my skin back there. I owe you," Clay thanked his newfound passenger. "That guy with the wrench looked crazy."

"His name is Santiago. He is loco. But, where are you going senior? I guess I should ask where are WE going, senior?" Enrique wanted to know the cowboy's name.

"My name's Clay. Clay Blevins. The way that camper unloaded, sure looked like a smuggling operation gone bad. You were planning to head north I assume?" Clay asked as he restarted his truck. Stalled lines of cars began creeping again.

"Yes I was. To Nevada. Many good construction jobs around Las Vegas and Reno, I was told," Enrique made known while glancing ahead toward the row of manned check stations and spotting a few ticked off guards manning the crossing.

"What kind of work do you do?" Clay asked Enrique, also looking ahead and wondering how to handle uptight crossing guards asking serious questions.

"I work on farms. I do just about any job on a farm. Irrigation, combine harvest, spraying, orchards, row crops, fix trucks," the farm worker listed his résumé of experience. Some in English, some in Spanish. "But higher paying jobs are in construction, I hear?"

"Kind of a coincidence. I was in Mexico most of the week looking to hire some help for my farm," Blevins stated, getting ready to tender a job offer to his new body guard. "I can use some reliable help."

Enrique felt much better about his situation now. Even thinking events may have been altered somehow, into his favor! "Where is your farm senior Clay?" he was still focused on the guards but suspecting this gringo cowboy was okay.

"California. San Joaquin Valley. Orchards near Mendota and Gustine. Are you familiar with the Valley?" Clay asked.

"Oh, si," the lucky refugee told him. "I have an uncle working on a farm in the delta. Not far from Stocktone," mispronouncing the delta city. "What do you grow on your farm?" Enrique asked just as another car alarm went viral, jolting the still high strung young man back into his current situation. All was not well just yet.

"Different crops. Mostly almonds right now. Some tomatoes, beans and melons. But I'm planning to expand into new acreage. Growing grapes." Clay's truck moved up another station. Soon to be greeting a friendly Mexican guard but the cowboy wasn't all warm and fuzzy inside. Likewise his partner.

"I tended nut orchards in Nicaragua with my mother and uncle. Pecans. I like working the trees," which caught the migrants attention when Clay mentioned almonds. "I hate tomatoes. Grapes in the Valley?" Enrique asked Clay with a quizzical tone. "Too hot?"

"Not the grapes I plan to grow, I hope. We'll see?" Clay observed the crossing contemplating his situation for a moment. He considered Henry's too. "What the hell. I have a good feeling about this guy. Let's gamble," convincing himself. "If I get you into the states, will you come work for me. I need someone to care for my almond and walnut orchards. What d'ya say Henry?" Blevins offered. With only two cars in front of his Chevy one-ton, Clay realized they'd be at the check station in a few minutes. Guards were passing more cars through without a strict check. Lined up vehicles were stretched too far and the guards were too aware of nothing worse than an agitated gringo, having to wait in line.

Clay's plan was to show his driver's license and entry permit with a C-note folded neat and clear on top. Hoping for a corruptible guard. If not, things could get pretty weird again. Thinking how much he needed a plan B, but nothing else was coming to mind. Blevins knew one of the U.S. border guards very well, making it easy for him to get workers into California. Clay never tried smuggling people across the border himself. Too much can go wrong, like tonight. His arrangements were always made to get workers into the States. It was up to the professional smugglers to get his labor out of Mexico. That was the deal. Clay wasn't about to spend time in a Mexican jail cell! Getting into California wasn't a problem. The trick tonight, was getting out of Mexico. This trip was growing risky.

Enrique jolted Clay back into the moment. "Do you treat your workers well, Senior Blevins? Pay them fair?" he asked as the Dodge in front of them pulled up to the check station.

An edgy cowboy ran explanation scenarios through his mind. Discussing job benefits or qualifications wasn't a top priority at the moment. "I think you'll find me a fair man." If nothing else, fairness defined the character of Clay

Blevins. Unlike most growers, Blevins understood the migrants position. Competing to enter into a foreign country illegally for the privilege of performing stoop labor day in and out, for low wages. Very little in terms of fulfillment but thankful for the opportunity nonetheless. Farm labor was their last chance to make a better world for their children and most jumped at the chance. Blevins knew he would get more production if he dropped his arrogance and gave the migrants a chance to settle in and feel secure. When hired help stayed on long enough and worked reasonably well, the cowboy arranged for families of his expanding illegal worker force to be smuggled north.

Something about the man's presence and tone seemed genuine to Enrique. Incapable to explain why he could trust this man, it became his turn to take a chance. "Okay Clay Blevins. You have a deal." Extending his right hand as the two of them shook. "But, we have to get across the border to make it happen." Enrique spoke quite a bit tense. Clay looked at his new employee with gritted teeth and raised eyebrows. He said nothing.

Enrique recognized the Mexican crossing guard knowing he might help get them through. This Federal, after all, had been bribed by American Express. Getting out of Mexico could be easy, thinking to himself. Getting into the States spelled trouble.

In front of the two border crashers, taillights departed from a busy Mexican guard station, heading north. Clay pulled forward to take his turn and set the Chevy's parking break but didn't kill a rumbling engine, hoping for a quick pass. He even let a quick idea pass to make a run for it. Just as quick, realizing what a simple idiot he would be.

"Good evening sir," a smiling, well dressed guard greeted Clay. Bending slow to get a good look at everyone. "I have to see both ID's and your entry permits please."

"All right," Clay responded. Struggling to sound as routine as possible and looking at Enrique. But before Clay retrieved his license and permit, Enrique spoke up.

"Senior, I was part of the American Express shipment. I'm sure you know it was disrupted tonight." Enrique informed an immaculate uniformed guard in Spanish. Clay picked up a word or two and was thrown for a loop when he heard American Express. A brief attempt to quiet his passenger failed, thinking it might be better if Enrique stayed quiet. Clay intended to handle this situation, just about to launch his bribe at the same time good luck showed again. Fresh commotion and loud screams flared from behind. More guards came running from the break room as another migrant worker scampered behind San Diego's two terrified shoppers locked inside a dented BMW. Their horn promptly blasted again, on cue!

A running laborer grabbed the Mexican guard's attention. He lowered his head in disgust and thought it might be better to pass these two through. In no mood to lose his job tonight. Swiveling his head back to Enrique issuing a stern glare right past the cowboy, who now judged it best to stay silent.

In English with just a modest accent, the guard responded, "I have no idea what the hell you mean by American Express? I should have you both arrested and thrown in a fucking Tijuana jail. Get this damn truck back to California, now. Don't say shit. Comprenda! Ondelay!"

Clay could only smile and say, "si senior!" Pleased he left the engine running, slammed the transmission into first and sped away. The cowboy swerved one lane to his left and said, "I don't have a clue what went down back there, but hell of a job Henry." Enrique, or Henry as he would be called from now on, could only laugh. "Let me handle the next one," Clay instructed.

There wasn't to be an incident passing into California. Jimbo, as Clay referred to the U.S. Border Patrolman, gave a hearty hello to his confidant and passenger. Just like his Mexican counterpart, Jimbo had been corrupted long ago too, passing them through in record time. Deal closed. A deal benefiting both men.

This evening's desert air hung especially warm as Clay's dented Chevy moved north on Interstate 5. Moving away from urban lights, stars burst forth in a dark night sky competing with a bright half moon glow. His truck's cab cooled as two strangers rode into the night, both at ease in each other's company. Their drive was a long one which helped two new acquaintances establish a friendship during a routine ride north. Clay preferred a fast run without stopping except for fast food and gas. Henry had no problem whatsoever with his strategy. The fewer eyes and faces he'd see in the near future, better his chances would be for a long stay in California. They took turns driving. Clay bought Henry breakfast and finally, his new Chevy pulled into a gravel driveway just as a lemon yellow sun rose above his almond grove, surrounding the Blevins' modest, white farmhouse.

Henry was thoroughly impressed. Right away, his experienced farming eye noticed Clay's well kept almond trees. An immense grove looked well trimmed as rows of trees stood productive and healthy. Inhaling deep, enjoying heavy morning air. Enrique breathed in again, reminded of smells like those of orchards in Nicaragua. Ambling among leafy trees, looking and finding a large one to his liking, spreading a wide canopy offering dense shade. Henry sat at the base, filled his nose and lungs once more, leaned back against the cool trunk and fell deep asleep. Clay never had his dented Chevy repaired.

•••

Regina always returns to a handful of vivid memories. One in particular she never forgets. A rare moment of bliss, has mama dressed in a loose fit, white cotton dress. "Another forced marriage, of yet another farm labor couple, due to another young girl getting pregnant. Husband and wife hurried to the altar of love, as a shamed bride committed to veil her showing pregnancy," Gonzalez imagines to herself. Most immigrant families couldn't afford to rent a hall for the never ending list of reception invitees, so tables would be spread among a clearing inside an almond or walnut orchard.

It was a gorgeous spring day in very early March as mild weather first arrived in the valley, forcing dramatic changes. Some years spring comes very early. Often ushered in on the heels of periodic droughts that leave California parched dry and thirsting for water. Temperatures climb and air becomes almost dead still during pleasant warm afternoons. A short two week window at best, will open as almond trees blossom with copious pink and white flowers dominating orchard canopies. Barren dirt below turns white, like a soft snowfall, as dropping petals cover the ground beneath. Regina can still see mama in that white cotton dress. Emerging even whiter against her dark skin and long coal black hair. Recalling her mother in vivid detail moving gracefully, silhouetted against rows of trees, catching delicate afternoon sunshine. Radiant smiles in a flowing dress. "Mama, you carried yourself so well," Regina said to herself. "You were dirt poor but you displayed so much spirit and charm." She knew firsthand how all the poor laboring families struggled. But spring weddings seemed somehow, to be wonderfully simple, yet exquisite and delightful. Almond blossoms and wedding parties hidden among an orchard's small clearing.

Regina was able to smile, a fleeting relief to have a few good memories of her bleak childhood. Family poverty, her mother's unexpected passing at such a young age, prevailing gringo prejudice, Dad's struggle and now her brother falling into a world of meth.

"Padre, how can I keep faith when my family is destroyed?" Regina moaned under her breath in a voice filled with honest anger. Another eighteen wheeler rolled by as she turned away to go unspotted talking wild eyed to herself and passing a sign announcing Highway 140, Gustine two miles ahead. To her right lay open pasture as if I-5 prevented cultivated land westward. Mostly scrub pasture as small herds of cattle, sheep and a few horses grazed among the dry brittle grasses. To her left flowed the concrete river, flashing the lone blue color visible, besides that of a cloudless sky. Water raided from the delta. A continuous shipment south, like semi tractors, like waterfowl and now like her. Further east, laying flat was her heritage. Her sadness. "I still hate these farms!" The detective reminded herself trying to put it out of her mind, upping the satellite radio volume and blaring music as loud as she could stand. Her car passed the Gustine exit. Recalling her suspect, Tom Ellis, lived in Gustine. She thought Mendota was a long way to go for work, shifting attention back to her suspect. "What would he look like," she asked? Ellis' bio described him as dark hair, blue eyes, Caucasian male. Six feet two inches tall and forty six years old.

"White guy, dark hair with blue eyes. Kinda unusual," Gonzalez said to herself? "So Ted," then checked her notes closer. "Sorry, Tom. Not Ted. Tom Ellis, where were you on this fateful morning in November, when Mr. Crosby was ruthlessly shot through the neck?" Talking aloud, overacting every bit, reminiscent of TV crime drama.

"Forty six years old, huh?" starting to question if, maybe he was her type. "Christ girl, this guy could be a cold blooded killer. Quit that crap right now." Regina said, leaning her head on the window as her other older, stinging issues crept in again.

"Yeah, yeah. I know. Female, thirty eight, never married, no kids and Hispanic. Not now," as she reached for the XM button set, changing to baseball talk. Anything to get her head clear.

"Always the same old talk this time of year. Yankees, Boston, Jeter, A-Rod and Big Poppy." Wishing she could listen to a game right now. "How sweet would that be." She'd even take a Giants game! "Can you mention Oakland just once. One time? They have much better young pitching than either of those big, bad east coast teams." Regina resurrected her fantasies of how much better the A's would be if they could afford a Tex, a Cano, a Cabrera. Baseball sports talk, deep into Hot Stove this time of year centered on trade rumors and free agent signings. Small market teams like Oakland, Tampa Bay and K.C. can't sign free agents like these. "I know Billy Beane will attempt some positive changes, working the free agent market this off season. Letting Zito go was a good move. Maybe he'll sign a third baseman that can play every day and take over for Chavez. Poor Chavey and his miserable back, shoulder, knee and arm. What's left?" chuckling to herself recalling how much she loved watching Eric play the hot corner. "His glove rocks. Mid November and I miss baseball already," she whispered her craving.

Santa Nella was next with its locally famous eatery, Anderson's Famous Split Pea Soup Restaurant and the rarely noticed, Korean War Memorial. Truckers filled the parking lot. This also meant Highway 152 was only four miles away. Her dreaded highway to hell, as she called it. Back to her early days.

"I should stop here, in Santa Nella," planning ahead to avoid trouble. "I can take a pee and pass on stopping in Los Banos. No way. No way at all, do I stop in Los Banos. Crum ball town!" All but demanding, to shun the pain. Somehow. First love gone wrong in Los Banos. Last love gone wrong in Los Banos, less than a year ago. Both breakup episodes, taking place at the same restaurant. Celia's Mexican Restaurant. Great food but an establishment Regina pledged, never to set foot inside again. "The guy was married for Christ sake," murmuring in shame while pulling into an antiquated Shell station parking lot. Sitting perfectly still for a moment, staring at the Split Pea Soup sign across I-5 filling her windshield. Two adult crows flew in and landed on the top edge of the sign. Come what may, as an image of freshness and excellence in dining, touched her funny bone. Bringing hands up over her face and rubbing both eyes firm with clenched fists. Shaking her head and hair, wanting to clear away some abysmal lingering memories while clearing her bladder of excess pressure. "Nobody, will ever know anything about that last debacle. Nobody. Not even Davis," she promised. "No way."

Regina purchased Milk Duds and bottled water, entered another on ramp once again and got the tail end of a sports update. Joe Mauer, a free agent, and the Twins were having trouble signing him.

"Oh right, like the Twins won't resign Mauer. There's a catcher I could fall in love with. Great body and batting average," Gonzalez was speaking out loud, checking side mirrors. Her attention snapped into place seeing a large eighteen wheeler approaching fast, hurling in the slow lane, hemmed in by two SUV's passing in the fast lane. The driver couldn't pull his rig over. Regina backed off her gas pedal allowing the metal monster to glide by. "That could've been ugly," she groaned.

"If only Oakland could afford a free agent like Joe Mauer. Justin Morneau will have a big contract coming too, if he bounces back from the concussion and Joe signs for big bucks. Interesting. Can the Twins afford both?" She considered the chances for a while as an exit sign for Highway 152 East, screamed out, one mile away. Her attitude soured even more.

Overall, anyone would have to say Regina's attitude and personality were very upbeat. Her partner was somewhat taken back by her optimism and playfulness. The latter often being at his own expense. Gonzalez felt fortunate to be where she was in her life. Off the farm, thank God. Her father saw to that and she would never forget. His children would be better off than he ever hoped to be. It became his mission. Regina knew too well papa's mission probably killed him. That was a guilt she stored back shelf and eventually would be forced to deal with later in life, after she had her own children, becoming time to pay up. For now, never forget, and be thankful for any opportunity to improve her life.

Regina understood, due to her poor childhood, the way many people feel entitled to a better than even chance in life. They expect it and when easy opportunities don't occur, all hell can break lose. Her brother fell into this group, leading to his drug use regrettably. Others feel grateful, lucky or maybe blessed by the least amount of good luck. Taking full advantage of minor situations when the tiniest of cracks fracture. Regina Gonzalez definitely falls into this latter group and it shows. She appreciates what's been given and knows what it takes to earn. Fortunate, yes. Persevering, much more. Transcending major difficulties during her young life means everything to her. This alone is her accomplishment. Not her job, her status, her stuff or money. Yet she appreciates how her farm life defines her character, each day, and carries her through. She recognizes accomplishment as mere determination. No magic, nothing decidedly intellectual, not God but almost always nurtured by a little luck.

Gonzalez had every excuse to be bitter. Every reason to give up and fail. She accepted the notion early on that life is inherently unfair and decided to thrive on it. A daily witness would be her father. Enrique was a man forced to work too hard each and every day. Never earning anything splendid from his grueling toil, other than sacrificing himself for a chance to make his children live better than he. A noble concept but the work remained daunting! Another value he taught by example, was not to complain or whine. To her father, that was the sign of limitation and defeat and he wouldn't stand for it. Either meet your obstacles head on or figure out a way around them. She carried a certain mindset allowing her to mobilize worthy principles into thoughts for constructing ideas, then using them as inspiration to keep pushing. To do the right thing combined with a stubborn drive had proved the difference in solving many crimes, as her partner can verify. Regina was by no means imaginable, a quitter.

None the less most of us are burdened to carry some baggage in our lives. She entered onto a long slow curving off ramp, arcing hard right. Driving into her baggage claim area, Los Banos. From the Spanish translation, The Baths. Early Spanish explorers and priests would stop and rest at nearby hot springs. Hot water for a warm bath. A Mission followed and the local Indians were soon under the spell or sword, of powerful Catholic invaders. The legacy of religious conquest is rooted deep within California's history, whose native tribes will certainly attest. Regina had her own history of bad memories also. For some reason, misbegotten love ruled Gonzalez in Los Banos.

"Let's see, mid November. That would put Spring Training about three and a half months away," running calculations on her fingers counting down each month, one by one to March first. "Pitchers and catchers report in mid February. Three months." Baseball was Regina's go to device, when trying to forget the unpleasant memories. It didn't work in Los Banos. Way too many reminders. Forced to look at so much torment while attempting to speed past the heartaches. Spaced stoplights haulted her fast advance.

Before a quick growth spurt commencing in the mid nineties, Los Banos was known best by waterfowl hunters and cotton farmers. Los Banos grew, quite fast, accommodating those wanting less expensive houses and willing to make a long crowded drive to Santa Clara County and Silicon Valley. Regina witnessed the city's growth. Another Valley town became more subdivided for more houses, more strip malls, more chain restaurants and long commutes.

Memories and traffic lights elevated her anxiety as she passed few of the remaining landmark businesses. The town continued spreading east and west along Highway 152. However one could see the vacancy signs littering unoccupied storefront buildings. Los Banos wouldn't be spared the decade's economic meltdown. Central Valley towns suffer much harder however, during recessions. Agriculture alone just can't generate enough high paying jobs to keep the state's economy humming, even though it makes up a big percentage of California's bottom line. The 209 area code became accustomed to ever rising property values, which unfortunately, stopped rather abrupt in 2007. Houses stopped selling or drowned under a network of bogus mortgage loans. Many businesses riding high two years before, were just wishing to stay alive, even now. Some drowned. Many more would pass away soon.

But ducks still arrive each winter followed by waterfowl guns. Migrating birds seem to hold a better understanding of the valley. Move in, take what's needed but always move on. The Valley is just a way station until spring. People choose to stay and many pay dearly for their choice.

Gonzalez made it through town, increasing escape speed as sprawling housing developments faded to standing water, both north and south of the roadway. Nearby duck clubs and Refuge Lands supplied wetland habitat for migrating birds, right to the banks of Highway 152. Regina looked left just as three Cinnamon Teal glided low in front, crossing her vehicle, trying to coordinate to one open water pond lying south of the freeway. Wings set but tipping hard toward her car showing their reddish-brown back feathers and light blue patches glinting off stiff forewings.

"Whoa, you better watch it guys," laughing out loud at the low flying assembly, clueless what kind of birds had just passed of course. "Very impressive."

Her Highway 152 trek would soon end as the exit south, to Mendota, was approaching fast. Hometown lay dead ahead. Maybe twenty more minutes. Wetland ponds gave way to fallow fields of cotton and trimmed alfalfa. Its yellow tips shining as early winter evenings grew colder. Regina couldn't feel much lousier or for some reason, more guilty. She considered a fast detour by one house she remembered well. "We'll see," whispering soft, exiting her highway to hell and entering the south bound road of tears. California State Route 33. It just got serious. She didn't have to go far before rundown ramshackle houses and dilapidated cinder block commercial buildings materialized. A two lane blacktop divided by dashed yellow stripes. Regina winced passing the neglected shacks and vacant houses. Recalling a friend who lived in one of the many old, weathered white homes. Her heart sank seeing Meg's house boarded up, wondering what ever happened to Megan Casilla. Miss Casilla sure liked to kiss the boys. "She must have a couple of kids by now?" Megan joined the army and served in the first Iraq War. "Came through without a scratch or firing her gun," Regina heard from friends, which seemed like such a long time ago.

First up was a short drive into Dos Palos. Nothing more than a few intersections flooded her mind with additional snapshots from a less than adorable childhood. Father and mother too. As usual the Padre's words came to mind. Faith, family and a brief run of haunting memories. "I hate it here," speaking out loud, unaware of her grinding teeth. Rolling to a slow stop at Dos Palos' first traffic light. Ethereal.

Butches Diner, still serving, situated to the right and across a wide intersection. Butches large sign easily dominating a rather narrow Dos Palos commercial area. "Not a bad cheeseburger," striking a chord which recalled many summer nights spent hanging out. "No appetite right now."

Next up was Firebaugh. "What an odd name for a town?" Regina thought to herself, unless one included the summer time heat. The detective never spent much time in Firebaugh but often hearing it was way better than Mendota. It took forever for the stoplight to turn green, due to a burned out bulb. Regina drove through passing a gas station to her left, easing out of town among barren trees and barren fields. Next stop, Mendota.

Making a long, slow left turn, plus about ten minutes later would reveal the outskirts and 'skyline' of the old home town. She broke into a warm sweat with clammy hands and a softball in her throat. The Bass Avenue sign came into view as Gonzalez turned left on the northern outskirts of town, drove past Blanco Street and spotted a green trailer up ahead. Surrounded by chain link fence. Slowed her car and slid up against the curb to the right side of the roadway, in front of two rundown buildings. Yet another vacated low end bar, unable to find enough customers willing to drink their jobless problems away. "So, here I am old home town," squinting to see S.R. 33 behind and S.R. 180 ahead. Suffering every sentiment except the warm fuzzy feelings of home. One underlying awareness still existed. No matter how far she roamed, lived or worked, Regina Gonzalez was connected to this land. Despite the bad memories, disappointments and heartaches, she recognized her connection to the San Joaquin Valley. It was good land.

"Grab the papers and let's go talk to Mr. Mazzaro," Regina told herself, pausing again for one more scan of home town streets and buildings. She needed to compel herself from sanctuary of her car, stepping outside just before a truck carrying two farm workers sped by. They issued a loud honk as the passenger gave Regina a male whoop, acknowledging her good looks. "God, nothing changes here," she observed, smiling then hurried across the pavement to a green trailer door. Letting herself inside.

"Hey, ever heard of knocking," came a stern yell from the far end of a dusty mobile office.

"Oops. Sorry," Regina apologized softly, feeling stupid by just barging in. "I thought it was okay to let myself in," at the same time, doing her best to see who was doing the yelling. "I'm here to see a Mr. Mazzaro," she announced. Through the small office door emerged a huge hulk of a man. His size took

Regina by surprise making her dark eyes grew large and round. Tense reflexes mandated a step and a half retreat as he approached. The entire trailer shook and swayed with each step of the four hundred pound plus, foreman.

"I'm Ted Mazzaro and who might you be?" he asked with little politeness.

"Regina Gonzalez. Tracy PD," showing the sizeable foreman her Detective ID and badge. "My boss, Captain Anderson, talked with you earlier this morning. I was told to meet with you before entering your jobsite," coming across cooperative.

Ted gave a quizzical smile at the Hispanic woman in his office. "Oh yes, you're the detective?" trying not to sound surprised. "Your boss didn't mention first names. I was expecting a man." Speaking abrupt.

Regina thought for a moment and decided to risk sounding aggressive. "Women not allowed on your site Ted?" she asked with as much attitude as she could bring, hinting at being insulted.

"Oh no, detective. Nothing like that. My bad, that's all." The large man attempted to render a genuine apology. Ted was huge. Grossly overweight, but in general a friendly man. Part of his problem was being stuck indoors all day. Checking, then rechecking engineering and architectural design plans as well as issuing endless change orders to construction crews. Ted Mazzaro had a reputation as a damn good foreman.

"You have to speak with one of the surveyors on site, I was told." Ted spoke with a much more accommodating tone in his voice.

"That's right. One Mister Tom Ellis."

"What's this all about mame?" Ted asked. "If you don't mind me prying, Tom's a darn good surveyor." Sounding congenial as a girl scout, caused Regina to smirk, realizing 'The Hulk' was eating out of her hands. As if the obese man needed more food!

"Mmm, not free to say at this time. But I'm sure it won't end up being anything major. Sort of routine questions," Gonzalez answered with one of her canned responses.

"Well, okay then," Ted shrugged his massive shoulders. "It'll have to stay a mystery," concluding he wasn't about to get any information. "Follow me Miss Gonzalez," instructing the detective gently with a smile.

Ted waddled over to the side door, shaking his office trailer back and forth, toe holding it open for Regina, together descending a small metal stairway. He led her across a tool laden dirt lot then out toward a busy work area. Ted's medium size construction site was fairly active at the moment. Two large yellow backhoes lifted dirt, opening a rather large, deep trench, about a hundred yards distant. Working in tandem. One mechanical dinosaur, deep inside the trench, excavating and lifting its load onto a growing pile of fill alongside. Another monster scooped away at the growing pile, delivering fill into waiting trucks. A high cost endeavor, removing dirt from a work site. As design cut and fill calcs yielded tons of leftover dirt after backfilling the trench. Once a large diameter pipe is laid, offsetting fill volumes require a great deal of dirt having to go somewhere.

"So, what're you building out here Ted?" Regina asked, raising her hand to block vivid sunlight, trying to get a better look at the machinery.

"Gees, hell if I know detective," Ted responded very dry, causing Regina to look dumbfounded at the large man, his strange statement not quite registering.

"Wow, I thought you were in charge." Then seeing a smile spread over his broad face with red cheeks glowing. Knowing she'd just been had. The grin on her face grew too.

"I love to do that," looking at Regina with a wink and a nod. "Actually we're laying storm drain and irrigation pipes. A new pump house is being built on a main canal to increase water flow to the Irrigation District. Moving water back and forth," he explained not really thinking she would understand.

"The West Valley just keeps sucking up more and more precious water, doesn't it Ted," Gonzalez responded looking at stacks of pipe, kind of sad.

"Maybe she does understand," Ted thought. "That's how we keep eating mame." They both looked at each other. She thought about his words, noting Mazzaro's massive size but kept her mouth shut.

"So, your man is right down," pausing to search the work site along his outstretched arm and fingers. "Right over there," pointing toward a quieter area away from the two mechanical shovels.

She could see a man on a small knoll, bent slightly, peering into a camera fixed atop a yellow tripod. "He's laying out stakes for the trench alignment. I hope he's marking our cut and fills. We're gonna need 'em soon." Ted's attention went back to his project again while mulling over a tight schedule in his head. "They should be digging over there tomorrow, I hope." Regina didn't know what he was mumbling but thought better than to ask.

"Tom's on the instrument." Then he explained further, "I hope this doesn't take too long detective. If our surveyor can't get hubs in the ground we don't know where and how deep to dig." Ted pleaded in a mild way at the same time handing Regina a white hard hat, hoping she understood his subtle request. Regina knew too well she'd be holding up their work.

"This shouldn't take too long sir. Three, maybe four days, at the outside," causing Ted to spin around and stare in disbelief at the female cop's words.

"Three days? Holy cow detective I can't stop this dig," just as fast realizing it was his turn to be skewered. Regina looked at the immense man and saw all the jiggling flesh as he laughed out loud at her clever prank. "You're pretty good Miss Gonzalez."

"Gotch ya Teddy," proud of herself. "I won't be long at all," the detective shouted back, already crossing the jobsite toward Tom Ellis, operating the thing on a yellow tripod. She adjusted a knob on her hard hat for a better fit. If she only knew the way her life was about to change, on this rather small, lonesome Central Valley construction site. "The guy looking into one of those yellow camera gadgets on the tripod," she confirmed to herself. "I always wondered how those things worked."

Small plumes of dust swirled around the surveyor and Regina, in a light valley breeze. Dry dirt spilled from excavation machinery while workman were hauling, digging, yelling and molding the site into a noisy, busy enterprise. Tom's back faced Regina and he hadn't a clue she was fast approaching. Gazing ahead she could see a fit figure with a significant neck tan below his hard hat. For some reason she looked forward to meeting Tom Ellis and her childhood memories were all but forgotten. Driving back into her past had filled the detective with angst and mild trepidation, but all her baggage suddenly cleared away like the valley's famed tule fog, lifting in late morning sunshine. Calm. It was mid November and it just occurred to her, Thanksgiving was next week. "Hello." Regina called out.

The Braden's

"Henry," Franny yelled out. "The detective will be here soon. Are we good with the information we're going to tell him?" she asked her husband wanting to rerun some questions and answers they anticipated being asked.

"Franny. C'mon girl, please. You're wound tighter than a banjo string. Calm down," Mr. Braden smiled at his beloved wife yearning for her to relax. "We've been through it all three times. There's nothing to worry about." As Henry moved to the other side of their living room gathering loose newspaper laying on thick carpet.

"Jesus Henry, nothing to worry about? I don't think the Tracy Police Department is sending a detective all this way to deliver condolences," pleading with her husband, apparent how shaken she'd become. Franny's biggest fear was speaking without thinking. She couldn't afford to give the police any indication they were involved in a revenge murder.

"Sweetheart," Henry's everyday referral to a sexy Franny. "We don't know what they really think. I'm betting it's all routine," getting tired of the constant ordeal with his wife, in a parental manner.

"The police certainly know we own one hell of a lot of guns, Henry. I'm sure they're aware we do some shooting. A lot of shooting." The middle aged woman paced the floor as hands trembled and suffering from extreme dry mouth. Obvious shaking when she raised her left hand to rub her forehead in an effort to relieve tension. It didn't help. "The fucking scum ball murdered our little girl," continuing her pace, struggling to clear her head wishing she wouldn't have dropped the f-bomb.

"Oh God, I'm going crazy," Franny gasped and ran to the window, peeking through the curtains. "Is that him?" she looked outside to see what caused a slight front yard noise. Turning to look back at her relaxed, but somewhat annoyed, husband.

Henry paused then shook his head slow. "Franny, it was just a passing truck. Please, you have to sit down and relax," Mr. Braden bellowed, leading his wife to her sofa chair at the end of a long, well pillowed couch. Sitting silent for just a few seconds then popping back up like a high strung cat and continuing to pace.

"You're making this harder than it need be," Henry told her pulling his lovely wife into sheltered arms, holding Franny tight against his body.

Mrs. Braden murmured, "I hope so." Wrapping arms around Henry's neck and shoulders, feeling some comfort.

Henry loved holding Franny close to his body. She became intoxicating as soon as he pressed his legs and body against hers. The sensuality she conveyed was overwhelming and sex with her was a special reward. Keeping herself in fine shape, willful of doing anything to maintain a young image. Running, walking and workout routines became a constant part of her life for many years. Time consuming but determined to pay any price to keep her husband coming back for more. Well into her late forties but passing for an easy thirty six. Lazy auburn hair, still curling at the ends, lay across firm shoulders like a twenty something. Jeans, skirts and blouses were fitted just right, showing off her firm rear end, and it didn't hurt a bit being blessed with ample breasts. The coup de gras as far as she was concerned.

"I always demo a little cleavage. It keeps them looking and not thinking." She believed, stressing 'them' with firm emphasis. In reality, Franny's bust line was much larger in her own mind then what actually existed on her chest. None of her early suitors ignored the endowment, but most were smitten by her sensual attitude and freedoms she routinely granted, to explore with groping hands.

"I think I'll change my clothes," she yelled out to Henry as she proceeded down a wide hallway to their bedroom.

"You look fine just as you are Franny. Sheesh," Henry yelled back.

Mrs. Braden decided on a dress. "Go conservative," she reasoned. "This detective will know I'm taking it serious. Don't take me too light Mr. Policeman!" Repeating mental messages over and over. Franny also practiced her canned responses, guessing at questions the detective may ask.

"Mrs. Braden. Did you and your husband shoot Marcus Crosby in a fit of anger?" Imagining a persistent cop.

"No lieutenant, we absolutely did not shoot him." Correcting and changing her response to Mr. Crosby.

"Mrs. Braden. Do you know who killed Mr. Crosby?"

"I have no clue who killed Marcus Crosby, but I'd like to shake the shooters hand," stopping abrupt with her train of thought. "Jesus Christ don't say anything like that," Franny scolded herself aloud, lifted the tan dress off her shoulders and threw it on the bed. "Don't give this detective one lousy reason to think I was involved in this mess," she repeated to herself. Moving in front of the mirror on her closet door to check close for any hint of bulging thighs or flabby rolls on her stomach. Turning slow, admiring the reflection in a tight nylon slip. Proud of her firm condition.

"Where were you on the morning of the murder?" mimicking a make-believe interrogator while fanning through a closet full of various dresses and skirts. Hoping one might jump out and strike her attention as perfect.

"I was all alone in my bed, sound asleep." Quickly rethinking her stupid response. "No, no, no, not alone you dumb fuck. Christ, don't give any impressions of Henry out shooting Marcus on his way to work or something." Franny thought out loud. Franny sat on her bed captured by the mirror once more, adjusting tangled hair and speculating how bad another murder would disrupt their lives again. Forced to handle a replay of her daughter's murder less than two years ago. "I am so sorry Sarah. You know all I wanted was a better life for you. For both of us. So you didn't have to live in fear. Like me," Mrs. Braden whispered, checking pairs of shoes for some time but going undocumented in her occupied mind. "Christ, not the pumps you dolt, he'll think I'm trying to seduce him. Go with the short heels," she decided, clearing her mind of murders and quickly deciding on the school teacher look.

"Uh, well detective, my horny husband and I were in bed having raw, violent sex at the time of the murder," smiling and wishing she could say it loud and hard. Her selected blue dress slid over bare shoulders without bunching and unfurling below a short black slip. Displaying a plain and business like fashion. Franny didn't go for an overly conservative look but decided this was perfect for their interview. Preferring red but choosing blue. A gray dress hanging to her left looked inviting at first but too bland. "No way do I talk like that in front of the cops," warning herself, making sure nothing was caught in her teeth before unbuttoning the top button on her blue V-neck collar. "We'll give him a tiny peek," Mrs. Braden snickered.

"Who do you think may have killed Marcus Crosby?" She continued her fake interview. A blank look came over her face. Resting on her large bed considering a response. She wanted a reasonable response here. Franny sat staring into the mirror looking deep and beyond her own eyes. Staring, thinking with a slight panic, but failing to deliver a proper statement. The mirror turned back on her, waiting for a response. Jarred from the trance, her body shook when Henry yelled out, loud from the hallway.

"Franny, I think he's here. Are you ready?" her husband dispatched, hoping she wouldn't be too late. Henry caught sight of his .243 leaning in one corner of his male themed den. Wanting to hide it from view but closing the door instead.

"Okay, I'll be right there," his wife answered intending to run behind schedule. "Try to make an entrance," Franny planned. "It helps me gain control of the meeting," she wagered, standing straight and firm, her outfit tight in the right places. "Not bad," she said. Someplace deep inside Franny wondered about her daughter once more. She wondered about her daughter's father too. Undoing one more button.

•••

Chris Davis pushed a lighted doorbell on the left side framework of Franny and Henry Braden's front door. "Kinda different on that side," Chris observed. Their ranch style house painted white with dark green trim and window shutters, matched nice with a brick mantle and well maintained landscape. Spaced redwoods further accented a spacious lawn reaching each side of the house. Birds chirped throughout high canopy as Chris picked up an unrecognizable sound. Not quite a drone but a rather consistent low pitched hiss. "What is that," he wondered, continuing to survey the residence. "Very nice. Very nice. Seems way too nice here. Cold blooded killers? I don't know." Chris realized he shouldn't draw conclusions, but?

The front door swung open, interrupting his analysis and Henry Braden filled the entryway.

"Hello. Detective Davis?" Henry greeted Chris.

"Yes sir. Mr. Braden. Henry Braden?" Chris greeted the homeowner with a question also. They shook hands as a nervous host motioned the detective inside. Chris mulled over layouts and appearances of the Braden house. "Much different than I thought it would be," examining everything from their recently hung, new front door, down a short staircase into a spacious living room complete with high ceilings and elaborate stone fireplace. "Nice place Mr. Braden. Just as I imagined," he lied.

"No, no. I hate formalities. Folks call me Henry," trying to be polite.

"No problem, Henry. As long as you call me Chris," lying again as the detective actually preferred formalities.

"Done." Mr. Braden nodded.

"Done." Wishing it wasn't.

Then came that inevitable silent, lingering awkwardness between two men meeting for the first time. Chris didn't mind as much as Henry, however. "I have nothing to hide," Davis said to himself. The uneasiness also granted insight how a suspect might be feeling or about to behave. Strung out or relaxed. "Not always, but sometimes giving a little something to go on," Chris often thought.

Henry on the other hand, was quite uneasy with strangers in general. First encounters were never one of Henry's strong suits. Not that he wasn't courteous or a diehard loner. It just took a while for Henry Braden to reach his personal comfort level. At the moment, he was clueless how to behave himself, deciding to just relax and perhaps offer the cop something to drink. Then concluding, under the circumstances, this wasn't an invite to a social function. Choosing to keep it more formal!

"Should we sit at the table?" Henry pointed to a long, dark mahogany, dining room table in the adjacent room. "Or would you be more comfortable in the living room?" Henry was quite uneasy by this time and hoped he wasn't coming across too inane.

Chris was about to say it didn't matter when Franny made her dynamic entrance into a dreadful conversation. She moved quick through the hallway striding face to face with the cop stationed in her living room.

"Oh, hello detective. I'm Deborah Braden, but everyone calls me Franny. A family joke sort of thing. It's so nice to meet you Detective Davis. Sorry, I'm late as usual and please forgive my husband's manners," greeting Chris with a warm handshake then throwing in a Hollywood style kiss on the cheek. "Would you like some coffee? Have you eaten yet? It would be a pleasure to have lunch together." Mrs. Braden offered. Standing poised, a wide smile, with one hand still connected with the detective's.

Davis was overrun by the woman and her powerful welcome. "Oh, no thanks." Chris stammered. "I've already had my lunch and please don't go to any trouble. Besides," quickly interrupted by the feminine dynamo.

"It's no trouble at all detective," Franny insisted, marching across the room into her kitchen. "I'll make coffee and we can get down to business."

Chris heard lids clanging, doors opening and water pouring. He also noticed the woman herself. Quite attractive, he observed, even at her age. Her fragrance lingered inside his nose and he enjoyed it.

"Would you like to sit outside Mr. Davis?" She yelled from the kitchen. "It's so nice this afternoon. Henry and I love to sit and watch the river flow by," presuming the detective was feeling a bit shoved around by now. Franny intended to control this interview as long as possible.

"River?" Chris looked at Henry with a puzzled sound in his voice.

"Uhm, yes detective. I mean Chris," Henry stammered. "The Stanislaus River. It runs along our backyard. Quite relaxing." He showed Davis to a cozy family room, opening fresh painted French Doors which retained a lingering aroma of latex paint. Once outside, Chris became struck by shear loveliness and surveyed the layout surrounding a rather plush backyard. Unaware their property bordered a river as a dense tree line partially obstructed its view. The Stanislaus River was a large waterway and Davis felt a little dumb, oblivious it flowed nearby. Oak and pine added a shaded canopy to a brick and redwood patio overlooking the charming stream. Chris had to pause to take it all in.

"This is pleasant," the detective said to himself but Henry heard him. Unusual for Chris to be stirred by nature but this setting was something even he could enjoy. Outdoor settings, civilized by a controlled environment was more to his liking. "I could watch the world go by out here," he told Henry. Mr. Braden nodded in confirmation offering Davis a seat at one of many Adirondack chairs surrounding a raised fire pit. Chris could feel himself becoming too relaxed. A cold, free flowing river carved a striking backdrop framed through the underside of a thick tree canopy, reconnecting on the constant hum in his ears, when he first arrived. Finally occurring, it was the river. To be more precise, a large boulder anchored solid in stream bed, favored Franny Braden's side of the river. Deflecting constant current, as the stream made a slow arcing turn forcing flows to the north side of the waterway. Water stalled in front of the rock then split, spilling on each side, churning into a bubbly white roil. Which caused the sound in Chris's ear and he stared for a while longer at the pleasant scene.

"Coffee'll be ready in a minute," Franny announced. She strolled onto the patio and gave Chris a long look. She seemed to be studying his face and Chris stared back. He wanted to look away at first but felt challenged, locking his eyes to hers and prevailed in battle. Franny's dipped head caused a slight stumble as she moved a chair next to her husband. Together, each man jumped to lend a hand but she stopped them both, resettled, perching unfazed into a cozy Adirondack chair.

"So detective, did we meet during Sarah's murder trial?" Franny ventured with an unexpected question.

"Uhm, no mame. The trial was held in Sonora? That county is way out of our jurisdiction. Couldn't be involved," Davis explained, struggling to subdue his quizzical look regarding her question.

"Oh right," she responded. "You're from the Tracy Police Department. How stupid of me."

"I did follow the trial however, and I'm very sorry for your loss but I must say," pausing then silent. Chris waited for a go ahead before offering an opinion.

"Please Chris," Henry spoke up. "I'd love to hear your take on the outcome. Speak free."

"I appreciate that," said Chris. "It surprised me. Closer to stunned, by the jury's verdict. Reminded me of the O.J. trial," he offered. "Your daughter was routinely abused, wasn't she?" Chris asked, with as much compassion he could gather, not about to reopen their healing wounds.

"Yes. Yes she was," Franny answered. "That lousy bastard often beat my

Sarah." She wasn't prepared for Chris's next question. Henry frowned, wishing Franny would control her emotions to prevent saying something the detective might take out of context.

"Did you intervene in your daughter's behalf at any time, during their marriage?" Chris asked calmly. This question marked the beginning of his investigation, as far as Franny was concerned. She peered at the cop again.

Very hard this time with little expression on her face. She was furious. "We chose to stay out of our daughter's marital affairs," Franny imparted a short response then sat back in her chair, arms folded low, supporting her full chest.

Henry sensed his wife's feelings and anger level rising fast, deciding he better run interference. "Do you think the coffee's ready yet? I could use some. How about you Chris?" Henry offered, looking at a pissed off wife. Aching for her offer to get the brew and take ample time to compose herself.

"I'd love a cup, Henry," Chris lied. Gambling Mr. Braden might do coffee service leaving him alone to grill Franny.

"I'm sorry. Let me get prepared," Franny uttered. "How do you like your coffee detective?" Rising from her slouching chair, making for the kitchen.

"Black." The cop said close to shouting. Chris noticed her shoulders tighten just as she exited the patio door.

Henry came to Franny's aid and offered Davis an apology. "Pardon her detective, my wife's still suffering over the loss of our daughter. We both are. Marcus' murder is teasing old pains. I hope you understand and sympathize with our loss?" Mr. Braden stated with a polite tone but was actually inviting the detective to perhaps, cut them some slack!

"Like I said before, Henry. I'm sorry for your loss but I have an investigation to conduct," the detective instructed. "Mr. Crosby was shot and killed in his driveway. Like it or not, it's my job to find out who pulled the trigger." Chris didn't intend to seem heartless, as Franny entered the patio carrying a tray of coffee and stacked piles of cookies arranged on an old fashioned serving platter.

Franny set the tray and poured a cup for whom she perceived as a prying guest. "I hope it's black enough for you Mr. Davis," she said, close to insulting the cop. Continuing to fill cups but spotting Chris go tense following her intentional remark. Normally she wouldn't be drinking coffee at this time of day. Caffeine wreaked havoc with her at night, but Franny needed something to keep her hands anchored.

"It's perfect Mrs. Braden," Chris responded with a grin, resuming his formal convention.

Reclaiming her seat Franny became comfortable again looking straight at the cop seated on her patio. Chris lifted his cup taking a long sip. Drank again, staring back at 'intriguing' over his cup. Lowering hands, then head, eyes glued to the patio floor. Out in mid stream a pair of adult pacific salmon were swimming past the midstream boulder nearing an end to their grand journey upstream. Goodwin Dam, above Oakdale, would see to that. Fall salmon runs were underway to produce new life and to die. Yet another example of entering the valley then moving through. Noble creatures. Either Braden would, without question, have traded life for their only child. In the present scenario, unlike salmon, the Braden's offspring has perished while both adults live on, grieving. No one sitting on the comfortable patio had a clue ocean going fish were nearby, in the Stanislaus.

"So detective, do you think we murdered Marcus Crosby?" Franny asked in a calm tone.

"Well, to be honest. We," Davis decided to correct his word. "Our department believes you have the means as well as motive to commit a revenge murder. Revenge for your daughter's death. We're aware however, any solid evidence is pretty thin." Chris admitted.

"Is that all you have detective? Motive." Henry chimed in.

Davis sipped more coffee and deliberately returned his cup very slow, leaning back into his wooden chair. Unnoticeable to the three was a warm, late fall breeze. Not blowing hard but enough to swirl loose ends of Fanny's hair. "The lady living next door to Marcus got a partial license plate number and identified the shooters truck. It resembles your rig." Davis said nothing more waiting a response. He looked at Henry now. Henry wouldn't dare look back. Chris sensed something wasn't quite right. Now hearing the breeze amidst swaying tree limbs, rippling the river's surface with passing squalls of air. An elegant setting alongside flowing waters, minus the pissed off parents of a murdered daughter of course.

"So it seems to me, if you have a license plate number, you've identified the killer. Correct?" Henry responded.

"Like I said, we only got a partial number from the plate and by coincidence your truck plate has a few of the winning numbers," the Tracy cop was attempting his best to sound convincing, but Chris knew the evidence was hardly substantial. Flimsy evidence isn't what brought Davis here. He was here for his own gut check. Just what sort of people were the Braden's? How would they respond to direct questioning? Would he be able to challenge them for new information? Could the Braden's offer something, by mistake, to help his case? Perhaps very simple, they're hiding something?

"What numbers did the lady see?" Franny asked. "Is this Mrs. Patterson by any chance?"

"Yes it is. You know each other?" Chris responded and went on. "She identified a number three. Letters N and I. Possibly the number six," letting it go at that and waiting for their reaction.

"Hell, I don't even know our truck plates. Do you Henry?" Mrs. Braden posed.

"My truck plate has a three, a one and the letter N. No six or an I." Henry informed Chris. "That seems like a real long shot for a plate ID to me detective. Don't you?" With a short chuckle in his response, just able to restrain a look of disbelief as he stared into his wife's eyes.

At this point Franny had to chime in. "Detective that seems almost ridiculous as far as a match is concerned? Mrs. Patterson is fairly old you know? Her condition can be unstable at times."

"Agreed," but ignoring Franny's condition statement. "Nobody would call it a perfect match and it's not much to go on. But numbers on a license plate are often mixed up. Some numbers and letters on your plate could've been misread." Chris continued. "It wasn't full daylight when the murder took place. We have to broaden our plate search when we only get partial identification." None of this unnerved the cop, knowing the situation better than either suspect. How would they react now, that's what he came to witness.

"A perfect match! I certainly agree it's not a perfect match," Franny exclaimed. "It's not even close." Pausing for a moment turning her head away from Chris. She looked out over the river. So much time was spent out here thinking about events over the last two years. Sarah's death and now her killer getting his just payment. "Christ, my life is so screwed up," she reflected to herself, sitting back, aching to relax. "Detective Davis, do you think we were motivated enough to kill Marcus?" Franny Braden asked rather bold.

Now it was Franny's turn to wait for a response. At this point Chris figured to be firm. He decided on polite also. "Could I have more coffee please?" causing Henry to jump from his chair, filling his cup from the white thermos container. Franny sat still, peering at Chris with a look saying, games are being played out here. "Thanks." Chris kept sipping his brew. "Do I think you killed Marcus? You may have," Davis stated firm. "There are some other things," stopping in mid sentence to see if one of them might offer to complete his words. A clever ploy Davis used with past success. Sometimes paying off with volunteered information.

Henry couldn't help himself and defended his passion. "It's because we like to shoot, isn't it detective."

Chris wasn't facing Henry when he made the statement. He expected Franny to respond and stayed fixed to her, almost hidden behind his coffee cup. Davis detected Franny's slight distress concerning her husband's remark. She reacted like there was something more to be settled and Chris couldn't help but sense she wasn't telling everything. Her hands were nervous. Franny knew something.

"Sweetheart, everyone knows we like our guns and we like to shoot.

A lot! That's no secret," his wife explained. "The detective was referring to other things, I think?" hesitating and realized she shouldn't offer anything unless asked. "Be on your toes damn it. This cop is smart," Franny commanded herself.

"What other things mame?" Chris pursued immediately. Continuing to stare, watching Mrs. Braden squirm in her chair contemplating a response, predicting this could be good. "You were saying," pressing her now. He couldn't look away if he had to as Franny's sex appeal began a surge into his fantasies. She carried herself both feminine and sensual while Chris observed her entire body language. Henry would need to say something in order to break this spell but he thought better. Mr. Braden didn't want to appear too anxious.

"I don't know detective. Why don't you tell us," with a load of attitude in her answer. Franny knew it sounded strange and wished she could've done better. Would the cop press his attack again?

"Is there something you should be telling me mame?" Chris phrased the question a bit aggressive hoping to get some emotional reaction from Franny. His thoughts shifted to and from her erotic looks. She was older than he, but all of a sudden, emerged forbidden sexy. Surprising how long it took to notice her appeal. Franny looked calm. Sitting back appearing relaxed and self confident, legs crossed with a soft dress clinging to enticing, smooth thighs. Reddish brown hair still caught a mild fall breeze and swirled around her face, complimenting that quirky smile. "So exquisitely feminine and in great form," Chris continued to fantasize. Henry seemed old for her, in his opinion. "How the fuck did he land this beauty?" Davis had to wonder. "Money and security?"

Franny was feminine. As a result she knew when a man took notice of her good looks. She could see it shining in the face of this detective right now. Here he rested, in her home, husband at her side, subtle accusations of murder and intentionally checking her out! His boldness both perturbed and flattered her self-esteem. "Go ahead and look detective," she told herself, squirming just enough to show a little more thigh while making sure her breasts were in clear line of sight, adding a casual arch of her back for effect. "Take it all in you bastard." Chris didn't miss a thing. Henry missed it all, fortunately, still caught up in his gun collection.

"I still don't know what you mean detective. What should I be telling you?" Franny Braden spat back close to yelling the words. This caught Henry's attention and he worried his wife may lose her temper. It didn't happen often. But when she was cornered or the least bit drunk, her tone could turn wicked.

"I'm not insinuating you're holding anything back. You mentioned other things. I was just curious about the other things," Davis spoke direct hoping she might lose some self control.

"Just empty words, I suppose detective. Nothing more." Holding a tight grip.

Silence embraced the threesome for the moment. Henry poured more coffee as Chris gorged on the splendid view once again. The river this time. It's rush was more noticeable at the moment due to the silence on the patio. It felt clumsy to Henry while the other two combatants seemed to relish the break. Chris couldn't help but think Regina would see it as an inning change. A short spell to relax and regroup. Offense to defense and vice versa for the other side.

"Tell me about your passion for shooting," Detective Davis requested in a rather flat tone. He looked to Henry for a response. Franny likewise.

Happy the cop asked. Henry started. "Well Chris, not much to it and like my wife says, it's certainly no secret. We both love to shoot for fun as well as competition," Mr. Braden spoke with obvious pride in his voice. "Franny's become quite the shooter also, I must say."

"Do you shoot shotguns too?" Chris asked.

"No. I don't even own a scatter-gun. I never could hit those damn skeet targets. Not our taste I'm afraid." Henry explained wondering why he asked.

"Pistols?"

"Uhm, Franny owns a pistol. Two if you count me," Mr. Braden joked, pleased with his quick wit. His wife blushed. "Franny has a nine millimeter she practices with once in a great while, but could stand much more, I'm afraid."

"Easy tiger, I'm not that bad. Only for self defense detective," Franny interjected. "May I call you Chris? I'm tired of using rank," she asked with a quiet smile, combining her blushing schoolgirl look. Intent on softening the gun association. "What do you carry Chris?"

"Fine with me. Franny?" Davis assumed to use her first name also. "And I carry a nine millimeter." Pulling aside his jacket to reveal the weapon strapped to his belt. "I can't hit shi," pausing to clean it up, "can't hit anything with it!" Both Braden's laughed out loud at the detective's irony.

"What type of rifles do you shoot? Caliber that is," Chris asked the couple.

"Henry will give you the details," Franny said. "Maybe I can find us something to munch on." Rising from her comfortable chair sure to face the cop straight away while bending over to gather the coffee container. "Be sure he gets an eyeful," she said to herself, unsure why she acted this way. Then she walked the patio like a stripper, into her home.

"Let's see. Do you want the entire list? It's kinda long," Henry said in a perplexed voice. "I prefer shooting somewhat larger bores. Eight and nine millimeters. I like a .270 also. Lots of kick but very flat shooting." Recalling his inventory and rattling off others in his private armory. ".22's, .222, .223, which Franny shoots very well. Two .243's. Seven mill, .308 and a .348 I used for deer hunting in Colorado. Good heavy brush gun. And three 30.06 Remington's. I still like shooting my odd six," Mr. Braden spoke affectionately of his last three rifles.

"Quite a collection. I hope you understand why some of us in the department have you both as possible suspects." Chris let the comment stand as he listed the firearms in his notebook. Adding a bold note to have both, the .222 and .223 checked for ballistics, doubting they would match. These two couldn't be that dumb. Finishing with a note about gunpowder checks in the bed of his truck, owning a camper shell matching Beatrice's description.

Franny returned setting out a plate of grissini and sour dough slices with local olive oil for dipping. A small tray of almonds and green olives accompanied her serving. "It's all I could find. Help yourself Chris," eagerly encouraging the detective, using his first name. It made her more at ease.

"What do ya think of Henry's gun collection?" Franny asked the detective. "Quite the firepower, huh," smiling at the cop. "I bet that'll raise a few eyebrows at Tracy's Police Department. Couple of gun nuts with a murdered daughter. Can you say armed and dangerous with mountains of motive," laying ironic emphasis on the last word. She checked Chris just finishing his last scribbled notes but paying close attention to her comments. Henry looked at his wife with jaws clamped, not appreciating what she just said.

"I mentioned to your husband, you both will be considered suspects. Not that you're the only ones." Chris was fully expecting Franny to ask whom the other suspects might be.

"Who else are you investigating detective?" switching back to formalities sitting graceful in her Adirondack. "Anyone we might know?" Franny asked.

Looking at Franny with an evil grin, "you know I can't say anything about possible suspects. But we are looking at," Chris decided to stop and think about his choice of words yet again and to end his comment. "Others." Adding a polite nod. He reached for a slice of bread, plunging it into pale green oil. Swirled and gobbled the snack in one bite. "This olive oil rocks, Franny. Where'd you get it?"

"Oh thanks. Normally I'd serve a red wine with bread and oil but I imagined alcohol might be off limits." Mrs. Braden explained. "I buy most of my oil at a few fruit stands just this side of Manteca. Kinda pricey but it tastes so good. Glad you like it." Henry began to wonder if all police investigations go like this?

Manteca caught Chris's ear and looked at Franny with wide eyes. "I get some great nectarines at a fruit stand in Manteca. Too late in the season to get 'em now unfortunately," Davis revealed, reaching for another bread slice, oiled up, tossed back and swallowed in pleasure.

"The stand at the corner of Jack Tone Road and highway 120?" she guessed.

"Yes," Chris said firm, sitting at full attention.

"Henry and I will drive down just to get a few of those nectarines. We love 'em. I can't find fruit like that anywhere else, but in that stand," she said.

This topic had Henry wondering about the meeting even more. "Maybe we can exchange recipes later on," keeping to himself.

"I hear ya," Chris added. Sat back and looked at Franny again, flooded now in the filtered sunlight. "Even prettier," he thought. "I've checked most of the food stores in Tracy. None of 'em carry fruit like that."

"It's a small world Chris," Mrs. Braden smiled at him for a long time. "Go ahead and get comfy Mr. Davis. Continue checking me out," still thinking and plotting to herself. "I'll be taking charge of this exchange. Soon enough, I'll be leading you right out the door with nothing to go on." Franny made sure the aroused cop had a clear vista of exposed thigh, resting just below her crossed leg.

"What the hell is up with this lady," Chris thought to himself. "Look at her. Showing it off like some bar fly tramp. What's she doing?"

Unaware of the body heat, Henry remarked how much cooler it was, with the sun so low in the sky. "Maybe I'll start a fire, since we'll be here a while." Franny and Chris agreed, partial to late afternoon fires in late fall.

Davis thought a fire was the last thing Mrs. Braden needed right now. Henry fumbled with firewood and matches trying to get hot flames. Franny's coaching only made things worse. Chris didn't mind, expecting the Braden's going all cozy might possibly let their guard down, tripping and spilling new evidence. If they had something to spill? He took in the Stanislaus backdrop again as a bird of prey called from a nearby sycamore. Fall hadn't completely stripped the sycamores of drying, yellow tipped leaves, helping conceal the hawk. Not much longer and every limb would be exposed. Chris opted to start questioning, wondering when the Braden's might be exposed too.

"Where did you say you were at the time of the murder?" Chris asked, realizing neither suspect had made a statement, explaining their whereabouts at murder time. Davis chose to ask this way, open to both suspects. Who would shoot? Always trying to stir the pot.

Henry Braden decided to bat first. "I was on my way to work and Franny was lounging in bed, I believe," verbalizing the remark with a toothy smile, grinning to his wife. She smirked.

"You work for the City of Oakdale, correct?" Chris asked recording a note in his binder. "I'll be verifying statements with the city. I hope you don't mind?" adding the comment anticipating another response. Tracy Police had already checked Henry's arrival time, the day of the murder. Confirming his arrival that morning close to an hour and a half late. Leaving open a rather narrow window, but a window nonetheless. Pulling trigger on Marcus and making work in Oakdale? All within his late arrival window? Close, but possible.

"I'm sure you know I was late that morning too?" Henry told Chris in a comfortable manner.

Chris expected the answer to his next question. "I do. I do at that, Henry. Why were you late, if you don't mind?"

Franny looked at Henry. Henry leaned back. Chris didn't hear anything as his head bobbed up. He noticed the older woman peering back at him sort of funny. Chris cocked his head as if saying, "go ahead."

"Uh, we were running late that morning, detective," glaring down the ridge of her nose at Chris clenching a tight smile while shrugging her shoulders. A whiff of gray smoke drifted around her face adding, "need I explain?"

Chris stopped for a moment. Almost asking to continue, but held silent. "Iron tight alibi!" Nothing he could do now. "What do you do for the city Henry?" the detective asked with no reason in mind.

"I'm a supervisor in the Public Works Department," Henry answered. "Keeping storm drains and sewers open for the most part. I also review and field check contract work."

Smoke billowed from the fire place and getting late in the afternoon, sunshine fought to pour through surrounding trees at low angles. Running east to west, the Stanislaus River was catching its share of full sunlight. Water reflections sparkled as a late season mayfly hatch developed below the large boulder. Up close, small gray wings floated like mini sailboats on a bank side slick, downstream to a handful of small trout feeding steady on free drifting nymphs struggling to make it to the surface. Emergence can be risky business for aquatic insects in their fight for life. All three resting on the patio couldn't help but breath in a superb river setting. Murder, even Sarah's, seemed far away.

Chris' experience led him to believe at this point, maybe the questioning was about over. Both Braden's for the most part, had all the right responses. He mulled things over, checking if he overlooked anything, making a mental note to search Henry's credit card statement. Maybe he wasn't making passionate love to Franny on that fateful morning. If he stopped for gas or bought something to eat, it could negate his alibi. Explanations would be required.

"Our department will be doing credit card checks for the last two weeks. I need to see your cards, if you don't mind," Chris spoke while writing notes and didn't see Henry's fallen look, cover his face.

"No problem," Franny responded. Quickly moving to retrieve her cards as well as Henry's, handing them all to Chris. Two Visas and two gas cards. "Security will be tight I presume?"

"What's that," Chris asked, not understanding the comment? "Oh, security. Yes, for sure. We'll just be contacting the bank for record of use. Just the last four numbers and names will be used," he explained. "I may have most of what I came for," he lied. Pausing, Columbo style, contemplating, analyzing details. "Before leaving however, I'd like additional info," coming across unyielding. "This will be uneasy for you two, I'm sure, but you need to tell me about your daughter and her murder trial, if you don't mind," Chris demanded, knowing he upset the couple. He turned the page of his binder and jotted a quick entry. 'Murder Trial:'

Franny seemed bothered after hearing his request. She didn't want to go over any more trial details, ever again. "Do we have enough time detective," she asked? "We really don't want to open this up again. It's so hard. On both of us."

"I couldn't agree more Mr. Davis," Henry sighed, standing in protest, entering the formal system once more. "You have all you need in the court transcripts. Open to everyone." Mr. Braden delivered his resolute statement with a long arm stroke for effect.

Chris could see Henry wasn't about to cooperate but he was undecided about Franny, considering her behavior earlier. It seemed to Davis, she was just slightly annoyed. "I have to hear the story from both of you. Every court detail can't be covered here, I'm aware of that. I want to hear the story from your point of view. Only so much can be gleaned from transcripts. Emotions are missing, which convey much more to me. It's hard recognizing a possible lie on paper. But spoken in tense situations can often come across as falsehood." Chris wasn't sure they understood but he held his ground. "I need more time with the Braden's. Especially Franny," Chris said to himself. "Some disturbing dialogue wouldn't hurt my investigation either," waiting for their reaction.

"You're not implying we lied about anything, I know that much detective," Henry said with emphasis on we. "Hmm. I don't know Chris, it's getting late. What do you need to hear that hasn't been said already?" Henry asked with somewhat less conviction. Franny stayed mum, then bent forward in her chair and looked at Henry with warm eyes.

"I'll get more firewood sweetheart," she offered, lifting a few narrow limbs, and one large piece from a pile near the corner of the patio. "This cop won't take no for an answer." Franny taunted the detective in a lighthearted but odd way.

"You're right about that," Chris said with friendly smiles this time. Nothing more.

Mrs. Braden carted the fuel while Henry poked the fire, scattering embers and glowing red coals. A couple limbs went in waiting for flames to build and crackle before centering the split log in place. Smoke drifted and lightly occupied Chris's nose with a comforting aroma of cedar. Franny stood behind her husband resting both hands on his upper back, rubbing and patting his slumped shoulders, trying to ease his outward distress. Reassuring Henry all would be fine and they hugged each other with affection. She had completely stopped her earlier show, going out of her way now to comfort Henry and acting with contempt when looking at the detective. Davis couldn't help but surmise, "she sees me as some sort of threat?" But then asked himself if he was reading her right.

The Braden's launched their story. Sarah Braden was born, in a difficult delivery some twenty eight years ago. Henry couldn't say enough how gorgeous Sarah was. "The most wonderful pale olive complexion, from her mother's side and dark brown hair from me. Her eyes were intense blue. We don't know where they came from!" Which struck Chris as odd. Franny didn't look at all pale, but dark complexion was a bit of a stretch. She had reddish brown hair for God's sake! Dye job? Maybe, thinking to himself. Examining Henry now, he seemed to have dark hair with salt and pepper gray beginning to win out. Chris held his tongue stealing quick looks at Franny. She stared hard at the patio floor which Davis interpreted as being miles away. Odd?

Both parents agreed Sara was not an outgoing child. Very timid all through middle school. A few close friends and avid reader. High school helped develop her budding social personality and she matured into an attractive young woman. So much so, the boys wouldn't leave her alone. "Sarah definitely inherited her mom's good looks," Henry spoke very proud. It took a while before his wife looked up, in appreciation. Chris could see, quite easy, the way Franny's mood soured just talking about Sarah, becoming more uncomfortable hearing Henry brag about his daughter. She squirmed and forced smiles to her husband but constantly rubbed the fingers of her right hand across her forehead. Was it Henry's fawning over Sarah making her uncomfortable? Maybe a normal reaction? "Maybe not?" Chris weighed the possibilities. "Wish I could get her alone and really grill her. She's not telling everything. I can feel it. I know it. I will," Chris vowed, "get it from her somehow."

Henry elaborated. Sarah went off to college attending University of The Pacific, in Stockton. Studied English Lit and History. Graduated with a lackluster college experience, but earned her degree. Took a part time job editing blogs and website ads at a small, local newspaper. "She continued working on her teaching credential up to the fateful day," he spoke with a mournful sigh.

"The fateful day?" Chris asked suspecting Marcus Crosby, knowing the chronology was too early for her murder.

"Car battery," Henry said annoyed slouching into his chair staring at the river.

"Come again," Chris said not understanding.

"Her car battery went dead," Franny answered this time, very serious. "A lousy, rotten Wal-Mart car battery determined her fate. "The lucky couple met in a Starbucks parking lot," she went on to explain. Telling Chris about Sarah's dome light left on one afternoon, draining her car battery. "Lucky little Sarah, rescued by non-other, Mr. Marcus Crosby." she groaned with a lethal amount of venom in her voice. His car happened to be parked next to hers. "Can you imagine the lousy twists of fate we're forced to endure sometimes?" Franny said with a heaving chest and wet rolling eyes. Shaking her head in disgust but continuing. "Sarah leaves her car door just slightly open, which never happened before. A dome light drains a cheap manufactured battery from China. An abusive maniac happens to stop to get a cup of tea. Tea I'm telling you. At a Starbucks coffee shop, not even close to where he lives. Somehow he manages to restart her car with a pair of jumper cables he didn't even know how to use." Chris could tell Fanny's story played like a movie in her mind, over and over, every day. Irony coupled with grief and aggravation.

"Some guy in the parking lot shows Marcus Crosby how to set the damn jumper cables!" Henry mumbles under his breath in a tone resembling a black-jack player, just losing, when the dealer made twenty one on a five card hit. "What rotten luck."

"Sarah and Marcus hit it off. They started going out and a few months later, the happy couple announced their spring wedding. It was way too fast. I thought Sarah might've become pregnant," Franny said.

"We were stunned at how soon they decided on events. She barely knew the man but we supported her judgment. We stayed happy for her. Friends kept saying Marcus Crosby, what a lucky catch," Franny spoke her words in a daze of sorts losing touch with the coffee cup which slid from her grasp, plunking to the patio floor. Cracking but not shattering. Reaching to retrieve the cup, checking its cracked handle but still talking. "Lucky catch? Shit. Like Henry said, rotten luck." Franny rested her wounded cup on a small wood end table and presented Chris with an ironic smile. "Only three months later when he first hit her!"

"Wow! Did Sarah attempt to end the marriage at any point?" Chris asked. "Did anyone have any idea that this jerk was abusive or had serious anger issues?" Davis wanted to hear what Franny and Henry knew about Marcus before they married. Also what they didn't know for that matter.

"I have to plead ignorance," Franny said with shame penciled in across her face. Chris could see she carried a lot of guilt. It didn't show at first but her pain appeared genuine right now. "I only met the maniac a few times and it was brief at that. Sarah mentioned one outburst right before their wedding, over some ridiculous issue about having to study so long for her teaching credential." Franny pulled at one smallish log on the fire and repositioned it. Flames grew and thick smoke cleared away. "Neither Sarah or myself had any idea. It seems we were in select company however. During the trial a lot of people testified to his short temper," she stated with a certain amount of disgrace. "Being her mother and last to know was humiliating. My husband wasn't as blind however. Henry remarked more than once, Marcus rubbed him the wrong way and speculated he was a cruel man." Mrs. Braden concluded.

"What did you see Henry?" Chris asked a bit surprised.

"I can't say for sure. Just a hunch. Marcus acted out pretty rude to Sarah," the older man said. Henry stared solid into spreading flames and Chris could tell he wanted to give something more. The detective waited. "One incident happened here. They were over for a short visit just before the wedding. We had a few odds and ends for them to take home. Sarah was stashing things in the back seat of his car when he went red faced and became madder than hell. I still hear his words to Sarah." Henry grimaced a tight clench of his jaw reflecting on the event. "What the fuck are you doing dumb ass! Get that shit in the trunk. You're going to ruin my fucking leather seats!" Repeating Marcus' pathetic rant.

Franny grimaced whenever Henry used swear words. He rarely swore in public but she believed her husband set the appropriate scene.

"I wanted to slap that boy. I wanted to tell that little prick, never speak like that to your future wife. No class. Over nothing for Christ's sake," Henry sighed disgusted with his own inaction. "From then on, I didn't like the man and didn't trust him." Mr. Braden paused. "To make things worse, I did nothing to help my daughter."

Franny gushed at Henry and was proud of her husband. "We just wanted them to be happy together, that's all," his wife spoke with nothing but simple honesty. "It's hard for parents to know what's really going on in their kids' lives. They have to learn how to work things out for themselves." Franny said in a way of hoping this may sound good but not a hundred percent committed to the concept. Deep down both parents knew they should've stepped in. Difficult to do in the beginning, but certainly by the violent second year of Sarah's marriage. When harsh beatings became more frequent.

"Did any of his beatings require Sarah to be hospitalized?" Chris asked while scribbling more notes into his binder.

"No, he was probably too smart to take it that far. I saw a bruise on her neck once," Henry added. "That should have been the clincher, but we delayed. Correction, I delayed. Can't speak for Franny on this one."

"I'm guilty of dragging my feet too and you can speak for me anytime, baby," Franny said rubbing his knee with affection.

"So. by this time they had moved to Tracy. Is that correct?" Chris asked.

"That's about right." Henry added, "we saw very little of Sarah once they moved to Tracy. We assumed she stayed away not wanting us to know about the abuse. To think she would be ashamed. It tears my heart out."

"The beatings continued and finally, everything came to an end over Thanksgiving weekend?" Chris inquired. Neither suspect said anything. Henry got up gradually, stood very still looking out over his beloved river while Franny lost herself in painful regrets. She stared deep into red hot embers. Davis held back, conceding he would be blatantly rude to say anything now. Patient but waiting for the pair to recompose themselves.

"Where's the bathroom?" Chris asked wanting to give the couple room and needing a break himself.

The Braden's maintained silence on a lonesome patio. Henry batted leadoff again. "What's your take my love? You think he believes us?" asking his wife with tender strokes to her cheek but all the while angling for support. "It's hard for me to get a read on this cop," Henry admitted.

"I'm not sure what to make of all this. We won't be hauled off to jail, anytime soon, I don't think." Henry's smiling wife spoke with an uplifting demeanor. "He's not too sure about us either?" The older couple looked at one another then embracing tight in a lengthy hold, trying to stay positive. Out over the river two wood ducks sailed through the trees. Moving upstream in search of a slow backwater to settle into.

"There they go Henry, see 'em? Your pair of woodies," Franny pointed upstream from the patio. Henry rose from his chair, leaned over the rail straining to get a glance of the fleeting ducks.

"Darn it. Missed 'em."

"Looks like that same pair," Franny believed. In reality, almost impossible to know one distinct pair of wood ducks at this time of year. Migrants had been winging south for a month or more. Quite a few birds were settling into lower river basins all through California's Central Valley. Seeking quiet water and plentiful food until winter concludes. But it felt good to Franny seeing such colorful birds nearby. Painted drakes, with their green crested heads cocked upward and robust screaming calls sounded wonderful.

Chris returned noticing Henry bent clear over the wood railing staring at something. "What's up? Spot a bear," chuckling to himself.

"Our pair of wood ducks just flew by. Right in front of those oak trees on the far bank," pointing her finger for direction. "Looks like they settled down just upstream from here," Franny explained while Henry continued to observe, hoping for a glimpse of the resting birds.

"Are these like, pet birds or something?" Chris stammered.

"No, no. Wild birds. Are you familiar with wood ducks Chris?" Henry asked the detective revealing an obvious affection.

"Don't know my birds too well, I'm afraid."

"Gorgeous ducks. Very colorful. The drake bird, that is," Henry informed the confused detective, trying to detail markings and peer through tangles of shrubs and trees at the same time. "They seek these riparian zones when migrating through in winter. Some breed right around here too," realizing he sounded too much over the top, perhaps.

"The riparian zone huh," Chris repeated Henry's reference to river habitat but vaguely understood its meaning.

"Okay Henry, let's sit down," Franny issued polite orders slapping his chair with her outstretched hand. "Detective Davis would like to wrap things up soon I assume," looking at Chris while rubbing her chin with cupped fingers.

"What are your impressions of the murder trial? Both of you." Chris was anxious for the couple to bring up the arresting officer, Douglas Sheets, who was a suspect too. Davis wasn't about to breech his name. It wasn't smart, in his experience, revealing one suspect to another. His personal experience anyway.

"We have differing opinions concerning the trial, I'm afraid," Franny offered, giving her husband a short jab with a feminine fist, solid to his left shoulder. Henry flinched but let her continue. "My take, on the whole mess, is the D.A. and his prosecutors botched their case from the beginning. The explosive atmosphere of that trial was overrun and scandalized by a fanatical press," Franny commented showing more of her raw feelings, it seemed to Chris. "Those small town prosecutors got caught up in the TV lights. Hell, they adored the attention. Their suits and haircuts went upscale after seeing themselves on the six o'clock news for the first time."

Her husband chuckled, nodding in support. Henry's opinion lay with family money. Simple, Marcus Crosby could afford better lawyers. "Marcus had to do it," Henry insisted. "His weak excuse of being away from the cabin all day wouldn't have been accepted in most trials. He had no proof. Those lawyers used this alibi and pleaded his case well. Convincing one juror anyway."

Passions left Franny searching for words to explain her individual belief, but brain lock set in when blood filled images ravaged her thoughts. Pain filled emotions just wouldn't permit the words to come forth. Too much bloody anguish. Too much hatred.

Estefan

At last, Estefan was making his way back. Lucky enough to finish his after school chores early, biking hard for nearly two miles and with any luck, maybe clever enough to retrieve his fortune. Stopping short of the bridge crossing to study traffic and survey what drivers might see from the road. "Not much," he concluded. Being too low for direct line of sight once inside the channel.

Traffic was on the light side, as the lion's share of valley harvests had been completed. An isolated truck rumbled past without a glance in his direction from a tired driver inside. Just what Estefan needed to obtain his prize. Thoroughly fixated, with a clear understanding to get the job done without being spotted would determine his success. An under aged immigrant, carrying a firearm, was a one way pass for him and his family back to Mexico.

Inside his ragged backpack was an even older, beat up blanket, cloth rags, wire coat hanger and one can of Three in One light oil.

"A rifle," the boy said to himself. "I always wanted a gun. Now I'll have a rifle." Estefan wondered what papa would say. "He'll be proud of me, I'm sure," bringing a sly grin to his young face. Checking all around, Estefan had the area to himself. He cleared his tracks nicely. Peddling closer to the bridge as relaxed as possible but hearing a car closing in from behind. They didn't notice. Dismounting to drag his bike off pavement and stashed in a patch of tall, dry shrubs. Estefan moved as far as possible from the road, slipping in behind a large sycamore tree just as two more cars sped past. Continuing along a sparse tree line in a medium jog, slowing to a fast walk, catching his breath, but alert, constantly on guard and checking for cars. He tripped and nearly flopped while climbing a rusted wire fence marking the western right of way corridor but able to scramble through loose rocks at the top of bank grade. Estefan took one final look for passing cars. "Nothing in sight." Reassured. The young boy slid downward digging his heels into soft sand, coming to a stop edging the muddied flow next to a large snag of dead cottonwoods. Two frogs jumped from the bank side into cool, murky water. His true mission was about to commence. Estefan had a clear sense for the gun's location, just downstream from the rotting snag he was hiding behind. Promptly removing boots, socks and pants. Desperate to start his search.

The boy eased his way into a languid water channel but was fast surprised at how quick the bottom slid away. "Wow, it gets deep fast. I'm gonna' have to dive down," frustration showing, talking loud to stay calm. Being late fall, the creek water was becoming quite cold as air temps weren't exactly warm. "I want that rifle." Visions of the person hurling the weapon from the bridge engulfed him.

Removing his shirt next and tossing it bank side, Estefan waded out up to his waist and dove in, headed for midstream. "Jesus Christo, it's cold," immediately bolting back to the surface like a frightened otter. He rose in thigh deep water and discovered, to his advantage, the creek went shallow the closer to midstream he went. Estefan was wading again and commenced a search. Probing a soft mucky bottom with each foot, extending his big toe like a dreadful ballerina, hopeful he'd find his treasure soon. He was getting colder. A few toe scans front to back revealed nothing. "I know it's here," vanquishing weak thoughts of someone beating him to it. Standing in place to survey his next search, something slithered along his left ankle sending the boy into soaring panic and high stepping for safety toward the opposite bank. "What the hell was that," he yelled out! "A snake? Probably one of those fucking frogs, I hope." Wading fast and churning mud into coffee and cream colored stream. Nearing the bank his foot came to rest on something altogether out of place. Hard and metallic. Panic subsided, sliding his ballet toe along the object. Smooth to the touch and fairly long, Estefan bent both knees, reached down into a swirl of mud filled bottom and pulled the object free. Keeping his prize submerged to rinse it clean of sticky mud. Once cleared, the young farm boy slowly raised the weapon above water, gazing with eyes wide open before wading toward the far bank. He went in over his head and forced to swim a deeper side channel but didn't mind. Once in shallow water Estefan forgot about being chilled even though he stood dripping cold, muddy water. Climbing above the channel, back to his hiding snag and checked again for any possible witness. All clear. Gathering clothes but not once losing sight of his trophy. Feeling proud, knowing his papa would be too. For some reason, murder scenes entered the young boy's thoughts.

Estefan cradled the rifle in his arms wiping layers of mud from a full wooden stock, still shiny underneath.

Chris

"In your opinion the prosecutor didn't present a strong case," Chris said while examining the couple's posture. Always studying.

"I thought Mrs. Patterson's testimony would've been helpful," Henry added with a somber tone. "The Tuolumne County DA assumed one of her unpredictable outbursts might alienate the jury. Whatever that means? Sarah confided in Beatrice and they became very close," Henry stated, sipping coffee.

"A little too close," Franny interjected. "I'm not sure how she would have acted on the stand. Nobody did."

Chris was aware of the issue, hearing about Beatrice and her potential liability. "After Sarah and Marcus moved to Tracy, Mrs. Patterson became very close to your daughter," trying to goad an emotional response from Franny.

"That's fair to say," Franny's tone and the look in her eye spoke volumes. "Sarah was my daughter, not Mrs. Patterson's." Adamant but appeared uneasy about the comment. "Playing second base isn't the proudest moment in a mother's life." Chris sensed something else was bothering her but couldn't put his finger on it.

"Do you think testimony from Beatrice would've turned the hung jury?" Chris asked Franny. "Would her testimony have swayed that single juror? What was her name? Mrs. Powell?" Who's identity was suspiciously leaked out after the trial.

Henry jumped in. "I think so. That entire case hinged on a direct witness to the constant beatings. The jury had to be swayed, beyond doubt, that Marcus was indeed an habitual wife beater. Our testimonies must have appeared hollow to Mrs. Powell." Mr. Braden said, then hung his head running both hands deep, through his gray hair. "We didn't do enough, on the stand, to avenge our daughter's death, I'm afraid."

Davis took notice of his words. Especially the word avenge. Scribbling notes into his binder.

"Please Henry," Franny began choking back tears once hearing her husband's words. "Don't. Please, don't."

Chris continued to ask questions, displaying little respect even though the elder couple had fallen grief stricken. Davis had experienced several edgy moments like these, which often reveals a lot about people. To him, Mrs. Braden was on the verge of breaking. Red faced, shaking and all but panicked. "Who else went on the stand?" Davis asked with a serious look, locking eye to eye contact with the extremely attractive woman. She held the back of her right hand over a quivering mouth. Clenched fists and clenched jaw. Her sexy eyes opened wide as they filled with tears.

Chris leaned forward on the edge of his seat, squirming. "C'mon gorgeous. You have something to say. Something to tell me. Let it out," he reflected in silence, convinced she held a secret.

Franny stood opened mouth as her face went pale with a look of shame and extreme sorrow. Chris never looked away as she appeared ready to say something. But Henry spoke again. "The arresting officer took the stand. He testified about probable beatings, as he put it. Those words did more to convince Mrs. Powell, perhaps, that Marcus wasn't abusive. Many of his responses seemed unprofessional and vague at best." Henry looked over to Chris, preparing to speak again.

His wife was regaining her composure and Chris thought he missed another chance to get something new from the woman. "Damn it, bad timing," infuriated with himself.

"Sheets' testimony to questions about a lack of blood on Marcus' clothes almost killed the whole trial," Henry said, then mimicked the arresting officers statement. "I can't say for sure," quoting Sheets and speaking with distaste, "isn't what a jury should hear from the officer at the forefront of a murder investigation." Henry paused to gather his thoughts. "He just wasn't convincing enough for the prosecutors case. Trying to prove by circumstance that Marcus was at the cabin that evening and murdered Sarah. So many times he misspoke, becoming tongue tied." Henry added in a disgusted tone. "Finger prints were even botched. Christ!"

"Hell the arresting officer's own prints were all over the house," Franny added with an obvious mocking tenor.

"The defense raised the possibility of Sheets being," Chris hesitated now, wanting to say romantically involved but opted for, "involved on a personal level with your daughter?"

The Braden's looked at one another, growing uneasy about this topic. "We knew nothing about an affair. The judge threw that motion out and he warned every defense lawyer about breeching the subject again." Henry recalled. "Unless some very serious evidence was brought forward, it was not to be raised again. But just mentioning an affair, I'm sure, had its affect on Mrs. Powell." Henry responded with Franny nodding her head in agreement. "The courtroom became a very strange place from that moment on, if you ask me."

"Strange in what way?" the detective asked scribbling more notes. Nothing but silence from the older couple. They were both at a loss of words for some reason and Chris needed them talking. "What about Mrs. Crosby?" Davis opened up a new topic to get the pair conversing again.

"What about the bitch," Franny issued her harsh statement as Chris secretly verbalized, 'go girl.' "That woman sure as hell learned how to manipulate the press in her favor," she snapped, displaying obvious hatred for the mother of Marcus Crosby. Mrs. Braden leaned forward into her Adirondack and rested to collect herself. Narrow rays of light cut through tree limbs and streaked across her face igniting her conspicuous beauty and Davis couldn't help but linger his stair. She caught his eyes and flashed a sexy glimpse in return. Chris, exposed and embarrassed, fumbled with his next question.

"Did her impact on the trial come from," but stopping quick. "Do you believe she had that much impact on the trial?" Chris asked, getting his question right on the second try. Wanting to hear their opinions of Abigail Crosby's antics around Sonora and during the trial. Chris recalled how Mrs. Crosby was able to get Assemblyman Wulffe, freshly elected from the Fifth District, to hold that wretched press conference.

Standing, sweating in direct sunshine, speaking in behalf of the Crosby family as if he was Marcus' older brother. So many voters lapped it up. Disgusting, as far as Chris was concerned but, what a coup for the Crosby family. Wulffe, the paid for politician declaring this trial must be held in Sonora. "The only place Marcus Crosby could get a fair trial," exulted a bought and paid for hack. "The only place Marcus would be found innocent," Chris thought to himself. Abigail knew how to pick the boobs she helped put into office. They existed on her hook to tell lies then instructed to appear proud of what they were told to say. The consummate politician. It worked in similar ways with her business holdings too. Maneuvering to propose cheaper water allotments for the family's corporate Ag empire in addition to lower pollution standards. Wulffe would be ever-present on the evening Network News, CNN and NPR, reciting the family line without balking. Why not have the elected stiff come to her aid personally too!

"We were in way over our heads. No match for the Crosby machine," Franny explained. "Our brief TV interviews just couldn't compare with her press onslaught and performances. "I have to admit she was way ahead of us. Smart ass woman." Franny hesitated and Chris could see she was reliving some memories of the trial. "Abigail understands theatrics are more persuasive than content, ethics or moral high ground."

"Well said good lookin'," Henry applauded his wife.

"Thank you. But it's true," Franny went on. "Joe public ate it up. They couldn't get enough of her mug and ridiculous outbursts almost every night on the evening news. Right there on the court house steps. The press loved her."

Henry added his own comment. "If the jury got wind of the Crosby public relations campaign, it's no wonder Mrs. Powell hung their decision. I give that Crosby bitch all the credit for derailing the trial." Shaking his head with amused cynicism, believing deep inside the jury had little chance of knowing what Abigail was doing.

"Henry, you mentioned before, the trial got weird. Can you elaborate on that for me?" Chris asked, hoping to keep the momentum going with another topic. Davis wasn't buying jury corruption either. Not entirely anyway.

"The rest of the case centered around forensic testimony. Prosecutors presented their evidence in a way," pausing to recollect, "that wasn't well thought out," Henry stated, convinced of his opinion. "Those fucking defense attorneys objected time after time with hear-say and the judge agreed close to seventy five percent of the time. County prosecutors just weren't up for the job."

Chris watched the pain in Henry's face grow severe. "Go on Henry."

"Sarah's murder took place inside their cabin and her murderer came from inside the cabin. Sarah and Marcus were alone, inside the cabin." Henry raised his voice an octave as he ticked off each allegation. "No sign of forced entry. No phone calls in or out. Marcus testified he and Sarah had a somewhat physical argument. Marcus leaves for an unknown amount of time, returning to find Sarah murdered in a gruesome manner." Henry turned to look at Chris. "Hung jury? You gotta' be kidden' me?"

"Are you okay darlin'?" Franny stood and walked to her husband. She knelt beside him and held both his hands together within hers. "You're my man," she said to him soft. Franny wished her husband wouldn't say anything more. Holding a special fear for his most profound nightmare. She only heard it once. "I don't know if I can handle that again," brooding to herself.

"You know what I keep thinking about," Henry declared while facing the river. He seemed to be talking through the gently flowing water as tender currents helped to endure his pain. The Stanislaus River's charm made it possible for Henry to talk without anguish.

"Henry don't," Franny insisted after scooting close and pressing her head against his shoulder. Her eyes briefly met Chris's gaze and hurried to bury her face into Henry's shoulder. She preferred to hide her husband's pain. "Please Henry. Not now." Placing her right arm across his chest. She begged him to stop. "Henry don't. Please. I love you."

One might assume Chris should be feeling quite awkward, but he didn't. Instead, with Franny and Henry mired in anguish, he coldly envisaged yet another opportunity presenting itself. His experience taught him how this becomes a critical moment. Emotions running high and in rare moments people tend to open up, running off at the mouth. Sometimes by mistake, many times to clear their own conscience. Often saying too much. Chris was dying to ask Franny what her husband knew. "Screw it," whispering to himself way under his breath, deciding to go for it. Scooting forward in his chair, starting to utter Franny's name when Henry spoke again.

"I keep seeing Sarah's horrified look, over and over. Some days it's hard to drive the image from my mind. Our daughter wasn't a tough person to say the least." Henry's words sounded like a wounded apology. "Sarah's personality and physical demeanor was extremely low key. That's what made her such a love and so attractive. Someone like Marcus, much stronger, took complete advantage of Sarah's frailty." Franny hid her face from Chris's view. Henry rubbed his wife's cheek, kissing the top of her head through silky hair. "My thoughts always return to my daughter falling to the floor with that maniac in full view. Somehow, inside her terror knowing she is about to die, fills me with fear and my legs actually go weak and tremble. She must have felt so alone in those final moments." Henry was in tears now. "Sarah's horror haunts me. All alone and life shifting to black. Experiencing your daughter's death is a cruel event." The older man was talking Chris through to his heart, like an artist, painting his most current feelings.

"That's enough Henry," Franny whispered into his ear. He leaned into her lips and it made him feel better. Her breath somehow warming him.

Mr. Braden ended with a remark that surprised Chris as well as his wife. "I could easily kill Marcus Crosby. That fucking bastard took our daughter away from us." Franny turned to glare into Henry's face. Somewhat astonished but impressed. She lowered her head and stared into the detective's face with thin squinting eyes and a smirk, as if to say, "now asshole, go ahead and arrest us!"

To Chris, the door opened and he barged through. "Henry, could you kill Marcus if you knew he killed your daughter?"

"You bet your ass I could," the elder man spoke very low key, without hesitating. Franny lowered her head a bit and Chris was taken at how attractive she looked right now.

"Did you shoot Marcus?" Chris asked direct.

Henry chuckled quietly. "I'm afraid someone else beat me to it detective," answering direct, back to a formal tone this time.

Franny kissed her husband twice on the cheek before standing, then offered in a relaxed voice, "can I get either of you anything?"

Chris declined and thought it best to end matters for now. In his mind the usual questions swirled in, out and through. Were they lying? Did they appear genuine? Alibis? A team job? Franny's attractiveness?

On the river, a late hatch of mayflies grew heavier. Below the mid stream boulder, three or four small trout, steelhead smolts most likely, established feeding positions and sipped helpless olive duns from twirling eddies. Circular swirls radiated outward from each gentle rise. Aquatic insects drifted and rose through moving water columns, determined by nature to carry out reproductive cycles. Predators are present too. By instinct feeding upon vulnerable prey without malicious intent. Life and death in watery poetic movements. Much unlike human endeavors.

•••

Estefan finished wiping his new rifle, rather his first rifle, clean while working a sticky bolt action back and forth. Each movement followed by a swiping rag, to remove watery streaks of mud. From his backpack, he gathered the last clean rag and light oil. Keeping well behind a scruffy old sycamore tree with peeling bark clinging to a wide trunk, oblivious from passing trucks as trickles of shiny oil were spread along the barrel, scope and action. Estefan worked oil around and rubbed the metal to smooth out a polished look. Most of the weapon seemed to be in very good condition. A few very small pits of surface rust began to form on the metal action's side and a short deposit down one side of an otherwise well restored barrel.

Grabbing the wire coat hanger, straightening it as best he could aided by his sycamore's wide trunk, Estefan fashioned a cleaning rod. He tore away a small patch of rag to act as a wad and forced it down a mud laden barrel. A small load of watery mud poured from the breech which forced another wipe down. Repeated swabs seemed to clear the choked barrel. It's chrome like finish would shine bright again once coated with oil. His biggest worry ended as the gun barrel looked fine. Almost shiny!

Timing was just about right with a setting sun helping to hide his new found trophy. Hidden in high weeds, he lashed the rifle, wrapped in a blanket, to the bike's crossbar. Only two cars passed, giving the impression of taking little notice at all. Estefan had to get home as fast as possible, peddling hard, unaware of his aching legs. He understood now the prize must be kept secret.

•••

Chris voiced his goodbyes, thanking his suspects, grateful for their hospitality but by no means forgetting this wasn't a social visit. He knew however, it played that way at times. Slowly exiting the driveway Davis looked back in his rearview mirror observing the Braden household fading away. In his windshield, a low, late fall sun, hung just above rising mountains to the west. Angled sunlight prompted local color spectrums to shift closer to warm tones. Drying leaves stuck to brittle limbs, shined bright yellow among groves of walnut trees. Shimmering as light breezes made them shake and flicker. Further away, parched grasses in fallow fields took on a winter season, reddish hue. Vivid blue skies commanded a rural 209 Area Code. Highway 120, his road home, felt comfortable and easy. Oakdale was quiet this evening.

Chris munched from a leftover bag of candied nuts with thoughts of having a drink later. Hoping it wasn't too late. Drinks rarely came too late for the detective. He wasn't sure about anything concerning the Braden's testimony. Especially Franny. Her good looks stayed imprinted on the forefront of his mind. "I don't know if they committed murder?" mumbling out loud. They would meet again however, deep in fantasy about Franny's sensual body.

Tom

"Five feet left," voicing direction but spoken firm into a radio mike. "Too far Anthony. A foot and a half right," waiting for correction. "Four tenths right. Okay, plumb up," instructing his chainman to straighten the survey rod while sighting the survey instrument's eye piece. Cross hairs focused on a point in Central Valley dirt. Tom's task was getting Anthony to locate his rod tip, as close as possible, to an imaginary position of design improvement. A point consisting of three dimensional coordinates entered into his survey instrument. Northing, Easting and Elevation. Still a theoretical spot on the ground until a wood hub or ginnie, bestowed the location with some sort of intelligence. For now it remained a speck of dirt on sun bleached soil.

"Let's see," groaning out loud and staring at the metal tip attempting to estimate a very small distance correction. "A tenth left," Ellis ordered. The tip became nearly centered in his crosshairs, but not precise enough as the chainman had moved the survey rod a little too far. "Good enough for a distance check. We'll take a shot," as Tom Ellis tilted his eyepiece upward until thin black crosshairs focused once again, on the business end of a survey rod. The reflection prism. Hundredths didn't matter much to Anthony knowing he'd reposition himself to find the correct distance from the survey instrument. He let the rod sink an inch or so into dry crusty soil and held steady, determining the tip's location. Tom's data recorder chirped a few audible notes signaling shot taken and point recorded. This time, the rod tip's relative location was compared to a calculated location. Tom's measured results displayed a distance too close to the instrument.

"Anthony, go away four point seven feet. Your pacing sucks today," teasing his burley chainman with his slighted remark. Anthony took it all in stride, visually estimated his error and prepared to move away just under a rod length. It's not a feet and inches game in the civil engineering world as tenths of feet ruled in field survey. 'Only whores and carpenters measure in inches!' Many surveyors were fond of saying.

"Fuck you," came a booming response over Tom's radio. Anthony moved away five feet, plus or minus, doing his best to stay aligned with the previous shot. Careless movements caused wasted adjustments, left or right, to get back on line. With the rod reset they went through a whole new set of measurements once again.

"Four tenths right," Tom announced. Anthony shifted his rod tip right, just above the dirt surface allowing Tom to call out any small corrections. "Right there," his chief instructed over the radio. "Excellent." Cross hairs from Tom's instrument aligned dead center on his chainman's rod. "We'll take another check shot," which Anthony already knew dropping his bag of tools nearby into dry dirt. Tape measure, paint, hammer, wood stakes and lathe. Tom adjusted his eyepiece centering prism once more expecting the data recorder's conclusion. His survey instrument seemed to be running slow, Tom concluded, perhaps due to low batteries knowing he'd need a backup before too long. Still waiting a signaling chirp but getting dead silence instead, except for low pitched, far off drones groaning from a front end loader. Peering through the eyepiece once again to check target, which Anthony had allowed to lean to left ever so slight, disabling their infra-red connection. Surveying, like shooting, can only hit what one sees!

"Plumb up Tony," Tom yelled into the mike. He saw Anthony jump, pushing the rod back to his right. His chainman hated to be called Tony for some unknown reason, which Tom knew all too well, using it often to get quick attention. Anthony made sure the rod bubble was centered as Tom listened for the chirp but kept his eyes fixed on the prism. Still waiting. Expecting a signal but hearing a woman's voice speaking rather soft, behind him.

"Hello," she almost whispered. "Sorry to interrupt you," Regina said to the surveyor taking one step closer. His back to her.

"One moment please. I'm right in the middle of a shot." Tom's eye kept a continued lock on prism as Anthony started to waver yet again. "Tony," alerting the chainman like a child getting out of line, just as his computer beeped and chirped soft. Recorded. "Got it," signaling his partner to relax.

"Okay. Let me know when you can break," Regina answered back but crept in closer to the yellow camera atop red and yellow tripod legs, the way a juvenile cat sneaks up on unsuspecting prey. Gonzalez found herself enthralled by all the technical code used between the two man crew.

"Will do," Tom replied to the yet unseen policewoman. "Anthony, go away point three five and I'll put the ginnie on line." Regina looked toward the chainman some two hundred feet distant trying hard to grasp their routine.

"Is he taking pictures of that other guy," she wondered to herself, confused but captivated. Anthony dropped to both knees marking the rod location with a metal scribe about the size of a common yellow pencil. Scattering items needed to set a hub and continuing his organized routine. Measured thirty five hundredths away from his marker holding the eight inch guinnie(a large pencil shaped wood stake) in clear sight, vertical to ground, next to his metal tape. Tip touching dirt for stability, waiting for final corrections. The whole routine, done over and over, to get markers set within two or three hundredths of a foot at designed locations.

"Can you see ground?" Came Anthony's voice crackling over Tom's radio knowing his chief watched every move close, from the instrument.

"Clearly," Tom verified. The stake was ever so slight off line. Tom estimated error and long experienced with his chainman, recognizing Anthony's corrections were always too long. "Two hundredths right," Tom said as the chainman moved the hub about four hundredths right, splitting crosshairs. "Put it in," crackled Anthony's radio.

"Yes mame," came Anthony's voice loud and clear from Tom's mike. Regina heard Anthony's remark but didn't connect on his crude joke, being too caught up in the proceedings.

Anthony hammered the stake flush to grade. Set his survey rod on center and imparted a firm push, forming a small dimple in the hub's flat head. This dimple became the true design point. Rod in vertical balance as Tony announced, "shot to guinnie," signaling his chief all was ready.

Back at the gun, Tom still hadn't gone face to face with the voice behind him. Regina didn't mind. Her attention remained square on the specialized dialogue between two field surveyors. Not understanding much, but fascinated.

Tom set the crosshairs on target one last time then focused on prism. Pushed a red enter button to record one final shot. Beep. Chirp, chirp. Catching Regina's ear making her smile. Remaining error of just over one hundredth. "That's good Anthony. We'll write up a lathe. Then I have to talk to someone." Ellis relayed.

Not expecting a response. "Is that your new babe?" Came the chainman's voice loud and clear over Tom's radio.

Regina fielded Anthony's remark clean, forcing a fake grin and feinting blushes. "Oh brother," whispering just underneath her breath.

Tom announced more scripted code, to be written on the marking lathe. A two foot length of flat wood about an inch and a half wide displaying: Elevation 26.77; Point number 412; Station 12 plus 50; Flow line, 18" water pipe. All data to be labeled on the wood stake. "And we have a cut of seven feet even, to flow line." Rendering Gonzalez even more curious as to what it all meant. She loved it.

Tom checked his field point result, comparing 'Cut Sheet' data, making sure it all made sense according to design plans. He was about to turn and address his visitor, but stopped and pushed his radio button. "Make sure that lathe faces west toward the road," instructing Anthony to position the wood marker to indicate an accurate pipe line location. Anthony was way ahead of him and felt insulted by another needless order.

"Already done. Go talk to your bitch!" Tom could only look at the ground in disgrace while hitting the radio button to cut off any additional colorful language. "Tone it down Anthony." Setting his clipboard on a makeshift table made from splintered plywood and empty ten gallon paint buckets. "Sorry," he told Regina getting his first look at the detective. His eyes opened wide and his thoughts changed from apology to maneuver. "Jesus, this lady is hot, in a strange way!"

Regina, arms folded across her chest, looked at Tom pissed off and disgusted. She hated the bitch word and Tom could certainly tell. Removing his hard hat and sweeping long thin fingers through thick dark hair. Making Regina step closer, for a clear view of her suspect. Not expecting at what happened next. Tom's short beard on a tanned face contrasted with his blue eyes and dark eyebrows just perfect.

Attempting to hide her surprise she turned away from the surveyor. "Guapisimo!" Gonzalez almost said out loud. "Jesus, this guy's gorgeous," mouthing words in silence, being sure he didn't see.

"Hey look, let me apologize for my chainman. He's a good guy. Kind of mouthy at times but a good man," the surveyor was backing his partner and good friend all the while taking his best shot at being a gentleman.

Regina remained in the middle of her, "okay, I'll have your baby," fog and couldn't quite formulate a thank you for his apology. So she reached out to shake the surveyor's hand. Still silent. His hand felt firm and warm but his grip was tender and she loved it. Still tongue tied, just managing to blurt out, "I've always wondered how these camera instruments worked?" Walking slow around the tripod, bending to examine every knob and marking. Lacking any apprehension she turned on the sensitive total station the way a child attacks presents on Christmas morning, fumbling with tuning knobs and looking through the eyepiece. She couldn't quite acquire focus but spotted Anthony moving back and forth, blurred, across her vision field. "I can't really see much?" Both hands pulling against the tripod legs to keep her balance and shifting the instrument's set. Then pushing her foot against the stomp for raised support.

"Uh, wait a second, please." Ellis reached out to help the teetering cop stay fixed, preventing a fall into his sensitive instrument. "Do you know what you're dealing with?" he asked while watching her hammer his survey gun out of balance. Regina was now standing on one of the tripods foot stomps, desperate to obtain a comfortable height to peer through the instrument eyepiece! Turning the tool back and forth, wanting to see something. "God just don't knock it over," Tom thought to himself, on guard to grab the instrument but willing to let it fall if he had any chance of catching the attractive detective. He was enamored with her looks. Combined with a bold and somewhat careless attitude, Tom enjoyed her curiosity immensely. She seemed composed in a strange way.

"Anthony, we'll be needing another back sight before setting anymore stakes," notifying his chainman with a subdued chuckle in his voice, forgetting about another possible rebuttal from his workmate.

"What the hell's that bitch doing to your gun, man?" Tom fumbled with his mike but couldn't cut it off in time.

"Hey!" Regina yelled out, prompting a sharp twist, facing directly where the bitch word originated but still hanging on the tripod. "Knock it off asshole," yelling loud enough for one wood framer to quit hammering and spotting the source.

"He can't hear you." Tom became more amused with her passion.

Regina looked back at Tom with her noticeable scoff. "What?"

"He's too far away to hear you detective. His hearing's pretty weak too."

"He'll hear me all right if he keeps dropping that damn B-word," Gonzalez scowled trying to take a step back from the mysterious yellow camera. Unaware her left pant leg had wrapped around a protruding foot stomp on the tripod leg. As she tried taking her second step, the tripod failed to release its grip. An upset and embarrassed woman fell to one knee, kind of hard. Her loose pant leg still tangled in a three legged metal trap. Her sustained balance began to fail then shifted right, however a left leg wasn't going anywhere. The hopeless detective rolled onto her butt, rather hard to firm ground, both legs spread wide open. Regina could only look up sheepishly at Tom, her left leg twisting even tighter to the tripod! "What the hell," trying to force an expression as if to say none of this is my fault, then looking away humiliated.

Tom bent down, smiling, to assist a funny looking detective. It was all he could do to squash a laugh. "Let me help you out'a there," he said, grabbing her upper arms as Regina clutched his shoulders to get a solid lock. Mr. Ellis enjoyed every enchanting moment.

Then it came, "Christ, did you just hit that bitch?" From his radio mike, loud and clear into Regina's ear adding to her rising frustration. Tom's hands were occupied lifting the detective from her snare and saw nothing but rage form over the cop's face. "Oh shit," is all he thought feeling her pluck his mouthpiece clipped to a blaze orange vest with as much deft as any well seasoned, Stockton pick-pocket. When the two dancers obtained vertical plumb, his newfound partner jerked the radio cord so hard, it forced Tom up against the seething woman. They bumped heads gently. So close now he smelled her. "Marvelous," he breathed in deep and exhaled slow. No doubt aroused!

"Listen up jerk," Regina growled into the mouthpiece. "I'm a cop. Got it? You call me bitch one more time and I'll throw your fat ass in jail." She paused for a moment, her chest heaving quite heavy now, sucking air. Tom assumed maybe that was it. "You hear me?" Obvious she wasn't quite finished. Regina held steady, panting in and out.

More than pleasant amusement filled Tom and thought the drama might be finished, starting a slow reach for his mouthpiece. Not yet, Gonzalez sucked in one more deep breath then exploded again.

"Next time you hear the word bitch, it'll be coming from a cell mate slob named Sammy." Another deep breath. "He'll be calling you his bitch! Got it?" Dead silence followed. Only distant whining from a solitary truck running south could be heard, away from Mendota, almost like an attempted escape.

Tom stood at a right angle to Regina's face. Still very close. So close, he could see tiny drops of saliva shoot from her mouth as she screamed into the mouthpiece. One vein expanded just above her left temple but below hairline. Jaw muscles bulging and tensing behind reddened cheeks. White teeth and messy dark brown hair. A perfect dark brown. Approaching black in some angles of sunlight. Tom hoped she would continue, enjoying their closeness the way children enjoy a mother's affection. He relished her cell mate comment. "Great word usage," he told himself. Regina kept keen eyes trained forward, covering the far off chainman. Her steady breathing starting to calm, but still audible.

Anthony's lame apology crackled over the radio, "Uh, okay. Sorry, my bad." Dazed and embarrassed.

Regina was tense, but regaining reality, turning to face Tom. They remained close, face to face with each other, tight and both breathing hard. Her, due to a stirring outburst. He, sucking air just standing so close. Regina lifted her hand, coming to a soft rest on his chest, offering a return of his radio mike and putting slack into the cord. Tom eagerly cupped his hand around hers as slow as possible and lifted the mouthpiece. They lingered, examining, finally stepping away from one another. She flashed a short quick smile, dipping her head for a moment. "Sorry Mr. Ellis. I guess I kinda blew apart there."

Tom blinked, smiled and said, "not a problem. Tony had it coming. But who's this Sammy guy?" Backing off another step, adding some much needed humor to the moment.

Regina adored his comment. Feeling relieved her suspect didn't take her for some sort of whacko. She couldn't help but giggle like a thirteen year old and beamed her charming face to him. "Ya gonna show me how your camera works?" asking Tom, rather innocent.

Tom fumbled around for coherent words not expecting the request, then committed a complete demo to his new acquaintance. Describing the instrument's function and in short order had her taking topo shots of various people and equipment scattered about the job site. "Most assume it's a camera too, and start acting all photogenic as if their picture is being taken." Regina felt somewhat let down realizing the yellow device wasn't a high tech imaging device. Although current survey instruments are every bit high tech and incredibly precise, logging points on the ground within a couple hundredths of a foot accuracy. This station did carry a small built in camera used as a log for complex features when mapping an area for redesign. "The instrument's main function," Tom explained, "is recording three dimensional coordinates. It's all about X,Y and Z, followed by a picture. Not the highest quality but enough to help a Cadd Drafter interpret data for drawing topo." Ellis took a quick picture of Regina and himself, standing close, then emailed the photo to her cell phone.

Not bad, she thought! "Hey, that's kinda like stop action replay on a called third strike," the detective replied to a somewhat confounded surveyor.

Tom looked at the well trained professional lady with a tilted head. "I guess?" not understanding her comparison at all, but enjoyed the moment nonetheless, becoming much more comfortable in Regina's presence. Imagining many different scenarios, having just met this woman who seemed younger than himself. One of which was fighting off a prevailing urge to buy her a drink later. "I kinda doubt you're here to learn about surveying, detective. What brings you out to my jobsite?" he asked. "Ted's email from your Captain Anderson I believe, was fairly vague."

"Well," Regina muttered, waiting a moment until selecting the right answer, not wanting to break their lackadaisical atmosphere. "I'll just say it," making quick eye contact then staring at the ground shuffling her left foot in loose dirt. "You're a murder suspect." Leaving it go at that. "Your move handsome," she said to herself.

Tom didn't know what to say. "So, what took you so long flatfoot?" holding a ridiculous look on his face like yeah, I'm a stone cold killer.

"You may not want to joke too much about this one, Mr. Surveyor."

Tom reached for his mouthpiece. "Anthony, today we'll be having a long lunch." Regina grinned, recognizing neither took the accusation seriously.

"Is she taking you to meet Sammy?" Anthony crackled over the radio.

"Good call partner. She might be at that!" Tom replied as Anthony heard them laugh out loud from his speaker.

A small flock of mourning doves flew low over the jobsite twisting in separate courses over the road through town. One turned sharp to the northwest and the others followed, continuing over a plowed tomato field. Dropping low they regrouped, tightened their stations and would be under fire soon from a shooter waiting at an adjacent orchard. Most would make it through. One, maybe two wouldn't.

"Okay detective, I confess. I shot him," Tom joked to Regina again, holding out both hands as if receiving handcuffs.

Regina grabbed both wrists but couldn't stop blurting out, "I may enjoy doing this!" Then immediately wished she hadn't. "Oh Christ," holding a hand over her mouth, blushing, turning away. "I can't believe I just said that! This guy thinks I'm some kind of sex crazed cop," scolding herself and turning deeper red all the time. Tom stared, eyes locked on, not letting go. Making her feel a little bit worse each time she peeked in his direction. Turning away, peeking, like a fresh scolded schoolgirl.

"I am utterly shocked by the nature of your expression, miss," going blank in the middle of his fake disapproval. It just occurred he didn't know her name! "What's your name anyway? I'd like to know who to charge when you cuff me too hard," Tom bluffed, still burning straight ahead at the red faced detective, taking great pleasure in every moment of her uneasiness.

Regina thought this may get her off the hook. "I'm Regina. Detective Regina Gonzalez. Tracy Police Department. Homicide." Rendering Tom slightly less secure and reluctant to dwell much longer on her handcuff remark. Opening her leather jacket and revealing a black 9mm sidearm hanging in her shoulder holster. She removed a business card from her inner pocket revealing a rather tight fitting knit shirt, which didn't hide much underneath. Handing her suspect a routine blue card, feeling poised and focused on his pleasant face.

Tom took close inventory of Regina's sidearm. Checking her business card but his mind was preoccupied with how well armed and shaped, the detective exposed. "Nice guns, I mean gun detective." Tom hurried to correct his gaffe and praying she didn't grasp what was really of his mind. "You dumb ass," he admonished himself. "Is that a forty five?" hoping Regina might take the bait letting him wiggle free of his own hook.

"Nine millimeter. Autoloader," Regina replied tugging at her jacket then crossing both arms over her chest acting with grave offense. Flattered in all honesty. The handsome suspect was noticing anyway, she told herself wondering how her next comment might shake things up even more. "I do own a pair, of nine millimeters, for your information," she said trying to hold a cop-like straight face. They both burst out laughing.

"Hey, you Tracy cops sure make interrogations a lot of fun detective," Tom remarked still chuckling.

"Oh boy, I know. I'm going to have to tighten things up here," Gonzalez told a relaxed suspect and reminded herself this rather handsome, nice guy, could be a murderer. Deep inside her gut however, she had already passed judgment. Not guilty. "So Mr. Ellis, I do have a few questions to ask," Regina warned, wanting to give Tom the impression that things were about to become much more serious. "Mostly routine," she added, inspecting the outskirts of the rough jobsite for a comfortable place to conduct an interview. "But, some questions," pausing for effect, "maybe not so routine." Eyeing the land surveyor, angling for any sort of facial response or body language which might indicate nerves.

Mr. Ellis shrugged his shoulders responding with a quick, "no problem."

He came across confident and relaxed. Nothing unusual, very attractive.

"Where can we sit and talk, Mr. Ellis?" Regina asked.

"There's a lunch area on the other side of the contractor's trailer. Nothing more than an awning and picnic tables. Hardly anyone uses it. We could be alone over there, if you like," wondering if his use of the word alone sounded too personal. "Or," powerless to refrain from a little humor, for some unknown reason, "we could head out to any one of Mendota's many dive bars?"

"Sounds perfect." Regina's comedy kept coming.

"Which one?" catching Tom off guard again.

"The dive bar of course. What could be more quaint?" Regina's zealous words steered her suspect on. "Let's see, which one? Mi Ranchito? The Busty Senioritas? Or wait, how about Town and Country Pool Hall? Are they still in business?"

Tom stared at the sexy cop pretty well shell shocked. "What the," stumbling for dialogue but incapable of a witty response. "Do you party in Mendota or what?" asking to some extent serious and amazed this detective could name three of six dive bars no less, flourishing in marvelous downtown Mendota!

Knowing she had Tom Ellis thoroughly bewildered by her local knowledge. "It's a long story Mr. Ellis," beginning to walk toward the trailer. "We'll use your lunch patio. Let me guess, dirt floors?"

"Uh huh. The finest eastern sierra red cinders money can buy. We opted to remove the white linen though. Nothing like eating on genuine sugar pine. All natural by the way." As they walked Tom revealed how he got into surveying and came to own his own business. A crew of two and change, when the economy allows. Anthony, himself and a seasonal aid managing his answering service. "All working together like a well oiled machine, keeping Ellis Surveys Limited, World Headquarters viable and flush with cash." In reality, becoming self employed ten years previous, a short time after earning his L.S.

"What's an L.S." Gonzalez asked?

"Licensed Surveyor. Number seven, seven, eight, four." Telling the detective with a taste of pride in his voice.

"Licensed Surveyor? What do you pay for that?" Gonzalez asked somewhat naive.

"Loads of blood for about ten years," Tom replied, feeling a modest insult but understood, very few people knew of the time and experience required in earning his professional license.

Regina told Tom, in brief, of her time living near Mendota. She didn't elaborate details, but Tom sensed the detective was pleased to be living away from this part of California's Central Valley. Still edging the 209 area code however, not entirely removed. "I gave about fifteen years of blood. All growing up around here," attempting to steal some of his thunder.

Clear skies and a slight cooling breeze covered most of the middle San Joaquin Valley. Overall the day was pleasant and a light sweatshirt would keep one comfortable, if occupying available shade. Another flock of doves passed near the patio just as Tom and Regina made their way to the trailer. Agricultural dormancy was in full swing with the patio surrounded by a number of harvested fields. Orchards were bare except for year round citrus groves bearing ripe fruit in the Indian Summer sunshine. Most farm activity currently plugging away was routine maintenance work. Repairing irrigation pipe and valves; Pruning nut trees and burning high stacks of dry branches creating huge pits of wood ash and sending carbon into the atmosphere; Tractor and truck repairs; Preparing vegetable fields for winter doldrums or plowed for winter crops.

"Are those gunshots I keep hearing?" Regina asked taking a seat at one weathered picnic table displaying loose planks on the opposite seat. Listening close, she heard another series of muffled blasts emanating from out of sight fields.

"Dove hunters probably," Tom assumed. Taking keen notice of the occasional bangs, wishing he could join in.

"Oh right. How could I forget. You gringos love your shotguns down here and it's open season on our consummate bird of peace. Only in the Valley, I guess." Regina lectured the surveyor, who was trapped in yet another loss for words. Seating himself opposite the detective, discovering a loose plank by accident and waited for the grilling to begin. "So Mr. Ellis," prompting Tom to interrupt the detective.

"How about Tom. Why don't you call me Tom? Mr. Ellis makes me sound so old."

"Okay. All right." Regina agreed. Preferring to keep her interview less personal. "This guy didn't kill anyone," she admitted to herself again. Becoming hard to keep the hammer down on an innocent suspect. "Mr. Ellis. Why did you shoot Marcus Crosby? We know you did it." Trying her best to sound like a red ass cop. Failing terribly.

"I hated that lousy bastard from the get go. You and I both know he deserved it. Tell me you aren't glad the world is finally rid of that son of bitch. Michael Crosby deserved to die a long time ago. End of story." Ellis performed well.

She wouldn't take the bait. Didn't say anything. Slipping a hand inside her jacket, careful this time, removing a small notebook. She couldn't help sneaking a peek at Tom when her jacket opened. Tom's eyes shifted away fast, but knew she'd caught him again. Second offense! Regina slapped her small paper notebook with a sharp crack onto cheap pinewood, jerking his attention back to the detective. Gonzalez was indeed enjoying his interest. She enjoyed toying with her innocent suspect even more, like a bored house cat teasing wounded insects.

"Marcus," she said to him with a palpable emphasis on the first name, making it evident he used the wrong name in his ridiculous confession.

"What did I say?" asking with innocence, gushing.

"Michael."

Ellis could see she wasn't taking it all serious. "He deserved it too," was all Tom could think of and added on, "I shot 'em both!"

"So, you'll be coming downtown with me. I assume you want to put it in writing?" Regina continued the joke another step.

"I'll go anywhere you want me to go," using his most feeble of sexy voices.

"Okay, okay." Feigning her disgust again, raising both hands over her head, waving them back and forth in pretend surrender. Tom thought it better to back off, unaware Regina was taking a lot of pleasure in their exchange. She looked around for a moment. Leaned forward with her chin cradled in both palms and stared at Tom for a few seconds. Biting her lower lip a couple times. Tom observed the playful lady transforming into a serious cop.

"Do you know what murder I'm talking about?" she asked with a somber tone.

"I think so," Tom answered leaving the comedy behind. "Some guy gunned down in his driveway about a week ago. In Tracy I assume," he acknowledged her Tracy Police Department association. "His name must be Marcus?"

"Yes sir, that's what this is all about. The Marcus Crosby murder. You're familiar I see. Did you know him by any chance?" the detective started mining deep for any type of incriminating comments.

Ellis swallowed hard, looking at Regina with eyes wide. "Did I know him?" asking in disbelief. "Wait a minute Detective Gonzalez. You think I had something to do with this don't you?" Tom acted very serious, but at the same time, Gonzalez judged him too calm. Way too calm for someone just accused of committing a violent crime. Ellis began rubbing his five day old beard, up and down his left cheek using the tips of his fingers. Waiting for a response.

"I'm here to let you know, you're a suspect," Regina informed the surveyor, speaking soft and very serious, dwelling for a moment. Letting her comment sink in, avoiding eye contact but watching him rub. "An eyewitness managed a partial license plate I.D. on the shooters vehicle," She said. "Your plate number came up on our search."

"Wait a minute. Your witness identified my license plate?" Emphasizing the word 'my' very loud. "Gotta be a mistake." Rising fast from the picnic table almost losing his balance. Tom grabbed the table top to keep from falling over, displaying an irate expression. Regina stayed relaxed and watched him close. Noting every move her suspect made. Gonzalez had witnessed far too many suspects trying to act their way out of suspicion. "She," Tom stopped quick, looking straight into the detective's face burning his stare thru Regina's eyes, "or he, got it wrong." Holding his sights on a most pleasant looking woman.

Regina stared back, as the will of both combatants to win over, continued. She focused on the shade of blue and intense darkness of his eyebrows, with little regard for his comment. "Like I said, she identified a partial plate number. What type of truck do you drive by the way?"

Tom relinquished his temper turning away from Regina. Bracing himself with raised hands gripping the tinny awning, his eye caught two more doves close to the construction site, winging for a plowed cotton field. They appear so powerful. Very small but so swift, streamlined with pointed airfoil tails enabling sharp, twisted patterns, working hard in flight. Shifting, diving, turning and sailing. Nothing effortless about their movements. Ellis appreciated the gauntlet these birds have to run during hunting season. Shooters take a heavy toll on dove populations but the durable birds continue to thrive throughout the valley. "Uh, what?" snapping back into reality. "I drive a truck. A blue Nissan," not offering additional details.

"Dark blue?" the detective asked.

'Umm, yeah. Kinda dark blue, I guess." Visualizing his truck. "Royal blue, maybe?"

"That's why I'm here. Your plate number and vehicle type matched the search criteria. DMV issued your name. You have a camper shell on your pick-up," the detective confirmed while scribbling a reminder in her notebook.

"I do have a shell on my truck," Tom was sounding more confrontational. "That's not enough to make your department press charges, is it?

"Of course not, but I have to be thorough. Just doing my job, Tom Ellis," Regina spoke as gentle as possible attempting to calm her suspect. She couldn't help feel a little curious about his character at the moment. "He's definitely lost some of his cool," contemplating his attitude.

"Am I under arrest?" Ellis asked, sounding worried in a sincere manner. "I've never been associated with anything like this before. I mean, connected to a murder. Not me!"

"No, you're not under arrest. I don't have nearly enough evidence for an arrest, just yet," adding fuel to keep the fire alive but making sure he saw her smile, letting him know she wasn't serious about her 'just yet' remark. "We're following up on some," Regina stopped, concluding it might be smarter if she didn't give the impression just how weak her case may be. "Some...kinda thin leads to be frank."

"Maybe I should hire a lawyer," Tom said knowing he didn't have much extra money for legal fees at the moment. "You know, this was a lot more fun when we first met about an hour ago." Tom focused more subtle details around her face. He became obsessed and intrigued with her beauty. "What the hell is it about you," he wondered. "Your simple act of eyes moving from notepad, to my face, back to notepad. It's killing me. She's extraordinary," thinking to himself.

Wagging a red pen flickering between thin fingers, she decided on a different tack. "Where were you on the morning of the murder? Working?" Regina didn't know what to expect. A quick response might indicate a canned answer. As many guilty suspects have answers memorized. Not always but now and again. She could see he was thinking back through quite a few days trying hard to connect the murder date. "It was last Wednesday. A week ago," she told him.

"Last Wednesday," Tom thought a moment longer and then his face lit up with an, I'm innocent look. "Of course. I was duck hunting," responding with a taut smile. "Did pretty well too."

"Duck hunting?" a skeptical detective asked. Her nose squished and eyes squinting, shaking her head slow, side to side as her pen tapped the pine tabletop. Regina never expected this defense. First time for this alibi, matter of fact. "You don't look like a duck hunter. I've known a few duck hunters and you don't fit the bill?"

"Good pun."

"What pun?" she squinted harder and tilted her head. Bewildered.

"Bill. Fit the bill. Ducks have bills, not beaks. Nice pun." Tom noticeably tapped his knuckles on soft wood waiting a reply. Silence from the detective except for an extreme low pitched groan. "Okay, so I don't have a long beard, no camo face paint, no duck calls hanging around my neck, no waders, no dead birds on a leather strap." Wanting some sort of comment. Hush.

Regina couldn't invent a snappy comeback but enjoyed her suspect's aggravation. "You finished?" she asked, rubbing his wounds.

"Maybe." he answered.

"You're too pleasant to be a duck hunter," she said, leaning away, head dipping, feeling self conscious about her personal remark. She expected him to deliver another clever comment but dreadful silence followed. Gonzalez had no reason to doubt him, deciding he was being honest. So many guys from this area enjoyed bird hunting. Doves, quail, pheasants, geese, ducks. None of these birds were safe during fall and winter. To Regina however, 'that crowd' had a certain look about them. More redneck! More gringo.

"Okay Thomas," Gonzalez pressed, perhaps resembling his mother as she scolded her young boy. "Where were you hunting and can you prove it?" showing a display of reasonable skepticism.

Tom thought about his answer, realizing the cop may not understand his response. "I hunted in Los Banos. A Wildlife Refuge in Los Banos. You probably know where it is since you grew up around here?" Ellis outlined his hunting area.

"I vaguely remember," the detective interjected.

Tom was more concerned about proving it to her. "I got a limit of ducks too. Huh? Not bad, huh?" Once again trying to keep the mood in a low key atmosphere.

"Prove it, oh brave, blue eyed hunter. Prove to me you hunted that day and maybe, just maybe, I will set you free." Regina sensed the interview becoming less of a question and answer encounter. "I don't think this is our guy." Reflecting on similar thoughts she had earlier in their meeting. "Tom Ellis you just don't seem the type to commit cold blooded murder." She told herself.

Their minor confrontation which developed earlier had subsided with Tom feeling the comfort level gaining momentum. Comfortable on rough wood tables under a metal awning, with the aid of a light fall breeze softened their situation. Ellis enjoyed Regina's company even after accusing him of murder!! She felt it too. "So, how do I prove it?" Recalling the refuge checkout procedures that evening, Tom was reminded of the young biologist collecting wing samples from harvested birds. "You can check my hunting permit. My license number should be on last Wednesday's hunting permit. I'll join you, if you want?"

"That won't be necessary. I'll get to the refuge later this week to verify your story." Writing a few notes about Los Banos refuge location and wondering if patrolman Buck could assist in her investigation. Remembering Buck hunted ducks also, jotting additional notes about the patrolman. She verified his hunting license and noted Tom's number. The letter H, for hunting, followed by a six digit number.

"This doesn't completely exonerate you, Mr. Ellis," speaking in force, perhaps too heavy for that matter, but intentional. "I still think you did it. Why'd you shoot him Tom?" Regina sounded way too close to an old TV cop show.

"All right flatfoot, I confess once again," playing along with her absurd farce. "Mike was a rat and a big meany," once again Ellis used the wrong first name for cheap effect.

"What type of guns do you own Mr. Ellis?" Regina did an about face and Tom could see she just double clutched back into serious.

"I own a few shotguns. For bird hunting." Tom replied.

"What kind?" Asking sober.

"I have a pair of Browning Citori's. Over and under. One twelve gauge, one twenty," Ellis stated. "Also an older Remington twelve gauge. Model Eleven Hundred autoloader. That's it," running through his arsenal.

Regina recorded the list of guns. "Hmm, nice guns," turning Tom's earlier hardball around for her own homerun! She smiled wide at the surveyor.

"Touché," complimenting her wit and good charm.

"Tom. Is there anyone who can verify you were out hunting?" she asked with an almost helpful tenor inside her question. "You were hunting alone I presume?" Regina was still persuading herself Tom wasn't the shooter, but in her position, she had to be meticulous. The detective inside couldn't help it. She maintained a modest heat, if for no other reason, maybe he'd trip and say something out of character. Anything, to make him seem a little more suspicious but she was betting it wasn't there. It wasn't going to happen. He was either very good or very innocent. Leaning toward the latter.

"Like I said detective, just me and my shotgun," Tom answered, running a visual loop of potential supporters. Deliberating for a moment but could only think of Anthony. "I gave Anthony the day off with pay. He knows I went hunting. He can vouch for me," sounding every bit like a young boy, out to fool mom one more time he didn't eat the candy. "See, that should clear me!"

"Was he there to watch you walk into the swamp carrying your gun and rubber ducks?" she posed with the perfect measure of sarcasm in her voice.

"Rubber ducks my ass." Tom sounded riled.

"Uh huh," the detective teased.

"Marsh." he added in.

"Pardon me?" Gonzalez asked. Unclear about her innocent suspect's last statement.

Tom shied away from sounding cross or ingratiating. "It isn't a swamp. We call it a marsh. A refuge marsh," speaking with a sincere level of pride in his statement. Not bragging but expressing specific terms instead to describe the places he held dear.

Regina didn't mind hearing his opinion at all. If nothing else, it implied a degree of respect for the areas he stalked which speaks volumes about hidden character in a man. "I like that," writing the words in her notebook.

"They're beautiful places and I cherish my time spent there. Much more to it than just shooting birds." Looking away from Regina's rather admiring face, Tom was feeling embarrassed for his exuberance.

"I can tell you're sincere about your pleasure Mr. Ellis. I must say, it sounds kinda cool. Are you married?" Asking another one of her patented, from left field, questions.

Turning back to her with a strange look on his face like, where the hell did that come from! "Single," Tom replied. Uncontrolled thoughts about his wife flooded his head. Similar in a way, how forgotten acquaintances pop into memory for no apparent reason. He tried for years to bury his pain and made progress. Tom hadn't thought about his wife since earlier that morning and Martha's image never returned, since the detective arrived. "I was married for a few months. A long, long time ago"

"Things didn't work out?" asking like a detective.

Tom had a quick impulse to tell her more, but decided against it, for now. "Uh, no. Afraid not," he simply stated.

"I don't think I need to go into it," Gonzalez responded as if familiar with the sordid details of another failed marriage. Infidelity, lying, too many work hours, not understanding, not listening, growing apart, falling out of love. She knew nothing of his ordeal, abandoning the dime store analysis.

Tom thought the subject may come up again someday. He could explain then, if needed. Regina, on the other hand, was quite relieved Ellis was single. She imagined his ex wife story would surface again someday too.

"How about you detective?"

Regina laughed. "I'm not a suspect." Lingering for a moment to see if he wanted a definitive answer. He did. "Nope. Never been married." She wanted to leave it at that but couldn't help asking, "Why?" The detective anticipated something unexpected from the handsome man, but remembering, still a suspect.

Tom wanted to offer a dinner date, right now. He wanted to spend some time with her, right now. He wanted to press her body tight against his, right now. He wanted her in his bed, right now. Looking away before blurting out something ridiculous, right now. He had to hold it back forcefully. Scratching his forehead searching, contemplating the correct words. Don't take that step. It's not the right time. She'll think you're some sort of loser. If she leaves, I may not get another chance. She's a cop for Christ's sake, accusing you of murder. What if I said...

"Cat got your tongue Mr. Ellis?" Regina charmed in.

Clearing runaway ideas inundating his mind, of a dumb ass request like, let's have a drink, babe! "Just curious." Tom replied, relieved he kept to the cautious side, having a hard time not staring at the detective. She, without realizing, had captured him and like teenagers, managed to swipe a glance or two at one another. Each one, veering away after a soft gaze and slight smile. Both needing to speak free with each other but couldn't. It wasn't their time. Nothing was said aloud in the exchange but almost everything was conveyed to each other with body language and intuition. They knew at this time anything could happen but silence dominated. In the distance Tom heard more gunshots wondering if lead shot was striking their marks. Hoping for some strange reason, they didn't. It feels good knowing the small fast birds were too swift this time. "Regina may be too swift for my aim," he told himself. Tom might have to take that shot however, sooner or later.

"I don't think I need anything else, except your truck," Gonzalez stated, sounding as though the department was about to confiscate his vehicle. "I have to see your truck. You have it here don't you?"

"Yep, in the contractor's lot. I'll lead the way," walking around the work trailer a short way with Tom pointing out his rig.

"So, this is the murderer's platform," delivering her routine sarcasm. "Our eyewitness described your truck very well Mr. Ellis. Dark color, camper shell, mid size and what else?" This time, with some genuine surprise. "You have a bumper sticker don't you?" Regina did a quick double take in Tom's direction then stooped to get a closer look. "Not really a badge shape. A duck head? What is this?" she asked picking at a frayed, white corner peeling from the chrome bumper. "What the hell is this? The Ellis family crest?"

Tom lowered his shoulders in modest disappointment. "Sheesh detective, it's a D.U. sticker." The suspect spoke with an implied tone of 'you don't get out much, do you'.

"Okay I'll bite, what's a D.U.?" shooting back, a bit bruised, after his display of bad manners. "I'm not the bumper sticker type, gringo," telling herself to stay calm while maintaining an irregular smile.

Tom peered at Regina with his wrinkled forehead. "Ducks Unlimited, detective. You know. I hunt ducks," speaking rather stern. "I support their conservation efforts." Ellis declared steadfast.

"Oh yes. Yes, I've heard of them. Sorry. The abbreviation threw me. It won't happen again Mr. Hunter, I promise." Regina tried turning the spotlight back on him. Imitating Tom's lack of patience. "They have a great reputation, I'm told." Making another entry into her notebook.

"Sorry. I went off a bit there. Won't happen again Captain," using his form of tit for tat. "They do great work. You might consider giving to the cause," Tom said.

"I'm not a duck hunter. Although, I did give it a try once, a long time ago in a galaxy far away," she said recalling her dreadful event. "Not one of my best memories from that far off galaxy." Bringing a raised eyebrow to Tom's face. "His name was Eduardo," causing Gonzalez to chuckle aloud, just thinking of the poor boy.

"Let me guess. An old boyfriend you loved to death at the time and would do anything to please, dragged you out on that cold, stormy, winter morning. You just adored him. But, more than likely, you ended up falling into freezing, muddy water hating the whole screwed up experience," Tom chronicled the episode as if he witnessed the entire event. "As well as seeing Eddy in a completely different light. Am I right?" he asked with boastful assurance.

Regina said nothing unwilling to give her suspect the pleasure. She acted as though his narrative went unheard. "I'm sorry did you say something?"

"You heard me," knowing the shrewd gal was putting him on again.

"Not bad. Not bad at all Mr. surveyor man. Good guess? Or, maybe you're drawing on a similar experience with one of your ex's?" Regina expected his next tirade. It didn't come.

Obvious they both enjoyed their exchanges. Gonzalez was close to finishing her interview and felt strange, almost dejected, knowing it was over. Tom hoped their meeting would last well into tomorrow morning. "I'd love to cook this woman some Eggs Benedict tomorrow!" Fantasizing an erotic morning.

"Maybe you should consider another try?" His query was extremely loaded. Clear in his words what was on his mind. Regina didn't quite make the romantic connection. To her, shooting waterfowl would in no way, relate to romance, for what she knew now. Watching the surveyor smile however, commenced some immediate second guessing.

"Maybe. Someday. You never know," her ambiguous statement which Tom read as no way in hell mister. He was wrong, failing to read between the detective's lines, at the moment. "Well Mr. Ellis, you have my business card."

Tom drew one of his cards too. In no way was Miss Gonzalez getting away without his phone number. "Just in case you need a property survey."

"Thank you," she said smirking and eyeing his number. "The two zero nine area code," logging a mental note to herself and slipped it inside her notebook. "Please, Mr. Ellis, feel free to call me anytime, if you think of something I should know about this crime. Anything at all. If you've forgotten anything, let me know," repeating her instructions one too many times, Regina thought. "I hope he doesn't get the wrong impression." Very soon realizing, she hoped he would call. For anything! "I'm going over to Los Banos Refuge. Will let you know what I find out."

"Miss Gonzalez, I didn't kill him. You must know that," Tom declared, assertive this time. Using his most serious tenor Regina had heard all day, from the pleasant looking man.

They moved toward a rickety chain link fence with gravel crunching under foot as silence prevailed. "I think, just between you and me, I'm believing you gringo." Reaching the gate, Regina turned and looked at her suspect one last time. "So appealing," she thought to herself again. "But, I've made a few mistakes about people before." They shook hands followed by an adolescent awkward goodbye. Regina was ready to turn away, but then stopped fast. "Oh, Tom. I forgot to ask. Where did you go to school?" she inquired.

Tom went unnerved by this sudden, unexpected probe. "I went to Fresno State. A math and field survey major."

"What about high school?"

"Uh, Los Banos High. Class of eighty five. Why?" A little on edge.

"Just wondering," the detective responded and turned away, issuing a short wave goodbye. Tom noticed the detective write yet another note once inside her car.

"No big deal," telling himself, watching Gonzalez drive away, speculating about the meeting. What would the sexy detective find in Los Banos? The Refuge? Would she even know where to look? She should be able to find the hunting permit. That should make it all a mute point, assuring himself. Next week will be Thanksgiving. "That could be worth a try," Tom speculated.

Regina headed north, through downtown Mendota, instead of taking a shortcut road west, connecting to Interstate 5 and all its eighteen wheelers. Highway 33 north once again. She had the time and decided to drive by Los Banos Wildlife Refuge. Not an official investigation. More like snooping around to see what the place looks like. The detective's bad experiences from her distant past didn't seem as intense this time, riding through the places she grew up. Due to the fact, most likely, she couldn't shake the surveyor from her head.

•••

Estefan concealed his treasure, as far as possible to the rear of the barn. Coated with oil, too heavy perhaps, making sure the barrel's bore was shiny and clean. Fascinated with the rifling spirals and more than once staring down the muzzle to see them glimmer. Estefan had reached his fork, becoming torn. On one hand dearly wanting papa to see his newfound prize but greed and mistrust even infects young boys. Estefan was captured by a soaring desire to keep the rifle for himself. Many different scenario's entered into the boy's mind. "Would papa take the gun away from me?" he wondered. "You're too young and a rifle like this is too dangerous. It should be taken to the police." Maybe he would try to sell his rifle? "He could get a lot of money for the gun," the boy thought. Papa needed money and our poor family was always short of cash. His parents argued over money many times. "I'm sure he would take it from me and sell it. Better to keep the rifle hidden for now," the young gun owner convinced himself. Changing.

Captivated and trancelike, the poor kid couldn't resist holding his rifle, shouldering the weapon constantly. Loving its feel of smooth wood and the way it smelled after applying a fresh coat of oil. Something about a boy's first encounter with firearms. Maybe not quite as sexy as his first well shaped girl would be, but comparable in the way raw power can seduce, by mere touch. Releasing so many different sounds, as flawless machined parts slid against one another. Clicks and low pitched rings from the bolt action transformed the boy into dozens of imaginary worlds.

Estefan sneaked his weapon into the barn's confined loft where a narrow split in weathered wood planks made a crease like opening. Holding steady as a make believe marksman, aiming through the crevice toward a far off almond orchard. His real attraction by far, lie with the scope. Amazed by the newly discovered optics but unable to comprehend how close, far off objects appeared through transparent lenses. Easily making out individual branches, twigs, leaves and cracks running along far off tree trunks. He enjoyed spotting crows resting in muted shade then centering crosshairs on the birds head, taking ample time to examine their eyes. Like glass beads sparkling wet and shiny. Staring long enough, his young mind fell absorbed into the distorted views, permitting the enlarged images to become reality. Convinced on occasion due to images so close and clear, the crow knew he was watching. Believing many big black birds were staring back! Estefan couldn't resist an occasional urge to pull the trigger until hearing a heavy firing pin click.

To a young sniper, thin crosshairs made the view port complete. Way back, someplace in Estefan's mind, those crosshairs represented the ominous power possessed in a rifle. Fearing it, but at the same time helpless in being drawn to it. "Maybe Papa's right," speaking soft as if Papa may be listening. Then the power would take charge again, like a gunshot, unwilling to share. It was his now. Forever. "Bullets." Estefan ached. "I have to get bullets somehow, for my rifle."

•••

Regina was able to locate the refuge check station with some help. Like always, Starbucks was calling, waiting with a jolt of caffeine. She happened to ask a young barista if he could direct her to Los Banos Wildlife Refuge. He couldn't but by surprise, another young female employee grinding coffee beans did know. It turned out the young gal happened to be a biology major at U.C. Merced and her ornithology labs visited the Refuge quite often, observing birds of prey. Giving Regina easy directions, pointing out Highway 165, known to locals as Mercy Springs Road, just past the coffee shop, followed by a right turn onto Henry Miller Road. "You can't miss the refuge signs and a plain white building less than a mile on your left. Ten minutes from here," her barista relayed directions.

"Thanks, very much," Regina said, leaving folding money in her tip jar.

A low mid November sun flashed her windshield when Gonzalez slowly entered the refuge parking lot. Appearing as though the refuge was shut down as no other vehicles occupied an empty parking lot. Exiting the car, a growing evening breeze blew long curls across her face catching a small bunch of dark hair between her lips. Short gusts of cool air moved in from the northeast making a late fall day feel cooler but by no means cold. Direct sun was being scattered and slightly obscured by high cirrus clouds streaming into the Valley, which helped to reduce the bright and shifted certain light spectrums into heavy ochre. A fall season tone. Not being a clear sky, subtle pinks began to develop. In an hour or so, reds and magentas would dominate the landscape, applying warmer colors among low lying scrub trees, marsh grass and tules. By sunset, winds would dwindle and as long as clouds continued stacking along distant western slopes, a remarkable Central Valley sunset would burst forth amid multicolored light shows.

Regina tried the office door. Locked. Computer printed signs taped to a metal door indicated the check station would reopen Friday at 3:00 P.M. Ending in bold letters, stating: 'NON RESERVATION LOTTERY NUMBERS WILL BE ISSUED TO HUNTERS BEGINNING AT 4:00 P.M.' "Whatever that means," Regina whispered under her breath peeking through a plate glass window. She cut the reflection with hands cupped around her face. Her visual scan yielded some dried out taxidermy behind a large wood counter. Various maps, warnings and hunting regulations were posted on the counter's lower panel. She continued her check around the building front, but all remained quiet. At one end of the parking lot sat a row of recreational trailers. Ten or twelve in all. Winnebagos, Streamlines and a lonesome Coleman tent trailer, parked side by side. All empty. "Employee housing maybe?" Regina guessed out loud then changed her mind. "Duck hunters?" Resting at her feet were two spent, twelve gauge shotgun shells. Bright green with Remington printed in bold along the plastic hulls. Reminding her what goes on out here. She kicked both shells aside continuing past the row of trailers toward a stout metal gate, blocking access to a dirt road leading northwest away from the paved parking lot. Stopping for a moment, gazing across a stand of thick tules waiving and bowing from each slightest breeze. Their sharp points dancing like Roman spears, forming arbitrary and irregular legions. Between green and pale brown covered canopies, open water flickered in front of a waning sun. Not large lakes or wide expanses of open water but small individual ponds. Low flattened waves ushered incoming gusts of wind. Regina was drawn to walk out wanting a close look of the wetland. To her, it appeared absolutely serene and realized she'd have it to herself. Glancing back to her car, hoping she remembered to lock the doors. Gonzalez climbed two bars onto the heavy metal gate giving her a better view of additional ponds and tules extending a long distance beyond. Ignoring a 'Road Closed - No Admittance' sign posted in plain view. "Wow, beautiful," she said and looked back one last time to the check station. "Oh well, still no one around." One foot on the highest bar, bouncing easy over an ineffective barrier onto gravel road. "I'm a cop for Christ's sake. What the hell can they do to me?" Whispering to herself almost silent. Then for some reason Gonzalez felt duty bound to proceed further into the refuge. Being Thursday, hunting was not allowed. No human activity or noise broke a calm silence apart from occasional rattles of tule spears from hurried breezes, providing a tranquil background to the area. Regina stopped to listen as barely audible sounds imparted a feeling of contentment, similar in the way her favorite music imparts a blissful atmosphere when she's home alone.

"This place is kinda eerie," smiling to stay brave, still advancing down the gravel road with a wide dirt canal running parallel on her left. She could just make out the check station rooftop fading in her wake. "Even if someone did come by, they couldn't see me now." Shrugging shoulders and walking on, expecting to reach the nearest pond at least. Small bugs swirled near her face as drops of sweat formed above her forehead. She took wild swings swatting at flies. "Crap, this better not turn into a mosquito infested swamp." Unknown to the detective, most of the blood sucking flies perished weeks ago in early November frosts. Onward, as noisy flocks of blackbirds began winging overhead. Squeaks and short squeals emanated from larger flocks and even their short flight feathers caught air, becoming audible. With the sun dipping lower, increased activity encircled the refuge. Colors changed and shadows extended. Harsh sunlight reflecting off rippling water seemed to soften with each step Regina took, unaware how far she'd gone. It didn't matter, feeling different and choosing to keep walking. Up ahead a dirt levee came into view. Not much more than a dirt berm angling in from her right, forming a raised barrier which created the pond she was seeking. Regina went right and found herself punching and ducking through tall weeds. They cracked like tree limbs from a small dead forest.

"Why the hell am I out here," questioning her decision in a frustrated tone. Pausing to glance back one final time toward the check station, completely out of sight now. She hesitated and even turned to go back but caught a display of two long lines of waving birds flying low over the marsh. Flocks of white fronted geese grabbed her attention as even longer lines of rising waterfowl started their daily mass exit from safe resting grounds. Needing high calorie feed, geese become regular evening commuters to nearby fields in search of grain or grasses. Longer and longer skeins of white and black birds vacated distant ponds, calling out, ending the rich silence. Gonzalez reached a levee breach which spilled water into an adjacent weed covered field to her right. It appeared intentional as two boards formed a make shift footbridge over swirling muddy water. High in a partly clouded sky, increasing V formations became visible. Looking harder, more flocks passed even higher reaching just beyond her range of vision. "Jesus Christ. Look at all the fucking birds? Where the hell are they all going?"

"I'm walking the planks," urging herself on, gathering balance and scampering across bent boards, arms outstretched like wild geese flying overhead. Spotting Regina's movements, birds banked left and right to avoid an implicit danger. The dirt levee appeared headed toward more open water drawing Regina in and pushing her forward, just as the same levee changed again with a slow turn left then back to the right. Off to her left, open water filled to the dirt berm, forming a large gap in the dense tules. She could hear geese calling, much closer now and hoped they might deter to cover her location. Their long necks and non-stop honking revived a sudden memory she hadn't thought of for a long time. A happier one at that. As a young girl Regina looked forward to the birds arrivals during winter migrations. She loved snow geese, their flight patterns, calls and black tipped wings. On winter mornings, dense tule fog settled in over Mendota so thick she couldn't see objects forty or fifty feet away. Low flying flocks of geese just above the fog, sounded clear and close but were never seen. Always intriguing her.

Settling to one knee between clumps of green and tan tules, Gonzalez stared out over darkening water. "What the hell am I doing here?" asking herself again. "There isn't anything important to this case out here? Is there?" Pleasant thoughts wandered back to Tom Ellis. His looks in particular were leading to an undeniable attraction. She imagined if Tom was familiar with this area. "Probably not?" Regina scooted on her butt, a few feet down into a makeshift blind close to the water's edge, trying to become a bit more hidden. High overhead but unknown to the detective, small, medium and large flocks of waterfowl raced well below a clouded sky. Sporadic wing beats were heard, as noisy diving ducks flashed by, coveting their preferred, deep water environs. Regina's dirt levee continued further into the refuge and she took a few more steps kneeling into dried out weeds. Shifting attention left into a red sunset, pleased with alternating colors but interrupted by a deep, rushing hiss knifing through the cool evening air fixed her awareness. She hesitated for a split second staying motionless, trying to comprehend the sound looking straight up, squinting eyes then checking behind her. Nothing? Beginning a one eighty degree scan to her left and catching sight of four birds with their wings locked in place and held very low, moving as one in a typical offset 'V' formation. Sailing left to right a bigger flight of twelve to fifteen ducks glided over the pond from the opposite direction but a smidgeon higher. Separate flocks crossing above center pond with the lower birds seemingly drawing down the higher flocks. Whistling noises grew audible as Regina guessed they originated from the higher group. Another pair, much smaller, joined the fray as well, shifting a quiet pond into an eruption of wing beats, rushing air, whistles, acrobatic flying but most of all, gracefulness. Crouching lower amid a tangle of tall weeds letting a smile form on her face, in a peculiar way, but never gave it another thought. Two gadwalls, whose narrow escape from Tom's gun last week, entered into the landing flight. They stayed a touch higher over this untested pond willing to let other groups accept the risk of suffering loud noises. A wary hen gadwall looked close however, covering this pond's perimeter meticulously and their experience showed by spotting Regina rather easy, rising fast, leaving these reckless flocks behind. Heading toward more familiar as well as secure water with the hen leading as usual.

Somewhat lower now, with open water underneath, the largest group of ducks were falling fast. Whistling broadcast calls to one another then swinging around in a tight, compact arc. Almost in free fall, their wings slung very low and tails lower, this flock appeared to be homing in on Regina's position. She thought the group may be aiming at her open bay which indeed they were. White feather patches covering the drakes forewings shined like beacons even in low light. Regina stared at the birds awed by maneuvers on their landing approach toward her. Ten to fifteen birds packed together at one moment then dispersed the next. Bodies and heads rigid but wings tipping wildly, side to side.

Two or three birds rose as others dropped, changing positions for preferred landing zones. In unison, they all went rigid. Still a loose formation stacked in two groups, deciding to lower webbed feet at once as the entire flight broke into wild chatter and staccato whistles. One hen bird, on the extreme right, fluttered in a strange position as her wings tipped way left. She must have caught wind and hurled away from the main group, nearly inverted. Forcing herself upright, she caught reverse air and rejoined the flock as if nothing ever happened. The detective was fixed on this bird, by chance, giggling at her biplane like maneuver. A raucous concert of warnings and greeting whistles filled the oncoming twilight. Beyond the approaching flight more ducks came rushing in from various directions circling, gliding, crisscrossing and picking landing spots scattered here and there. Regina scrunched down again trying to curl into the smallest ball she could profile. Smiling ear to ear at the scene unfolding in front, captivated by some crazy acrobatic displays. They sailed in closer and closer, able to see individual markings on the male birds. White forewings, white crowns on raised foreheads, black rumps and brown body feathers. "They're wonderful," Regina whispered crouching low, almost prone, peering through dense weeds.

Two birds broke away from their secure flock heading straight for her location. The flock seemed to sense a protected confidence, for some reason, in both birds with feet slung low. Prompting ten or more widgeon to drop their inside wings at the same time, shifting the entire flight path into the detective's direction. Just as fast shifting again, radically, hugging the levee but acting nervous with increased whistles. Three ducks exploded upward while most birds maintained their elevated positions, swinging in a powerful spin back to open water and regrouping. This well rehearsed routine of edgy waterfowl moved closer in tight formation with no idea of Regina's presence. Subdued sunlight angled in from her left. She expected a flight of widgeon, not knowing their breed, about to pass very low and straight overhead. Her heart raced a little faster anticipating an unusual sight. But as ducks are prone to do, they braked. Banked sharp in her direction, flipping bottom up to display white under-wings and cream colored bellies before settling into a splashy landing. Their noisy whistles went dead silent. Each bird stretching long necks, with heads spinning to spot potential danger. Regina didn't move a muscle, just staring at the flight bobbing composed over tiny waves. Gaudy waterfowl. A single male bird let loose a timid whistle, as if signaling, landing complete!

"Damn." Laughing with her wide grin still intact, not quite knowing what to do. Remaining still, admiring the delicate waterfowl showing off in front of her. "They give an impression of being strong, sturdy birds in flight," she thought to herself. "On the water those ducks look kinda tender?" Staring intense now, examining colors and shapes. No splashing, preening or tipping up in search of food but several birds relaxed their necks and rested heads as danger didn't seem imminent. Regina continued close observation from her makeshift blind.

The sun's rays were diffused by coastal mountains and low clouds, but sparse enough allowing beams to penetrate in a loud glow, tinting the evening red. Tules caught the faint light, adjusting their hues, waving like rusty brown needles against a dark blue pond. Willow trees, spaced along the levees shimmered in various tones of yellow and orange. Their dead leaves helped to cast dense shadows onto the ponds with an entire wetland, as far as she could witness, set in motion. Behind her, subdued gurgling from a gate valve indicated water flowing from one pond to fill another. Continuous flooding increased resting water thus preparing for escalated arrivals in the coming weeks. Swelling breezes pushed tules and different species of birds in several directions. Songbirds, blackbirds, shorebirds, raptors, ravens, cormorants plus geese and ducks. All on the move but few in the same direction. Even two tiny titmouse, scurried from stalk to stalk along her dirt berm within hand reach of the hidden cop.

This watery expanse, from a distance, appeared to be stolid and fixed like a man made reservoir. Similar, in a vague manner, the way a distant peak appears on constant guard but never fluid. Neither are ever still. Mountain streams and marshes, with watery movements and seasonal transformation will change as much as Central Valley rivers and the Delta they form. Night and day, year after year, water and dirt mix notes, playing out as an orchestra in constant motion.

Regina peeked over to the flock and noticed a pair of birds nibbling each other's necks, showing affection. "Nice having a mate to curl up with." Recognizing how ridiculous the word mate sounded at the moment. However, the widgeon pair looked awfully content bouncing together on rolling waves. Life seemed pleasant out here in mid November, but knew very well, some days the ducks didn't see it as contented existence. Becoming a life and death survival for three months each year with many birds in front of her likely dead in a few weeks. But some, those smarter and faster, would make it through. She thought of similarities in her own life and the death struggles, surrounding her career. The wretched criminals and murders. Crime victims so pathetic they broke her heart. Children became especially difficult for the detective. Seeing a child beaten, abused or just terrified, weighed on her more with each occurrence, making it harder to show up for work many mornings following child abuse arrests. One particular gruesome crime had Regina close to reaching for her 9mm ready to execute the young boys father as she led him to a patrol car, just able to stay in command of deep emotions, that time. Then, out of nowhere an unknown civilian materializes, initiating noble actions and helps to solve an investigation, rescue the innocent, comfort injured victims, complete a distasteful job. Her shaken faith is restored. Life goes on.

In a few hours the refuge would change again. Hunters will be present with waterfowl and upland birds filling varied bag limits. Some people see a blood sport as murder. Not a sport at all. To them it's simple animal cruelty. The same folks who gather around barbeques on summer evenings or fine restaurants lining city boulevards serving well prepared chickens, pigs, fish, cows and even lambs. Those with blood on their hands take the heat. Chefs and consumers are given free passes, as life and death struggle on, in different locations.

Regina's crunched legs began to cramp. She shifted but had to stand, causing the flock in front to shift also, exploding airborne among watery spray and beating wings. She was taken just how quick the startled widgeon roared up and away in a few short seconds. "I had no idea," she said out loud watching the birds rise followed by other spooked ducks as well, all across the pond.

So much was going through her mind right now. The murder case. What did Chris learn about the Braden's? Do we have a case against them perhaps? Together, we will be questioning a possible rogue cop next week. Does Beatrice Patterson know something more about this investigation? Now enter Tom Ellis. Regina couldn't help but feel she could be getting to know the refuge area a lot better, turning her slightly giddy. If so, Tom would play a leading role in the arena soon to be opened to her. Ellis and steady flocks of settling ducks coming in to rest were forefront on her mind, throughout a satisfying walk back to the dimly lit check station. Darkness ended this remarkable day before reaching the car, her enthusiasm re-established.

Mrs. Crosby

Abbey paced her dining room like a hungry panther. Dressed in black, some would say she looked and acted like the actual feline. Chief Yung refused to return her many calls and the mayor, her paid for politician, was too stupid to get any new information back to her. She wasn't used to being tolerant by force. Waiting and patience wasn't her style, in the least. Abbey had to be forcing most situations. Yelling, screaming, belittling, swearing.

"If I don't hear something soon I'm going to split right down the middle," fuming out loud, both arms folded below sagging breasts as her left hand stroked loose skin under a wrinkled chin. Mulling over various options. Mrs. Crosby considered one girl's position. "Perhaps it's time to talk with my reporter, Miss Bailey."

Buck

"Thanksgiving is next week already," Regina mumbled under her breath not looking forward to the gringo holiday. She loved four day weekends but without a boyfriend in tow, most likely meant over eating again during the festival of gluttony. "Holidays suck!" Grumbling to herself upon entering the station parking lot. Friday morning following a sound sleep, had Gonzalez getting to work early for a change.

Her partner sitting at his desk took notice when Gonzalez entered. Surprised to see his partner. "Hey girl, it's not even eight o'clock. What're you doing here?" knowing she hated to be teased about her constant tardiness.

"Whoa, Gonzo. What's up?" Anderson checked his watch for time. "You're in early," Billy tagged on with little concern, giving the hard working girl as much rope as needed.

"I'm not late every day," tossing her jacket to a vacant chair. "Here today on time. So what!" responding rather shrill causing Anderson to blink and raise his hands in mock surrender.

"Nothing implied at all. Good morning," Billy returned with a direct reply, coming across as if to say, "don't go there."

Regina lowered her head, embarrassed, aware how juvenile she must sound. "Sorry Captain. Good Morning. And good morning to you too, partner," Gonzalez kidded with an extended gawk toward Chris using a tone of severe pleasantness, which neither cop was buying. "How was your day yesterday?" she requested, referring to the Braden meeting.

"We'll brief each other later," Chris answered.

"Good enough. I need some caffeine," Regina nodded affirmative to Davis then straight to a coffee pot before rerouting to Anderson's office. Upon entering, Billy signaled Regina to sit down having just answered a call from Patricia Bailey.

"I'll have to call you back later." Captain Anderson dispatched his caller. "One of my detectives just walked in. We'll talk later this morning. Okay? Bye." Which to Regina, sure sounded like the chief was talking to a woman. "What's on your schedule today Gonzo?" Billy asked.

Regina gave the Captain a peculiar look. "Somebody I might know, stud?" she asked her boss in a way that would've crossed way over the line, with most captain to detective relationships. In here business as usual. Anderson didn't much care, even flattered of sorts, the way Regina took a gossipy interest in his potential love life. He needed a love life, bad. Like Gonzo!

"When something happens, you're the first to know," speaking with fondness, but her boss was lying all the while, of course.

"Oh yeah, I'm sure," Regina said, paging through a busy notebook after delivering a tight smirk. "Anyway, I have to take Buck with me today." Checking notes to get the Refuge name correct. "Los Banos State Wildlife Refuge. I told him to meet us here in your office," looking through the glass window trying to spot the patrolman.

"Uh, why do you need Buck?" Billy asked.

"He's a duck hunter, I'm told," the detective answered.

"You two going out to shoot some birds, are ya?" Her boss did his best to act as smug as possible. Billy loved throwing it back to her, the same way she enjoyed cutting him.

"Yep. We're a gunnin' for our limits, whatever the hell that means?" Regina extended both arms, hands clenched together, holding an imaginary pistol locked in a tight grip, dry firing twice then framing the pose! "Actually, it's about our man Tom Ellis. His alibi is waterfowl hunting, believe it or not. Claims to be out shooting ducks the morning of our murder," dropping her imaginary guns. "I have to verify his story and look around myself." Gonzalez went on, explaining to Anderson she could use Buck, not knowing much about bird hunting. "Buck knows the game and maybe he can ask some pertinent questions. I don't want to miss anything," pleading her case as strong as possible.

"What's your read on this guy?" Anderson asked seriously.

Regina paused. "Umm? If you only knew what my true read is on this guy!" Gonzalez appeared to be in deep examination to Billy.

"C'mon Gonzo, gut feeling." The Captain proposed.

"He's not our boy. Ninety nine point nine, nine percent sure," Regina conveyed speaking in her typical confident tone.

"So why the trip to Los Banos today?" Anderson wanted to know.

"That last point zero, zero, one percent," she told her boss. "I want to clear my mind about this guy before moving on. I hope that makes sense to you Captain." Regina wished she hadn't used the 'this guy' phrase.

"You went one zero too far and it makes perfect sense to me Gonzo. But my budget's already strained. Can you, maybe, get by on your own?" Anderson asked his detective, hoping to save the department some much needed dollars.

"Like I said, I don't know anything about the routine. Buck can hit clean-up if I overlook something important. We're talking about giving this suspect an all-clear Captain." The detective was speaking very sensibly but also keeping her personal wish hidden away. She intended to get Tom Ellis cleared then reminded herself about showing too much passion for any suspect's innocence.

"You wanted to see me Captain?" Officer Buck announced his entrance into the meeting. "Sorry I'm late. Good morning Detective Gonzalez." Running fingers through medium blond but thinning hair.

"Morning Buck," Regina greeted the patrolman.

"Uh, yes Charley. Sit down," Billy offered the twenty something patrolman a seat next to Gonzo. "I'm told you do a fare amount of duck hunting?" he asked without any judgment whatsoever, stifling criticism regarding Buck's bird hunting activity. The patrolman was indeed sensitive around people when it came to talk about hunting. He learned to stay quiet.

"Yes sir, I do," the officer responded straight away. "As many weekends my wife will give me," following with an earthy retort. "Is that okay with the department sir?" Sending Gonzalez a sheepish frown wondering if there were complaints about his hunting.

Regina did her best to keep from frowning at the remark, lifting a mug of hot coffee instead. Covering her facial expression with two or three long sips and peered over to Anderson. She fired off a quick wink to her boss notifying him to disregard his question. Her opinion of officer Buck was an eyelash above ridiculous incompetence. "This guy is so dense." Inward, running many thoughts through her mind but outward, drinking more coffee and staying mum. Regina could care less about his hunting. That was his business.

"Detective Gonzalez needs some help confirming a suspect's story." Anderson explained then asked, "where do you hunt Charley? Duck hunt specifically?" Regina wiggled then leaned way back into her chair, taking one more long drink from her steamy brew. It was easy to tell she wouldn't miss a single word from the patrolman and hoped he could demonstrate some real duck hunting experience. If so, the patrolman might be of some help.

"I hunt where the ducks are," Buck unloaded, eager to get some kind of reaction. Regina rolled her eyes and studied floor tile patterns. "That's a joke sir." The young cop's jest had him smiling at the Captain then checked to see if Regina was laughing too. She just nodded very polite, faked a tight lipped grin raising her mug and looking at Anderson too.

She had to jump in now. "Have you ever hunted in Los Banos?" Regina asked after swallowing a mouthful.

"Oh, sure detective. Many times," he responded.

"At the Los Banos Wildlife Refuge?" Gonzalez followed up.

"Just once," Buck answered firm, which made Regina blink and wonder about the officer's response. She looked at a strange patrolman remaining calm, steering clear of appearing trite. "All right. You said many times first and now, just once?" Regina and Anderson shared a common misunderstanding. They both remained still, hanging on what the unorthodox officer might say this time.

"Oh. Sorry. Well, you see detective and Captain Anderson," making sure to address his Captain, being the ranking officer. Buck was troubled at how he came across. Attempting to show some poise, then acting surprised when both superiors seemed confused with his answer. "You see, I'm a freelance hunter."

"A what?" Regina blurted out, head tilted and recoiling her neck an inch or two, growing irritated.

"What's a freelance hunter, Buck?" Captain Anderson inquired flat but giggled at the way Gonzalez responded. He enjoyed seeing her become riled.

Buck, who had a problem reading his own wife's mood, thought both officers were enamored by his answers. If he only had a clue. "I hunt refuge areas not duck clubs," Buck added matter of fact.

"Gotcha," Anderson confirmed. He recalled hearing how some duck hunters paid a heavy price to lease blinds. "Club hunters shoot on private property, right?"

"Yes. That's right Captain," Buck confirmed with a nod of his head as each cop saw the young man growing energized. Regina stayed somewhat vague.

"Are there private refuges? Is "refuges" the correct word?" Regina asked, laughing to herself. "Let's try refuge areas, for one hundred Alex." Getting a laugh from Anderson, picking up on her Jeopardy correlation, but nothing more than a blank stare coming from Buck.

Buck had the floor. "No, not a private refuge. Farmers and cattle ranchers will flood fields during winter, making smaller habitat areas. Some can have fantastic shooting but big bucks to get in," Charley explained, with Gonzalez recognizing his 'Bucks' pun. He continued, "my hunting is almost exclusively in Los Banos. Volta Refuge, San Luis Refuge, Merced Refuge if I can ever get a reservation, Grasslands and Kesterson. Those refuge areas," accenting areas, "are all close to Los Banos." Which did wonders for Regina to clarify his earlier remarks. "I don't hunt at Los Banos State Wildlife Area. Don't really care for the place. Never seem to do well there?"

"Okay, now that makes sense," Regina acknowledged the patrolman's efforts, as well as feeling a bit thick headed herself. "That's good to know. Don't you think?" She sat staring at Captain Anderson with a told ya so look in her delivery. "If I'm on the bump, pitching in Los Banos, I need Buck as my catcher."

Anderson sighed. "Good baseball comparison, Gonzo. All right, all right. I'm convinced." Billy relented. "You and Buck head out and see what's up with the damn duck hunters."

"Thanks boss man," Regina replied, sincere in her comment. "Buck. How soon can you be ready? The refuge will be opening soon. "She stood up showing more enthusiasm after getting the go-ahead.

No response from the patrolman. He sat in his chair, thinking hard and looking glum. "I can't make it today Detective Gonzalez," Charley Buck had some difficulty announcing his decision to the pair of higher ranking officers, expecting major disappointment.

Captain Anderson spoke up, interrupting Regina, who looked on the verge of showing way too much frustration. "Why not Charley? I can rearrange your agenda if you have training or a meeting scheduled," his boss made clear.

"It's not that Captain," bowing his head then gazing somberly at Anderson as the cop's whole disposition changed. Very sober. "It's my wife," Buck said gently. "She has a medical exam today and I have to go with her. She won't be able to drive home alone. I'll be leaving at lunchtime today. Sorry."

Regina spoke up, quite embarrassed for becoming so impatient. "I hope it isn't serious Buck. What the hell, we can wait 'till Monday," she said.

"Thanks detective. But I'm off all next week too, for Thanksgiving. My wife and I will be spending the week at her sister's in Mariposa. I don't want to seem like I'm flaking out here but. Uh," very embarrassed, as the patrolman stumbled for the correct words. "My wife's having a biopsy done today. Possible breast cancer," Charley said with deep frown. "I really must be with her."

"Oh Christ, Buck, I'm so sorry. Absolutely. Don't worry about this refuge stuff. I can go by myself. You have to be with your wife today," Regina almost pleaded. Her mom came to mind, passing away very sudden, feeling extreme regret for Buck's situation. Cancer robbed Regina from her mother's love.

"You know what detective, I just had a thought," with an unexpected buoyant sound in Buck's voice. "We're planning to leave tomorrow anyway. With a slight detour, we can drive through Los Banos on our way to Mariposa."

"Go on." Regina listened close.

"Well, we could meet at the Refuge tomorrow." Buck proposed. "It shouldn't take long to check things out. Maggie won't mind if we stop." Looking at Anderson now with eyes opened wide then continuing with his best part. "If we go down tomorrow, being Saturday, is a shoot day. You can see the check station in action which could help with your investigation."

"Good idea Buck." Regina weighed his offer for a few seconds then agreed a hundred ten percent. "Great idea. You're sure Maggie wouldn't mind?" she asked in all sincerity. "Her condition is more important." The detective wondered what the small check station would be like on a hunt day. Hoping not too hectic, making a mental note to contact the refuge later in the day. She wanted to meet face to face with the manager in charge. "What time?" Gonzalez asked Buck.

"Noon works for me if it works for you," Buck answered as Captain Anderson reclined deep into his chair listening close but with no intention of interrupting. "This early in the season most guys will be coming in around midday. It's supposed to be a clear weekend, I think?" Buck added. "Hunting will be slow I'm sure, unless the weather turns bad."

Both cops thought for a minute then agreed on a meeting time. Captain Anderson was impressed with his staff, willing to work on their off days. For the sake of courtesy, Regina made sure it was perfectly all right for Buck to cancel.

"If Maggie doesn't want to stop, for any reason whatsoever, you let me know. It's fine by me. Better to go down tomorrow anyway. I'm curious how that place works." Regina concluded and holding Buck in a somewhat higher light. "Please, tell Maggie I'll say a prayer for her."

"Thanks Detective Gonzalez."

"Regina." She issued a soft order to use her first name. When they stood, she offered the young patrolman a delicate hug for moral support. "Call me Regina, please." Buck departed Anderson's office and left Regina feeling a little guilty. They expected Chris at any moment.

Anderson preferred both detectives to brief him, as well as one another, on their previous day's examinations. Chris was running late and Billy took the time to let Regina know, going to Los Banos tomorrow was a great idea. "It saves me a few bucks too. No pun intended." Anderson confirmed, as Chris strolled in taking a seat.

"So kids, what's happening?" Davis showed his partner a toothy smile.

She responded with her dead pan stare, uttering in brief, "can't wait to hear your scouting report."

"More baseball lingo?" Chris posed with a stifled laugh. "My batting lineup looks weak right now. I don't think the two I scouted yesterday could hit in the lead off position." Staring at his partner, who was taken by surprise but did a great job of hiding her shocked face. Gonzalez searched deep for a comeback, but could only stare, very quiet. Problem, nothing came to mind. Like taking a called third strike! "What'd you find out Gonzo?" Chris asked before his partner might respond. Knowing how mad it made her, relishing his minor victory.

"My man hits with power but not average," Regina come up with something at last, but knew it sounded lame and made little sense regarding Tom Ellis' situation. Swinging hard but missing.

"Heard enough from you two," Anderson chimed in letting it be known their amusement was over. "Let's hear about the Braden's," Billy spoke directly to Chris.

"Okay. I guess I'm first," Davis sounded annoyed. "I met with the lovely couple, and had a nice visit for most of an afternoon. Conclusion. They may have done it and I have to emphasize, they. As a team. I can't believe, at this time, either one is capable of doing it alone," going quiet, Chris decided to let his assumption sink in. "Henry Braden sure has enough firepower on hand, as well as expert marksmanship skills to carry out the murder. But he doesn't fit the cold blooded killer type." Chris continued briefing his partner and boss thoroughly, with meeting details. "The only weak link in their alibi is a verifiable location at time of the murder."

"Didn't we confirm Henry Braden being late to work that morning?" Anderson responded. "Where did they claim he was?"

Looking at Regina about to enjoy his next statement immensely. "His wife, Franny," Chris stated simply, "claims to be getting laid at the time." Davis continued to observe his partner, smirking.

"By her husband I presume," Gonzalez said with a forced calm, not about to give Davis the satisfaction of seeing her uncomfortable. "Likely excuse," she said, whispering loud enough and heard by both cops.

"Motive is still high, I suppose." Anderson spoke, unwilling to write the couple off so early.

Chris was waiting for this issue to surface. "Motive is the one big issue with the Braden's. They couldn't be happier over Marcus Crosby's death. Ecstatic wouldn't be an exaggeration." In secret, Chris thought their pain alone wasn't enough motivation for a middle aged couple to carry out an assassination. Gonzalez sensed his hunch. "I plan to follow up with another meeting. Maybe if I get Mrs. Braden alone, she would be more revealing? Who knows? She seems the type to go off like a loose cannon when the heat's on." Chris gave his account as if thinking out loud, expecting no response, soon realizing all the sexual innuendo in his last statement. "Get her alone; more revealing; the heat on. What the hell is on my mind?" Davis was interrogating himself but managed to focus his concentration.

"What's she like? How does she carry herself?" Regina asked.

"What does she look like?" Davis was caught short handed by her question, unclear of what she asked and complicated by his own persistent sensual feelings for Franny Braden, which he struggled to force from his thoughts.

"That too," Regina followed.

Bewildered and uneasy, Chris proceeded to offer an answer. "Umm. Franny's middle aged but she takes good care of herself. Dresses liberally. I wouldn't say provocative but trying hard to look younger," wondering how Regina and Billy might interpret his last remark. "Probably not the most confident person, without her husband present and I suspect she's kinda high strung for the most part. That's my read. Oh, and Henry says she shoots very well too."

"Your type of girl?" his partner probed with an evil smile on her face.

"What the hell does that mean, Gonzo?" Chris shot back knowing Regina would say anything to even the score. "She seems like a typical, contented, married woman." Eager to chop Regina off at the knees and bring the personal subject matter, to a close.

"Do you have a thing for this lady, Christopher?" his partner shot back with a peculiar tone of voice, which sounded quite dubious.

"What's on your mind Gonzo?" Captain Anderson cut in letting Regina know he wasn't in the mood for more games.

Regina preferred to continue chasing, but thought better. Knowing very well her own situation mirrored the last few curveballs she dished out, attempting a feeble mask of the prickly Tom Ellis state of affairs. "Is she the killer type, is all I'm asking?" With no desire to explain her previous remarks.

"Killer type?" Chris answered, this time making a killer label sound a bit incredible. "I don't think so Gonzalez, but," he stopped cold to think, wanting to deliver a clear opinion. "But maybe holding back some information? Possibly knowing who shot Marcus Crosby?" Stopping. Wanting to emphasize his next statement. "An angle I plan to pursue." Davis promised.

"What about Henry Braden?" Regina asked.

A long drawn out sigh followed before Chris spoke. "Certainly capable to be the shooter. But for some reason I can't explain, Henry's demeanor seems to be a real long shot. No pun intended." Davis thought of the older man and concluded Mr. Braden just didn't convey killer instinct. "Unless the old dude has me completely fooled and took up a rifle to exact revenge for the murder of his daughter, which can't be ruled out yet, my impression is Henry will grow more and more bitter over his daughter's death. Unable to have rescued her. Unable to make Marcus pay. It'll eat him alive in the long run. That's my two cent, psycho-babble diagnosis." Chris finished.

"How about showing up late for work. Does that carry any weight?" Anderson asked, enjoying every second of his team arguing opinions, hunches and strategy.

"Not to me Captain. Not at this time at least. Probably pure coincidence." Which was typical in the way Chris approached his inquiries. Location alibis are easy to manufacture and hard to disprove when investigations just begin. "I intend to nail Franny down later, regarding their location, when the pressure's on." Chris told himself to never say 'nail Franny' ever again. Silence ruled for what seemed a long time as both Regina and Anderson appreciated Chris' innate ability to force information from suspects, even when they're holding back. "What about your man, Gonzalez?" Chris inquired, looking at his partner with a firm stare, serious and concerned.

Regina sat in her chair wondering what to say. "Our suspect, Tom Ellis, is very handsome," escaping from her lips just before wishing a do over. "I can't believe it," scolding herself. Afraid of what her partner might say now?

Chris peered at Regina straight faced, squinting slightly, anticipating something more. He had to speak up. "So, he's not our guy?" asking without a hint of sensation. Davis rubbed his cheek with an index finger, up and down, calculating their next move. Addressing his boss, "that puts a lot of pressure on our cop in Sonora, don't ya think, Captain?"

"It does at that," Anderson responded. "Mr. Ellis stays a suspect Gonzo. We'll see what the refuge folks say tomorrow."

"Where was your lover boy at the time, partner?" Chris wondered aloud.

"Duck hunting."

"Shooting ducks? You're kidding?" Davis chuckled, speaking with a disbelieving attitude and body language. "Can he prove that?"

"I'll let you know tomorrow, after Buck and I meet with folks running Los Banos Wildlife Refuge." Feeling better about her 'handsome' observation a minute ago. Both cops paid no attention to her Mr. Ellis comment so why not jump in the fire. "The man I'm going to marry one day, claims they have proof he was hunting that morning." Gonzalez said, upping the ante with her marriage plans.

"Anything else?" Davis wanted to know, ignoring her wedding announcement.

"No record. Field surveyor. Self employed. No connections. Very nice guy." Checking to see if she left anything out. "Unless something comes up tomorrow, entirely unexpected, I have to call Tom Ellis a dead end." Regina announced with confidence.

"Okay folks. Starting Monday we're hot after Sheets. Our first meeting and I want you both on him, together, at the same time. We go after Douglas Sheets hard," Anderson proclaimed with a determined voice. "Maybe Mrs. Braden eventually gives something? Who knows?" Billy's words struck Detective Davis hard, hoping Franny Braden gives him something.

...

Both detectives left Anderson's office, walking the cubicle hallway side by side but saying nothing to one another. Regina began to feel somewhat awkward, expecting Chris to deliver his standard jabs regarding her comments, at any moment. She knew from their meeting, Davis had to have picked up on her peculiar handsome remark. Her Latin intuition decided to wait.

"So, it's you and Buck tomorrow, working together. I'm jealous," Chris' comment went well beyond sarcastic. "Duck hunters. Man, they seem like a strange lot, don't ya think?" giving Regina ground to feel even more awkward.

Regina shrugged her shoulders offering a faint, "I guess."

"What time do you meet in Los Ba," Chris tried asking about tomorrow's schedule but Regina butted in on her partner, about to go irate but stayed mostly under control.

"Why don't you just ask and be done with it?" Gonzo squealed, stopping at a corner hallway with a look of demise, arms folded, weight on one leg, eyebrows raised, presenting her best 'I know what you want to say' look on her face, holding it.

Davis was stumped. "What?"

"Go ahead, ask me."

"Ask what?" Chris honestly wondered what the hell his partner was referring to! Regina held fast but dropped each hand to her hips. "I have to plead ignorance Gonzo," replying with a smile and short chuckle, making Gonzalez even madder.

"Whatever. If you can't ask, that's your problem. I have to use the lady's room," sticking out her tongue and turning sharp to retrace earlier steps down the hallway.

Davis, mesmerized by his partner's actions, hadn't a clue what to make of it all but desperately rethought what was said or what was missed. "Hey, say hi to the girls for me," yelling quite loud, knowing it was meeting time with the gang. She walked with long strides and twisted her head around, delivering yet another tongue lashing. Failing in direction for a few strides, bumping off a cubicle wall causing a slight trip over her own feet. Catching herself after both knees buckled deep, driving a rush forward to prevent a sprawling fall realizing how preposterous she must look. Regina loped down the hallway listening to Davis hooting all the way. Reaching the bathroom, she broke into embarrassed laughter.

"Damn it, he gets me every time," Regina admitted, murmuring aloud as another gal exited her stall, checking out the red faced detective with a curious expression.

"I'm sorry?" a confused woman asked.

"Oh, nothing. Sorry. Just talking out loud," suffering ridiculous once again!

Gang of Four

Regina's beeline took her to one of the many 'gourmet burrito' shops spread around her part of the 209. One convenient location was right across the street from Police Headquarters and Regina Gonzalez wasn't about to miss out on a Gang of Four lunch meeting.

"All right, Regina! You made it. Where've you been girl?" Maria asked, always glad to see her detective friend again.

"You know. Usual stuff. The chase never ends for murderers, scoundrels, thieves and boyfriends," Regina joked, watching each member of the gang laughing with fists held aloft, offering high fives among a couple subtle hoots. "How about you ladies, what's juicy right now? Give it up."

Maria broke out laughing hard making her cheeks roll like small ripples across a still water pond. Looking at Pam made her laugh even more. "You better shut up lady," Pam warned the large Mexican girl desperate to avoid explaining her situation. "Just ignore her Gonzo, she's being an ass." Pam knew the more she fought to suppress it the more each gang member had to know.

"I don't know Pamela," Regina flashed a big smile for the Gang's rather loose girl. "Maria has real dirt on someone?" Pamela covered her face with both hands wallowing in severe embarrassment. She lowered her head to the table top hoping it would all go away. "Uh oh, let me guess Pam. You picked up another guy this week? I thought you were steady right now?"

"Steady!" Denise bellowed out, going above the busy restaurant noise. "Pam's steadily dating, I should probably say screwing, half the guys in Tracy for Christ's sake. You won't believe this one."

"Mmm, I love it. Who is it this time Pam?" Regina asked, as a cold quiet enveloped the table. The entire gang sat like Supreme Court Justices, in waiting for someone to start proceedings. "Come on, who's the lucky man?" Smiling with great expectations, Gonzalez believed a juicy story was about to come forth.

Maria couldn't hold back a high pressure giggle. Out it came with more jiggling flesh. "Men." Maria leaked.

Her word didn't register. "What?" Regina asked.

"Plural!" Marie added.

Gonzalez thought hard for a moment, no doubt missing something. From left field, it hit her. "God Pam, you didn't? Tell me they're lying. Say it ain't so, Joe!" Robbing the baseball quote.

Pam turned her head peering from under one arm at the detective. "Oh, I wish. I wish I could Gonzo," the loose gal confessed.

"Two guys?" Gonzalez remained in doubt. "Not at the same time though?" the detective asked amused.

Pam never raised her head from the table. Her dark eyes staring at Regina delivered the unspoken confirmation.

"Shit! How was it?" Regina asked lowering her head too but laughing much too loud. Maria and Denise were both taking large bites from drippy burritos as Regina launched her question. Denise nearly choked while Maria squealed a high pitched laugh with a mouthful of beans, rice and tortilla showing. They wanted to hear Pam's answer. Bad!

Pam raised her head and plopped her chin onto stacked fists of both hands, strutted on spread elbows, gaping straight away from the group not saying a word. The surrounding gang giggled and munched on high calorie lunches at a much higher rate. Cheese, sour cream, tortillas, avocado and hot sauce scattered about the lunch table. All three ladies waited intent for their partner's retort. "I'm in trouble girls." Pam confessed. "I loved it!"

On queue, three wraps went down. Three hands then came up to cover gaping mouths trying to stifle teasing snickers. Denise spilled her Pacifico all over the table.

"Pam, you're nuts," Denise scolded the red faced young gal. "You better stop this shit right now. You need to settle down, and soon. It's dangerous."

"I know," the guilty brunette whispered. "I can't go there again. I could get addicted to that stuff!" Pam admitted.

"I'd love to give it a try." Maria blurted out restoring their lunch table to snorts and hoots again. As nervous laughs faded away the gang sat in comfort and clumsy silence, like schoolgirls. Peeking at one another, it secretly occurred to them one by one, Maria's consent received a unanimous endorsement!

Pam spoke up, "I knew all of you would be into it too." As one they rose, preparing to leave.

"Let's get out of here before this goes any further," Denise ordered. Four girls returned to work with a lot more on their minds than just their jobs.

Estefan

Estefan's father made sure his young son would be helping his mother around the house. It was getting late and gathering firewood was one designated chore. Tree limbs and split trunks were always spilled or stacked into high piles around orchards. It took some time but in due course, a fair size load of almond wood kept a stove and fireplace blazing for a few days. Estefan hated farm chores but it beat the hell out of cleaning items inside their family's rundown home. Dust being the never ending infiltrator. Clean and shiny furniture one day and coated in dust the next. Another signature item of life in the orchard business.

Front and foremost on Estefan's mind was ammunition. "I need to get bullets," repeating bullets, over and over to himself. He kept seeing those .222 numbers stamped on his rifle barrel. Knowing this designated the correct ammunition but he also understood, too well, his age was a problem.

Bullets would have to come through someone else, however. He knew only one person up for this kind of assignment. Carlos. The drunk. The tweaker. The deadbeat. The bandito. The Jackal! Washed up at twenty, Carlos! "Just the sort who could get my shiny new bullets," the young farm worker weighed his only option. It must be done quietly too, so no one could find out. The Jackal was one of those types who attracted trouble and Estefan hated to get near him. Best way to deal with this outlaw had to be through someone else and everyone knew Carlos liked Angelina. A lot.

Chief Yung

Stacks of folders and paper memos covered his desk top. The damn phone too. Constant ringing was getting under Alex's hide, growing desperate to leave his office, letting it ring. Tracy's mayor was calling yet again for updates and Alex had nothing new to report on an early investigation. If it wasn't for Abigail Crosby ringing the mayor's office each day, Chief Yung's work would be quite a bit easier. Abbey kept the heat on. In her mind, it was purely checking up on one of her investments.

"Yes Mr. Mayor. How are you?" asking a phony politician with the phoniest greeting he could muster.

"Any news Alex?"

"Nothing." Not about to offer anything else. Chief Yung was dying to ask the mayor how Abigail Crosby was treating him, but knew a smart-ass comment like that would ignite some unneeded fireworks. Alex heard a brief, but no doubt intentional sigh, come over his end of the line. "I'll check with my staff on Monday and brief you if anything substantial pops up," the Chief offered.

"Good. Maybe I'll just check in myself," pressing the Chief hard.

"Feel free, Mr. Mayor. But this case is off to a crawl so far. It's a tough one to say the least, I'm sure you're aware," Alex replied knowing how this political hack loved being referred to as Mr. Mayor. Somehow making him feel as though he actually held high office. Self centered son of a bitch! "I'll talk to Anderson as well as his detectives directly. They do a great job. Right now they're searching for evidence with very little to go on. It's still very early."

"Have a good weekend Alex," as the rude politician hung up without saying goodbye.

"Up yours, ass wipe!" Chief Yung slurred the mayor, slamming his phone down. Yung's rattling desk, sent a stack of folders to the floor.

Patricia Bailey

Being late Friday evening, Billy Anderson made sure his docket was clear. Everything was covered which needed attention. Both Davis and Gonzalez were pursuing leads and questioning suspects. Department budgets were being met, just barely, bet being met. The Crosby murder case was going nowhere fast and the arrest horizon appeared far off to clear. His phone rang and Billy gave it the identical disdain as his Chief. An outside line he had to answer. "Captain Anderson here."

"Hello Captain, Patricia Bailey. How are you?" the newswoman asked, out of the blue, as Anderson bounced between excited and tongue tied.

"Well, Miss Bailey. Hello. What can I do for you?" hoping he didn't sound too formal.

"Just calling to see if I could buy you a drink," hoping she didn't sound too forward.

"I get the feeling you're fishing for information. The Crosby case by chance?" Billy posed, testing her motive.

"Maybe, but I would still like to buy you a drink. Even if we don't talk business." Coming across quite provocative to the Captain.

"Sounds fine by me," Anderson agreed, aware he couldn't say no. Billy knew the reporter was out of his league. "Let's meet in about an hour at Moss's on Third Avenue," he proposed.

"I'll see ya in one hour, Billy," Patricia dropped a throaty sex bomb on top of Anderson's first name. Her way of signing off.

The Captain's imagination was painting a variety of crazy pictures, at the moment.

The Braden's

Franny and her husband were out for a leisurely walk, along their beloved Stanislaus River. Flat, slick flows meandered around rocks and gravel bars along the seasonal low running stream. Numerous runs glided by smooth, almost thick, shining with a virtual oily appearance. Former noisy rapids interspersed with various plunge pools had long been tamed and their currents emerged gentle, compared to spring torrents. Each season has its own appeal. Franny enjoyed the spring drama, noise and violent white water. Henry favored the fall river character with its quiet gurgle, long slow tail outs and riffles which beckon to be waded and explored. Late afternoon shade delivered a slight chill to the air making Franny huddle up close to her husband and squeezed his hand firm to rob any available warmth. Stopping on occasion to absorb the river's charm, trade kisses and allowing Henry to grope his lovely wife like a schoolboy, as Franny squirmed and giggled with pleasure.

"I wonder how far along the investigation has progressed?" Franny queried her husband. "Do you suppose they've discovered anything firm yet?" She looked close at Henry, hiding the indecision and confusion weighing on her mind. There was so much she wanted to tell him, considering the river to be the right place and time. But her approach floundered, deciding to pass once again like a hundred times before. "This isn't the right time," Franny concluded, thinking to herself. "Not here, in this place we love."

Henry followed a pair of gray colored raptors sail above the river, turning to drift low along dense willow trees. He reached out for blackberry vines growing thick near the path. Too late for ripe berries. Only dried out remnants remained. "Hard to say my love. We don't have much to be worried about," Henry said then slipped his arm around Franny's waist moving her in close. She felt very sexy to him at the moment becoming cheerfully aroused.

His wife played along but had far too much dancing about her mind. Ideas which developed delicate and tricky plans. Like the tricky currents developing on their beloved river.

Douglas Sheets

"Hi sweetheart, coming home soon?" Loretta Sheets appealed to her husband over the phone. Her use of sweetheart didn't come off too endearing, once she heard rock music blaring in the background, creating a painful, dispirited reaction. Her self-esteem degraded. She knew his answer, but held a minuscule amount of hope for the best. To Loretta, her husband stayed away from home on a regular basis. In reality, Douglas was out a few nights each week but when a relationship deteriorates, one partner's loneliness usually grows profound. Reeking of beer when he did arrive, tore at a heavy heart making her feel ashamed. Some nights never coming home at all, obvious her husband must be mixing it up with another affair. Loretta Sheets was trapped and knew it. A stay home wife and now full time mom, Loretta lacked vital job skills and much more. The self confidence necessary to make a go of it on her own.

"Is daddy coming home mommy?" Lucy, her four year old asked in a sort of neutral tone, while brushing long strands of counterfeit, red hair on Bee-Bee, her black spider baby doll. Lucy had grown accustomed to her father being away and eating dinner alone with mom. Fast-food filled their diets as Loretta succumbed to her third year of a loveless marriage. Making bona fide efforts to win her husband back while her marriage slipped away as each week passed. Lucy enjoyed the fries and cokes however. What better than sugary food when you're young and taste is honed on sucrose or salt. Mom's teary eyes had become so common, the young girl was bothered less and less by the outbreaks anymore. An obvious problem for the child.

"Don't cry Bee-Bee, it'll be all right," stroking the doll's long blood toned hair as Loretta raised her index finger to signal quiet please.

"I'm going to be out a little longer," her husband replied already sounding every bit tipsy. "Me and the guys are having an impromptu work meeting. We need to discuss some," but Loretta interrupted quick.

On the other end of the phone Douglas could tell his wife was upset in the way her voice quivered. "Lucy and I have barely seen you this week, Doug. When do you think you might be home?" Hearing his wife's mood change from sad to mad in a heartbeat. "Maybe we could all go out for dinner. I know Lucy would love it," Loretta begged. Willing to try any sort of guilt trip to get her husband back into his normal routine.

"Kiss Lucy for me. I'll be late. You two get something to eat without me. We'll be eating here," her husband said as more loud music blared among the laughs and yells.

"That doesn't sound like much of a work meeting to me Douglas. How about Lucy and I, coming down and having dinner with you?" Loretta challenged, knowing first hand she was about to be sloughed off or start receiving his intimidating threats again.

Silence filled the sheriff's end of the phone. Doug paused, racing his mind to come up with any sort of alibi at this point. "Look, you two will be bored stiff. I'll be home later," Douglas dodged.

"It can't be any more boring than staying home alone again," swallowing her compelling urge to break down and cry.

"Don't Loretta," Doug ordered with force, letting her know his agitation was growing. "Just go have something to eat with Lucy. I'll see you both later."

The sheriff killed an unwanted connection before his wife conjured up anymore ideas.

Loretta heard the click. That appalling, terrible, lonesome click, signifying affection couldn't be less interested. Her heart sank even deeper when she turned to see Lucy stroking Bee-Bee's hair. Over and over again, the toy brush passed through the spider's hair, telling her not to cry.

"Are you clear?" a rather short brunette wearing a baggy, revealing, cut away tee-shirt asked Douglas. She locked her anticipation on the deputy setting two cold beers on a wood table. Sheets all but fell into the padded chair feeling guilty as well as drunk. He also noticed how the young tee-shirt didn't seem as attractive just a few minutes previous.

"Clear." Doug certified, clutching the heavy glass of Ranger IPA, guzzled, looking long at the hard living floozy across from him. For some unexpected reason a lucid image of his daughter grabbed and held his attention. The young brunette guzzled beer too, growing more unpleasant with each gulp. It wouldn't matter as long as the IPA kept coming.

Loretta was close to breaking down. She thought of the Crosby case. "If it wasn't for those lowlife idiots, my life might be a lot fucking better right now," mumbling to herself but not loud enough for Lucy to hear. "Jesus Doug, not another affair. Please. I won't make it through another affair," she whimpered, wiping plump tears dripping from her chin. "Sarah Crosby, I hope you're burning in fucking hell." Loretta snatched a half empty white wine bottle from the fridge. Lucy continued combing Bee-Bee's hair.

Beatrice

Resting in her backyard, Beatrice moved close to a small fire crackling in a raised metal bowl. Late afternoon sun filtered through three aging sycamore trees, displaying persistent orange leaves on crooked limbs, scattering partial shade around her brick patio. If observing the scene from indoors one could imagine a late summer afternoon, typical perhaps of mid fall Valley weather. Verging on a tad warm. But the sun's low angle in mid November couldn't overcome a growing, intact chill. Smoke coiled vertically indicating dead calm, keeping the stinging carbon from swirling into Betty's face and eyes. She could sit close to the warmth allowing for a comfy setting.

Mrs. Patterson wasn't completely relaxed however. Her thoughts bounced from Tracy's police investigation wondering if they were close to identifying the shooter. Images of that morning's slow moving truck driving by haunted her dreams. Lifeless faces, similar to grim reaper caricatures prevalent around Halloween night. Just a few nights before, she suffered a rare nightmare about a faceless shooter returning to kill her. Beatrice looked forward to meeting with the Hispanic detective again. Regina turned out to be a rather nice gal, even after their rough start over morning coffee. "I hope she calls soon," Mrs. Patterson whispered to herself, poking hot coals, stoking the fire. Sudden sensations of warmth covered her face as hot flames erupted from the blaze.

In her right hand Beatrice couldn't stop twirling her prize. Its shiny part was reflecting firelight off the surface and it fixed her gaze. Finger to finger, never veering from the object's captivating, yet menacing allure. How long would she have to wait before returning her find, to the original owner. Maybe then she'd know the killers identity.

"Perhaps it's time to talk with Franny?" Beatrice contemplated.

Los Banos State Wildlife Refuge

Saturday morning's drive south on I-5 began rather ordinary. But just past the three quarter mark to Los Banos, things changed to awfully painful. South of the Santa Nella exit, two semi-truck long haulers decided to dance with one another. Traffic rolled to a standstill. Gonzalez had arranged to meet with Buck and his wife Maggie, a potential cancer patient, at Los Banos Wildlife Refuge. Meeting time was agreed at noon but getting out of bed late, as usual, then trapped inside a Starbucks drive thru line found the detective running way behind and dead stop at the moment. Regina didn't have Buck's cell phone number and she left her notebook laying on the kitchen counter. 11:45 A.M. and she wasn't moving.

"Oh Christ, I can't believe this crap," Regina scolded herself, rubbing a clammy forehead and downing a long slug of her morning caffeine. She saw lights flashing ahead. Coming from behind, a siren bellowed as an ambulance and Triple-A tow truck lifted dust from the slow lane dirt shoulder. As each vehicle roared by, Regina thought they moved way too slow.

Next to her in a large SUV a middle aged man was taken by surprise ducking his head like a turtle seeking self protection. He looked at Regina sheepishly, mouthing the word, "Wow!" Offering his opinion of the emergency trucks speed! She looked away in disgust.

"Wimp," Gonzalez muttered. "C'mon, I've got to get moving." Another geologic five minutes would pass before slight movements started beyond the flashing red and amber lights. Hope was elevated by a line of cars beginning to snake into the fast lane berm. One by one, brake lights dimmed as a long, slow single file line of vehicles crept south on the Golden State's main thoroughfare. Regina's attitude rebounded, taking another long drink from her hot mug. Moving again.

"Maybe Buck will call? Did I ever give him my cell phone number?" she wondered moving toward the collision scene. One Roadway trailer with a

Peterbuilt tractor had flipped onto its right side lying grotesque in broken glass, engine coolant and chunks of failed tires. Victim number two saw its tractor facing north in the south bound fast lane. Severe dents, scrapes and a large windshield completely shattered. "That can't be good for the driver." Regina winced and those waiting in line mulled over similar opinions, fast becoming less impatient.

The big rig's tandem trailers stayed upright somehow, resting at right angles to the roadway in a complete block of Interstate Five's two southbound lanes. Regina passed the collision site as two medics wheeled a stretcher toward the flipped trailer. Powerless to detach her eyes from the grisly disaster but glancing behind while Highway Patrol officers waved cars through, imploring them to keep rolling. Soon enough finding herself at the Highway 152 exit ramp and sailing into a hard banking curve which dropped onto two lanes, en route for Los Banos, at last. Thirty minutes late if nothing else gets in her way. Reaching the western outskirts of town, a faint vestige of low clouds lingered to the northeast after a notorious Central Valley tule fog formed just before sunrise. Lingering patches of the low clouds caught vivid sunlight and reflected various shades of faint yellow and pale orange. Dead calm and warmer. Another typical mid-day setting in Los Banos, which curses duck hunters way too often.

Turning right onto Henry Miller Road from Mercy Springs, Regina finally reached the check station. Half past noon and couldn't feel more embarrassed. In complete understanding if the patrolman didn't wait for her to show. Her car bounced through an uneven entrance, relieved to spot Buck talking it up with two hunters dressed head to toe in camouflage. "Oh boy," Regina observed in absolute sarcasm then whipped hard right landing next to a white Dodge Ram.

In the passenger's seat, Gonzalez believed, sat Charley Buck's wife, Maggie. She held a glaring scowl on Regina longer than someone exchanging pleasantries, rolled her window down and yelled to hubby, "the A's fan has finally arrived." Then nodded to Regina for added effect.

Freezing the detective in her seat, embarrassed, feeling like a careless, heartless loser. "I wonder if Maggie received bad news about her breast cancer?" the detective thought. "God I feel like crap." Building enough fortitude to open her car door, she climbed out conveying greetings and apologies. "Hi Maggie. I'm late and very sorry. I had so many hold ups on the drive down. You haven't been waiting too long, I hope?" Regina sunk even lower with her lame excuse.

"Hey Charley, she's here. Let's hustle things up now," Maggie yelled once more to her husband, louder and getting his undivided attention. Her dyed blond hair complete with dark roots shined in the afternoon light as blood red lipstick spread unbalanced over her thin lips. Buck turned, lifting a short wave to the ladies who appeared to be getting along swell.

"Detective Gonzalez, come on over," Buck called out which gave Regina the out she needed to extricate herself from a lousy situation.

"I hope you're feeling okay Maggie," Regina offered, backing away, in reference to her condition.

"I'm fine," the grumpy woman spit out looking away for effect, rolling her window up.

Regina hustled toward the three men spotting several ducks swinging from a metal strap. Repulsed and forced to cover her mouth by the unwitting site of bloody birds hung by their necks, but compelled closer by colorful feathers and broad bills. She strolled next to both hunters and leaned forward to get a better look at the birds. Both men noticed Gonzalez' enthralled gaze on their unusual waterfowl. Buck, now holding the strap, lifted a heavy bunch into direct sunlight providing Regina her thorough inspection. For some reason, entirely captivated with the birds and dried blood dripping the length of one bird's short leg, crossing its webbed, gray foot. A tiny coagulated droplet still hung from the pebbly skin.

"What kind of ducks are those?" pointing to a pair of sleek, white breasted drakes. Their pointed tail feathers, vermiculated gray flanks and characteristic white 'sprigs' climbing up behind chocolate heads, were marks as beautifully displayed on any animal she'd ever seen. One bird appeared unmarked except for the crooked line of dried blood blemishing it's right foot. The other showed pink stains tarnishing an otherwise snow white belly.

"Those are drake sprig, as hunters call them," Buck chimed in. "Pintails to lay people," speaking proud as if harvesting the strap of waterfowl himself. "These are widgeon, here's a ringneck and those two small birds are teal," Charley ran through the dead birds lifting each one to give Gonzalez a clear look. "You know this one," Buck assumed, cradling a drake mallard in his hand, turning it slow to show off hues of iridescent green, chestnut and blue.

"That's a mallard and the only duck I know," Regina acknowledged then scanned the group close. "Those small ones. Tell me they're not baby ducks?" Standing in surprised recoil, Gonzalez was expecting an explanation from the nearest middle aged shooter.

"No mame. Those are full grown teal," hunter number one explained with a slight chuckle but not in ridicule. "Small ducks and full grown. Nice colors." Holding one green winged teal, hunter one permitted the detective to appreciate a vivid, iridescent green eye patch covering its reddish brown head.

Developing enough nerve, Gonzalez reached in to stroke each teal's green eye patch outlined with a thin, creamy-white border. "They're spectacular," Regina concurred.

"Charley, we don't have all day," Maggie's voice shrieked again, causing all four heads to turn in her direction.

"She sounds serious," hunter number two said in a dry tone with a joking attitude.

Buck registered her second warning, so he got moving. "Nice birds guys. Good job," complimenting both shooters. "We should get inside detective." Charley Buck decided to speed it up.

"Buck. What about Maggie?" asking the patrolman. "How did her biopsy go?" Not wanting to pry but feeling guilty for keeping his wife trapped out here. "You don't have to stay Charley, if Maggie wants to leave." Gonzalez relented, wishing Buck might have something encouraging to say.

"Oh yeah. Actually, things look great. Doc's needle placement to locate her tumor popped a cyst instead. Fluid was drained, which means negative for cancer," explaining Maggie's condition while most of his attention stayed on hunters coming and going from the check station.

"Let's go," Regina stated resolute, assuming this could be Maggie's normal attitude. "What a bitch!" slamming Buck's wife to herself.

Inside the check station two hunters lingered, waiting for any late arriving information on productive shooting areas. Peppering Fish and Wildlife personnel with questions of bird numbers, water conditions and harvest averages. One older man entered, wanting to go hunting and was promptly checked through then sent on his way.

"Shooting time ends at sunset," an attendant called out just before an exit door closed behind an anxious hunter, brimming with confidence. Many shooters had called it a day and left the refuge despite a better than average morning shoot. Check station personnel were much more active than Regina imagined they'd be, as departing trucks, camoed sportsmen and dead waterfowl shuffled through the parking lot. Each one handing in his or her permit card with tallied kills or empty handed. Who left a bit uncomfortable for getting skunked.

A modest cold snap ushered in fresh birds to the Los Banos region, down from northern refuge areas surrounding Willows and Colusa. Uneducated ducks, helpless in locating safe, closed zones, were falling for decoy spreads, producing much better shooting than expected. Cold air moving in overnight formed dense tule fog before sunrise and right at legal shooting time. That anticipated half hour before sunrise when new arrivals are most vulnerable. First light often proves as the benchmark between success or failure for novice shooters. Conditions this morning provided varied success. Typical of the valley at this time of year, morning fog will lift during late morning hours. Sometimes lingering past noon, if it stays cold enough. Experienced waterfowlers will stay patient, waiting for the lift to occur. New birds having a rough time locating safe resting water or confused in the high fog, become easier to deceive into shooting range just as clear skies burst forth. But usually for less than an hour. Bright sunshine lights up bobbing decoys, compelling these new flocks to fold wings and plummet into shooting range. Guns roar, ducks splash in watery demise as shooters relish forty five minutes of fast action. As quick as they come, these same birds easily fooled less than an hour before get wise, fly high out of range, searching out real birds at rest. Quiet returns once again and understandably most hunters call it a day.

Buck introduced himself to Jennifer Sweeney, working hard behind a high wooden counter. She scarcely acknowledged Charley focused on writing up permit tags, counting active hunters and running a tally of birds killed this morning. "We're from the City of Tracy Police Department. Homicide Division," Buck announced seeming very official to Regina who preferred to keep meetings more low key.

"What the hell, he's doing fine," Gonzalez supposed.

Buck continued. "We scheduled a meeting with your Refuge Manager. I believe her name is Kelly Crisp? Unusual name," he added not intending to sound flip.

Caught off guard, Jennifer looked up from behind a tattered countertop, diverting attention away from a stack of papers and red tags. Somewhat confused. "Yes, yes, yes. Sorry, I was expecting something more hunting related," the clerk responded, pushing permits aside and closing her counter drawer. "Kelly mentioned you were coming to visit our little refuge. Welcome," playing it a touch too country hospitable for Regina's taste. "Something about that awful murder in Tracy last week. Gunned down in his own driveway. Whew, that's weird," the attendant replied using very soft words, staring at two cops who had nothing to say in return.

Regina stepped to the plate, not letting her chance to scare the bumpkin get away. Gonzalez knew she could get in trouble but couldn't resist. "Don't play that innocent crap with me Loretta Lynn. Why'd you shoot the poor sap?" Regina concealed a big smile while setting eyes straight on the awestruck woman.

"Hey, wait a minute," Jennifer mumbled, visibly shaken, stepping back from the counter and raising both hands, fingers splayed, head turning side to side. "I was working that day and you can't accuse me," Sweeney stopped cold, her lips quivering. She surveyed Regina and Buck laughing now. Jennifer realized she'd been played.

"Oh man! You're very good," pointing to Regina. "You got me, big time." Jennifer relaxed but continued unsteady, returning to her counter. "Let me get Kelly for you." Disappearing into one of a few rather small offices making up the rear structure.

"Thanks," Regina said to Jennifer, spotting Buck's broad smile.

"Great job," Buck acknowledged. "Great job."

Kelly Crisp had Jennifer in tow rounding the office corner, greeting Regina with handshakes and cooperative attitudes. "Hi, I'm Kelly. We talked yesterday. You must be Regina Gonzalez?" asking the detective in her dry manner, not even politely recognizing Buck's presence. Kelly Crisp, a fairly young refuge manager, didn't seem like a homespun woman as displayed by Miss Sweeney. Polar opposites in fact. "Why don't we meet in my office where we can talk in private," Kelly proposed, levering up the counter access board, allowing both cops to enter.

"What can I do for you detective?" Kelly offered after settling into her work area. Cluttered about the room were various topo maps, engineering plans, piles of loose papers stacked next to an antiquated computer and a few specimen jars lining a small metal sink. "You're interested in how we do things here," the manager said, waving a pencil in her fingers and scrutinizing both cops in front of her.

"If I may, Kelly," Regina began, "my department is investigating an individual who might've been involved in a murder about ten days ago." Gonzalez wanted to explain her motive as simple as possible. "He claims to be duck hunting here on the day of the murder. Also, just to be clear, in no way shape or form are we investigating anything you folks do here. Nor anyone employed at the refuge." Further clarifying her request for their meeting today.

"That's a relief," Miss Crisp responded, showing a slight trace of emotion but still appearing as though her time was being wasted while obligated to assist in murder cases. The refuge manager began her outline. "Okay, our routine is simple. Hunters show up Wednesday, Saturday or Sunday to hunt birds, filling a sign-up sheet the evening before shoot days. They're after ducks mostly, but pheasants too. We begin around four in the morning, collect passes, issue permits and off they go to shoot waterfowl" Dictating her simple sketch of refuge operations.

"I was told, you issue permit tags to every person hunting each day?" Gonzalez asked the all business like manager. "I'm not familiar with a sign-up sheet however?"

"Uhh, let's see," Kelley gathered her words. "Sign-up sheets are for those hunters who don't have a reservation. They're permitted access, only after shooters with reservations are checked in. The sign-up sheet just logs them in the night before on a lottery basis." Miss Crisp could tell Regina was having trouble following the process. Not surprising however, if one hasn't been through the system a few times. "We still have the permits and sign-up sheets for that day, on file," confident about her record keeping. "What's the suspect's name?" wishing to get this inquire over with promptly.

Regina handed the refuge manager a copy of Ellis' vital stats. "Tom Ellis. Gustine, California. Here's his hunting license number and vehicle tags."

Ms. Crisp paused and deliberated, twirling her pencil, deciding the best way to handle things. "Let's go back up front. Jennifer can help us pull these tags." As all three rose once again, leaving her office, Kelley stopped the train's motion to instruct. "Before we go up front, let's keep the murder talk quiet, if possible," the manager cautioned. "I can't afford to alarm any of these hunters around here. They're our customers and this department needs as much revenue as possible these days. Is that all right?"

"Understood," Regina agreed, making their way toward Jennifer's work area. Filing cabinets were opened, dates located and a small stack of records were removed. "Finding this guy's tags may take a little time," Jennifer instructed just as the station door swung open, permitting two successful hunters to enter. A woman this time, joined by her husband, each carrying a pair of green wing teal on duck straps. Kelley checked them through, quick, as Jennifer continued searching.

"Kelly, I'm told all hunters have to go in and out through this check station?" Regina asked.

"Correct. Permit in and permit out. If we have his record filed, he was definitely here," Kelly confirmed. "All hunters drive out from the check station, after check-in, to various lots on the refuge. Loading up their gear, hiking or biking, out to favored ponds in the middle of the night, foolishly I might add, just to shoot birds. Don't ask me to explain this behavior." The refuge manager was speaking straightforward to Regina for a split second but the subtle laugh emanating under Buck's breath, exposed the sardonic dig from Ms. Crisp. She was capable of her moments. Kelly continued to show Gonzalez more procedures, passes and how various types of permits were filled out.

"Once a hunter goes out, they can't come and go from the refuge?" Regina asked as another pair of shooters funneled inside, to be checked out. A father with his young son.

"Verboten!" Crisp answered, smiling this time, but additional details were swiftly cut off.

The young boy, still wearing heavy streaks of camo painted on red cheeks, scurried to Jennifer's counter with dad holding two mallards and a spoony. All drakes. The proud shooter, not much more than eleven years old. "I got this one," an excited young hunter shouted, grabbing a full grown mallard in both hands around its soft belly, showing off to everyone now peering over the counter. The room's attention shifted to a young boy's infectious excitement. Including Miss Crisp!

"Great job," Jennifer congratulated in high volume, checked both permits and flashed a quick wink to the boy's father to say good job dad. Regina couldn't help but giggle too and Buck was once more caught up admiring a brace of waterfowl. He paid almost no interest in the investigation going on. Too many ducks.

The young interruption ended with Kelley getting back to business. "What was your question detective?" Crisp asked Regina.

"Here he is," Jennifer announced valiantly, jarring Regina from her admiring gaze upon the cute boy and his mallard. "Tom Ellis," Sweeney read his name and license number. "You know, I think I remember this guy," Jennifer added. "Yeah, I remember him now. He limited that day. That was the only limit brought in since opening weekend."

"He limited?" Kelly asked kind of surprised.

Regina, wanting to know why, asked, "Is that unusual?"

"For this time of year, you bet it is," Kelly affirmed staring at a tattered kill record and ticking off each duck killed. Buck nodded in agreement staring over Ms. Crisp's shoulder, impressed by the quality of birds taken that day. He held a map of the refuge and pointed out numbered parking lot locations laid out along a winding refuge access road.

"Your boy hunted from lot four, checking out after shoot time. It was after dark if I remember right. He had to be here all day," Jennifer assumed, judging by the number of birds he took that day. "No question."

Buck, attempting to further clarify directions to Regina was tracing his finger along the access road leading out to parking lot four. Gonzalez nodded, sending Buck a disparaged signal, just to let him know she could comprehended a simple diagram.

"If it's who I'm thinking of, this guy was pretty hot," Jennifer whispered to Regina, examining his permit card intently, trying to remember clear details of his face.

"God, I know," Regina confirmed bowing her head on the counter top attempting to hide her face as well as her passion. Before she could say anything more, into the room strode Maggie Buck, searching her husband like a female lab.

"Are we going to be here much longer?" Maggie asked, addressing a startled group, burning a hole through Charley's face. Everything stopped as the entire group stared at her husband.

"Not much longer sweetheart," Buck answered like a scolded boy, knowing Maggie would be a lot more anxious after her stressful medical procedure. His wife always had run of their relationship, maintaining constant pressure because Charley offered very little resistance.

Maggie turned, opened the door and proclaimed to all, he had five more minutes.

"Who the hell was that?" Kelly asked Regina with a baffled expression on her face.

"That would be my wife," Buck said with a sheepish voice, back to a shamed Miss Crisp. "She's not feeling herself these days."

"Sorry to hear that," she offered quick condolences, but thought this guy shouldn't have to take her kind of behavior. "What's your name again?" Kelly asked Buck, forgetting her original impoliteness when they first arrived.

"Charley Buck," he answered fast, accepting Kelly's business card.

"Feel free to call me anytime, if you have any questions Charley," Crisp added as Regina and Jennifer glanced to each other in a curious way. Sweeney shrugged her shoulders as if to say, 'was that a pass or what?' Each gal smirked while Buck slid Kelly's card into his thin wallet.

Regina took a deep breath thinking over the sum total of their meeting thus far. Overall; the truck accident, her being late, Buck's impatient wife, a constant parade of camo clad hunters carrying dead ducks, Buck's undivided attention on hunting and a refuge manager wondering what the hell does this have to do with us. All total, a meeting which accomplished very little.

"Not enough here," Regina stood quiet thinking to herself. "There's not enough evidence to say keep the heat on Tom Ellis." Desperate to expose something, which in her mind might scream, "he's involved."

"It seems like a fair alibi to me detective," Kelly Crisp said to Gonzalez. "Anything else I can help you with?" she asked in her neutral tone.

"I don't know. It all seems so simple," Regina admitted, scratching off each item from her laundry list. "A signed hunting permit with a record of birds killed that day. Paid pass. Same license number. Nobody in or out without a tag. Confirmed identification. How couldn't he have been here?" she presumed.

"We have his plate number and truck model, from our sign-up sheet," Jennifer added, as Gonzalez checked her notes to confirm.

Regina remembered her picture of Ellis. "Is this the guy you checked out that evening?" showing Jennifer a DMV picture of her suspect.

"Mmm, oh yeah. I was checking him out. That's him all right," nodding positive to Regina with a sexed gaze in her eyes. Crisp heard Sweeney's remark and rolled her eyes too, annoyed.

"Buck, you have anything to ask?" Gonzalez shouted over to her cohort. He shrugged his shoulders and shook his head no. "Why don't you and Maggie take off. She's ready." Regina ordered.

"That's for sure," Buck agreed then chuckled. He left the room making a beeline for the love of his life.

"Nice meeting you Charley. Come back again," Kelly said to the rushing patrolman, leaving to console his angry spouse. Charley waved goodbye just before catching his hand in the closing door. Regina and Jennifer made eye contact, surprised again but staying mum.

"Ms. Crisp. May I take a ride out on your refuge? I'd like to look around if I could." he asked, hoping it wouldn't become a big issue.

"Sure can. Jennifer, would you issue the detective a non-shooting permit please," Kelley instructed. More than happy to get the search party out of sight and bring this caucus to a close. "It's a good time to go out. Most hunters have quit for the day anyway," he said, hoping she might get back to some real work. "Please tell Charley for me, it was nice meeting him."

"Uh, will do Kelly." Gonzalez obliged. "Now, access is through the front gate?" Pointing through the check station window across an empty parking lot.

"That's it," Jennifer replied handing Regina her permit. "That guy's way too sexy to be a killer," Sweeney urged the detective, causing both women to laugh. Regina peered out the window thinking, then gazed back to Jennifer in full agreement.

Gonzalez left the parking lot driving toward an open gate this time. Inside the now quiet check station, Kelly rushed from her office asking Jennifer if the detective had left. She pointed to Regina's car with a pistol like point, just as her car approached the entrance gate. Kelly made a mad dash outside in a losing effort to stop the detective. She forgot to tell Regina, parking lot four access was from Henry Miller Road. "I guess it doesn't matter?" telling herself out loud.

Crisp went unnoticed trying to wave Regina to stop. Gonzalez focused on a bumpy gravel road ahead, impatient to revisit the ponds from last Thursday evening. This afternoon was calm with clear skies between puffs of light clouds. Midday sunshine bathed her surroundings giving the refuge a whole new appeal. Deep blue sky contrasting with ground and cumulous. Approaching the first familiar ponds, Regina fully expected flocks of ducks floating on a calm surface. Not today. This was a shoot day and skittish birds reacted by seeking safe water or left the refuge entirely. Loafing away a pleasant day on calm waters of nearby reservoirs, backwater lakes or secret river channels.

She proceeded down the gravel road going slow over ruts and bumps. Her car handled the all-weather access road but still jumped and bounced on occasion, passing over holes in need of grading and fill. A few trucks passed in the opposite direction, as more hunters had finished for the day. Each driver giving a short wave as they passed. She didn't know what to make of it. Perhaps a salute of sorts amongst the bird hunting fraternity.

One long open field to her left held three figures walking in dense weeds. Out in front of them two dogs, both white and dark reddish brown, appeared to be leading the group forward. Regina stopped to watch, assuming they were hunting pheasant. They were. Red hats and yellow vests have no part in water-fowl shooting. Not much happened except for two dogs jumping high weeds with occasional whistles and yells from the line of pursuers coming up behind.

Gonzalez moved on soon reaching parking lot one. A single green truck resided in the dirt lot. "Probably the pheasant hunting conga line back down the road," Regina told herself. Checking the refuge map and verifying her location, she pushed on for lot two. Coming upon another group, further away in red and yellow working an uneven field between two low water ditches and high tules. They disappeared into dense, tan vegetation, reappeared, only to vanish again within a dozen or so steps. Fluorescent red hats shined bright reflecting intense afternoon glare. Compared to his partner whose yellow vest, at Regina's distance, blended in with thick, sun bleached weeds. She slowed to watch again, hoping to see some action. But like the other hunters, nothing much happened except the depiction of a hunting scene resembling a brightly lit landscape painting. Complete with soaring birds of prey, still water ponds and low foothills rising in the distance. Shadows dwelled very short in mid afternoon sun, as a single band of wispy cirrus clouds rested above the eastern horizon, and cumulous burst in from western hills. Two distant thumps sounded off, from somewhere, as Regina identified gunshots.

"Somebody's still hunting out here," she mumbled out loud, wondering if a few more ducks had been downed. Her car bumped and shimmied, before long spotting a sign for lot two as sweeping dry fields gave way to more flooding. Ponds left and right supporting thick expanses of tules, blocked her view into open water. Lot two was vacant. Regina had an itch to explore on foot but growing inside, was an urge to see some duck hunters in action.

"Let's move on to lots three and four. Someone's still out there?" Continuing her one sided conversation out loud. Gonzalez reached to turn up the volume as a Lucinda Williams CD belted out her sandpaper voice. She thought how the mature vocalist's current ballad, in a strange way, matched this watery environment she occupied. Following gravel ruts along a slow arc to her right, Regina spotted two white trucks shining bright, like beacons still far away near a small clump of trees. "Parking lot three," she concluded, getting anxious to begin hiking. Closing in, both trucks became clearly visible but stopping at the entrance, debating which way to proceed. Lot four was her destination, but Regina had to consider whether anyone would be there. Contemplating odds, the decision was made for her. She spotted two figures to her left in dark green camo, pushing a fairly large cart along a small levee road.

"What the fuck is that?" whispering to herself, squinting at two pushers, unable to comprehend the image of a large cart, sporting bicycle wheels, being pushed along a dirt path. They're route would pass right in front of her so she waited. Close to three o'clock reminded Gonzalez it was getting late. Shooting time ended at sundown which Jennifer said was just after five. Only two hours to find someone shooting out here. Lot four is out of the question.

On they came, pushing their cart along at a slow but steady clip, akin to defeated soldiers in retreat, salvaging gear and wounded. Each man looked tired. Regina scooted forward in her seat to check the contents while two shooters labored their contraption just beyond the car's hood. The nearest pusher looked her way and nodded in appreciation. She waved in return glimpsing decoys, guns, ammo belts, some sort of rotating wing device, jackets, packs and of course a few dead birds. Quite a load, she thought!

Gonzalez veered off into lot three, excited and forgetting lot four alto-gether. "It's too late," she reasoned, choosing to look around here knowing at least one hunter was still in the field. Pulling her car forward next to two sweating hunters unloading their cumbersome cart, now just beyond her car window. The elder of the two turned his head and said hello after flipping a pair of hard body decoys into an open truck bed. She smiled climbing from her car. "Looks like fun, guys," Regina stated. Deciding to pitch her sarcasm, not knowing what else to say, to see if they were approachable.

"You can help out, if you like," belting sarcasm in return, from the younger.

"Can I interrupt? I need some help from you two big, strong, hunks," the detective was stacking even more sarcasm onto her proverbial pile.

"How can we refuse?" emerging from the younger hunter while lifting a mesh bag of plastic decoys from the cart, flopping it into the truck bed with a thud and loud clanging from lead weights.

"You can't," Regina quickly responded for effect. "So. I have no idea what I'm doing out here," trying to figure an easy way to ask questions.

"You're in trouble miss," the elder responded.

Regina laid her smile on thick, saw the elder smiling too and beginning to enjoy these two. "Just hear me out, okay?"

"Okay," the younger.

"I'm wondering. Let's see, how to ask this," Regina was stumbling bad. "Do you know?" looking stupid.

"Just say it sweetheart," the elder said in a calm tone which relaxed the detective.

"Do either of you know where, perhaps, the guys in that truck might be hunting right now?" Finally asking, knowing how dumb she must sound, turning radish red.

"Yeah, that's Gordon's truck," the younger informed. "Don't know his last name. He's hunting a pond we planned on shooting today," imparting the exact answer she needed.

"Oh, great. How do I find that pond?" Gonzalez inquired, afraid too many turns would make it impossible to find Gordon.

Her answer came direct and from younger once again. "Very easy. Stay on that levee from the parking lot," pointing to a gap between two small willow trees. As if on cue, two gun shots thumped in the distance right where younger was pointing.

"See," the elder smiled proud, "he's still out there. That pond draws the birds. Especially late afternoons. You'll see his spread set up in the first big open water pond, on your right. Can't miss him."

"His spread?" Regina spoke with an obvious question in her voice.

"His decoys," the younger said, as they finished unloading, not in the least interested why she wanted to know Gordon's whereabouts.

"Hey, thanks guys. I see you two got some ducks today." Gonzalez noted, receiving a mumbled 'yep' in return from elder, as both hunters paid Regina little attention. Finished for the day. "Okay, see ya," she bid farewell.

"Okay," from younger, offering aid. "Mame, you might need this." Tossing this odd lady a half filled bottle of water.

"Thanks." A grateful detective replied. "Told ya I don't know what the hell I'm doing." Elder grinned. Regina checked her watch. Almost 3:30. "I only have an hour and a half left," she supposed, beginning her hike between two willows and officially entering hunting territory. Stumbling bad at first in thick mud, the levee dirt soon dried out, growing wide enough but choked in dense weeds. Dead and dried out tules, scattered between thistle shrubs, armed with long sharp spikes pricked her skin. The detective's route developed a narrow, winding path leading around and through a stand of choking brush. Granting slow but steady progress with only a few more wet spots on an otherwise dry levee, Gonzalez worried her path might become too muddy or continue to a water break altogether. Scanning ahead appeared to be high and dry as far as she could see. Moving on for a half mile she reached open water to her left. This pond, noticeably shallow, showed grasses and tules emerging through a tranquil surface. Further on, ducking and dodging weeds, another levee, much smaller, intersected at right angles. Open water laying beyond made Regina think out loud, "Gordon should be on the other side of that ditch," and picked up the pace. Succeeding the intersection, forming Gordon's pond, she stopped to rest, drink and look around, as a low sun to her left created intense glare on a smooth surface. Beyond this corner, maybe seventy five yards on her levee, stood a medium size dying tree. The trunk was submerged into open water where a patch of dense tules formed, jutting out and away but toward Gordon's pond.

"Should be a good vantage point," she concluded, investigating muddied waters for any sign of her hidden duck hunter. Staring hard, her eyes caught a blinking object near another clump of tules just a bit off center in open water. Straining to see it clear, she focused on the device, uncertain what it was. Gonzalez surveyed the scene. "That could be him out there," whispering to herself while dropping to one knee continuing a visual search. Once her eyesight adjusted she could see the spinning motion, presenting a strange impression of black and white blinking.

Regina relaxed, resting, watching and enjoying her newfound situation. Various blackbirds and a few snowy egrets glided beyond the pond heading somewhere. Their wing beats appeared fairly slow and methodical, noticing how each bird dropped, ever so slight, between every dozen strokes. Almost bobbing in flight, unlike waterfowl, staying in high power mode throughout their advance. She guzzled from the Younger's cool water. In a tranquil eerie silence she took a deep breath, absorbing her surroundings and the way it took on a soothing atmosphere. That was about to change however.

Before long, she made out faint whistles and chirps, similar to those heard two days before. "From the birds or from Gordon?" Regina asked herself, spotting a flock of large birds in a rough V formation, gliding slow, way above the pond. She knelt, sliding under a low slung branch holding a sparse collection of dry leaves offering decent camouflage from ducks on obvious lookout. Whistles and low pitched grunting seemed to originate high overhead but untrained ears had difficulty in verifying their true origin. Each bird turned, all at once, before reaching heavy cover spread along a muddy shoreline, dispersing the tight formation. Powerful wing beats resumed and faint whirring could be heard, enabling a suitable altitude required for safe searches. This flock lost a number of young members on their flight south to dark upright figures and many loud noises. Two older birds, one hen and drake, kept close vigilance for movements below. In fact, all seven birds making up the flock were very skittish about this area. Except one. An older drake carrying two steal pellets near his abdomen, one inside the rib cage.

Last Wednesday morning found him committing to a usually safe but small piece of water, rich in swamp timothy. Two loud booms roared from below as another drake nearest him, crumpled, splashing to a bloody heap far below. Errant steel shot found its way to his lower breast area but didn't penetrate deep enough to damage vital organs or break bone. It caused some pain over longer flights and the drake was in desperate need of rest. Open water, quiet and resting birds all appeared inviting as the wounded bird began to abandon caution. The flock veered left passing well out over safe water then turned hard once again, honing in on Gordon's spinning wings. Lower on this pass. Intermittent breezes managed to briefly twirl each wing but came to a stop as calm air resumed once again. Gordon cussed himself for his bad luck. "Not even a little fucking breeze," he squealed.

Chirps streamed out again but more rhythmic this time. "That's gotta be coming from Gordon," Regina thought. "What the hell is that spinning thing?" she wondered out loud. "I don't get that one at all," trying in vain to comprehend any sort of usefulness from such a ridiculous device. "That stupid thing can't attract ducks," she whispered with a short laugh. Kneeling lower, under two overhanging limbs, but keeping a clear line of sight to Gordon's patch of blind. "Act One seems to be unfolding right now," Gonzalez murmured, slumping lower to remain unseen.

Once again, over Gordon's pond, the medium flock banked and turned hard. Rolling long and steady with some birds dropping slightly but just enough erratic flutters kept others from getting too low. A characteristic searching flight common to northern pintails. Each bird scrutinized individual decoys but more important, searched every patch of tules scattered throughout the pond for subtle movement betraying any dangerous figures below.

Regina had the sun almost behind her but a steep angle failed to complete a covering shadow. She froze stiff when the group sailed low in front of her. They cut through thick air with distinctive rushing sounds, white breasts almost glowing by bright sunshine. She made out every long, needle like tail feather terminating the streamlined drakes. Continuing to circle overhead, but never losing much altitude, which didn't surprise Gordon at all. Four times now, repeating their sweeps. Four times yet still not close to committing a full out landing. Beginning pass number five, the wounded drake slumped one wing making a sharp left turn which initiated a sustained but controlled drop. Regina caught sight of the falling pintail and focused her attention, guessing Gordon was doing exactly the same. Like a magnet, every remaining bird moved close together, flocking up, preparing to chase the loner. Loud chirps and female chuckles broke out sending the flock higher, as if choosing to observe the outcome of their valiant or foolish member. A single drake with wings locked in place picked up speed as he fell. This same event playing out over and again, each hunt day.

In fact, his pain had been increasing for close to an hour. Knowing a low pass was risking life, but the pain exaggerated a gamble he was willing to play, betting this pond would be free of loud booms. If he landed in quiet and safety, the flock would follow in, making him feel secure with familiar birds nearby. Especially a certain hen he'd been courting the last few weeks and beginning to accept his daily passes. Closing in on Gordon's decoys and lowering his wings a bit more. Air released and blue water was coming up to meet him now. Well within range and gliding over a patch of vegetation hoping for the best at this point. Reaching an edge of thick tules the drake began to lower webbed feet when abruptly, he became pain free and the resting water he needed came up very fast.

"Spectacular," Gonzalez said out loud with subdued chuckles, eyeing the lone bird, wings tipping from side to side, gliding straight into that stupid spinning thing flying right over an oval shaped patch of tules. Fixated on her single drake, she lost track of the main flock. Sensing danger from the sprig's bold maneuver but admitting a strange compassion for an unknown man named Gordon hidden in a bunch of tules, all alone. Finding herself cheering for a faceless shooter but still admiring a fearless single sprig sketching a bold picture as he plunged lower. All alone. "Act Two!"

Gonzales watched, almost trancelike, as the pintail's angling descent brought himself closer into killing range. Playing out in front of her from right to left, as the bird closed on Gordon's blind and decoys. Then for no apparent reason the pintail dropped. Not oblique, like a controlled landing. Instead a sudden, uncontrolled free fall. Steep. Appearing unnatural, Regina didn't grasp what happened in the brief instant, forcing in a deep breath of surprise. Now came the shotgun blast and more surprise. Loud, even at this distance between her and Gordon but far enough away to delay the sound wave. Regina witnessed the bird killed in flight a split second before the decisive gunshot registered. Nonetheless she gasped slightly, due in part to an unexpected blast and because her regal pintail lay dead. Wings folded, it fell to cold water exploding into a large splash, reaching her ears a split second later too. Everything played like an old movie with a soundtrack slightly out of sequence. She couldn't help feel a slight amount of empathy for the downed sprig but Regina smiled when Gordon emerged from his blind, waded into deeper water, lifted the dead bird by its neck and returned to his makeshift blind. No cheering, no laughing, no celebrating. End of act three and the curtain closes. "That's something you don't see every day," Regina muttered to herself.

Gonzalez leaned back on her knees waiting for another flight of ducks. Keeping a sharp look out, spotting one other lone duck fly by, very high, but not interested in stiff decoys or loud calls coming from the lone shooter below. Twenty minutes later she decided to head back. It was late, not many birds were in motion and she was out of water.

A few seconds later her cell phone rang. Ringing three times before she acknowledged an incoming call. Standing to remove her phone as Gordon did likewise. She, getting a clear view of the faceless shooter from his waist up. He, scanning empty skies for more waterfowl.

"This is Regina," failing to check who was calling. "Hello." Gordon turned in her direction handing Gonzalez a courteous wave.

From the other end, "Regina? Miss Gonzalez. Hi, Tom Ellis here." Her suspect caught Gonzalez off guard, similar to the gun blast erupting not long ago. She waved back to Gordon.

"Mr. Ellis. How are you? You wouldn't believe where I am right now," Regina greeted the surveyor, not about to reveal anything of her adventure, after considering today's events.

"Okay, I'll bite. Where are you?"

Anticipating his question, "never mind. What can I do for you?" she asked with a slight eagerness in her voice.

"Uhm, all right. I'd like to get together," Tom spoke, nervous of course, wondering why she snubbed him about her current location. "I have more info about the murder case you might be interested in," he added, out to grab her attention.

"I'm interested in anything new," the detective consented. Then feeling a rush of excitement in the pit of her stomach, leaving behind her hiding place and beginning a fast pace back to lot three. "Just say where."

Part II

Tracy, California

Chris

Saturday night and alone once again. Chris Davis wasn't intentionally avoiding people but difficult murder cases brought his relentless dark side to the surface. Acute brooding then escalating deeper into alcohol.

"One more time Benny," Davis requested sliding a wet rocks glass forward allowing his well-situated drinking pal and bartender to tip a bottle of Bullet Bourbon, refilling Chris's drink. Benny skewered three ripe berries, dropping the plastic sword with impaled fruit, recharging his glass.

"One Blackman," Benny declared.

"My man," Chris acknowledged.

A rather tall middle aged woman entered the lounge earlier. Chris noticed her arrival and thought it a little odd as his watering hole failed to attract many single woman inside. She refused a quick but clumsy advance from one of a few drunk patrons but made eye contact with Davis more than once. He glanced over to 'flying solo' after she settled in and chased away her first admirer. Nowhere near a vigorous pass but typical in the way most red blooded, intoxicated men take notice of any single woman in a hard drinking establishment. Events started changing however, as 'going it alone' stared right at Davis for a lengthy measure, nodded her head in approval and announced a bold hello. She maintained a strong female confidence which frankly made Chris quite nervous.

Davis backed down. Shying away, letting Benny grab his attention and sidetracked from a possible liaison. One more lousy NCAA football game played out on a big screen TV as classic rock filtered through the bar. Chris wasn't interested letting his thoughts drift to Regina, wondering how her duck hunting field trip worked out. "I bet that was sorta weird," he assumed, conjuring images of his partner up to her butt in mud and Buck!

His real interest kept returning to Franny Braden of course. Recalling her appearance during their meeting. The way she dressed, her smell, that innocent tone in her voice and how she slinked throughout the room. As if each movement became a sensuous tease distracting him from a job to be done.

Chris knew Franny's charm had gone way too far. "Can't keep going there," reminding himself a few times over the last few days.

Henry Braden popped into his mind, promptly spoiling Chris' previous fantasies he'd been painting about his sexy wife. Henry forced Davis into deep meditation, replaying some of his statements over again. So deep in fact he almost failed to notice when 'little miss sunshine' changed bar stools, now sitting alone next to him. Accidentally on purpose bumping his arm causing Davis to spring from under his secret crime world. Studying her wide eyed and surprised, but smiling this time. She giggled how fast his head jerked around, sensing the rather attractive man was miles away from the tavern. Liking that too.

"Welcome back," joking but refusing to remove her scrutiny.

"Maybe I'm lucky tonight," Chris hoped. It had been a while.

Business being so slow this evening had Benny glued to a lopsided football game. Not a moment too soon another college blowout was coming to a merciful close. "Boise State whips up on another Western Athletic Conference dog," mumbling out loud to Chris. "Boise's schedule is a joke," concluding even louder as the Broncos run out forty two final seconds while racking up fifty two final points and only giving up three field goals. "What drama," Benny grumbled.

Chris couldn't help but inquire, "I don't follow the college game too close Benny, but is Boise State that good or is New Mexico that bad?" asking the bartender while his 'current love' leaned against his arm, waiting on Benny's opinion too.

"That bad," Benny boomed too loud and killed the broadcast. "And I lost this damn game on my parlay card. Which is all that matters." Revealing his real interest in this game.

Chris turned to see 'free and easy' laughing it up and amused with Benny's perspective. "I'm sorry, can I buy you a drink?" Chris asked the fortyish lady with dark hair. Being a gentleman but also trolling for trophy fish later this evening. No sooner had 'miss one or two night stand' moved in on him, Chris' cell phone vibrated with an incoming call. Not answering right away, deeming it rude to take a call this soon in front of his new playmate. "I can always check it later." Charting strategy unwilling to jeopardize any late night possibilities. After all, he found himself in good standing with 'lonesome dove' and he hadn't talked to her yet. Didn't even know her name!

Settling soon into quiet, easy conversation and before long, becoming more than comfortable as Chris welcomed his new love rubbing a thigh, squeezing hands and wrapping his arm. Davis loved it. They both drank more as Benny even chipped in a round for the romantic couple. She liked her gin as much as Davis enjoyed his bourbon. A good enough match as long as 'willing and able' followed Chris to his or her bedroom this evening. "Things seem to be going very well tonight," sensing victory, then excused himself for a fake bathroom run. His real intention was to check the earlier call.

"Holy crap," Davis squealed aloud after hearing the voicemail. It was Mrs. Braden of course and she wanted a private meeting. "Additional information," Franny explained! Chris could feel a level of excitement rush through his stomach. In part from the potential evidence she may have withheld but much more from his sexual fantasy. Realizing he was more or less falling for this woman. Maybe not quite head over heels but enough perhaps to cause interference with his investigation. "Be careful," whispering caution to himself.

"I better get back to 'cat woman' before some lowlife tries his luck." Chris made tracks to what he imagined would be his own personal masseuse, wishing for a warm greeting from both hands with sensuous fingers opened wide. But, rounding the corner like an amorous black Cadillac, he saw some other tall, dark and handsome being massaged by HIS middle aged, flaming two timer! "Christ, I was only gone for ten minutes," Davis muttered, pacing quick across his watering hole open space. An intentional noisy flop atop his wood barstool got the full attention from 'miss behavin'.

'Missy' grinned wide at Chris while pointing to his cell phone. "I thought maybe your girlfriend called." Commenting with a 'sorry but you were gone way too long' manner. Tall and handsome just refreshed her gin.

Chris knew when he'd been outdone and right now he felt vanquished! "I can't believe I'm out of this game so fast," looking at Benny with deflated shoulders.

"Sorry bucko, but that's how fast they come and go these days. You must feel like you just played Boise State on the road?" As the barkeep offered to refill his empty glass.

"Thanks my man but I'm outa' here. See ya next time." Chris departed his social club as 'middle aged' slipped a peek over a clear shoulder, at her preferred rendezvous. "Gin drinking floozy. I should know better." Chris scorned, letting his thoughts return to Franny. He wondered if Mrs. Braden had hands like the masseuse he just lost.

Anderson

"Okay, Okay. We'll have another glass of wine. Remember, we both have to drive tonight," Anderson warned Patricia Bailey who had every intention to push a bucket of alcohol down Billy Anderson's throat. Patricia needed any information she could get about the Crosby murder, betting Captain Anderson would speak candidly once the wine kicked in. One problem with Patty's plan however, Billy could drink with the best of them and imbibed quite heavy in red wine. Italian reds. He preferred Barbera but keen on Sangiovese and Primitivo too. Tonight the bar belonged to Billy and a rich, nearly ink black Barbera from a small but accomplished Livermore winery just over the western hills.

Bailey was on the hook here. Mrs. Crosby had pulled a mile of strings to further her career and Abigail expected payment on occasion. This was going to be major compensation. Trying to goad information from a cop could be risky business for a woman in her position. The reporter had to be extra careful but was forced into dropping her guard, little by little.

"Thank you," Patricia acknowledged to an older woman tending customers, whom almost to a man, were drinking only wine. Red wines at that. Captain Anderson's watering hole was on the southeast side of town almost into the sticks of Central Valley farms. Billy preferred people near his own age and he loved sipping reds. White wines didn't register on his radar screen referring to them as nothing more than Cool Aid.

"Look at that color." Displaying the contents of his tipped wine glass. Billy confirmed how dark in color one of his favorite varietals appeared, holding his glass almost horizontal. "Take this Barbera," swirling the Italian variety sharp. "Lightly filtered and aged longer to contract that deep, rich oak flavor. RM Winery in Livermore. They produce a good wine, don't you think?"

"You should write commercial advertising Captain." Patricia Bailey, on the other hand much preferred sipping cocktails. Margaritas, daiquiris on occasion, a chocolate martini. Doing a fair share of investigation around bars, mixed drinks became her specialty when needing to loosen up a District Attorney or Chief Investigator. Always a struggle to get inside information, as Captain Anderson was proving tonight. More times than not Bailey was able to get her story. Tonight however, was going rather different. Tonight she plied herself with liquor, or at least wine. Miss Bailey's second problem was proving to be something out of her control. Patricia thoroughly enjoyed her work this evening. Even minus the alcohol, Billy Anderson's personality turned out to be a pleasant surprise. Much more than anticipated. Easy going for the most part, clever with a tease and fun to talk with. Proving to be a funny yet weird sort of character. "Maybe he's my new type," thinking then questioning herself. They both relaxed in comfortable but more important, adult conversation which stimulated Bailey. Enjoying the gab and comparing Anderson to some of her recent dates. Out with men who were more accomplished in careers and well healed but lacking in basic social skills. The reporter welcomed a comfortable rapport to talk issues freely and with conviction. Expressing coherent opinions on a variety of subjects from politics, current events and sports, for Christ's sake. As of late, unable to say why, she yearned to just sit, drink a little, and talk with someone intelligent. Simple debates or a challenge to strongly held opinions and capable of changing her point of view perhaps. Not another mindless litany of where I've been and how much I've made. It felt easy tonight, engaged in a tussle of enjoyable exchanges. Bailey decided to change the subject and tone however. A challenge of course but with a designed ending.

"So Captain. Let's talk about Marcus Crosby's murder instegivation," Patricia garbled, mauling bad her drunken pronunciation, intending investigation.

"I don't think so Red," Billy shot back chuckling at the bold effort as well as her inebriated speech.

"Okay then." Stopping abrupt, pondering her next move as red wine took a stronger hold of her concentration and at the same time relaxing inhibitions. "Okay then, what do you drink of me, I mean think of me Billy?" Showing full affect of her third large glass of Barbera sporting a lofty alcohol content.

"Let me think about that one," Billy replied, somewhat serious but with a wide grin. Sipping more grape. "I suppose, just maybe, we were made for each other! Two aggressive forty year old pros always on the lookout for that vertical step up." Billy stopped quick, taking in Miss Bailey's profile, liking very much what he saw. Around the lounge, drinking and socializing began to grow as 'his place' seemed more appealing at the moment. Miss Bailey added to this appeal, he thought to himself and added to the subject matter, "What can you tell me about the Crosby murder?" handing her the ball and wanting a reply.

"You're the chief instevigator, I mean investigator," slurring yet another load of consonants. "Holy shit, I can barely talk!" Both her and Billy laughed together and stroked each other's arms. "What the hell are they putting in this wine anyway?" struggling in vain to shift her speech failures away from her own drunkenness. "You better know more about this case than I do," Bailey delivered coherent this time, facing the cop with a frontal display of sexiness. "Captain Anderson." Laying it on thick.

"Seriously, what have you learned so far? I'm extremely curious," Billy asked knowing it would be a long shot to get all she might know.

"I have exactly what I left the crime scene with. Plus what your Chief of Police gave at his two short press conferences." Bailey conquered her drunkenness by force, wanting to add more but decided to stop there. "You're supposed to be questioning suspects who matched the license plate search, I'm told," she said, reaching out to touch Billy's shoulder, letting her hand drop slow along his arm coming to rest at his elbow. Not a seductive response but more of an automatic impulse when first aware of heartfelt friendship.

"We've talked to a few suspects," Anderson responded in quiet review of his case, assessing what to give away then decided what the hell. "Frankly, not much more to report." Which, in reality said volumes. He just told the attractive reporter his case had nothing so far. "Maybe the hottie thinks I'm holding back or trying to decoy?"

"Who's been questioned so far?" the reporter asked, attempting to burn her stare into Billy's eyes but flinched when the Police Captain smiled back. With genuine affection.

"Can't say," speaking flat.

"The Braden's?" still pursuing.

"Can't say," still smirking. "Why do you think someone shot Marcus Crosby?" Anderson invited a different scheme leading to a whole new direction of questions, emphasizing why. He was curious to hear Patricia's remarks which were merely surface observations so far. Wanting a small taste of her deeper hunches.

"Why? Uhm, Why?" Bailey considered the cop's question, deliberating as hard as the alcohol permitted, wondering why he was asking. "Haven't thought too much about it, to be honest. Assumed somebody was out for revenge?"

"Maybe. Seems likely to me. I wonder if it might've been a mistake?" Billy appeared to be thinking out loud. "How about a decoy?"

His follow up remark seemed odd too. Patricia squished her face and squinted light blue eyes. Not understanding. "A mistake? Like maybe the gun was aimed in the wrong direction, accidentally blowing poor Mr. Crosby's head off. No way copper!" Adding a quip which Anderson enjoyed, then paused to consider Billy's remarks further. "It can't be a random murder, can it?" turning to look at the cop then added, "a serial killer? Unlikely, but I'm simply a purveyor of weird news."

"You do it well, I might add." Billy drank more wine.

"Hey Captain!" looking at Anderson with her mock scowl. "I'm not sure if that was compliment or what?" not expecting a follow up response as the Captain indulged in a long pour.

Anderson stayed determined to withhold murder case information. "It could be the start of some new serial killer? Not likely however," he admitted, taking a long slow drink of wine. Followed by inserting his nose over half way into his wine glass, enjoying the deep oak smell. Alex prized the variety of smells in a simple glass of wine. "Maybe there's something more than just revenge?"

"Go on," Bailey encouraged.

"Uh," wondering if he should be telling a reporter his unfounded random thoughts. "This is all way off the professional level. I can't have one bit of this repeated on your news report. Ferstanzig!" Almost deciding to keep his mouth shut from here on, regarding his wild opinions about this murder case.

"I understand. Tell me what you're feeling," the reported blurted out.

"For God's sake Patty, you sound like a shrink," letting her know how lame that last request sounded, causing Bailey to step away from the bar, lower her head and break out in rather loud laughs. Gaining full attention from a bartender and two patrons enjoying their late harvest Primitivo.

"I've had way too much wine," confessing to Anderson but enjoying their meeting more and more. "What do you mean exactly, by a decoy?"

Billy studied Patricia now, maybe a bit too long wondering if she was too young for him but becoming rather attracted to her now. Especially the way she touched him. It felt great but held back on a sudden urge to reach out and stroke her soft face. Unable to fabricate enough courage "I don't know, maybe this murder is a way of covering up something. Taking cover-up to a drastic level I admit. But this isn't your classic hit and kill payback." Anderson sounded a bit vague to Bailey. To himself as well. "An awful attempt to draw attention away from something else?" He examined Patricia once more. This time she looked back. "Maybe I've had too much wine too?"

"I'm not following you all the way on this one Captain. Who the hell are you referring to?" she asked, wishing to get lucky with a knee jerk response of withheld information. Billy Anderson wasn't about to slip now and reveal something important.

"I was talking more about motive. Whom perhaps, did you think I had in mind?" Anderson asked the reporter, sipping Barbera.

"Like perhaps, a police officer in Sonora?" Patricia took a relaxed drink to avoid direct eye contact this time, after pitching her wild hunch. Captain Anderson went silent and Bailey wondered if maybe she hit a nerve, checking him out.

Billy was admiring the attractive reporter now, biting his lower lip and removing a tiny bit of skin from inside his mouth. When Patricia ended her gaze, Billy asked himself how she could know about Sheets. A wild guess perhaps? "I don't know who you're talking about," speaking serious to see her reaction.

"I ain't buying that one Captain but you're holding all the cards right now," Bailey responded, deflated. "But not the entire deck however," dealing again as Bailey reached out once more, this time rubbing her hand over Billy's thigh causing his leg muscles to quiver. "I'm unable to drive myself home tonight, William Anderson," slurring words but finishing off the remaining third of her wine in one gulp. "Are you going to be a gentleman and offer me a place to sex, I mean stay the night," acting as though she made another drunken stumble of words.

The Captain went wide eyed, red faced and warm but ended with an embarrassing loss for words! Conjuring up all his wits to suggest, "how about one more glass of wine?" Launching a feeble plan to lower the reporter's defenses, once and for all.

"Really?" Patricia asked in surprise. "I'm pretty toasty. But," unsure if the good Captain wasn't interested in sharing his bed with her. "What the hell, I'm driving with a cop tonight. How much trouble can that be? I'll have another red with ya." Wrapping her arms around one of his and holding tight. Her head slid next to his and they lingered, waiting while their glasses were filled with a robust Sangiovese. This last glass would prove to be, symbolically speaking, one for the ditch. Billy became very drunk talking way too much about the merits of red wine which bored the hell from a drunk Miss Bailey who slow but sure, became nothing short of plastered.

Following an eventful drive across town, both drunken dates stumbled into Anderson's townhouse, where Patricia promptly out classed herself by throwing up in Billy's bathroom. Spending most of the night passed out on a cold tile floor. That last glass of red was not a good move on Billy's part. Both dates woke up in an awkward, hung-over state the following morning, wanting to be rid of each other fast! Their first sleep over didn't go as planned. One glass too many.

Gustine

Regina eased her car away from Los Banos Wildlife following a hurried checkout from new refuge personnel. The evening shift came on duty relieving both Jennifer Sweeny and Kelly Crisp. Gonzalez regretted missing them, wanting to thank each woman, face to face, for their help and information. Just one more eye opening experience on the refuge.

Pulling to a stop and sitting motionless at a stop sign controlling east-west traffic onto Highway 165, better known as Mercy Springs Road. A relentless debate roared through Regina's principles. Straight ahead for home? Right turn for Gustine and rendezvous with Tom Ellis? "Which way," she asked herself? Lumbering in from her right came a well lit heavy duty pick-up truck. "What the hell," she said aloud. "He's too damn good looking." Stomping the gas and turning right, turning her life perchance. She passed through farmlands reviving brief childhood memories once again. More orchards, grasslands, ranches and spotted wetlands. Flooded areas falling under wildlife jurisdiction of the San Luis Wildlife Area. Regina wasn't overly familiar with this stretch of road as ventures north from Los Banos in her younger years were rare.

Taking barely thirty minutes to reach Gustine's outer fringes. A small town, even for Central Valley standards, anchored by a well kept city park complete with pond, dominated Gustine's town center. Rising on Gustine's western flank one can't miss Hillview Packing Company with its conspicuous warehouse buildings. While northeasterly, bathed in bright floodlights each evening, sits Saputo Dairy Foods. Two firms making up Gustine's largest employers. Food is grown nearby, processed, packaged and sent on its way north and south, consumed by suburbanites in the Bay Area and Los Angeles. An Ag town lying dead center in California's agricultural region, Gustine remains tidy and also retains an authentic, old fashioned appeal hearkening back to the sixties.

Appearing that way to Regina at least, going left at a three way stop. One more left turn would put her onto Gustine's main downtown boulevard. What else but Fifth Avenue! She followed Tom's directions keeping right and stopping in front of their designated meeting place. The Pastime Bar, since Nineteen Fifty Four!

"Yikes," Regina mumbled to herself. "I was hoping for something nicer. A place resembling the nineties at least!" Deciding quick to drive the block one more time, thinking hard of what she might be stepping into and desperate to foster a brighter outlook. "Maybe seeing more of Gustine will make me feel better?" Grasping for just about anything to get some sort of positive spin.

Pressing down on a sticky gas pedal Regina launched her search for better feelings. Down Fifth Avenue once more. On her right, Pioneer Drug occupying an old, two story, brick building reminiscent of a fifties style drug store. "I bet there's still a fountain in that store," reflecting back to her own Woolworth's days. Further on, achieving the universal apex of Fifth and Fifth, housed what appeared to be one of Gustine's senior firms. Scooter's Car Repair. "Charming," scoffing but smiling benign. "Old Mr. Scooter had to have something to do with naming these streets."

Advancing to La Mexicana Food and Deli off to her left and impressed with the firm's large plate glass windows which, "kind of welcome's a customer inside," she told herself, beginning to catch that better feeling and growing more comfortable. Continuing down Fifth Avenue for a right turn, intending to leave Gustine.

"Maybe another time," speaking out loud but battled strong impulses to stay and risk buying what Tom Ellis was selling. "Crap. I don't know what to do." Gliding to a stop at First Street which faced another large commercial building, ablaze in harsh glare by two large spotlights. Shining bright in cold November air was the Pusateri Nut Company. "My God," Regina whispered to herself. "Pusateri Nut Company," reading aloud, awestruck. "I know Frankie Pusateri, from Dos Palos. That has to be his company. He always worked in those walnut orchards west of town." Bringing out yet another smile, sitting in an idling car staring at the company name. "That's really cool," feeling proud for Frankie, turning left to make her meeting under a starry night sky. "Pusateri Nuts. This town has to be okay." Moving down Fifth one last time finding an open parking slot opposite The Pastime Bar. Sitting strategic and adjacent to the future site of Gustine's City Hall. Catching Regina's attention in a comical way. "This place will do land office business when Gustine's city fathers relocate!" She approached two deep red, wood doors. "Okay, let's do this Regina." Belly nerves tingling, anticipating another episode with her quite attractive, former suspect.

"Why in hell am I so nervous?" doing her very best to appear confident and calm, picking up on a Beetles song playing inside. "Let's go," pushing through double doors. Entering a well lit bar room complete with slow motion ceiling fans, padded chairs, hardwood and neat maroon table clothes covering a few round tables and booths to her right. Shiny brass rails trimmed a modern light oak bar situated to her left. Surprised and pleased with The Pastime appearance. Ten or twelve patrons were scattered about a comfortable dining area with another half dozen sitting on stools at the bar. All men, minus one, admiring the attractive late twenties gal mixing cocktails and pouring micro-brews. Gonzalez caught sight of a man sitting alone, relaxed in a smallish booth for two. Tom looked up and locked onto Regina standing in the entryway. Rising to greet her, stumbling bad, embarrassed but all smiles, taking a step or two in her direction as she approached him.

••••

Regina's suspect waited patient at the bar, chatted up by Satchel, a self described independent harvester contracting out combines and orchard harvesting services. Specializing in almonds. Tom enjoyed listening to Satch explain his mechanized collection and the way they operated. However, other matters occupied Tom's mind besides almonds, at the same time avoiding any insults to a friend. Ellis constantly checked his watch wondering if Regina would show. Tom allowed the harvester to ramble on, listening patient on subjects covering vacuum machines, tree shakers, ripe almonds and weather conditions.

Required to harvest alfalfa early in the morning, Tom was relieved when Satchel called it a night. Giving his courteous goodbye, Ellis slipped into a vacant booth preferring to be alone until Regina arrived. She was running late and he couldn't prevent the emerging assumptions Detective Gonzalez wouldn't show. Unaware, tardiness was a big part of her makeup. He considered calling again but decided against. "Sounds too needy," speaking quietly just as a middle aged waitress delivered his beer and one glass, which represented all that remained of his confidence.

"C'mon detective, you're curious. You want to be here," talking himself into an even higher state of nervousness. "My decoy of additional evidence forces you here detective," in a deep, Joda type concentration, missing two red bar room doors swing open followed by his squeamish cop standing alone. Attractive to Tom Ellis to say the least, with dark hair relaxed and hanging loose over angled shoulders. Her leather jacket hugged a fortyish waistline, covering a deep burgundy blouse complimenting an olive complexion. Faded jeans, snug, smoothing a pair of aging legs with smatterings of refuge mud clinging to her black leather boots. Tom shot up like a foul ball, banging his right knee underneath the wood table.

When they converged Elly reached out for the detective's arm pulling her elbow soft, bent forward and lightly kissed her pink cheek, saying hi. His warm greeting caught Regina off guard but Mr. Ellis smelled great and without thinking, gathered up his hands in hers unable to stop staring. They managed to get themselves seated after a long, warm, awkward greeting.

"I'm glad you made it Miss Gonzalez. No trouble finding the place I hope?" Tom gave it his best to say something coherent, always having a hard time initiating conversation with attractive women.

"Nope. No trouble at all," Regina said, noting his behavior. "At least he had enough courtesy to stand up when I arrived and good God, he looks so good!" His smell remained with her and wished it would stay a bit longer. Regina Gonzalez had just taken step one into someone and perhaps something new. "So Mr. Ellis we meet once again," thinking how dorky she must sound right now. Tom just nodded, holding a broad smile which she appreciated.

"Is this your usual hangout in Gustine?" she asked, attempting to be polite but quite nervous. Tom seemed very relaxed, unaware to her just how fast his thoughts were racing all over hell! Both secretly admitted to being very attracted to each other but acted like teenagers on homecoming night, waiting on the other's first step. Tom volunteered to shoot first.

"Wasn't sure you'd show Regina, but I'm glad you did. I come here once in a while for a beer and fish and chips. I'm by no means a heavy drinker however." Letting her know for some odd reason he wasn't drunk all the time. "I demand a red wine with dinner however." Close to empty on small talk and switching into food gear. "Hungry detective?" guessing she hadn't eaten yet. "The fish & chips are great here." Wanting to buy dinner.

"Um," squirming in her seat to send the suspect a message she wasn't comfortable being here. Which in turn caused Tom to perceive his own unease. "Why am I even here?" Gonzalez questioned herself like a suspect, wishing she'd made that right turn. "Damn Pusateri Nuts!" Mumbling under her breath.

"What was that?" Tom asked, not hearing her muffled comment just as the middle aged waitress returned to take an order.

"How are you two doing here? Can I bring you a drink miss?" Middle aged asked, giving Regina her raised eyebrows, recognizing Tom as an occasional patron and pleasant on the eyes. The detective exhaled, growing a tiny bit more comfortable. The Rolling Stones' Satisfaction, filled the bar now.

"You know, I think I'll have a beer. Yeah, a beer sounds great." Regina appeared to be calming and perhaps coming alive. Perhaps. "Pacifico, with a lime. A glass of ice water too, please."

"No problema," middle aged confirmed using one of the few words she knew in Spanish. "Sir, a refill?"

"Absolutely, another Fat Tire please," Tom nearly yelled in excitement concluding their meeting had taken a positive turn.

"Wait a minute," Regina had second thoughts once again. This time about her drink order. "A Fat Tire? How is that? I've never tried that beer. Change mine to a Fat Tire too, please."

"Okay, two Fat Tires it is. I'll be right back. Let me know if you'd like to order fish," middle aged announced before shagging drinks.

"Fish? Is that all they serve here?" Regina asked in a curious way.

"That's it. But they do it right," Tom answered soft, scrutinizing Regina's face once again noticing her smooth, clear complexion then turning away, afraid to be caught staring.

"Why don't you order Tom. I'm not that hungry right now," lying to Ellis, actually famished since returning from her refuge workout. "I might have a bite or two of yours, if you don't mind."

"I don't want to eat alone," thinking about her, bite of yours, comment. "I'm kinda hungry."

"No, no. You go ahead. It's fine. Order, please," Regina implored expecting to get a bite or two or three, not allowing their meeting to become, in her mind, a date. Tom was still too close to being a suspect, even if she had established his innocence today at Los Banos Wildlife. Middle aged returned laying down two beers.

"Who's hungry?" she asked.

"I guess we're having one large order of fish and chips," Tom answered going back to Regina with a, "last chance?"

"Just one order?" Middle aged confirmed. "I'll bring you an extra large order with two plates." Sending Regina a wince this time and frowned as if to say, "what the hell are you doing girl?"

Tom sensed the waitress's mind-set and cut in. "Sounds good," responding quick, to avoid confrontation. Gonzalez loosened two belts. One to remove a dark brown leather jacket and the other removing nerves, intending to get comfortable.

They both suffered from embarrassing high levels of excitement and nervousness. Tom kept returning to his doubts of getting involved with a cop who just a few days previous, accused him of murder. Albeit in a nice way! Physically drawn to say the least but was Miss Gonzalez the type to be interested in someone like him? Did she trust him? Was she attracted to him or prospecting for more information concerning her murder case? "I'm attracted to this woman," was a phrase which continued to surface in his head.

Regina couldn't calm herself either. In part due to additional information promised to her investigation, but more so due to Tom's sex appeal. She found herself examining every speck of his good looks. Glancing on occasion when he wasn't looking. "I'm walking a thin line here," became her repetitive phrase swirling through clouded thoughts. "I can't help it, but I'm kinda into it too!" Fleetwood Mac filled The Pastime now. Regina felt herself warming up and glad as hell she made this engagement. Across the lounge a medium size fire burned with loud cracks inside a stone mantle helping to build her comfort. Their get-together began drifting away as a formal meeting along with a growing awareness, her and Tom were about to sanction their first date within a mood of satisfaction.

"So Miss Detective. Everything okay?" Tom inquired, amused with Miss Gonzalez, seeing how she appeared much more relaxed. Just what Ellis needed and would do everything to keep the mood growing. "I noticed your shoes and jeans are muddy. Where the hell were you today?" attempting to keep their conversation alive. If he only knew.

"Yeah, I've been out," searching for the right words to use, dying to continue with, "up to my ass in mud and tules!" Speculating how Tom might respond while taking a long drink from her micro-brew, helping to hide her face along with any surprised reactions. Regina noticed Tom's face light up. Like a sunrise it just occurred to him, Gonzalez had been out to Los Banos Wildlife Refuge checking his alibi. Regina stayed quiet however, giving her suspect a chance to say something. Anything that might add to the case.

"I know where you were today," Tom declared, studying Regina's eyes then inspecting her hair, mouth, lips and ears, wishing to stare a while longer. Ellis jerked himself back to reality. "Sorry. I must look pretty scary right now, gawking away like some sort of perv!" Shifting his admiration toward the lounge fireplace. "How'd it go?" Tom asked, intentionally acting reserved.

"It went okay, I guess," Regina offered. She wanted to continue but stopped short waiting for Tom to finish a deep gulp from his brew. She knew it was going way past protocol to discuss case matters. With her suspect no less, running a slow hand through thick, dark hair beginning to feel foolish. "This guy isn't capable of killing anyone," compelling herself toward, 'no harm in taking the next step.'

"Los Banos Refuge. Kind of neat huh?" doubting she found the area interesting and wiping a small amount of foam from his upper lip.

"Some parts were um, very revealing," Gonzalez disclosed, focusing inside his bright blue eyes. Regina smiled, nodded and sent a quiet signal, indicating obvious attraction to her handsome suspect. "Very helpful folks over there too. I was impressed." She waited to see if Tom might display some sort of nervous reaction. He didn't. Which made Regina more uncertain about her next comment. "A certain Miss Jennifer Sweeny certainly remembered you!" Head lowered, staring into a drying beer glass rethinking strategy, wondering, "maybe I shouldn't have spilled that one out? Oh well?"

Tom kept silent, recalling faces of refuge personnel from Los Banos check station. Drawing a blank on names except for Suzuki, the young biologist for some reason. But his memory did retrieve an older gal who checked him out the evening of his limit. "A problem I've had for so long. Who could forget me?" handing Regina his most deadpan stare over a relaxed face, annoying but quick.

Regina sipped beer. "She was impressed by all the birds you killed that day." Granting no praise for his last joke.

"Oh, I thought it was a little more personal," Tom said, enjoying their exchange.

"No. Nothing like that. Just birds." she said, hiding a smile and giggle behind her beer glass again. She knew Tom had picked up on Jennifer's attraction toward him that evening. Gonzalez dug in, refusing him the pleasure.

"Maybe you misinterpreted what Heather said," Tom remarked in a sly way.

"Jennifer," Regina corrected

"What did I say?"

"You said Heather. Mr. Ellis you're sounding similar to our first meeting. Botching names then too." Obvious he toyed with her now. "I do like the way he plays around," thinking to herself.

For Tom, his gaff was good news. She remembered a minor detail from their first meeting. "That's right, Jennifer. Now I recall. Nice gal," sounding chivalrous, hoping Regina wasn't taking him serious. "She sure knows how to check a guy out. Through the check line, I mean." They both grinned to each other again, enjoying the skirmish and began to laugh gently. Tom believed the situation was becoming more agreeable. Almost normal. He planned to get as close as possible to the detective needing to learn more about her.

Gonzalez settled in even more by motioning for another beer.

"Put that on my bill please," Tom instructed as middle aged poured out a dark beer at the table and announced their food order would be up soon.

"Oh great," Regina responded wholehearted, smoothing out her long dark hair then pushing it all behind her shoulders. "I'm hungry!" Forgetting she hadn't ordered anything to eat but prepared to help herself. Tom remembered however, as background music changed from Fleetwood Mac to Neil Young.

Shifting his mood more upbeat and positive, sensing Regina's swelling comfort. "I love Neil Young's music," he thought to himself. They both listened.

"So Tom. I watched someone shoot down a duck this evening. Mr. Gordon. Quite the spectacle, I must admit," compelled for some reason to announce the event.

Curious in how she was able to witness someone hunting. "Really. What kind of bird?" Testing the cop to identify different species of waterfowl.

"I said, a duck!" Perplexed.

"What kind of duck?" Tom chuckled.

"No clue. It did have a white belly and long tail feathers. Whatever it was, that duck sure hit the water with a major splash." Enjoying a long guzzle of beer.

"When are you taking me out duck hunting?" Regina asked in all seriousness while stealing a peak to see the reaction he might have. Right on cue, middle aged returned carrying a steamy plate mounded with fried fish fillets, cole slaw, tartar sauce and a pile of fries. She lowered the hot plate in front of Gonzalez lighting up the detective's eyes, who deftly snatched a few hot potato slices. Verifying they tasted great.

Tom received an empty plate with napkins and silverware but failed to notice anything placed in front of him. Even the appetizing aroma of fresh fried fish, could capture his attention. He was still absorbed, head over hind-end, into Regina's hunting proposition. "Did she just ask me out in some weird way?" Ellis asked watching her pick up a piece of fish and tear it apart. Subtle plumes of vapor floated from tender white flesh. Regina slathered a generous helping of spicy tartar biting off a healthy chunk which slightly burned her tongue, inhaling deep and leaving a small drop of white sauce on her lower lip. Tasting superb as Neil Young continued singing.

···

Food. The great equalizer. Regina and her partner learned long ago, food owns that perfect intrinsic capacity, in its ability to soften the most stubborn of suspects. Food tends to decrease tension and often compels folks to talk without restraint. Openly. Tom and Regina's sudden reception of French fried potatoes and mounds of fish, golden, just slightly greasy, salty, taste bud satisfying, was doing its job. The cop and her waning suspect continued to unwind in one another's company. Neil Young gave way to The Doors as Riders on the Storm played without notice from either member. They focused more on one another and Morrison had to take a back seat for now. Relaxation set in.

Talk went wide open as Regina devoured Tom's order with abandoned eagerness. He watched but didn't care. Finding it perfectly fine to nibble here and there like his conversation, but couldn't keep from raising her hunting offer once again.

"So, detective. You're up for shooting some ducks, are ya?" Attempting to sound casual and flippant reaching across her plate, expecting to snatch a particularly large fillet of codfish. Only to have Regina sever it in half with a lightening quick knife. She was in high gear now taking over dinner. Tom watched, sucking down beer and waiting patient for her response. But wouldn't mind a morsel or two.

"Mmm, maybe? I could use something new right now. Out of the ordinary. Looks like," stopping to smother another bite in tartar sauce and choose some sensible words. "I have to admit, it intrigues me for some reason. What do you think? You up for it?" Inhaling the piece of fish being waved back and forth skewered to her fork then washed down with more beer.

"Uhm," Tom thought about it too. "I might be. Yeah I'm up for it, I guess," sounding a little unsure. "Are you okay with killing animals?" asking Regina a serious question, as she chomped away on a large morsel, forcing wipes of dripping tartar sauce from the corner of her mouth. "My goodness girl, slow down," Tom said to himself, covering a broad grin watching the detective's vigorous jaw bones work up and down!

Taking another drink of beer, Regina reflected for an instant. "I think I'm okay with shooting a few ducks. It's not like I'm vegan." Picking a batter flake off an oily chin.

"That's for sure," Tom interjected, unable to resist a dig, reaching over to wipe a smear of oil left on her cheek. Regina missed the catch on his sarcasm.

She continued, "I've eaten a mountain of animal parts in my life. Yeah, I'm good with shooting birds." Knowing she may need a few outings to get comfortable with the kill. "Are you having second thoughts already?" Noticing Tom deep in second thoughts assuming he'd back away from his offer. Ellis stayed silent.

Tom was nudged back into their conversation by Regina's gentle kick to his left shin. He remained quiet. Looking straight at her sipping Fat Tire. "You seem to be kinda spooked? What's wrong Mr. Ellis?" Spooning out a large helping of cole slaw before sliding what remained his way.

"Uh, nothing's wrong. I'm sorry?" Tom shivered.

"We were talking about duck hunting," she said as middle aged reappeared offering more service.

The waitress got his attention quick. "We'll have two more beers please," Tom replied receiving a thumbs up from Regina.

"Coming up." Middle dished Regina a sly smirk. "How's the fish?"

"Wow, very good. My compliments to your kitchen," Gonzalez praised, while the waitress cleared around a rather cluttered table, made that way by a hungry cop sacrificing most of her table manners. Middle aged hustled back to the bar for more beer.

"So what do you think? Are you up for it?" Regina asked picking her front teeth at tiny bits of cabbage.

Tom had a neutral look on his face. Not good or bad, but simple indifference. "Yeah, sure. I was thinking about Thanksgiving next week," Ellis contemplated his schedule out loud. "What're your plans for Thanksgiving?"

Heaving back into her seat and palming one hand over a reddened forehead in a way people often do after realizing forgotten promises. "Oh Christ, I completely forgot. Damn it." Staring off toward the rousing fire, flames licking a stack of burning wood. "Shoot!"

"What's wrong?"

"I was supposed to call my Aunt Sophie, to let her know I'm coming over for dinner Thursday," the detective recalled, clearly upset for failing on a minor promise.

Tom observed an upset policewoman, as Regina slammed down another heavy drink of chilled beer. He couldn't quite figure her issues with aunty. "Can you call her tomorrow?" chuckling. "Let her know you'll be there?" It didn't seem like a deal breaker to Ellis? "What's the big deal?"

"Oh crap," she said, holding her head with one hand while slapping the table top repeatedly with the other. "What?" her head came up, dazed or drunk, Tom couldn't tell. "I'm sorry Tom," apologizing and looking at him a bit embarrassed. "You don't know my Aunt Sophie. Protocol and deadlines with Aunty must not be broken." Once again, Regina's sinking feelings of holiday blues resurfaced. "I hate Thanksgiving," she thought to herself, staring hard at Tom's plate of fries, stealing two more bites of salty potatoes.

Tom saw an opening and decided on a wild shot. "How about letting me, make you, Thanksgiving dinner?" Waiting to see her reaction, after speaking very slow and ready to be shot down.

Regina's head jolted back just as she bit into a few fried potatoes. Two hangers slipped from her mouth and fell clumsy back to a messy dinner plate. One managed to flip a few inches off the rim sliding across a cleared table. Regina eyed Tom, holding a napkin to her lips but with no words in reply. "What a nice offer," was all she could think. "Oh gees, I couldn't. Are you serious? We hardly know each other. You must have family to be with and all that. I couldn't," getting cut off.

"No family this year. Just me and you, if you dare. We'll get some hunting gear set up too. What say you detective?" waiting to see if he sold his plan well enough. "Maybe I connected?" Tom assessed, noticing how the detective's face shined, opening her brown eyes wide beyond appreciation. Delighted and surprised.

She tried thinking of a reason to decline, knowing her position demanded a refusal, coming up empty. "What a nice offer Mr. Ellis. Are you sure?" Regina went uneasy and rather shaken by Tom's generosity, at last deciding to accept. Knowing she shouldn't but, "what the hell, being alone on the holidays sucks," thinking herself into submission with quick reasoning. "Having a guy cook for me would be a welcome change," pondering her thought with a gentle smile.

"I'm positive. Besides I have no dinner plans for Thursday," rethinking his schedule to make sure. "No family get-together this year. It'll be fun detective. Just you and I."

Tom's offer began sounding better and better to Regina now. No meeting the family sort of thing. "Just the two of us. You're sure?" asking again to make certain.

"Sounds good doesn't it Miss Gonzalez," Tom stated, watching overtly as her eyes locked onto his, looking away then back again. He admired her soft lips and every Hispanic feature of her face.

"Seems perfect," she agreed, growing excited at the concept of an intimate Thanksgiving dinner with a handsome man whom the day before was a serious murder suspect. All history now. "Can you cook?"

"Not Really!"

Her jaw dropped as it hit home. Maybe Tom expected her to make dinner? "Uhm, okay. I'm not the best cook either," Gonzalez disclosed trying to stay positive, at the same time feeling rather let down. Remaining silent, but couldn't help fidgeting on her nervous side of the booth.

"Gotchya again detective. Now that's a look of being rung up on a called third strike Regina," Tom ribbed the cop, using her first name for a change. "That was almost too easy. Don't worry about a thing. I'll take care of dinner. Appetizers to dessert," noticing as concern grew across a charming face. He laughed as she began to squirm, twitch and twirl her dense black hair in nervous fingers. "You bring the wine. Deal?"

"That's it? Just wine?' she asked, expecting to carry a bit more of the load but not complaining. "This is getting better and better," she told herself.

"That's it, but I prefer red," Tom added.

"Me too. Done." In a pretty good mood about her spontaneous engagement. "So, National or American?"

"Come again?" Tom squinted.

"American League or National League? Your last comment. I take it you're a baseball fan too?" The detective leaned way back into the booth, comfortable with a change in topic. Drinking more beer waiting to see where he stood.

"Mmm, this could be a toughie?" Tom replied, wondering what major league team the detective might be aligned. "We haven't even dated and I'm already being asked my baseball preferences." Wanting to swing away but chickened out. "She has to be a Giants fan. Growing up in the Valley," debating hard for a moment. "I don't know if our relationship is ready for questions like these!" Loving every second. His next date loved baseball too.

"C'mon Tom. Have some guts. It's an easy question. I won't hold it against you for too long." Regina laughed soft, watching the lines under his deep set eyes change lengths. She could tell he must be an avid fan too, enjoying the contest. "I'll bet National League. You look like a Giants fan to me," she announced with her subtle grin this time, wanting to hear a response. Tom appeared quite uneasy, at the moment. "He must be into the game too."

"This can be a deal breaker sometimes, you know," telling her but holding back a nervous laugh.

"C'mon orange man, tell me I'm wrong," Regina prodded.

"I can't detective. You have me by the fly balls! Oops, did I say that?" noting it was fine by Regina's toothy grin. "I'm a Giants fan. Is that good or bad for you?" acting sheepish, followed by a long sip of beer examining Regina over the brim, unsure how she'd respond.

"Let's go Oakland," whispering her team's staccato cheer, chanted during A's games at the Coliseum. "Let's go Oakland." The remaining rendezvous went on for a little too long with each participant enjoying the low key atmosphere and a new encounter. Regina had a longer drive home with perhaps too much beer consumed, but managed to decline Tom's invitation to spend the night at his house. That offer was a hard one to turn down.

Estefan

"I need two boxes of .222's. Can you get them to me?" Estefan realized his voice sounded like a plea for the merchandise. He told himself to speak calm and act bored. "Don't give Carlos the upper hand," scolding himself. "I have to dictate terms to a lowlife like Carlos."

"Of course I can get 'em. Not cheap you know, but I can get them." Carlos tried in vain to sell what little machismo he could carry on his scrawny but tall frame. Drawing hard from a burned down cigarette, inhaled deep, which irritated his throat but managed to bluff a normal look. "Who's the ammo for, Estefan? You don't own a gun like this?" Challenging his young customer to offer some information, all the while doubting if Estefan somehow mustered sufficient nerve to steal a gun. Perhaps from one of his many relatives? "Tell me Melon Head, do you have a new gun?" Tossing his smoke on the gravel road and grinding it down with his left foot. All show to reinforce things to come, if anyone would dare try deceiving Carlos.

Estefan did carry a rather large head on his young but growing broad shoulders. Years ago, another soon to be criminal type pinned the tag on Estefan. Too small and frail at the time to do much about it, the label stuck. Unfortunately for Estefan it fit. No denying the lad had a rather large head and melon shaped to boot! "No. No, not me. The bullets are for someone else. That doesn't matter," reciting his rehearsed lines knowing the Jackal would want to know about any gun owned by Melon Head. "How much will they cost me, daring creature?" playing to get Carlos' mind off his gun and onto money.

The Jackal switched. "Let's see. Probably seventy dollars for two boxes," testing the water for Melon Head's threshold of financial pain. Fast forgetting about Estefan's weapon and back to where the ammo was going. As a shrewd business man, he must be cautious with his buyers. Careless customers could put them both in jail. "Who's buying ammo Melon? I have to be assured this doesn't get to one of your foolish friends."

Estefan prayed for this question. Holding a trump card and deciding to play it, reasoning even Carlos the Jackal would succumb to love. "They're for

Angelina. She sent me to get the bullets. Angelina doesn't know bullets from a bulls balls." Seeing the way Carlos' eyes lit up, Estefan knew he had the simple minded bandito by his balls. Carlos was hopelessly smitten with the well endowed Angelina. All the boys from nearby farms were in love with Estefan's cousin. Long black hair, long legs, long on sex appeal, short on patience. How could the Jackal resist? He couldn't and Estefan knew it.

"Angelina!" The Jackal howled. "She owns a gun? I don't think so Melon Head?" Carlos became an easy read for Estefan now, knowing he wanted to believe the bullets were for her. One or two lingering doubts had to be shot away.

"Not for her, brave one. Her new boyfriend, I think." Letting his lie sink in for effect. "You know, she mentions your name sometimes, Carlos. Maybe I can put in a good word for you. I think she likes you." Estefan witnessed The Jackal melt into a poodle. Love can conquer the most crooked and felonious. "Back to business," he told himself.

Carlos stumbled for words and forgot his business principals as well as his offer. "Wow, really Melon Head? You'd do that for me? Tell Angelina about Carlos. How could she resist?"

Estefan laughed inside. "How could she resist throwing up you snail brain!" Deciding to move quickly back into business. Shuffling away a half step for effect. "C'mon, you know I can't afford thirty five dollars a box. That's stupid," Estefan sneered, doffing his own businessman's hat. He could see Carlos was somewhere between his wedding day and a romp in the hay with Angelina. Forgetting guns and ammo and money. "I'll give you thirty dollars for two boxes, that's all I have Carlos," Melon offered, which was close to factual, holding but another ten bucks in reserve.

Carlos turned to face Estefan and mounted a lofty smile. "Angelina," he whispered. "What a wife she would," stopping dead as Estefan's offer finally set in. "Thirty dollars? Total? Don't even try offering that to me," Jackal grumbled, erasing his grin. "Where else are you going to get ammunition like this?" aiming to continue his bluff.

Pushing down on his right side bike peddle, rocking back and forth on a beat-to-hell bicycle, Estefan pondered his situation. "I'm patient," he said to himself. "I'm the customer too. Carlos needs my money, I'm sure." Staying mum to see if this skinny mobster might speak up. Very little was heard now. No droning farm equipment or trucks working crop laden fields. An occasional far off call from a lonesome crow barely broke the nervous silence. Estefan faced the crow's position conveying a lack of interest in Carlos' last comment. "If he speaks up now, like the crow, Jackal will reveal his lack of patience," plotting, staying aloof, squinting across a vacant tomato field anticipating a ridiculous comment at any moment. Sure enough, Carlos the Jackal spoke.

"I might be able to get them for, umm, maybe fifty? I doubt forty five dollars, but maybe?" Flinching ever so slight as Carlos knew he shouldn't have mentioned forty five.

"You idiot. What do you think you're doing?" Estefan thought to himself, dying to say it too! Glaring at his rival with a full grasp of how easy the Jackal could punch him out. But also aware, Carlos was no match in icing a good business deal. "Forty five dollars is still way too much for .222 bullets Carlos. You know that."

"Forty five is the going rate Melon Head," jumping back into business. "Don't act like you know the market on illegal ammo," the Jackal sounded agitated and flustered.

"He didn't even attempt to stay at fifty. Stupid snake." Estefan contemplated, twisting to the black crow again preferring to keep his smirk secret. He played the leave-it tactic now. "Well Carlos, if that's your best price, I'm out of the market." Faking a push on his rusty bike pedals. Melon Head began a slow tight circle around the future small time delinquent. "Thirty five dollars will get those damn bullets. You watch Jackal," Estefan spoke under his breath. His provider swore he heard Melon mumbling and watched his payday push down the dirt road away from him. "Thirty dollars Carlos, which is all of Angelina's cash. Take it or leave it." Pedaling slow but steady expecting to hear a counteroffer, not his footsteps, actually being chased down!

"You or Angelina have forty bucks, I'm sure. Give me forty for two boxes," Carlos continued to pursue and negotiate at the same time on sparse gravel, grabbing Melon's rear bike fender to stop his fleeing customer and fix this deal. Wal-Mart stores only dream of dedication like this. "I need the cash," Carlos reminded himself, out of breath from the smoking habit he adopted two years ago.

"What?" Estefan quit pedaling as Carlos had a firm grip on his rear tire now. "How much did you say? Thirty five?" Knowing almond brain would eventually agree to his offer. "Watch how this weasel retreats to thirty five dollars." Propping himself and bicycle on one foot, while the other foot constantly spun a red pedal sprocket, striving to show Carlos, "I can leave this deal behind at any moment." Estefan kept his face stoic, not uttering a single word but telling himself, "don't even try getting forty dollars. We both know thirty five is the going rate, which happens to be what I can afford to pay. The market works out here too," Estefan reminded The Jackal, hanging firm in silence.

"Do we have a deal Carlos the Wise?" Melon Head asked with a straight-forward gaze, adding a jab at his adversary too.

"Thirty five bucks. That's as low as I can go Melon Head," Carlos dished out his own retort and outwardly coming across as if he set market terms. Inside, knowing little Melon Head got his price, feeling foolish.

"Next week. If Angelina's bullets aren't here by next week, the deal's off Carlos." Not about to miss another opportunity at rubbing more rock salt into this ignorant hack's sore prestige. Estefan kicked down on the pedals, standing upright to push as hard as he could, sending him away fast down loose gravel.

"Make sure you have the money," is all Estefan heard from a careless Jackal, riding off in a mini cloud of dust and small flying pebbles. It felt good to beat back on a bully for a change.

"I'll be shooting soon," Melon Head repeated to himself, pedaling faster and faster.

Patricia

"Hello, this is Patricia."

"Miss Bailey. Abigail here," Mrs. Crosby articulated a clear greeting into her cell phone. Both parties knew what was expected from each other.

"Hello Abbey. I was expecting a call from you but not quite this soon. What's on your mind?" doing her very best to sound relaxed and aloof.

"You're on my mind dear. Any news from the keystone cops?" conveying a sense of anticipation or impatience over Patricia's phone, accompanied by Abbey's slightly labored breathing.

"Well," Mrs. Crosby's heavy breathing made the reporter uncomfortable. "Not really Abbey. I was out with Billy Anderson last night. He didn't have much to say about the investigation." Feelings of cheapness began to surface again and wanted bad, to simply hang up the damn phone. Her own uneasiness induced a few steps backward without looking, near a family room desk as if Abbey was stalking her in person. Patricia knew very well, Queen Bitch was waiting to hear something but the reporter wasn't about to offer information for free. Wishing Abbey would just make it short and sweet tonight. After all, Miss Bailey enjoyed Anderson's company and looked forward to seeing him again. Sober this time and on less professional terms if possible. "Mrs. Crosby will not hear any of this right now," Patricia assured herself taking one last step backward struggling to feel wood on her foot, indicating desk location. Not tonight however.

"Billy Anderson!" Abbey laughed, bellowing into her phone.

"Abbey please, for Christ's sake," Bailey shot back.

"Anderson huh. Well, he's one of the slower ones at least. You and Billy dating these days, I take it?" Abbey's sarcasm came across loud and clear. "For crying out loud, remember why I sent you there. Does Billy," emphasizing Anderson's first name very deliberate, "seem to have any hard suspects yet?" Pausing and breathing into the phone again. Almost a rhythmic pant. "Have you found out anything at all?" Abbey expected some sort of an answer but from the other end of the line Bailey ridiculed Abbey by flipping her middle finger at the receiver, in a make believe gesture of the electronic bird! Her foot wagging, still in search for that desk corner but failing to find home. One more half step back. All the while nothing but livid silence coming across from Abbey's end.

"I'm sorry Abbey, my phone keeps dropping our connection. What did you say?" Lying but she enjoyed sticking it to her boss for a change.

"Shit Patricia, what do you have for me?" sounding tense.

"I told you Abbey. There doesn't seem to be much evidence in this case right now. My reporter instincts tell me Billy is," Bailey heard laughter coming from the Queen Bitch and was subsequently cut off in an uncouth manner. Patty moved back again as Abbey stalked her via phone signals, now using one hand in search of a missing desk while holding her phone close, not to miss anything.

"Your reporter's instincts. Now that's laughable young lady," Mrs. Crosby snarled. "Your reporter instincts!" Clearly Abbey's patience vanished and sounded as venomous as Patricia had ever heard. "That's just ridiculous. You, Miss Bailey. You work for me. If it wasn't for my generosity you'd still be serving bad food in some lousy East Bay dive!" Stopping to catch her breath.

Patricia knew better to say anything. She needed to sit down but still couldn't locate the damn desk and chair. Her hand shook noticeably, but stayed locked hard around a small cell, pressed to her ear, quivering due both to anger and shame for letting herself get hooked in this situation. Hopeful it would end soon. She knew it wouldn't, regretting now the way Abbey pulled quite a few strings to get Bailey into the Channel Forty newsroom. All those 'exclusive' interviews during the Mountain Murder are coming home to roost now.

Silence from the other end caught Patricia off guard. Abbey then spoke up. "Patricia. Look kid, I'm sorry for that. But I need your help on this one," coming across to Bailey now in a first ever apology. It didn't mean much to the reporter right now, still stinging from her rant. "My son's head was nearly blown off. I have to make sure they find the bastard who did it." Patricia's reporter instincts noticed a sad hint of honest remorse spilling from Queenie.

"Probably just another clever tact," Bailey thought. "The clever witch," mouthing words, then waiting to hear what might come next. She waved a foot in a wide sweep behind her still searching that chair to sit into. Waiting but remaining in retreat from a ghostly Mrs. Crosby.

"Look Patricia. I plan to keep pressure on Tracy's finest," adding yet another sarcastic jab at a police force, she determined to be incompetent. "You have to help me," phrasing her comment in uncharacteristic begging, which caught Patricia's attention as she slowed her foot search and concentrated too keen on her phone call. "If you help me out here, this will." Abigail stopped in mid sentence to reconsider her offer. Silence. Sweeping the reporter up even more into each word. She sensed a slight scrape against her foot, locating the desk. Anticipating a chair close by, Patricia stepped back full, bending legs slightly expecting a seat just under her tush.

It was nervous silence from Mrs. Crosby. She intended to prod her reporter into higher motivation but didn't want to burn down the barn too.

Patricia had to ask now. Bending more, holding an outstretched hand behind as a brace. "This will what Abbey?" She asked in reply without a clue as to what her boss might say next. Mrs. Crosby stayed quiet. Still deliberating. "Hello Abbey, you still there?" Bailey queried. Halting her stoop she wondered what the older lady might say next.

"I'm still here darling," Abbey answered back with unusual softness.

"Darling? What the fuck?" Patricia could only think this was going way out of character, resuming her stoop, her hand catching firm wood, slouching to finally sit in comfort. Phone never leaving her ear.

"Look. Marcus was all I had left. My husband dead, a daughter with her brains scrambled on drugs and now my son," her voice shivering, gripped with emotion which Patricia had never witnessed. Abbey had buried her son earlier in the morning, in a small intimate ceremony, making clear her anxiety. Bailey went all ears but estimated herself being way too low and losing equilibrium. "I thought I'd make a deal with you. Get what I need from these chumps and," stopping to take a deep breath, "we'll be even." Pausing for Patricia to comment.

She couldn't. The reporter heard the words and wanted Abigail to repeat it. Lying somewhere between amazement and waning balance, Patricia spun around in near free fall but clutching her cell. She'd take a slam to here Abbey say it again. "Even," she thought, seeing her chair now, making a feeble lunge toward it's padded seat. Coming up short with a torso and elbows landing, sprawling in front of her desk as the prized chair skidded then flopped to one side. Thud! So did Bailey. She lay outstretched on the carpet like a wounded carp but her ear remained pinned to Abigail.

Abbey continued, unaware of her reporter's posture but heard commotion from her end. "Hell, it sounds like you already have Billy in your confidence!" Delivering a slight accent on his name. "Keep grinding, so to speak," chuckling soft. "I need suspect names and anything else about their investigation." Abbey immediately felt she may be paying too high?

"Even?" Patricia had to keep from yelling the word into her cell phone. She rolled onto her back and looked straight up at an ugly popcorn ceiling with every awareness remaining focused on Abbey's deal now. Having no reason to move and feeling quite comfortable, Bailey had to respond and at the same time ice this bargain. "Okay. Okay Abbey, I'll see what I can dig up. But," realizing her volume and intensity were both running a bit high, "I'm holding you to your word. This will make us even." Cutting it off right there, now hearing her own deep breaths emanating through the phone, tipping the cell from her face.

Abbey realized her reporter recognized a good exchange when she heard it. "We have a deal. Just get me those damn names," back into her more familiar, snarling voice. "I'll be talking to you soon Patricia." Just like that Bailey's phone went blank followed by dial tone.

Patricia didn't move. Lowering the cell to her chest and flipping it closed, she could only lie still. Arms fallen to her side with both legs raised and bent at the knees. Sensing uneasy relief. "Even!" Murmuring her agreement out loud. "Queen Bitch be gone!" Checking her watch.

"Billy boy, you don't know it yet, but you're getting me out of this mess. Like it or not you're giving me what I need," talking loud, flat on her back and feeling a bit less ashamed of herself. "Maybe? At last? Over?" Bailey knew it wasn't coming cheap however. Yet another chunk of her integrity would be lost, most likely. "I'll pay it."

Franny

"I shouldn't do this," Franny cautioned herself just before pressing the green button on her I-Phone. As ring tones ensued, she couldn't squash her conflicted desires, both wishing Chris wouldn't pick up but in dire need of a meeting. A private meeting. Her first attempt last night turned out to be a failed relief. The detective didn't answer and her message ended rather convoluted to say the least, due to a serious case of jitters.

"Hello, Detective Davis here," Chris's rather loud greeting boomed into Franny's ear, shaking her from deep inspection and the endeavor she had to carry out. Still no response from her end, mired in debate with second thoughts again, then tried to compose herself. "Hello," Chris spoke into his phone a little softer this time helping to ease her anxiety.

"Detective Davis? Hi, this is Franny Braden," deciding to take that first step into unknown areas leading perhaps to unknown desires.

"Yes, Mrs. Braden. How are you?" Chris felt a slight combination of adrenaline and testosterone surge into his stomach and legs. Rising quick from a soft chair at home, beginning a pace in his living room. "Sorry I missed your call last night," Davis apologized, sounding serious and softer yet in volume. I was planning to call you back," which was true, but more than glad to hear from her now. "What can I do for you Mrs. Braden?" wondering again why she called. But in the back of his mind a bizarre notion and images came to mind. Franny was up to something. Chris could tell, somehow. His instincts told him this lady was about to launch into a serious deception. A decoy maybe? "It's way too early to confirm anything, but I'll play along and see what develops," telling himself, determined.

"First, please don't be so formal. Call me Franny for starters," craving to retract the statement immediately. "Christ lady, slow down." Mrs. Braden had the urge to hang up, rubbing a nervous neckline to ease some awkwardness. "Could I be more fucking obvious?" Franny thought.

Chris' assumptions just became more valid following her request. "Okay, Franny. What's up?" Davis then quickly asked himself, "could she be more obvious? This woman is something."

"Detective Davis, I'd like to get together with, I mean I'd like to meet with you again," preferring her correction, sounding more businesslike. "To discuss the Crosby case naturally." At this point Franny was close to shaking, not knowing how much she might tell Davis if he pressured her. Images, thoughts and doubts were spinning her mind around so much, she craved to hang up again, right now. "He must think I've lost it," she thought in silence, then reluctantly agreed with her own assumption.

"Umm, well Mrs. Braden. Franny," leaving out the formalities, "I'm all ears to hear anything new about this case. If you overlooked something from our meeting, I'll listen." Chris' thoughts jumped back to her home. How she dressed. How she carried herself. How she looked at him. Admitting to some extent, he was captivated by this older woman. "Get these images out of your head," demanding himself. "Shut them down, now," forcing his mind to cover the intrusion. "Do you have some new information?" Davis asked, which helped to bury any more interference.

Franny realized the detective wanted to hear what she had to say right now, over the phone. "No way," telling herself, "can I give away anything now." Her plan was twofold. Plan A had to be carried out with care, face to face and it must be convincing. If not, Plan B will initiate. Desperation time. Franny raised her now shaking hand, rubbing a blushed forehead, visualizing Plan B. Reckless. Scorched Earth. "Plan B should never come to pass," imploring herself, suffering quick fixes of panic which did nothing but develop higher anxiety about her whole scheme. "I have a few things I'd like to discuss with you. About Sarah, mostly. You might find it important," she told Chris, acting as confident as she possibly could.

"Can you tell me anything now, over the phone?" Davis asked, almost longing they would meet face to face again. His request being an half-ass attempt to bury a vivid image in his head. Striving not to surrender to a few random fantasies running amuck.

"I'd rather meet again. Face to face. Just you and I if at all possible?" she sounded a drop or two beyond mysterious.

"Sure. One day this week is fine with me." Davis responded knowing Franny meant just her. Alone. Henry wouldn't make it. He decided to ask anyway, wanting her to say it for some reason? Titillation? "I can come out to the house. It'll be kinda nice sitting around your deck with you and Henry once more." Jovial.

Franny didn't hesitate. Speaking firm as Chris read her excitement and well prepared to handle this issue, Chris assumed. "Uh, no. I'd prefer to keep my husband out of this. Besides, he'll be out of town a few days before Thanksgiving. Visiting family." Feeling pretty good about Henry's explanation. A meeting place would be more dicey she thought. "Actually detective, I'll be in Tracy Tuesday afternoon. Perhaps we could meet someplace, in your area?"

"In Tracy?" shaking his head for a moment. "Yeah, that's fine with me," Chris approved, not surprised at all she preferred to stay clear of home. "Early or late in the day?"

"I thought maybe," Franny paused to appear thinking hard, "how about after work hours?" asking a trifle sheepish. "I'll be tied up most of the afternoon and you won't need to rearrange your workday."

"Christ lady," Chris thought to himself. "Let me think about my schedule this week," Davis said to Franny, watching a busy Tracy street below. Cars moved faster as the holiday approached. People seemed to move much faster too. Heads down, less courteous, less giving of thanks. "You're killing me lady." His sexy thoughts lingered with images of her full breasts roaring back into focus, putting a hand to his forehead striving to hide from an overwhelming hunger. "Hmm, after work. I guess that works." Chris shook his head, desperate to put a positive slant on their next encounter, continuing to stare out over his busy street. He barely noticed Franny speaking on the other end.

"Great Chris. I'll call you again Tuesday evening around five o'clock. We'll meet then," Mrs. Braden confirmed, sensing things went better than she thought it would. "Good bye Chris."

"What? Oh, yes. Goodbye Franny." Chris hit the red button on his cell to disconnect. Considering he should've done it earlier. Back away and disconnect. Similar to folks scurrying away in their cars right now, disconnected. Davis was still shocked by Fanny's boldness. A murder suspect wanting to rendezvous with a lead investigator. Contemplating a briefing he should give to Captain Anderson and Regina tomorrow morning, then deciding rather hasty against it. "No interference on this one. I'll let them know if anything substantial develops. When something develops," he whispered, leaving the window view behind. "One way or another, there will be a development here. I'm sure. Painfully sure I'm afraid," muttering in a low voice while searching the fridge for beer. "I know this lady has something to tell. She knows something we're all in the dark about. I'm getting it from her somehow." Opening a short neck draft and talking to himself in full voice now. "Somehow, I'm going to get what I need from her." Davis thought how this private meeting might very well start the ball rolling. "In more ways than one." Taking a long drink from his beer, aware of the tightrope he just stepped onto.

Franny stood frozen holding her phone tight, staring out over the river.

"I can't believe it's come to this," she contemplated. "My God, don't let it go all the way." Surprised, then startled as Henry's car pulled into the driveway.

Headquarters

Monday morning. Thanksgiving week begins. To most workplaces and employees, it really means a short work week, families barging into town, leaving home to visit relatives, too much food, some good, some bad. Added family pressure always seems to reveal a variety of unknown, disturbing baggage.

Tracy's homicide group had its own share of extra baggage to deal with this week too. Regarding Marcus Crosby's murder case, both lead detectives were about to meet in secret, with otherwise primary suspects. The Police Captain in charge of this homicide group had met twice already, in secret, with a network newswoman. Channel Forty news, a network affiliate! Even Tracy's Chief of Police met with the victim's mother. Not by choice however

Outside, away from the warm offices inside headquarters, late fall turned cold. Dead calm combined with cold arctic air funneled in from a northeasterly direction this time, bringing frost, icy windshields, more tule fog and fresh flights of waterfowl. If anyone cared to listen or observe new arrivals of snow geese and pintail migrants could be heard. White geese calling and sprig chirping. Unfortunately, most folks never pay much attention. Going way over their heads, so to speak.

Lacking wind, which usually advances northern air masses, left no swirling leaves or bent, barren trees. As the valley winter cold settled in soon after Thanksgiving, California's Central Valley inverses from its normal crushing, daytime heat to fog shrouded daytime cold. Different from those intense arctic blasts that sweep through Midwestern states like unstoppable frozen invaders complete with high snow drifts and ice. Dead of winter in the Golden State interior valley ranges from low twenty degrees on colder days to balmy mid fifties. After tule fog burns away and flooding sunshine has a chance to warm the still air. Larger Bay Area population centers to the west are warmer now, essentially flipping the usual valley routine. San Francisco will see more sun each day in fall and winter, minus pacific rainstorms sweeping inland, than during foggy summertime months. For wimpy coastal Californians, valley cold combined with the slightest breeze, cuts to the bone!

Regina scurried to get inside warm headquarters looking wide awake and unusually cheery. "Morning partner. Feels like winter today, huh?" Getting situated at her desk and logging onto her computer.

"Anderson wants a meeting as soon as you've settled in," Chris told Regina sounding very much like, "you're in trouble now lady."

"Oh, who me. Well I'm just fine today, thanks so much for asking,"

Gonzalez deadpanned, semi-scolding her partner for his lousy manners. Concerned however, if Anderson somehow got wind of her meeting with Ellis on Saturday night. "This could get kinda weird," she thought. "No way. Nobody knows," persuading herself. Realizing her investigation team, to a certain degree, was being deceived and considered opening up about her meeting. Maybe?

Chris stopped. Smiling very thin at his annoyed partner. Davis wrestled with his own decision and slim deception, to meet with Franny Braden. Deep inside, two images he couldn't shake played again and again in his thoughts. One was Franny. The other had Captain Anderson admonishing him for setting up unauthorized meetings with any potential murder suspects. "He can't possibly know short of my phone being bugged?" Knowing there was even less chance of that happening as he lifted his cell phone from the desk, examining it for any telltale tampering. "No chance," mumbling under his breath, tossing the cell to one side admitting how stupid he acted. "No chance. Anderson can't possibly know." As another image of his boss letting him have it, crept back into his mind.

"I wonder? Do they suspect something? Do they know anything?" Anderson asked himself after leaning back in his squeaking chair, hands clammy. "How could they know? Nobody knows," convincing himself for now, he was probably in the clear. "It could sure look bad. An attractive newsperson this close to a murder investigation," Billy counseled himself rubbing a palm across his chin helping relieve a little tension. "Shit, they don't know a damn thing. Tighten it up for Christ's sake," trying and succeeding to shake some worries for now. But understanding he, the person in charge, would be deceiving his investigation team in a slight but peculiar way. "Not good leadership methods," Billy whispered aloud.

"Okay I'm ready," Regina announced, standing quick, waiting for her partner to get moving. Chris seemed to be in low gear this morning. "Tough weekend?" Gonzalez snickered to Davis full of goofy smirks and sexual innuendo.

"What the hell is that supposed to mean Gonzo?" her partner barked with way too much force, causing Regina to step back then tripping into a clerk passing behind. The lucky office worker reached in, grabbing Regina full around her waistline, cuddling close to keep her from falling.

After a second or two they both salvaged equilibrium. "Watch it detective. They'll be talking us up all over headquarters," a happy clerk joked, releasing his helpful clench, expecting a warm thank you.

"Sorry, my bad," Regina apologized, red faced as her rescuer continued his way down the hall feeling great at work for a change. "What's your problem?" glaring at Chris with screaming eyes, who appeared quite embarrassed for his outburst and cause for a near tumble.

"Sorry partner. My bad," joking with his copy-cat apology. Davis realized he needed to relax, strung too tight and brimming with guilt over his decision. "It might be better to come clean about my upcoming meeting with Mrs. Braden? Maybe I will?" running the notion through his dishonor a few times. Like always, her image would flood in, roiling his decision once more. "Maybe?" Chris already forgot about Regina's close call starting his march down a crooked hallway.

"C'mon, let's get over to Anderson's office," Regina said jogging a couple strides to catch up, laying a gawk that asked, 'what the hell was that all about?' She stayed locked on her partner and added, "like you were just rung up looking at strike three!"

Rolling eyes at his partner they continued to their meeting. "Always the damn baseball Gonzalez," Chris mumbled just loud enough, making sure his partner heard. "That didn't even make sense," Davis snarled. Forcing Regina to look away, concealing her wide smile.

Strolling into Anderson's office with Gonzalez leading and making small talk now about their routine weekends. All three passing off the two free days as mostly routine. Chris went on about a football game as Captain Anderson flipped open his leather binder, saying nothing and paying little attention to his detective's ramblings. Both cops understood the meeting was underway.

Anderson scribbled a few vague notes delaying his first remark, in case either cop mentions anything regarding a Channel Forty newswoman. Chris and Regina remained hush anticipating his first comments or questions. "I think I'm in the clear," Billy assumed, getting relaxed. "So Gonzo, on Saturday you and Mr. Buck made your joy ride to Los Banos Wildlife Refuge. Please, enlighten us," Billy said, watching Regina nod in concurrence. "How many mallards did you bag?" Captain Anderson joked waiting for her comeback.

"Limited out. Big time! Nothing but webbed feet and feathers when I was done," Gonzo replied, which drew a discrete laugh from both colleagues. "I met with the Refuge Manager, a Miss Kelly Crisp. Nice lady and very helpful."

"Cool name," Chris interrupted, wondering who'd name their kid that way. Anderson said nothing but glanced at Davis in agreement.

Regina ignored his comment, continuing instead to explain hunter check-in routines, kill records, paper chase, check out rituals, shooting times and how difficult it can be to limit in a day. She concluded the report with her opinion of Tom Ellis being innocent. "No doubt he hunted ducks on the morning of Crosby's murder. Eyewitnesses, paperwork and dead ducks all in a row," smiling at the easy pun. "Sorry Captain, he's not our shooter," sounding convinced. More important, convincing herself.

"Was Buck helpful?" Anderson asked.

"Yeah, it was good to have him there. Buck likes his duck hunting," Regina added getting stirred up. "Miss Crisp took a liking to him too." Listening for remarks from either guy. Nothing.

"Okay, we'll pass on Mr. Ellis for now. But he remains on the suspect list," Anderson instructed. "She has the hots for Buck?" Billy asked in unbelievable tone.

Regina thought she'd get some form of a rise and just like a guy, there it was. Opting to let it pass. "That's your call Captain, but for myself, Ellis is clear," choosing not to plead her opinion too strong feeling how an all clear would be perfect for a very relaxed Thanksgiving. "I got to watch a guy shoot a duck on Saturday. Kinda cool." Getting prompt attention from both men now.

"Come again Gonzo?" Chris demanded.

"Where?" Anderson followed up.

"Out on the refuge. Duhh!" Neither man batting an eye as Regina mocked them, both taken back by her disclosure. "I wanted to look around the place. You know, get a better sense for this guy's alibi," she explained. "Went for a hike and stumbled across this guy hunting. Gordon. Had decoys out and the whole bit."

"Didn't Gordon care you were around?" the Captain asked.

"I don't think he knew I was there, hidden under that tree," she continued, realizing both men found her exploit rather engaging and decided to ham it up.

"Crouching real low in thick vegetation," Gonzalez stood up slowly with arms spread out, wanting to maximize her overblown act. "My heart raced like an ugly boy on his first prom date! I could only hope one of the keen eyed fowl wouldn't spot me." Trying in vain to hold back a belly laugh as Davis and Anderson leaned forward and waited for more melodrama! She couldn't believe how they ate it up. "Guys," she called out. "You can stop me anytime," laughing at the intensity on each face.

Chris realized first they'd been had. "Damn you Gonzo," was all Davis mustered as he and Anderson snapped, chuckling at each other. "You had me hooked partner!"

"Boy, I'll say. You were both pretty intense for a minute there." Captain Anderson stayed quiet, leaning back shaking his head. Regina sat down laughing at each man's expense and resumed her account. "Like I was saying, I found someone set up for hunting and stayed back, under a tree, to watch for a while. Some ducks came around and this guy started calling 'em down, or in I guess. They kept circling and circling and for some reason, one bird dropped away from the flock and BAM!" Shouting for effect, flinching two cops slightly, still keen on every word. "He nailed it. Poor thing fell like a stone and hit the water with a huge splash. Exciting stuff!" Both guys staring and squinting, waiting for more.

"What?" she asked.

Neither responded for a quick second. "Hmm, okay Gonzo, thanks for that," her boss sounded amused and intrigued at the same time. "What about you Chris?" turning to Davis hoping to get the meeting back on track. Chris remained locked on Regina wondering what to make of her story. She sat back, comfortable, wagging a crossed leg back and forth in cheeky disregard.

Captain Anderson waited for Davis to continue. But Chris' eyes stayed fixed on Gonzalez. "Chris you were about to explain." Unsure if his detective even heard him. "Davis!" Billy said much louder snapping Chris to attention.

Davis grimaced at his boss and stammered, "uh yeah right. Mr. Sheets and I," halting a broken phrase then peering back to his partner. "Exciting? Shooting ducks? What the hell is that Gonzalez?" Convinced she was putting them on again.

Regina had a mouthful to say but knew better to stay mum. Cocking her head slow and brushing back a handful of loose, dark hair, aware that Chris was still watching her. Perplexed to say the least. "C'mon detective, can't a girl enjoy the thrill of the kill, once in a while?" proud of her rhymes and easing back into her wooden chair with folded arms framed over her chest, sporting a smug expression. Lips tight. "Yeah, I could get into it," Gonzalez showed minimum attitude. Alex sighed out loud, tossing his pen onto the binder. He saw Chris move into hot pursuit realizing his meeting had been sidetracked again. He'd have to wait it out.

"Is this one of your curveballs coming our way or what? Shooting ducks?" Chris charged with a heightened voice, not letting go, only to be stung by another of her occasional pranks.

"No sir. No junk ball here." Shooting back.

"All right you two. Let's get through this and cut the baseball, right now." Anderson knew his investigators would joust way too long when baseball metaphors commenced. "Back to your investigation Chris. Save the duck hunts for another time."

Davis shook his head, stared at the floor for a moment and dragged his notebook into view. Regina squirmed in silence and re-crossed her legs for impact, feeling quite comfortable. Chris would pursue his partner and her ducks at another time. Back to business. "Sheets," Davis said out loud. "I'd like both of us to grill this guy."

"I'm down with that," Regina agreed, steering this meeting away from killing ducks. "Are we still a go for tomorrow morning?" she asked her boss.

"Yep, ten A.M. in Sonora," Captain Anderson confirmed.

Chris nodded with confirmation adding a quick reminder into his notebook. Cursing himself the whole time, remembering Tuesday's meeting with Franny Braden would most likely be broken. He wanted to keep their meeting. More than just the Crosby murder was at issue with Franny. "Damn it," he swore to himself a few more times.

"What approach will you take in questioning our deputy?" the Captain asked, open for both detectives to respond.

Regina wondered if Sheets would have a lawyer present.

"My last conversation with him was on Thursday. He said no attorneys would be permitted," Billy responded. "Permitted! A strong conviction," Anderson winced. "I'm calling him again today just to confirm our meeting. I'll sneak in a lawyer question."

"Without lawyers, we shouldn't start out too bold. Try it soft at first then finish strong," Davis tagged on.

"Kinda like a starting pitcher," Regina added in all seriousness. Both boss and partner looked at her, as if to say, "would you please knock it off with the baseball." Nothing was said. "Too much pitching, Captain?" sneaking a peek at Anderson then toward Davis. She gave Chris a squished up face and stuck out her tongue too! Davis played it straight controlling his laughs.

"You kill me Gonzo," Billy gave Regina a dry observation. "Anyway, I have partial copies of Sheets' investigation reports from the Sarah Crosby murder case. Take a good look. He seems to be." Anderson stopped abrupt, thinking over his finishing statement.

"You were saying Captain?" Regina interrupted.

"Yeah. I know," Anderson replied gently. "Well, the man seemed to be exceptionally thorough. To a point of repeating some routines two or three times." Billy stared blank into the distance and both detectives could see he was bothered by Douglas Sheets. "Hell, the guy dusted for fingerprints four times. "Why would he do that?" Looking at Davis for an expected comment.

"Messed up maybe?" Davis presumed.

"Maybe?" Anderson said, taking a drink of coffee. "Or, looking for something he knows is there, perhaps?" waiting to hear his team's opinion.

Regina cut in fast, "Captain, you sound like Sheets might've been involved in Sarah Crosby's murder?" Chris sat up in his chair.

"Do we question him about the Sarah Crosby murder? Seems kinda' late for that?" Davis checked his boss now, waiting for an answer.

Captain Anderson weighed the odds of a long shot success they might have in a murder case, already tried. "What the hell, why not. I wouldn't focus on Sarah Crosby's murder but let's voice some of our concerns. Maybe we'll get a base running blunder on his part." Billy's use of a baseball metaphor made Regina's smile unfold, handing each cop a sizable stack of paper from the Sarah Crosby investigation. "Look over the reports today and let me know what you think. I might be reading too much into them."

"Wow, this is a you know what, load of reading," Gonzalez responded flipping through pages of detail.

"I'll never finish all of this before tomorrow," Chris added holding his head in both hands wishing he had at least one more day.

"Yeah I know," Billy said taking in a deep breath. "It's kinda sudden. Do the best you can and be ready to brief me about your meeting next Monday in detail," Anderson explained, thinking of the upcoming holiday. "I'm out of here tomorrow afternoon. Before you two get back, I hope."

"So am I," Chris added, unable to stop speculating about his meeting tomorrow evening. "Although, I might work a day over the weekend to clear some loose ends," adding his disclaimer to cut off any possible inquires about Thanksgiving plans.

"After lunch on Wednesday, you won't see me until Monday morning. Can use the extra sleep," Gonzalez said, wondering about Thanksgiving Day. Growing nervous.

•••

Both cops worked well into the night, going over Sarah Crosby murder reports and debating strategy. Thinking out loud and bouncing ideas off one another, trying to develop a game plan to make it easy for Sheets to talk openly. Well aware this would be a tough interrogation. Chris and Regina anticipated short quick answers with little detail or emotion from Douglas Sheets, being an experienced investigator. Chris sensed he'd be tested tomorrow but looked forward to a new challenge. It had been a while since the detective had interrogated a possible bad lawman.

Sonora

Driving east Tuesday morning. Very early, very cold. It came on like silent seduction, gradually building momentum until blocking out the sun and cloaking everything in a wet, drippy shawl. Central Valley tule fog formed after midnight. Thick as clam chowder this morning, forcing reduced speeds for those cutting across flat roads through valley towns, by orchards and fallow fields. Relief from the gray blindness came in two ways. Waiting for the late morning burn off or an elevation gain. Two detectives were headed to higher ground but Gold Country foothills lay more than thirty minutes away, east.

Chris demanded a stop at his fruit stand cornered on Jack Tone Road and Route 120, not too far east of Manteca. Regina rolled both brown eyes, letting her partner know she didn't think fruit stands offered a great deal. "I bet you can get most of that produce cheaper at Lucky's or Safeway," commenting and asking at the same time.

"Not the nectarines," Chris stated, matter of fact, leaning left to check their speed. Regina traveled a bit high on this stretch of undivided road. "It's up ahead on the right, better slow it down Gonzo."

"Don't tell me how to drive. I hate that," Regina objected, adjusting both hands along the steering wheel offering a look of complete control. "I still can't see shit," she hissed, blaming Davis' for the dense tule fog but refused to back off on the accelerator for some reason. She was able to shift to the right lane as Route 120 divided into two lanes. No landmarks, signs or street lights helped illuminate a long gravel parking lot preceding the stand. Chris instinctively began a slow push into the floorboard with his right foot, simulating an imaginary brake pedal, knowing Regina was driving way too fast. They just passed the leading edge of gravel parking lot as Gonzo clipped along above fifty.

"It's right up here partner," Chris warned, bracing his left arm with hand planted firm on a padded dashboard, eyes wide open. His only mistake was pointing right, which the driver interpreted as an ordered change of direction, now! Regina took Chris' outstretched finger literally, swerving right, off smooth asphalt onto course gravel. Loose rock pelted metal wheel wells and underbody sounding like small caliber gunfire scaring Chris even more. Regina hadn't a clue they were bearing down on chain link fencing, two large sycamores and a small wood structure. Much too fast, which Chris recognized.

"Uh, brakes partner. Now," Chris barked as Regina shifted into second gear just before hitting the brake pad a tad too stiff. Car tires lost what little grip they held which started a rather smooth slide over mixed stones and shifting left on its own. Emerging faintly out of thick fog like multi-winged dinosaurs, each detective made out tree trunks and an obscured fence line. At Regina's current speed Chris estimated an unavoidable collision. Imagining oranges, pumpkins, almonds and jars of olives exploding throughout his small produce stand. Two Tracy homicide detectives speeding reckless, out of control on a fog shrouded roadway, would make for titillating reading in tomorrow's newspapers. Then reminded himself at an odd time, "remember to cancel tonight's meeting with Franny Braden!"

"Mary Jesus, hold on!" Regina suggested rather than shout, very calm, knowing well her passenger could see the two large, leafy obstacles dead ahead, growing increasingly clear. Chris obliged in silence, bracing both hands this time, square to the padded dash. Breaking a little harder Gonzalez slammed it into low gear and turning the steering wheel left a half turn. The car's rear end spun sharp right, front end left, all the while keeping steady brake pressure forcing a full sidelong skid! Straight into a gap between two substantial California sycamores. Blind luck took control as fate decided to cut them some slack. Splitting the uprights, coming to rest less than a foot and perfectly parallel to a locked chain link gate. Blanketed by tule fog outside, all quiet inside except for the steady engine idle. Regina maintained a tight grip on her left turn wheel. Any tighter and liquid resin might seep from the plastic ring!

"Whew," she bellowed. "That was close," excited, shaking her head, hair flying back and forth. Smiling intense. "I saw that in a movie once. Can't believe it really works." Chris, just able to peek out behind squinting eyes, couldn't understand how they avoided an embarrassing catastrophe. He could reach through his side window and open a padlock had he possessed the key. Helping himself to delicious varieties of Central Valley bounty.

"Shoot, they're not open yet," Regina said flatly. "Afraid it's no goodies for you today Chris," she quipped, treating Davis like a parent apologizing to her toddler.

"I see that. Up close and personal."

Able to turn a sharp left, she inched by one tree to her front right. Both cops felt an ever so slight jiggle as the bumper nicked thin, flakey tree bark. A fitting end, one might presume, after dodging a mammoth impact. "No harm no foul," Gonzalez came across almost stoic, trading gravel for smooth asphalt, accelerating through tandem green stoplights and leaving Jack Tone Road behind. Chris bowed his head, marveling at what just unraveled a minute before.

"Just slow it down Gonzo," Davis gritted speaking firm. "Please."

"Okay," chuckling. "Try and relax," she joked, goosing the gas pedal, streaming through soupy gray once again. Rows of barely visible walnut trees outlined extensive orchards edging their roadway. Speeding past empty brown fields and numerous fruit stands not yet open for business either. Passing through Escalon brought Franny Braden back into Chris' interest. This same route, flooded with sunshine little more than a week previous contrasted sharp with his current undertaking.

"Hell, we might pass one another anywhere along this road today," Davis imagined, preoccupied and on edge as cars sped by heading west. In reality they did just that, oblivious to each other however. Two cars, Franny westbound for some quick shopping in Oakdale and two Tracy cops on an eastbound hunt. Unaware but slipping alongside just before the Oakdale Café where California Route 120 takes a sharp turn due east, joining with State Route 108 from Modesto. Like two ghosts rushing through a haunted mist.

For the most part Davis and Gonzalez drove in silence, which wasn't unusual for them. Often, hardly saying a word to each other during any given work day. Neither detective felt the least bit awkward about their restful quiet. In fact, Chris needed these spells, more than Regina, to concentrate on case proceedings and strategies. Regina on the other hand excelled at bouncing ideas off her partner, hypothesizing or counterpunching concepts and tactics. Sometimes unlocking clever creativity which opened new paths helping to solve demanding murder cases. At the moment however, following her near crash debacle, she knew better to stay quiet. If she only grasped the reach of what her partner was considering.

They continued east leaving Oakdale behind. Silent. Slow. Thankfully, dense fog grew thin giving way to extended visibility and a clear roadway appeared. Gaining just enough elevation to glimpse bright blue skies between low clouds and splashes of sunshine. Another mile or two would place them above it all. Ascending higher and puncturing the earth bound mist visible in her rear view mirror as dry foothills beneath a crystal clear sky filled her windshield. Regina pressed down on the gas pedal, making up for slow going and crazy driving.

State Route 120 heads southeast, leading to Yosemite National Park, perhaps California's foremost wonderland and eventually into snow topped peaks forming a natural wall called the Sierra Nevada! Highway 108 carries on, coursing a twisted, up-down route, leading directly into Sonora. Continuing east to gain altitude also. Dry tan grass, sparse oak tree clusters and various shrubs of manzanita, chamfer and poison oak give way to ponderosa pines with their long hair like needles and bulging cones. Neither cop taking much notice of what passed by outside. A shame as these dry interior hills capture yet another subtle charm if observed close with an eye for detail. Plenty of signs remain, similar to vague clues, revealing previous settlements and occupiers.

Regina and Chris had something else to think about now. A deputy. Possible murderer. A rare event, questioning one of their own for a capital offense. Each feeling nervous and stimulated, wondering how Douglas Sheets will react to tough questions. "Can I keep the heat on?" Chris knew he'd most likely be matched against a skilled investigator. "Sheets will know very well how to handle himself on the defensive side of investigation. Experience playing the attack side teaches careful preparation for playing strong defense," Davis reflected, aware he and Gonzalez would need their A games today.

Regina entered Sonora at a crawl realizing it had been a long time since she last visited. Sonora, bathed in bright sunshine today, displaying its typical makeup of Sierra foothill communities. Huddled groups of fast food outlets, small independent businesses, retirement developments, chronic unemployment, picturesque scenes of rustic buildings holding on to better days long past, as well as an eastward vista to snow capped peaks.

On the surface, Sonora being one of a handful of gateway towns to higher elevations, gives every impression of being trapped between valley and mountain. Between a plush arable landscape and true alpine beauty. Individual foothill towns retain a certain look and feel all their own but as a whole, they exist in vaguely similar ways. Economic struggles make for tough survival but still attractive for some odd reason, to highly independent and self reliant types determined to make a life of it here.

"A person has to be a pretty hard ass to survive, let alone thrive in the foothills. Just like many of the ugly animal creatures dwelling out here," Regina commented, aiming for Tuolumne County Sheriff's Department parking lot. Chris wrinkled his forehead and quietly ruminated on his partner's animal remark. She managed to hit this parking lot dead center unlike Chris' fruit stand. Douglas Sheets would be found inside an old brick building standing a little above and beyond their windshield, well renovated but not completely modern. "Nice digs," Regina mentioned before leaving the car. Chris didn't notice.

Once inside and checked in, Tracy's two detectives were escorted by a uniformed female officer, bound and determined to make small talk with Davis and ignore Gonzalez. Deputy McCarthy opened a door to a rather small room. Not an actual interrogation room, after all Sheets hadn't been accused of any crime yet. More like an empty office. One desk, four chairs, small movable blackboard minus chalk and a curious wood stepladder leaning against the wall, just below an air vent. Regina didn't like the accommodations one bit however, Chris said it would be perfect giving officer McCarthy a genuine thank you. One door, no phone, no foot traffic, no interruptions. Simple. McCarthy left the room gushing at Davis without even acknowledging Regina's presence.

"Sweet girl," Gonzalez snarled.

"I thought so too," Chris agreed, recognizing his partner's sarcasm. Then climbing the rickety ladder for a peek inside the air vent. Nothing unusual.

Douglas Sheets

Sitting, getting comfortable, waiting, quiet. A dark room, poor lighting, stark, anticipation. One minute later, enter Douglas Sheets. Strutting a casual smile and shaking hands with each detective. Very firm then stating flat, "shoot away."

Standing six feet two inches and only thirty six years old. Blond hair with a slight curl, just a little long, blue eyes leaning toward hazel with a face someplace between rugged and gnarly. His lighter complexion sported red cheeks. When-ever his temper or anxiety grew, so did the redness in those cheeks, forehead, even his ears! It had to be exceptional however for his ears to light up.

Douglas Sheets joined Sonora County's Sheriff Department as one of its few legitimate homicide investigators. Hired away from one of California's foremost murder capitols, Stockton. Received excellent training with plenty of hands on experience, serving over six years commendably. Slow to work his way up through a police force in a city well established with promotions based on political favors, race and lingering nepotism. Douglas saw his chance for quick advancement landing somewhere between nil and nothing. Deciding to apply to various East Bay cities, Northern Counties and the Feds. At one point believing he landed a decent position with the FBI, only to be told he didn't make the cut. Due more to budget than a lack of qualifications. A setback lighting up his ears up like a Christmas tree! Reeling from what he viewed as a major letdown, Douglas would connect in Sonora County, accepting a minor pay raise for a title.

Deputy Homicide Detective. Disregarding all the professional shortcomings, Sheets concluded a small town atmosphere might do himself, his wife and their marriage some possible good. Small town, nice setting, cheap housing and far less crime than Stockton. "Almost any town, USA had a lower crime rate than California's two-o-nine," Sheets always told himself, glad to be leaving that part of the valley and delta behind.

Sheets wanted to believe Stockton had potential to become a desirable place to live in Northern California. Situated on the eastern flank of the delta with its intimate access to boating and recreation yet short drives to San Francisco, Sacramento and Lake Tahoe. "It's a shame Stockton can't shake its earned reputation as the drug and crime center of California's interior," Douglas often told his wife following another demoralizing crime.

Sonora would fail to be of much help with Douglas spending more time away from his wife and newborn baby girl. A short time passed. Not even two years from move in, when the deputy drifted into a series of short intense affairs. Compounded by an ever increasing attraction to cheap gin and his first meeting with Sarah Crosby, on a domestic violence call.

Following a quick introduction, Regina opened the interview. "Well Doug, you know why we're here today? Not to make an arrest or to accuse you of anything. I assume you understand?"

"Do you really think I shot Marcus Crosby, detective?" Sheets asked attempting a display of calm pose. But Chris and Regina detected a thin vale of nervousness with constant tapping of his left hand fingers on the wood tabletop.

"Nothing too unusual," Chris assumed to himself, "maybe a bit edgy, for a seasoned investigator?"

"We'd like to determine that, deputy," Gonzalez said, emphasizing deputy to mimic Sheets' initial retort directed at her. "Did you?" Fixing her stare into his eyes without blinking. Douglas blinked a few times, then turned away.

"Very direct. I like that," Sheets responded, leaning back into his sturdy chair, going quiet. After a moment of lingering stillness, Chris couldn't wait any longer.

"Did you detective?" Davis asked abruptly.

Sheets stayed mum, his head lowered with eyes closed. Regina was about to ask again but checked her partner. Chris shook his head. Instructing her to stay quiet, without saying as much.

"I've never been asked this before. Not in a million years," interrupting himself while contemplating this abysmal situation. "I never thought, for one second I'd ever be on this side of the table. Christ!" Never regaining eye contact with either detective, Douglas reached slow into his jacket retrieving a cell phone followed by a black leather wallet holding his symbol. Laying his coveted badge face up on the table. Regina didn't know what to make of Sheets' gesture. She even faked an itch on her neck to see what might be on Chris' mind. Davis raised his eyebrows indicating a blank also.

Chris even started to think Sheets was about to confess and unable to stop his dumbfounded stare. The longer Douglas stayed quiet, the more tense Davis became. Regina assumed the badge presentation was his way of saying, "I'm a cop too and didn't kill anyone." She decided to continue questioning. Chris wondered why his partner didn't let their suspect turn in the wind a little longer.

"How long have you been an investigator, Mr. Sheets?" Regina asked with respect.

Sheets breathed in deep followed by a snorted chuckle. "Almost eight years," sounding bored now with Regina's line of question. "All of this is available on my record. You know that detective. How long have you been making a difference?" he asked, using a rude, sarcastic tone.

"Some days way too long. I'm feeling that way today," swinging back, Regina turned herself slightly, preferring to face the Sonora Deputy square.

Both sides felt the tension soon after saying hello. Nothing but confrontation ensued. Chris read Sheets' discomfort, deciding to let his partner keep swinging away. "This guy appears a little strung out to me. Just let Regina keep going tit for tat and maybe he'll tire of fighting. Get someone good and tired and they'll make that big mistake?" Chris mulled over his strategy assuming Douglas would start to cooperate before too long. "The question is, like always, how long can a person hold out?" Davis speculated. So far not much accomplished. Nothing was revealed and Chris understood they hadn't even started to bear down. At this point, just rude small talk.

"Why don't you begin by telling us where you were on the morning of Marcus' murder," Regina boomed in with her first pitch, beginning the actual interrogation. Chris peaked up wanting to see Sheets' reaction.

"I'm sure detective, you already know I didn't work that day. Why are you even asking?" Sheets responded while his finger tapping grew louder. "Big deal, a day off!"

"I'm aware you didn't work that day," Gonzalez responded without a shred of surprise in her voice. Nor looking up as she entered a fast note in her binder. "Where were you?" returning a locked gaze onto her professional counterpart, without flinching. The deputy glared back. This time with obvious anger on his face.

Chris noticed how strong Sheets' display of temper captured his entire focus. Redness almost glowed over his features. Knowing this was hardly incriminating behavior but he found the sudden display very odd, for an investigator with his level of experience. "Maybe a normal reaction from the opposite side of the table?"

Not answering Regina's question, Sheets realized he appeared way too defensive, going out of control displaying his emotions. Doug leaned back, relaxing tight jaw muscles permitting a small but noticeable smile develop, giving off an agreeable exterior. Neither Chris or Regina were buying it, but knew the deputy from Sonora would have something to say.

"Look, Detective Gonzalez, what can I tell you. I was home, feeling like crap. Just a coincidence," Sheets made clear, coming across much more relaxed.

"You were home?" Regina followed up. "Our records show you don't miss a day of work Douglas," speaking matter of fact. "Two sick days and a one week vacation in six years, total! Coincidence?" waiting to see his reaction.

"Pretty good work ethic for a government employee, wouldn't you say madam," inserting a slight insult at the same time showing about half of his broad grin.

"Sure is. What was so important on the day of Marcus Crosby's murder?" Regina continued slight pressure on her confident suspect.

"I just told you detective, I was sick. Pure coincidence," Doug's attitude level rising a bit. "Are you suggesting I might be lying?" His voice rising now.

Gonzalez wasn't fazed by his modest bullying. "Some cops do a great job of lying. Are you lying to us Douglas?" she asked in a controlled, mechanized manner but still expressing a sense of belligerence. Regina had a gut feeling Sheets would have to be pushed very hard to give up any real information. Her partner came to the same conclusion when Sheets first walked through the door, acting very self-assured. Chris opted to stay in the background observing close, while his partner prodded and poked their suspect.

Douglas Sheets, working in the Sherriff's Department after all, had to be handled aggressively but with a certain amount of latitude. Bad cops were perceived as traitors to honest working police officers. Going back on his oath, commitment to fellow officers and the department. If found to be crooked, pressure can and will be applied viciously, whenever necessary. Sheets was all too aware of the unwritten rules knowing he could play games to a certain level. But also aware, cooperation in high criminal investigations comes with the job. Being asked point blank if he was lying or holding back information was certainly at, but not over the deputy's limit line.

"If you have something to prove I wasn't sick that day, just say so." Sheets challenged, switching looks between Regina and Davis in his most serious demeanor. Sounding every bit like he didn't merit this sort of questioning or its implications.

Regina scooted back into her chair then leaned forward, glancing brief at Deputy Sheets, writing notes as if uninterested in his small tirade. Chris studied his mannerisms. "He's acting and his face is way too red!" Silence filled the room with Sheets the only person squirming in his chair.

Gonzalez broke silence with a step into his personal life. Their report held a small side note about possible marital problems. "Okay, let's see. You're at home all day, too sick to work. This should be easy to confirm with your wife?" Avoiding direct eye contact after bringing his wife into play. Both Tracy cops noticed his finger tapping stopped dead. The deputy cleared his throat groaning, started to speak but shut up fast. Chris meanwhile studied every move he made, never letting go. This became bothersome to Sheets but he stayed determined, not to give in to Chris' inspection. Regina played her part, aware of what her partner was doing.

"You were going to say something," Chris jumped in with a tone in his voice sounding quite tender and helpful. Almost fatherly. Douglas, taken by surprise, quivered ever so slight not expecting Davis' voice. Regina couldn't look up now, grinning ear to ear pretending to log a few notes in her binder. She adored the way Chris chose to enter the fray. Smooth, like soft rain. Suspects couldn't help but be drawn into his venomous charm.

Douglas Sheets took a deep breath, clenched his jaw, seized by Chris' lair and chuckled mildly. Conscious now of Davis' tactic, cursing in silence to allow himself taken by surprise. Head spinning in anger knowing he had to respond but wanting to stop the questions at once. "Hey look, uh," mumbling. "No need to get Loretta invol," stuttering, clearing his voice. "No need to get my wife involved." Knowing as soon as he uttered the stupid phrase, these two would be after her like leopards to a bloodied springbok! "I told you I've been seeing another woman, didn't I?" Sheets asked, as if he wasn't sure of his own immediate reality. He examined two cops who seemed to be thrown way off guard.

"Holy shit, is he having a meltdown or what?" Regina asked herself.

"Oh boy! Don't I look stupid?" Sheets blurted out, realizing he was turning various shades of red. "Uhm, what the hell. Me and my current girlfriend spent that day together," Doug admitted, keeping his head down. "You know how it gets Chris," hoping for sympathy from Davis. Using his first name and some rather clumsy man to man commentary.

"I'm single," Chris said coming across neutral, shrugging his shoulders. He followed with a quick stare into Doug's face, read by Regina as saying, "not okay!" Going over Sheets' head somehow. Chris Davis liked his girlfriends as well as the next guy but marital infidelity wasn't acceptable. Especially his own. Regina didn't proceed as expected. She waited to permit a tense silence eat away at their suspect. Chris picked up on his partner's tactic, giving Regina a silent message, "I like what you're up to."

Sheets would break silence this time by restarting his fingertips. "Hopefully we can leave my family out of this. I don't see any reason in getting them involved," almost pleading with both detectives for a break. Douglas became an extremely nervous individual right now. Ears turned red and he fidgeted like a nine year old boy at Sunday Mass. The last thing he needed was his wife suing for divorce. "She wouldn't keep from telling these two about my affairs. One in particular," reminding himself. Doug's mind began to race almost out of control, wishing for an attorney at his side now.

Regina saw the opening, wanting to chime in and did. "We'll have to talk to your wife at some point, Doug," she paused briefly, just before using his homey first name.

"Your girlfriend too, what's her name by the way?" Chris asked in a sharp unsympathetic tone.

"Well, what else do you want?" strumming his fingers even louder. "I mean, anything to keep this from getting to my wife. Believe me, I hated that bastard," their suspect hissed, losing control of his thoughts and capable of saying just about anything. "I hated that man enough to shoot him. But," forcing himself to regain control. "You have to believe me, I didn't shoot Marcus Crosby!" Seeming absolute desperate to Regina and Chris, both surprised by his wild remarks. Neither cop was sure where to go next.

Estefan

No school for the Thanksgiving Holidays. Standing behind a leafless walnut tree, Estefan waited for his pin headed confidant, Carlos slash provider, to deliver Angelina's ammunition. Far off toward the south, bending around a slow arcing dirt road bordering one of Clay Blevins' orchards, came a sound clearly recognized by the young farm boy. A narrow cloud of dust, backlit in bright fall sunlight, escalated like a smoky serpent hiding trees then vanishing among crooked limbs and brown leaves. Mourning doves began vacating their hidden rests, whistling among trees with various pairs twisting across open fields of dirt and alfalfa. From the opposite side of the orchard two muffled pops from secret shooters, unheard by Estefan, downed one gray bird.

"Oh Christ, he must've fixed that lousy mini-bike. Somehow getting it running again," Melon Head mumbled out loud, disgusted. Estefan had grown to hate the noisy contraptions spewing dust, scaring children and churning through plowed fields leaving behind rutted scars and busted irrigation. He witnessed his father, mad as hell, forced to stay late in the fields mending PVC after the mechanized demolishers completed their deeds.

On he came, growing louder and louder. Speeding along dirt curves, Carlos leaned hard to his left to keep from sliding sideways and flying into a concrete irrigation canal parallel to his route. Closing, Estefan could see Carlos' right hand twist the throttle wide open, traveling fifty miles plus and flying fast. Dust, dirt, leaves and gravel flew to each side.

Bolting from trees to his left, concealed from the Jackal, three doves couldn't stand any more high pitched whining and flushed for open air. One of three birds, still navigating between narrow rows of trees, failed to realize Carlos was coming up so fast. Dove number three, intent on keeping pace, had to swoop very low in order to miss a dense cluster of outstretched tree limbs. This trailing bird, anticipating correction away from the ear splitting din was forced into a low flight path, failed to spot the mini-bike. The bird's reeling senses flickered by high pitched screaming. Carlos too, his senses distorted by blasting air into his face and eyes, never saw the dove. They met in force over screaming exhaust and flying dirt.

Estefan watched all three birds exit from his side of the orchard, clear and visible, surprised at the low altitude dove number three maintained. Like magic, a huge puffball of feathers exploded in front of Carlos, obscuring head and shoulders for a moment. Changing fortunately, from flat out throttle to dead flat throttle. The bike seemed to clear a detonation of fluffy down just as Estefan witnessed a glimpse of twirling wings, which had to be the dove carcass being hurled to its watery demise. Carlos stunned, scared, unsure what just happened, had a hard time breathing after intercepting a fast flying bird a few inches below his neck at fifty plus! Still upright and slowing but leaning too far left in Estefan's modest opinion.

"If he doesn't upright soon, my ammunition will be wrapped around a lone walnut tree one row over." Estefan projected the itinerary while thoroughly enjoying Carlos' gutsy predicament. His bike started to veer one way then jump and buck with fierce resistance back toward the uniformed tree trunks, edging a Clay Blevins' orchard. It turned out to be a small stack of pruned tree limbs which ended pin head's wild ride. Cut walnut rounds rolled left and right as a red, motorized death trap reared up on its hind wheel, faded awkward to starboard, just after throwing Carlos dead center between two walnut trees. Not more than twenty feet from an hysterical Melon Head. Neither boy could speak, wondering if severe injuries had ensued.

"You better have my .222 ammo," the young Hispanic boy yelled out walking over to inspect damages. Carlos being a little dizzy, unable to form coherent words lay face up in warm dirt, left hand rubbing a bright red patch already forming on his chest. "You killed that dove you know," Estefan jeered, unable to resist a cheap shot.

"Fuck you Melon Head," Carlos scolded his young customer still lying flat on his back. Slowly rolling over to his least aching side, a valiant but defeated rider looked back to his ride. Akin to how a brave cowboy might look upon his trusty stallion after being thrown! Twisted handlebars, severe dents in the gas tank, battered headlight and a walnut branch jammed through rear spokes. Both arms dangling on raised, bent knees, observing heartbroken carnage from a sitting position. "Fucking bike is trashed again," speaking loud enough for his customer to hear. "A long walk back home too!" Estefan elected to say nothing, peering down upon a shaken pin head, relishing the devastation around him.

"Okay Melon Head, you have my forty bucks?" Getting to his feet, wobbling some, removing two bright green, narrow boxes from his jacket. Handing them over businesslike to his client.

To Estefan they felt heavier than expected. Forcing open a cover sleeve on one end then sliding out a foam cartridge holder. He smiled, unexpectedly pleased and filled with a sense of power too. Each brass case shined bright below vivid copper bullets. In perfect accents to a metallic color scheme. Lifting one round from two rows of resting cylinders a young boy examined close the butt end primer, fingering its sharp point, growing more and more seduced by the precise, balanced lines. Estefan reached into his pocket this time, removed three bills and handed them to Carlos. One twenty, one ten, one five. "Our agreement was thirty five dollars."

Franny Braden

Midday had Franny walking bank side along her beloved river, a short distance upstream from home. Stanislaus flows were still mild with murmurs, soft hisses and timid gurgles, doing wonders to aid her rare, relaxed mood. She needed to be calmed. Surrounded by cottonwood trees still hosting a sparse canopy, changing from bright green to yellow and disappearing soon. Most of the Central Valley waited for late fall kindliness to turn hostile into cold winter. She leaned most her weight against a wide trunk charting a strange task ahead. Wishing instead, to just be alone with the soothing river. End the fear once and for all. A smile brought on by a small trout splashing behind a loose stack of small boulders, slurping besieged midges, turning a swift tail flap sending water droplets in her direction. "Two fish with one hook today," a troubled older woman mumbled after exhaling a long puff of smoke.

"Good God, I've gotta handle this carefully," talking to herself then inhaling deep on a menthol cigarette. An infrequent smoker, except in nervous situations like this one. Franny would never consider smoking near Henry. Simply put, her husband forbids anyone to smoke in his immediate presence. Leftover memories of his mother gasping for air on her hospital deathbed, would always haunt him. Especially in ongoing nightmares, often awakening in violent shouts, gasping for a lungful of air and begging his wife to save him. At first she could hardly cope with his, as well as her own absolute terrors, but managed to accept Henry's episodes much better now. Cigarettes being Henry's number one revulsion.

But, Mrs. Braden had seen her husband off an hour earlier. Henry was meeting later in the day with a number of engineering colleagues, in Colusa of all places. He and various Northern California city departments were arriving to compare new and old guidelines for awarding projects as well as bid sample streamlines. Nothing bored Franny more than listening to her husband recite job qualifications and timetable projections. After the meetings, Henry planned to spend the night with his younger brother and sister-in-law in Chico. Her husband's way of staying in touch with family during the holidays. Franny never saw eye to eye with Henry's brother and chose to keep her distance. Henry understood.

In royal comfort of her streamside retreat, Franny suffered second thoughts about meeting with Detective Davis. "What am I doing?" she whispered, staring into clear water windows seeing smooth rocks and grains of sand picked up, swirled and deposited between stones a few feet away downstream. The ever present movement of rock, sand and water grinding mountains into a moveable size. Returning to the Pacific. Always moving, always changing like the valley where she lived. "I don't want any changes right now," speaking above a peaceful, spilling current.

An hour later Franny locked her front door and left for Tracy, deciding to play the game today, very attractive in her tight outfit. Black of course.

Sheets

Chris and Regina continued their assault on Douglas for two solid hours. Gonzalez stayed firm asking the lion's share of questions as planned, enjoying the heavy role. Chris preferred it that way, giving him time and resource to study their suspect's behavior, motions and analyze answers. Especially answers to repetitive questions. The same question asked two or even three times but worded just slightly different. Each cop built on this tactic learning to exploit the subtle deceptions. Regina became quite good at the wording routine and combined with Davis' ability to read minor nuance in repeated answers, proved an effective technique to tangle suspects in outright lies. Unfortunately for two Tracy cops, Sheets was aware of this technique as well. Using her best skills to conceive repeated questions and more or less every answer from the deputy was identical and unwavering.

Douglas Sheets wasn't cooperating much to help their case since his confession of infidelity. Both sides grew tired and hungry, like out of shape ballplayers in the late innings of an August day game. They decided on a cease fire, voting in a lunch break. Chris signaled Gonzalez using his sliced throat finger motion, indicating time to break it off. Pit stop, some food, sun and rest would help evaluate what the two had learned or failed to discover, then bounce ideas off each other. Sheets had no argument, wanting out of this room fast.

A short walk from Sonora's Police Headquarters to a typical foothills strip mall found a small deli secluded to a lonesome side. Brisk business inside implied the shop's location didn't hurt a well earned reputation. Simple, sell good food.

"We're not getting much partner," Chris stated point-blank to Regina. "It'll take a major screw up on his part or else he has to cave," Davis conceded taking a large rip from a pastrami and Swiss on ciabatta, overflowing with condiments. Mustard streaked his left cheek as Gonzalez pointed to the smeared mess.

"Clean your face young man," she joked.

Both cops relaxed on stone benches, alongside a small fountain and fake pond, listening to gentle water splashes. Flanked by valley oaks with sturdy trunks and prolific limbs, appearing as monstrous arms intending to gather up nearby folks loafing out a pleasant afternoon. Late fall shadows stretched from individuals enjoying intense sunshine without the overwhelming summertime heat. Instead merely warming those willing to dine outdoors feeling splendid to the cops from Tracy.

"We have to talk to Mrs. Sheets," Regina spoke with an almost sinister tone. "I bet, if we isolate her and open the throttle, we'll find out if her husband is involved in these murders." Shifting to her wide-eyed glare at Chris affirming their plan, followed by a huge bite from roast beef and cheddar on sourdough. Jaw muscles and full cheeks flexing as Chris noticed her ears even moved a little bit with every chomp.

"This lady kills me. Just something else sometimes," thinking how lucky he was having Gonzalez as a partner. They could count on one another. "Maybe I'm just too laid-back today, on a fine afternoon and pastrami sandwich," almost dreaming now. But, out of nowhere his mood switched realizing he'd be doing the same thing later in the day, with Franny. Full throttle!

Relaxed in calm surroundings they continued to rip bread and meat, washed down with bottled water and iced tea. Moods nothing but first-rate. Lounging, stomachs full with a warm thaw spreading over arms, shoulders and back of the neck. Pines and oaks dotted hillsides leading to rounded peaks above steep ravines, thick with brush and stunted trees fighting for survival. Nothing like steep grades to make for pleasurable changes to flatlanders and each cop relished their break from the ordinary.

Long narrow shadows protruded from each tree as they intercepted low angled sunshine trying to penetrate a high semi sparse canopy. Easy to be drawn into such plush scenery, which both detectives were, but also hung up to a great extent, on Douglas Sheets. What does he know?

"This guy has information about Crosby's murder. He must know something the rest of us don't, about Sarah Crosby's murder. I just know it, somehow," Regina told her partner picking distasteful with a pinky fingernail, removing stubborn bits of wedged meat in her upper front teeth. "Damn roast beef sandwiches!" Forcing fibrous remnants between her teeth. Chris took note of Gonzo's flagrant oral hygiene, saying nothing for fear of retribution, fixed on her jaw muscles flexing again but those ears remained stationary.

Davis reconsidered Regina's sense of blind conviction. Nothing concrete but convinced nonetheless Douglas Sheets knows something. The same impression he carries about Franny Braden. "She's holding back too, I know it." Chris told himself but uneasy to mention her name today.

"Our case is running fast toward a dead end Gonzo unless we break down the Braden's or Sheets," Chris told his partner in a peculiar, almost apologetic manner. "There isn't much left?" Davis avoided her dejected look, scanning a small clearing where two small deer walked through shadows almost unnoticed, except by him. Regina spotted Chris' serious look which was new to Gonzalez. It was pretty rare to witness her partner with a serious, blank stare suggesting failure. "We're down to three suspects. Two if we count the Braden's acting as a team and not much testimony to hang our hats on. We've got to start forcing the situation," Davis implored, glancing back to the clearing but seeing only one deer moving now. The other was in plain sight but Chris's eye failed to draw him among shadows and shrubs. Analogous to this shadowy murder case. As detectives, they hated the notion of a brick wall. Unsolved murder cases became personal and professional failures not unlike a lost trial to a lawyer or faulty design to engineers. To Chris they became obsessions. His white whales.

Regina, finished with her dental cleaning, could tell Davis was formulating ideas. "What route do you have in mind?" Predicting he was about to change tactics.

"How do we break this cop if he has to be broken at all?" Davis thought privately. "Shotgun, I think," Chris responded.

"You sure?"

"I seem to be outta bullets partner!" he admitted. "You have any ideas?" he asked.

"I'll come up with something. Be ready to follow my lead," Regina instructed, betting she could develop some sort of tactic to get Sheets talking. Back to the drawing room.

Both deer lay at the edge of the clearing in thin brown grass. Fallen tree limbs and thick shadows helped veil their charisma, even to those walking by not fifty feet away. Every now and then the eye just isn't permitted to discover those obvious shapes, laying bare in the proverbial grass.

■■■

Franny skidded her black Yukon from the driveway, beginning the departure to Tracy, clueless how events would go later today. So, with fears buried low and music volume high, she prepared for an otherwise safe drive west. "I better not get stood up," mumbling in a subtle, worried voice. "Might be better if I did?" Her fears surfacing then brushed away by resolve. She wondered if the fruit stand at Jack Tone Road would be open?

···

"Hi detectives, any more questions?" Douglas Sheets announced his bold return to their small room, fifteen minutes late. "Let's get started," seeming to order his two investigators. "Beautiful day, that's for sure." Appearing to be in a good mood following lunch. Regina had a hunch he might've spent lunch with his girlfriend? Chris and Regina made fast eye contact as Davis raised his eyebrows, rolling eyes upward signaling his partner how stupid this cop seemed to be.

"Since you say so, question number one, deputy Sheets. Tell us about the Sarah Crosby murder investigation," Regina boomed across the table getting Douglas' attention rather fast, combined with a tiny, surprised shudder from her unanticipated loud voice. Even Chris feigned a ducking head at her volume.

"Good move Gonzo," Davis said to himself.

Regina turned her head and bore down on Sheets. "I'm waiting," she said with anger, jerking her head back, flinging long hair to one side then tossing her pen firm into a waiting notebook, for effect.

"Sarah Crosby's murder?" Sheets asked, scrunching his face wondering why she asked about that case.

"If you don't have the case files already, I'll get them for you. Read 'em," Sheets presented the most aloof performance as he possibly could but the Tracy detectives read through his nervous body language. Doug rose from his chair acting as though he lost something and looked both right and left. "Oops, not in my office am I? That's why there's no coffee pot to be found," losing touch for a moment as the automatic reaction kicked in. Which seemed clear to Chris that Sheets was working hard to stay one step ahead.

Regina said nothing about imaginary coffee. "We did some reading of the files and have a question or two to ask. About techniques," Regina said to a mounting uptight investigator.

"Go ahead, ask away," Douglas responded using up the last round of his cocky ammunition.

"Okay, there is something I'd like to know Doug," Chris asked, finally saying something, with an almost school kid like enthusiasm. "Yeah, one thing about that case bothers me," turning in Sheets' direction but not seeing him as the detective's thoughts were somewhere else. He paused. Silent.

"Go ahead," Sheets said, almost imploring to ask his question.

He got Davis' attention. "What I don't quite understand. Why in hell would you dust the murder scene for fingerprints four times? I've never heard of any crime scene being dusted that many times. Was it just sloppiness?" Chris leaned back, absorbed into his uncomfortable chair as a fleeting pain jolted his lower back. He winced and scooted around to find comfort. Douglas did the same. Regina shared smirking lips with her sharp stare. A worried deputy began to strum his jumpy fingers again, stalling. Which Gonzalez read as a delay for more time, desperate to think of a reasonable answer.

"What the hell does that matter Detective Davis?" shifting to formal gear, returning his confused startled look covering a red face. "We're not sloppy in our investigations. I wanted to be thorough." Doug was looking down at the table top instead of facing his interrogators. As all three participants sensed a shift into a more formal inquest. No longer an uncomplicated, civil question and answer. His mood changed considerably. Quite dramatic in fact from his post lunch aloofness.

"Thorough to say the least," Regina interjected with her typical acerbic tone. "Then you end up lifting a number of your own prints at the scene. That seems to me," pausing for effect to convey a little more contempt, "to be kinda' sloppy!" Without moving his head Douglas swung his eyes abruptly over to Regina, processing a sinister gaze. She enjoyed his contempt for her accusation. He waited once again before speaking.

"I was the first one at the murder scene. It uh," stumbling over his own thoughts and mumbled words, "took me by surprise when I saw the situation." Douglas spoke in a stop and stuttering manner failing to sound convincing in the least. Not a shred of cockiness armed him now and uneven answers didn't sound anything like the morning Douglas. "I should've been more careful, I suppose?" wanting to add something more, but decided to check his bet and stay quiet.

Regina attempted to goad him along. "A bit sloppy I suppose?" expecting some sort of reaction. Sheets stayed quiet. Failing his own training and experience briefly and he knew it.

"Short answers," the deputy reminded himself.

Davis carried on the attack. "First upon the scene? No phone calls or any notices? You just happen to arrive, minutes after Sarah Crosby's murder. Explain that to me please." Davis realized he sounded somewhat paternal as if questioning his own teenage son, if he had one, on trial for flicking school. Regina loved it.

"It's all in the files Detective Davis, you should look it up," choosing to let that stand. "I have to use the bathroom folks. Be right back," excusing himself in an awkward exit.

"Sure, go ahead," Davis said, slouching into his chair intent on revealing some outward frustration. Douglas read his body language before leaving the small room.

"That's more like it, you black bad-ass!" Regina hissed from across the table leaning far forward with her jaw sticking out and face flushed. Chris understood when Gonzalez included racial earthiness, it was always in her most endearing way. "This reminds me of the North Side Murders," Regina referred to one of the more publicized cases they broke open a few years ago.

"Another bad cop involved with one too many women," Davis added with his partner in agreement. Two cops believing perhaps, they finally had a suspect worth pursuing. Until now not much was coming to light. Sheets, being a deputy, was a hurdle that had to be overcome.

"Look, let's keep hitting him on Sarah's murder," Regina told Davis, quite excited, eyes wide open. "What do you think?"

"Absolutely. He's pretty nervous talking about his murder case. Stay focused on Sarah's investigation." Chris just finished his observation when Sheets stumbled back through the doorway. Catching his shoe tip in a metal divider separating hallway and room, sent Douglas skipping and hopping, bent over and reeling toward the table. Regina leaped to help catch her fellow cop before crash diving into sturdy wood. Sheets managed to catch his left hand on the table then easing a right shoulder into Regina's waiting arms. She leaned in, crash prevented. Douglas went red faced but breathed in deep when Regina's fragrance penetrated his nose. Her smell was intoxicating, aroused him and didn't want to let go. Gonzalez stepped back not realizing her own magnetism. Sheets stepped back too, slow to let go, managing to get seated but missed the chair ever so slight scraping a butt cheek over one arm rest, almost tipping over.

"So, where were we?" Sheets returned to sarcasm. Knowing full well he couldn't look cool if he had to. Spotting Davis' face, chin settled above thumb and forefinger, head swaying back and forth. Transmitting his analysis of, 'you dumb fuck!

"We were at Sarah Crosby's murder scene. You just arrived at the cabin," Regina reminded their suspect, eager to regain the momentum. "Not alerted," adding on a little more with a hint of derision.

"I thought you two were here investigating Marcus Crosby's murder? Why all the interest in Sarah's murder?" Sheets asked, a flustered look with face, neck and ears glowing red. It was all Regina could do to save her giggle from bursting out loud.

Chris and Regina concluded separately, unknown they had the same idea, to stay mum and allow Douglas to twist in the wind. It was clear as plastic wrap how easy he became aggravated. "How well did you know Sarah Crosby?" Regina asked, setting up her next question. Fastball, fastball, slider, thinking to herself in simple amusement.

Douglas knew he would be negotiating tricky issues now. "I first met her on a spouse abuse call. I came out to her house with a uniform in tow, to see if she was all right. Over two years ago," Sheets answered then added, "it's in the trial transcripts." Annoyed.

"You made a few more visits to their cabin without being called. Why?"

Regina just delivered a nasty fastball. Chris observed close, enjoying the way she was throwing today.

Sheets thought he might be asked about this. "I liked Mrs. Crosby." Douglas immediately wished to take back his last words, noticing Chris look up and wince ever so slight. "She seemed very nice and I wanted to make sure she wasn't suffering continued abuse. We became kinda friendly." Another slip of the tongue he sensed. "Just a good sheriff making sure a nice lady wasn't getting knocked around."

"You two became fairly good friends?" Davis asked a shaky hand deputy.

Douglas shrugged, "I'm not sure if I'd say good friends," as Regina cut him off in mid sentence and presented her slider.

Gonzalez, arms folded and leaning back to appear outright composed. "During Marcus' murder trial, the defense attorney asked if you and Sarah were having an affair," hoping with all she had Sheets might offer at her pitch. He swung away.

"That was stricken from the trial detective," pointing his index finger to Regina with an outstretched arm rendering himself quite aggressive. "How did you know that?" Douglas asked, cheeks glowing. Aware he over reacted and cursed himself once again. He didn't know what to say, deciding to sit back and stay silent. "Try to stay cool," Douglas told himself looking at both detectives with a stern face. Silence crept through the shabby little room.

Not one to be intimidated, Regina stood this time and pointed her finger at Sheets. Douglas could tell she was pissed. "I'm fully aware it was stricken from the court records deputy," letting him know she'd done her research. "However, someone present at the trial heard the defense ask you about this," scolding her opponent with force as Chris sensed Regina's anger growing also. He loved it when that vein started to pop out just above her right temple.

"No comment," Sheets said, feeling both livid and intimidated at once, but most of all without discretion. Both Tracy cops, dumbfounded by his response, watched the deputy fidget and tap fingers. Douglas Sheets understood he screwed up again. Knowing each detective assumed him now, to be a murder suspect. They would presume motive. "I'm not on trial for Christ's sake," he told himself and attempted to correct his situation. "I meant to say, not correct, Detective Gonzalez," Sheets amended, facing Regina bearing a sheepish manner, eyes darting about the room, unable to stay focused on her.

This may well be the break Chris and Regina needed. Both cops sensed it. Sheets expected they'd be gnawing at his wounds for a while. They feasted. Asking hard questions for more than an hour, covering his alibis again, pestering him over Sarah Crosby's sloppy murder scene, obtaining more investigation files and in the end examining his truck and double checking license plates. After all, that's what led them to Sonora in the first place.

...

Moving along sprawling oak trees, dry creek beds and flattened ridgelines neither detective had much to say on their drive back to Tracy. Leaving brown foothills behind and entering softer, rolling fields of knee high grasses splattered with boulders and small rocks. A testimony to ancient volcanic eruptions, blowing earth's molten lava from areas now geologically inactive, at rest for the time being. Similar to the way a small town sheriff may have blown a hole into their favor. At least something new and something else to build on. Nowhere near a possible arrest just yet. But maybe, just maybe they've found someone, possibly, connected to their bizarre murder case. Chris's mind was set in the cast of characters making up this drama. One of the strangest, he'd be meeting with later this evening occupied his mind nonstop. Her looks and sexy build wouldn't leave his thoughts easily. "Nothing's going routine so far. It's verging on ridiculous," telling himself in silence of course.

Cresting a small rise on Highway 108, Oakdale lay west a few more minutes and returning once again to straight and level roads. Oakdale, one of California's imaginary edges separating foothill from valley. Separating rich and poor. Separating migrant and desperate. Davis seized on yet another odd feeling about passing through Franny's home town, since they would be connecting in his home town before long. Chris had a passing urge to tell Regina of his upcoming meeting. But no, not this time either. Deciding against. "It would sound too strange keeping this under wraps for so long," he concluded. "I'll let her know at a better time." Reminded again about this cast of weird characters making up the drama. Franny Braden and her older husband, Regina's refuge gang, Mrs. Crosby, Mrs. Patterson, a duck hunter and now a probable bad sheriff in Douglas Sheets. "What a mob," Davis mumbled quietly. Chris wasn't even aware of all the infidelity running amuck!

Regina had something else on her mind. She drove steady, taking in shadows, tree shapes, orchard rows and to her left a heavy flock of Canada geese, drifting low and slow over alfalfa fields searching out resting water after a generous feeding. Their same tracks would intercept Highway 108 straight ahead if she kept her speed constant. Sure enough two dozen geese, give or take, came into full view not twenty yards off the ground. Wings all but locked except for an occasional quiver indicating landing zones close at hand. Her brain turned off the murder case for the time being. The detective had a Thanksgiving date set up and most of tomorrow off from work. Unlike Chris she possessed an indispensable gift. Able to leave work behind and out of mind, for a while. To forget, rest and recharge. Gonzalez wasn't consumed by obsessive addiction, of never letting go until fatigue eventually wins, followed by collapse. She learned from early training it was vital to her performance to step away on occasion. Time off lasted a few days at best however, before her brain begins that slow churn, permitting testimony and evidence to seep back into her consciousness. Soon in hot pursuit. This holiday would be a lucky break however. Chris could pull the ox cart, reviewing transcripts and Sheets' testimony

Not her. Their murder case will wait. Regina had to see Tom Ellis, soon. In reality, most of her attention away from the investigation entertained risqué thoughts about him. Holding him close, discovering his body, exploring his lips, he breathing hard, pressing back very hard. After Thanksgiving, "things would be entirely different," Regina told herself. If she only knew how different.

Franny

Occupying a small round table alone, Franny wished for a double vodka over to keep from jumping in her car and scampering back to safe and cozy Oakdale. Sorry to say, no baristas in this busy Starbucks could deliver the much needed courage. Already past five thirty and Davis still hadn't made contact. Six o'clock was her first deadline. "If he doesn't call by six, I'll have to bag this lousy idea." From behind a glass plated counter emerged a young teenager and an older woman, each armed with pitchers of steaming coffee, refilling cups of customers lingering in the store. No empty tables remained which made Franny wonder, "why free coffee when vacant tables were needed?" However, a rare nice touch for appreciated clients. The absolute last thing the edgy woman needed right now was more caffeine but she accepted graciously, checking her watch yet again. Dinner hour was closing in and still no call. In a way, being coddled with a sense of relief. Thoughts that her plan could be mortally flawed began to surface, leading to a huge disaster. "I can wait a few more minutes and finish my coffee," telling herself, just as the middle aged computer nerd, two tables over, began another move. "Oh Christ, he must've hit the repeat command," Franny joked as mister skinny took two steps in her direction. I.T. was just about to log on and say hello when her phone rang. Lucky for her the cell lay exposed. Ringing clear and reaching for it fast, watching Google's approach. She gave him a shrugging wave off signaling an important call.

"Hello," she answered as another disappointed techie attempted to exit in grace. At the adjacent table another gal sitting alone took in the desperate scene and chuckled into her coffee mug. If both ladies only knew how much this software developer had in his checking account, they might reconsider a warm greeting. "Hello, this is Franny," answering loud.

Chris's connection wasn't the best but recognized Mrs. Braden's voice. "Hello Fra," Chris promptly stopped, deliberated and changed his address. "Hello, Mrs. Braden? Is that you?" shouting, as if speaking louder could improve a lousy connection. "Are you there Mrs. Braden?" glad his car windows were rolled up.

"I'm here detective, thanks for calling," Franny struggled to keep her volume low in the crowded coffee shop but becoming much more concerned with her thorny game plan. "Calm down," she told herself, nerves clicking, snatching her cup of java almost wiping it off the table. Swabbing up a small spill. "Are you still available Detective Davis," playing it formal for now.

"Um, yes. Sure, I have plenty of time," Davis responded. "Let's see, where can we go? I have a small watering hole. Kinda' quiet with decent food. If that's okay with you?"

"Sounds perfect. I'd love to buy you a drink," Mrs. Braden offered, perhaps too personal but feeling it was fine. "How do I get there?" explaining her location, Franny was only a few minutes away as it was, so Chris offered a ride. "Great. That's nice of you detective. See you soon."

Closing her phone then off to the ladies room wanting to look her best. Franny posed for a long inspection in the mirror, turning sideways, making sure her butt looked tight then loosened a button to show some cleavage. Fluffing hair and pulling down an auburn lock, getting it to hang loose just below her temple. In doing so, Mrs. Braden glimpsed a few unnoticed wrinkles flanking the extreme edges of her mature eyes. For some reason it forced an impulsive stop.

"Christ Franny, don't let this end in one big pile of stupid blunders!" She cautioned herself. Erratic thoughts becoming a whirlwind of competing images. Bringing back younger days and a few very stupid mistakes. Her time with Henry for whom she fretted most of all, if this plan blows apart. Loosing Sarah. But most of all tonight, stuck between a police officer investigating her for murder and a bold scheme engineered to keep from being exposed. Mrs. Braden was still a tough person. A devious woman, sexy, clever, full of common sense with an ability to take charge of a situation and forcing it to work in her favor. More than all her inherent qualities, Franny is determined and rarely permits her optimism to wane. Staying in the game, somehow. Her mirror image looked back in confidence lowering tense shoulders and shifting ever so slight to offer an oblique profile then relaxed without thinking about it. "I'll do what I have to do tonight. I've come way too far to let it all unravel for nothing," Franny said, bending at the waist while leaning closer to a determined reflection. Reflection with beauty, plan and resolve. "Too far," she repeated a few more times resembling a rally call, tweaking lipstick on her lower lip.

Chris drove collected into a well occupied parking lot. Safeway, Starbucks, Office Depot, H&R Block, two or three restaurants and a smoothie shop rounded out one of many strip malls shaping a large part of Tracy's economy. Not the highest paying work but the commute is easy on young locals. Detective Davis' thoughts bounced back and forth between questions to ask about this murder case and vivid fantasies involving Mrs. Braden, sporting various themes of red and black lingerie.

Pushing through glass doors as roast coffee filled his nose. Breathing in deep aromas, Chris spotted his suspect rising to greet him. His eyes lit up spotting firm legs glide through a tight black skirt and blouse clinging to waistline and ample bust. A pinch of cleavage at the moment but not too obvious however.

"Save it for later, if more ammunition is needed!" Mrs. Braden told herself.

Chris walked closer trying not to gape but taken by surprise as Franny grasped his offered hand, continuing to move in close. Pressing her cheek to his followed by a quick but firm hug. Davis instinctively slid a hand behind her waist, with a gentle pull hugging back. She felt firm and wonderful losing most thoughts of his murder case. If given consent he'd take this woman to bed right now, unable to resist temptation. "It's nice to see you again detective," Franny spoke very calm. "Tank you," misspeaking but this time catching herself. "Oh God, excuse me," she smiled, turning pink. "Thank you, for giving your time to meet with me. Oh boy," Mrs. Braden laughed her words knowing she was still nervous. Chris laughed too.

"Call me Chris," Davis offered without much thought, wishing to take it back. The detective in him reemerging, wanting to regain control and filled with a sudden fear that it all was getting dangerously close to a tasteless affair. "With a murder suspect no less!" Never remotely close to anything like this before. Davis had met with beautiful woman many times, on many different crime scenes. "Why was this particular woman having such an effect on me?" asking himself. "You've gotta be kidding," as another forbidden urge flooded in to capture erotic impulses once again. Chris scrutinized her mature but still lovely face, loose hair and soft body curves supplying him those much needed doubts. "How could she, looking this superb, be a murderer?"

"I'll ride with you if that's okay," Franny inquired, seeing Chris, whom frankly appeared somewhat dazed. She grinned and raised an eyebrow for confirmation. "It's working."

Davis melted and stammered but managed a coherent response. "Sure. Yes, that sounds fine. No use in taking two cars," babbling in a low voice.

"Let's go," Franny announced, handing away the lead away from our country's more interesting social phenomena. Mrs. Braden always reminded herself, "who could've predicted how the utterly mundane ritual of buying coffee, would be transformed into such a big part of daily life? Amazing!"

It began. Heading to Chris' out of the way tavern, where Franny had to conduct a private meeting and keep everything confidential. Since the detective didn't mention official police business, she assumed for now anyway, this conference would be clandestine. If her plans were going to work, "it must be secret," calculating strategy. She made sure to show a little extra thigh, crossing her legs while riding shotgun in Davis' uncomfortable seat. The detective noticed more than once. They managed brisk small talk centered around Tracy compared to

Oakdale. Mrs. Braden took this opportunity to let Chris know Henry would be out of town until late tomorrow. Davis couldn't help but wonder if this was an easy way of declaring, her husband will never know.

"Good God man, get a grip," muttering to himself, sliding into a very familiar parking lot and vacating as fast as possible. Needing fresh air to dilute an intoxicating smell and hoping to relax a dreaded, noticeable erection! "This lady's making me crazy." Davis took ample time to circle around, crotch tweaking, before opening her car door as if Mrs. Braden had become a quick pick-up date. Swinging both legs boldly across a narrow door opening, skirt riding somewhat high but nimble enough to avoid the awkward, spread eagle departure. Resting two clicking heels on solid pavement. Chris offered his hand to assist, completely dark outside now with a clear sky full of stars. Neither observing flickering points of light tonight. But both did feel a sudden wind blow across the lot pushing against Franny's loose blouse, outlining a lush body as well as her smooth movements.

"I have to keep this professional somehow. Why in hell didn't I just tell Gonzalez about our meeting? It would've kept me in line," scolding himself, holding her chair at a vacant lounge table. They made themselves cozy next to a blazing fireplace.

"Good choice detective," Franny liked the bar setting. Not too formal and perfect for a possible Plan B.

"What are you drinking Mrs. Braden?" Chris proposed wanting to sound businesslike, but in absolute failure.

"I don't know, what are you having?"

"A Blackman," Chris responded forthright.

"Come again?" Franny asked polite, unsure if he was referring someway to his race?

"My drink. It's called a Blackman. Manhattan over with three blackberries instead of a red cherry. Blackberry Manhattan. A Blackman, for short," explaining in length. "I invented it," performing his best Rocky Balboa for effect. He assumed she didn't catch the humor.

Franny shook her head positive. "I like it Rock!" Smiling loud, letting Chris know she approved of his wit. "So it has no racial connotation, you being black of course?" hoping she didn't reek of bigotry.

"Of course not. Nope. Pure coincidence," Chris answered smirking, deceitful, rising to order cocktails.

"I'll have one too," Franny responded with a tone of 'how can I refuse.'

Chris placed his order getting thumbs up from Benny on his classy date. Davis had thoughts of explaining her away as all business, although delivering drinks made it a very hard sell. Choosing to stay mum, nodding affirmative.

"Three sweet blackberries into each glass," Benny confirmed, dropping ripe fruit, collecting cash and pitching the leftover into a skinny, Tuesday night tip jar. "Enjoy yourself my man," delivering a wink to one of his more enjoyable regulars.

"So tell me. Why three blackberries?" accepting her deep copper colored drink with two hands and spilling a few drops onto her skirt. "Symbolism or flavor?" Franny asked.

Davis sat quietly while checking his suspect. "She even looks good under the bar's dim lights," not missing a detail. "You noticed. Very observant," Davis commended lifting a drippy glass, clinking it against Franny's in an impromptu toast. "Those blackberries taste great smothered in sweet vermouth, don't ya think? To me they symbolize three people." Taking a long slow sip peering over his rocks glass.

"I'll bite. Who are they?" she wanted to know swiveling in her chair so an attractive detective could examine the goods, up close. "C'mon detective, give it up." Enjoying the sweet flavor.

"Okay. Three berries for my top three heroes. Frederick Douglass, Martin Luther King and Jackie Robinson," Chris listed the names, taking another short taste, acknowledging Benny's good work. "Perfect!"

"Oh man, I like that. Very clever Mr. Davis," Franny applauded, giving Chris' her most sexy smile. "Aren't you the insightful man. Blackman, very clever indeed."

Davis didn't respond. Sizing up the room but didn't recognize anyone. Benny was knee deep into another NCAA football game of the week, but appeared disappointed with his current investment. Chris turned back to Mrs. Braden enjoying her desirable allure once again. Without thinking, the detective realized he could take control right now with Franny especially calm.

"Are you a clever woman?" Chris asked direct, seeing her face switch to dead serious. Chris knew he'd just changed the current mood tonight. It's back to cop versus suspect, for now. Franny sensed it also.

"I'm very clever, Christopher," attempting boldness. Franny lifted her glass near trembling lips, still able to sip sweet alcohol. She studied her opponent's face, noticing one more time his pleasant looks and sipping again, wondering what might happen later tonight.

"I concluded that too. At your house not too long ago," Davis decided to wade in deeper with bluntness. "So clever lady, what are we up to tonight? Is this business or pleasure?" remaining optimistic she wouldn't close the door right now. "I think you like it this way, Mrs. Braden. You seem typical of a strong woman thriving on contest," Chris told himself wanting to speak his mind but deciding against wading in too far, possibly floating his hat. He looked close as a smile grew just right, over a charming face.

"I'm here to plead my innocence once again detective. You know that.

You're curious, I'm sure. What else can I say to prove my case?" Franny leaned forward sliding her drink on the small table, anxious to see what reaction Davis might present now. She dug a blackberry buried under small ice cubes and crunched down hard, spurting a seed and small drops of juice on one side of her chin. Chris took his paper napkin and gently wiped it away. "Who'd I just eat detective?" Franny asked, wanting to be clever.

"With that splatter I'd have to guess Jackie," answering brave.

"Why's that?" twisting in her chair.

Chris slouched in his chair at this point with arms folded. "Have no idea. Thought it might sound provocative?"

"You have no idea how provocative." Franny grinned.

Davis didn't give much regard to her comment. "Okay Franny. Tell me how you and Henry are innocent," emphasizing her husband's name, anticipating legitimate news.

"I wasn't home on the morning of Marcus' murder." Mrs. Braden stated firm, swirling her Blackman listening to ice cubes click and ring at the bottom of sweating glass. "I wasn't home with Henry having passionate morning sex," stated matter of fact.

Chris didn't speak right away. He wanted to let her words sink in and presenting Franny the chance to offer more information. Without being prodded, Mrs. Braden wasn't about to say anything more. Chris responded, "you and Henry lied to me at your house?" pausing again to think over his situation, not equipped to charge head first into her last comment. "She might be lying right now," reminding himself, aiming to keep her talking. He wouldn't mention repercussions for lying to a police investigator. Just yet! "Go on," he told her, as Davis became consumed by second guessing his awful strategy of keeping this meeting undisclosed.

Franny was growing more and more nervous about Plan A. "I should've just launched Plan B. He may well have plunged headlong into it? God, if I screw this up," thinking she better stay on her toes, continuing new testimony to Davis. "We weren't together that morning," Mrs. Braden repeated herself. She sat still tapping her cocktail glass rim with the bottom of her wedding ring. Neither noticed.

"Okay, where were you? Christ, where was Henry?" Chris imagined if Mrs. Braden was about to throw her husband under a bus. "She can't," Davis told himself. That concept sounded ridiculous right away. Noticing his drink was empty.

Franny continued. "Henry spent Tuesday night, the day before Marcus' murder at his brother's house. That's why he was late getting to work that morning." Feeling strange at the moment, tugging a neckline, scratching her chest, opening a scenic view of cleavage without realizing. Chris took in the exhibition. She didn't know how to proceed so, like a clever girl, "can I have another drink please?" Franny asked, catching Davis off guard, guessing another shot of booze might help to complete Plan A.

"Uh, sure thing," Chris agreed. Needing time to mull over her statements. Franny craved a quick break needing time to regain her composure.

Benny threw his hands in the air for a second time as B.C. had just intercepted Colorado for the third time. "Good God, I gave up nine points thinking the fuckin' Buffalos would roll this team. I'm already down by nineteen, partner." Reaching for two fresh glasses. "Two more Blackmen, marching in?"

"You got it," smiling at a busy bartender.

"You and miss sexy dress getting along all right?" Punching keys to ring up another round. "I'm almost out of blackberries."

"No comment Benny. But your Buffs need some big time defense," Chris nodded to his friend, teasing, just before turning back to miss sexy dress. Davis arrived sitting fast, dying to hear Franny's next move.

"I need this," Franny said, smiling gently back to her detective. "I love these berries," plucking another soft fruit aided by a plastic stir, holding it between her front teeth, sucking off the sweet vermouth before squishing with a firm bite. "Mmm," she hummed, flashing Chris a delayed wink. They both laughed out loud. "I can't believe I just did that," Franny giggled between laughs.

"Henry was late for work, Marcus was gunned down and you were where, Mrs. Braden?" asking assertive and peering through the lady's inviting eyes, expecting truth and emphasizing her title rather heavy.

"Well," Franny exhaled knowing full well, Chris meant business now. "I stayed at," stopping, turning away from the detective. "I stayed at a friend's house," she revealed, pulling a pack of smokes from a black Coach purse.

Chris squinted at Franny's idea of lighting up inside. "Benny won't let you smoke in here," he stated calmly.

"I bet he will," wagering firm then striking a red plastic lighter, firing her cigarette, exhaling a small cloud of thin smoke hanging above their table. Chris didn't move a muscle but clenched his jaw waiting to hear protests from the bar and Benny, expecting a clear cut-off sign. Instead, Benny shrugged his shoulders, reached below his wooden bar and set a small glass ashtray in front of him.

Franny turned to check the bartender, spotting an ashtray. Benny was leaning over the dish, head propped in hands with both elbows anchored firm to the bar with a funny looking smirk covering his thin face. "If you don't mind detective," nearly commanding Davis to fetch her tray. Smoke rising in tight curls like mini campfire spirals up and away on a calm evening. The red hot end of her menthol laden cancer stick glowed bright.

"Yesim missy," Davis responded, connecting a slight bit of racism to Franny's coarse demand.

"Oh right, gimme' a break," denying his notion, watching Davis roll two eyes upward in a show of mock disdain. "It's about manners, not race. You know I'm not the least bit racist," Mrs. Braden assured, never removing her lock, watching him slide a glass dish in her direction. Franny tapped her cigarette, brushing ash along a shiny clean ashtray. She blew smoke between her lips from deep inside her lungs upward, away from Chris. "See, I knew he wouldn't mind," presenting a clear victory facade across her contented face. Davis never stopped sucking up her middle-aged beauty.

"You're very clever," Davis said showing a combination of sarcasm and compliment. Staying quiet for a moment to ponder his next move. It was important to let Franny know he still meant business. "So, you mentioned a friend's house? Spent the night?" he asked blind and as if taking a hit from a vodka bottle, Davis just figured why she wanted this meeting. Mrs. Braden was going to tell him about an affair. "Jesus man, how thick are you?" disappointed for not realizing her motive.

Chris squirmed, wanting to make sure his thoughts were in sync. "I don't know if it's my place to ask but it sure sounds like you're admitting to a affair. Am I off base here?" Davis ventured, waiting to see her react. Franny kept still, staring off toward another room avoiding the detective. Pulling deep on a half finished cigarette. It seemed evident to Chris, Mrs. Braden was thinking hard but her façade stayed calm, maybe even calculating. "You are a clever girl," Chris sensed. The clever girl failed to respond forcing Chris' hand.

"What's his name?" Davis asked pulling a small notebook from his coat pocket, ready to write him in. "You know I have to confirm this. Does Henry know?"

"Oh, no way," answering without hesitation.

"I need his name," Chris requested again, polite but feeling sympathetic and uncomfortable. Waiting. Franny stayed silent, smashing out her cigarette, sucking her half empty Blackman.

"His name?" she said with a question and commentary in her manner. Although not demonstrating tension, Mrs. Braden had no clue she'd be this nervous. Even beginning a brief bout of nausea. "I can't do this," she warned herself shifting back and forth, confined, more like a prison cell, running a hand through her hair twice, twirling her drink, digging someplace for that last drop of potential guts. Chris asked for a name once again. "Oh what the hell," she said subdued but audible to Davis. "Evelyn, her name is Evelyn." Taking a long drink this time from her sweet cocktail unable to face the detective but noticed how the news stopped him cold. Franny still didn't look into his face, choosing to stay aloof, appearing calm under fire. She knew he was staggered. Like a closing pitcher just giving up a late game homer. Unable to think.

Chris, putting it mild, was dumbfounded! "Are you serious? A woman? I don't know if I believe you Fra....Mrs. Braden?" His mouth drooped noticeably. The murder case vanished entirely as a whole new scene of erotic images rushed in. An excited, overworked libido became overwhelmed.

Gadwalls

Nestled in a narrow opening between two stands of thick tules, both gadwalls floated relaxed and secure. At last, locating safe areas on two separate refuges. One at Los Banos Wildlife Area and another a few miles north inside the San Luis Area complex, with preferred shallow, open water and plentiful food. These ponds were located in areas of refuge closed zones where hunting and public access of any kind was prohibited. Safe tonight, but each gadwall was always on guard for loud noises which might erupt any morning. The hen suffered from strong urges to continue their journey south, moving into southern California before winter's main migration took hold. She felt more secure in their own abilities to locate safe water and food, with less chance of being decoyed into dangerous fields by large flocks of stupid ducks.

Her dilemma grew this evening. She sensed the drake's comfort level building each day. Comfort that leads to mistakes and careless approaches. The hen had to stay on guard and stay connected to her mate. She nuzzled in close, rubbing her small bill against the drake's soft, warm neck. Nibbling then biting tender at small feathers to reinsure their bond. Feeling good as a pair.

Chris and Franny

Detective Davis felt awful about his rude comment which he considered to be just another brainless outburst. "You have my apologies Mrs. Braden. That was uncalled for."

"It's still Franny, Christopher."

Chris knew she was upset, refusing to look at him direct. Even after trying to lighten things up with her attempted drollness. "Please Franny," following her lead, "I apologize." She rolled her eyes upward, which Chris presumed, could lead her to an emotional break. Instead, Mrs. Braden lowered her gaze to meet his, square. Davis was clueless how she might react now.

"Oh, c'mon detective. It's all right," Franny reported, speaking very low but unconcerned, which surprised the detective once again. "I'd probably respond the same way," she spoke with all smiles. "I won't hold it against you. Hell, I feel an ounce of relief finally telling someone. It's been my secret for too long." Unusual calm covered both her tone of voice and body language.

Chris' attitude changed and decided to press on with Franny unruffled and completely composed. "I will have to confirm this with Evelyn. What's her last name and where does she live?" Chris asked pulling a pen from his jacket and fumbling for a notepad.

"Oh no. Oh no. No way detective," Franny instructed a wide eyed cop, signaling a stop with her waving hands mimicking traffic control. "I'm not under arrest and I don't have to give that information. Not yet." Unsure if she was correct, legally, desperate to make Davis see her side. "Besides, this isn't a formal police examination," speaking firm. "I'm here to tell you, neither Henry or myself had anything to do with Marcus' murder. But please, what I just told you must remain in your confidence. Henry can't find out and I know you don't want," searching for a proper word but in the heat of the moment, never came. "You don't want to expose me. That's why I came here tonight." Franny was ringing her hands sweaty, nervous, stopped, then reached across the table to embrace Chris' hands. She stayed quiet knowing Detective Davis fully comprehended her plea.

"Henry has no idea about you and your partner?" Chris asked, making every effort to uphold sensitivity.

"As far as I'm aware, he doesn't know and it must stay that way," Mrs. Braden answered direct and honest.

Chris understood Franny was right. Unless formally charged, "and no judge in his or her right mind would issue an arrest warrant on my flimsy, hearsay evidence," Chris reasoned to himself wishing for another drink. "She doesn't have to give more information. If I got something significant tonight in this manner, it's unlikely to demonstrate probable cause anyway." Deciding not to pursue for now.

"I'm not about to ruin a marriage tonight," Chris told Franny. She tilted her head sideways as Davis immediately saw her relax. "She's won this round," speaking to himself, biting his lip, staying quiet. "I kind of hoped she was here tonight for other reasons." Once again eyeing the elegant older woman, admiring her soft face and subtle flaws. His mind turned wild, conveying images of her and Evelyn and how they looked together, how they dressed, how they spoke, how they moved with each other, how they enjoyed one another, staring intense. Franny stared right back with a fragile but inviting glow. Not a bit of animosity or threat in her eyes. In fact, Chris could read her inviting look like large print. By instinct, Davis recognized the sexy woman was aware of his imagination buried deep in scenes of her and a faceless lover. They stayed connected for a few moments, she shifted her legs, then together broke into controlled, soft laughter. Chris was much more embarrassed than Franny!

Mrs. Braden, red faced, swept a cluster of drooping hair to one side of her pink cheek. "What can I say Mr. Detective, I am what I am." Franny morphed into feeling warm and fuzzy now that Plan A seems to have concluded better than expected. "Hell, he's kinda into it, I think?" Speculating. Now she recognized Plan B. Should I initiate Plan B? Like some sort of balls-out field general consumed by a surprise victory. "Keep up the attack," held everything running through her mind. She believed a successful Plan B could keep her and Henry clear until this whole murder ordeal passed. A more confident, mature player willing to gamble a little more. Tingling sensations of dominance and success ran up her legs, hips, stomach and the back of her neck! More than confident, she felt very sexy sitting in front of her handsome black detective, enjoying the moment immensely. "How could I lose now?" assuming her plan flew way above the detective's good sense. "I'm the one in control here," she reminded herself, admiring Chris' features, growing aroused.

Little did she know, after Chris recovered from his initial shock, he retreated back to his usual state of dissecting statements and observing body vibe. He refocused on Franny's proclaimed infidelity and innocence. "I wonder, is she one hundred percent believable? Obviously she can't be trusted. How will I verify her claims as legit?" Asking himself just as the sexy woman, fresh removed from the proverbial closet, squirmed and wiggled in her chair. Mrs. Braden leaned back lighting another cigarette. A pall of smoke exhaled through her puckered lips and drifted just above Chris' head. She sustained an 'I'm going to eat you alive' presence which Chris found humorous but at the same time, very arousing.

"Whatever you are, I'm finding you interesting Mrs. Braden. How about one more drink? Are you hungry?" Chris asked hoping she wanted to stay longer.

"Please detective. It's Franny."

Tom

Gonzalez flipped her cell to receive a call. "Hello."

"Hello. Regina?" Tom's voice came across to some extent excited but not urgent.

"Is this Tommy gringo?" Knowing it was and glad to hear his voice again. She fancied a call for no other reason than to say hi. Following, for no apparent reason, with a shiver of apprehension concluding his Thanksgiving offer was about to fall flat. "All right, what's up?" droll and let down, breeding empty feelings of Mr. Ellis leaving her hanging.

"Hey, I was thinking about Thanksgiving," giving Regina her first bad impression of a guy she really started to like.

"Okay, I'm guessing something's come up," she responded limp, disappointed and pissed off for backing out on a promised date. "Men suck so bad sometimes." She wanted to scream, bursting red faced and stalking her kitchen. Hushed!

"Well yeah, sort of." Ellis turned sheepish and Regina expected his regret. "I've been kind of busy with work and haven't had time to pick up any wine. Would you mind bringing a decent bottle, when you come down Thursday? It's hard to get much better than Manoschevitz around here. Be glad to pay ya for the trouble.

Tense shoulders dropped as relaxation invaded her bloodstream. "That's sort of cute," Gonzalez told herself, undergoing a day-night change of relief. "Oh God, heck no. But you told me that already in Gustine. I think you just wanted to call me, gringo," laughing into her phone.

"You know, I couldn't remember if I mentioned the wine or not," Tom stumbled for his words, "but you're always nice to talk to." Gushing into his phone

"I have a few Livermore reds on hand. I'd love for you to try them." More release set in. They were still on and Gonzalez couldn't help but think how stupid she acted. "I'm looking forward to Thursday," speaking with a genuine, soothed tone. All was good again.

"Great. Hey, me too. Just don't expect a traditional Thanksgiving menu. I'm working up surprises," Tom alerted, feeling good after sensing Regina's lively interest. They exchanged small talk for a few minutes. Each one growing more at ease the longer they spent chatting. Their friendship, which all it was at this point, was becoming comfortable to them both. So far, not much worry what was being said or trying to impress each other. The first hurdle of a potential romance had already been breached as an easy calm set in, much like old friends falling in love. Regina kept thinking how pleasant this Thanksgiving could be. Finally, a holiday spent alone with someone quite uncomplicated and more than easy to be around. Her mind wondered as Tom broke into details about extra hunting gear he managed to scrounge up. It eventually got her attention and she was impressed.

"Some might be a little baggy, but it should be fine to start out. We're still on for Saturday, I hope?" Which was his real reason for calling. In fact, Tom had all the red wine he needed, never running too low on the enchanting grape. He wanted to make sure she wasn't all talk concerning their hunt this weekend.

Regina relaxed even more. Relieved. She wondered if Tom had been blowing smoke about his offer of duck hunting. "You bet we're on. I'm gitten' me a limit of them birds!" Using her best redneck imitation. She expected some sort of reaction from the other end, hoping a small laugh, but barely received steady breathing from her future dinner date. "You still there Mr. Ellis?"

"I'm still here Miss Gonzalez. Please, no more hick impressions," Tom begged, hoping he didn't insult her with his humor. "Maybe she takes me to be a country bumpkin?" Wondering if this hunting invitation was still a good idea.

"Uhm, that didn't go over too well did it? How about we let it go at that, so I don't come across any more the fool," she giggled like a child, failing her attempted gaffe.

"Sounds good Regina," agreeing and laughing too, letting her know he wasn't too serious.

"Git some shuteye." Gonzo revealed a small slice of her personality to Tom, quite unable to avoid an additional jab.

"Oh boy, good night."

Regina hit her red button after a short wait. A loud dial tone made her wish for more conversation. "Why not?" she prodded herself, pushing the redial button. When Tom answered hello with a sizeable laugh, it was easily read as affectionate. "I'm really looking forward to Thanksgiving," she whispered without the slightest hint of inhibition.

Tom translated her comment as sincere, giving him good reason to feel great for a change. "Me too. You git some shuteye gorgeous," he waited for the detective to say good night, listening for dial tone before hanging up. "I hope this goes the way I need it to go," Tom said to himself.

Franny and Chris

The unusual pair ate a laid-back dinner. Chris, finishing only half of his rare steak sandwich. Franny nibbled away at a side of seasoned cole slaw, accompanying her hot and spicy fried clams. Chris recommended the deep fried onion rings. Many nights he and Benny would put away a stack of beer battered Vidalia onions while griping loud during football games, among dead glasses of micro-brew. Chris and Franny continued nursing cocktails and turning slightly numb from excess alcohol, thus disposed to speak free of charge. Talking of their pasts, young loves, children and marriage. Franny dished out even more secrets between spoonfuls of a caramel sundae shoveled to a gulping Chris. Not quite matching her disclosed bombshell of sexual alternatives but still handing out small morsels of insight into a high strung but controlled woman. Chris decided, "now was probably as good as ever to press on her again."

"So, Henry doesn't know about your," Davis pondered his best choice of words to use, "your other life?" speaking the last two words with opinion but also courtesy.

Franny had to move the focus away from her, fearing she might say something stupid or at least suspicious. "I must turn tables on you mister detective. With some charm however," plotting her quiet strategy in a devious mind and spooned the final scoop of vanilla into Chris' mouth, licking the spoon clean with her red lips and tongue. Chris noticed the procedure but didn't know what to make of it. "I don't think Henry knows anything, but one is never a hundred percent sure," she was trying someway to change this discussion.

"What about you detective. Any hot secrets you wanna share with me?" Franny maneuvered to shake Davis loose with some sharp prodding. At first, seeming like it might work as Chris pushed his plate away considering her question. Lips puckering. "I'm nowhere near your league madam!" Drawing a deep but covered laugh from Mrs. Braden, followed by a soft clap of her hands. "Nothing exciting about my past. Usual stuff, married, happy for a while, an affair, divorced with a daughter I rarely see." Davis cut it short right there, suspecting Franny's intention.

"Mmm, an affair," came her juicy response which Chris expected. Franny leaned way forward resting full on both elbows. Her heavy breasts positioned on the table top with generous cleavage exposed, catching Chris' rambling eyes take in the view with quick peeks. She waited, permitting her open viewport to linger before speaking and letting it all sink in. "Tell me about her," she inquired polite.

"My affair?" Chris responded, looking away embarrassed, ill at ease about a topic he avoided to discuss. Seeing Benny smile, holding one arm straight up. "His team must be back in the hunt," he said, hearing the announcer yelling, "touchdown Buffs!"

"Not her. Your wife," Franny said in a character new to Chris. Almost a concerned tone similar to a person yearning to console a dear friend.

"My wife?" he wondered, caught off guard this time.

"Yes. What's her name?"

Davis was forced to think for a moment, unsure how much to tell. "Uhm, well let's see. Attractive, good mother, didn't trust me," as Franny cut in to stop him.

"What's her name?" She requested once again, louder.

"Her name," Chris sighed bringing up flashbacks of both good and bad days. "Nora," answering deadpanned, catching a glimpse of Benny, still excited, indicating Colorado must be threatening to score again. Franny issued Davis a strange look once more turning her head sideways, squinting, grinning, biting down on her lower lip.

"What now?" Chris wanted to know why Mrs. Braden wore a mocking expression. "Her moods were all over the place," Davis told himself.

"Nora!?" Franny paused. "Kind of a plain Jane for a black girl don't ya think? You don't seem the type to hook up with a Nora?" She accepted a refill on her coffee from an older waitress, waiting on her to finish before continuing their awkward discussion.

"For a black girl? You're getting very close to the racial line, don't ya think." The detective was poking fun at her choice of words while making it known, old attitudes about race wouldn't be tolerated. "I don't know what you're talking about." Davis concluded it might be best to stop right here.

"C'mon detective, lighten up. You know I'm not the bigoted type," redeeming herself of any prejudice against the black woman but strange enough, willing to launch an attack on her character. "I'm betting it was a boring marriage. Was it?" Mrs. Braden spoke in a restrained volume, hardly described as bellicose. But coming across well aware what a boring marriage was about. Another loss for words from the detective. He tweaked his neck a few times trying to relieve some useless stress, thinking over Franny's assessment.

"It was a boring marriage." Chris stared through the bottom of his coffee cup. Almost empty. Associating his vacant cup with time spent married to Nora. Empty. No passion to remember. Boring was the perfect word. He knew Franny had his marriage figured spot on and she wasn't the least bit racist. "I guess it was at that." he replied wistfully. "Nora tried her best. I made it boring however. My commitment was lacking and then I turned cheap, with a low life affair." He stopped talking but Franny knew he had more to say. More he wanted to tell her. More blame to relieve.

Franny kept to herself. She regretted for coming across so cavalier about his marriage. "I shouldn't have brought it up that way. It's mean to make light of another person's marriage. I shouldn't have done that." She repeated to herself. "It's interesting however," permitting her scheming side to peep back in. She thought again why she was here tonight then told herself to stay on target.

"Enough about my personal life. You're still the suspect Mrs. Braden." Davis had to let Franny know he wouldn't be manipulated for long. "Could you pull the trigger? That's still up for grabs."

"You know I didn't do it detective," speaking right away, removing her bosom from the table and folding arms in front like a no trespassing sign, giving Davis a stern look. "I thought we moved beyond all that Chris?" Mrs. Braden asked.

"I'm not so sure Franny. Just not so sure," Chris said truthfully glaring straight into her surprised wide open eyes. "I do know one thing Mrs. Braden."

"And what's that Mr. Davis?" Displaying her not so scared smirk.

"It probably isn't the best time to bring this up, but what the fuck, I've had enough alcohol tonight and I don't really care anymore." Franny sat back in slight recoil at his curious F-bomb then sort of giggled at Chris' crude language.

"Kind of cute actually," she thought to herself.

"I am positive Mrs. Braden you know something," Davis said very serious. "You're hiding something and I'm going to find out what it is. I believe you have important information about this murder and sooner or later you're going to give it to me. In fact lady, I think," pausing to elevate the drama, "you want to give it to me!" Watching her movements and expressions for incriminating reactions to be unveiled. Franny reacted swift and rather calm, bringing her ample cleavage back into play. Resting her chin atop two clenched fists, delivering yet another warm sexy grin. Chris identified her look and everything behind it, admitting to himself. "Not what I expected."

"Christopher Davis, now I'm the one who doesn't have a clue," delivering her own dramatic pause, "what the hell you're talking about. But, if you like, I could show you one thing I've been hiding away." Telling herself Plan B had been launched and yearning, somewhat hard, Chris would turn her down. But Franny's skilled acting this evening left no clue, indicating an ounce of trepidation. Holding the detective in her sight, fixed hard like a sniper, she leaned back appearing casual. She waited his next move but could tell, easily, Chris debated her offer. Serious too! "What's it going to be detective?" Desperate to ask him aloud but continuing to hold her cards, letting her policeman choose. "I wonder?" Franny's mind raced at this point. "I didn't fuck it up, did I?"

"Shall we go?" Chris responded, with little emotion detected but rather anxious. Rising fast, which Franny assumed signaled an abrupt end to their evening. Standing next to his suspect in a gentleman like manner, assisting with her chair, she stood and let Chris help with her jacket. He brushed her shoulders after a delicate pull of trapped hair from a wedged collar. Both hands sweeping along each side of a bare neck causing Franny's skin and thighs to tingle with excitement. Mrs. Braden thanked Benny for the Blackman cocktails and Davis offered fast condolences on yet another poor gambling pick, bidding goodnight.

A tipsy detective held her car door and once more shapely legs were flashed prior to seating herself. They maintained perfect quiet tracing their way back to a now closed Starbucks. Franny rubbed her hands together to get some circulation into cold fingers. Nighttime temperatures were dropping fast throughout the Central Valley. Halfway back, she tucked her balled up fingers under his chin and slid a bit closer to maintain constant contact. Shoulder to shoulder. They both wondered what would happen next.

"Good God, should I bed this woman tonight?" Chris wrestled with himself, as out of control sensual urges approached a decisive state. "Should I?" debating pro and con, indicating a final degree of self-discipline, turning sharp into a near empty parking lot after running a stop sign which neither player noticed!

"Here goes," Franny assumed. In her mind a well placed heated kiss or two might have the same result as an all-night stand. Davis killed the ignition, hesitated, not yet ready to say the right words. It didn't matter, as her fragrance filled his senses followed soon after by a hand probing gently along his stomach and chest, causing side muscles to flex and quiver. He was losing control and caving in as Mrs. Braden's mouth moved close to his neck the way a predatory lioness intends to silence entrapped prey. Her hand slipped up from his breast, fanning fingers outward, wiggling around his neck and pulling closer. He could smell her deep breaths pushing hard to his lips, covering a willing mouth. Both breathing fast and hard. Franny was struck by how aroused she became as earlier fears seemed to evaporate, permitting erotic impulses to take over Plan B. She shifted out of control wanting to feel this detective deep inside. Fantasies cascaded into her mind containing raw images of sweating nude figures, his black skin in perfect contrast with her pale body. Desire racked Mrs. Braden. Wanting hands, lips and tongue to flick aggressive across her heated breast, nipples, stomach and lower still. Pulling harder to remain locked in place while her investigating tongue probed at liberty, inside, bold and unashamed.

Chris, caught fixed in the moment, lost all thought of Franny being an older woman. Tasting every bit as sweet and soft as any other women in his sex life. Her aggression filled him with passion as blood flow between his legs grew even further, building an exciting spectacle of her being this aggressive with Evelyn. Elaborate fantasies of two women pushed his control to the limit.

Reflected light flashed bright from passing headlights, reflecting off their mirrors, illuminating the car ever so slight. Just enough, allowing each occupant to capture a flash look at one another. Chris reached over to caress a blushing cheek as they glimpsed each other between sexy embraces. Distant vehicles provided a faint glow like soft candles. Franny panted deep forcing an affectionate smile. She lowered her eyes, then pulled her black lover close again, craving his soft lips. Chris allowed his hand to drop to her heavy breasts, fondling her firm. Rubbing and exploring both, filling two hands as fingers gracefully pinched and swirled along tight, raised nipples. She pleasured in his touch and knew it couldn't stop now, being long ago since aroused to this level so fast. She breathed deep again helping his hands explore, imploring Chris' touch, forcing his lips apart with her maddening tongue. Neither wanted to separate as sensual erotic impulses grew higher and higher. She tried forcing his body even closer, wanting to feel his full weight crush down on her. Plan B became something of a farce at this point, realizing this idea could become a regular event if it felt this good every time!

The words rolled out like something from an abysmal country western song. "Mrs. Braden, we have to say good night." As Franny seized his hand keeping it situated to her breast, peering up to see Chris and a pair of disappointed, sorrowful eyes. Their heads and shoulders swayed as every outward pant exhaled a large volume of breath. She returned with a dumfounded, rag doll gaze wondering what went wrong.

"What? Are you sure?" straining her neck outward to reach his lips, hoping he might cave in altogether. Not so much to complete Plan B anymore. Franny's game plan had been transformed into fulfilling sensual wishes. Her essential objective was to keep his touch in place and pulled his hand in desperation, further down between her spreading legs. Moaning pleasantly before forcing his fingers to slide in vital contact where it compelled her most. She exhaled loud into Chris' ear, letting him know how much she hunted his body now.

Chris wouldn't permit her lips to linger this time, sliding his hand away albeit pretty slow, from Franny's warm, moist upper thighs. With anyone else, Chris knew he wouldn't possess the stamina necessary to stop now. His career put an end to what certainly could've been a bizarre evening of disloyal gratification and absolute pleasure.

"You have a long drive home. Besides what about Evelyn?" Exhibiting a friendly smile unable to refrain from commenting on her lifestyle. Imagining himself as Evelyn's competition, striking a funny note how Henry didn't factor in the same way?

"She'll understand," Franny replied moving closer once again. Letting her hand fall along his inside thigh, moving all five curious fingers about his critical zone, grasping firm and holding on.

"Okay, let's call it," Davis reached a warm hand just in time, looking straight into her eyes with implied seriousness. But once lowering his stare Franny felt unconvinced he was able to stop. She continued her upward advance as a quick flash of reflected light revealed a surreptitious smile covering her face. Chris forced the situation now, devouring her smaller hand, folding all five fingers back into a tight fist.

Mrs. Braden caved in, understanding Plan B must be suspended, withdrawing smiles, dropping her eyes and feigning slight embarrassment. All the time telling herself, "that's fine, I've accomplished what I needed." Scooting away from the detective just after delivering a rapid kiss on his warm cheek. Composing herself, fluffing auburn hair in the mirror, tugging a ruffled flimsy blouse, pulling her skirt down to proper depth as Chris came around, opening her door once again like a gentleman.

Feeling a vague broken heart but in reality he suffered more of an unfilled craving, seeing his prospective lover exit. Compounded by a steady breeze, icy cold, forcing Mrs. Braden to lurch close struggling to keep warm. The slightest whisper of moving air blew wisps of reddish locks over cheeks and forehead. To Chris, Franny appeared to be all legs and titts moving graceful through his mind, unable to stop intense sexual urges eclipsing his entire body. It became arduous and painful knowing distance was about to grow between them while a sudden urge to grab her up into his arms and take her to his bedroom had to be defeated. Not tonight. It wasn't possible on this night.

"Goodnight detective. Maybe another time?" not offering much of a goodbye as the lioness slithered into the driver's seat fastening her belt, preparing to leave.

"Maybe," Chris whispered.

Franny nodded holding her lips pursed, shifted into drive offering only a sly look from the corner of her eye. Glowing red tail lights amplified Chris' urge that much further.

"Who has a date and who has family tomorrow?" Maria solicited the luncheon committee, happy faced as always, dying to know what was happening within the gang over Thanksgiving. Wednesday's lunch marked the end of their work week, having the remaining afternoon free to begin a long holiday week-end. "Denise, I'm sure you have family, like myself," the Mexican gal added. Observing the only married woman at their lunch table with raised eyebrows waiting for a response, heaping in a fork full of cheese enchilada and sour cream.

"Family it is for me. My sister and her two children are joining us," Denise reported to the gang. "It's Sabrina's first Thanksgiving since her messy divorce. We'll see how she does." Churning a robust pepper mill above a plate full of Shrimp Caesar. "Arthur's grilling the turkey this year," stating proud and taking a small bite of crisp romaine, chewing slow, all the while displaying a genuine look of concern on her face.

"What's wrong Big D?" Pam jumped in challenging her friend, knowing without a doubt Denise had zero confidence in her husband to get the job done. "C'mon, cook the damn bird for four hours and cut into the thigh. If you see a lot of pink, continue cooking. It's that easy," Pam insisted twisting her head back and forth while giving Regina a subtle wink. "I'm sure, between you and Arthur, the bird will be cooked just fine."

"And what are you up to Pam," Regina butted in changing the sensitive subject between two polar opposites.

"I'll be breaking bread with his family. Nothing but my best behavior and cautiously dressed." Pam noted.

"Boo, boring," Maria bellowed out. "We were hoping for turkey and a threesome. Perhaps a little something weird with a Thanksgiving drumstick!"

Raising Pam's eyebrows as an innocent look covered her face, saying, "I'm really not that type of girl," joining muffled laughs squeezed from Denise and Regina, well aware her threesome episode would continue to haunt for some time.

Maria's aim then turned squarely on Regina. "Okay detective, your turn. To Aunties again?" achieving full attention from everyone at the table. Lengthy silence ensued as Regina made a clumsy lift of a stout fish taco turning her head sideways to try a polite mouthful. She licked her index finger dripping with white sauce before letting go of the soft tortilla. All the while weighing how much smarter it would be to just confirm with tradition, avoiding any undue hype. She couldn't resist however, leaning back in a hard smirk, finishing her last bite. Pam knew going away the detective had something fresh.

"Regina, you're pink and trying to act to 'sereno'. Que pasa senora de la casa?" Maria demanded shifting into Spanish feeling something new was in 'al aire.'

"What the hell," Gonzalez declared in silence. "Denise you might appreciate this?" Shifting only her eyes toward the married gal who just put a finishing touch on one last cherry tomato, still all ears.

"Met a guy. A little older but very cute. He's cooking Thanksgiving dinner tomorrow. All I have to do is show up with a couple bottles of red and a low cut blouse." Regina laughed, red faced, eyes wide and glowing. It made her feel great but noticed Denise presenting a face full of combined doubt and surprise. Pam and Maria were still chuckling, each offering high fives to a blushing detective.

Denise was first to respond. "You never mentioned any new guy. We're all supposed to let the group know about new men we might be sleeping with." Lowering her head but glaring at Pamela sitting across from her.

Pam responded with eyes wide open, tongue hanging out and her head shaking like a zombie. Everybody, including two construction workers at a table behind, got a kick out of her sarcastic reaction! She flashed each guy a sexy smile, proud they were watching. Denise couldn't help but break down at her friend's ridiculous face, telling Regina, "I expect a full report on Monday morning."

"Mmm, me too," Pam whispered which all three girls knew very well what she wanted to hear.

"I'm talking about dinner you skanky bitch," Denise blurted out a bit too loud, getting more attention from the construction workers and surprising the gang into a full round of snickers and giggles. It was rare to hear the married lady talk in such low brow editorial.

"I'm not," Pam shot back stealing a peek at Regina in her way of conveying, " enjoy your sex young lady!" Maria, not to be outdone, demanded itemized particulars on both food and sex. The former being number one on her list.

"We'll see ladies. But I may be keeping things mysterious for a while." Knowing absolute, she had to keep Tom under wraps until the murder investigation concluded.

"Not fair," Denise shouted out. "Local boy?" following up, eager to get any info.

"Uh, nope," Regina answered smoothly twisting her head side to side in negative mode.

"Where's he from?" Maria chimed in.

"Uh, nope," Regina cut it off right there, unwilling to offer another scrap. "Let's go girls. It's the holidays."

One by one four women made their goodbyes, offered best wishes and looked forward to meeting again on Monday. Tomorrow morning The Gang of Four would head in opposite directions. One staying put, one north, one east. Regina would be the only one heading south.

■■■

Midday and bright sunshine filled the valley. Dissimilar from summertime day to day glare. A string covering ten days of calm, dry weather followed by predictable foggy mornings. Each day's high temperature dropped a degree or two, transpiring a comfortable, inviting, relaxed Central Valley. Forecasts called for a pleasant but cool Thanksgiving Day with a change due later in the evening. Friday would see a noticeable transformation with high clouds streaming in, pushed across by strong northwest winds. Winds that will change everything. Colder air, more clouds, light rain with snow in the Sierra.

For now it was all satisfying as Regina breathed it in deep. Unaware of an impending winter storm and didn't much care. More important would be the welcomed break in her uneventful routine with perhaps, some wicked immoral behavior thrown in for good measure. No research, questions or meetings. Chris will handle their investigation over the holiday. This weekend was about Regina and her change. One quick stop to check on a new friend, before going home.

Sheets

"Are you nuts? What the fucking hell is wrong with you? It's the day before Thanksgiving and you're going out?" Loretta Sheets, was growing more and more distraught, realizing their severance increased almost daily. Her marriage was failing fast and Doug was acting as though he cared less.

"I'll be home tonight. Just a few hours. It's important I meet with someone about a case," Douglas' half hearted appeal to Loretta intended to sound convincing but he knew she wasn't buying. In his fractured mind however, it no longer mattered. He trusted in his detached abilities to eventually wear Loretta down. She continued her argument almost begging him to stay home. He didn't pay much attention, letting her words spin about the room like dry leaves swirling on a breezy afternoon. "You don't have the money, the strength or the confidence to go it alone," telling himself with a dead blank stare and very little to stop him. "You go on, and on, and on lady. I have a few things to do," thinking how pathetic his wife appeared at the moment.

Loretta cried out, "don't do this to me. I'm your wife and Douglas." She stopped abrupt, cutting off, overwhelmed as a combination of emotional sting and intense menstrual cycle filled her heart and metabolism to a boiling point. She had to stop and sit. Tears welled up, stomach trembled, the back of her throat sensed immediate vomiting could be possible. Mrs. Sheets lowered her heavy head into open hands, eyes facing down and odd enough noticing a myriad of small food stains scattered over the table cloth. Douglas observed her form from a long distance, no empathy in sight. "If you continue like this, my husband," almost yelling the last two key words and shaking her head in a mocking tone to get his attention, "I'll be forced to go to the police." Stopping her husband in his tracks just as he reached the front door.

Douglas whirled, stretching two potent strides toward his shaken wife. "Police? I am the fucking police Loretta!" Breathing heavy in and out with both fists clenched tight. "You don't have anything to tell the police. Do you understand, my dearest wife?" he said, holding a combined look of venomous hostility and heightened concern. Delivering the last three words with his own sarcastic malice. Right now, Douglas realized he'd have to intimidate Loretta to keep her in line. "Eventually you'll surrender, you stupid bitch," talking to himself in a reassuring way. "Don't even try standing up to me," stating his warning calm, clear and matter of fact.

"I'll be back later tonight. Tomorrow we'll have Thanksgiving dinner," Douglas told Loretta in a low pitched, commanding voice while gathering keys, wallet and watch. His wife said nothing, too scared and intimidated to tender any sort of battle. As Douglas left the house, Loretta could barely keep up with a flood of tears flowing along a reddened face and almost trickling into her left ear.

Attempting comfort, telling herself it was fortunate Lucy wasn't home to witness mom and dad behaving so poor. She would be picking up her daughter soon, at a neighbor's house, after playing with her one good friend. "I can make Thanksgiving happy for Lucy at least," Loretta sobbed out loud. "No use in wrecking her holiday. She deserves that much, and more." Lighting a brief image of her much too young heartbroken child. Which triggered yet another crying episode as Loretta Sheets conceded her marriage was certainly finished. Wiping tears and rising from her chair, she had to refresh. Reflecting on the violent outburst, her husband became more than merely upset or angry. Douglas, a sworn protector of the law, ventured into a sudden state of violence and from his last words, as well as looks, Loretta understood the man she married was now capable of anything.

"Hell, he probably could kill us both and not care in the least," frightening herself with a stark realization how vulnerable her and Lucy had become. Wiping both cheeks with a cold wet towel, sitting to recompose and swab wet eyes. Without warning, the prior urges for tears disappeared, as Loretta's attention focused solid on her predicament. This time she didn't recoil into her usual bubble of nervous trepidation. "I'm going to learn how to fight this psycho, for Lucy's sake," swearing and surging with a small amount of new-fangled fortitude and a dose of a mother's reckless obligation toward her child's well being. Getting herself ready to fetch the one real love of her life, Loretta strode throughout their home, muttering words of regret and revenge. "I'm going to bide my time quietly, until the moment's right. You're going to pay for all this Douglas. Somehow, I'm going to burn your ass, you lousy fuck!"

...

Douglas exited a long bumpy driveway steering his dark blue truck toward Highway 108, planning a westward ride in search of someone or something, no clue as to what he might find. Possessing only a full tank of gas and two blue lined paper stick-ups. One with two addresses scribbled in. Not too familiar with the city of Tracy but his Google directions on the second page, illustrated a routine course. Tracy Boulevard exit south, followed by two left turns, a right turn halfway down Portage Drive to Arlington Street and a quick left onto Anaheim Drive. Left side, two houses down. Mrs. Patterson lived right there and with a lot of luck, "I might just catch her coming home," Douglas told himself passing a slow moving mini-van lumbering its way to grandma's house, someplace west. Thoughts, images and ideas whirled in and through his mostly eccentric head. Possibilities bloomed. One had him following her to a front door, just about ready to close but able to force entry. Maybe two quick gunshots at very close range would silence the old bag, thereby keeping a secret hidden. A secret lying in tomb. A secret known only to Douglas and Beatrice. A secret Mrs. Patterson promised never to reveal.

Ideas surfaced ever more wild. "Perhaps waiting 'til dark with a simple knock," Sheets mumbled, rehearsing peculiar scenarios over and over in his ever mounting, flawed rational. "Hello, Mrs. Patterson, Tracy police. I'd like to ask you a few questions about the Crosby murder." Conjuring up morbid images of a quiet kill. His imagination continued with scenarios of stolen items of value. Cash, jewelry, purse, a wallet perhaps. Leaving her residence ransacked, an obvious case of theft gone weird and bad. "Yet another tragic example of Tracy's ever growing senseless violence. Now, an elderly woman murdered most brutal, inside her own home." Douglas thought for a moment how a headline searching press, might cover the scene. Drug related and gang violence would invariably enter into this latest example of vicious crimes racking a long gone safe and bucolic Valley town. Coupled with recent news of prison gang paroles linking up with Mexico's powerful drug cartels throughout many of California's Central Valley cities. The migration of crime, this time, away from Bay Area and L.A. Basin cities, into a more subdued lifestyle around farms and poverty. One more example of temporary migrants in and out of Valley regions. All this troubling news leading to a quick reasonable explanation residents will understand. Wanted to understand. Needing to understand it this way. Drugs and violence mixing together, causing the storm, making it all fit together perfect.

"No chance of Mrs. Patterson telling that snoopy bitch from Tracy's Police Department her most sworn secret. However, maybe a secret buried under her, soon. Then, down to only one, who knows anything at all. Free and clear." Uttering his words with a merciless smirk.

Winding further west, Sheets and his fertile mind continued dream scenarios. Some simple, some detailed. Deep within his devious plus injured prefrontal cortex, Sheets developed crafty approaches in ways to kill the elder woman. The act of killing no longer bothered him. Becoming closer to a curious challenge or sport for his own survival. "Either she goes or I goes!" Telling himself in full voice, complete with bursting grin acknowledging a rather foolish verse. "It's almost a turkey shoot," his words whispered soft as his truck left behind rolling foothills, stretching north and south, and well beyond any earthbound horizon. Entering now into his zone of personal distaste for the Central Valley's mundane flatness. To Douglas Sheets it was simple Central Valley repugnance. Inching ever closer to his naive prey. Hearing the high pitched voice screaming out again, struggling mentally to bury the nightmarish scene and sounds. A voice resurfacing, like that of a struggling, drowning child. Wet, gurgling, gasping for one more life sparing breath. Just about any time the sheriff found himself alone, his event surfaced, trying scores of tricks to erase the haunting sound from memory. But unable to do so. He was however, learning to exist with it. He had help. A low resting heartbeat allowed Douglas to stay under control, ignore his fear, rarely experience regret and feel no empathy. This sheriff appeared in command. In reality his violence lever was close to being engaged.

"Murder? Am I a simple murderer? Maybe I'm closer to being a hunter? Stalking a shrewd animal or waiting patient, hidden, prepared to spring on unsuspecting prey? Better yet, unsuspecting game!" More dissolute and criminal notions infiltrated his warped philosophy for justifiable murder. "Killing it before it can kill you?" He was sworn to prevent anyone willing to play out a role in this way, doing his duty admirably. But, being on the verge of absolute derangement, his own actions became acceptable, justified, even reasonable. Continuing with his twisted self debate, "I'm no more or less a sportsmen. Bringing down hapless deer or elk, spraying rabbits in high weeds with lead shot or dropping birds that wonder to close into shooting range. My only difference is food. I don't eat what I have to kill!" Sheets was even capable of talking himself into a distorted unbalanced corner, from which he had nothing to offer as a counter argument.

Doug's journey west passed fewer dormant farm fields as more homes and commercial parks emerged. Not long ago, these expanded developments occupied former expanses of fertile ground. A constant stream of holiday headlights passed in the opposite direction. Family seeking family, long weekend vacationers, holiday movement, tradition. Douglas Sheets however, wasn't headed toward anything remotely cordial, pleasant or thankful. He headed straight to another nightmare. Unlike his haunting memories Douglas wasn't burdened with remorse. If he was, he wouldn't be capable of carrying out this horrifying action. Strange, but he didn't actually long for another deed, telling himself, "I'm not a serial killer. I don't have to kill." Somehow putting his conduct above those other nuts and weirdo's running amuck with uncontrolled blood lust. "Hell, those are the types I'm paid to capture." His defective brain able to soften the tiniest bit of guilt and without doubt turn back the slightest feeling of empathy. He realized what steps he'd taken and the lines he crossed. Murder became understandable. Permissible. "It's them or me," cold-blooded whispers under his breath, gunning his truck as much as a small engine vehicle allows. Increasing speed, entering Highway 120 further west, connector to I-5. "Not much longer now."

Mrs. Patterson

"Reggie, I am so glad you stopped by my dear," Beatrice gushed lifting a bright, decorated beaker refilling Regina's cup with a delicate pour, not permitted to spill even one drop. Very bad taste on her part to splash coffee like some over worked pancake waitress.

"You're English but prefer afternoon coffee instead of tea. Why's that?" Regina asked, enjoying French roast much more than milky tea.

"Oh gosh, I don't know," Betty answered, topping off her own cup before sitting down to enjoy her welcomed visitor still clinging to a nationality secret. "I became addicted to the dark brew years ago. With all the coffee shops in town, I never find myself boiling tea." Smiling at her guest, almost consenting to one of her most personal secrets, deciding against, way too grateful and happy Regina found time to visit. "Do you prefer tea darling? If so, I'll be happy to share a few tea bags on your next visit," Beatrice promised, sipping deep from her hefty cup of black caffeine checking Gonzalez quick, hoping she didn't disappoint her guest.

"Nope. Nope. Not at all," reaching out, grasping her host's frail arm, in a gentle display of gratitude. "I prefer coffee, being Hispanic and all, of course." Looking at Mrs. Patterson with a sly grin. "Muy caliente!" Squeezing the elder woman's arm once more ever so slight. Both giggled, forcing Beatrice into a reflex action, clutching her hand over Regina's. The older woman's fingers felt cold even in afternoon sunshine.

Beatrice permitted their touch to linger, just as a torrent of images flooded her memory. Reminding her of moments like this spent with Sarah. Knowing it was too early in their friendship to have that easy feeling like mother and daughter. But Mrs. Patterson mused if they might be a natural pair. "In time, this wise cracking cop might become my other daughter? She's not like Sarah that's for sure, but fun company," the older gal whispered, eager to be in the initial stages of a close relationship. Just as the two girls became comfortable and relaxed, Beatrice sprang from her chair like a flushing quail, moving faster than her aging legs should allow. Making a beeline toward a rear fence corner, Betty's unexpected movements jolted Regina into keen awareness, causing a loud laugh and to sit up straight.

"Get the fu, get the hell out of here you mangy killer," correcting a bit of foul language choosing to keep things polite. Staying on track while deftly extracting a rock from her garden apron front pocket. Like the British, she always had ammo on hand. Without losing a step Betty hurled her stone fiercely at a reddish-gray striped flash. Being a southpaw combined with an acute left to right angle of attack her aim was a wee bit high. Striking one fence line with a severe left to right fade, ricocheting over to the adjoining side. Both strikes echoed loud, like hard foul balls getting full attention from 'killer kat'! "Shoo you damn little monster," Beatrice yelled, as Striper leapt clean to the fence top in a single elastic stride, seizing dovetailed redwood with expanded front paws. All the while scratching and pushing panic stricken rear legs desperate to clear the wooden line of departure.

Regina, relishing the display, cupped one hand over her drooping jaw, laughing and fairly awestruck by the older woman's fervent attack. She rose to run toward Mrs. Patterson hoping to offer some sort of aid laughing the whole time.

"Sorry sweetheart, but that damn cat really does a number on my visiting birds. I hate Striper!" Accenting the cat's name which brought more laughs from a surprised Gonzalez. "Hell I hate most cats. I'm not much of a pet lover if you didn't know already." Betty expressed. Regina could only shake her head and admire the feisty woman.

"C'mon Betty, come sit down. Striper will be hiding for a while now I'm sure. Nice throw by the way." Regina ushered her senior friend back to tables and chairs, chuckling soft, asking her to save on ammunition for a while too! "You move pretty fast when the moment strikes, don't ya," the detective observed, helping to seat Beatrice, giving her bony shoulders a brisk rub to get a worked up lady calmed down.

"Oh, bank it. I've still got plenty left girl. Maybe the coffee helps out some, who knows?" Beatrice acted serious for a lengthy moment before dealing a sly blink from her teasing left eye. Things calmed again letting the afternoon go peaceful and still. Both girls enjoyed more coffee and Regina brought Beatrice up to speed on her former neighbor's investigation.

"Not much to go on I'm afraid," Beatrice commented. "I had a feeling this could be a sticky case. I mean, the lack of identification on my part and all. I just wish I hadn't been taken so much by surprise."

"Well, maybe next time the shooter will donate a warning shot just to get you ready!" Gonzalez joked.

"Don't get too smart ass with me, young lady. You witnessed how well I can throw rocks," Mrs. Patterson felt good about getting one over her young cop. "Maybe some hidden evidence will surface, giving you and your partner that needed break." Mrs. Patterson's words sparked Regina's attention.

"Maybe? I sure hope so? We could use a break." The detective stopped to think about asking her new friend direct, for any first hand information. She aimed to handle it appropriately. "Is there something you have to tell me?" wondering if the older woman had something to offer, perhaps revealing. Beatrice remained still in a nervous quiet, lifting her cup, sipping steady, a blank stare in the direction of Striper's fence corner. Regina could tell she wasn't seeing much and knew very well Mrs. Patterson was deep in thought. The way she bit on a fingernail revealed a little about her current mood. "C'mon Betty, let it out," Regina said to herself repeating her wishful hope a number of times before Betty spoke again.

Mrs. Patterson's facial appearance exhibited complex sorrow while her head swayed side to side. "I just can't think of anything, my darling," articulating her veto with a heavy dose of compassion and mystery. Without looking away, even in the sun's angled glare, a distressed woman reached out with trembling hands, inserting her wrinkled fingers into Regina's palms. Compressing gently. "I wish to hell I could offer you something Reggie. But I just can't." Squeezing her fingers a tiny bit harder.

To the young detective her touch felt soothing, so secure. With no warning, Regina focused a tender image of her long passed childhood. Young again, moody but calm, slipping easy into long gone childhood days, momma at her side, held secure. Stoic, safe, trust, love. Gonzalez, the capable cop she is, comprehended her look, her touch, her words with their hidden meaning. Beatrice told her clearly, without saying a word, she knew something but couldn't or wouldn't disclose. At least, not inclined to tell her now. Regina understood and wouldn't push the troubled woman any further, fearing a stone chucked into her ear! It was time for her to leave anyway with less than thirty minutes of daylight remaining. She had made contact knowing a return date wasn't far away.

Opening a wooden gate leading to the front yard, Beatrice led the way pointing to fresh planted shrubs lining a small corner of raised beds for spring vegetables. Walking out onto her concrete driveway, Regina caught site of a front yard fountain semi-hidden amongst older, dense landscape. Brown finches flocked, squeaking and fluttering from basin to tree limbs then back to the basin. Gonzalez turned away, her back to the street admiring the lines of fleeting birds with Mrs. Patterson standing alongside, facing Anaheim Drive. Her aging eyes caught a familiar site. Once again low light conditions painted a reddish glow, reflecting glare from the side of another small, worn, dark pick-up truck. Beatrice gasped just as the vehicle drove by, passing slow from right to left. Another invisible face stared back. Beatrice froze, like Striper caught trespassing, recoiled, gasped then stumbled backward. One hand reached out to latch onto Regina's shoulder while the other covered her mouth. Regina felt Beatrice tugging her arm just after hearing a loud gasp but failed to recognize what transpired. Lucky for Mrs. Patterson the detective turned just before the elder woman was ready to keel over. Eyes gone blank when Gonzalez suffered her full weight against one arm, helping to break the fall but Beatrice still went down to one knee.

"The shooter. He's back," Beatrice forced out between panted breaths.

"What?" Regina didn't quite comprehend the words, concentrating on her stumbling fall. "Careful now," Gonzalez screeched as she looked toward Anaheim Drive where Mrs. Patterson pointed. Regina's glance spotted a dark pick-up truck passing very slow beyond the Patterson yard in front of Marcus Crosby's fateful driveway. Barely glimpsing a silhouette peering back, window rolled up, like someone lost perhaps but also not missing a thing. Alas, another faceless driver in poor light.

"Go Reggie, see if it's him. I'm okay," Beatrice implored her, "quickly."

Regina responded, loosening her grip as the older woman managed to stay upright on one arm. Running down her driveway she got a brief glimpse of the truck's side and rear end, just as it sped up to leave the area. Gonzalez could tell she must've been spotted. "Doubtful a routine passing vehicle would act this way," the detective told herself. Distance grew between them and Regina failed to get any sort of license plate identification. The rear of the truck revealed nothing as her eye honed in on a camper shell rear window. Rolling steady, further out, disappearing like a bird flying straight away vanishing into thin air. Nervous adrenaline surged into her stomach and upper thighs as her first thought went direct to Tom Ellis. Close resemblance to Tom's truck. She was inclined to give chase but looked back to see Beatrice rolling over, laboring to get on one knee

"Too late now," telling herself, retreating fast to help her aging friend. "Stay down Betty. Don't try getting up yet," Regina ordered, as Mrs. Patterson reached for Gonzalez, feeling stronger, balancing on one knee and holding steady.

"I'm all right. Sorry for all this. I'm okay now, really." Wanting to receive Regina's concern.

"That's fine, just stay still," Regina warned, keeping Beatrice steady and opening her cell phone. Scrolling to Tom Ellis and pushing the green call button. "Don't move Betty, let me make this call." Hearing the connection and second ring tone loud and clear. "Perfect connection, I wonder?" Regina thought to herself.

"I don't need an ambulance Regina, I'll be fine in a few minutes," Mrs. Patterson directed the detective.

"I'm perfectly aware you don't need an ambulance you old mule," Gonzalez joked. Looking at Betty as two excited ladies laughed out loud.

A greeting came across her small phone, no doubt hearing Tom answer. "Hello," followed by a sharp yell of Tom's voice away from the receiver, much like a job site? "Hey Andy, get loaded up. I've gotta take this call," Regina heard a far off voice come thru the phone answering positive amid muffled truck engines. Tom checked the incoming name before answering with a decent hunch to who was calling.

"Hey flatfoot, you better not be calling to break our dinner date tomorrow," Tom responded, yelling into the phone due to background commotion.

"He must be working," Regina told herself before answering back. "Whoops. Tom is this you?" trying to play calm.

"It sure as hell is," he shot back.

"Sorry to bother you Tom, I hit the wrong number." Turning away from Mrs. Patterson wanting to cover her words.

"Yeah, right. I think you're getting hooked on me."

"Uhm, we'll see," blurting out a poor choice of words. Cringing. "You're working late?" in her devious manner to get the confirmation she needed. Hoping for verification.

"We're just wrapping up. Back in Mendota. Setting out emergency construction stakes all day." Tom spoke free and relaxed, giving Regina no cause for doubt. "What's up?" he asked while whispering to someone else. "Hey, Anthony's right here. Wanna say hi?" chuckling into his cell.

Regina smiled looking down at her feet. She shuffled her stance knowing for certain Tom was working, squashing a minor guilt spasm rippling through her mid-section. "Tell Antoine, Happy Thanksgiving for me. Nothing's up. My bad. See ya tomorrow. I'm in the middle of something here," she said, trying to let go without seeming nervous. "Tomorrow."

"See ya tomorrow. Can't wait," Tom finished before hanging up.

Regina felt a sudden rush of calm and relief with his final comment striking a high note too. She waited too long then responded, "Tom, I'm really looking forward," but too late. Dial tone. Already hung up. "Shoot. Waited too damn long!"

Regina moved back to her patient who was up on both feet now but wobbly. "Maybe Mrs. Patterson's imagination was a bit overloaded?" she thought.

"That was the truck. I'm almost sure of it," Mrs. Patterson told Regina, trying to stop shivering.

"Let's get back inside Betty." Gina flashed her an uplifting grin. A sudden image of Douglas Sheets filled her head. A tingling sensation filled her stomach. A look of possibility filled her face. "Son of a bitch," Regina mumbled under her breath, realizing for the first time if that was Sheets, they may have finally caught a break. "Why would he be here now? Returning to the crime scene? Why now? Was he here maybe, to confront Beatrice? Planning to harm Betty?" Attempting to sort through the plausible. "This is all too damn strange right now," the detective's mind flared, knowing she'd have to tell Chris later tonight.

"C'mon young lady, let's get inside with ya. We'll see if you need a doctor," Regina said walking Beatrice back to her front door.

"Don't be stupid child. Sorry. Don't be silly detective. I'm fine," Betty's homily getting a pleasant laugh from Regina as they retreated back inside. "Just taken a bit by surprise, I'm afraid. I'll be okay." Giving her friend every visible indication she didn't need a doctor. "Regina," Mrs. Patterson started to speak then seated herself slowly, "that sure looked like the shooter's truck."

"You know Beatrice, I'm beginning to think you could be right. It's still a long shot but who knows?" Regina told the elderly woman hoping she didn't scare her. "A phone call to the department? Maybe someone could ask for his whereabouts?" Regina thought, keeping it secret. "Beatrice if you're okay, I've gotta get going. To look into this."

"Go on. Go," shooing the detective away like telling a child to get outside and play. "Go. Get him," Beatrice encouraged, letting Gonzalez leave, watching her run down the driveway. Mrs. Patterson closed and locked her front door. She lifted the sherry bottle, poured a shot and a half, then dampened a dish towel with cold water. "Why would the killer be coming back?" Beatrice stopped, rolled her eyes and leaned back against her counter top appearing dumbfounded. "For me, I assume!" Mrs. Patterson checked her doors making sure they were all locked.

···

"Gonzo, slow down. You didn't even get an I.D. on the truck let alone a plate number. We may look kinda foolish calling to check the location of an investigator," Captain Anderson questioned Gonzalez on her strategy asking to rethink her idea. "Hell, it might've just been average Joe driving down the street for all you know Gonzo."

"You may be right Captain but it looked like Sheets' truck. Captain please, a simple call. Make it sound like some sort of formality or paperwork." Regina kept the pressure on hoping Anderson would give in. "A wrong number. That would look legit?"

"Look Gonzo, even if it was him, we don't have a thing to make an arrest. Douglas Sheets you're under arrest for driving by a crime scene in your truck? For now, let's just assume it was our sheriff. If we start making some wild ass phone calls to the County we're just going to spook him." Anderson dug in his heels as Regina started warming to his point of view. "I can scrounge up enough budget to put a car out for a few days. They can keep a close watch on Mrs. Patterson. If Sheets happens to swing by again maybe we'll get a firm identification?"

"Oh shoot?" his detective voiced her disappointment, "you're probably right Captain. I might've spooked him as it is. If that was Sheets, another five fricken' minutes sooner would've found me inside armed to the teeth." Regina considered calling Chris to get his opinion but the Captain made good sense. "Let's feed him some more rope," she remarked to Billy.

"Good idea. He's just the type to hang himself," Anderson agreed with his detective.

"Maybe. Maybe. Okay Captain, we'll play it your way. Happy Thanksgiving," offering Billy well wishes for the upcoming weekend remembering her own dinner date tomorrow.

Captain Anderson let out a low sigh, glad his detective called him before she moved on the deputy but also relieved to be getting out of the office on time for once. "Gonzo, you have a nice, long, restful weekend. See you Monday morning." Ending the call, while reaching fast for his cell, reading an incoming text from a certain red haired woman.

Regina gave up but couldn't help feeling short changed, wondering if more action might've helped determine this mystery man. Before heading home she couldn't help cruising through a half dozen neighborhoods and parking lots from two nearby strip malls. Spotting one truck, a dead ringer in fact, soon to be occupied by an early twenty year old Hispanic girl. Her boyfriend arrived too, both enjoying some lively action in a cramped front seat! Nothing found as Gonzalez decided she had enough, called it quits and made her way home. She thought about Tom. Worried about Betty too.

Sheets

"Fuck! I can't believe my lousy goddamn timing. How in the hell did that broken down old bitch have a cop in her house today? Today?" Douglas repeated louder each time as he turned off Arlington Drive and sped as fast as possible without bringing attention upon himself. He wouldn't be surprised to see that damn cop coming up hard from behind any moment now. "Shit! That bitch blew the whole damn plan for me. I've gotta get back there but not too soon though." Turning right with a slight tire screech and then left, before heading north out of town. Douglas checked his mirrors constantly making sure nobody followed. Toward Highway 205 entering at Eleventh Street, "all clear behind me," Sheets said aloud, speeding his truck further on. "Get back home and regroup."

Traffic was at a standstill eastbound. Typical of the Bay Area on Turkey Day getaway Wednesday, clogging roadways with families headed south preferring not to make the trip by air. It only added to Sheets' frustration and increased anger. Loretta would be in for a rough night if Douglas couldn't settle down during his ride back. New ideas to deal with Beatrice Patterson were already fermenting deep within Sheets' insidious mind.

Anderson

His weekend was gradually arriving but Captain Anderson suspected she wanted to be with family tomorrow. Flipping his cell open, not expecting any surprises in her response although quite disappointed with Patricia Bailey's text. The reporter anticipated an intimate dinner together this evening but would be heading to San Francisco tomorrow morning for the annual, Bailey Holiday Extravaganza. Her rich nephew threw the party each year. Sometimes at Thanksgiving, sometimes at Christmas.

"You're welcome to join me, Pretty Boy!" The newswoman ended her message with a polite but informal offer.

Billy thought about saying the hell with it and accepting. But, like a good cop, he landed back on earth knowing it was pure fantasy. "No way can I attend your party," Billy responded, fumbling with keys and a sensitive 'send' button. Captain Anderson made a mental note to inform the night shift to add extra patrol around Mrs. Patterson's house. He noted her address just as his phone chimed with an incoming text.

"Suit yourself colonel. Are we meeting tonight at our usual place??" Came her response causing Billy to wonder how Patricia could text so fast. Especially since he often found himself fumbling like a child with simple yes responses. Like now, frustrated and confused changing routine caps and number settings! "I'll see ya @ 6:00," came her lightening fast confirmation, before Anderson dialed in the patrol sergeant's desk number, commanding Tracy's night shift dispatch. He directed stationing of unmarked cars at four hour intervals, on and off, for the rest of the weekend. "Stay well to the south of her house," instructing them to watch for small, dark pick-ups cruising the neighborhood. "Anything suspicious, pull 'em over and get full identification."

"Got it Captain," a skinny sergeant confirmed as another text came across.

"Will be spending the night Lover Boy!" Anderson read it mumbling and smiling. He couldn't stop an aroused stimulus, surge into his lower extremities. "Finally, some decent holiday news," he spoke soft, beaming to himself. Billy reclined, rubbing chin stubble, squirming, with images of Beatrice Patterson home alone.

Abigail

"Happy Thanksgiving," Patricia Bailey answered her call with open sarcasm knowing who was calling. She setup Abby's incoming ringtone to

Darth Vadar's March! Bailey's loud and rather extensive exhaled sigh put an exclamation mark on her personalized hello.

Abbey wanted to reach through her phone set, grab the gaudy redhead about her long neck and squeeze very slow until constricted. Hesitating a response, allowing her thin emotions to settle before speaking. Patricia smiled with evil satisfaction knowing her sardonic greeting had struck a nerve, like a power hitting right hander knows it's gone, over the wall in left as soon as contact is made. Gratifying awareness. "Happy Holidays to you too," Abbey bestowed just about including the bitch word, but refused herself one more time.

"We're getting together tonight, but I don't think he has anything new," Bailey responded before giving Mrs. Crosby a fair chance to snarl her repetitive demands.

"Don't give me that lousy attitude. You, do what you do best and find something. Anything. I don't care how insignificant you think it is, get me something." Coming across as sinister as Bailey had ever heard the elder matriarch.

"Don't dare talk to me like that, you lousy witch," Bailey returned fire, her first attempt to stand up to Abigail, eager to start a shouting match but only hearing an unruffled, brief retort.

"Get it done," came Abbey's cool response followed fast by her harsh dial tone. Mrs. Crosby wasn't about to sit back listening to an 'employee' bad mouth her.

"You low life ass," Patricia screeched out inside her black BMW. Like steam venting from a thermal geyser. The street light turned green allowing her to proceed toward Tracy, undecided if she'd make a play for new information tonight. This will be a good way to stick it to Abbey one more time, talking loud and accelerating. Besides, she was looking forward to seeing Billy again.

Gadwalls

Wednesday morning, the day before Thanksgiving was a shoot day. Loud noises and dark figures greeted the pair as they sailed into Los Banos Refuge, seeking food, remaining high before sunrise over two inviting open water ponds. Small islands covered in sparse vegetation were scattered about each small lake offering dry ground. Perfect for dry resting, preening or afternoon naps. Each bird angled one wing, tipping ever so slight resulting in a long slow turn and selecting the larger pond's interior. Never failing to maintain safe altitude the hen kept her dark eye in close study on a medium flock of small bright ducks. Green-winged teal soaring in a tight group. Wings low, banking hard left then harder right. Dark back feathers from the gadwalls perspective above and whitish-gray bellies under nervous wings from two concealed hunters below. Dropping low way too fast, the flock was favoring a shoreline covered in small trees, shrubs and thinning cattails. They banked left in unison, drifted away from a dangerous edge and retreated to safe center. Turning hard right in a spiral curl, on a gradual track to their desired landing zone. Closing in, soft whistling chirps emitted throughout the flashy pod of colorful drakes. Fiery bronze heads, green eye patches and distinct white shoulder crescents were subdued in the predawn light. In a few minutes brilliant sunshine would paint individual birds with color detail, depending on turn direction and angling light.

Overhead both gadwalls descended, still observing as the hen wasn't convinced of this pond's safety. Never taking rest or feed in these waters, due to being sidetracked by numerous flocks leading away from familiar resting water. Below, the small ducks made one more quick turn beginning a steady glide toward the shoreline. Committed and dropping further with wings and webbed feet tipping side to side. Loud noises rang out repeating again and again as two birds fell in awkward cartwheels before splashing into gray dirty water. A third bird dropped slower, wings outstretched twisting downward, gravity winning, mortally wounded but still alive. Delayed but wounded too, a fourth teal was able to leave the flock, higher in flight then descending slow but away from two dark figures. It too would be unable to fly in short time, carrying three number four shot in its abdomen and wing muscles. Most likely dying in high weeds or taken by a natural predator. Certainly wasted due to poor shooting decisions.

Each loud shot startled the drake gadwall causing a sudden rise for safe air, as the pair remained on a close watch. A small wounded duck scooted across open water. Struggling harder with each movement. Pain inside her tiny body cavity interfered with life giving air, helpless as droplets of blood spurted from each nostril smearing a leathery gray bill. One dark figure emerged, hidden somewhere along the covered shoreline, moving with splashes toward the hen teal. She managed two or three feeble wing flaps before completely engulfed in watery spray followed close by the somewhat muted boom. Once the scene calmed each gadwall circled above. Below, a white belly stayed visible, bobbing on dark water, deadly inert. Sunshine knifed in now lighting up the dark figure, leaning over, lifting the small duck clear of its sodden grave and turning to make its way back into dense cover.

Enough. Both gadwalls whirled together tight, away and rising higher making for safe water and late morning feed.

Thanksgiving

Wishing to sleep late for a change but unable, Gonzalez was out of the house sooner than expected. "Room for cream?" came the standard morning question.

"Please," the detective replied to an older woman manning one of Starbuck's cash registers. Her smile appeared genuine begetting Regina to respond in kind. "Happy Thanksgiving," she added, accepting her bold coffee.

"Same to you," from the upbeat cashier.

Regina exited this noisy coffee shop, opting to sit outside at a vacant sun drenched table and chairs. A venue of cool morning air, dead calm at the moment but wrapped nicely in a shroud of warm sunshine stirred her curiosity. On the verge of spending Thanksgiving with an unknown ending named Tom, elevated a sunny mood even higher. She was expected in the early afternoon and considered going earlier, sipping with care at her steamy French roast. "No rush," telling herself, watching a young mother giving chase to a sugar hyped three year old. The toddler sped right through two lingering opened doors, turned right almost crashing, completing a nice getaway around the courtyard fountain. He adjusted course slightly which caused Regina to set her cup down a second before rushing headlong into Gonzalez' outstretched arms. They bumped firm, wrapping two short arms around Regina's shoulder and laughed joyful into her ear. Giving the detective giggles too. For the moment a bonded pair. His fluffy red hair smelled of chocolate cookies as the detective pressed her chin against his soft, pink cheek.

"Gotchya," Regina hissed her joke, holding the squirmy catch tight before a red faced mom jogged up from behind.

"Stop Jacob," she shouted. The young escapee looked back quick only to see his mother approaching, knowing she wasn't too upset but reading mom as meaning business. Jacob stammered both legs and feet in place, gripped his accomplice even harder letting fly with another nervous laugh. Regina accepted his embrace and made eye contact with Jacob's embarrassed parent. The detective's face signaled all was perfectly fine. In fact she couldn't resist clutching the sweet boy, squeezing and rocking him soft. His third laugh and hug brought out Regina's maternal sensations which seemed to surface by the most unexpected triggers. Heartfelt instincts of incomplete love badgered her life.

"You certainly have your hands full." Peering at Jacob's mother while turning the boy around. Jacob faced mom, his small body shook releasing an overload of built up adrenaline accompanied by yet another low squeal. Dropping both hands from Regina's arm, he lurched back to his exasperated mother. Gonzalez had to refuse a reflexive urge to reach out and coddle the young boy once more. His touch, ever so brief was warm and consoling.

"I'm so sorry. He gets away sometimes and does keep me hopping." As mom picked up the giggling, thrashing boy kissing the top of his hair covered forehead.

"Believe me, it was great. Your son is adorable," Regina gushed passing glances at the youngster one more time. Both women understood somehow,

Regina's slim envy of the young mother. Equaling the young mother's envy for Regina's independence, slightly.

"Happy Thanksgiving," a reunited parent bade Regina, seeing a tender loneliness in her face. Mom tilted her head and smiled again before telling Jacob to say goodbye.

"Thanks so much, same to you and Jacob," spoken in a way revealing her desire to someday have a child. This simple encounter launched a flood of family memories. Always her mom first, in the kitchen, in the orchards, in the white dress.

•••

Driving south again. Interstate 5 traffic was light and quiet compared to last night's mess. Hurried drivers and backed up tail lights always caused a few tragic crashes on I-5's Thanksgiving rush. Made all the more dreadful with an unfortunate family suffering heavy losses.

Regina cruised her way along easy however, without episode skirting jagged hills to her right and a soft open valley stretching far off to her left. Dormant trees, dirt fields, blue skies and two never ending canals still carrying water south. This drive wasn't spent dwelling on past years. Her mind raced between Jacob's indulgent squeezes and what Tom's touch may feel like. Not so much about sex but as simple affection. Hopefully?

"You can't sleep with him tonight," giving herself orders like a strict mother laying the law down. "I hope I can't." Cracks already showing in her own conviction, passing the first rest stop south of Tracy. In the distance, two hundred yards to her left, a flock of large white birds with black tipped wings made an easy push south too. Six or seven snow geese forming a small tight flock. Regina spotted the birds admiring their snug formation, long rigid necks and smooth nearly effortless wing beats. Her exit lay only a few miles away setting butterflies free to stir wild inside, in contrast with the uniform flight of geese over alfalfa fields. An exciting degree of anticipation swirled about. No thoughts of murder now. Not much concern for her partner, her boss or her murder case. Today was about Tom Ellis. "I hope this guy is cool." Checking her directions one more time. "Sure could use a decent man right now."

Exiting into Gustine, noticing a handful of landmarks from her last visit in town. Like always a little different in daylight. "Better in fact." Spotting West Street a hair late forcing a fast right turn including the soft wail of sliding rubber. "Hope the neighbors won't mind," Regina winced, locating his brick house and entering a gravel driveway under full control. "Nine forty one West. That's it," she said out loud, for the most part still under control.

•••

Tom had to leave the kitchen with prepped food lying all over his counter to field a phone call from a favorite nephew and now his dinner date arrived.

Early of course. Tom opened the door slow causing Regina to lean right, peering around the door's edge at her date with a wood spoon in one hand and a phone tucked on an awkwardly raised shoulder. Pointing to his cell mouthing the word relative and shrugging, still able to catch the falling phone in his right hand. "Sorry," he whispered.

Ushering his guest inside, giving Gonzalez the one minute sign. She whispered back, "no problem." Regina scanned the living room for first impressions unable to stop peeking around a doorway into Tom's kitchen. Mouthwatering aromas filled her taste buds with a combination of sautéed onions, garlic and a deeper bouquet wafting from a covered cast iron pot, on a slow simmer. Regina lifted two bottles of wine she carried in a cloth bag, setting them on the counter top. Tom heard the heavy ring on tile turning to see two bottles of Italian reds. Sangiovese and Barbera.

"Happy Thanksgiving Mark," Tom signaled an end to his phone call. "Tell your mom and dad the same, okay. I'll call you in a few weeks with a hunting report. Bye." Closing his cell and lifting a wine bottle for close inspection. "Sorry but I had to take that call. My nephew and he loves to hunt ducks."

"Hey, no problem. It's the holidays," Regina said with her nervousness diminishing somewhat.

"Mmm, this looks great," Tom sighed, studying the Barbera with a soft rub of its label, grinning to Regina in approval. She nodded as two uneasy people stood together, clueless what to do next. Tom began his tentative approach, planning a polite hug sliding his cheek to hers for a simple greeting. "I'm glad you're here." Starting to separate but feeling Regina's arm slide behind his neck and pull, taking him by complete surprise. She kissed his lips once, quick but full. Kissed him again, very firm this time, pressing into his chest enjoying Tom's grasp and tug on her hips. They stayed together a few enticing seconds before grudgingly breaking apart. Regina's hands slipped down onto Tom's chest clutching onto loose shirt pockets.

"Happy Thanksgiving," the detective whispered unable to look straight into his face. She preferred an immediate return to his lips and embrace but stepped back instead, deciding to stop anything ridiculous from happening across his kitchen floor. Tom regained his reluctant self control albeit, still awkward. He also wished to touch, smell and embrace this unusual, sensuous woman once again. Regina's dark hair flowed over part of her face. Tom noticed the contrast between her rich coffee toned hair and olive skin. Slightly wavy locks covering her smooth, almost shiny complexion.

"Much better than being smart," Ellis whispered.

"Come again?" Regina asked.

"Your kiss. Someone once said, kisses are a better fate than wisdom. How about a glass of wine?" His only thought which made sense inside Tom's jumbled mind. They both understood in the last minute, something new and exciting had just occurred. Regina perceived a comfortable closeness. Not immediately serious or compelling but without a doubt desirable. She grew relaxed enjoying Tom fumble through two kitchen drawers, hopeless and lost in search of a wine opener. She enjoyed even more, pointing out his gadget sitting at the end of his cluttered counter like a lighthouse beacon shrouded inside mental fog.

"Of course it is," Tom mumbled, red faced stumbling into an open drawer. He heard Regina snicker which made him feel even more ridiculous. Turning to see Gonzalez, folded arms on her chest, weight shifted left.

"Need some help?" Regina shot out holding tight to a laugh behind pursed lips. Tom exploded, seldom being caught up in personal embarrassment. He laughed loud, tilted his head back and laughed again relieving a large portion of anxiety and clumsiness.

"Just call me Mr. Stupid. Ha, ha, I should be able to handle it," he vowed shaking his head back and forth, twisting the screw into rich, solid cork. "Let's begin with Sangiovese."

They began to relax and breathe easier after a touch of alcohol deadened their nervous symptoms. From here forward it proved pretty simple, for each of them. An easy going first date with calm chit chat between a variety of jokes and laughs. Regina enjoyed Tom's company thoroughly, just as she hoped.

"So what's on the menu?" a curious detective asked pouring out her first refill, inhaling rich oak scents from a dark red swirling in her glass. "You can probably tell I'm your typical, gringo, turkey slob." Noticing Tom's eyes light up following her slob comment.

"You're gonna love my turkey leg from an ancient family recipe smothered in slobbery smashed potatoes," Tom answered back, sarcastic and waiting to hear her response.

Regina squirmed just a trace in her chair knowing her slob insult hit home like a knuckles ringing fastball off the handle. "Uhm, of course I wasn't including you Mr. Ellis," showing her teeth both mentally as well as expression. Waiting quiet for Tom's rebuttal knowing he wasn't insulted. It evolved into a standoff as each gun held their ground. She thought for sure Tom would blink. He didn't, but alcohol was winning over her resolve. "Gees sorry!" Gonzalez announced, drawing her gun first. Tom grinned wide. "You rat," she said, kidding, taking another sip of wine. Tom glowed in his minor victory then began to rattle off his Thanksgiving menu.

"First a small cup of clam chowder to get in the mood. Not too thick with plenty of carrots for color. Followed by grilled pablano peppers with a garlic, olive oil rub, spicy tomatillo sauce, and parmesan cheese. Garnished with grilled pineapple." Sounding every bit like the aspiring chef with his own cable show.

Regina tried following his descriptions, "tomatillo what?" squinting her glossy eyes wishing for a repeat but Tom preferred to continue.

"Grilled avocado halves with green taco sauce smothered in melted mozzarella. Seared scallops and spicy coconut cantaloupe over a bed of asparagus risotto, duck breast scaloppini" pausing his menu to take in Regina's dumbfounded look. "Braised short ribs in a sweet peach salsa verde. You have the red wine but I'm forgetting something," Tom's squinting eye helped him remember what's missing. "Oh right. And hot, fresh cornbread," speaking with a exclamation mark.

Regina held steady, centering a searing stare on Mr. Chef Surprise, shuffling nervous in her chair followed by crossing legs. "Yeah right! Spicy coconut, what the hell did ya say?" Drinking heavy from her wine glass wondering if Tom was just pulling her nipples!

"Sea scallops with spicy coconut cantaloupe. Have you had it before?" coming off innocent enough but Tom knew he'd taken the cop by surprise, enjoying every second. Ellis loved cooking and the last few years he experimented like a madman with off center combinations of seasonings and creative inspiration. Wild game forced the probing chef's instincts out, which overflowed into his daily meals as well. Entertaining became more fun finding his varied dishes succeeded more often than not. His occasional new dates, especially blind dates for which Regina almost qualified, were always impressed. Knowing most of the girls he dated wouldn't last but a few lingered on due to his cooking more than passion!

"I like experimenting with new food combinations," Tom explained. "It's fun but kinda challenging, testing some unusual fruits to go with fish or veggies. I hope you like what I put together but be warned, the salsa verde peach sauce is my first attempt. So be direct with your comments."

Regina's dumbfounded gaze appeared to look straight through Tom' face! She failed to deliver a comment as one thought kept running through her mind. Denise, from the luncheon gang, often said, "it's great when a man cooks for you. Especially when it takes some time to prepare." Regina smiled at Tom. Not a full grin but the kind of smile that says, 'thanks for your effort. I appreciate this.'

"No dessert?" Spoken with playful cynicism.

"Glad you asked, my dear. My mom's fattening but delicious walnut tart including homemade, late harvest Zinfandel cherry ice cream." Tom held a blank face for upshot.

"Wow, can't wait to try it all. I'm impressed to say the least," Regina responded seeing Tom very pleased. "Not your usual Turkey Day, gringo dinner Mr. Ellis." Once more departing back to her lunch gang and thinking, "they won't believe this one!" Smirking to herself.

Tom invited his guest to help him in the kitchen to which Regina obliged, impressed with various cooking details. In particular, the way some dishes finished so simple while others in dreadful complexity. "I can do that," was heard more and more by Gonzalez as preparation faded closer to dinner. A constant shuffle of dishes, in and out to tend the charcoal grill new menu items and at last, their taste buds challenged before each course served. Regina savored every minute as Tom sweated each dish. Of special concern was his short rib sauce and tenderness. Each serving seemed to lighten the mood, turning dinner into a shared experience. Regina's comments were blunt but by far steeped in praise and eaten fast for proof. When over half of the cornbread fell to the floor, both just laughed while salvaging two or three clean slices claiming good on the five second rule. Uncorking the Barbera didn't hamper their looseness, indulging heavy in the above average alcohol content.

Thanksgiving dinner continued beyond merely satisfied. Regina, on the verge of stuffing herself enjoyed Tom's creations with an impression of culinary surprise and bulimic pleasure. Just unable to stop eating! She adored it all as they ended Thanksgiving gluttony, breaking away from food to an easy slip into relaxed conversation and mild affection. Tom passed on the dirty dishes preferring not to break their momentary playful charm. Regina, limbering even more with another dose of Barbera was having second thoughts about not sleeping over. Her tipsy attitude concluded the kitchen floor might just be an erotic episode worth trying!

Fortunately, conditions changed by her host. "We're still hunting on Saturday?" he asked, plugging a hole in a brief moment of silence. "I dug out some gear you can use. It's a little old but in good condition," Tom verified, assuming Regina still planned to hunt this weekend.

"Well why not," talking loud as deep red moved ahead of her metabolism with each sip consumed. "You seem to have a knack for surprises. Shooting at ducks with you might just turn out to be what's missing in my love, I mean life," realizing one word too late how much influence the wine was having. Tom chuckled, in subtle refrain from sarcasm, deciding the timing wasn't fit to tease her 'surprises' remark. He did find it appropriate to replace the cork in a half empty wine bottle, knowing she needed to drive home tonight, sober.

The remaining evening was spent very much warm and cozy, planning Friday and Saturday's hunting schedule, making out again on Tom's uncomfortable living room sofa and updating Regina on her must have list; hunting license, duck stamps and refuge pass. All seemed in order for the weekend outing. Soon enough, breaking into one more intense, heavy petting and face licking session to which Regina applied her passion brakes, hard. Not allowing the great day get out of hand. "Gringo, you're going to have to wait." Regina thought it best to leave before letting any additional romance rekindle. She rose to get her jacket, preparing to make a polite exit.

Tom stood also, reluctant to end the evening. Wanting another chance to change her mind. Thought better of it and switched to a professional question. "So how's the murder case coming along?" Clearing plates from the dinner table without looking at Gonzalez. Stacking bowls, cups and wiping down before helping with her jacket.

Regina was a little unnerved for some reason. She didn't expect any questions about the case, fumbling bad for a cheap response. "Not much new as of late. You're still a suspect however," she bellowed wondering how Tom Ellis would react.

"Wheeeww, I'm scared," Tom joked. Opening his front door, descending a porch staircase.

Regina didn't know what to make of his question at first but concluded he acted fairly unconcerned. She snickered, shrugged it off, descended the stairs and in one motion hugged the newest man in her life. Kissed him goodnight wishing pleasant dreams, would see him tomorrow around six o'clock, then drove off into a breezy and cold Thanksgiving night.

Elly kept watch until taillights faded away. "That went better than expected. Much better," speaking out loud. He couldn't force a holiday feeling however. "I hope she shows up tomorrow."

Chris

Late Friday morning, Chris came into work even though it was an off day. He received a short text on his cell from Captain Anderson. "Sheets might have been spotted driving by Mrs. Patterson's house Wednesday evening. Suspicious circumstances??" End of message. No more details.

It was just going this way for Davis, spending most of Thanksgiving Day trying in vain to touch base with his elusive daughter. Indeed, becoming harder and harder to talk to her and as usual, Chris' ex-wife proved to be of little help. "Oh well," he told himself in a leftover, Turkey Day drunken fog, "another holiday spent solo. What else is new?" Which was the main reason why Davis came to the office on his off day.

Another reason was Anderson's text message. "Suspicious circumstances," kept repeating in his head. "This seems way too coincidental," talking himself into a stubborn resolve all but forgetting his lousy family holiday. "I have to get some additional information on this deputy," Chris said logging onto his work station, going straight to the Sarah Crosby murder files. He decided to research the investigation files yet again. Rereading reports, findings and conclusions. Probing, aching to stumble over something, anything he might've missed on three previous scours. Nothing much caught his eye beyond previous observations. Irate and shoving his chair away from his computer grumbling in frustration.

Realizing the need to confront Douglas Sheets face to face. He thought about tailing him for a while if he could. "Risky business for cops following cops around," reasoning it unlikely to reveal much unless tracked twenty four hours a day.

His mind wondered. "What's the best way to win some reliable information on this cop?" Then shifting wild over to Franny. "I wonder how the Braden's Thanksgiving Day went?" Envisioning her soft touch and full body shape. Believing for a moment, somehow receiving a whiff of her fragrance, fostering deep cravings which ignited a fantasy world of them together. Groping, breathing hard and feeling each other rise with pure excitement. Chris kicked the chair this time. Graphic images drained from his libido like an empty Blackman, replaced by another idea. "Why not? Maybe Douglas and his wife don't get along? Hell, look at Franny Braden. She's even hot to get it going with an investigating cop! Why not Mrs. Sheets?" Considering it for real now. "What the fuck, maybe all the women surrounding this case are screwed up? It couldn't hurt." Composing preliminary plans for a possible meeting with Mrs. Douglas Sheets ASAP. "I'll run it by Anderson on Monday morning. Get his and Gonzo's opinion," Chris talked to himself quite loud, raising his excitement level a notch or two. "Forget it, I'm going up today!"

Now he considered his next two days. Saturday and Sunday, eavesdropping, peeking, watching, observing. "An old fashioned surveillance," speaking out loud as if someone was standing by his side listening intent. Dampening his spirits somewhat, knowing he'd most likely get one opportunity to question Mrs. Sheets without Douglas being present. Chris understood, once Sheets discovers his wife being questioned he'll shut her down with a lawyer and that'll be it. "Or he'll just shoot me!" Joking to himself but in truth, unable to put it past the sheriff. Davis returned to Sarah Crosby's case files one more time, reading notes carefully for something unusual but the fingerprint sessions kept shouting back over and over again. "All those repeated dustings for fingerprints that never materialized. Why? In some peculiar way these dustings mean something to both murder cases. I'm sure of it," Chris told himself, letting the faint words roll off his lips without making a sound. "What is it?"

He knew this weekend would offer plenty of free time to think it over. Sitting in his car, bored, waiting, waiting and waiting. Davis made a note of Sheets' address and left the office. He could be in Sonora by early afternoon, easy. "Mmm, I can get a few bags of toffee almonds on the way up."

Anderson

Bailey rolled over bumping her cheek against Billy's forehead. "Ouch," groaning soft to avoid waking Billy from a supposed deep sleep. Anderson stirred, rather slow from another night of light snoozing and sporadic tossing. Patricia scooted in close to Billy's warm body, throwing her right arm over his sparse hairy chest. She arrived late, Thanksgiving night finding Billy awake and waiting. He refused to join the reporter at her family's Turkey Day Bash. Once seeing the guest list and press coverage, Billy was glad he declined but aware he missed quite a party at the Mark Hopkins. The glitzy event brought out quite a few local celebs, politicians and wealthy San Franciscans. If anyone from Tracy's P.D. had spotted him, Chief Yung would've had a fit. Anderson realized the Chief would go ballistic if he had any idea who shared his bed right now. Patricia moved in closer yet, wrapping a bare leg over his then allowed her hand to settle over Billy's lower stomach. She felt his reflexes jump, emitting a sexy giggle and moved her fingers slowly lower, holding him in full grasp hearing a short breath followed by a pleasurable moan.

Bailey prized his reaction accepting her lover's touch over each humid breast. They continued their soft touches exploring bodies with reckless indulgence, building into passionate groans and intense orgasms. Lying together for a while longer, resting, panting, caressing, holding. Patricia welcomed Anderson's body, feeling satisfied and a comfortable intimacy with their sexual play. She wasn't sure if they were on track for a serious relationship but Bailey pictured them together in a way that appealed to her at this time. After all, Billy was crucial if she was ever to earn her freedom.

"You know, let's sleep in a little longer," Anderson whispered, rolling over and dragging Bailey's arm to cover his torso. Grasping her hand and holding tight, Billy rolled away slowly drawing Bailey even closer. Feeling her full breasts and hard nipples pressing into the small of his bare back. He pushed back taking pleasure in her body heat.

Bailey enjoyed the cuddle and took this moment as perfect opportunity. "So how's the investigation going? Anything new?" she asked, neutral as possible, wiggling her smooth legs in even tighter. "Any new suspects?"

Anderson responded, with little consideration coming from his sexed up drowsy wits. "Uh, let's see. Gonzalez swears she saw Douglas Sheets drive by Mrs. Patterson's house Wednesday evening," trying harder to stay awake.

"Why? What would he be doing there?" Bailey asked, aware of whom Anderson referred from Sarah Crosby's murder trial. She had to contain a bit of excitement, finally receiving some news about the case. Not prepared however, to hear of the sheriff acting strange. None the less it could be fresh news Bailey needed. "That seems kind of odd. Is Sheets a suspect?" asking in monotone trying to avoid coming across like an investigator.

"Yeah. We need more info on him but he's being treated like a suspect for now," the Captain offered failing to consider Bailey's personal and professional attachments to his murder case.

Patricia mulled over his last statement. "Why the hell would Sheets want to shoot Marcus Crosby? That sounds like a stretch?" needing to keep her boyfriend talking. She began a slow back scratch with long fingernails. Anderson let out a hefty sigh indicating delight.

Billy rolled over coming face to face with Bailey, her red hair falling loose along bare shoulders and chest. To Anderson, Patricia's pale skin tone, lightly freckled, contrasted just right with the color of her hair. He found her look sensual in the extreme and reached out to enjoy her body once more. "If I didn't know better, I'd think you were trading sex for murder case info?" examining Bailey direct. She was down to one option and moved in close to kiss her Captain firm, forcing her forked tongue into her lover's mouth, plying every corner she could reach. Anderson's mouth slid close to a coddled breast allowing the other hand to slip along her stomach eventually reaching warm, wet inner thighs. Obtaining a soft moan. "Okay, I'm sold," Billy said getting a low snicker from Bailey as well as a long kiss pulling hard with an arm around his neck. The detective thought it harmless to give away some case details. "This is just between us?" Billy waited for the reporter to confirm.

"We think Sheets might have murdered and at this point I can't stress enough, might have murdered him for simple revenge. Douglas Sheets was in charge of getting the evidence needed to convict Marcus of murder. Crosby beat the rap, Sheets failed, Doug got pissed, putting a bullet into Marcus' neck." Anderson kept his hands working fluidly all over the reporter's lower margins.

Bailey had to verbally respond quick. She was growing ager for a double play this morning and it wouldn't be long before Patricia was responding to Billy's touch. "Do you think Sheets may have killed him for another reason? Maybe trying to keep something hidden?" but Billy's touch guided her into more sexual activity instead of analysis.

"Funny you should ask Miss Bailey. We've been discussing that topic ourselves. You'll just have to trust in the Tracy P.D. for now. By the way, I better not hear any of this on tomorrow's evening news," Billy warned. Shifting on top of his red haired passion, loving how she moved beneath him, breathing hard. Patricia Bailey got part of what she came for this morning. Now she could refocus on coming once this morning. She sensed, perhaps a loose freedom from a formidable tyrant. She also sensed a man in her life. For once maybe even legitimate.

Estefan

Gleaming. Almost a glare when the sun's angle was just right. Estefan lifted a few rounds from the foam shell holder arranging two neat rows of shiny ammunition. Like always, rolling them through his fingers the way a jeweler inspects final cut gems, perhaps viewing reflections, checking lines, hoping for enchantment.

Unrolling the blanket holding his rifle and draping the wool cover over a wood bench. Pulling up and back on a worn bolt action, Estefan loaded the magazine with four picture perfect cartridges. In and down on the bolt. Up and back. Metallic clicks as one shell is pulled back then launched away, tumbling at Estefan's right foot. Each sequence lands a new round upon the wood plank floor with a solid thud, unlike spent brass cases hitting with slight ring tones. One severely captivated young boy anticipating a special occasion.

"What are you doing Melon Head?" The Jackal's voice whispered causing Estefan to jump. Two rounds slipped from his hand, juggling the rifle too, close to losing his grip altogether but catching the forearm before falling away. Carlos stood rigid on the third step taking in the scene. "The rifle is finally unmasked," Jackal observed, taking two small footsteps closer to Melon Head, eyeing close a glossy scope more than the rifle itself. "You have a shiny new gun and a box of bullets but haven't fired it yet, have you?" Advancing two more strides, reaching out for the rifle barrel inspecting a few small scratches and a minor dent on an ample forearm. Carlos pulled the weapon around wanting to gain control but Estefan wouldn't dare release his treasure.

"You have me again Carlos. I need your help to get it out of here, quietly. You got a car I hope?" Estefan verified while straining to see an old silver gray Honda parked in front of the barn. "I'm almost afraid to ask where you got that car."

"It belongs to my sister's boyfriend. They're in a walnut orchard going at it right now and won't be back for a few hours," encouraging Melon Head with a winking eye.

"Oh man, this gets worse and worse," Estefan growled. "We have to get it out of here in secret!" Estefan ordered a careless looking Jackal who wasn't nervous in the least. "Why should he be scared? It's not his rifle. Why do I partner so often with this criminal anyway?" Estefan cringed turning away in disgust.

"Should be easy man. I'll back into the barn," Carlos started to explain but was fiercely cut off by a riled gun owner.

"No, no. I don't want to explain what your stolen car was doing in Mr. Blevins' barn," conveying his serious side on this one to Carlos.

"The car's parked real close to the front door. Nobody will see anything if you keep it rolled in that blanket," Carlos instructed grabbing Estefan's green ammo box leaving the loft, hopping down squeaky wood steps. "C'mon Melon, no one's around. I get a few shots too," sounding as reckless as ever.

Estefan wanted to call it all off now growing a sick feeling of getting caught today. "If he does anything stupid while on that main road, we're dead.

Dad will kill me," telling himself, but frightened more with the thought of losing his rifle. He stopped cold. However his desire to shoot the rifle took over, put four rounds in his pocket, rolled an oily .222 in the blanket and proceeded down squeaking stairs also. Fast! His criminal accomplice waiting behind the wheel.

Facing Estefan was a wide open passenger door as his blanket roll slipped easy into a worn out backseat. Ordering, "let's go," checking the barn and dirt road. Nothing but a far off tractor churning dust along an open field of harvested beans much too far away to even notice. Carlos hit the gas pedal as Melon Head's door swung close with a loud crunch but didn't latch. "Slow down Jackal," telling his fast driving partner. "Don't give anyone a reason to stop us and how do I close this damn door?"

"Pull up on the handle then release when it shuts," Jackal instructed, bumping down a dry road sending out thin dust plumes, headed for paved highway.

Two gunslingers driving an empty road seeking a right turn through an open gate, back to dirt which leads away from pavement. Finishing in a small grove of oaks scattered among several very old sycamores. The grove flourished in a convenient location beyond two medium sized knolls hiding roadway views and muffling gunshots. Carlos' small Honda bumped and heaved over rough gravel, little more than a one lane path. Arriving at a closed but unlocked gate, which Estefan opened then secured behind them, keeping cattle from wandering onto paved roadway. They continued along the nose of a grass covered mound, arced right and chose to park under a massive horizontal limb stretching from a four foot diameter oak. Estefan felt adrenaline shoot into his legs and torso knowing very soon he'd finally be shooting. Selecting a large fallen limb as a shooting bench, endowed with one remaining branch poking straight up. A convenient fork about two feet above their makeshift seats, created an ideal gun rest.

Estefan withdrew sheets of paper to act as targets complete with one inch diameter bulls eyes, hand drawn of course. He began a pace toward three different trees.

"Hey Melon Head, why not over here," Carlos yelled out pointing to a stand of trees one hundred eighty degrees opposite.

Without interrupting his stride Estefan shouted back, "we'll be shooting toward the road," mystified how the Jackal had made it this far. "What a bean brain," mumbling low.

Near a hundred yards out, Estefan lifted a fist sized rock and pounded small roofing nails to mount one target on a smooth section of fourteen inch oak. Starting another pace he reached a wide sycamore close to one hundred fifty yards. Another target mounted. Ending somewhere near two hundred yards stood a huge oak tree, still catching sunshine. His last target blazed like a beacon. Three goals mounted had Estefan barely under control and jogging back, excitement growing even higher listening to dry leaves and small twigs crackle beneath his running shoes. Nearing Carlos, he spotted his pea-brained partner swinging the rifle and trying to get a clear fix thru the scope. Bringing aim right across Melon Head's path! Estefan ducked sharp behind a large tree without noticing a juvenile rattlesnake slither its way to a partially hollow limb.

"Put it down Carlos. You're pointing it right at me. If that gun's loaded, I'm going to kick your ass," taking Jackal by surprise with his unusually threatening remark.

"Remember Melon Head, I have the rifle," Carlos responded knowing he held a bluffing upper hand. Estefan reached an intimidated Carlos snatching his prize away, drawing back on a weathered bolt action. As expected, one glossy round flipped from the chamber.

"Don't ever load the gun before you're ready to shoot. Never, never point a gun at anyone," Melon growled, giving Carlos a stern look, wanting at the very least to slap the idiot silly!

Estefan snatched the ejected round laying inside a curled, brown sycamore leaf. Conducting one last assessment, determining all was ready. Calming, Estefan loaded the gun, placing it in the forked limb, cleared scope, focused crosshairs, swung the muzzle a couple inches, lowered aim on a large dot one hundred yards distant, firmed his shoulder fit, held his breath, closed both eyes and flinched bad, previous to squeezing a jumpy trigger finger. BAM!

Estefan's eyes popped wide open. Taken by surprise at how loud it fired but fooled by how little it kicked. Peering back at Jackal, sporting a clear wide-eyed look.

"Jesus man, that was cool," Jackal whispered. Each boy breathing in the sweet smell of burnt gunpowder.

"Let's see where it hit," Estefan said sighting thru the scope, trying to see anything like a bullet hole on the paper target. "Clean miss." Already reloading. "Try again."

Knowing what to expect an excited boy sighted with more confidence, held steady and squeezed under control. BANG! He smiled this time like a low average second baseman sliding in safe with a double. Spotting a small hole about an inch up and to the left from the bulls-eye. Reloading and firing again. This round landed just under his previous shot.

"My turn Melon Head," Carlos implored half asking, half begging.

"Wait, let me adjust the scope," uncapping a small metal knob and turning the screw two clicks counter clockwise, moving the rifle's aim left. "Try it now," Estefan directed.

Carlos readied himself and fired quick. Estefan saw the round hit a few feet right of the tree holding the one fifty target. "Clean miss. Way right," confirming Jackal's result. Carlos fired again, much more controlled this time. His round struck just below the black dot's edge. Estefan peered through the scope to check their grouping, in vain. One fifty was too far away to confirm. "Fire one more round and we'll check targets," speaking excited, breaking a sweat.

"That should be good. We have two high, one low but all near center," Estefan replied, studying each page of notebook paper and rubbing a frayed edge of one tiny bullet hole. Estefan couldn't afford to waste all his ammo sighting in the rifle, limiting five rounds at each target. He shot three more at one hundred fifty yards letting Carlos shoot two, after making another sight adjustment. Lower this time as all three shots were high. Carlos put two bullets inside the circle. One a bit high, one slightly low.

"You're good at this Jackal," giving his accomplice a rare compliment. Carlos nodded like he knew this game! They finished at two hundred yards with the gun shooting quite a bit low. "Bet this gun shoots best at one fifty to one hundred seventy five yards. Two hundred yards might be kinda long. Who knows?" responding like a seasoned bench shooter, impressing Carlos with his apparent knowledge.

"We have to get more bullets Estefan and shoot again," Jackal reacted. Estefan noticed Carlos suddenly drop the Melon Head slur. Carefully wrapping the rifle like a swaddling infant, they departed their target range being sure to drive slow but getting back to the barn as soon as possible. Friday night could find more than a few farm workers sharing cervasas and tequila at the barn. Jackal and Melon Head arrived in good shape finding no one inside. Estefan decided to change his hiding place to the other side of the loft, for security and access to a small square opening facing south over Mr. Blevins orchards. "See ya around Estefan," Jackal fisted up before pulling away. Melon began to feel much taller now. Guns having the strange effect of doing that to people.

First Hunt

"Jesus Christ, maybe I should turn around?" Gonzalez passed the first truck and fast food stop along I-5. Hesitating for a split second on the gas, almost applying brakes to catch the exit and make a scared beeline north, back to Tracy. "What am I doing? Duck hunting for God's sake. Am I nuts or what?" struggling to talk herself out of this lunatic commitment but keeping a steady seventy mph south. She couldn't ignore Tom's embraces. Certainly loved the way he kissed, imagining his body pressed hard to hers and, "letting me do most of the probing," she reflected, twisting strands of dark hair tight around her left index finger. Gonzalez remained south bound. Nearing sunset but the valley extending to her left fought off the reddish hues, changing from bright clarity to soft warm tints. Direct sun lit up most building faces, even those laying far to the east. Dark gray shade covered steep hills facing west beyond her passenger window, allowing thin slivers of sunlight to catch the steepest draws and cuts like cracks emitting fiery streaks from underground furnaces. Regina sped by a large green sign. Gustine, two miles.

"What the hell," she sighed. "Over a hundred bucks lighter anyway. He better appreciate this, damn it." Smiling and wondering but with no idea what the day would be like. She continued talking out loud. "I hope I don't have to wear a camo hat."

•••

Less than an hour later, Tom and Regina were driving east on Highway 140 from Gustine then turning south on Highway 165 to Los Banos. Both secondary back routes. A clear evening with stronger than expected winds out of the northwest. Not intense enough right now to excite most waterfowlers, however adequate to spread cold air throughout the Central Valley. For this hunt, Ellis would take any weather he could get.

Tom appeared calm but the detective could read his excitement, anticipating tomorrow's hunt. Regina grew more and more nervous, almost to the point of being nauseous, jammed with a slew of questions but felt uneasy being a nuisance. "So where do we hunt tomorrow? Los Banos Refuge I'm guessing?" she asked, wondering if Kelly Crisp might be working. A strange notion suddenly entered the detective's mind. How would she look to the Refuge folks, hunting now with her recent suspect? Not cool!

"No, not Los Banos. I have a reservation for San Luis Wildlife Refuge. It's a few miles north of Los Banos. We'll be checked in early. Out and long gone before the sweat line goes in." Tom illustrated.

"Sounds good to me," no clue what Tom just detailed but Gonzalez felt relieved knowing she avoided an awkward situation. Tom checked off her essentials one more time. Making sure Regina had her license, duck stamps, ammo and refuge pass.

"Looks like you have it all. We'll have dinner in town then head back to the refuge," Tom directed just as they approached a brown road sign ahead indicating San Luis Wildlife Area. "Have you ever eaten at the Basque Restaurant in Los Banos? My treat. Hope you're hungry."

Regina was almost spinning at this point. "This isn't what I expected," she scolded herself. "But oh boy, he's taking me out to dinner tonight," hoping it's not all that bad. "Is this what you do on all your first dates?" looking at Tom before letting loose with a sharp laugh. Tom smiled but stayed quiet. One nagging concern trickled into Regina's thoughts but too afraid to ask. "Where the hell do we sleep tonight?"

•••

Dinner proved quite unromantic, but plenty of it. Great home cooked food with plenty of it. Family style seating, checkered table clothes, large portions and plenty of it. Regina felt a tad awkward as Tom chatted non-stop with a lady planning to shoot on her husband's duck club in the morning. All the while a substantial over weight fellow insisted on enlightening Gonzo with his subtle secrets on the art of shooting ducks. She was trapped but kept nodding polite, making eye contact with Tom every chance she got. "I wish he'd rescue me damn it!" Following a dessert of chocolate brownie with butter pecan ice cream and plenty of it, Regina reconnected with Tom. Finally getting in some deserved, relaxed conversation and poking fun at one another. She warmed to the casual atmosphere accepting a refill of after dinner coffee. Almost sorry when they headed off but making sure to thank her robust dinner partner cordially, for his advice and plenty of it.

A quick ride found the happy and well fed couple arriving back at San Luis Wildlife Area. Tom conducted a brief check-in at the refuge check station, getting a better idea about tomorrow's time schedule. Regina waited in the truck, becoming her moment of truth. "Where in the hell am I sleeping tonight?" She asked herself looking behind to see an enclave of small travel trailers, half of which had lights burning inside. Off to her right, forty yards out, stood a kelley green port-a-potty which ignited prayers. "Oh God please, let him have a trailer. Please! I promise to say a full Novena, attend three high masses and light a river of candles at St. Mary's if you let him have one of those trailers!"

Tom returned to find an open parking area killing the engine just after muttering, "this looks about as good as any." Regina scanned both sides to the rear of the pick-up to no avail. Not a single trailer hidden from her view. "Okay, let's stash most of the gear up front and get the sleeping bags laid out for bed." The very words Regina dreaded most to hear. Her prayers went unanswered tonight.

"Oh Christ, we're sleeping together in the back of this God damned truck!" Prompting more anxiety, acting with a happy face while helping to store waders, decoy bag, guns and all the other stuff needed for tomorrow's hunt. At least Tom came prepared with a rather thick foam cushion laying throughout his truck bed. She hoped his intent was a comfortable night, sleeping! Ellis smoothed out one sleeping bag, full and open. Then proceeded skillfully to zip together the other bag on top. Her pulse rate went up in significant digits once realizing they'd be sharing one cozy bag tonight. Together! Her heart sank a little also. "Can I just call this whole thing off right now?" she prodded herself with serious misgivings.

Tom Ellis on the other hand seemed to be right at home drafting lax comments about a soft mattress, warm sleeping bag and cuddling for a few hours. Not in any way demented but seeming almost second nature. He had it all in place with a cell phone set to ring at 3:45 A.M. Flashlight, water bottle, two pillows, shirt and pants removed looking back at his lady, ready for action! "Hop in Regina. Close the tailgate behind ya," sounding purely innocent, without gushing in sexual innuendo.

Regina remained frozen at the back of the truck noticing how cold it seemed to be, all of a sudden. Both hands inserted in front pockets staring weird at Tom.

"What?" Tom asked, scooting to one side giving Regina room to climb in. She started to step up but stopped.

"Tom, I don't know about this," she replied softly, almost whimpering.

"About what?" responding without the least bit of discontent in his voice. Almost childlike.

Gonzalez stood outside wagging her bent arms in a vain attempt to shake loose some stress. "I really wasn't expecting it to be quite like this. I thought there might be a motel, cabin or trailer at least." She paused and looked at Tom with sad eyes and quivering lips.

"Oh shoot," Tom said leaning up with a apprehensive look on his face. "You want to bag it all and go back home? Now?"

"Well, no not exactly," stumbling to get the right words out. "Look, I'm not going to sleep with you, I mean make love to you for the first time in the back a damn pick-up truck. I just can't do that." Stopping to regain her composure. But before saying anything more, she heard Tom break into repressed laughs, trying in vain to contain himself. Regina rubbed her forehead wondering where her comedy materialized.

"I don't blame you Regina. I hope you don't think I was expecting or demanding for Christ's sake, you screw me tonight. Really. It's not what I had in mind at all, believe me," Tom pleaded. Red faced but still smiles and chuckles. "C'mon, hop in. It's getting cold outside. I'll kill the light and we'll just go to sleep. You're going to need it."

"Wow," Regina said to herself, which relieved the entire situation. Feeling much better and noticing the temperature drop. "You won't be mad?" rubbing her arms to shake the cold.

"No, now get in here. I'm freezing." Tom responded wanting to sound reassuring as Regina finally climbed in bumping her head on the camper shell's low ceiling.

"Damn it," she hissed, rubbing her miscue. But at last, inside Tom's mobile bedroom.

"Ouch, that one hurt," Ellis joked at a red faced detective. "Go ahead and kill the light if you want to slip out of those jeans. If not, I certainly understand."

Regina opted to stay inside her pants this night but rocked and wiggled down to her T-shirt. Getting comfortable then slid gingerly into the enclosed sleeping arrangements, sure to keep on her side. "I can't believe this," nervous, having all sorts of weird images strafing her fretful mind. She tried to settle in and keep still for a few minutes coercing a gradual calm down.

"Better?" Tom asked. "Sorry but I just assumed you knew the sleeping arrangements," trying his best to comfort her a bit. "My bad."

"No, it's okay. I'm much better now," she lied, curling up tight as her left knee glided along Tom's butt by accident. No reaction.

"Good night," Tom relayed a fake kiss to her with an exaggerated smooch.

"Night," Gonzalez sighed. They went silent for but a few minutes when Regina heard Tom's deep breathing. Sleeping breaths. "Man, that was quick," Regina whispered, not quite believing how sudden he passed into heavy slumber. "Didn't even make a pass at me you jerk!" she fantasized to herself. It took a good hour before falling asleep. Truck lights from new arrivals would illuminate their bedroom with bright headlamps and muffled voices of hunters preparing for an early rise, kept her stirring. Regina relaxed completely, drifting into light siesta, rolling a few times, waking, then at last surrendering into a deeper sleep. She woke again, around two o'clock and by instinct curled in close to Tom. Dragging one arm over his chest, snuggling firm, then collapsing back into deep sleep. Comfortable and warm.

Gadwalls

Flying almost due east led by the hen, both gadwalls left the safety of open refuge water well after dark. A bright moon assisted the small flight of a half dozen birds to locate a large field of coarsely picked seed corn. Roaming flocks of geese and resident mallards, those remaining after opening day slaughter, fed well for a couple weeks or more. The large field lay seven miles or so east of the refuge bounded on three sides by large, older poplars and eucalyptus, acting as wind breaks. Each gadwall could feed heavily, returning to safe waters before sunrise. Knowing somehow, the dark figures with their loud noises would show up in the next day or two, if not this oncoming morning. They could feel a slight chill intruding inside soft down as many pin feathers hadn't developed yet which provided additional insulation needed to fight off winter's cold. Tonight many birds sensed an impending cold front sweeping into the valley led by prevailing northwest currents of air and aware of harsh winter months laying ahead. Colder air and fewer grain fields added up to less accumulated calories needed to grow critical fat reserves. For the gadwalls thus far, all was good in terms of feed but they suffered narrow escapes on three different occasions, when close loud noises had spared their lives for some reason. Their real threat now.

Three pairs, made up of four gadwalls and a cinnamon teal twosome, traveling in a loose flight managed to locate the corn field without event. The hen gadwall was fully satisfied with ample grain and supplemental seeds loading her stomach, as ducks are one bird not endowed with a true crop. She wanted a return to secure water before sunrise sensing danger when attempting to navigate a safe flight in broad daylight. Her mate sensed the anxiety grow, beginning to feel nervous himself should they get started late. Both cinnamon teal loafed in the corn for over an hour before starting an eager feed. They were scratching for much needed grain and wouldn't make it back to their pond before sunrise, at the rate they fed. Low chirps and muted grunts signaled a contented hen teal not ready to leave any time soon. The drake gadwall expected a flight signal from his mate at any moment. A nervous feeling of imminent danger was building, unsure where it might come from.

Across the field calls from three large flocks of Canada geese filled the feeding ground with noise and flapping wings. The gadwalls called them fat black-heads due to an obvious large size, sporting charcoal necks and heads. Thirty five to forty birds glided low over the corn, wings steady, feet low and necks stretched forward looking almost tense. This was all the hen gadwall needed, quacked soft and launched into darkness angling right. Her mate followed as abrupt loud noises rang out in deafening blasts, shattering the feeding zone. Geese fell limp, ducks sprang into flight, more geese fell as shots continued to roar, two mallards crashed back to earth as the lucky gadwalls lifted away just in time. They struggled harder for altitude as more loud noises thudded but sounding distant and less menacing, still climbing however.

It was a small but insidious group of poachers hidden well in a rough pit blind, waiting for geese to arrive before opening fire. They took six or seven large Canadas and a few ducks before leaving the field in running flight. Two rednecks and a Mexican illegal, all in their mid twenties had been scouting the field for days. Setting a timetable and sneaking in after dark to dig a large hole in the field. Sitting quiet this night and waiting, knowing the geese would come eventually and they'd kill a portion. Not to feed a hungry family or ease some strain on making ends meet. They did it for the simple act of doing it! Tonight they got away with it. Tomorrow they'd eat one bird and trash the rest. Fish and Wildlife would soon get wind of their bragging and drunk talk. They'd be caught, arrested, fined and set free. Soon to do it all over again, possibly?

Leaving the cinnamon teal and others way behind, both gadwalls flew a cautious route well above refuge boundaries. Encountering noises from dark shapes and small lights scattered in tules, ponds and along dirt roads. Coming down, slow however, close to Regina and Tom above dark rippled water, flooded in moonlight glare.

...

'Beeeep... Beeeep... Beeeep,' Tom's alarm went off loud enough to disturb him from deep sleep. 3:50 A.M. sharp. 'Beeeep, Beeeep, Beeeep,' continuing to fill the camper shell with annoyance but finishing four cycles before Tom's squishy sensations registered. Sleep time was now over. Reaching out to kill the shrill noise before noticing Regina draped over his back and chest. She issued a faint stir, smacking dry lips but still drowning in deep slumber. Tom noticed her deep breaths and thought it odd how anyone could sleep right through all the irritating noise. "Deep sleeper," he assumed.

Elly turned gently onto his back, relishing her closeness and how warm she felt while trying to wake his body and head. "Whew, this lady can cut some Z's," seeing her scrunched face pressed firm on his bare shoulder. Enjoying their arrangement a while longer, wishing for an intense round of erotic wake up. But knowing time was short and the detective would have none of it in the back of his truck. He issued a soft nudge. No response. Waited, nudged again.

Regina never moved a muscle but her eyes popped open wide, reminiscent of a zombie or vampire awakening in a seventies low budget horror film. While close to awake she needed another ten or fifteen seconds to gain some coherence. Her expression went wide eyed again, jolted into reality but way too self conscious to make any sudden moves. Frantic groping ensured her jeans and t-shirt intact, relieved to find them both in place. "God, what time is it?" being the most she could comprehend at the moment.

"Almost four A.M. Time to get up lover," Ellis enjoyed relaying the info way too much.

Regina didn't reply verbally. Moving a stealthy hand over Tom's left nipple, squeezing it hard between long thin fingers until he squirmed and yelped like a teenager. "Don't call me that," Regina said with her head still resting calm on his shoulder. Tom sat straight up brushing his head on the shell's top.

"That's going to leave a mark," Ellis responded in his most feminine voice, rubbing a cherry red nipple as Regina curled in tight to stay warm. "C'mon detective, time to go hunting."

Regina was just too sleep deprived to get moving and thinking she may not make it. Grabbing her sleeping bag and diving under she prepared to offer new terms. "Tell you what," speaking like a car salesman.

"Oh Christ. What?" Tom wondered trying to get stuff squared away for an orderly gear-up.

"We cancel this whole undertaking, go back to sleep, make violent love later this morning, then go hunting just before noon. What say you lover boy?" having no intention what so ever delivering on the violent sex part of course.

"Let's go," Tom's edict included a pull on her sleeping bag driving Gonzalez to curl even tighter then burying her head into a small red pillow. "What happened to your standards about love in a pick-up truck?" shoving bags of clothes, waders and boots into place for easy access. "C'mon baby, let's go," trying his hand at a little sarcastic humor.

Regina rose, leaning on one elbow. Dark brown hair flowed across her face, t-shirt pinched tight against her upper body outlining firm breasts and frozen nipples. Her sultry act, generating an adult invitation. Tom took it all in, glad to accept her offer if only she was half serious. "At four in the morning you have me a little over a barrel, stud," emphasizing her own sarcasm. "Hell, I might say yes to anything right now," talking sexy and appearing coy for a brief moment only to see Tom on all fours, crawling, grunting and ready to pounce on his sensual prey.

"Really? Anything?" Tom joked, moving in close completely covering his desire.

"All right, all right!" Regina yelled out pushing her would be lover to one side. "I'm gettin' up. Let's go waste some ducks!" A noticeable smirk on her face wondering what the devil she'd be wearing and how the hell to put it on. "What do I need in terms of clothes?" she asked holding a fist over her big yawn.

Tom already started to dress. Standing outside the bed on a small square of carpet where he dropped his jeans, pulled on black, loose fitting fleece pants and wool socks then stepping clumsy into olive green waders. Regina watched close. Poking her head out from the mobile bedroom seeing two young gringos on the left and three older men to her right. "If you think for one second I'm stepping out there and dropping my pants in front of all those rednecks, you're insane." Tom laughed out loud pulling a wading boot over one neoprene booty. "Give me another option sweaty," she commanded but chuckled too.

"Here," Tom lifted a pair of red fleece tights from a clothes bag. "Put these on inside, then come out and we'll get your waders on. But let's move it. They'll be calling reservations soon." Flinging the tights with every intention of hitting the cop full in the face. Regina feinted her mocking fall back with a high pitched squeal, forcing Tom to close the tailgate. She shimmied and squirmed, struggling from one outfit then into another. He helped get her into baggy waders. She laced up well worn wading boots as Tom readied his decoy bag, checking time often to make sure they didn't fall behind.

"You'll have to carry this daypack. It shouldn't be too heavy."

"I don't carry nothin' gringo. Got it!" Looking at her hunting guide with a make-believe frown while trying on the camouflaged backpack. Made a simple strap adjustment and had it fitting just right.

"Just one question sexy," Regina turned slightly presenting Ellis with her best profile, bending one leg, hands on hips. Feeling giddy from a combination of light sleep and a curious anticipation of what this hunt may bring. "Do these waders make my butt look big?" trying to maintain a pose someplace between humor and super model.

"Believe me, your ass looks huge in those waders!" Elly jabbed, tucking in miscellaneous items before closing the tailgate.

"Hey bub," Regina shot back, slapping Tom firm across his right bicep ready to demand respect when Ellis interrupted, knowing a good shot was landed.

"Let's go. They're calling reservations. Got your license and pass, right?" Tom confirmed once more as they headed toward a small mobile trailer.

"Got it boss," Regina answered, following Tom, peering over a shoulder to see just how wide her rear end showed in a pair of baggy, olive green waders.

"Reservation seventeen. Number seventeen," came the early morning call from a small loudspeaker mounted above the trailer door. Department personnel did their best to keep a line of anxious hunters moving along. Verifying hunting licenses, duck stamps, reservation cards, passes and issuing permits to various parking lots scattered throughout four or five separate hunting areas with a limited number of hunters permitted in each lot. "Reservation seventeen please, last call," announced one more time. Soon to be assumed reservation seventeen was still enjoying his sleep somewhere in the parking area.

"We're up next darling," Tom informed Regina as they moved past a group of camo laden hunters filling out the proverbial 'sweat line.' That unfortunate majority not selected in a weekly lottery system. Reservations guaranteed entrance for a day's hunt. Non-reservations entered into a group of hopefuls waiting to be permitted early enough to make shooting time. At this point in the season, all those waiting would likely receive entry.

"Number eighteen here," Tom held the door for Regina as he announced their number, seeing a few hunters take notice of his rather attractive shooting partner.

"Oh yeah, that's us," Regina stated, still lingering in a state of silliness. Predicting her casual wisecrack would draw laughs, but instead, summoned a deadpan look from a bored counter person. He verified her pass quickly directing a rather wide eyed customer to the next station.

"License please," a drowsy middle aged lady summoned Regina to present her hunting license.

"Yep, right here," Gonzo flipped through a jumble of computer generated paper. Holding it open on the counter top.

"Duck stamp?" The fatigued agent looked at Regina over her eyeglasses, smiling disingenuous. Gonzalez produced one large stamp from her wallet, displayed proud to an impatient employee. "Now that needs to be fixed to the back of your license," the clerk instructed, rubbing her forehead and looking down at the counter in annoyance. "Rookies," the agent thought to herself, reaching smartly for the stamp, licking then mounting it on Regina's license. "Please sign the stamp," directing Regina while handing her a pen.

"Where do I sign?" Gonzalez asked.

"Over the face," holding her finger at the signature point beginning to display an air of edginess. As Regina signed she couldn't stop initiating small talk, oblivious that she was slowing things down.

"Do you know Kelly Crisp? She's the refuge manager over at Los Banos Refuge," handing back her pen, expecting a reply.

"Day Pass," the sleepy employee requested all but ignoring Regina's question.

"Yep, right here," Gonzalez handed over a well worn print out. "She's a really nice gal," referring back to the manager once more.

Handing Regina a tag, the weary attendant pointed to the detective's left. "Never met her. Next station please," hoping this hunter would please step aside. Tom moved over helping to usher his gabby partner along, amused but motivated by a group of hunters growing agitated by his partners slow progress. Ellis displayed his documents hearing another female agent manning station three.

"Where are you going today?" asking in a tone which implied 'why are you looking at me and not saying anything!' She waited to fill out Regina's hunting permit and log a parking lot.

Regina couldn't resist. "We're duck huntin' today!" Gonzalez responded, one last attempt to get a laugh from this early morning crowd. Agent three, unable to contain herself, laughed out loud along with two hunters waiting behind Tom. Gonzalez held a ridiculous pose, her right elbow leaning hard on the counter, weight shifted, right knee bent, gushing at Tom.

"We're together. Lot three." Ellis answered swift to cut in as Tom was thankful the staff enjoyed themselves. "That's it, let's go Regina," almost shoving his partner through a narrow metal door, reaching back for his permit.

"See you guys later," Regina shouted over Tom's shoulder just before the trailer door slammed shut. "Nice folks," she commented needing a slow jog to keep steady with Ellis' pace. Tom couldn't help but enjoy every second of the detectives antics.

"Hop in madam. Next stop, parking lot three," Ellis whispered in high spirits.

Pavement gave way to a maintained, all-weather gravel road. A handful of water filled pot holes and deep ruts bounced the couple riding inside a squeaky cab. "I hope we don't get stuck," Gonzalez uttered under her breath somewhat nervous, buckling a now useless seatbelt not used to driving dirt roads in the middle of the night. She looked through a dripping door window into pitch black barely seeing tules and small trees just off the roadway. Feeling much relief when headlamps illuminated a bright yellow sign, indicating parking lot three.

"Make it every time," Tom joked pulling his truck forward onto matted grass and weeds. "Before we get going, let's put on our make-up." Ellis knew how to draw yet another goofy look from his partner. Pulling a plastic tube from his shirt pocket containing two different shades of green on one thick waxy crayon. Lit the dome light and started applying streaks of olive green followed by a darker shade of olive green. Soon, her face looked every bit a special forces soldier. "Do mine now," Tom said handing her the camo tube and shifting his face forward to offer an easy application.

"Kinda into this aren't we," Regina commented rubbing blobs of color over his white skin. "I think I'll give ya the Pedroia look," smearing two large patches below each eye similar to major leaguers. She continued with vampire eyebrows and vertical zombie lines of light green. "Lookin' good man," Gonzalez joked holding back her laughs.

She just about finished as Tom spoke up. "Thanks for coming out with me." His absolute sincerity tugged at Regina's heart. She gave Tom a wink and positive nod, drawing her last lines. She couldn't speak and her eyes became extremely wet.

"Let's go baby doll," Tom declared grabbing food, water, flashlights and two gun cases. He was trying to keep Regina moving, planning to set up in a pond about forty minutes out, walking. Not sure how Gonzalez would fair hiking in waders but glad to see temperatures had dropped into the mid thirties, aware the cold air would help a lot in keeping them cool. This was free roam area on San Luis Wildlife. Those first in had the best chance at best waters. Causing Ellis to grow antsy knowing others would attempt shooting the same pond also. An underlying competition between hunters, was always present on any California Refuge.

"I'm freezing," Regina said strapping on her daypack but spotting two gun cases illuminated by a glowing dome light, resting on the truck bed. She reached for the nearest bag and pulled on exposed stock.

"You won't be cold for long, guaranteed." Tom threw a large decoy bad over his shoulder noticing the extra weight. He wanted to keep Regina's pack light loaded only with food, water and shells. "I'll have to carry the rest," was his plan. The bag seemed heavy none the less, adjusting shoulder and waist straps keeping the load as high as possible.

"Whoa, awesome. Double barrel," Regina exclaimed in a throaty voice holding the shotgun, admiring it's balanced lines and engraved receiver. Shouldering the gun, swinging easy, tracking flight of imaginary birds across the night. "Tom, I love this gun."

Ellis' heart sank. He should've made known his shotgun, never occurring the detective would lay claim. "That's an over and under. Not a double barrel," telling Regina, too late to take the gun back now.

"Right, over and under," Gonzalez agreed, unconscious as she continued to swing the firearm noticing its light weight and compact fit.

"Twenty gauge. You'll love it sweetie," Tom chided with an air of loss she failed to notice. He dearly wanted his gun back. "Oh well," mumbling and clipping a flip buckle over Regina's wading belt then closing the camper shell. Tom slipped a gun strap on a Remington 1100, lifting the shotgun over his left shoulder then adjusted Regina's strap to fit her favorite gun. This night just became first-rate seeing her all smiles. "Let's go seniorita." Pointing out a dirt trail leading away from lot three.

"What's this?" Regina asked holding up a tethered wood rod.

"It's a wading staff slash hiking stick," Tom answered as they walked side by side flipping wood sticks back and forth. "Helps keep you dry when we begin wading."

"Cool, just like fast water trout fishing in the mountains," Regina said, raising Tom's eyebrows, not at all expecting her connection. Another pleasant surprise.

A night walk, served in a bright moon over dry levee roads but with a share of mud and small potholes for splashing rain water. Cold morning air lent to dampness beading up on gun barrels as they dripped condensed moisture. Regina stayed mostly quiet, enthralled by the moonlight hike and didn't complain at all to Tom's relief. He knew too well, how duck hunting can turn into a dreadful labor of sweat, determination and sometimes disappointment. "It's not for everyone," crossed Elly's mind a few times this night but Regina seemed to be enjoying what she experienced thus far. He noticed her look of resolve and enthusiasm to risk something new. Then making occasional small talk and joking, even after slipping and falling twice. Once right off the levee where it narrowed holding a patch of thick, sticky mud. "So far so good," Tom told himself helping her to stand upright and remain steady.

"There's our pond straight ahead. Not more than ten minutes." Tom pointed, stopping to take a short rest and drink much needed water. He sweated heavy now and Regina breathed deep. She gulped on the water bottle too.

"I can't see a thing so lead on bwanna," Regina grunted, flashing Ellis a quick smile then patting him on the butt for effect.

Tom felt like they had it licked, setting a fast pace without stopping. He worried about someone else reaching his pond before them. If so, more hiking would be in order to locate decent shooting water. Always stiff competition on the refuge.

They resumed. Regina was startled favorably, when a great blue heron flushed with a noisy takeoff from a flooded depression next to their levee. Silhouetted against a falling moon and squawking loud she focused on its long bill and dangling legs. Oohed and giggled at the sight, "that's pretty neat. Remind me to bring a camera next time." Tom took her 'next time' remark as a sign things were going well. Reaching a small gap in dense tules, which gave way to a large expanse of open water split by a shimmering streak of bright moonlight.

"Is this it Tom?" Regina asked, somewhat gassed and glad the hike was almost over. "Walking in all this gortex really sucks." Her words promptly sent four mallards flushing from the pond's center. Two loud hens crying alarm calls as the foursome labored in a vertical climb.

Tom watched the flock disappear then glanced to Regina, eyes wide open. "We're here first," is all he said.

"Okay, here's the deal. I'm going out to that large clump of tules," Tom pointed the staff over 'his' pond. "I thought I saw flashlights moving along the opposite levee. We need to make sure someone else isn't trying to set up in here." In a rush to leave the dirt road he splashed into knee deep water. Tom waded through a narrow winding slot in the tules, disappearing after making a hard right turn. Regina removed the daypack needing to give her sore shoulders a quick rest.

"What's up with the pond power already?" Not understanding why Tom had to have this water all to himself. "Should I wait hear quietly for your return? Darling!" Making sure he understood she didn't appreciate him leaving so fast.

"You can follow me out if you feel okay with it. If not, I'll be back in five minutes to give you a hand." Tom was already up to his crotch in muddy water and rather gooey mud. Regina's vision was compromised by darkness, thick tules and Tom's glaring headlamp. She didn't know about the sudden drop-off either, some forty or fifty feet into the pond. A narrow but plunging channel paralleled the perimeter.

"I think I can manage," Regina shouted out, wading with care into muddy water. Her first impression was positive. "Seems easy enough," she said, sliding across firm bottom held together by low growing swamp timothy and sparse tules. Tom had just climbed out of the hidden grade break standing knee deep once more in open water. He just heard Regina say, 'easy enough' when struck by the strange sensation of 'this is all going too well?'

Regina rounded one last turn in the tule channel and reached open water. Seeing Tom standing careless and firm in shallow water no more than twenty five feet away, assuming all clear and safe going. One more stride however, would put her into deep water. Tom turned to cry out alarm but Regina didn't hesitate stepping with confidence off the steep bank. Her left foot went down. Way down without finding bottom, trying in vain to swing the wading staff forward but her weight leaned too far forward, to make the prop useful. All one could do now was pump each leg as feverish as possible, for a run to shallow water.

"Watch for the drop-off," Tom yelled, two seconds too late.

Down she went in a light brown spray of thrashing and splashing, having to reach out to forestall an all out breast stroke! Ellis splashed his way forward attempting to grab outstretched fingers. Just a bit late. Regina half plunged, instinctively turning on one side offering more reach as her right hand finally touched bottom on the other side of the narrow drop-off. Forcing her left leg forward hurled Gonzalez into more splashes, flogging with a high pitched yelp cursing Tom's name. Momentum finished into Tom's grasp. He bent over wrapping arms around Regina's waist, lifting the detective clear of pond water. Losing balance as the decoy bag shifted from his catch, they almost went down together butt first into cold water! Saved by Regina's wading staff being shoved into firm mud. The whole noisy episode lasted only five or six seconds but the damage was done.

Regina emerged coughing and spitting pond water, mad as hell. "What the fuck! Why didn't you tell me about the goddamned hole?" Swinging a hard right hand, slapping Tom stiff on his upper shoulder then glancing across an exposed neck.

"Ouch, gees sorry," Ellis muttered in disgrace rubbing a reddened neckline. "Don't swallow any of that pond water, you know what ducks do in it," asking for more trouble.

"Shit Tom, I'm soaked!" Feeling steady trickles of cold water seeping around a cold butt and down along her right leg. Regina waited a second and confirmed a small amount puddling among chilled toes. Hitting Tom again, square on the elbow with a fisted hand this time. Tom flinched then started squeezing wet sleeves as water fell free from soaked camo.

"You'll be fine. A little water is expected when you're hunting ducks," needing to assure her all was still good. "Hell my waders leak in both feet," Ellis lied, willing to say anything to keep this hunt going forward.

"Damn it. Damn it! Are there any other holes to fall into out here?" Gonzalez yelled at her red faced partner, who became relieved she didn't want to end the day.

"No, it's shallow with a hard bottom out to where we shoot," Tom assured her but still a hundred yards away.

"Stay close this time. Let me know about any trouble. You got that, sweetheart!" Giving Tom a look that said, 'you really screwed up this time.' Regina used her staff to get steady then issued a vigorous shake of both arms in front of her, deliberately spraying Tom with a light shower of pond water.

"Yes dear," Tom turned fast to keep moving toward the tules and wiping pond water from his cheeks.

Moving together neither had much to say after the debacle. "I hope your Citori didn't get soaked," the detective acted as if she cared about his gun at the moment.

"It's okay. I saw it the whole time. You kept it pretty clear of the water. Nice job," lying again and drawing Regina closer, wiping her face clear of muddy streaks and forcing a sympathetic smile. "Sorry. My bad but you'll hardly notice it in a while. Those sleeves will dry out in no time," Tom was becoming way to good playing the deceitful part. Elly heard widgeon and pintails whistling overhead. High flying groups unseen in darkness but their chirps snapped Tom back into hunting form.

"You owe me on this one," Regina sneered poking her index finger into Tom's chest, forcing a tiny leer.

"C'mon, it's almost six o'clock. Shooting time starts in a half hour. Let's get set-up." Tom grasped Regina's hand walking side by side toward the tules without incident, reaching their make shift blind breathing hard and just in time. Across the pond almost straight away, Ellis spotted two headlamps entering his shooting water. "I've gotta chase those two out of this pond. If they get set-up in here none of us will get any birds," Elly warned, having Regina start unloading decoys to make it appear this pond is already well covered. Tom began pursuit direct at two lights bobbing up and down a couple hundred yards away.

Regina stashed some gear and removed a few decoys admiring their looks and painted detail. Figuring out the pliable anchor weights twisted around each neck and began unraveling plastic lines. She removed two mallard dekes but kept an ear tuned to hear Tom's voice. "Get a few boys together with all that testosterone flowing and you're bound to have some pushing and shoving," talking to herself, further inspecting a small teal decoy appreciating it's tiny bill and uplifted tail feathers.

"Hey, this pond is taken," Tom yelled to unseen faces and glowing headlamps. Regina stood to get a look. "This pond is taken," shouting out his trespassing caution even louder.

"Ah crap," one flashlight said out loud. "Someone's already out here," the other flashlight confirmed.

"Maybe we can shoot at the far end," light number one wondered, clearly audible to Tom still on direct approach.

"No way guys," Tom came hard-ass again. "I've shot here a few times. This pond's not big enough for two groups," almost screaming now as each backlit figure came into outline view. "Try the pond on the other side. It shoots good too. Especially in the afternoon," untruthful once more, referencing both flashlights to open water opposite the levee they hiked in from.

"We can hunt the other end of this pond," second light announced beginning a move to Tom's right.

"It's too close guys," Tom said firm, demanding them to move out.

"C'mon, let's move up," number two light couldn't quite finish his thought when from behind, Regina's voice roared out.

"Both of you assholes better move on. I'm a cop and I'll have wardens out here to arrest you for crowding!" Tom was caught off guard looking back to see Regina wading in force, leaving the tules in a march toward three flashlights and churning splashy waves.

"I've heard this one before," Tom mumbled. "Let's see what happens," squinting back into bright headlights.

Number one light stopped. "Let's go back. We have time to find some other place to set-up." Number two turned in mid stride, giving in and made his way out of Tom's pond.

Once again Ellis stood in awe, thoroughly impressed by the detective's boldness.

"Nice work partner," Tom applauded Regina as he returned to 'their' clump of tules. "You're pretty good at laying down the law, aren't you." Working a couple decoy lines to remove tangles separating mallards from pintails.

Regina chuckled softly. "I am a cop after all," laughing the words.

Beginning their setup by hauling decoys, grabbing each deke by a rigid neck and launching them underhand like distorted oversized softballs. "I'm not too anal about decoy spreads and patterns," he told Regina lobbing the small teal next to bobbing pintails.

Regina stopped moving abrupt. "Oh, that's a relief Tom. I was so scared you might be one of those, every decoy has to be in just the right place, kinda duck hunter!" Letting Tom know how ridiculous he sounded. Ellis pretended to ignore her swipe but came to a halt and let loose with a belly laugh. He made his way back in a hurry removing the wind duck decoy for setup. Assembling wings into ball bearing tubes and mounting the awkward looking windmill atop a section of PVC pipe. Its wings rotated sharp as he waded into their landing zone and shoved the contraption into firm mud.

"You have one of those whirly gigs too," Regina commented flipping a hen pintail decoy to one side and moving close to get a better view of this mallard, wing-flapping object. "Does that thing really decoy birds?" She asked, bending over to inspect its elements. Intrigued.

"I know all this stuff sounds goofy but you can't believe how fanatical some hunters can get," Ellis explained still giggling but continuing on about extensive decoy patterns and using specific species in certain areas. "I just separate the mallards and pintails into two groups creating an opening between decoy sets, making for a clear landing zone. Hopefully we'll get some birds to commit inside this open area."

"A killing zone," Regina observed.

"That's it," Ellis concurred. "We'll be hidden right at the front door so to speak." Launching the last of two teal dekes adjacent to the sprig.

"We'll see," Gonzalez scoffed, splashing her way back to the tules. Hearing a slight clanking from the spinning wing decoy as ripples on the water indicated an intermediate wind. It hit her in the face cold, not realizing Tom intentionally set the spread downwind from their blind, knowing ducks almost always land into the wind. She was wide eyed now and enjoying every minute. The entire scene of darkness, strange sounds, water, fake ducks, spinning wings, shotguns, hiding, camouflage and Tom's closeness added to her sense of expectation. "I wonder how all this will unfold?" she asked herself feeling almost giddy. Shooting time was little more than five minutes away. Gonzalez completely forgot about her wet toes.

...

Circling high over an extreme end of a rather large pond, the two gadwalls began a methodical search for inviting but safe resting water. Well fed this morning and only needing a quiet backwater to loaf the remaining day away. However, both remained on high guard following their near death episode in the corn field. Looping around but staying close to his companion the drake gadwall advanced on more open water intending another close search. His eye made out very clear surface detail and a shrub filled outline. Nothing unnatural detected so far. Small loose flocks of mud hens favored the pond's center resting peaceful with slight, undulating bobs. Flying lower he caught sight of a single hen mallard gliding below well inside the pond's perimeter. She seemed encouraged by two groups of resting ducks with fluttering wings flashing in muted, light. The drake gadwall spotted them also, descending but swerving hard to his left. He considered a better approach crossing against building winds to make a lower pass. If any loud noises happen to erupt, they could escape to safe height with wind in their wings. One more sharp turn allowed his mate to draw even. They aimed for a patch of tules stretching behind bobbing ducks just as the hen mallard veered from her approach, landing safe and secure further out amid smaller clumps of tules, as mallards often will. Each gadwall dropped faster favoring this quiet pond for a morning's rest.

...

Reaching inside her coat pocket retrieving three inch magnum loads, two yellow shell cases slid secure into well oiled chambers, loading her acquired over and under, checking its tang safety for proper position. Regina turned, scanning dark skies. But lacking any experienced nighttime vision, to her pitch black remained. Sunrise over thirty minutes away, the detective lowered her Citori, resting it over bent tules on the green decoy bag. Waiting time.

Tom heard a low pitched quack from an unseen hen mallard. Straining eyes to spot any ducks flying low enough for an easy, legal time kill. Way off to one side he spotted two birds, wings set in a nervous glide on an up and down flight path crossing into the wind. He could tell they sensed danger maintaining repeated searches from side to side but on a wide track to pass near their blind.

"I can't see a thing," Regina chuckled sitting quite high on her marsh seat. Tom had fastened wooden seats, little more than two boards nailed into a crude 'T' and stabbed into thick mud. Presenting just enough support to offer a break from standing all day in a sticky bottom.

Ellis dropped slow to one knee, very low in pond water right in front of Regina. Staring directly over her right shoulder. Regina glanced at Tom wondering what he was up to now. "Are you proposing to me gringo?" she giggled, clueless of developments behind her.

Shifting his gun across a bent knee appearing tense. "Don't move," staring bug eyed.

"What is it?" Regina whimpered scrunching shoulders tight, drawing her head down like a fretting baby bird.

"Don't move," Tom whispered bending lower, holding an intense stare just above her right ear.

"What?" Gonzalez whispered, frozen in place and too afraid to move. Perceiving Tom's focus above her ear she tried in vain to shift her eyes as far as possible, straining to find out what it might be. "What?" whispering but still not moving her head.

"Don't move." Tom said slower yet. He appeared haunted.

"Jesus Tom!" Regina yelled out in a shrill scream, leaping off her seat right into her companion's grasp. She cared less about the splash close to knocking him into muddy water. "What is it!?" shrieking again, holding trembling arms around Tom's shoulders, head buried in his chest, panting scared gulps of air.

The drake gadwall saw Regina's movements, flaring in a vertical rise. Hearing the high pitched scream sent him even higher. His mate followed suit banking sharp left and rising fast. "Two mallards, I think?" Having a hard time discerning the species in scarce light. "They were coming right in," Tom delighted, holding Gonzalez close making sure she didn't slip or fall again. Giving her time to calm down.

"Oh my God, you have to tell me." Regina unlocked from Tom's tight grasp. "I thought a spider or snake was creeping up behind me. You scared me half to death!" Forcing a thin smile, peeping back at Tom, shaking her head feeling quite stupid and completely red faced. Falling back into his grasp for additional relief.

"Sorry," Tom apologized. "But, a spider? That's wimpy."

"I hate spiders," Regina confessed. Tom knew immediately she was a hundred twenty percent serious. They both resettled, drank some water, calmed down, resuming their watch for targets.

"Okay, let's keep an eye out. Maybe we can get a shot or two," Tom said just as four booms roared from the pond opposite the levee road. From various directions more gunshots rang out. Some quite loud and some scarcely audible in the distance. Nearby shooting would spook birds working their pond but the birds seemed aware far off noises were of no danger. Saturday's hunt was in full swing now.

"There's a flock of teal off to the right," Tom pointed across the pond to a tight bunch of small birds churning rapid wings. Low, but out of shooting range.

"I can't see a thing. How can you see ducks flying in the dark?" Regina half commented and half asked.

"Give it time, your eyes will adjust," Ellis said, reaching for a sprig whistle to blow short, high pitched beeps. Attempting to mimick teal chirps. He knew how hard it was getting adjusted to spot small birds in low light conditions.

"I still can't see much," Regina sounded lost and grew frustrated.

"Still there off to the right. Four or five birds. They're dropping lower, turning our way now." Tom squatted into water. Regina stared intense. She finally picked up white flashes moving low over the pond, making out three birds.

"I see 'em now," she responded. Excited. Crouching, keeping her gun low and the muzzle pointed over swaying decoys. Gonzalez felt comfortable and ready to shoot. All three birds she locked onto veered in closer increasing her pulse rate, sparking arms and legs into tiny shivers. "Let me know when to shoot," squealing a whisper as Tom nodded while blowing peeps and chirps. "They're closer," she felt but Tom still didn't give the go sign. "What's he waiting for?" Regina thought to herself, needing to leave her crouch as muscle tension set in. "He doesn't seem to be looking at the birds?"

The first of three birds just passed beyond the farthest decoy, angling in low, directly over their spread. "Get ready," Tom spoke at last and Regina pushed the safety forward, raising her head above swaying tules to watch the lead bird sail through the killing zone. Tom stayed focused to the right and up, however. "Now," speaking clear.

Regina stood, trying to catch a lead on the second bird. It's white belly and under wings contrasted nice with various black marks across a dark black tail and back. Three stilts right in place, preceding a winter sunrise! Tom shifted behind Regina for safety's sake and to better watch her aim. She was swinging the twenty gauge too low however. Below the horizon in fact. Five teal had locked up. Each diminutive bird tipping fast, left to right, trying to force a quick landing but still some twenty yards overhead. Tom noticed a glimpse of white in the killing zone as Regina fired her first barrel. White spray erupted well behind and under the second stilt, veering away sharp after being paid a heavy blast.

"Whoa girl, not those." Too late! The detective fired again swinging on the trailing bird. Another splash exploded right next to a drake mallard decoy but far to one side of an outbound, petrified stilt. Lucky and unharmed.

"What'd you say?" Regina asked chuckling, lowering the over and under with smoke curling from the muzzle, watching three stilts fly off and land on the opposite side of the pond. Which struck her as odd checking Tom with a blank stare.

"Those weren't ducks," said Tom, laughing once again seeing Regina swallow hard.

"You said shoot," Regina replied, a little bewildered but exhilarated.

"I meant at the teal, off to your right," pointing to where she should've been aimed. They looked at one another in silence. Tom grinned first, like always.

"Oops," Regina said laughing easy.

"No harm done," consoling his partner, settling back into the blind. Gonzalez couldn't wait to take another shot.

So it went for the next two hours with a number of flights approaching, fixed on their decoys. Regina still couldn't quite establish the low flying birds on most flocks and way too late on others. Not quite enough light, even after sunrise for untrained eyes to adjust on low, fast flying waterfowl. In her defense however, she made time to admire a winter sunrise over swaying expanses of rapier tipped tules, framed against red outlines of thin clouds and deep blue water. Her concentration waned which Tom noticed but refused to interrupt her enchantment. "It's more than just shooting birds," he told himself on every hunt.

Gonzalez began sighting higher flocks as her eyes made the correction to waving V formations and hearing calls from passing birds, constantly asking, "what kind are those?" Ellis enjoyed offering his best guesses.

"Gringo," she said direct. "You take the next bird. I'll watch. I need some visual aid." Making perfect sense, realizing two or three good set ups on close birds had failed. Tom was willing to back off from shooting, not wanting to dampen Regina's enthusiasm. Maybe now would be a good time to teach and learn through example.

"You're sure?" asking sincere.

"Yep. Go for it," Regina affirmed. Which started the inevitable waiting game. Two flocks of teal, one a large group of fifteen plus three birds following a pair of widgeon made close passes but spooked after two nearby gunshots. Skyscrapers from novice or just impatient shooters unwilling to let cautious ducks work in close. A common problem on slow days. Refuge hunting will often go this way unfortunately, as groups of inconsiderate hunters crowd onto productive ponds flaring ducks throughout the day. Frustrating rookie hunters until boredom, surrender or better sense prevails. Leaving the diehards to their secluded locations.

After eleven o'clock subtle changes were set in motion, slightly. Casual hunters began moving out and a stiffer breeze seemed to wake up a sleepy marsh. Shorebirds, egrets, mud hens and stilts come forward working shallow water along watery edges for insects, snails and small fish. Hawks and harriers hovered above grass fields searching vulnerable rodents or occasional reptiles. Overhead two fast moving flocks of diving ducks pierced the wind head on leaving a noticeable blast of air in their wakes. Like magic, out of nowhere two drake pintails sailed in high over the pond, catching Tom off guard. Regina heard them cutting across a growing breeze generating sound like stiff winds blowing through tall trees. She stooped lower, settling still as they passed straight overhead. Causing Regina to ask Tom, "what kind of ducks are those?" Both shooters crouched even lower in unison. Watching close as each sprig turned but flying very fast above open water showing their backs this time. Circling further behind them, two elegant pintails became framed against billowy soft clouds. A characteristic scene of late fall and early winter in Los Banos. One bird banked hard, turning fast.

Gonzalez, glued to this bird watched wing feathers ruffle slightly. It's long thin 'sprig' tail waved like a conductors baton as head and neck stayed rigid, looking side to side. To her this bird became an illustration of fluid life, speed, agility, grace. The second bird tried to catch up but its wide turn dragged him over open water giving him a different perspective of their set-up. Both birds on separate searching paths getting two clear views to scrutinize potential danger but remaining safe, completing another high pass.

"Don't move," said Tom, barely loud enough squatting as low as he could. Breathing harder.

Regina looked at him grinning fierce, "more spiders!" They had to cover their mouths to hold belly laughs inside. Tom chirped a few notes as the lead sprig passed again, his partner close behind and always lagging, higher but interested. Regina remained motionless tracking the second bird's pass, its bright white breast and belly catching sunshine like fresh snow covering a ridge line. As if planned, two pintails eventually merged with one another, regrouping as always above open water but setting wings and dropping. They swung in unison this time, back and forth studying every inch of the pond, tule bunches and shoreline. Rising higher to acquire one last safe, wide arc. Testing any unforeseen hidden shapes keeping guard for loud noises or giveaway movements below. Tom sensed the birds were focused on the landing area but maybe away from their decoys, letting loose with a series of loud hailing calls to get their attention. Regina flinched upon hearing Tom's piercing blasts wondering if the volume might actually force the ducks away. Blowing again from the wood call dangling on a lanyard and she noticed at once the way each bird swung around, returning to a searching path for calling ducks. Tom handed Regina a sprig whistle giving her a try at calling, sparingly. He followed up with a long series of feeding chuckles. Rising and falling in tone as each bird dipped and turned, in and away, caught by the fake chattering. Regina blew a few chirps every so often complimenting Ellis' feeding calls. Keying in a little more on the combined calls, two inbound birds dropped lower, freezing each wing for a slow glide and close inspection. Tom could tell by their motions the guarded pintails were feeling more at ease. It was critical to remain still and hidden but also to keep an eye on the pair as much as possible. Watching for unexpected direction changes as well as sudden rises out of gun range. Sailing overhead almost in range, Regina grew tense hearing wind empty from stiff wings and cricket like chirps from the trailing bird.

They played the part well as two adult sprig passed over without noticing two hunters below then banked sharp downwind. Descending even more but gaining speed in another turn. The next pass would take them straight across their decoys giving Regina a backlit profile of sleek, fast moving birds. They were both chirping more excited, indicating a potential landing. Tom could've taken a long shot on this pass but decided to risk a possible closer attempt. He gambled on one last close inspection before landing. Right on cue, like tied to a string, two sprig turned even sharper. Wings locked and dropping lower. This bank would bring the trailing bird on a path straight for the blind. Regina blew the whistle soft causing the lead drake to signal back as if announcing all clear. All Tom had to do was wait for the lingering bird to drift overhead. He stood up easy, raised the shotgun, pointing in front of a blue gray bill letting his gun fire. The drake took a number of pellets throughout his belly, wings and two in its long neck. Never feeling pain, folding slack in mid air crashing with a large splash among mallard decoys to the right side.

"Oh wow," Regina called out. "He looks dead as nails!" Leaving the blind fast to get a glimpse of Tom's kill. Ellis followed, joining her just in case the bull sprig was still alive. It lay belly up, head to one side, eyes open, wings relaxed, still, except for two feet pushing air fore and aft. Final nerve impulses relaying messages to keep kicking. Keep swimming. Keep struggling. The way a light bulb flickers right before the filament burns away. Darkness wins.

Regina stopped a few yards away radiating small waves, causing the pin-tail to bob on a clear surface. Dispersing a faint trail of blood in the water exiting its lower abdomen and a small flow from a gray trimmed bill. Regina fixated on the blood not exactly sure how she felt about a gorgeous bird laying dead in shallow water. Her mind switched unexpected, to a bloody Marcus Crosby crime scene. Vivid recall from long, dark streams of flowing blood. It occurred how fate connected her to this hunt, by someone killing Marcus Crosby. She stepped closer.

Tom fixed on the sprig's gray, scaly, webbed feet, still pumping. After so many kills this one minor occurrence remained, relaying a curious but lingering feeling of guilt. Unknown why but it always passed gently. Ellis approached, firmly lifting a hefty bird by the neck. Regina stared at the chocolate brown head accented with white neck sprigs, soft gray flanks and long tail.

"Incredible." Regina continued to stare not knowing what to say. They waded back to the blind developing a sloshing rhythm, filling silent air. "It seemed like a clean kill to me," she declared, handing Tom some deserved praise. "That whole scenario was," searching for the appropriate word, "it was pretty cool!" Her best word. Then handing Tom a fleeting look that he read simply as, "I can see why you hold this so near." Gonzalez jumped her pace grabbing the pintail from Tom's hand, admiring shape, size and detailed markings. A ruffled section of scarlet red feathers staining a snowy white patch of breast from a blood trickle, failed to dampen her approval. Quickly coming to terms with performing the inevitable role of shooting waterfowl. Blood and killing and death. It didn't seem to bother Regina to any great extent. She held no feelings of revelry or circus and certainly didn't hold any urges to yell out in celebration. Like Tom, a quick wave of respect passed with the bird certainly appreciated in death, much the same as when alive. Once a kill became food which Tom deemed as inflexible, all kills had to become food, ended the hunt entirely. Becoming another fond memory. Nothing evil. Nothing noble.

"I have to get one more shot, at least." Regina pleaded, handing Tom his sprig. He slipped the bird's head through a metal ring joined to a canvass strap. For now, it lay belly down on a bed of tules with a thin drop of blood oozing from one side of its bill. Soon going stiff.

Noon would pass without event as a breezy wind remained. Two teal showed interest for one pass but lifted away gradually on the second and never returned. Tom prepared lunch with both hunters growing hungry as the number of ducks passing by grew thin. Nothing fancy. Splitting a sourdough turkey sandwich smothered in scratch made cranberry relish, added a nice touch. They shared a sweet naval orange and Regina gulped down her Snicker's Bar in a few large bites. Noon rolled halfway past one o'clock capturing Gonzalez in her lack of sleep. Sitting on a hard seat, she slumped and swayed at times with her head down, withdrawing into light sleep for a few minutes at a time. Tom followed suit, relaxed and balanced, feet spread wide with head rested in both hands. If it got bad enough he'd wade to a levee road, find a comfy tree and sleep for an hour. Deep. Fully recharged after a sound rest. Today he stayed in the blind knowing Regina was intent on getting one shot. One good chance. She kept rousing with a shudder swearing she heard sprig whistles and once a faint hen mallard quack. Unlucky for the detective, all budding from her drowsy imagination.

They seemed to get their second wind just past three o'clock. The hard breeze developed into a fair wind spinning Tom's wind decoy in a steady, turning flash. Clouds increased into dense groups permitting streaks of sunny rays streaming between and under gaps in fluffy billows. Becoming colder too forcing zip-ups on their camo jackets. No rain but a definite, albeit minor weather change. Sometimes just enough to trigger groups of willing birds, becoming much colder as the day lingered. First hearing very faint chirps as high flying flocks of pintails were on the move in a variety directions. Followed soon by low groups of widgeon and noisy diving ducks. By four o'clock many ducks were on the move as Tom commented, "the last hour will bring some birds in." Just as the sun slipped behind a large building cloud changing bright blue water to gunpowder gray. Tules appeared darker changing from their normal loud green. Sudden gusts of wind bellowed, surging swimming decoys into a common direction, as they each registered a faint quack. Unquestionably heard the second time. They changed to kneeling positions together like genuflecting at Sunday Mass. Sneaking peeks behind thick tules to see three mallards flying low, gliding a tight turn, searching for an empty corner to settle into.

"Should I call," Regina whispered, her turn to transform wide eyed and very serious.

"Just a little. I'll try the mallard call. Get ready," Tom said without looking at Regina but enjoying their latest decoy. He tracked the flock sailing over open water intending to land somewhere on Tom's pond. Descending lower with intermittent glides and wings set as the hen began hailing in loud drawn out calls. Almost screeching in her typical sandpaper voice. Low volume reedy quacks emitted from two drakes in slow repetition. Three birds committed. In the distance but not far enough away, two gun blasts went off sending each mallard scurrying for altitude. Flying right over two well hidden shooters, way too high for clean shots. Regina chirped her whistle getting a handle on rippling her tongue to better imitate drake pintails as Tom blasted three or four hailing calls trying to seduce the birds back. All three ducks seemed to give up their search and Tom assumed another failed chance. Likely gone. In frustration blowing again even louder, watching three ducks make a wide circle returning near the front edge of the pond. Continuing to turn, accelerating as two shooters noticed a promising flight path. Strange enough heading right at Tom and Regina. The hen leading this time, hailing and chuckling all the way letting her wings drop to a weak flutter. Much lower too.

"Not this pass. We'll wait for the next one," checking to make sure Regina was on board. She nodded, never removing her fix on two drake mallards catching sight of bright orange feet folded below extended tail feathers and a white band on the drake's extended neck. Into the wind, sailing overhead low with a slight whisper continuing halfway to the back edge of the pond before swinging back. "They should pass directly over the decoys, across the wind, into our kill zone," Tom said to himself.

"You take the bird on the right and I'll shoot the left one," Tom directed. Again Regina nodded, excited with tension churning in her stomach. Another gust of wind blew across the water as bright sunshine emerged from behind drifting clouds. Lighting the entire stage, providing Regina an easy display of the drake's yellow bill and blue wing patches reflected off rigid wings. On they came, in complete decoy swinging right to left. "Get ready," Elly whispered. Regina pushed her safety off ready to fire. "Now," speaking calm.

Both shooters rose to fire. Regina brought her gun up fast aiming right to the closest drake gliding over decoys but moving faster than expected. Her gun blasted first but well behind a stunned drake. Hearing Tom's gun explode as both birds rose fast, unhurt. Tom fired again winging the hen, dropping straight down. Regina's upper barrel unloaded behind and under this time.

"Missed, damn it," Gonzalez announced as Tom bolted from the tules.

"I wounded that hen. Shit! C'mon, I may need some help," sounding dissatisfied as Regina splashed thru the pond. "There it is," pointing to his left, floating low and paddling hard going away but upright. "Stay to the right side." Tom had to keep the wounded bird in open water as he gave chase. The hen was able to keep the gap steady, by flapping one good wing every so often to make ground, even as Tom's strides were long and hard over a sun drenched pond. Regina, quite spent now, stumbled in thick mud and almost fell watching as Tom continue to pursue.

Ellis, pissed at himself knew the hen would reach the shoreline first thus able to slip into dense tules and weeds, probably lost for good. He had to shoot again. Gonzalez watched on as Tom stopped and aimed steady at the swimming bird. It's head and neck dipping on each leg stroke in pain, getting as much push as possible. The shot went off, subdued by low aim. A violent spray engulfed the mottled brown hen. One pellet striking her upper neck off center. Another entered through flank muscles piercing upper lung tissue. Two more struck her lower abdomen severing intestine as the other barely punctured heavy skin and fat. She flailed her wing in pain, spasms splashing water as Tom arrived, still alive but mortally wounded. Then lifted from the pond where she dearly wanted to rest.

Ellis hated wounded birds. "Shit!" he growled as Regina approached. She wondered why he seemed so mad. "All right," he told himself. "Damn I hate this," grimacing as blood ran from the mallard's spotted orange bill and wings flapping wild. Moving both hands around the hen's neck, pulling slight then pushing and twisting decisive, feeling vertebrae separate as the hen flapped in one last violent defiance. "I'm sorry. Please pass on." he said, holding tight, disappointed and lamenting his poor aim. Her head grew limp in a slow droop then stillness, indicating unpleasant death. For the hen as well as Tom.

Regina watched close, unable to say anything but understood the bird had to be put out of its misery. Not sure however, if she could complete a finishing task with her own hands? "That wasn't pretty," she thought, pinning an uneasy look on Tom right now.

"Not exactly the bright side of hunting," Tom confessed, holding his kill in both hands admiring its shape and deep blue wing speculums edged in black and white. "I hate screwing up an easy shot like that. It's not fair to the birds. Shit, I hate that!" Spurning himself again as they turned back to the tules. Regina walked behind focused on the dead bird. As it flopped and spun she noticed color detail on dark back feathers and how smooth they transitioned to a softer, tan breast. Orange feet and legs almost glowing. Somehow out of place?

Tom stayed silent hoping Regina didn't think lesser of him in light of what has to be done to wounded birds. Wondering if the episode may have altered her attitude on hunting? In reality, it wouldn't change anything at all. By the time they reached the blind she was replaying her own missed shot and admired how perfect Tom's two birds looked side by side.

"I want a pair of ducks like those," mumbling to herself already forgetting about the neck ringing taking place just a few minutes before. Under fifteen minutes remained in shooting time as Tom knelt down yet again, blowing sharp feeding chuckles. Regina, on instinct now clutched her whistle bending deep without noticing pond water up to her waist. "Where?"

"Straight out. Four teal working this way." Tom kept watch in their direction. It was all Regina needed as she froze, picking out four zigzagging ducks. Very low, very fast. Right at her. Her call chirped twice. "Get ready," Tom said as the flock kept coming. "Now."

Regina stood faster this time and four teal paid no attention, remaining in formation. She wasn't prepared for the speed a group of small waterfowl could manage. Shouldering her over and under clean but unable to get enough lead required on a tilted, fast moving green wing. She fired as the muzzle just cleared a black bill. Nothing. Pulled the trigger again pretty fast, knowing both shots were into open air behind a passing male bird.

"Too fast. Way too fast," Regina spoke a soft laugh showing a toothy grin that Tom read as pure enchantment. He was well experienced how misses can be every bit as fun as hits, most times. "Teal are quick aren't they?" Breaking her gun in half as two spent casings popped from a smoking breech.

Tom moved his head in positive motion. "They are at that, gorgeous!" Looking over dark water as a red glow and pink horizon was the last light remaining. Birds continued to move but most flew too high to show interest. Many of these flights were leaving the refuge foraging for high calorie food. Little appeal in resting water for hungry waterfowl but that was about to change soon. Rested, well fed ducks and geese would be returning to safe refuge waters soon after sunset. A fall sun dipped behind clusters of thick clouds just above ridgeline, blushing a red and light blue sky. "We're about out of time. Let's call it a day," Tom said almost sad, which held a duel viewpoint. Dusk being a fleeting time of appreciation and rare beauty. It was also the end, similar to ninth innings with cheers for a winning game but sad it was ending too.

"It's glorious out here," Regina whispered, admiring the entire scene. Ducks flying in without caution, geese honking, undulating flocks of songbirds, raptors hunting watery edges, faint gunshots, evening sunset, water, weeds and mud. "Next Saturday. Bring me back out here next week," the detective issued a serious demand.

"You got it," Tom agreed.

"Promise?"

"I promise." Tom smiled, knowing what a day like this meant to him. "It's working," he thought to himself. "Let's grab the decoys. You can carry them back," wading in, joking next to his new hunting partner.

Regina hauled in a few deeks wrapping cords and soft lead weights around thin necks. Together pitching plastic ducks back to heavy tules near their shooting blind. Gear collected, decoys stashed in a heavy decoy bag, wood seats left behind for future hunts, guns in slings and Regina wearing a strap of dead birds. Now for the long walk back. By far, the hardest work of the day. Not much conversation ensued after the first ten minutes. Weary legs and heavy breathing took over. Tom helped out by carrying the ducks for a while and telling her lies, "not much further." Before long they spotted headlights at the end of a long dirt levee. Almost there.

Gonzalez wasn't struggling nearly as much as Tom imagined however. Her slow, steady pace appeared to be exhaustion but the detective's mind was in other places. Understanding this had become more than a new experience. She was wading into a new relationship, literally! Feeling excited and more than a little scared, all at the same time. They were almost there.

Estefan

Before darkness fell Estefan wanted to check his trophy. From his high perch, Melon Head held a clear view covering more than half of Clay Blevins' productive ranch. Orchards stretched far off to the south and west teased by dimming sunlight on the uppermost branches only. Estefan held a loaded rifle in his hands. Knowing it wasn't the safest thing to do but he loved how smooth and quiet the bolt action worked with live ammunition. Not as many hollow pings and rings but much softer clicks controlling each delicate metal on metal stroke. He wondered if it might be soft brass and copper helping in some way to cushion machined parts during the reloading process. Sitting comfortable and high on a wood produce box, Estefan shoved his last four rounds into the magazine noticing each sharp bullet point nestled inside their spring loaded resting place. Every .222 round possessed metallic reflections with their nuanced attraction. Perfect shapes compiled of tangent curves and slight tapers emitted an oily coating. The young boy became seduced by every small detail of lines, workmanship and power.

Having a difficult time initially, to seat some ammo into their proper click points and locked in place. In time, with plenty of practice, Estefan worked these quirky problems out becoming hooked on running bullets in and out of his rifle. Lifting sharp then pulling back on a polished bolt action watching each load extracted from the firing chamber, snared by a small metal claw and flipped clear from a spring loaded lever. Ejected rounds somersaulted in brisk fashion a few inches up and away from the breech, clanging sharp to a wood floor below. Reversing the procedure, Estefan pushed the bolt forward enabling the next round to shift into position, caught rearward and shoved at an upward angle into an empty chamber, followed by a downward plunge locking the bolt's tarnished ball. Once again loaded. Melon Head in a mindless state, repeated the loading exercise over and over becoming more addicted on each turn. By reflex he loaded again, caught up in a movie reel of moving metal parts, shiny copper, twisting shells and floor rattling ammo. Estefan lifted his prize, pushed the stock firm into his shoulder and peered into a narrow scope attempting to clear focus. Since he and Carlos fired the first shots in the sycamore grove, Estefan advanced to a new association with his rifle. No longer afraid. More at ease but maintaining respect for a loaded weapon.

Scoping through a wood gap, Estefan spotted movement and locked onto a figure moving deliberate just inside the outermost row of almond trees. One of many nut orchards belonging to Clay Blevins. Able to register thin crosshairs above his target then covering a narrow midsection before aiming hairlines centered on a man's chest. His target being an older man needing a cane to keep himself on a steady pace. "Mr. Blevins, you're in my sights," a tense sniper whispered aloud. At the same time allowing his unconscious index finger to slide from trigger guard to an unsafe trigger, back to guard. Continuing to follow Clay Blevins make his way along barren trees and unaware of being tracked. Estefan wiggled his trigger finger up and down, almost like caressing the guard's face. Clay stopped, in need of a short rest near a substantial almond tree. One hefty branch from a low split trunk partially obscured the older man from the young man's narrow view. Deadly crosshairs intercepted the limb forcing Estefan to raise his sight, resting now at the base of Clay's neck along the shoulder line. Both remained still aside from Clay's head twisting side to side. Two adult crows lighted in a tree twenty yards beyond the target, showing as blurred motion in the scope. Melon Head didn't notice.

Estefan went uncontrolled, caught in the moment. Absolute focus on his stationary object without thought. Extending his most important digit through the guard and curling soft around a deadly lever. Not unlike a small python slithering along an undersized tree, curling among its thin branches. His finger joint began a slow steady constriction. Unaware.

The young farm boy's world flooded with vivid sensations and spread transformed into military sniper, hired gun, assassin. Everything in place. Everything in alignment. A few deep breaths then holding, attempting absolute stillness. Clay turned his head full to the left viewing his large red barn. Inside the sniper world an elderly man appeared to be staring right at Estefan enabling a gentle flinch, tightening a curled finger ever so slight. The fantasy world gave way to a shudder of terror when the gun fired.

"Jesus Christ man," Melon Head gasped. Followed by a deep breath. "What the fuck happened," yelling at himself, recoiling a tense body while concentrating on a loose trigger finger, being sure his right index moved no closer to a positive trigger. Estefan lowered the weapon. "Shit," continuing his scold as light smoke drifted from a dreaded muzzle. "The damn gun was loaded? I didn't know it? I didn't know it?" telling himself. Head down, ashamed then hearing faint shouts and noise from the farm. Estefan peered thru the scope once more to see if Mr. Blevins had been hit.

Sensing a warm stream of liquid running down his right leg as the young boy lost temporary control of some body functions. Blevins' lay in cool dirt. Not moving. Looking closer, Estefan clearly observed splattered blood over Clay's rear shoulder.

"Don't ever load it until you're ready to shoot. Not until you're ready to shoot," he scolded himself as a grotesque image of Mr. Blevins laying on the ground covered in blood repeated in his head. Gaining control of his senses Estefan ran down the squeaky stairs to get help, screaming wild, desperate to deliver his emergency. He led a group of alarmed farm workers running hard to where the wounded man lay. As they approached he could see Mr. Blevins trying to move his legs. "Thank God he's alive," Estefan repeated a number of times, wiping tears streaming down his reddened cheeks.

Chris

Two hours plus and not so much as an opened door from the Sheets' household. "It's the holiday weekend for Christ's sake. You must be doing something," Davis muttered, digging out yet another small handful of toffee almonds. He couldn't stop eating them. Chris made a quick drive from Tracy half believing in what he referred to as his quarter baked plan. He and Anderson agreed on a stakeout of Douglas' home. Chris proposed the idea at the outset but Anderson failed a vigorous agreement, instead displaying little more than bad attitude by saying, "what the hell it can't hurt!"

Davis located a convenient location about a hundred fifty yards away from the Sheets' household. Parked in a small gravel parking lot used by county road crews with a convenient open gate and clusters of valley oaks offering a buffer line of concealment. This narrow county road turned sharp just before the lot entrance which forced driving attention to the road and away from Chris' isolated hideout.

Angling his car for a clear view between three heavy oaks, Davis observed a large, covered red porch with front door and stairs leading to a gravel driveway. Anyone coming in or going out couldn't be missed. Friday afternoon turned into evening which turned into a cold night with no one leaving the house. Fast food provided evening dinner which always lead to slight indigestion. Chris was lucky to have an unlocked porta-potty on the lot with plenty of toilet paper!

Late Saturday morning warmed after a cold night. Morning lingered way too long before late afternoon finally appeared. "C'mon folks, let's look alive in there," Davis implored, tuning the radio to another NCAA football game. Ohio State was doing a number on the Wolverines this year. "Just give me a game. Anything close. I'll take Lehigh and M.I.T. if they're within ten points of each other." Receiving scratchy signals but able to hear most of the action.

"Virginia Tech at the Tarheel twenty eight yard line. Third and short for the much needed first down. A Virginia touchdown ties this game late in the third quarter," Chris' radio was speaking southern play-by-play dead clear, announcing the situation behind constant background noise.

"That's much better," Chris sighed reaching for another scoop of nuts, never losing contact with the sheriff's front door. "Okay Tech, tie it up. I'm sure Benny has money on this game." Listening close as the color man analyzed each play.

"Two wide outs split way to each side spreading the Tarheel defense. Backfield in an I formation with Allen calling signals. He takes the snap, faking the middle to Sizemoore, drops back fairly deep." Davis' head twitched ever so slight, surprised to hear the Tech quarterback about to throw.

"This coach has balls," Davis grunted. Entire boredom had taken over. Trapped inside a small car on a lousy watch, waiting. Waiting. Nothing happening. "Let it fly kid," whispering words of encouragement as if Chris had a personal stake in this far-off outcome. He wasn't even one hundred percent sure what college these Tar Heels represented!

"Allen pump fakes right, feels pressure, scrambles left, launches a long throw down the left side, has a man out there," a short silence from the play-by-play man followed waiting to see what takes place. Davis looked at a backlit radio dial as if he could see on-field action in progress. A roar went up from the fans just as Sheets' front door swung open. Chris jerked, fixing on a mid thirties woman with a small child in tow, presumed to be her daughter. Davis instantly focused on Mrs. Sheets, he presumed again, oblivious to Virginia Tech's touchdown pass. Cheers and accolades emitted from his radio all but ignored now. The detective had a decision to make. He and the Captain agreed, call headquarters and keep in touch with Douglas Sheets at all times while driving. Mrs. Sheets was optional. If it appeared Douglas wasn't moving go ahead and follow her.

"How the hell do I know if Douglas is even home?" Chris asked himself, thoroughly frustrated.

Mrs. Sheets settled her daughter into a child seat as Chris turned the ignition key. Remaining motionless in quiet idle, waiting to be sure his car remained hidden. Lucky enough Douglas showed, standing on a shaded front porch acting like a big deal in town yelling to his wife. Not in a usual way as if saying goodbye. His arms waved and fingers pointed while his face contorted in obvious anger. "They are indeed fighting," Davis spoke aloud, lowering radio volume and his side window. He could hear shouting even from his distance. The sheriff grew more angry each time Mrs. Sheets yelled back. "Get after him lady. Don't take his crap," Chris mumbled, ready to follow Loretta Sheets when she leaves.

"Damn it," Chris said aloud dropping the car into drive but holding the brake firm. Douglas was leaving too, making a bee-line for a dark colored truck. Mid-size. The same one checked out after their interview. Douglas pulled from the driveway rather slow for some reason, waiting for his wife to catch up in her white mini-van. Chris left his parking lot turning hard right cutting distance to the van. All three vehicles sat delayed at a traffic signal controlling an intersection at Highway 108. Douglas turned right. Mrs. Sheets was blinking left. Davis could only laugh at his predicament asking himself aloud, "which one?"

For some reason Chris' hunch leaned more to Mrs. Sheets for potential new information. Sonora County's Sheriff Offices were to the right. "I'm betting Douglas is going into work." Davis wanted bad to believe his assumption but knew it was risky. Green lights blinked on, the mini-van turned left, Davis hesitated. "Let's gamble today," he said aloud remembering the Virginia Tech quarterback going for it all. Chris turned left just before the light turned yellow. Bright sunshine filled his car as higher elevations equaled clear skies. He wouldn't stop wondering about Douglas, driving east right now. "He's gotta be heading into the station," trying to reassure his decision but second guessing also. "Should I break the game plan? The hell with it, I'm going with Mrs. Sheets. Let's see what happens. Go deep."

Chris tailed the mini-van westerly on Highway 108 through two sharp turns. One right the other left. Settling back to back, waiting a traffic signal change, Chris watched his objective check her rear view mirror twice. "She has no clue," the detective reassured himself. They both proceeded another short distance as the van turned right into a Safeway parking lot. Davis kept straight, entering the lot at a distant corner driveway, not wanting to press too hard. Loretta parked and the detective found a spot two rows over.

"Okay, what do I do now?" Davis asked himself, brooding how so many investigation decisions were off the top of his head, while Mrs. Sheets exited her van, daughter in tow. "Shoot, I can't approach now, not while the kid's with her. Maybe I'll just wonder around the store." Knowing he'd look like some low brow stalker. "I'll sit tight for a while. See where she goes." Loretta and Lucy made their way inside Safeway somewhat slow, vanishing behind automatic doors. Chris sat silent for almost thirty seconds. "Hell with this," bolting from the door but forgetting to unbuckle his seatbelt. Halfway out he was pulled back bumping his head, close to falling. "Damn it man!"

Chris grabbed a shopping cart for effect marching into Safeway for who knows what. Searching the 'produce' isle first, in vain. No sign of Mrs. Sheets as an older gentleman lingering alongside issued a courteous glance. Waiting to select fresh asparagus currently on sale and which Davis was blocking. "Oh yes, pardon me," Chris apologized hurrying to clear space. It occurred he should have something in his cart, bagging a few honeycrisp apples, breadsticks and a large handful of fresh green beans. He also stocked up on ready to eat food should this stakeout last longer than expected. Passed through 'produce' and 'bakery' and navigated the busy isle in 'meat and poultry' without a sign of Mrs. Sheets. He made his way to 'international foods' then decided to take 'bake time' toward the store front keeping an eye out for packaged foods and candy bars. As Davis rounded an end display of wine and discounted plate ware, he continued to look down 'snack-time' to his right until his cart hit something solid. Another cart.

"I'm sorry," a woman's voice spoke soft, jumping Chris back to attention. In front stood Loretta and Lucy Sheets staring puzzled but smiling. They waited for Davis to move his cart. Chris nodded, apologized twice, skidding his rickety shopping cart sideways. Loretta, avoiding eye contact as usual allowed Davis to study her face close. Seeing heavy make-up behind her rear left cheek and the tip of black and blue skin peeking over a white shirt collar.

"Douglas Sheets, the wife beater," Chris told himself. "Could be an opening?"

"Sorry," Loretta apologized.

"No no, my fault. Gotta watch where I'm going," Chris spoke gently, noticing her rapid eye contact submerge. Easy to see something was wrong from a glance which displayed surrender and shame, evading one to one contact. Loretta was compelled to turn her head briefly toward Chris. He gave away a small, crooked, sympathetic smile as they passed. Davis continued slow down 'bake-time' adding a couple more items to his cart. He had to give Mrs. Sheets more time to finish shopping but needed to synchronize her checkout with his, planning to approach Loretta in the parking lot. Knowing it would be risky. Maybe even too soon but on the other hand with that fresh mark still glowing, she could be ripe to offer valuable information on her abusive husband. Just maybe a perfect opportunity for a battered woman to strike back. Chris also realized Mrs. Sheets may have nothing to give. "We'll see," forcing the notion from his head. He turned right, down 'breakfast-time' throwing a box of Krusteaz blueberry pancake mix into a growing cart. 'Frozen foods' loomed left, leading to a bank of available checkout counters. Nothing could stop him now except a burgeoning display of small personal ice creams. On sale of course. Searching through bins of various flavors until finding Dryer's Butterfinger, putting all of the remaining five in his cart. Failing to consider how to get them home before melting! Leaving the last freezer door behind, Chris made it to a routine line of waiting customers. Checking left and right he spotted Loretta and child approaching the express checkout.

Two carts were ahead of Davis in his line and one just finished paying. "Have a nice day," coming from an older man working a courtesy clerk position teamed with a younger gal checking. Davis hoped to leave the store just ahead of Mrs. Sheets thinking it would appear more spontaneous?

A middle aged woman in front of Chris emptied her cart, then flashed the detective a curious smile. Catching him completely off guard. He turned quite embarrassed when she did it for a second time. Usually a calm detective, Davis couldn't face his admirer and looked away in a hurry. In luck, there they were. Loretta and Lucy third in the 'express lane' with more than fifteen items!

Chris' admirer finished unloading and stepping forward to the ATM reader. She peeked another longer look making him feel very uncomfortable. "Mature weird," he said way under his breath turning back to Mrs. Sheets. "I'm still one ahead of her," the detective observed, concluding their positions to be just right.

"How are you today? Did you find everything you were looking for?" a dark haired gal asked from behind her check stand scanning Chris' items. Davis kept his eyes glued to Loretta. So much so, when his vision returned to the checker she was in fact, expecting an answer.

"Hmm? What?" stumbling bad. "Uhh. Oh yes, yes. Found everything just fine. Right where it all should be," attempting humor but knowing he sounded like an idiot. Chris peeked toward Mrs. Sheets, checking her progress, as the bill was tallied and the elderly clerk loaded most items into a waiting cart. He separated the ice creams placing them into double plastic bags.

"Club card?" cashier asked.

"Yep," handing over a red plastic card earning hefty savings of about a buck ten.

"That's seventeen dollars and fifty-four cents."

"On ATM," Chris responded seeing Loretta still stuck in a slow line. He punched in his four digit code and withdrew twenty in cash.

"Do you need help out?" the clerk offered after loading his groceries.

"No thanks. I'm fine," turning back to receive his Jackson.

"Mr. Davis you saved one dollar and fifteen cents today," handing over a receipt, twenty bucks and fake grin. Chris wasn't paying much attention right now, planning operations, forgetting to say thank you.

"She'll probably use this entrance," walking to his left through a set of doors leaving the cart. Davis took a seat on a wood bench in a small patio shaded by lattice cover. Waiting, not sure if the timing was right or if he'd even make contact. Hearing doors open behind, Davis turned, expecting Mrs. Sheets but watched instead as two young boys exited laughing at one another for some reason. Chris turned away perpendicular to the doorway, as it opened again hearing a cart roll.

"Lucy, don't run sweetheart," recognizing Mrs. Sheets' voice, attending her daughter.

Chris rose casual as possible, waiting for Loretta to walk by, finally making solid eye contact with each other. "Mrs. Sheets?" he spoke straightforward but kept the gentle tone.

"Yes? I'm Loretta Sheets. Can I help you?" Loretta didn't quite stop but pulled Lucy close, holding tight. "You and I crashed into each other just a bit ago," recognizing Chris pushing his cart inside.

"Yes mame. Can I speak to you?" making sure to ask as decisively as possible but not wanting to scare her away. Mrs. Sheets came to a slow, gradual stop.

Looking close at Davis, examining clothes, squinting nervous eyes. She raised a hand pointing her index finger close to Chris' chest. "You're a police officer aren't you?"

Regina and Tom

"I made soup yesterday. You up for a quick dinner?" pulling one arm away from his lower waist and the other from his breast.

"I'm up for something that might take longer," Gonzalez whispered into Tom's ear licking his lower lobe then biting sharp, too hard, with a pointed incisor. She kept a body search going with both hands as Tom made a feeble attempt to lift them away.

"Ouch," squealing like a twelve year old but Ellis was determined to keep his French onion from burning. "That hurts babe. Go wash the camo off your charming face," speaking with a smirk, reaching back with his left hand fondling Regina's breast with a shallow grope. He squeezed one nipple between his fingers.

"Ouch. Hey bub, watch it. Do it more sexy," Gonzalez whispered again, nibbling softer this time. Her hands rubbed below Tom's belt and across his stomach. Ellis maintained his continuous stir but getting seriously sidetracked with all of Regina's sensuous strokes. "So that's why the counter girl at Starbucks was looking at me so strange." Lowering her aim while kissing and working her tongue across Tom's lower neck. "Maybe I'll go freshen' up, since someone is interested more in hot soup than a hot babe," she said, relaxing her grip but grabbing Tom with both arms around his neck pulling his lips to hers. Tom let her tongue explore his mouth at will. He loved it, managing to stay with his pot of soup, stirring as small bubbles began to surface indicating almost dinner.

Sitting together in cushioned chairs they enjoyed a cheese laden soup and garlic bread. Regina relished yet another dinner she didn't have to prepare. "Denise is gonna be pissed," telling herself as Tom slurped spoonfuls of his favorite soup. Gonzo wasn't overly hungry, her mind and libido occupied elsewhere. Ellis was starved. Filling another bowl three quarters full and biting hard into a crunchy piece of French bread full of minced garlic and parmesan shavings. One thing they did have in common, bone tired. Regina and Tom lingered after eating. Talking, recalling the day's shoot, teasing, touching and always asking a few personal questions of each other.

Tom refilled two loafing wine glasses swelling their fatigue with each sip. "So, where's your faithful dog Mr. Ellis? I thought all duck hunters had a dog?" Regina asked feeling her alcoholic glow rise upward. Tom paused, contemplating her question. "I don't know. Not really a dog person anymore, I guess. If I had more time to work and train a dog," he stopped again rubbing his whiskered cheek. "Maybe I'd try it again."

"Again? I take it you had a dog?" Gonzalez asked, prying harder.

"Some time ago. My long time friend, Fudge. Good looking chocolate lab. Perfect size, perfect lines, perfect pet, average hunter." Tom stood, moved to the living room adding an almond round to a dying fire. "She died two and a half years ago. Broke my heart." He poked the fire releasing a small eruption of red sparks swirling through a warm hearth. Tom stared into growing flames. "Damn animal was one of a very few that close to me," feeling uncomfortable telling Regina any of his inner-most secrets.

"Weird name for a dog?" Gonzalez walked to the sofa, sprawling on her side still clutching a wine glass. She felt kind of privileged hearing Tom open up for a change. "I'd say you're a dog person, Tom." Locked solid into Tom's face and eyes. Her crooked smile signaled sex. She wished he'd come over with certainty, strip her, and make love to her. Hard.

"I'd say I'm a dog person too," Tom agreed, approaching the sofa. Looking down at Regina, deciding to act slow but firm. Enjoying a mounting urge to take this wonderful woman into his arms kissing her lips and breasts in a rough kind of way. "I wonder if she likes it that way?" asking himself, with no clue what she wished from him. He regained control wondering if the red wine had captured some libido? Like always playing it safe. Sitting next to Regina, rubbing her neck with soft finger strokes and messaging the small of her back. Her skin was smooth and barely on the oily side after their day of hard work forcing Tom into a higher, sexual playing field.

Regina relaxed, becoming more and more aroused by his strokes and touches. She began breathing harder and unbuttoned her shirt inviting Tom to enjoy any part of her body. Squirmed, then pushed into her lover's chest. Tom leaned back into the sofa's armrest feeling comfortable and delighted in exploring Regina's full breasts. His hands passed easy inside her shirt fondling at will, feeling her chest heave with heavy breathing signaling pleasure in each stroke. Kissing her lips with almost rude force and twirling each dark brown nipple between his fingers, feeling them grow longer and hard.

Regina moved for position, wiggling onto her back offering full access to her warm inner thighs showing no sign of inhibition. Tom took advantage letting his hand and fingers rub her softly. She moaned, breathed harder and squeezed her thighs together trapping his venturing hand. Laying together comfortable and relaxed like a warm blanket. Regina reached back and pulled Tom's face to hers. She kissed him in a long spell but much softer, with much more emotion this time. She dropped her head into Tom's chest. He lowered his head too, resting content on hers letting a delightful fragrance fill his senses then closed his eyes. Regina breathed hard, waited then closed her eyes also, anticipating sex. They remained this way for a few seconds too long. Much too cozy and way too tired. Sleep deprived far too long, pausing their strong sexual urges and without warning, captured by a heavy, still, waterfowler's sleep. Neither would hardly move until early next morning. Quite different from a routine slumber normal on any night. This was different. A deep, sound sleep from near exhaustion, wrapped in each other's arms, the fireplace providing warmth, body heat providing affection and comfort.

Chris

"Yes mame, I'm a homicide detective with the Tracy Police Department. How did you know?" Chris asked as a light breeze waived a lock of Loretta's hair revealing a light red bruise. Mrs. Sheets sensed this cop examining her wound.

"I'm married to a cop. You probably know that already," Loretta answered keeping her left hand raised to a nervous temple, catching loose hair caught in persistent breezes. "I can spot the police most times." Loretta spoke with an injured, regretful tone. She looked away often, avoiding lengthy eye contact and pulling Lucy close to her hips.

"May I ask you a few questions?" Chris inquired in a respectful, sympathetic tone.

Loretta scanned the parking lot as if planning to inspect each and every stall for something specific. Chris could see she was thinking it over. "Uh, you know, you look friendly enough detective," with a brief stammer, acting nervous. "I don't think so detective. If my husband finds out," as abrupt silence filled in and Mrs. Sheets glanced at Chris, quickly veered away then turned again with a look seeking sympathy written on her face. "If he finds out, you see what can happen." Guiding Lucy into the mini-van. Warm air moved across Chris and Loretta just before she looked back still holding her nervous but available smile. Lucy was buckled in as mom closed the sliding door. She paused at the car's side looking through a large window at her lovely daughter. Davis had a notion she might be reconsidering. Mom waived Lucy a playful kiss, walked around the car head down until reaching the detective once more.

"It won't take long Mrs. Sheets," Davis said. Loretta stood next to Chris admiring two small trees with dry golden leaves covering thin branches. Setting sunshine captured them square emitting long gray shadows stretching over grass and a red brick sidewalk. Loretta moved brisk, putting her arm through Chris' and turned for the driver's side door. They walked arm in arm catching Chris off guard, being led to the van.

"Fuck it detective. I need to talk to someone and you look like a sensible cop. If I need protection will you be able to help me?" Mrs. Sheets asked, very calm now.

"I'll shoot him myself, if he touches you again," Chris responded with watery eyes.

"Can we meet here Monday? Say one o'clock?" Loretta asked, fishing car keys from a brown leather, Coach handbag.

"Monday afternoon. One o'clock sharp," Chris assured her.

"See you then, Mr." Loretta realized she didn't know this man. "I don't know your name detective."

"Chris Davis," speaking soft, waiting for Mrs. Sheets to slide into her van and buckle up. Just before driving away he asked her to wait a minute, separating a plastic bag from his load of groceries. The side door opened as he handed Lucy a bag full of ice creams. "I bought these not thinking how to keep them frozen, duh. They're for you now sweetheart," Lucy giggled with pleasure giving away two thank you's.

Mrs. Sheets thought how long it had been since her father took them out for ice cream. She mouthed the words, "see you Monday," and pulled away, thinking the ice cream would have to be their little secret. Loretta felt better than she had in a long, long time.

Chris walked back to his car dreading how boring Sunday would be.

Gustine

It wasn't a lot but enough drool seeped from the corner of the detective's mouth soaking a wet spot on Tom's shirt. Her eyes sprung wide open as Tom squirmed, easing Regina's shoulder weight away from his left ribs. Neither had budged much from restful sleeping positions for the better part of seven hours.

Gonzalez sensed the light moisture running down her cheek, but her sleep induced state didn't quite permit an easy explanation. Nor did she have a solid bearing on her current location. Tom moaned, then sighed with a long, loud breath, tensing legs and torso needing to reactivate stiff muscles. Instinctively, Regina tried sitting up feeling a little anxious but relaxed, staying in Tom's grasp. "Where the," she muttered, reaching up to feel wet spit running down one side of her chin.

"Mmm, that's lovely," Tom said all smiles, stretching his shirt tail upward to wiping Regina's chin soft and clear of any remaining saliva.

"Oh God, thanks. Wow, talk about sleep." Regina yawned, laying her head back onto Tom's chest. She especially enjoyed his warm body, soft hands rubbing her back and the way he was moving his thigh between her legs. Sensuous, applying erotic pressure forcing her to snuggle in closer kissing his neck and cheek. Regina felt warm hands slide around her body and move across her breasts messaging each with a supple touch. "Mmm, that feels good," loving each subtle stroke. She wasn't about to stop anything from happening now. Instead, demanding it all now. Moving in then on top of her lover as both breathed hard, ripped away clothes, hands and fingers caressing hidden wet members, intense movements combined with oral pleasures. Each one convulsing into sweaty moans of pleasure and satisfaction.

For Tom it finally came to pass. Since they first met he heldback on his strong sexual desire for this woman. Waiting for her to feel ready. Every time he saw he he willfully had to deny himself that lingering kiss, those caressing touches over her tempting body and feeling her response under his full weight. The wait paid off in an experience Tom could only hope would be repeated often. Regina gushed in her intense orgasm falling just short of another. It was a rare lover who would bring her to climax on their first session. Ellis nearly homered twice in his first two swings! Later on, following another couple hours of deep sleep she would test this man to see if he could deliver two more times. "One would be easy," telling herself unconcerned, closing both eyes, contacting as much nude body as Tom could give.

Davis

"Ouch!" Davis squirmed and stretched his legs to return decent blood flow back into his numb calves. "I should've gotten a room," Chris moaned, starting the car to get some heat generated inside. "Fuck its cold out here." Spreading a small, thin jacket across his chest. Davis was lucky for stashing a wool blanket, although too short, in the trunk of his car. "Just in case of emergency, kinda like this one," whispering as his breath showed, chilled and frustrated. "I don't know if I can last much longer," complaining as sleep began coveting his tired body more and more. The previous night didn't seem so bad as Chris chose to follow Douglas on two separate occasions. Once on a routine trip to Safeway for groceries and another for a return trip to County Sheriff. Davis stayed at the sheriff parking lot for an hour before cashing in to resume his watch.

"Why the hell did I offer to stay? What can I do anyway?" Chris' thoughts moved back and forth between his earlier commitment and a hasty decision to go it alone on this poorly conceived stakeout. "Two nights are bad enough. Three is way overboard," the detective mumbled out loud in a rare mood of self pity. Reddish skies were building, backlighting Loretta's home as sunset closed in. Davis welcomed his final evening but didn't relish another cold night attempting sleep in his cramped car. "Buck up. This lady probably holds all the secrets we need to shed some light on a stalled case," coaxing himself along, trying to be tough. "She must be a strong woman," the detective noted as headlights appeared around the curving road.

Earlier, Chris followed Douglas yet again to County but waited barely twenty minutes this time. "Is this all you do Douglas? Work every day?" Sure enough on he came, pulling his dark green truck into the driveway and killed the engine. He stayed inside the vehicle however.

Only a sliver of red remained over the house. Not quite blood red, however dark enough to know the sun had set. Chris could see Douglas clear but unable to make out Doug's raised hands to the cab's roof, assessing his situation and working off inner tension. Sheets prepared to re-enter home, no clue what to expect from his wife after the serious threats he issued yesterday. No beating took place, "but Loretta had a curious look on her face this time," Douglas clued himself. "Almost defiance," speaking aloud, in a low voice. Perhaps why he didn't act out with violence?

Chris kept a tight lock on his fellow professional and suspect. "I hope she blows a big hole in your fucking head when you open the door deputy," Chris spoke in a normal tone of voice but recognized unfortunately, something like that would turn this case insane!

Sheets climbed from the truck walking to his front door in a three quarter trot, slid in his key, no explosion ensued, letting himself inside. Two lights went on, just as one on the second floor went out. "She must be in bed," Chris told himself unsure, nothing but a decent guess at best dropping the window to listen for any sounds for some reason. All quiet. "Whew, it's cold out there." Feeling thick, low forties cold air flood across his face filling the cab with double blanket temperatures. Needless to say his window went up fast! From inside the sheriff's home Davis detected electronic blue flashes emitting from their rear most room. "You get to watch a little TV Douglas," Chris muttered comparing his current lower standard of living. He had the feeling Douglas wasn't hell bent on battering Loretta this evening. Too tired or maybe the holiday atmosphere had finally won him over. "What a great guy," Davis said with his usual dose of heavy sarcasm.

The stubborn detective continued into very late hours fending off boredom, cold and sleep. Big screen lights continued flashing as Davis nodded off for a few seconds, increasing to minutes, jolting himself back into surveillance. Convincing himself Douglas decided against doing harm tonight. "Hell, he probably fell asleep in front of some lousy fuckin' B-movie?" Leaning back on a thin padded door, heavy head lowered into his chest, diminishing into sleep, waking, falling back to darkness. "Hell with it," Davis surrendered, shutting weary eyes just after one o'clock falling into shallow slumber, his protective watch had concluded. In time, achieving sound sleep like his partner did the night previous.

Outside temperatures continued dropping. Crystal clear skies dominated California's foothills as unrelenting fog smothered most Central Valley farm towns, wetlands and barren fields. Lacking any serious storm fronts sweeping inland from cold Pacific waters, stabilizing cold, calm air would dictate terms for a while. Stars glistened against a coal black background. So many in fact it took a trained eye to pry apart confused and hidden constellations much the same way this murder case proceeded. Maybe tomorrow will blow in some fresh clues. Fresh northern flights of waterfowl trickled in tonight building populations within foggy valley marshes.

Douglas Sheets

Inside his family room Douglas stared blind into the family's Hi-Def, plasma based brain juicer. Another science fiction slash fantasy slash vampire slash zombie drama played out. He wasn't following the film, contemplating what had gone bad a few days ago. "Somehow, I must get to that old woman and shut her up. Permanently." Running various scenarios through repetitive, fouled logic just as a teenage vixen vampire flew from a balcony connecting to an unsuspecting young lad's exposed throat. In broad daylight no less! Douglas watched but didn't see. Many bold ideas were being stymied by images of bursting inside and delivering one or two quick shots to Betty's head. His clouded mind changed direction, starting to obsess if that Tracy cop Gonzalez, suspected him? "She had to get a fairly clean look," compelled to keep talking to himself. Sheets pondered a police watch on Mrs. Patterson's home, anticipating Tracy cops protecting the old woman. "I bet they don't have a clue?" asking the question over and over. At one point surging with confidence nobody expected a thing. The next moment, rushing into a low stupor with wild images blinking through a shattered intellect; I'm being followed, close to arrest, finding everything, ending life in prison. All of his nonsense and flawed schemes eventually lead to frustration making the sheriff pissed and dangerous. These sessions became Loretta's most vulnerable situations. Douglas Sheets would sink into extreme gloominess, fostering intense misery, then allow deep anger to take charge. His one release was to strike out. Unfortunately for Loretta she had to suffer her husband's violent release.

Tonight, being so late and Loretta already sleeping, Douglas lacked an outlet. Anger throbbed within. Pacing the TV room like a jaguar he backed down three urges to bolt upstairs. Pulling himself out each time somehow. The look Loretta presented today stayed in his mind. "That look," whispering soft but with intensity, as if displaying humiliated failure. "She knows something," Douglas admitted, realizing he didn't have it in him to wake his wife just to beat her senseless. All of which added to his growing frustrations and unstable actions. "If only she'd come down and say something. Complain, bitch, moan, drink some water. I'll take anything." Permitting more crazed reasoning to pour free through warped ideas.

Douglas sat quiet for a short time watching a zombie bite into pink flesh of a middle aged vampire. He turned away interrupted, trying to think clear. His mood would shift again aided by three straight shots of cheap vodka. Not relieving tension altogether but his aggressions began to dull. Douglas Sheets wouldn't deliver a beating tonight. Sunday night, holiday over, work tomorrow. Two more hefty vodkas would put him to sleep.

"Maybe a drive by this week? See if the old gal is being watched," he thought almost out loud. Rubbing a stubby chin Sheets began to mull over Gonzalez in his cloudy senses. "Turn the tables? Stake her out. Watch where she goes. Who knows, maybe I can get something on her? Hold it over her head? I'll think more about it tomorrow." Douglas leaned back, attempting to relax but soon to pass out on a cushioned sofa. Before drifting off he made a mental note to look up the Tracy cop's personal info on his police data base. "Find out where the bitch lives," he told himself.

On television a zombie and a vampire were fighting over an attractive female victim. The victor would receive her warm body. Blood for one, flesh for another. Swinging clawed hands a rather young blood sucker missed as a surprisingly nimble zombie was able to duck the blow. As expected, lethal claws struck the poor girl's throat. The last thing Douglas saw was a large stream of dark red blood gushing from an exposed artery. He took notice then fell asleep. Electronic plasma would play the same movie all night. Over and over and over. Like hideous plans from the diabolic deputy.

Outside in a dark cold car, Davis watched without a clue what went on inside. Trusting for some reason, Loretta would be well tomorrow morning. Thanksgiving football ended hours ago, growing colder as the hours passed, disruping Chris' sleep off and on. Springing awake around four A.M. from a zombie nightmare, swearing he was chased through snake infested swamplands.

Gang of Four

Gonzalez sat at her desk on Monday morning almost alone. Davis hadn't arrived which to say the least was quite unusual. To make it even more peculiar, Captain Anderson couldn't be found either. She passed Buck in the hallway who had to tell her about his hunt on Saturday. Taking four good birds and, "damn, I missed four more easy shots. Should've limited," Buck insisted, at which point Regina wished dearly to compare notes, deciding instead to hold her tongue for another time.

"Sounds cool Buck." She avoided asking any hunting questions fearing too much detail in return. "Say, have you seen Davis or Anderson?" feeling free to ask about work. "Can't find either one?"

"Haven't seen 'em," Buck responded, not in the least concerned still reveling in Saturday's shoot.

Regina proceeded to the front offices. She came across Denise and Maria filling coffee pots for morning brews. "Regina baby, how was your weekend?" Maria asked, in a jovial mood.

"Oh, not bad. Not bad at all. Calientito!" triggering a red face while hiding a sly grin.

Maria turned and stared at her Hispanic friend exhibiting an even bigger smile. "You little slut," speaking soft but raising Denise's attention. "That's it, lunch today for sure. I'll gather the Gang." Maria set the coffee to brew, glaring at Denise.

The married woman squinted, peering at Gonzalez like a high school nun. "I want to hear every gory detail, girl. He better have cooked you a Thanksgiving dinner, at least." Forever concerned about a man cooking food and reaching out to touch the detective's shoulder the way a mother consoles her troubled daughter. Regina stayed quiet allowing her fellow employee's comments stand, knowing lunch would be loads of fun today.

"I think I'm inside today but I can't find Anderson. Have you seen him this morning?" Gonzalez asked.

"No, not yet."

Regina drew another blank. "Well, lunch will be juicy anyway," she said, leaving the kitchen area to find her partner or boss and listening to Maria giggle from well down the hallway.

···

"Hey, there you are," Regina spotted Anderson, now at his desk on the phone. She didn't want to interrupt taking a seat as each cop nodded good morning.

"Come on. It can't be that cold. Suck it up man!" Anderson laughed into his phone, but listened close. Regina heard a man's voice coming over the receiver due to excessive yelling on the other end. Unable to make out the words coming through she leaned back smiling, getting a rise from her boss's good humor.

"Just stay put and keep an eye on that house. I'm sure you two will be meeting again in a few hours. We've come this far with your wacky idea, let's not give up now," Anderson coaxed then switched to Regina, giving her the one minute sign, seeing she was honing in on the conversation. "You know I don't have any overtime budget. This weekend gets chalked-up to being one helluva' dedicated cop."

Words reached a higher volume coming over the small phone set. Anderson swiveled a full circle in his high back chair chuckling at the poor guy on the other end. Gonzalez leaned forward, further interested with a bubbly smile.

"I'll give your partner a hearty hello," Billy said, taking Regina by complete surprise, changing her face to mild shock.

"That's Chris?" Regina asked, leaning in close, unaware of the situation.

"Lighten up, it's bound to get warmer soon. We'll discuss the lady's comments tomorrow. Wrap your blanket a little tighter, bye." Regina still heard shouting after Billy's wisecrack just before killing the connection.

"Was that Davis? Where the hell is he? On stakeout?" Regina asked staccato, "what the hell is going on?"

"Yeah, that was your partner all right. He's been watching the Sheets residence all weekend," pausing for slight effect. "Loretta, that's Mrs. Sheets, says she'll talk to our detective this afternoon," seeming quite proud of the news.

"No kidding. Some good information for a change," Regina was almost gushing. "Way to go partner. Why's he so cold?"

"He's been camping out the last three nights, in his car, freezing his ass off," giving Gonzalez reason for a good laugh. "It's good for him." Billy stretched both hands behind his head, reclining slow like an executive basking in business glory. Looking every bit corporate.

"Do I head up to Sonora?" Regina ached for the chance to ask Mrs. Sheets quite a few questions.

"No, not now. Davis has Loretta trusting him. I don't want to do anything that might jeopardize this meeting," her boss displayed good judgment and Gonzalez agreed. "I need a report from you Gonzo. Write me something on Sheets' possible drive by last week to visit Mrs. Patterson." Billy emphasized possible. "I want something in the file for now," Anderson concluded with future investigation ideas cluttering his mind.

"You got it, boss man!" Standing when Billy's phone chimed. He checked the incoming number and Regina turned to see if her partner might be calling back.

"It isn't Chris," Billy confirmed to Gonzalez. Patricia Bailey this time.

"I'll leave you two alone," Regina teased, hurrying from her boss's office setting out to write a half-ass report on Douglas Sheets. Logging a possible encounter in the way an obituary might describe some poor, anonymous deceased. Time, who, what, time. Where, when, time, how, time. Very dry. Martini dry. Thinking she may well put anyone who reads it, right to sleep! She kept one eye on her computer and one on her watch, dreading the wait for today's Gang of Four luncheon. Her turn to climb the bump today. Her first real start as a pitcher in a long, long time. Her, in the rotation now.

Chris

Sunshine poured into Chris' right windshield. Just past 7:30 and warm radiation covered one side of his face, at last. By far the warmest part of his body. Away from direct sunlight light frost coated windows with intricate streaks of paper thin ice. Davis' breath helped to fog the inside. He couldn't have set his alarm any better catching Douglas Sheets back out of his driveway. Chris leaned forward to clear away a patch of humid mist, staying wrapped in a blanket.

"There he goes," talking out loud, laying back in his seat. "Off to work Dougy. Don't be late." Chris reached forward to start his car. "Let's get some heat in here," speaking in shivers, wiping away more fog to get a better look at the whole house. Nothing moved except Douglas driving away. "Christ, five more hours to go. Damn, it's cold as fuck in here," Chris whined, pulling the blanket up and over his head, almost Islamic, blinking both eyes firm needing a few hours of sleep.

Another hour passed with Chris sleeping lousy. Stirring in consistent intervals, peeking toward Loretta's home, hoping for something to happen. "I'll take movements of any kind for one hundred dollars Alex," Chris knew it was trouble when he resorted to a Jeopardy reference, followed by prolonged yawns. Nothing. He would move from sleep to reality then back into sleep. By 10:00 concern for Loretta's safety was priority. "Hell, maybe Douglas killed the poor woman last night or beat her to the point of scaring her off." Thinking less and less about his cold sore back, generating ideas of kicking in the front door. Direct sun had long ago cleared the car of frost while inside the cold retreated a bit. Remaining cold outside. Near ten forty five Chris' eye noticed something. Not a person or car this time. He wondered if he'd seen the smoke earlier but failed to make a connection. Gray puffs of acrid smoke drifted from a lone chimney, rising at the rear of the house. Chris thought about native Americans. A smoke signal, perhaps?

"Finally," Davis exhaled deep. "She must be all right," he whispered, relieved. Watching as smoke continued to pour, then swept clear by frail breezes. "That fire must feel great right now," wishing for a warm seat next to crackling flames. "Man am I hungry." Reaching into the back seat for another apple and orange juice container. Almost out of food and a cup of hot coffee seemed extravagant now. "I look like shit too," checking himself, bloodshot and all, in the rear view mirror. He wished for a hotel room, hot breakfast, hot shower, toothpaste. "Good God, my breath must stink." Which made him think of Anderson's phone call. He still heard his boss's words. "Suck it up Davis," ringing in his ear! Eleven forty five and still no sign of Loretta moving from the house. Her daughter must not be school age yet, I guess? "Kids are back in school today? Aren't they?" Chris asked himself searching the radio dial for anything but sports. Reception was proving to be almost nil but he heard more about Thanksgiving football games than he cared to know.

Around noon, hungry for lunch, down to a candy bar and some leftover pasta salad, a small sedan pulled into Sheets' driveway. Two doors swung open and launched from one side was a young girl about Lucy's age. From the other door sprang her presumed mother out to catch a rambunctious child before running into trouble. Loretta appeared at the front door welcoming inside her apparent friends.

"She's been waiting for a babysitter," Chris thought, hoping this woman's arrival would set free his newest witness. Davis decided on another chance. "I've gotta get to a store for some mouthwash, water and maybe a fricken' cup of coffee. What I'd pay for a fucking donut right now," muttering the mouthwatering words as he started the engine. "She'll be there at one o'clock. No problem," he gambled, exiting his weekend vacation site making quick time for downtown Sonora and a bucket of caffeine. Positive anticipation and almost smiling for a change.

Gang of Four

Slightly past noon, three quarters of the gang showed at Regina's cubicle. As usual, Maria had everyone laughing and ready to go. "Let's go Gonzo, our table's waiting," Maria's way of letting the gang know patience wasn't on her menu today.

"Perfect timing." As the detective pulled her three page report from a laden print tray. "Looks great," Regina said, admiring her work without real examination. "I'll drop this baby off with boss man on our way out," flashing her pack of co-workers a let's do this sign.

Billy knew right away what was up with all four ladies assembled near his office door. His detective stepped forward to hand over the morning work load. "Big session today?" Anderson asked with a wide smile, paging through her report.

"Uh, I may be a little late getting back," Gonzalez admitted to boss man.

Billy looked away from the report, his wide grin distorted into a mischievous smirk. "Okay, go ahead and catch up. I'll mark some changes and leave it on your desk to be completed today," letting Regina know he wanted it finished by workday's end.

"You got it boss," Gonzalez replied, as the detective turned fast to rejoin the group.

She heard Billy yell out, "hold nothing back Gonzo." With the foursome marching away eager for fresh scandal. Way back somewhere in Gonzo's dark, suspicious mind, she wondered if Anderson knew something about her weekend. Denise, Maria, and Pam on cue, looked at Regina and giggled.

It was Maria and Pam's turn to decide on appetizers while Denise and Regina ordered up a pitcher of margaritas. "On the weak side," instructing their waitress.

"So, I know we have one juicy weekend," Maria led off staring at Regina without uttering her name. "Mine started okay but fizzled like warm coke. He seemed too good to be true and I should've known. Long distance runner," saying those three last words like a plague but getting a roar from her three friends. She smiled and bowed, "the food was still good." Maria finished to deep condolences from everyone at the round table including their waitress spreading plates to accept mounds of potato skins and hot wings.

"I'm starved," the Hispanic gal grande gushed, enjoying a large bite of baked potato skin, cheese and sour cream. Pam took aim on the pause and jumped in next.

"My holiday went chummy," was all she got out before Maria issued her silly laugh and Denise interjected.

"I'm almost afraid to hear this one," blurted a laughing Denise, red faced with a cupped hand shielding both eyes.

"Oh baby this weekend was," pausing to sip her margarita to grow a little more expectation. "Juicy!" Pam played the room perfect with all three women hanging on her next words. "Do any of you know what sort of sensual feats," pausing again for an added tease, "can be done with turkey drum sticks? On her mark she raised a chicken wing drummette vertical. Enjoying immensely all three bug eyed stairs and slack jaws. As usual, Denise would respond first.

"Oh my God," was all she could muster. Even Maria stopped chewing. After a short silence Regina smelled out her prank.

"Pam, you're so full of bullshit it isn't funny. Quit acting like your world is all sex and drugs," Gonzalez said aloud, drawing a winded sigh from Denise but disappointment from Maria.

Denise had to speak up. "Regina, that's her whole life. Getting laid by someone or something! The more the merrier." Whispering to her colleagues seated around the table. Entrées were being delivered as Pam asked the married gal if she wanted detailed instructions.

"There are no details," Regina chimed in. The younger loose gal confessed to a rather typical Thanksgiving dinner with her current boyfriend and his family. Maria was simply disappointed once again. "Denise, how did Arthur's bird turn out?" Regina asked.

"Short version please," Pamela cut in, looking at Gonzalez expecting big thanks. "I think Regina has breaking news."

"To keep it short," Denise scowled. "Burnt bird, drunken husband, open argument, pissed off relatives, over cooked vegetables, lumpy gravy, wife yelled upon, verging on spousal abuse, followed by kinky sex late in the evening! Concise enough?" The married woman said nothing more cutting through a cheeseburger with castration scowled on her face.

Deathly silence resulted, to be filled with a gradual round of minor applause by all three gang members plus an eavesdropping waitress. Denise leaned back with a new appearance of calm and confidence. "Details Pam?" Leering at a smiling co-worker, shaking her head no.

"Regina. What's news?" Maria asked.

"Not too much. Hoping to be married by early summer." Unable to look away from a steamy soup bowl but wanting dear, to talk long and hard of her weekend. With details! Knowing however she was in no position to say too much. A verbal shootout was about to commence.

"How was your turkey?" Denise opened fire.

"Didn't have one," Gonzo retaliated.

"Did you cook or did he?" Denise shot again, missing high.

"Oh boy. Did he cook? Big-time." Gonzo returned fire, winging a married gal.

"So?" Denise reloaded.

"So what?" Gonzo shot her again.

"Are you going to tell us what he cooked?" her opponent asked, bleeding bad, out of ammo.

Maria squirmed in a padded chair intending to put the finishing bite on what remained of her chicken enchilada. Pam sipped her icy margarita savoring the gunfight.

"Sure," Gonzo replied. "Let's see, he started us out with clam chowder. Not that pasty stuff everyone serves these days. This was nice and thin, almost brothy, with lots of carrots. Homemade, from scratch. Did I say that before? Everything, from scratch," speaking firm, looking at Denise. Her gun arm folded, not missing a word.

"Go on," aiming sharp.

Regina had it all premeditated, all planned, all memorized on her drive home from Gustine. "Then grilled pablano peppers with a garlic, olive oil rub, tomatillo sauce and parmesan cheese, garnished with grilled pineapple. Grilled avocado with green taco sauce smothered in melted mozzarella cheese. Seared scallops and spicy coconut cantaloupe over a bed of asparagus risotto." Gonzo paused to see the gang's expressions. Denise was somewhere between fuming mad and disbelief.

"Go on," Big D ordered, holstering her six gun.

"Okay, let's see. Braised short ribs in a peach salsa verde. That was really good. Duck breast scaloppini. Fresh cornbread, plenty of red wine and a walnut tart with homemade ice cream for dessert." All three girls remained quiet now as their plates were collected and a bill placed at table center. Three gang members sat unsure if Gonzo had finished describing her Thanksgiving dinner or had she manufactured an elaborate ruse.

"Are you jerking us around Gonzalez?" Denise asked, unsure if the detective was capable of inventing food like that.

"Did you hook up with a chef?" Pam wanted to know with a bright chuckle.

"He even made the ice cream!!" Maria shouted in disbelief looking as if she could taste the walnuts inside a candied tart!

"Zinfandel cherry. Not bad huh?" Regina concluded knowing she carried the day.

"Are you kidding Regina?" Denise had to ask again.

"Holy shit Gonzo," Pam exclaimed. "If this guy followed it up with hot sex, you better sink your talons into his neck."

"Some pretty intense oral," Gonzalez stopped it right there. "I can't believe I just said that."

Denise peered over to Maria, waiting for comments. "Why look at me? I had my orgasm right after the seared scallops and coconut whatever!"

•••

Inside, Loretta scurried to gather clothes, toys and Bee-Bee. Everything Lucy could possibly need for the next four hours. "I really appreciate this Michelle," thanking her friend as everyone shuffled to the front door. Two youngsters were already laughing, in full play mode by now.

"No problem Loretta. Believe me, you're doing me a big favor. The girls will have a great afternoon together." Michelle opened the door just as Chris drove by. His small black car went unnoticed by Loretta and Chris was oblivious to the noisy foursome. Mrs. Sheets checked her watch. "I'll make it, no problem," she told herself, smiling for a change also.

•••

"Detective Davis? I must say, you look terrible!" Loretta greeted a worn out detective with brutal honesty.

Chris smiled, able to hold in a soft yawn. "Honesty. That's why I'm here. Perfect." Reassuring himself. "Mrs. Sheets, I can't thank you enough for meeting with me today," coming across a little canned but Loretta Sheets was well versed with police protocol. "I'd like to offer you Tracy Police Department protection for you and your," Loretta, with arms folded cut in and stopped Chris' offer cold.

"Detective, you couldn't stop Douglas from reaching me or my daughter and you know it!" Loretta pushed her light red hair back and to the left. More to relieve tension than attempting to arrange her attractive looks. Chris easily saw the appealing woman in Mrs. Sheets along with a great deal of strain unfortunately, dominating her appearance. Davis slipped into nervous silence. Two complete strangers standing in a moderately occupied parking lot. One searching for a safe way out of a violent marriage the other desperate for concrete information.

"Can I buy you a coffee or tea? Maybe we could go somewhere? What would you like?" Davis offered, trying to make Loretta as cozy as possible. Hoping she'd begin talking and never shut up.

"Detective, thank you. Thanks a bunch. I appreciate your offer and I know this isn't easy for either of us," Loretta spoke with a calm, firm voice. "But, too many people recognize me in this small town." She stared at the detective with sympathetic eyes making him appear somewhat naïve as a lack of sleep was taking its toll. "Why don't you get us each a cup of coffee? There's a shop right over there," pointing toward a row of storefronts across the asphalt lot. "They serve a pretty fair Italian roast. I'll meet you back at my van."

Chris was impressed the way Loretta took control. "Sounds right to me. How do you take your coffee?" he asked.

"Black, detective." Quickly realizing a poor choice of phrase. "No offense," Loretta apologized. Her embarrassed smile broke thru with her head cocked to one side, exposing the faint bruise just below her ear.

"None taken Mrs. Sheets." Chris turned, trotting a bee-line for Motherloads of Coffee. He returned soon with two steamy cups, hopping into a well padded front seat. Coffee was a good pal to him now as the detective wondered how this might all play out.

"Buckle up detective. Too many cops stop in here for afternoon caffeine. I can't risk it." Backing up way too fast and speeding away to Highway 108, reminded of his partner's reckless driving methods. "We'll go to a quiet park I like next to a small creek. A mile or so off the main drag." Loretta turned right a few miles from the outskirts of town, dropping down a steep grade to little more than a gravel turnout. "It's quiet here detective," Loretta said. Positioned underneath two large ponderosa pines.

"This is just like the open lot down the road from your house. Sure could've used some of this last night," Davis told Loretta taking repeated short sips of rich, hot Italian roast. "Good coffee."

"Down from my house?" Loretta asked. "Not the road work parking lot? You were down there all night?" Loretta peered over to Chris with tender approval on her face. "No kidding?"

"No kidding. I told you we offered protection. Had to keep my eye on you until our meeting today," explaining his presence on a cold night, including a slight beg for added praise.

"I'll be damned. It's been a long time since a man watched out for me." Loretta turned her head away. Staring out over a small rocky stream with little more than a trickle of flow. Sunlight bounced from water spilling across weed covered chunks of flat granite, hiding a slender, black water snake sound asleep in fall sunshine. Chris could see she was choking up, becoming distressed, perhaps unpredictable, wiping away tears, refusing to look at him. "Thanks detective. You don't know how good it feels knowing you were there for me. I had no idea how Doug might react last night. He's been very unpredictable the last two weeks. I can't stand it anymore," she told a concerned detective dabbing teary eyes and clearing her throat. Chris decided to be patient and kept quiet. "Sorry detective," Loretta cried. Pulling a few kleenex from a middle glove box, tending eyes and nose.

"That's perfectly all right Mrs. Sheets. I understand. Take your time," Chris replied.

"Loretta. Call me Loretta, please." She offered.

"Okay, Loretta it is." Another long wait ensued.

"Then you have to call me Chris," hoping to keep Mrs. Sheets calm.

"Oh, Okay. Chris. You see Chris," nodding her head. "Douglas and Sarah had quite the hot, little love affair going on. Quiet though," Loretta spoke her words without much pain. As if reading from a newspaper. Davis found it odd.

Which ushered in another repeated thought. "Good God, every woman associated with this ordeal is so fucked up!" Ticking off the names, each stranger then the last. Sarah Crosby, Franny Braden, Mrs. Patterson, now Loretta Sheets. Even my partner has been acting weird. "You know for certain they were having an affair?" Davis asked hoping for convincing details. He would get them.

"Oh yes, for certain."

"How," Davis had to hear more.

Loretta paused, tapping a tight fist on the lower steering wheel trying hard to choke off a flood of emotion. No use, as big salty drops dripped from the sides of her chin. "He told me," barely able to squeak the words before breaking down. Mrs. Sheets lowered her head and sobbed. Chris moved toward Loretta putting one arm around her shoulder. She lowered her head to his chest. Crying. On impulse, Davis rubbed her shoulders feeling sorry for the betrayed woman. "It gets better detective, I mean Chris," just able to speak.

Davis was afraid to ask. He glanced away and muttered, "what happened?"

"He proceeded to beat the fucking crap out of me. First my husband tells me bluntly he's having an affair with this woman, then he beats me senseless. Some love fest in my marriage!" Loretta sobbed like a ten year old into Chris' heart with his own emotion beginning to rupture. Teary eyes, knot in his throat and quivering lips. He listened to many chilling stories and confessions through a long career, not often becoming unglued. Today, suffering from lack of sleep combined with this tragic story, poignant memories of home came rushing in. His mom was brutally beaten also.

"Good lord Mrs. Sheets. I'm so sorry," whispering his words before kissing her forehead. Allowing Loretta all the time she needed to recover. Davis didn't know how long but it took a while. Loretta reemerged.

"Tell me you're not making all this up," Chris pleaded, but without any real suspicion Mrs. Sheets was lying. He almost always asked this simple question, letting the witness know he wouldn't stand for deception but stayed removed from their testimony.

Chris received a fast eye glance from Loretta sending him a stern message. "Don't screw with me asshole. I'm pouring my heart out and putting my butt on the line," she told herself

"What else can you tell me?" Davis approved but had to keep her talking now.

"I can tell you a lot more when I'm safe from Douglas. When Lucy and I are safe from him." Loretta made it clear she had more information but wasn't ready to talk. "I know I'll be safe when he's finally behind bars, locked up, double guarded, in solitary confinement. Then I'll tell you the whole story. His story. But not before."

"I'm not sure I understand?" Chris asked, confused.

"It's simple," Loretta spoke, demonstrating unexpected poise. "You make me safe, I'll tell you a story."

Chris thought about her last comments. "Why have you chosen to stay with Douglas? You should've left him a long time ago," Davis queried. Loretta didn't answer. She shimmied in her seat considering his question. Not prepared to discuss this topic but wanted to give a clear response.

"I'm not your classic career girl as you probably know. My work experience is extremely thin. It's a simple matter of money. Lucy and I still need the jerk. His money anyway." Mrs. Sheets paused for a few seconds more. "For a while anyway, I have to live with quite a bit of fear. He can kill me whenever he sees fit," adding the words in a quiet tone while staring out her window. Loretta maintained an attitude of complete vulnerability.

"Will you testify to everything you've told me today?" Chris asked, writing a scribble or two in his notepad.

"I'd like to," Loretta consented then hesitated. "I mean, I will. But it has to be safe for me and my daughter."

"Okay, I'll relay your offer to my boss and we'll see what he says. But you have to promise me you'll tell us everything," Chris demanded as if putting final touches on a business deal.

"Do you think your husband murdered Marcus Crosby?" Chris asked, ready to write her response in his binder.

"Uhm," Loretta stopped to think yet again. Fingers rose to her lips biting a nail, staring straight ahead. From the other side of the creek near smooth granite, a glistening water snake slithered into thick weeds. Ambush position.

Part III

Station 3009

"We're waiting for my partner to show. He had a long cold weekend. Suspect stake out," Gonzalez relayed to Tom, a keen listener on the receiving end of Regina's cell phone.

"Stakeout? Really? Where was he hiding?" Tom asked, his voice unusually dry. Almost blasé.

"Can't tell you that Mr. Ellis. Confidential police affairs," Gonzalez came across with her mocking, official business.

"Whoa, aren't we the little Miss Elliot Ness," Tom joked. "Le'me guess, someone near Gustine?" Lingering silence oozed from Regina's cell.

"You're way too curious about this case Thomas Ellis. Maybe we should put a tail on you?" Regina taunted.

"You've already put your tail on me detective," Tom fired back hoping to hear Regina laugh on the other end. She didn't, betting silence would annoy him to no end. "We're still on for Friday night?" confirming their weekend hunt.

"You betcha. Not trying to renege are ya?" Gonzalez kept the pot brewing.

"Never. We might make it a day hunt. Go out around nine or ten," Tom proposed.

"Why's that Mr. Ellis?" poking fun at Tom as usual.

Tom hesitated with his real reason, trying to invent something he should tell her but caved in. "Screw it," telling himself! "I've been thinking. Wouldn't it be more fun spending Friday night feeling you up. If you don't mind of course!"

"Mmm, good plan gringo. I'll be down early. But I have to be fed well or no bra and panties for you." The detective was growing way too comfortable talking sex with Tom knowing how well he became aroused by it, which spurred her into action. "I have to go lover boy. My partner just walked in," waving hello to Chris hoping he didn't hear any of her raunchy conversation. "Stay ready for me baby doll," she whispered to Tom, throaty, signaling goodbye.

"I'm ready now," Tom said much too serious.

Regina's sexiness giggled forth. "Go rub one out if you have to gringo. I'll see you Friday night, bye." Gonzo signed off laughing.

"Hey partner," Regina hailed, swiveling her chair with plenty of mischievous looks covering an amused face. Still glowing from Tom's conversation, standing to further greet her antsy partner. "Wha's up?"

"What's up? I'll tell you what's up. My ass is probably frost bit. That's one thing up," Chris was close to yelling at Regina now. Davis stopped cold, glaring at his partner, insinuating it was all her fault. Regina stood her ground half smiling half smirking, each hand stuffed into butt pockets.

"Sorry I wasn't there to help out. Anderson tells me you got Mrs. Sheets to talk?" Regina paused, seeing Captain Anderson work his way into their cubicle.

"Let's go. In my office. Briefing." All three cops marched like soldiers, Billy leading, entering the boss' office.

"Chris, I trust you're feeling warmer today?" Gonzalez was getting a rise from Davis' dry look coupled with Anderson's caustic smile.

"I'm doing much better. Much warmer. Even cozy. Thanks so much for asking partner," Chris replied staring right through her. "It freezes up there at night."

"Oh, poor baby," Regina teased, noticing Billy's pleasure in the way she handled her partner.

"That's enough," the boss ordered. "No baseball talk either. Chris, tell us about Mrs. Sheets."

Davis made it pretty fast, informing both cops of details regarding his interview with Loretta Sheets. "It wasn't testimony, just yet," Davis relayed. "Mrs. Sheets repeated a number of times she has information but demands security first."

"Security? We can give her all the security she wants," Regina assumed, failing to understand the woman's needs.

"No. Loretta's security lies somewhere between Douglas behind bars or with a bullet in his head," Chris explained. "Mrs. Sheets doesn't believe any police force can stop her husband from killing her and perhaps her daughter as well?"

"That's gonna' be tough to do!" Regina's sarcastic voice moaned. "Arrest him first, then we get the goods. Wouldn't that be nice," a cynical Gonzalez looked to Captain Anderson who showed quite a bit of pessimism.

"Did she give us anything at all?" Anderson asked as Regina looked to her partner.

"One thing. She told me Douglas and Sarah were having an affair," Davis relayed the information sitting back, waiting for comments.

"Holy cow! Interesting. Is she sure about that?" Anderson asked tapping his desk top thinking about motives.

"She didn't hint this might be a rumor, did she? I wondered about an affair myself, when we questioned Douglas. Holy shit!" Regina's head was whirling with scenarios now. "This could be something of a breakthrough not to mention conflict of interest on Sheets' part, being the lead investigator." Billy and Chris said nothing, mulling over Regina's comments.

"Loretta seemed firm about the affair. No rumor." Davis continued to reflect on their meeting in the park. "I'm not sure if this gets us anything for our case, let alone what it might have to do with Sarah's murder. We need Loretta's information," giving his boss a long hard look.

"I can't run to Sonora and arrest Douglas tomorrow," Anderson told his detective, knowing Chris expected the department to lend some help to Mrs. Sheets. "It'll take time just getting an investigation up and running. That's if our department chooses to pursue it."

"Crap. We're being held hostage by this lady," Regina added, disappointed in Loretta's terms.

"Did you tell her a judge can make her talk with a court order. Hell, we should arrest her for withholding evidence," Gonzalez went on. "She'll get all the security she needs behind bars!" Amused at her own commentary.

Chris stressed once again, it wasn't testimony just yet. "Who knows how she'll react after a few days. She could turn a one eighty and deny our whole conversation. However, Loretta Sheets seemed committed as of right now." Chris stopped to give his partner a chance to comment.

"This throws a wrench into our investigation. I was convinced Douglas killed Marcus Crosby," Regina commented. Appearing perplexed to say the least. She turned silent shooting Captain Anderson a blank stare, expecting him to respond. With a slow shift she rested her watch upon Chris. Davis waited.

"Do either of you think Sheets committed both murders?" Regina asked, but not in a way of inviting comments. More like thinking out loud. Uncomfortable silence filled the room for the moment. Anderson was first to speak.

"Until Loretta Sheets discloses something new, I don't see why not. He certainly has motive," Billy said rather hasty, without much thought.

"What motive did Douglas have to shoot Marcus?" Chris asked failing to see a clear connection.

"Revenge? Revenge for beating and murdering his mistress? Maybe Marcus threatened to kill her? Maybe Marcus knew something? Maybe to keep Marcus Crosby quiet forever. I can think of a few more maybes," Billy responded, in unconvincing mode to say the least.

"I don't see it Captain," Regina leaned back debating motives. "Why in hell does he kill the woman he's screwing, then turn around a year and a half later, and murder her husband? Something's way too strange about all this," Regina spoke in a quiet, level tone now.

"Hell, Marcus had more motive to kill Sheets if he knew about the affair. I don't see Douglas' motive either," Chris Davis agreed with his partner, as his thoughts raced with various scenarios. All ending in confusion. Much too complex. Most murder cases Davis investigated were not that complex. Easy to read motives involving lies, infidelity, jealousy, simple brutality or money. A suspect or two rooted out and case solved. This case had grown quite foggy. A simple investigation completely hamstrung by motives from a previous murder. "Hamstrung by Franny Braden too," Davis thought, suffocating the comment. "That lady is going to break this case open sooner or later. I know it?"

"We shouldn't get too caught up in Sarah Crosby's murder," Anderson warned, rubbing his eyes knowing it would be hard to separate the two after Loretta's statement.

"I don't know if we can separate them," Chris said, noticing Regina nodding in agreement.

Scenarios started running through Anderson's mind once more. "Jesus Christ, I hate to admit it but you're right. Maybe Sarah was going to leave Marcus? Now there's a little something to motivate murder. Let's get it all fouled up. How about Loretta killing Sarah Crosby? She found out Douglas and Sarah were going to," Anderson stopped abrupt. "Good God, I'm not even going to unchain that possibility."

Billy got to his feet looking at each of his detectives. They frowned in return. All three knew at this moment they had very little concrete evidence concerning Marcus Crosby's murderer. His case wasn't getting any closer to making an arrest. "We have to focus, for now anyway, either Marcus Crosby or Douglas Sheets, killed Sarah. We stop right there, until something from left field drops in. That gets us back to who shot Marcus?" Anderson squirmed, contemplating his own scheme, wondering if his strategy would prove sound. Chris and Regina stayed quiet contemplating Anderson's proposal.

Right on cue Regina set it aside. "An accident maybe?" speaking soft.

"How's that?" Chris asked.

Captain Anderson released a long slow breath, knowing his team would be working on new scenarios. "No. No more wild ass speculation. We could spin these murders off to a hundred different scenarios. Not today." Billy demanded.

Chris nodded. "Maybe," he said with no emotion what so ever. They all knew anything was plausible. At this point their own meeting had turned on end. Chief Yung entered the office. Billy had a hunch he might drop in after briefing him on Davis' contact with Loretta Sheets. The Chief behaved in a casual manner with a steaming cup of French roast in hand, like usual.

"Good morning Chief," both Chris and Regina stood, greeting Alex Yung at the same time.

"Good morning Gonzalez," Chief Yung shook her hand firm. "Detective Davis, how are you this morning?" Shaking Chris' hand too. "Sit down, relax. I'm only here to eavesdrop. The fricken' Mayor, City Council, District Attorney, the Chamber of Commerce and an older woman named Abbey are all riding me about the Crosby murder. They want some positive news to pop out of thin air. You know the routine. What can you tell me?" Tracy's Chief of Police took a seat, sipping hot coffee with care while Regina and Chris both went quiet. So Anderson jumped in never feeling intimidated by his boss. They worked well together in his mind.

"Frankly Chief, it seems this case just got a little more cloudy. Chris' meeting with Mrs. Sheets hasn't shed much light on either murder I'm afraid." Billy went on to outline Loretta's demands. "We're having reservations about Sheets murdering Marcus Crosby." Anderson knew the Chief didn't expect, nor want to hear, this kind of news. Billy Anderson however, had no problem delivering bad news. It was part of his job.

"I'll look at the budget one more time," Yung said, already displaying a tone of failure in his voice. "If I had an inkling of what she knew," but stopping there. The Chief wasn't about to go too far out on this limb. Too risky. What if the lady didn't have any real information? "If Sheets attempts to harm his wife and child again, we can step in then. But she'll have to press charges," Alex added in a rather pathetic tone. All four cops knew it was a lousy situation for Mrs. Sheets.

_____Alex scratched his forehead and sipped more coffee. "You know, it amazes me when a case like this comes along, tough as hell to unravel. But the more we pick at it, new wounds open bleeding all over a previous crime." Yung's analogy drew a razor-sharp glare from Regina. "Shit, I was hoping Mrs. Sheets might have something substantial. We need solid testimony to pressure her husband legally." He stood up, hands in pockets trying to think of a positive spin to give the mayor. "Let's turn the heat on both Sheets and the Braden's. Do whatever you see fit to get them to screw up and reveal something. Anything." Alex Yung just told his homicide group to force the situation, recognizing this case was going nowhere.

Pointing with his mug, Yung continued. "Maybe one of 'em will fuck up!" Excusing himself for another meeting leaving three cops wondering where to go next.

Chris Davis felt disappointed in himself and Tracy's police department. "I didn't get much accomplished to assist a threatened woman and child. My department seems willing to use them as bait," scolding himself. Chris would drink too much tonight.

Beatrice

"Well, hello Beatrice. How are you?" Mrs. Braden asked, nervous, surprised by the elder woman's phone call.

"Just fine Franny, thanks for asking. I'm not interrupting anything am I?" Mrs. Patterson wanted to be polite but her timing needed to be just right.

"What can I do for you Beatrice?" Mrs. Braden offered, feeling certain this wasn't a social call by any stretch. "Is everything all right? I mean since the murder. Are you okay?" knowing Beatrice needed time to recover after witnessing the terrible killing.

"Thank you again but yes, I'm doing fine. I still miss Sarah not being around, that's for sure. It would be nice to have her company. I miss her dearly," Mrs. Patterson admitted wondering if she should even be talking about her daughter.

"Don't we both, Beatrice. Don't we both," Franny answered without saying more, hoping to hear the reason for Mrs. Patterson's call.

"Deborah, would it be possible to meet with you? Sometime soon? I've acquired something you may be interested in seeing," Beatrice told the younger lady, using her real name in a deliberate way to arouse curiosity. She stopped there, waiting to hear Mrs. Braden's reaction.

Franny spoke after a few seconds. "What is it, Mrs. Patterson?" asking serious. "Does this have something to do with Sarah?" wanting to know more. She almost asked if this had something to do with Marcus' murder then decided to leave that subject alone.

"Franny," the older woman spoke into the phone, acting concerned and apprehensive. "I must sound mysterious but it may not be safe to discuss it over the phone," she explained, knowing this should arouse her interest even more.

"Safe? What's this about Beatrice?" Franny replied with an elevated manner. "Are you safe darling? You're not in danger are you?" she asked, rubbing her elbow hard to relieve growing tension.

"Yes dear. I'm perfectly safe. How soon can you come down to see me. We need to talk," telling the younger woman to avoid any theater melo-dramatics.

"Okay Beatrice. You've indeed piqued my interest. It sounds like something to do with Marcus' murder, am I right?" dying to get some sort of clue. "I could visit on Thursday afternoon. You can make me lunch," trying to plant a calmer tone with a little humor.

"Perfect and I'd love to make you lunch." Beatrice grew relieved, realizing she may finally be rid of her curious possession. "We'll see you Thursday around noon." Refusing to give away more information.

"Noon sounds good Beatrice. Good bye." Exiting the phone slow, trying to imagine what the older lady has to give? Henry will be gone until late Friday anyway. I'll be back before dark," she assumed. Her thoughts turned to Chris Davis which was happening more and more lately.

"Any ideas partner?" Chris passed Regina a long stare. "Where do we go from here?" asking in a low mumble, "I wonder how Loretta Sheets is doing right now?"

"Douglas. What's Douglas Sheets doing about now? He needs to be tracked somehow," Regina added, conjuring her only idea to possibly open a door on their case. Both cops appeared wedged in. An investigation standstill regarding the killer of Marcus Crosby. Chris still leaned heavy on his suspicions of Mrs. Braden hiding evidence or information. He knew by instinct and experience unfortunately, she kept her secrets in custody. What was it? Eventually, maybe even very soon Chris would find out. Either get it from her or get run out of the profession for carrying on a sexual affair with a key suspect! Each time Franny's image entered Davis' thoughts, he smelled her body, smelled her warm breath, smelled her hair. Craving her touch and eager to press against her full body once again. Davis doubted his resolve in saying no to the woman's advance, fully aware at the right time and place, he'd find himself ripping clothes away from milky white skin and fondling sweaty bodies together for hours on end.

"Chris," Gonzalez tried getting his attention. "Chris." Louder the second time. "Hey! You have a visitor," Regina yelled out this time. "Earth to Davis!" Once again, Davis found himself in cruel separation from a delightful fantasy.

Chris' shudder was noticeable. "Sorry, I'm a million light years away." Turning in his seat to see officer Buck, waiting for Davis to tidy up his deep thoughts.

"Sorry Detective Davis, but this just came across my workstation," handing Chris a copy of printed emails.

Davis smiled. "No, no. It's on me Buck. My mind's wondering all over the solar system today. What's up?" Letting the officer know he did nothing wrong then reading the first email. "What do we have here Buck?"

"They're crime reports from Merced County. Item number three caught my eye." Buck pointed to the bottom half of page two, triggering Gonzalez to stand and peer over Chris' shoulder. Davis began mumbling aloud.

"Hmm. Yeah, I think heard about this. Some kid shot an older man on a farm south of here. This past weekend. Right?" looking back to Buck not sure what significance it held.

"What?" Regina murmured. "How old was this kid?" attempting to scan the report from above her partner's arm. "Where did this happen?"

"Down near Newman," Buck answered.

"What's it have to do with our case Buck?" Chris asked examining the printout.

"Check paragraph three, I believe. Uhm," squinting deep trying to read from over Chris' other arm. "See, look right here," pointing again to the center of a long paragraph. "Where it says suspect's comments. The kid admitted retrieving a gun, an older .222 rifle with scope from a creek near his home."

"I'm listening," Regina said, staring at words on the printout.

"Holy shit," Chris belted, finally comprehending the next sentence as Buck painted a miniscule but proud smile. Chris continued, "that's what, less than an hour away, after Marcus was shot?"

"C'mon partner, read it for me," Regina demanded, her excitement building too.

"The kid testified he saw someone throw a rifle from a local bridge into the Merced River." Chris swiveled in his chair before completing what he read. "Early morning, the day Marcus was shot." Davis calculated a rough estimate of mileage and distance. "It falls into place just perfect," he told himself, knowing something had gone their way at last.

"That's gotta be our rifle. Gimme' that." Regina reached over Chris' arm grabbing the printout, continuing to read. 'Additional Confession' was one titled area. Out of nowhere a recognized name caught her eye. "What the," Gonzalez stopped reciting abruptly, falling loud and hard back into her chair, hand over mouth reading more testimony.

Chris' cell vibrated with a fresh email. He looked at the message and fell back into his chair. "What the hell?" Davis went cold, presuming to be thrust together for a second time, against his fantasy girl. He stayed quiet and still.

Regina could only mumble, clearly shaken. "Clay Blevins shot? No way?" Staring at the printout in shock.

Estefan

From the start, Merced County's Sherriff Department would prove to be quite rough on the young Hispanic boy. One uniformed thug managed to slam Estefan's forehead into a cinder block wall, after their suspect failed to understand a question asked in miserable English.

Estefan would do nothing to hide information or minute details, except to mention The Jackal. Melon Head, in a noble gesture after suffering his rough treatment decided to keep Carlos safe and hidden. Questioning himself often why he covered for his sometime friend. Little to be accomplish with the Jackal's face bouncing off wood and concrete.

"You dug that rifle out of a creek?" a particularly rude questioner asked. "What creek and don't lie to me spic," a red headed as well as red neck cop, spat to a helpless boy. In tears, a frightened Estefan attempted to answer. Retelling his account of slipping into cold water, searching by foot, retrieving the weapon and into hiding.

"The bridge is on the small road not far from home," Estefan said quietly, trembling.

"What's the name of the creek dumb shit," red hair yelled back. Estefan jumped in his chair, looking up to the red faced lawman unable to offer a correct answer. "What the fuck is wrong with you spic? Give me the name of that damned creek or I'll snap your arm like a crispy taco," the burly deputy grabbed Estefan's arm, beginning a sharp twist. "The name of the damn creek Jose or your right arm will be throbbing soon," the sheriff was spitting his venom louder and louder when the door to the interrogation room swung open.

"It's the Merced River, Mr. Barton. Drop his arm and drop the ridiculous intimidation. It isn't 1963 for Christ's sake," Captain Weeks scowled. A full six foot six inch County Sheriff ordered a much smaller, red headed interrogator. Weeks surveyed the room counting three deputies, all appearing to be caught with the cookie jar wide open.

"What's that?" A surprised Mr. Barton asked. Turning fast to see a very large black man with higher rank, staring like a panther.

"Take your grubby hands off the kid. We already know where our young sniper got his rifle, Mr. Barton. Our boy dragged his gun out of the Merced River. Near the bridge on River Road, east of Newman." Weeks informed an overbearing and now embarrassed deputy. "The victim knows who shot him, convinced it's all a careless mistake. He demands we go easy on the boy." Sheriff Weeks surveyed the room of hanging heads realizing he made his point. "All of you in here go take a long break. The last thing we need is prisoner abuse allegations suffocating this case at the get-go," letting each deputy know, loud and clear, they were finished with Estefan. Weeks didn't have to re-check his room or repeat orders. He simply kept a close watch on Estefan who was busy wiping streams of salty tears from stained cheeks. Hearing the large black man relay Mr. Blevins' kind words only made the young boy feel abysmal about his bone-head mistake. Relieved at the same time, knowing this large black man wouldn't be too rough on him.

"Estefan!" Weeks snapped, wanting the boy's full attention. Fixed onto his young face. "Can I get you some water?" offering the frightened boy with a fatherly tone this time.

"Please," Estefan replied. "Is Mr. Blevins going to be all right?" asking uncertain.

Carrying a paper cup of cold water, Weeks told the boy he had to ask a few questions. Estefan drained the cup asking for another.

"Mr. Blevins will be all right?" Estefan repeated.

"Yes sir," Weeks conveyed, moving back to a large blue cooler of cold water refilling the cup. On return the tall black man began to question his scared captive, firm but civilized. He let Estefan know his father was at the station, which caused a fresh round of tears and regrets for papa's disappointment. The young Latino started his story once again from the beginning, more than willing to tell Weeks everything. Estefan's mind kept returning to his father when Weeks jumped the gun.

"Did you get a look at who threw the rifle into the creek?" Weeks waited patiently for his prisoner's reply.

"I don't know who it was sir," Estefan answered.

"Man or woman?" the sheriff asked.

"I thought it was a man but it was thrown like a woman. I can't be sure," a more relaxed boy told his questioner.

"Threw it like a woman," Weeks repeated.

"Yes sir," the young boy mumbled.

"Not sure?"

Estefan paused. Looking hard at the floor in a desperate attempt to remember that morning's details. "Sorry officer," raising his eyes, delivering an honest impression to the sheriff. "I can't say for sure," hoping the intimidation wouldn't start again.

"Uh huh," Weeks grunted, scribbling a few notes onto a yellow legal pad. "Okay Estefan," Weeks said exhaling deep, then leaning so far forward he forced the young boy to sit back into his chair. "Tell me what you do know. Tell me this story." Letting Estefan know without a doubt he was to reveal everything, to the imposing black man. Which he did of course. From the morning his prize was hurled into muddy water, to a secret hiding place, to target practice, to sighting a rifle completely unaware of it being loaded. Once again however, never mentioning the Jackal. Estefan chose to keep his dim-witted friend safe and away from this stupid mess. "My only friend right now," the young farm worker told himself.

"Am I going to jail?" A frightened teenager cried to Weeks with a look of shame. "Mr. Blevins is going to be all right," Estefan mumbled. Half asking, half thankful.

•••

"He's not dead?" Regina whispered to Buck, as pale as her olive skin would allow. Stumbling after she stepped back from Chris' desk.

"No. Shoulder wound." Buck answered. "Are you all right detective Gonzalez?" The cop asked.

"What's with you Gonzo? You look like you were just shot at. Do you know the victim?" Chris finished sending a text and walked to his stressed partner, making sure Regina was steady. She couldn't move. Her mind flooded under acres of budding orchards, a serene mother and father and the man most responsible for what Regina Gonzalez was today.

"My father worked for Clay Blevins. He brought my dad into California. About the nicest man I've ever met." Regina whispered.

Beatrice

Being so far out of control was starting to weigh on Franny Braden. Her drive to Tracy included yet another drawn out plan, wild assumptions and cravings for sensual touches with passionate gropes! It also included a quick last minute stop at her favorite fruit stand. A bag of ripe apples and late season cherry tomatoes for Mrs. Patterson just to show good manners. While checking out she noticed a shelf brimming with various nuts. Toffee covered almonds caught her eye and jogged her memory. "Detective Davis mentioned butter toffee," reminding herself smiling. "Better get some mixed nuts too," telling a young dark haired girl ringing groceries.

"Those nuts are so addictive, they're better than boyfriends," a smirking clerk told Franny while bagging her goods. She sparkled with muffled laughs thinking how the intended man had become addicting too.

Heading west on Highway 120, Franny sent another text. "I'll call you in a few hours. Maybe Benny can serve us a few 'Blackmen' tonight?" still waiting for his response however.

Mrs. Braden continued below a burdened sky cluttered with clouds. A mix of white and gray mushrooming cumulous dominated by an elevated, extremely dark gloom, loaded with water. Every so often small gaps developed separating cloud cover, permitting slivers of vivid coral blue and bright rays of exposed sunlight. Close to magic appearing, vanishing, suddenly reappearing like a shy child. Reemerging in moments even brighter, only to be submerged again behind an opaque, watery curtain. Cresting a small rise after crossing the lower San Joaquin River, Franny looked off to the west over a varied land-scape. Patches of shadowy ground directly below dense clouds contrasted with extensive ribbons of sunlight. Lighting trees, dirt, houses and shrubs like giant spotlights.

Small raindrops splattered her clean windshield, growing heavier with each quarter mile. By the time Franny left Manteca behind, central California's first serious rainfall of early winter drenched farm fields, orchards, wetlands and valley rivers. She moved on, straight in the face of two approaching storms. One very real watery tumult with its usual potential for major destruction, flood and perhaps loss of personal property. But almost always in the long run, leaving dividends in return. It was a different story concerning her personal storm. Should Franny's dark clouds burst open, she knew very little would be left in return. Sensing for some reason, her world rapidly changing in the next hour or two.

Small windshield splashes turned to heavy droplets, transforming into long cascading sheets of California's vital blood. Anyone spending a few years in Northern California and spoiled by a perfect climate, learns to deal with annoying wet weather delivered by a cold Pacific Ocean. A collective sigh is usually delivered however, when early rains develop and widen into key northern counties as the abundance of water equals plenty of agriculture. Nearly forty billion dollars worth annually! Rain, which provides plenty of food, plenty of salmon, plenty of ducks, plenty of money, plenty of illegal labor, plenty of easy living. Franny drove along flowing roadways and fifty five mile per hour fountains of spray. Her central Tracy exit wouldn't come too soon.

···

"Franny?" Beatrice was taken by surprise with Mrs. Braden's absence on her front porch, positive she heard a robust knock. "Are you there?" peering around the door jamb seeing her guest wipe sheets of water from rain soaked sleeves. "There you are dear."

"Hi Beatrice. Sorry, but I'm a bit drenched at the moment," swatting away more water, smiling at the older woman.

"Give me that coat and get inside lady. We'll get warm by the fire." Beatrice helped with a dripping jacket making sure it didn't pass beyond the hallway entrance. "Everything's hot and steamy. We'll have coffee. If you like, a shot of brandy floated in helps to speed the warm up." Beatrice smiled at Sarah's mother to be polite before returning to her kitchen. "Make yourself at home dear."

"Thanks Beatrice, I'm fine," Franny stated, weaving long thin fingers through damp, reddish brown hair attempting to dislodge any remaining raindrops. Sitting comfortable on a built in bench seat bordering a robust fire. Feeling cozier by the minute, permitting her eyes to scan a heavily decorated living room. Made up by far with various photos of her late husband. Portraits, poses, professionals, postures. Striking her odd how very few frames included them both. Adding fuel to a mystery of what the woman had in store. She checked her phone. Still no response.

"Here we are dear. I'm glad you chose the fireside seats. That's a cold rainstorm. We're almost sure to get a dusting of snow on the foothills tonight." As the elder woman lay a tray of full cups, cream, cookies and a pint of brandy. Two women sitting relaxed, sipping coffee with brandy, making small talk, speaking of the murder, speaking of Sarah, speaking of Marcus, enjoining a mild intoxication on sweet booze. Which was Beatrice's plan all along. Wishing to loosen Franny's tongue before giving away her secret.

With brandy flowing free so did their conversation. "Sarah and I talked openly about you at various times," Mrs. Patterson told her guest in a confident manner. The younger woman was taken by the frank comment, weighing how much information her daughter may have known and passed on.

"I'm sure you did. Sarah and I talked our share about you too, Beatrice," sounding a bit tit-for-tat at first. "She loved you very much. Sarah was lucky to have someone close by. Someone to go too." Franny sipped hot coffee, glancing outside to see a heavy, pouring rain. "I must admit to being jealous of you two." Both women shied away from one another in an awkward mood. "In a good way however," Mrs. Braden added with a show of class. They women gazed at each other, laughing this time while Beatrice floated another shot of brandy. Mrs. Patterson reflected on a handful of short stories about Sarah. Her guest listened close. They each shared a few tears over the young girl, cherished by both and growing perhaps, too comfortable. The elder woman had to stop pouring booze as each lady cultivated a good high.

Franny stoked the fire, rain continued falling, gusty winds kicked in, driving flocks of resting waterfowl from nearby delta lakes and broad sloughs. Pintails, diving ducks and geese headed inland seeking shelter and protection to sit out the storm. All quite unknown to the ladies inside. Mrs. Braden enjoyed her visit. Beatrice served a late lunch of split pea soup and homemade bread. Opened a bottle of Macchia Zinfandel, made more coffee, without the brandy and sliced a few apples Franny brought to her.

Their afternoon continued with Franny growing anxious about that 'something' Beatrice promised her. She felt it rude to ask, just deciding to let her daughter's friend breach the topic on her terms. They sat with each other chatting light, when out of nowhere Beatrice changed the mood.

"We think the killer drove by my house last week," Beatrice blurted out noticing Franny's open mouth reaction.

"What?" she asked disbelieving.

"Yes. Lucky for me the Tracy cop was here. A dark truck kept moving by, very slow, just like that horrible morning. Scared the shit out of me!" Unleashing wide eyeballs from her guest. Franny thought Beatrice referred to Detective Davis, never having met Chris' partner. "That cop was ready to hop in her car and chase him down if I hadn't nearly fainted."

"Her? I thought Chris Davis, the Tracy detective, was in charge of this case? A black man? Have you met him?" Franny asked, reminding herself she hadn't checked her phone lately.

"I've met him. He was here the day of the murder. Matter of fact, Mr. Davis was the first detective I met that day. A black man indeed and quite attractive I might add." Beatrice noticed how keen Franny was listening now. "I take it you know him too?"

"Oh, do I know him. He met with Henry and I for questioning at our home. What's his partner's name?" Franny asked.

"Regina. Regina Gonzalez. She's been hounding Douglas Sheets. He was the lead investigator on Sarah's murder case." Beatrice told her. "You must remember him?"

Franny reflected, but only for a moment. Thoughts of Sarah's trial came rushing back to her. "Yes, I remember him. From the trial," she told Beatrice. "He's a suspect?" asking Mrs. Patterson in complete surprise.

"I guess so," Mrs. Patterson told her. "She also questioned another man from Newman or Gustine. Merced maybe? Someplace down there." Stopping to let the comment settle. She could see the change envelop her guest's face as a concerned woman arose.

"A man in Merced or Gustine?" Mrs. Braden asked. She walked to the window and looked outside. The winds settled somewhat into a steady breeze, still pushing falling rain to a slight angle. She thought about Los Banos, Merced, Gustine, rain, Sarah, fog, unhappy nights and Henry, continuing to gaze outside with a blank stare. Completely silent.

"Are you okay Deborah?" Beatrice walked to Sarah's mother and grabbed her hands. "Come. Sit down," the older woman almost had to compel Mrs. Braden into her warm bench. She took her napkin, wiping away the younger woman's thick tears. As Franny was slowly seated Beatrice held her hand firm, sliding the object into Mrs. Braden's shaking hands, cupping warm fingers around rather cool skin. Mrs. Patterson rose, looking down on Franny waiting to see if she might have an immediate reaction. She didn't. Franny stared and twirled the object in her palm. Cradling it. Beatrice put another log on the fire, stoking flames while bright red embers flew in every direction. Beatrice needed Franny's napkin one more time.

Chris

Three ripe blackberries were speared then dropped with a small splash into a second fiery brown, cocktail glass. Sitting near Benny's mixing station, Chris offered the bartender easy service. "Your tab is now open Mr. Davis," Benny confirmed, smiling at Chris in his way to say hello. Davis expected her call at any time, becoming a touch nervous why she hadn't made contact by now. Benny's lounge was fairly quiet tonight, following a Thanksgiving holiday with no football games scheduled this evening and preoccupied by stocking his bar. He was also pitching hard to a new cocktail waitress. Another patron sat solo at the middle of the bar, sad and intoxicated. A middle aged couple acting very serious occupied a table off in the opposite corner. Chris suspected a cheating husband hard at work, the way Mr. Smoothy scanned the bar every few minutes expecting someone.

Still no phone call behind a drink half empty. Benny came over after slicing a dozen or so limes, talking up Davis, checked his drink and expressed warm feelings for an extremely hot waitress, in his opinion.

"I couldn't agree more Benny. Good luck," Chris sanctioned his pursuit. Each man grinned just when another person entered the lounge. Chris didn't notice. Benny did.

"Good luck to you too, Mr. Detective," as the skinny bartender turned away to prepare another 'Blackman.'

"I take it this seat's open," Franny said to a startled Davis, squirming onto a cushioned barstool with her premeditated brush against a frozen cop. More or less on instinct Chris breathed in her smell, took notice of deep cleavage, wanting only to touch and explore her inviting body. In the briefest of moments he was hooked again.

"I've gotta be careful," Davis scolded himself as Benny slid her drink on a napkin, front and center. She accepted with pleasure, thanking Benny for reading her mind and taking a long sip, letting the barkeep know it was perfect. Inhaling a second sip for liquid nerve looking at Chris above the rim, winked and smiled. "What brings you here Mrs. Braden?" In truth, not knowing what else to say.

Mrs. Braden didn't like Chris' tone. Assuming he might've just sent a quiet message, "this being as far as it goes." She couldn't be further into left field. "Visiting an old friend in town and bringing you a small gift with deep desires for a Blackman," Franny stated, sliding Chris a bag of toffee almonds, just realizing her sexy word play. She needed another sip of alcohol after that but managed the sexiest of looks at her target. Chris understood Franny's obvious, double intention, but chose to stand pat, offering no comment. He did accept the candied almonds however. Almost ravenousness, tearing the cellophane bag apart with crude force spilling nuts across the wood bar. Chris didn't care, munching his favorite candy. Franny shook her head at his childlike display wondering if his stern wall might be crumbling a bit.

"Are you here to tell me something?" Chris asked, crunching nuts very loud, even offering a handful. Franny declined, laughing to herself. "You weren't visiting Evelyn by any chance?"

"Maybe. To both questions," she answered in a mysterious manner. "What interests you more detective?"

"We better stick to the murder investigation," Davis responded but debated if she was serious about a possible female rendezvous. Split second fantasies added fuel to his already passionate desires.

Franny hoped Davis wouldn't chase on one of her most bold confessions. He didn't and stayed quiet. She wanted to ask the detective about officer Sheets and his investigation, thinking better of it, however. This evening was going to be all about Plan B and the plotting woman assumed once again, this would probably be her last chance to pursue, subdue and corrupt Detective Davis. "You have an apartment in town. Maybe we could discuss some details of the case," pausing to consider her final thought, "at your place?" Forcing a naive, erotic look toward Davis with her head tilted.

To Chris it sounded perfect, partially overcome with sexual energy and forcing himself to stay seated. He wanted the woman, right now. Wanted to be inside her, right now. Wanted to hear her moans of indecent corrupt pleasure, right now. "Maybe," Davis answered with his voice cracking ever so slight. Neither said much for a while giving Franny cause to believe she wasn't able to knock down or burrow through Chris' formidable bulwark. Sipping cocktails, watching Benny pursue the new waitress, he even began wishing for a football game. From nowhere, Chris burst forward. "Let's go Mrs. Braden, you follow me." Heard by Benny, the help and a few patrons as cop and suspect bounced from the bar and left in a hurry.

"Good night you two," Benny just got in as the door closed behind Detective Davis.

"I'm parked over there." Franny pointed to the far end of a rain soaked parking lot just before Chris grabbed an outstretched arm, pulling her in close to his body. She laughed nervous, then took a deep breath. Davis pushed himself hard, up against an uncomplaining body. They kissed one another very hard as Plan B was put on the back burner. She wanted to screw this cop in a nasty way and made a few fast steps toward her car to avoid the showers. The detective parked in the opposite direction.

"Damn rain!" Chris hissed between his teeth. "I'll meet you at the lot exit," yelling out, pulling his jacket overhead for cover.

"Okay," Franny shouted without looking back.

"Damn rain," Davis repeated, speeding off to his vehicle. The asphalt had been pelted non-stop since early afternoon, gleaming in evening light and growing very slick. Chris rounded his own tail lights occupying the next to last parking stall, sliding somewhat while going into a hard turn. One more stride led him into a forbidding slip but he managed to grab the car's rear fender, regaining stability. As he reached out however, his jacket fell over, covering his face and blocking eyesight just long enough to miss a large bulging crack of offset pavement dead ahead. Due to faulty construction work, water was able to seep in below grade causing uplift and splitting. Chris' left foot made awkward contact before lifting his leather eye patch, slipping out of control now. Into the car door he lunged around fifty degrees from horizontal. One hand slipped off a wet window while the other slid helplessly down a dripping car door. Regrettably, Chris' cheek made solid contact with a chrome door handle just below the left eye, igniting bright lights on purple blackness. Feeling water seep in through his wet jeans, the detective was startled back into reality just before a solid ache engulfed the left side of his face. "This fucking rain," he scowled out loud, lifting himself from a drenched parking lot, crumpling into his front seat. Rushed into a short recovery Davis managed to make the exit, seeing Mrs. Braden in a patient wait. The wounded detective flashed high beams on and off, leading the way in pain.

•••

"Are you sure it doesn't hurt?" Franny asked Chris, lying flat on his living room sofa. She recovered a small amount of ice from a rather paltry stocked refrigerator, wrapping it inside a hand towel. Administering gentle presses below Davis' left eye. "It looks kinda bad right now," holding back as best she could with a slapdash smile. "You sure know how to take a fall Chris," she added with a slight giggle.

"Do you always break into comedy when folks get hurt?" Davis sneered, raising his throbbing head as Mrs. Braden scooted her lap underneath. She continued the cold press as her patient silently admired full breasts hanging just beyond reach of his drooling mouth. Leaning over to rub his shoulders for comfort and a possible slender tease, Franny permitted her chest to give a faint rub across Chris' good cheek. She was pulling out all the stops, hoping with a growing desire Plan B was about to unfold. She saw Christopher Davis not only as pure sex at the moment but also someone she might grow fond of. Committed also. Possibly falling in love. His race wasn't even an issue as she couldn't perceive the color difference any longer. It didn't matter. Only a desirable, fit, courteous, younger man who stirred her feelings. A fleeting pang of guilt shot through a throbbing body like electricity when Henry's image entered her mind however, Plan B had taken over and became her out of control monster. Franny managed a deft move to undo a couple blouse buttons, which Chris noticed, with little trouble. Her cleavage bulged wild. Which Chris noticed with no trouble. For some reason however, Davis recalled addressing Franny as Mrs. Braden just before leaving Benny's bar. "What the hell man she's a married woman for Christ's sake." Davis realized at this moment, tonight could be the night of ultimate sex. A night of definitive sex. A night which finally places the ending note to their opera of sexual pleasure. A night of no sex at all, matter of fact!

After the jolt he'd just taken Chris convinced himself passionate sex would just hurt his face, instead of helping. "Franny, I think we're going to call it a night. You understand don't you?" Becoming the second time Chris walked away from his fantasy. A most deep seated fantasy.

"You're sure?" she asked, disappointed but relieved at the same time. Mrs. Braden knew as well, if Chris proceeded she would do nothing to stop her pure animal satisfaction. Lucky however, severe guilt ensued once more. Henry appeared once more. Her monster reared once more tingling upper most thighs with a forlorn craving. She looked close into the detective's face.

"Good night Mrs. Braden," Christopher Davis spoke soft. Putting another sword into the monster. "I promise you this much Franny. You and I will be seeing each other again. There's something I need to know," sounding somewhat sinister and vague at the same time, to a reeling Deborah Braden.

She left the detective holding a soggy cold press knowing Plan B had become an utter failure. Most likely for good. Leaving his apartment and hit hard by dry, night air. Cold air however, as the day's rainstorm continued east into the Sierras leaving ample snowfall. Clean snow, eventually transformed into drinking water for California's thirsty residents, parched agriculture and the left over's for migrating waterfowl and spawning salmon. Hard on the storm's heals charged a cold air mass. Fresh from Canada, bringing fresh air, fresh winds of seasonal change and fresh flights of ducks and geese. Franny cloaked herself in a dry, warm jacket and without hesitation set about her next move. She chewed over Henry's return tomorrow around midday but knew he had to leave again Sunday morning. "More meetings. The poor boy," talking to herself. "Sunday morning sounds good to me," she thought as her truck rumbled with a warming idle. Franny Braden decided the time was right to send another important text. A simple message which could change everything. "I wonder if I'll get a response?" she asked herself, speeding away from the man she'd rather be sweating against right now. "Goodbye Christopher Davis. Hopefully?"

Station 3009

"Captain Anderson," Chris addressed his boss in a sheepish tone, Merced County will be running ballistics on the rifle recovered from the Merced River. We could get results by the middle of next week," Davis updated his boss hoping very much Billy wouldn't look away from his cluttered desk. Chris turned right, intending to hide a swollen, black and blue cheek, knowing everyone would see the damage by mid-morning but didn't want to start this Friday morning explaining an embarrassing blunder. "They also started a background search, unsure how long it may take."

"It's an old gun and will probably take a while to run that one down," Anderson told Davis glancing up to see his detective's profile, reading from a printout. "What's up for the weekend?" Billy asked, back down on the desk full of overwork in front of him.

"Not much. Definitely no stakeouts this weekend," Davis answered holding broadside. His boss paused and looked up again for just a moment. Staring across the small office, Anderson thought it peculiar to see his detective checking the printout almost trancelike.

"Kinda odd," Anderson said to himself, without giving it more thought. His cell phone rang handing Davis, more or less the exit needed.

Chris started down the hallway at a very fast pace, hurrying as long as the office was clear. Rounding the final corner his heart sank. "Awe fuck," he mumbled very subdued wishing he could go on patrol. Regina rounded the opposite corner at the same time. Davis pulled a sharp left, almost pivoting, attempting to shadow his injured side away from his partner's view. "Gonzalez will have a field day if she sees this now," Chris chided himself, nervous about the unfolding situation.

She greeted. "Good morning Mr. Davis."

"Morning partner," Davis obliged. Unknown for sure if Regina noticed the bruised cheek. "Maybe she missed it," Chris reasoned due to her lack of slicing comments! They sat in silence for a few minutes with Chris swelling more relaxed and comfortable. Regina jolted him.

"Merced is doing ballistics. All right! We have that decent size fragment from Marcus' neck," Gonzo said somewhat loud. "That should be enough to confirm if it's our murder weapon or not," tapping multiple fingernails along her space bar key in apparent thought.

"We should know next week," Chris replied almost turning to face Regina, positive he maintained his secret.

"You know Chris, I've told you so many times. If you're gonna insist on crowdin' the plate, don't stand flat footed in the batter's box." Regina couldn't refrain from an elfin giggle.

"Ohhh shit," was all Chris could gather. His partner swiveled in her chair like a dust devil, faced Chris head on, slumped in his chair, wounded head propped on his left hand and elbow imbedded in the armrest. "Jesus," he said again, knowing there would be more to come soon.

"You get too settled in the box looking for that one pitch to drive." Regina barely held back a fat laugh. "Bang," she shouted. "You can't get out of the way of Mr. Inside fastball. Bang! Right on the cheek." Regina went silent for added effect. Rocking back and forth in her repaired chair. Just enough to generate a rhythmic and continuous metallic click, guessing Chris waited for a final salvo. She kept laughing but able to speak. "You right hander's have to stay loose in the box," Regina's snickering words were like a foul tip off Chris' face, off his left cheek!

"Enough Gonzo," Davis whispered loud enough for his partner to hear. "It hurts bad, when I smile." Regina stood to check her partner's face. He resisted at first but caved when he realized Gonzalez had turned serious.

"I'm afraid to ask how you did that?" bending over to examine the battle scar, wanting a closer look, carrying her distinctive smirk, however. On impulse, she poked the swollen, red cheek with her index finger. "Too much to drink?" Regina asked rather hushed, leaning even closer to the wound, squinting, examining, like she had insight to his injury.

"That's enough partner," Chris asserted, standing to flee his partner's curiosity. When he stood however, who should be walking by but Captain Anderson.

"What the? What in hell happened to you?" Davis' boss asked, also bending down to get a closer look at Chris' popular cheek.

"Took a bad fall Captain," Davis answered with a swift excuse.

"You don't say, detective. I hope to hell this wasn't from a fist fight?" Anderson asked without a speck of comedy in his voice.

"Nope. No fighting here Captain. Slipped on wet pavement," Chris stayed the course.

"I'll vouch for him," Regina chimed in helping to protect her partner. "High inside heat. Locked in, waited too long to bail."

"All right, all right. A bad fall," Anderson relented. Let's talk in my office. Five minutes." Billy landed another sobering look at Chris' cheek smiling at Regina on his way out. He enjoyed her version.

"Don't go any further Gonzo," Chris ordered his partner knowing it was likely futile. "I'm going to hear enough about this bruise as it is. Cut me some slack for a change," Chris almost begged but sounded serious enough. When he looked back at Regina however, she delivered a dead blank response showing very little in the way of malice or sympathy. Her simple stare continued for a dozen long seconds then fabricated a faint grin. Almost a, "yeah right," smirk. Causing Chris to snort a series short chortles. He couldn't help it. She had him by the short hairs most of the time and he knew it.

"Okay Gonzalez, let's see what the Captain has in store," laughing through each word. Regina didn't have to say a thing.

...

"Any ideas how to raise the heat on Sheets or the Braden's?" Anderson asked with a simple tone of low expectations. "Everything's stuck in neutral. I hope we haven't missed a suspect? We should have more going for us by now," Anderson spoke in fragments and disengaged thoughts.

Regina couldn't help but notice her boss' rambling thoughts were all over the place. "Maybe Chris and I should have another Q&A with Douglas? More heat in our interrogation. He might slip up?" Regina offered to Captain Anderson, not fully convinced of her own idea.

"I want to nail Franny Braden," Chris declared in a threatening manner, seeing the other two cops adorned in squinting eyes and perplexed faces. A second later it dawned. More sexual innuendo. "I meant, nailing her down with extreme pressure." Recognizing that statement came across kind of heavy on strange desire too. Chris squirmed, sitting straight in his chair to explain noticing Regina's wide eyed gawk and suspicious grin. His sore cheek all but forgotten. "I want one good shot to pressure Mrs. Braden with her husband present too. I know she's hiding something." Chris became a little consumed by his own speech. "She's been acting too damn strange," as Davis realized he just stepped over the line. Regina and Billy had no clue about his rendezvous with Mrs. Braden but Chris still felt very dumb, letting his guard down that way. He thought over his gaffe.

"What's she been acting like?" Anderson asked, innocent enough. "I wasn't aware we had any contact with her or her husband, since your interview?"

Davis suffered a quick panic, scolding himself for not informing Anderson or Gonzalez about his meetings with Mrs. Braden. "All of a sudden it's Mrs. Braden! I never should've let it go as far as it did. Thank God I stopped things last night," telling himself while struggling to reach a sensible response. Regina stayed quiet but she held a look on him similar to the earlier stare, when Chris asked her to ease up about his cheek. He spotted her suspicion right away. Chris had to say something.

"She's called me a few times," striving to appear calm. "Once to ask how the case was going. Another to tell me she thought her daughter's murder might have something to do with Marcus getting shot. Which seems a little obvious," using sarcasm to deflect his spontaneous remark. Davis hated his decision of withholding information, cursing how he and Mrs. Braden went way out of control. On the tip of his tongue he almost said fuck it, willing to tell everything then caved in to fear. "I feel like a fool," scolding himself, slowly sitting back into his chair filled with sudden anger, conceding he'd been tricked. He realized Mrs. Braden might be smarter than he cared to admit as Chris' mind reeled with ideas and scenarios. "She's hamstrung me. Intentionally shut me up! Franny knows something. I know it. I know it now," as the detective kept repeating the thought over and over in his mind. "I must've said something about the calls," Davis finished in a rushed manner hoping to bury the issue.

"Uh, no. Nothing was said to me, that's for sure," Billy Anderson answered very calm however, with very little concern in his voice, Writing a note in his binder.

Regina on the other hand, kept her eyes fixed on Chris. Not to burn a hole through him but with understanding written on her face. Her thoughts turned to Tom for a quick moment of truth. "You may have mentioned something to me a few days ago. I never gave it much thought at the time." Regina appeared casual about her last remark, pretending to study a note or two in her notebook. She checked her partner's face. Bruised, somewhat bloody but gently grateful. Partners help their partners.

"Be sure to let me know if she happens to call again," Anderson instructed. Head lowered, continuing to refer to yesterday's notes. "You two need to go through the investigation files and trial transcripts for Sarah Crosby's murder once more. If you need some weekend time, use it." Billy faced his detectives. "Get ready to confront Sheets again by next week. We have to get after him." Silence crammed the office. Billy excused his staff, to field a call from his familiar partner.

Davis walked fast. Leaving the room like he dodged a bullet. His thoughts shot back to Franny. Her body and her touch just made him angry, at first. Sensual attitudes followed soon. Interrupted by his partner's face. Thankful for her support.

Gonzalez couldn't help but feel proud on one hand, coming to Chris' aid and bailing her partner out of trouble. "I owe it to him," Regina appeased herself. On the other hand, "do we need to talk about Franny Braden?" she wondered.

Outside, temperatures continued to drop. A slow moving cold front penetrated south into the lower Central Valley. Following a day of rain, saturated soils and standing water would help to form fog tonight. Becoming colder tomorrow thick tule fog would strangle California's lowlands for a few days.

Chris and Regina studied court testimony once more. The murder investigation files grew much more suspicious this time through. Each cop wanted to nail Douglas Sheets.

Second Hunt

Regina became a smidgen antsy as her Friday afternoon came to a close. She had everything; change of clothes, toothbrush, tank of gas, refuge pass and determination. A quick load up and off she went. To food, sex, company, food and marsh. Another drive in a close routine to the previous hunt but adding a steady, increasing fog. She could tell by the Valley's ritual indicators, deep, thick tule fog would fill in tonight.

Sunset, outside her passenger window was impacted by fog. Dense blankets of low, mobile clouds crawled in and spread along the east slope of hills, bordering the San Joaquin Valley's western flank. Sunshine withered as the murkiness grew. Instead of a bright glare filling Regina's peripheral vision, a perfect white disk hovered above the lengthy ridgeline. Direct and visible, plain and viable, painless and viewable, for a few more wonderful minutes anyway. Not often is one able to stare directly into the earth's star, free of repercussion. Night will win out early this evening with layers of mist building in density, preventing the solar energy's strength to penetrate. Just before absolute darkness, neutral and gray dominate with no reflected light carrying various wavelengths to producing a range of colors. It appears like a single wavelength, a narrow bandwidth, middle ground. Gray. With less contrast than a black and white movie reel the valley appeared painted in gray. What remained visible. Water, orchards, fading skies, crops, dirt, road. Neutral gray. Twilight Zone gray. Consenting only to darkness.

Gustine fast approached. Regina hoped for a warm fire, good food, sensual touch, plenty of high school petting and sleep in a decent bed.

■■■

West avenue was dead quiet. Not one person walking, nobody jogging, no kids playing, not a single dog barking, nil to the number of cars driving by. One porch light lit. Just one. "He left the light on," Regina noticed. "He better," she said to herself. Gonzalez pulled into a narrow driveway missing close on a fender to fender kiss. Grabbed her vinyl A's bag, jogging at a fast pace, climbing five wooden steps with hurried strides almost pounding on Tom's front door. Regina carried a much different view into this meeting. She was schoolgirl excited to see Tom again. Realizing tonight would be more about sex and excitement from her newest connection. "Love?" Running at light speed through her most inner thoughts. "Let's wait a while for that crap," telling herself. Simple enough, Regina was more preoccupied with tomorrow's shoot. "I can't wait to get out there again." Rewinding images of constant shooting, bobbing decoys and birds splashing hard into cold water played like a reel in her mind. Memories of last weekend kept her taste wet for more shooting, calling, passing waterfowl, muddy water and tules.

"Is anyone home or what?" she muttered to herself, getting ready to pound the door for a second time. Just before knocking she heard Tom's voice on the other side.

"Who's there?" he asked in a voice reminiscent of Mrs. Ward Cleaver.

"Who's there?" Regina asked herself. "Who the hell's he expecting?" Taken by surprise. "It's me Tom, Regina." Speaking in a dead serious tone, eyes squinting and brow wrinkled wondering if she somehow had the wrong house. The door cracked open while Gonzalez peeked around the jamb seeing Tom's single eye staring at her.

"No shit," Tom whispered, his sarcasm unmistakable. Smiling strong and swinging the door wide enough for his head to fit through. "It's really Regina Gonzalez, here for dinner and duck hunting!" Sweeping the door open.

Regina knew she'd been had, feeling like an absolute moron. "Okay, you got me," she confessed, blushing pink. "You had me worried for a moment but here I am. Miss Regina Gonzalez, total ding-dong," barging through Tom's door into outstretched arms. Tossing her bag on a big sofa after removing a bottle of RM Primitivo. "Just for that, no wine for you." Regina's attempted retaliation faded when whiffs of cooking aromas drifted by her nose.

"Jesus Christos, that smells good." clutching the wine bottle like it was her evening's date. "If I can taste whatever you're cooking I'll share my wine." Regina turned in time to see Tom's advance. He gently lifted the bottle of red, inspecting a simple label.

"Very nice," Ellis exhaled, peering into the woman's eyes obvious she was being admired more than the wine. They moved in close on one another, fitting thighs between open legs as Tom pressed hard against Regina's chest. He loved her hard breaths letting warm mouthfuls of air pour across his face. She hugged harder, kissing each other with more than affection. They kissed in a more sexual way, feral, anticipating naked bodies, excited sensations, orgasms. Regina's hands moved slow, down along his chest and stomach causing Tom's muscles to reflex in surprised convulsions. Her hand moved between Tom's legs rubbing his erection somewhat firm. Making him gasp in pleasure, letting her lover know she was more than glad to be here.

"I missed you," Tom said in heavy, raspy breaths not wanting to separate. His hands slid around her waist, under her shirt and across her quivering belly. Drawing close for another taste of her Hispanic lips, Hispanic breath, Hispanic heat. Finding her breasts she moaned with pleasure as he pinched her nipples tight. It didn't matter. He wanted to take her right now. So did Gonzalez.

Tom forced himself to break apart, barely. "Roast duckling for my lady tonight," telling her quietly about dinner. Regina moved back into his arms and raised her reddened face to capture his soft lips. Food was no longer at the top of her list. She could feel it stirring now, swamping her in euphoric sensations. This man was trending deep into Regina's emotional core. "Love," shot throughout her body for another quick appearance. "Sex," reinforced her feelings letting hands peel away clothing and permitting an open mouth to complete Tom's most animal desires. Descending on each other again and again, for one more taste, another smell, added sensation. Their second hunt begins.

Dinner would be served late in the night. 'Served' might be one way to describe the way they shared this particular meal. Two lovers verging on perverse, famished, devoured roast duck like wolves at a winter kill. Ripping small shreds of breast meat off early season kills. Warm juices gushed from reddish-pink flesh through extended fingers onto lips, cheeks, breasts and shared to each other's mouth. Regina couldn't decide whether to eat or have sex. She found herself more than once, wanting to press lips and naked, trembling body to Tom's while shoving rich meat into an open mouth. Having both would be her one satisfaction now.

Small but rich seasoned mallard legs were bent then broken and pink meat torn away from fragile bones, dipped into warm Béarnaise, tipping heads back to accept their luscious delights. Together, downing a mound of waterfowl, skewers of chipotle shrimp, steaming bites of Potatoes Anna and lettuce wraps spilling smoked salmon. Becoming like Roman gluttons, inhibitions abandoned at all levels. Patches of exposed skin were smeared with a combination of saliva, sweat, Béarnaise and olive oil. They turned on the red wine like parched field hands to cold water. Using alcohol from very good wine, to achieve new depths of depravity. Sex, food and drunkenness. Even Regina's mild but noticeable burp, caused Tom to lurch to her side and nude body with reckless lust. Still chewing a mouthful of meat, he fondled her spread legs raking aside a short cotton robe all the while gleefully teasing aroused nipples with greasy hands. On top of her, below, at her side, they finished a night's meal with grunts, moans and sweat covered bodies, across the dining room floor. Closer to barnyard swine than human tenderness. Even Regina's luncheon gang would be appalled by her display of depravity! Maybe not Pam?

...

"Beep, beep, beep, beep," Elly's alarm sounded. Not quite as early as their last hunt but plenty premature for Ellis. Dinner, wine, dinner and sex lasted way too long this time. Lust and gluttony kept him from precious sleep, deciding to reach over once and punch the snooze button. "No hurry. Just a day hunt," groaning the words forth, half asleep, snuggling close to a stretching, yawning hunting partner. Tom's arm relaxed across Regina's warm butt. She slid sideways and sat up.

"Hey, hunter. Get up. Let's go," Regina ordered, pulling on metal window blinds peering outside. "Ohh, it's gotta be cold outside. Thick too! Like clam chowder out there. Perfect duck day." Releasing window blinds with a metallic pop. "C'mon lover boy, let's get going," Gonzalez begged then made a direct line to the bathroom.

"What's the rush?" a groggy Ellis moaned, preferring to linger in his warm bed. Morning sex sounded much more appealing right now than tule fog. He sat up clutching a thick comforter.

"You may as well get up lover. I'm not coming back to bed until tonight," Regina yelled out through a cracked door opening, while taking her morning pee. "Remember, you promised." Flushing the toilet then opening the door a few inches. "You promised. Now get up!" She yelled out, closed the door and loaded her toothbrush.

"What the fuck?" Tom whispered, crashing backward onto a warm mattress. Getting one leg out of bed as the alarm screeched again. Ellis reached over to kill the offensive shrill but instead, knocked the clock off a small nightstand. Continuing to clang as he fumbled to stop the din, tempted to rip it from the wall.

"Let's go. Get up Mr. Ellis," Gonzalez yelled through a mouthful of toothpaste.

"Okay, Christ. Let me get this damn," Tom mumbled until finally reaching his morning noise maker. "Shut the fuck up," he squealed, pushing the off button extra firm, in a way to hand out some imaginary punishment to the timepiece! He gaped at the 7:00 digital readout, shook his head and yawned. "Good God I need more sleep."

Regina bounded from the bathroom all smiles, fastening her bra and zipping up black fleece tights. "I'm finished in the bathroom lover. Go for it. We kinda need to get a move on, don't we?" asking Tom while slipping on her hunting shirt and camo turtleneck. "You have my jacket, waders and boots packed away, don't you?" interrogating a somewhat stunned hunting partner.

Tom babbled, "yep." Hobbling through the bathroom door, kicking it shut with a fairly loud thwack! Regina noticed, smiled and yelled out, "hurry up sweetheart. I'll get coffee going." Giggling soft, snapping her last button in place, fluffing dark brown hair then checking two mirrors before heading to the kitchen.

Tom splashed cold water on his face, brushed his teeth and hair, looked in the mirror, laughed at his sorry looks, laughed at Regina's eagerness and got excited about hunting waterfowl.

••••

"Hey, I'm back!" Gonzalez announced to the same Fish and Wildlife employees manning a quiet check station.

A rather board, sleepy woman looked up after reaching out to review Regina's hunting license, vaguely remembering her from last weekend. "Trying to be cute, funny and goofy, at four thirty in the morning. Good luck," the sleepy agent thought to herself in no real mood for another drawn out session of lousy jokes and inanity.

"Here you are," Regina handed over her license as Tom looked on. In rigid silence and praying for a routine check-in with no attempt at comedy this morning. "How's huntin' so far," Regina blurted out causing Ellis to hang his head, aching she wasn't about to resurrect her routine. Regina maintained a sappy grin thinking the woman would appreciate a little redneck humor this morning.

"I need your pass," the agent responded, desperate to dodge her question at first. But as dry as gunpowder she responded with a show of force. "Well since it's only eight thirty," pausing for more drama, "AM!" Speaking the letters a little louder. At this point, Tom handed an agitated employee his hunting tags in attempt to redirect a potential confrontation. Fish and Wildlife continued however. "The fog is so thick I can't even see your truck and it may not lift at all today. No wind, no rain and you can't shoot what you can't see. I think it's safe to say, today will be a slow day!" Tossing back Regina's tags and report card. "Anything else?" the agent sneered!

Ellis moved over and cut in. "We'll be going out to Salt Slough today. Lot B if it isn't full?" Pushing and nudging on Regina's side with his hips and left shoulder then instructing her move to the next window. "I've gotta separate these two," Tom told himself. Regina couldn't tell if the counter lady was upset or merely offering information. Lucky for Tom, the second agent sensed danger too and he ushered the two along.

"Good luck," he relayed with a wink to Ellis on his way out.

Regina and Tom jiggled along a narrow muddy road toward lot B. Tule fog made it slow going with heavy condensation flooding the windshield, which ended visibility a few yards beyond the hood of a bouncing truck.

"Did you sense a little attitude from that lady back at the check station?" Regina asked with genuine blameless.

"Attitude? Hmm, I didn't notice. Not really. Maybe just tired from being up so early?" Tom lied, trying his best at traversing an unfamiliar road in near zero visibility. "Crap, this is thick. No reason to start hunting early today," wanting to change his partner's train of thought but having to concentrate on a road he seldom passed.

"I hope to hell you know where lot B is," Regina chimed in finally taking notice of the blind weather conditions.

"It's at the end of this road with a small canal almost perpendicular to the lot. If we miss the parking lot we're in big trouble. Wet!" Tom smiled and checked his partner. She didn't seem the least bit concerned.

Reaching their lot without incident, they slipped into waders, boots, strapped on fanny packs, backpacks, decoys and guns. Beginning a rhythmic gate with wading staffs swinging fore and aft. Due to a couple days of chilly rain sweeping through the valley, cold air had all the ample moisture it needed to form unusually dense fog. Extreme calm combined with a cold air mass might be capable of trapping the cloudy soup all day. Filling a hushed refuge in a peculiar envelope of solid gray. Trees, shrubs, ponds and tules became invisible beyond thirty or forty feet.

Regina warmed up with almost every step, excited to be out once again, anticipating ducks gliding into decoys, various calling and piercing gunshots. She absorbed the surreal setting, beginning to revel in the colorless world surrounding her. Resembling an old black and white movie. No lights and little to fix an alignment, she stumbled twice from slight dizziness with no horizon to coordinate a relative balance line. "Like walking on a hard cloud," she told herself. However, her sense of hearing seemed to deepen. Their footsteps seemed louder, far off voices from other hunters seemed audible, honking geese seemed extremely low, songbird and raptor voices screeched much more intense. "Does fog help carry sound with less effort or are my ears making up for blindness?" Mumbling soft, listening and alert to each soggy step. Her lover just laughed.

"Not much further," Tom replied. "We take a right turn soon and set up in a small pond off to the left. I bet my seats are waiting for us."

"You sure someone else won't be set up there too?" Regina asked, reminded of their confrontation last time out. "I don't mind using my cop status to kick a little ass again, if needed!" She was breathing harder feeling her chest heave in and out. Tom labored too with long streams of vapor pouring on each exhale.

"I doubt it. I'm the only one who hunts this area. This pond's not much more than an opening in thick tules. If we're lucky we might get a few mallards or teal sneaking in through the fog," Tom said not expecting much action. He strained to see into the pall, looking for a telltale patch of tules indicating their wade in point. He couldn't help repeating to himself, "if this damn soup doesn't clear sometime this afternoon, we're screwed." Walking on, not saying much, both inhaling very deep and noisy. One felt great anticipation. The other, merely glad to be in the detectives company.

Central Valley fog can be quite amazing when first experienced by outsiders. Thick and opaque. Overwhelming at first. Most often a general nuisance when hunting waterfowl. Until it begins to lift! That precious half hour to forty five minutes when blue patches of sky first appear. Trees and subtle landmarks are exposed, sunshine streaks in, shy ducks seem to be caught in open danger. They show themselves, gliding for a brief prospect of choosing to settle in only to disappear into low clouds with hissing wing beats. Fog breaks, reforms, dissipates like a raised curtain. Flights of widgeon and sprig, just moments before whistling through dense clouds, sail in and sometimes free fall to exposed decoys. Hunters shoot, call wildly, miss, get caught off guard, miss again. If lucky, taking one or two birds. Then, like the clearing itself it's over. Remaining flocks pass high and away. Soaring pintails heard chirping but unseen, invisible against a bright blue sky. Clear air prevails. Like magic a curtain of fog rises, fades and disappears. Poof! Like a magicians crafty hands not a trace remains. Forgotten ten minutes later. Similar to police investigations like the Crosby murder. Clues and evidence are in the open, to be observed but clouded in foggy secrets and deception. So much fog, dishonesty and fraud encircled this case like a small flock of waterfowl teasing their captors below.

If a cold wind chooses to stay away the wait grows long for evening flights of mallard and gadwall to present themselves. Most hunters give it up by noon making their way to bicycles, hand carts, back to trucks. In a slow exodus like retreating soldiers in organized withdrawal. One thought in mind now, home to bed. To sleep.

A determined few wait it out however. Getting whatever sleep they can and winning large areas of refuge to themselves. Enjoying the birds, surroundings, waiting, alone, thinking. These can be addicting, lonesome afternoons as if you own the refuge yourself. Your private club yet different from the club shooters. Duck clubs need to draw large flocks. Keep high numbers of ducks coming in to keep high paying members coming back. Sometimes, not often enough but sometimes, mallards decide to trickle back into refuge ponds. Usually seeking heavy cover. In need of specific food source, preferred resting water or tired from southerly flights. Singles and pairs. Maybe small flocks of sprig too.

Challenging but superb waterfowl hunting. Location, calling, camouflage and decoy placement take over. Two to three hours engaging birds to commit. Out of nowhere a lone bird or pair will materialize, looking close to find safe landing. Probing for the dark shapes and possible loud noises, always wanting to do them harm. Looking close for that out of place movement, sound or barrel flash. Shooters below must stay concealed, keep calm, patient and call sparingly. Sometimes they come into range. Sometimes they don't. No reason why the birds do or they don't, nonetheless wonderful to get the chance.

If it's good. Real good. Two, maybe three mallards at best. Big three year old drakes, fooled and killed clean. The competition is asleep and a couple of clear afternoon birds belong to you. Golden. Regina worked her cases this way too. Murder cases. Patience and constant attention to detail. Trusting no one and suspecting just about everyone. Even loved ones. Trying not to miss the obvious.

...

Very few practiced hunters would call this day golden. Regina and Tom were positioned and wailing calls by ten thirty. Ellis was lucky to discover the tule patch he wanted and their wade in went uneventful. He almost made things interesting, charging into pond water again, leaving Regina behind.

"Hey pal!" Gonzalez yelled out stopping him dead. Ellis turned about face. "I'm letting you do all sorts of sexy things to my body. At least help me stay dry this time." She motioned Tom back to calf deep water, becoming her handy crutch at two difficult spots, reaching their dense patch of cover bone dry.

Noon and fog still owned the San Joaquin Valley. From north of Stockton to well below Visalia, tule fog lay like an inert blob. One hen spoony glided across their decoys in the early afternoon from a direction they weren't covering however. The jittery thin female spotted both movements among low tules, veered then climbed away without a loud noise exploding. Regina's previous enthusiasm slowly diminished. Tom grew sleepy.

If this fog was ever going to lift, noon and two o'clock would offer the best chance. At one fifteen three faint slivers of blue appeared at a pair of five minute intervals. Unveiling low tree lines across the pond just as three flights of sprig and one flock of widgeon sounded close overhead. Chirping drakes and grunting hens gave them cause to believe ducks might drop through the fog at last. Gonzalez, by instinct crouched low, scanning the surrounding murkiness. Calls faded however as Regina grew more despondent and Ellis grew sleepier. Silence and a lack of birds overcame.

What else can two good friends do in a blind when birds fail to cooperate? Talk. Pass the day talking to one another. For Regina and Tom, question and answer time.

"What about club shooting? Tell me about duck clubs," Regina asked, draping her over and under across a makeshift table of folded and bent tules.

She wasn't holding out much chance for bird shooting right now as her eyes became heavy.

Tom leaned over to make sure his Browning wasn't resting in pond water. It wasn't, giving her question some thought. "I've been in two clubs. Low end pasture land that didn't shoot all that well. Even on late season picture perfect days," Elly revealed, perceiving a drake mallard's faint quack nearby and pausing to listen. All quiet, concluding he must be hearing things.

"What was that about?" Regina asked, laughing and snorting on a finger held under her nose.

"Don't laugh at me. I thought I heard a mallard. Nothing now." Tom justified, peering into deep fog holding back a snicker. "This lady kills me," telling himself, smiling back to his partner. He continued. "Never having the bucks for a high end club forced me to learn hunting on the refuge. I prefer to shoot out here now. For some reason I must admit, there's a competition in me," staring at Regina with fake bulging eyes.

"That's from a movie Tom," Regina blurted out with mock disgust. "No Country For Old Men." Guessing at the title. "Which may start applying to you old man!" Delivering the sharp jab.

"There Will Be Blood," Tom corrected her guess. "Great flick."

"You're right," she shot back. "What else," Regina pressed, wanting to hear more. "Gimme' your rules Ellis."

"All right. Since you asked." Tom got ready to spell out his ground rules, after one more quick listen for any possible waterfowl. All clear. "No electronics. All these battery powered spinning wings, swimming decoys, whirling kites. They're all a load of unethical bullshit. Using powered decoys should be made illegal, today."

Tom hesitated, thinking of another pet peeve. "Not taking the time to learn how to call. Just laziness I guess?" Tom insisted with cupped hands around his mallard call and blew a series of loud hailing calls. "It leaves out an interesting part of the shoot. Some days calling makes a big difference. Other days a minimal amount seems to work best. You never quite know for sure which is part of the challenge."

"I'm buying. We need to work on my calling," Regina said, blowing a few chirps from her sprig whistle. "Keep going," she demanded not knowing for sure if Tom was finished.

Ellis leaned way back on his stool and grabbed his uplifted leg at the knee, staying rigid but balanced. "Let's see," mulling over his gripes. "I know. Three or three and a half inch shotgun shells suck. More Cabella-ing of hunters. More, bigger, fatter, taller loads. They suck. Goofy hunters are convinced they shoot higher and farther. Not so." Tom paused once more to listen and hope. "Just let the birds work in close and you only need standard loads. If you learn how to shoot birds, standard twenty gauge ammo is plenty," he argued.

"Don't know what you're talking about but I'm still buying," Regina played on. "I do like the close in comment."

"I'm rollin' now," Tom delivered like a comedian. "Levee shooting scabs, guys crowding into popular ponds, skyscrapers and the designated hitter. They all suck." Ellis looked in Regina's direction. She smiled wide and scanned the fog behind her attempting to hide her laughs.

"The DH is not that bad. They need it in Oakland. Bad!" Regina disagreed but without conviction. "I have to admit I was a bigger fan of the DH when it first started. Now, only the large market teams can afford to buy those big bats. Loading up their batting orders. It's impossible for the A's to compete with that kind of money."

"Kinda like three inch magnum loads. Only those rich punks can afford to buy that ammo," Tom joked in return. "But c'mon," hesitating again for the phantom mallard calling. Nothing again. "Play the damn game. Everybody hits and everybody plays the field. Simple." Ellis let loose with a wide yawn needing ducks and sleep. "Hell, it was your team that got it all going. Charley Finley wanted more offense in the game. More hitting. Less defense. Don't get me started on the DH!" Tom argued then closed his sleepy eyes.

"Fishing?" Gonzalez asked. "Are you an angler?" Ellis lifted his head and yawned. "I can see you're not into fishing," responding with low giggles."

"Never been much of a fisherman. Don't like sitting and waiting for a bass to bite my worm. Boring," Tom spoke, rubbing sore eyes and checking the dense fog in vain.

"Oh yeah, unlike this hub of excitement," Regina teased. Tom grunted, realizing his words sounded ridiculous at the moment. "You're showing me the hunting thing. I'll show you the fly rod next season," Gonzalez offered, reflecting back on her trout fishing trips with dad and Clay Blevins. Telling herself she needed to get out more often. "Bait fishing sucks."

"You're on sweetheart. Fly fishing with girls sounds cool," Tom murmured, no idea what his words meant before dozing off again.

"What about kids?" Gonzalez dared, after a fifteen minute pause.

Ellis emerged from a restless nap. "Why are you still single?" he queried, hoping not to infringe on a sore subject.

"Never could find that honest man." Regina's answer contained an air of humor but her feelings ran true on this subject. Most of the men in her life had been liars, cheats or both. She never came close in a relationship to consider marriage let alone having children. She changed the subject. "I would love to have a daughter someday," Gonzalez added looking away from Tom's face, embarrassed about her last remark. She hoped Tom didn't take it as an offer to, "please get me pregnant."

"How about a boy? Boys are sorta cool too," Tom replied, not sure if Regina was serious about her gender preference.

"Boys are mean and girls are cool. You know that," Regina answered without a laugh and coming across very unconvincing. Tom stayed quiet, lowered his head to resume sleeping acting as though the words didn't warrant a rebuttal. Gonzalez looked back to Tom, wondering if she nicked a nerve. Too quiet.

Tom moved to rub his ear, folding arms on his chest. Giving in, "I couldn't agree more. Girls are very cool." Then dozed off. His response gave her a smile. Regina beamed and watched the pond for ducks. Ten minutes later she dozed off herself.

"Politics?" Regina asked. "I'm guessing you're a Demo?"

"Reformed Republican," Tom answered, detesting politics.

"What the hell does that mean?" Regina asked.

"I try to walk the center these days. Both Parties can fuck themselves. Just set aside more habitat for waterfowl. End of discussion." Tom tried to act severe but hid a desire to burst out laughing. He hoped for a response and spirited debate. Lucky for Ellis, not to be.

"Jesus, sorry I asked," Regina exclaimed, giggling all the while. She sat perched on her wood seat like a throne. Face full of streaky camo, crunching Tom's sunflower seeds, swinging boots through splashing water, cuddled in an oversized hunting jacket, enjoying herself. "When's the fun begin anyway," she wisecracked, oblivious to Tom's appraisal.

Ellis couldn't help but stare. He studied her for a long two minutes or more and knew he'd been captured. This moment. This one simple, ridiculous moment. Just like that, a crush of need for Regina Gonzalez! He wanted to keep her in his life. He had to now. Tom Ellis felt very good and a little sorry, all at once. He never thought it would get this far but couldn't help it. "She's too good to let go." He wondered if these feelings would lead to huge mistakes. "A blunder? Perhaps? Fuck it," he told himself moving in close, grabbing his over and under, handing her the shotgun. He kissed her soft and let his nibbling lips linger around hers. She nibbled back. Tom held steady for a while longer. Sinking in and just like that, he loved her.

···

Damp cold air continued to blanket a dull gray valley at 3:45. The sun itself became nothing more than an off white disc hanging low, settling west. A bulb of low light without its blinding glare held hostage by idyllic fog.

Tom slept. Steady on a narrow wood seat, slumped over, somehow managing balance, emitting soft snores every so often, as sound as one of his lifeless decoys. No wind, no water chop, no movement, no life. Regina didn't know how he did it, coveting his ability to fall asleep while slumped forward, head in hands and staying seated. Her own naps lasted no more than a few minutes of light slumber. Leaning further and further over the water, shuddering awake just in time to catch her fall. Startled back to consciousness by drastic bends to one side. Once even breaking a full backward flop with an arm flailing grab into a clump of tules! Over an hour of intermittent naps, at five minute intervals but in due course surrendering on sleep, standing to stretch out stiff joints. She lifted the Citori to feel it's balance, shouldered the stock, swinging on imaginary targets. Marveling at how seductive the weapon felt in her arms.

Two teal wheeled over the decoys unseen by Gonzalez, barely audible. She stared into the murky air freezing solid. Both birds fixing wings low before commencing a long, slow turn. In ruffled glides they made a fast turn on a direct line toward narrow water, phony ducks and Regina. Ready, all ears, staring in the right direction. The pair materialized over one side of the decoys. Very faint in a foggy haze but Regina made out the unmistakable silhouette. Set wings and a long neck swerving to get a closer look at the counterfeit resting birds. Gonzalez had little time to think, however she did react. Raised her Browning, pointing the muzzle just in front of the trailing bird without even noticing the gun's small aiming bead and fired. All reflex. Folding in a small puff of body feathers and relaxed webbed feet, a dead cinnamon teal went head over tail feathers in a listless, single summersault, falling beyond low weeds with a tall splash. Unfolding so fast Regina could only stand in a fixed stupor, a bit dazed, glaring at the pond.

Tom jumped at the gunshot, unsure if he was dreaming, but getting a glimpse of the teal splash down. Both hunters made their way to small water rings radiating from a dead bird. "Good shot," Tom praised, pumping hard toward low weeds. They reached a mature drake, belly side up, motionless except for a single webbed foot twitching. Dirty yellow webbing in swimming motion, nerves reluctantly firing. Tom observed the fragile motion, burying any subtle feelings. Powerful wings spent, suspended from a deep reddish brown belly, black rump and bill. Regina noticed its small size.

"Oh Mother Mary, tell me I didn't shoot a baby duck? It's so small?" She recoiled slightly when Tom lifted the bird. Cradled breast down in his hand.

"No way, full grown cinnamon teal," admiring feather detail as the bird's neck and head slumped, flopping side to side, limp. Tom extended each wing revealing distinctive powder blue fore-wings contrasting with vivid bright green speculums.

Regina reached out, taking her first kill, examining detailed back feathers and scapulars, fixating on the delicate bird while returning to the blind. "Congratulations. First bird. Everything okay?" Tom asked, checking if Gonzalez held regrets about taking a life. Regina held the bird, feeling its last warmth and soft belly feathers course through cold fingers. Continuing to examine the drakes deep reddish brown color and intricate highlights. She felt perfectly normal and calm. Finally.

"What's that?" responding to Ellis' inquire, not paying attention.

"Never mind." Tom concluded the detective would be fine. The last hour of shoot time stayed foggy and cold. A flock of ring neck ducks, six or seven total, worked their pond showing white breasts for a brief glimpse then disappeared. Wheeling a sharp pivot, air released through short wings both hunters heard the flock but couldn't gauge direction. Rushing air, rising louder and louder, Regina raised her gun halfway, expecting the flock to show straight overhead. Tom heard them from a different bearing, turning around. The flock emerged in the opposite direction and too low for Regina to adjust her sight and take a crossing shot. They vanished once more with wing beats soft then silent. Nothing visible as shooting time ran out, Tom and Regina took their time gathering decoys and sorting gear, in no real hurry to leave. One shooter a bit disappointed while the other couldn't be happier. Right on cue a light breeze developed out of the west, helping to erase some fog. Little by little stars popped and patches of deep blue evening sky appeared. A gibbous moon offered bright glow as low clouds continued to speed along. Tom took Regina's hand, holding firm all the way back to lot B. He squeezed cold fingers periodically catching his lover's attention. Regina smiled. Walking together, side by side, framed in moonlight, slipping along a muddy path, shotguns slung diagonally across tired shoulders, talking, joking, enjoying a great pleasure as the drake cinnamon teal swayed to and fro, at Regina's side.

Loretta

Things weren't going as well for Loretta Sheets.

"Who did you talk to Loretta and don't try lying to me anymore," Douglas screeched with a smoothly raised left arm, turning a backhand toward his cowering wife threatening to slap her again. Loretta braced herself for yet another blow across an aching jaw and forehead. No longer in a state of terror for herself, Loretta worried about Lucy. Her daughter had witnessed too much violence from a deranged father tonight. Loretta sensed Douglas' left arm about to make contact, just able to throw up a right forearm hoping to deflect some of the incoming blow which she did. But not entirely as her husband's anger, frustration and madness breached her defenses. Bright streaks of light and sparks filled her vision as the blow glanced off her rear jaw. Regaining senses, finding herself on both knees looking into crackling flames filling an inviting fireplace. Her pain went unnoticed as thoughts of Lucy played out one more time, hoping the door to her daughter's bedroom would be locked and closed tight this evening.

"Tracy PD wants to question me again. You talked to someone. Who?" screaming loud! Loretta felt liquid dripping from inside her nose. She spotted a thick drop of blood splatter to the hardwood floor directly below her face. Warm, slow flowing blood from her uppermost sinus cavity, formed heavy droplets before releasing upon high finish, oak plank. She noticed how the color contrast fit well together.

"Who did you talk to Loretta?" Douglas squealed, grabbing a fistful of his wife's hair and twisting the lush locks slowly, tightening against her scalp. Loretta's head was forced back until looking square into her red faced, raging husband. He appeared more comical somehow than intimidating. Eyes bulging wide while a thick purple vein protruded from his right forehead. His expressions grew closer to bad acting in a B-Grade horror flick, doing his best but failing to appear menacing. Douglas had morphed into a foolish character to Loretta, forcing choked laughter right in the middle of her possible termination!

"Go fuck yourself, ass-wipe!" Loretta hissed, spitting a fine spray of blood from her bleeding lower lip. "You gonna kill your wife tonight, sugar!" Succumbed to the fact he planned to murder her, maybe soon, driving Douglas even more severe by her insolence. Loretta's true concern remained in Lucy, probably crying in fear behind a bedroom door. "If I could reach a kitchen knife," Loretta longed to defend herself just before a stout metal fire stoker came into view. No more than three feet away.

"Tell me Loretta. Now." Douglas said in a calm voice. He sounded odd but extra sinister. "Just tell me who you talked to, my darling, and I'll leave. Quietly." Releasing his grip on thick blonde hair, pushing her head away forcefully.

"You can't let me live Douglas, I know too much." Loretta stood her ground, firm. She was beyond caring at this point. Douglas realized his wife was probably right. His problem. What to do next. Continue to beat information from Loretta or kill her now and fabricate some sort of wild yarn about his wife's grizzly murder. Even in his swelling irrational mind, he knew murder would be a tough sell but crazy enough to believe in pulling it off. They stood a few feet apart, Loretta breathed hard in and out. Douglas panted at a slower rate needing time to think.

Mrs. Sheets stayed head down but with the stoker in sight. Her only viable weapon nearby. "C'mon Douglas, get careless for mommy. Look away. Take a step or two sideways," she yearned to herself, silently craving for a tiny crack of possibility. "Maybe I did talk to a Tracy cop. I know what you're thinking Douglas. You're in a corner and you know I have to die," gambling a little more brazenness might cause the madman to misplace his focus for a second or two.

"Shut up you little bitch. I know exactly what has to be and hasn't need to be done," her husband seeming more out of touch with his use of bad grammar.

Loretta shifted her head sideways as another drop of blood followed the lower rim of her right nostril. The droplet paused at the lowest corner of her nose, accumulating, tickling ever so slight, falling to hardwood planks with a barely audible plop. She adjusted her gray eyes right, proud to see Douglas move over two steps facing away, for some reason peering through their large living room window.

"I'm not about to kill the mother of my child. Just tell me who you talked to," Douglas repeated his litany. "Was it those two bullshit Tracy cops? Loretta, tell me. Now!" Screaming the last word very loud. Sinister. Causing Loretta to flinch. She could tell he was looking down at her, holding position. Noticing his breathing quieted as he started shifting his weight rhythmically to each foot. His attention went back to the window and Loretta sensed an opening.

Douglas caught site of movements through the back yard shrubbery. Quail, in two small coveys moved in and out of brick patio landscaping, just as evening sunshine peeked over a far off foothill. Cultivated by more fanatical, delirious plans, his alertness decreased to fully diverted. It took a faint metallic ring to catch his awareness as the covey broke, flying low and fast, single file across thick grass into a small stand of young oak trees. Douglas initiated a relaxed turn back to his beaten wife. Rotating right unfortunately, intending to resume interrogation and determine what caused that ringing sound. "Tell me who you talked," was all Douglas could mutter.

His peripheral vision scarcely discerned an object coming into view and his brain even managed to compute, it traveled at a high rate of speed. The object moved in too fast however, connecting before a protection reflex commenced. The metal stoker bashed Douglas square on his forehead. Just above the right eyebrow with the poker's spur angled into Douglas' eye socket.

Loretta swung the metal tool like a baseball bat. Stepping in toward her victim, two handed, resembling an attempt to catch up with a high nineties fastball out of the strike zone. The lady could tell in her hands and arms she made solid contact, following through while staying in balance. Douglas hovered for a moment, arms flexed a little out and away from his torso then fell off to his left and back. Unable now to break his fall as faint sparks still flashed across a blackened field of visualization. Dropping faster, striking his head square to the corner of a heavy wood coffee table. Loretta knew right away her husband lay fully unconscious. Wondering perhaps, if she had committed murder!

Mrs. Sheets lowered her metal fungo bat, still clenched in both hands, pointing a sharp tip into Douglas' chest. She held it steady for twenty seconds just to be sure. His right pinky finger trembled ever so slight.

"Douglas," Loretta yelled out, checking for the faintest response. He didn't move a finger, except for one pinky. She moved the stoker to within a few inches of his chest. Held it straight, then poked him on his right breast twice, rib cage and upper abdomen, like a downed elk in a backcountry shoot. She expected her husband to leap up at any moment but Douglas Sheets lay perfectly still minus heavy breathing and a twitching digit. Loretta finally dropped her bat with a loud clang on the wood floor, jolting her back to reality. Then backed away slow, hearing Lucy's quiet whimper from her bedroom. Loretta was jolted back into reality a second time. "I hope you're out for about ten minutes asshole," she murmured, backing away two steps planning what she needed to pack. "Not too much," scolding herself while running upstairs, straight to Lucy's room. Hurrying at first down a long hallway, Loretta began to slow down, not knowing how her young daughter might react to the recent violence. Touching the door knob and listening for any sounds, she barely made out Lucy talking, turned the handle finding it still locked. "Thank God," she told herself.

"Lucy. It's mommy sweetheart," Mrs. Sheets yelled through the heavy wood door. "Open the door honey, for mommy, please. We need to leave sweetheart," hoping her daughter would open soon.

Following a short stillness, Lucy responded. "You said to keep it locked mommy. It might not be safe." The words landed on Loretta's ear with profound sentiment. Mom's heart sank and spilled over, flooded with guilt and pity for her deprived girl. "She shouldn't be exposed to this," Loretta whispered to herself, clutching a locked doorknob all the while falling to her knees and pressing her cheek against a painted wood door, in a rush of heavy tears.

"I know Lucy and you did it just right. But it's okay to open the door now. We have to hurry sweetheart," choking her words, wiping salty tears from red cheeks. Loretta leaned her head forward resting on the warm wood, trying to keep from sobbing. She heard Lucy walk to the other side of the door. Separated from the one love in her life by a mere inch and a half. Unfortunately, solid hardwood.

"I'm afraid mommy. I'm afraid you might be hurt. Did daddy hurt you?" the scared child asked, placing her cheek on the door opposite her mom's. Loretta had to control herself from slipping into breakdown. There wasn't time and somehow she must keep from succumbing to emotions. Lucy's words were more than just a sad song piercing Loretta's inner core. Ripping any lingering apprehension limb from limb. This was the moment in her life, right in the middle of unspeakable violence, the moment she realized another person cherished her. Loved her. Unconditional love. Loretta knew she would never be far from Lucy, for the remainder of her life.

"Lucy, listen to me. I love you darling. More than anything in the world. Mommy's fine." As she rubbed away a streak of dry blood from her left nostril with trembling fingers. "It's okay. Daddy can't hurt either of us. You have to open the door for mommy. Right now baby." Loretta listened very close but silence followed for the next ten seconds, growing very anxious, afraid to think what might happen if they were caught in the house by a wounded Douglas.

Like trumpets announcing a grand entrance she heard Lucy unlock the door. A brass doorknob turned slow, clicked twice followed by the door, little by little swinging open. Lucy stood motionless in the doorway, cradling her spider doll in both arms, relieved. Mom nearly collapsed, feeling light headed, but retaining control. She knelt to one knee holding both arms open to catch her daughter, who came running, hugging mother tight, crying on mom's shoulder, squeezing hard.

"It feels wonderful," Loretta told herself, craving to freeze the moment. She stood up lifting Lucy as well. "I need to pack some things Lucy. Help me. Get your pillow and blanket for me, okay." Mom implored. Lucy nodded, smiled and cleared a runny nose. The two girls rushed through the small bedroom gathering clothes, some toys and a few books. They scampered down a carpeted hallway into mom and dad's bedroom. Loretta slammed as much as she could into a pair of suitcases before heading downstairs, sure to shield Lucy from seeing her dad lie motionless on the living room floor. She ransacked what little remained from a disastrous looking kitchen, pulling her love through a side door leading to the driveway and waiting minivan. Loretta checked her watch. Just past five o'clock, not quite dark. Douglas had been out for almost twenty minutes.

"Let's go baby doll," kissing her daughter twice on pink cheeks before buckling her seatbelt. Mom scampered to the driver's seat, glancing back to the house of pain she was leaving behind. "Fuck this place," Loretta whispered, backing from the driveway a little too fast, ramming the opposite curb with both rear tires, spinning a steering wheel full right and punching a loose accelerator. "Where the hell do I go now?" Mrs. Sheets asked herself, exhilarated and scared, glancing in the rear view mirror to look at Lucy, safe in her possession.

Franny

Mrs. Braden left home early Sunday morning in a move to confront her biggest threat. Franny thought how she was driving way too much the last few days. Fortunately for her, Henry was having the same problem traveling in opposite directions however.

"One last time," Franny urged herself. "I hope it's the last time," knowing this was awfully risky. But, she must deliver the item, in person. Hand it over, let it be known, without a doubt, she held the proof. "I know. It's that simple," mumbling the words to herself. Thinking. "Get me the hell out of all this," repeating the phrase nonstop.

Rolling by were the relentless disked fields, picked orchards and distressed small towns, which remained just about oblivious in the world beyond her windshield. "I have to keep my marriage together. God knows I've gambled with

Henry, with our lives, with his love for me. It all ends now." Franny confessed. Sunday morning saw few cars on west bound highway. Soon, traffic would grow, as Bay Area weekenders begin their return trips from across the fall Sierra and foothills. Not congested traffic like high summer or dead of winter. Most of the camping and hiking crowds had dwindled away more than a month ago and too early for winter ski crowds. Those that know and appreciate a lingering fall in California's Sierra are rewarded with small crowds, cool days and a subtle but noticeable foliage change. Of little concern to Mrs. Braden. Her mission lay in the middle of a dormant San Joaquin Valley. Past Tracy then bearing due south on I-5. The morning fog would be thick and soupy, slowing her approach.

Tom and Regina

"Where do you think you're headed?" Regina pleaded in a voice filled with sleep, wrapping both arms and one leg around Tom's torso, squeezing while displaying a sexy smirk.

"I was thinking about making you blueberry pancakes. I once heard they help tits grow bigger!" Ellis snickered, turning back to face his love interest with a smirk of his own and inserting a bare thigh between her legs, rubbing gently. His hand massaged her bare breasts forcing Regina to moan in soft arousal, enjoying his warm fingers.

She scooted in close kissing his ear presuming her breath was way too feral for face up panting. "Blueberry pancakes are an old wives-tale. It's buttermilk pancakes that grows boobs. Like you!" She rolled in closer, all wiggles, feeling her belly and thighs press against his welcomed body. "You're so nice and warm. It feels too good." The detective moaned, closed her eyes allowing Tom's use of a moist tongue. Licking her neck, chest, stomach, hesitating as Regina pushed his head further south. She spread her legs catching breaths in a sharp inhale followed with a supple moan as sharp reflexes rolled through her thighs and belly. "I love waking up like this," whispering out loud and pushing Tom's face firm, lower still. Spreading even wider. His tongue found every groove, sweeping each lip, indulging a firm appendage over and over. Tasting every sensation as Regina writhed, whimpered, gasped and climaxed. They rested together in one another's hold for a short while. Regina moved into place to return the favor, soon starting familiar movements and sounds all over again. Pancakes would have to wait as both contestants enjoyed each other followed by a deep, hour long nap. Covered by a warm comforter, neither hunter stirred. Late morning would arrive before venturing to a hot shower. Tom patted Regina's back dry when a truck pulled up outside, parking opposite of Tom's house. The driver noticed two cars in the driveway, deciding on patience, laying in wait.

Loretta

Overweight, nursing a slight hangover and sleepy, Ricardo gunned a coarse sounding tractor engine, intending some response from a woman sound asleep inside the dew covered minivan. It worked. Loretta Sheets sat straight to see what caused the noise. She hurdled from complete sleep immersion to wild eyed awake in a split second. Her bulging eyes meeting a pair of bloodshot eyes atop a blue, coarse idling, John Deere tractor. Instinctively dropping her left hand to check for locked doors. They nodded, smiling at one another before the Hispanic laborer rumbled away to his morning chores. The senora seemed fine.

Mrs. Sheets rubbed hard on tired eyes then stole a peak into the rear view mirror. "Ugh. Shit!" she whispered with a slight twinge of soreness after viewing a deep lavender crescent below a puffy left eye. Then examining the left corner of her mouth revealing a bright red cut and dry blood. "I look ridiculous." She turned to see her daughter fast asleep, wrapped in a heavy blanket. Lucy slept sound as mom continued to stare.

Loretta fled from home Saturday evening just at dark. She drove for close to an hour trying to ease her panic and Lucy's fright. Her daughter immersed in tears for half an hour or more, worried for mom and dad. She couldn't understand how daddy could hurt mommy. Loretta was able to calm Lucy, then herself. Relieved that Douglas wasn't somehow in pursuit. She decided to stop for food at a rural diner outside of Lodi, betting he wouldn't search for her there if he could. Mom and daughter were permitted to linger until midnight, drinking coffee and diet cokes delivered by a sympathetic waitress. The young employee could see this customer was an abused woman from her own pathetic experience. Lucy didn't mind, with free soda and a nearby television. Loretta spent most of her time fighting back tears, depressed emotions and fear. Without a trace of what to do next.

No family to run to. No sister to rely on. Her only real friend lived too close and guessed Douglas would search there first. Uninformed and leery of which government agencies might offer help but knowing county social could be a nightmare. She left the restaurant driving north on Highway 99 for an hour then turned one eighty for the same ride south. In a state of mental exhaustion she exited just south of Highway 4, followed a county road east and decided to hide herself by sneaking along a secluded dirt road splitting two walnut groves. Lucy was deep asleep by this time when Loretta killed the engine, crying herself to sleep under foggy skies, a hazy moon and falling leaves.

Loretta Sheets had to do something now. One person kept coming to mind. Chris Davis. For some reason Loretta felt the detective would be willing to help out. He made a point to tell her, often enough, he'd be there when she decided to tell her story. Turning on her I-Phone aware she risked her location, rubbing a nervous thumb over the call button, hesitated, then heard Lucy stir and call out for mom. She pressed the button.

"Hello Mrs. Sheets. This is Detective Davis. What can I do for you?" came across loud and clear. Loretta knew, by instinct, he would move to her aid.

...

"How long do I sit here," the driver asked, expelling a long sigh while scooting deep into a large comfortable driver's seat, examining the house for any movement or life. All calm. Before long, glimpsing a shape move across the front porch window. Curtains were pulled to each side revealing white shears, permitting a thin veil into a rather large picture window. The driver looked away for a moment, seeing a lone woman walking the center of West Avenue, being led by two chocolate labs, one small Dalmatian and a beagle. An obvious dog walker doing her job. Inside the parked car an impatient individual wondered how the lanky girl kept all these canines under control. As she passed, still navigating West Avenue's centerline, the driver could see she was holding on for dear life.

"Those dogs are working you out young lady." Locking onto the lone beagle spotted in tan, white and black. "That hound dog is adorable," talking out loud in the front seat before glancing back toward Tom's house. Noticing lights burning in the living room and leaning forward to stretch body muscles upward. Staring. No doubt, just spotting a person silhouetted in the window standing rigid, looking straight back in return.

Tom

Regina checked her phone, seeing a recent text from Chris. Closing the cover as her initial reaction was to view it later. "It has to be work related," she presumed, not quite ready to part from a pair of blueberry pancakes browning just right on Tom's griddle. "I ain't leaving now." Receiving whiffs of cooking batter made her mouth water in a delicate way. She bolstered some resolve for a moment but caved and reached for her phone, flipping it open to check Chris' message. Reading the text triggered Regina to stand and turn on the light, inside a dim living room. Tom completed his browning flips and waited as the microwave heated maple syrup, glancing to Regina noticing her serious expression. He stayed quiet, knowing it had something to do with the murder case but couldn't help watching her face change, until three fingers slid over a hot griddle.

"Ouch," he yelped, waving his hand up and down trying in vain to ease the burn. "Damn, that hurts!" Shoving his hot hand under a cold water faucet and grabbed a dish towel to wrap three burnt fingers in wet cloth. Tom looked to his lover in need of affection, who displayed no interest whatsoever.

Regina walked to the picture window, staring outside through a veil of drifting fog clutching her phone. She didn't speak but caught a sudden movement from someone inside a parked truck across the street. Four dogs marched in the avenue held in check, barely, by a slim girl. It was hard to tell who was in charge! The person Regina discovered just now stared back. Car and driver had captured all of Regina's attention. "Kind of odd," the detective told herself.

"Your boob jobs are ready," Ellis called out, hand wrapped in wet cloth and feeling edgy. Regina didn't move a muscle and Tom didn't force it. He set their breakfast table, sliced oranges, rinsed a handful of pomegranate seeds and poured coffee. Stealing quick glances in her direction to keep tabs on his hunting partner.

Tom walked forthright to the detective, slid his hands over tense shoulders, leaning into her back. She shuddered soft but sudden, turning her head upward to accept a long serious kiss. "Breakfast is growing cold, me lady," in a poor British accent Tom took her hand, pulling his love back to the kitchen. They ate a filling meal in a relaxed manner but Ellis remained tuned to Regina's smallest movements. Reluctant as she grew less and less aware of him. Gonzalez responded to a couple texts, taking time to ponder each detailed reply, becoming silent and more distant. Tom had never seen her this way. He was only a few feet away and stayed almost completely out of touch with him. It felt awkward. Not quite rude but uncomfortable.

The detective tapped her phone on the table top between sips of coffee, deep in her own thoughts. Ellis cleaned the breakfast dishes and put on another pot of French roast. He expected to hear Regina's next words.

"Sorry Tom but I have to leave," Regina murmured, being of little surprise.

"Right now? I thought we could," Tom suggested, pausing and smiling, "we could, you know, hang out in my bedroom this afternoon. My mom and dad won't be back until later tonight." Elly grinned to his warm friend hoping she might find his charms engaging. Regina stood, wiggling in her sexiest gate toward her infatuation, throwing an arm around his neck. She kissed him hard but not serious.

"Sorry, I have to leave Gringo." Still holding him close. Looking at his agonized smile. "I'll call you later." She grabbed her bag and kissed Tom goodbye in the living room. Regina felt guilty about her hasty departure as well as disappointed, planning to stay close by Tom today.

"I'll walk you to your car," Tom offered.

"You don't have to," Regina said, making her way to the door. Tom didn't say anything but issued a stare that spoke, "yes I do!" Regina emerged first onto the front porch and Tom trailing. Walking a slow pace in silent, heavy steps, each had issues on their minds but afraid to discuss them now. Cutting across the front yard to Tom's driveway Regina had all but forgotten about the stranger parked across the street. The driver on the other hand, took a long hard look at Regina. Burning her image into memory. Wanting to remember this woman's face with keen eyes locked onto the unsuspecting detective.

Tom got Regina settled, kissed her rather passionately, wished she would stay and grumbled while watching her back down the driveway. Kicking at pebbles on his walkway like a designated hitter after swinging and missing at strike two.

Staying absolute still the driver managed to get an even closer look as Regina backed up. Cutting wheels full right, Regina's side window paired even with the metallic truck just perfect. The detective kept both eyes glued to her side mirror avoiding any scrapes but failing to notice a potent stare. Regina shifted gears looking right to wave goodbye to her dejected boyfriend, driving away with Tom watching from the sidewalk. First her car, then the glowing tail lights soon disappeared into a foggy wall. The invisible car still audible as she drove away. He continued watching until the engine drifted into background noise. Not so much listening as he was thinking. Considering the new possibilities his love may discover, regarding her case as he climbed his brick stairs.

"Hello Tom," came the words from behind. A soft shudder climbed the back of his neck.

Chris

Slowed by dense fog after entering northbound I-5, Gonzalez became racked by sudden stomach pains and was forced to halt by an unexpected throw-up. Symptoms passed as quick as they arrived affording Regina little alarm, resuming her drive without another episode. She arrived back to Tracy late in a state of curious excitement. Presuming their much needed break in a murder case, which proved frustrating and lacking direction came with a heavy toll. An innocent woman seriously beaten with her young daughter confused and terrified. Entering Chris' apartment, Regina noticed how fast Lucy ran away to hide in unfamiliar surroundings.

"Loretta has no family," Chris told Regina. They could talk in private, after Mrs. Sheets left to comfort her troubled daughter.

"You can see the bruises and marks on Loretta's face. She took a serious beating," Regina said, checking to be sure Mrs. Sheets was still in Chris' spare bedroom. "We'll talk to Anderson tomorrow. Maybe he can put them into a witness protection housing?"

Chris looked at his partner yielding a serious frown swinging his head back and forth in negative territory. "I already tried our Captain. He claims the budget isn't there to provide housing unless Loretta's willing to talk now."

Chris spelled out, coming away extremely disappointed about the department letdown.

"You gotta be kidding?" This sucks. Is the department expecting you to house them indefinitely?" Regina asked sounding painful and letdown. "Is she willing to talk? You think we can convince her?"

"They don't recognize her as a witness right now. She won't issue a statement and nothing's happened to get a warrant issued to arrest Sheets. Not yet anyway," Chris explained taking a long chug from his diet Coke. Davis decided to keep away from alcohol with the young visitor sharing his home.

Regina was thinking. Time to get creative but sorry to say, nothing much developed. "I can take them to my place for a while. Give you a break," she offered, knowing it wouldn't be much help.

"Thanks Gonzo. Anderson offered to open his place too," Chris said. "I just don't have the heart to slough 'em off to County. Those places can get kinda scary. I can't do that to a little girl." Chris looked away, embarrassed to show his emotion.

Impressed once again with her partner's generosity as well as his compassion. Regina approached, rubbing his anxious shoulders, at the same time resting her cheek into the small of his back feeling lucky to be working with this man. She rubbed her cheek further in, caressing both arms. "Something will break open soon, I'm sure," attempting to comfort her partner.

Chris stood still swimming in Regina's affection. "I must admit, if it does take some time, I won't mind too much." All smiles, turning to face Regina. "Lucy keeps me jumping," her partner declared without shame. Regina wrapped her arms around Davis' waist and hugged him tight.

"You're a good man. I hope you know that." Complimenting a blushing detective as best she could, still tangled in a long hug when Mrs. Sheets entered the living room.

"Oh, excuse me. I'm sorry," Loretta apologized, retracing her way toward the bedroom to offer some privacy.

"It's okay Mrs. Sheets. We're having one of our many work moments. Strictly business," Chris assured his new roommate.

"You're sure? I can go for a walk if you," Loretta was cut off sharp by Chris' interruption.

"No, no. Really, it's fine. My partner has to get all sappy every so often," Chris laughed, nodding to Regina, indicating his joke. "It's fine."

"I was just getting Lucy something to drink. You two keep working." Loretta forced an awkward smile, filled a glass with water, departing in haste while Chris and Regina snickered at the idea of themselves involved in any way other than work.

"What about Douglas? Any word on location?" Regina asked.

"Anderson called Sonora earlier. He talked to a staffing sergeant. Our boy has conveniently requested this week off, unscheduled of course. He just phoned it in on Friday claiming family matters." Chris told Regina with a palpable tone of disgust.

"He's searching for Loretta right now. We have to keep her hidden," Regina added.

"If so, he's looking through big black eyes and a plenty sore forehead," Chris exposed with a wide grin. "It seems my roomy clocked him pretty hard last night. With a fire stoker no less! That's how she got the hell out of there," Davis concluded like a proud father.

"Way to go Loretta," Regina hissed, pumping a tightened fist upward.

Douglas Sheets

Douglas was in a bad way now. He didn't stir after receiving the metal rod to his head until early Sunday morning. Sunshine splashed through a large kitchen window, brightening an otherwise dark interior. Outside, rolling foothills ranged clear, well above stubborn fog suffocating a rather cold, westerly San Joaquin Valley. Douglas Sheets however, remained trapped inside dense fog, physically speaking. His face, in particular a red inflated forehead ached with throbbing pain to a point of lightheaded stumbling, following three or four shaky steps toward the bathroom. He had to see the damage Loretta inflicted yesterday first hand. Pausing in the doorway to keep from falling over, staying upright with outstretched arms and each hand gripping the doorway frame. Sheets held steady, resembling a crucified Christ complete with bleeding forehead. His crown of thorns administered by an enraged spouse instead of an angry mob. Head hanging low he shifted himself in front of a vanity mirror with one hand, braced against a marble sink with the other hand. Raising his head inches at a time Douglas was taken by the deepness of color surrounding his right eyeball. Blinking and poking around a swollen face, soon realizing he suffered complete blindness in the battered eye, accounting for his awkward balance. Sudden upwelling oppressed his throat followed by intense sweating and light headedness. Sheets bent over his toilet shooting a stream of burning vomit into a porcelain bowl, most of which found the tile floor. He heaved and groaned two more times. Spitting, coughing, gagging back to his feet, peering into the mirror. Yelling at himself as if someone else stared back into his eyes.

"I will rip both arms from your shoulders Loretta, before I kill you," Douglas fumed at the image. He looked and acted like a wounded animal. Revenge filled his heart and mind, tearing apart whatever remained of coherent logic and rational behavior.

"It had to be those fucking Tracy cops," Douglas squealed, wetting a washrag to wipe his mouth, chin and dried blood that flowed from a gash above his eyebrow onto a white shirt collar. Losing the fluid's deep red color, to a rich brown tone in its current dehydrated state.

"Use your phone Loretta, just once and I'll find you. My GPS track will locate you." Sheets dabbed at his wound scrunching face muscles in pain with each stroke. "I will find you, silence you, be rid of you," Doug preached, going on further and further out of control. "I'll get those two fucking cops while I'm at it." Sheets continued to convalesce himself making a bad wound worse, as treatment continued.

Patricia

"I'm not an official member of the investigation team Abby, for Christ sakes!" Bailey yelled over a non–stop talking Abigail Crosby. "The Captain is handing me info as he sees fit. Once in a while he gives something away without knowing it. As far as I'm concerned we're done. This makes us even." Patricia Bailey was panting into the phone by this time. Clear, deep breathing could be heard on the receiving end.

"How do you know for sure Miss Bailey? There could be another investigation going on. Some other suspects?" Abbey tried a more civil tone. She felt the reporter gaining confidence, sensing the entrapment beginning to shake free. "I can't afford to lose her now," Mrs. Crosby told herself.

"Abbey, listen. Billy's told me everything he knows. The investigation is pointing toward Douglas Sheets," Patricia pleaded to the older woman. "He's convinced the damn cop is crazy, probably killing both Sarah and your son. From what Anderson says the other detectives still need persuading. They're both leaning toward Sheets as Sarah's murderer but neither consider Douglas having motive to kill Marcus." Listening to herself she sounded like a six o'clock news anchor aiming to convince a watchdog audience.

"That other detective. The black guy. He's the one I'm concerned with. What the hell does he know?" Abbey's question come across quite ridiculous to the reporter.

"I can't ask Anderson to allow me a direct examination! He's exposed almost all of what he knows, I'm sure." Patricia Bailey sounded even more frustrated.

"Why doesn't that detective believe Sheets committed both murders? What's his name again?" Abbey asked in a bewildered way, as thoughts appeared shaky and a bit scattered.

"Uhm, Davis. Rick Dav," Bailey stopped dead, correcting herself. "It's Chris. Not Rick. Chris Davis is his name," finally getting the name right and sat down hard. Flopping into a padded chair, on target this time, becoming more perturbed by the minute.

"Right. Davis?" Abbey recalled. Your lover boy doesn't say much about what's bothering his detective. Can you talk to Chris Davis?" Abbey asked knowing full well the chances would be remote, unaware it wouldn't happen in any police department! Abbey waited for a response hearing Patricia's deep breathing in her phone again.

"Abbey, for Christ's sakes, please. I can't just set up 'interview day' at the City of Tracy, Department of Police, to find out where their murder investigation is going!" Patricia stopped. Her cadence had grown louder with each phrase, holding the phone facing her mouth yelling uncontrolled! Still stopped, rubbing a wet forehead while trying to untie a few tense neck joints. "I can't believe I have to explain this shit," Bailey yelled to herself.

"Hello? You still there Bailey?" crackled an aged voice into an aggravated reporter's ear. Patricia waited, letting her silence convey what's on her mind.

"Still here Abbey," speaking with her lowest, most even pitch. Filled with contempt, refusing to offer anything more.

"Bailey," Mrs. Crosby recommenced. "I need more information. I must be sure. If this cop killed my son he's going to pay and pay up soon." Abbey sounded as if she would be delivering justice herself! Patricia's attention peeked even higher.

"Abbey, I hope you're not talking about taking revenge yourself? Tell me. Tell me right now," Bailey was yelling in the petite cell once more which barely covered her sweaty palm.

"Hit a nerve, did I?" Mrs. Crosby responded loaded with sarcasm.

"I'll tell you what you hit, you crazy old bitch. You just hit the walk-off bomb. This ends it all, now!" Patricia Bailey could hear herself clear as a bell. Liking her newfound guts and kept on swinging. "I'm blocking your phone number. Don't call anymore, stay away from me or I'll take legal action against your ass. If I have to I'll pull your God damned gray hair out with my bare hands!"

Abbey was put back in her heels to say the least, almost staggered then heard a resounding click. Her connections, including the investigation, was now over. "Fuck you. You little whore. I don't need your sorry ass anymore." Abbey continued to speak into her phone held below a trembling chin like it was some sort of cosmic transmitter. "Time to contact the Chief again." Mrs. Crosby envisaged various scenarios on how to approach her old flame one more time.

Station 3009

"Where the hell is Gonzalez?" Anderson barked, acting hamstrung with an open phone in one hand and a handful of e-mail printouts in the other. He glanced at Chris whose back faced Billy, but still expected some sort of reply.

Checking his watch yet again. "Shit it's almost nine o'clock."

"Right behind you boss," Regina signaled, tossing a large purse to the floor and flopping her leather jacket over a padded chair. "Shit, I'm in early Captain," joking while keeping a straight face. She had an early appointment that couldn't wait.

Captain Anderson turned sharp, "didn't see you Gonzo. Sorry!" her boss apologized feeling awkward. "Let's meet in my office for another of our," dwelling in silence for a tease, "productive meetings! Say about ten minutes?" Checking his watch once again, flipping printouts then storming back to his office.

"What's up with Anderson?" Regina posed to a laughing Davis, squinting eyes and scrunching cheeks.

"I don't know," Davis answered. "Maybe he has some fresh news?"

"How was your weekend partner?" Regina was hinting of Chris' house guests, hoping it wasn't all bad.

"Can't complain except for listening in on two girls crying a lot. I didn't know if," Davis searched for suitable words.

"Didn't know what?" Regina asked, clearing items around her desk.

"You know. Should I offer a shoulder?" Chris lifted a notepad appearing concerned to Regina but unable to come across face to face for some reason. Choosing to stand at his desk like a lost child and quiet as falling snow.

Regina approached noiseless from behind and delivered a prolonged but gentle poke into his back. Twisting her hand for good measure. "You played it right. Mom and daughter need to work things out for a while," Regina offered support but wanted to say, 'lend the shoulder big guy!' She didn't of course, knowing Davis' first night watching over the Sheets girls would be a training exercise at best. Gonzo laid her head on Chris' back letting him know she treasured him. She could tell somehow, he was thinking of his own daughter. "Let's go partner, Anderson's waiting," speaking soft, tugging on his shirt sleeve, guiding him from their work area. They reached Anderson's office after a bubbly Maria informed Gonzalez, The Gang of Four luncheon, will be held tomorrow afternoon. Regina might just deliver an attention grabbing disclosure.

"Christopher, how's mom and daughter doing?" Billy asked, causing Regina to cringe. Posed in a manner however, each detective understood. Anderson appreciated Davis' offer to open his home to Loretta and Lucy Sheets.

"They're doing okay. We'll see what happens in a few days," Chris responded glancing toward his partner for quiet support. "Any news on safe housing for them?"

Anderson frowned, "same story I'm afraid. No funds. Yung's talking to County trying to shake some money loose." Billy revealed, knowing it was a lousy situation

"County scares me. Especially for the little girl. I'll keep Lucy at my house before turning her over to this county's relief," Davis responded but lingered a serious stare into his boss' eye.

"You know we'll help out if it goes too long," speaking for himself and Regina too. "I'm borrowing from a couple select department funds for your out of pocket expenses. Food, clothes or any other stuff like that." Anderson informed with a nodding Gonzalez in support. Billy halted for a moment to check his notes.

"Okay," Davis responded, signaling an end to the housing issue for now. "What about Douglas Sheets? Any location yet?"

"Haven't heard a thing," Captain Anderson answered somewhat gloomy. "Calaveras County has been briefed, saying they'll look into all accusations starting tomorrow." Emphasizing 'tomorrow' with a disappointing attitude. However, Billy understood their problems. Prefering to deal with a bad cop quietly like any other police department. Plus, being embarrassed enough with a probable wife beating cop, Calaveras didn't have a suspect charged with murder, just yet.

"They will never find him Captain," Regina spoke in her typical confident tone. "He's a hunter now. Stalking his game to silence her once and forever." Regina studied each man's face, appearing to be in agreement.

"Do you think he suspects Davis taking her in?" Anderson asked. "Hell, he probably does," answering his own question.

"She probably needs twenty four hour protection." Gonzalez added.

"I can't afford any more people living in my apartment," Davis interjected with just the right amount of sarcasm.

"Nice change up partner," said Regina. Giving Chris a fist bump lauding his disrespect.

"We need a safe place to house Loretta. Some place he wouldn't expect," Anderson was thinking out loud, trying to force himself to conceive a perfect location. Resulting in a feeble strike out however.

Like a ringing double it occurred to Regina all at once. She may have the perfect place while asking herself if Douglas would suspect this location. Visualizing and pondering the site. "Way too close to the murder site we're investigating," telling herself. "It's perfect. Almost perfect anyway if the landlord buys in?" Gonzalez rubbed her cheeks trying to construct a negative. Resulting in a feeble strike out. "I'll see the owner later today," she mumbled under her breath, returning attention to Douglas' whereabouts.

"Where do you think Douglas is now? Is he still near home or out on the street prowling like a crazy animal?" Regina opened the topic for discussion.

Chris didn't speak right away, wondering the same thing himself. Anderson carried a straight face but noticed his cell phone receiving a text. It wasn't Sonora or department case information. Patricia would have to wait scooting the phone far to his left. Regina sat up straight, waiting. All three detectives had their own ideas and each of them realized it too. Chris was certain Douglas Sheets killed Sarah Crosby but not convinced he murdered Marcus Crosby. Davis never let go of his gut feeling about the Braden's. He'd bet the farm they held some vital information, if not the killers of Marcus themselves in revenge for their daughter's death. Chris wanted to pressure Franny Braden very soon. His intuition told him the time to do it was coming into focus very soon.

Regina leaned heavy toward Douglas Sheets being the killer of Sarah Crosby. A lousy marriage, violence toward women, an affair, a cop gone crazy. But remaining in the dark as to whom shot Marcus Crosby. Was it a crazed Douglas or did the Braden's execute him in a cold calculated scenario? Could it be someone not even suspected right now. She doubted the latter.

Anderson desperately wanted to believe Sheets murdered both Sarah and Marcus Crosby. In his mind, somehow making this murder case appear simple. One killer for two crimes. Easy! Except for the Loretta Sheets' wildcard, which offered nothing to confirm his skeletal theory on who the hell killed Marcus Crosby.

All three detectives shared four opinions in common about this case: The Braden's have crucial information; Loretta Sheets may have crucial information; The case continued to be stalled; It would remain stalled until Doug surfaces.

Their meeting continued another twenty minutes and a couple more wild scenarios invented, dissected and promptly discarded. Not too much accomplished during this summit. They adjourned, all in accord to protect Loretta Sheets and review court records one more time.

■■■

"What is it now?" Regina answered, acting as though Tom might be a bother. Exiting her workspace, not yet comfortable speaking with her lover-slash-hunting partner near Chris or Billy. Stepping outside before greeting Tom, "what's up?"

"How are you sexy?" Just calling to tell you how much I miss your warm, sweaty body." Tom's flattery sounded genuine and a bit over the top at the same time! In truth, he was very much in the mood for some long drawn out foreplay.

"Oh thank you, Mr. Ellis. Would you care to inform me, exactly just what it is you'd like to do with my tingling body," panting into her cell phone, playing the part of phone sex lady again. "What should I wear for you my hard lover boy. I know how you adore my black bra and panties. Spiked heels this time? Hmm?" Gonzalez played her part almost too convincing, feeling Tom shuttered in silence but hanging on every kinky description. "Should I wear black or red sweetheart? Maybe you want to see me in my thigh high nylons? That always makes you hot." Regina was getting into her part. Soft breaths and sensual moans played just right, in each sexual fantasy. "I'll let you peel them off my quivering thighs. Would you like that Mr. Ellis?" Silence continued from Ellis' end. "Are you there Mr. Ellis?" Regina whispered low and slow into her phone waiting for Tom to reply. Silence. Wondering perhaps, if she was doing so well, had Tom taken things into his own hand? In her deepest of enticing voice, "tell me what you're doing Mr. Ellis."

All at once in high volume, Tom replied. "Regina? Is that you? Sorry." Tom apologized in high capacity. "My chainman's been shouting in my fricken ear. I can't hear a thing? What did you say?" Tom asked in an aggravated tone.

"Nothing important. How's it going Ellis?" Regina left phone sex lady behind, once again failing to get interest. She felt as though her act rated very professional, erotic and believable. Thinking she had a future on a part-time basis at least!

"Hey, I'm calling to see if you can hunt Wednesday? The forecast is for strong north winds and very cold. Should be a good hunt day," Tom informed his lover, holding his index finger taught to keep Anthony quiet and at bay for the moment.

"This Wednesday? Day after tomorrow? I thought we were hunting on Saturday?" Gonzalez asked a little confused. "I forgot all about hunting weekdays to be honest."

"Oh yeah. Wednesday, Saturday and Sunday," Tom explained. "C'mon down tomorrow night. We'll get in some feel ups, dinner and a quick Wednesday morning shoot. What do ya think?"

"The feel me ups sound great. I'll check my schedule for the week but I don't see why not. One day of work shouldn't be a big deal?" Regina considered her case load, deciding fast to take Wednesday off. She wanted to see Tom again soon. "Let's do it big guy. You, me, sweaty boobs, dinner on you of course and a duck blind. What could be better?" Inelegant and laughing like a high school girl. Regina needed a day away from the Crosby murder case.

"Great," said Tom. "This could fun. If the forecast holds we should get a lot of shooting, I'm sure," stating positive and excited. "Try to come down early, We can," Tom stammered for a second.

"What?" is all Regina said causing Tom to explode into laughs.

"I gotta run lover. See ya naked tomorrow," Ellis said goodbye and hung up.

"Lover. Sounds great to me," Regina whispered into a dead phone, making plans to visit Beatrice for a drop-in lunch.

Beatrice

Regina forged a slow drive across Tracy. Deep in planning strategy which almost resulted in a broadside, T-bone collision, at one of Tracy Boulevard's many hectic intersections. Lacking road concentration Gonzalez glided straight through a no doubt red light, needing two blaring horns to jolt her attention back to the wheel. A slight screech of braking tires with faint smoke but no scrapes. She made it to Mrs. Patterson's quiet home amid a slight case of jittery nerves, not all of which stemmed from her near crash. Regina had an off the cuff game plan in mind, deciding to take a subtle approach. Hoping Beatrice might produce the generous offer herself. Deep inside the detective was afraid to ask her friend upfront and direct, for this kind of favor. "I don't have the courage to be that rude and blurt out a straight request," Gonzalez told herself just after knocking on her older friend's red door. "Oh shit, maybe I should've thought this over a little more. She may think this idea is nutso?" He bowed his head and rubbed her brow with a nervous hand.

"Regina my darling, what brings you here?" A pleasant air enveloped Mrs. Patterson like a surprise visit from children away too long. Guiding her friend inside to a backyard raked clean of dry leaves and cut back landscape.

"It's not too chilly out here, I hope?" Beatrice asked. "I'll start coffee." Not waiting for an answer by rushing inside to her kitchen.

"Don't go to any trouble Betty," Regina yelled. Playing the name game again, but hoped her mother like friend would return with food. Gonzalez passed on lunch today and grew very hungry.

Like a mind reader, her host returned with a tray of warm bread, olive oil, grapes, slices of crunchy apples and a medium size glass bowl, containing fresh salad for each. "Way to go Betty!" Regina burst out with a small hand clap. Laughing. "Perfect timing!"

Mrs. Patterson exhibited a sly grin while arranging plates, cups and silverware as two friends sat comfortable in afternoon sunshine. The valley air remained cool after a brief pastel fog dissipated near ten o'clock. "You look famished my dear." Beatrice was eyeing her guest with a discreet side view as the detective wolfed down large bites of tomato and lettuce. Sporadic breezes scattered loose hair from both ladies as they dined, talked, joked, relaxed. Hot coffee fit spot on with growing shadows and fall temperatures. Regina began to stir inside wanting to breach the topic and reason for her visit. Leaving her chair, stretching both arms before walking among the last remaining fall flowers. Smelling, finger touching, admiring, thinking.

By chance, Beatrice launched an unexpected question. "How's the murder investigation going?" Still seated pouring out a refill. "Any news?"

Regina didn't stop walking or reviewing the landscape then answering calm, "oh, some new development, like always." Trying to maintain a fake, blasé appearance about the case.

"Tell me about it," Mrs. Patterson insisted. Regina turned, after bending to sniff one unusually large gardenia, facing the patio table. She forced a lean smile.

"Our case is bouncing back and forth between both Crosby murders. They seem to have grown inseparable. The investigating officer in Sarah's murder has captured our focus of investigation. He's getting in the way of investigating Marcus' murder." Gonzalez stated, reaching her chair but didn't sit. "He seems to be driving way off the mental highway at the moment."

"Never liked that man," Betty's stern words caught the detective off guard.

"Have you met him?" Regina asked, with a vague understanding of her meaning.

"No. Not face to face," Beatrice replied sipping with care from a blue cup. Her answer indicated something more, hiding someplace below English proper. "Sarah told me about him," as the older woman locked eyes onto Regina's. Seeing her detective pal perk up and knew she wanted more. "Sit down Reggie," she requested, pulling her hand toward a chair. Gonzalez complied hoping for details. All was quiet except for cream swirling into Regina's cup and a handful of sparrows playing inside a fountain. "They were having an affair you know," Beatrice conveyed with slight emotion.

The cop was caught off guard again, waiting a moment to digest her revelation. "You're sure about this?" Regina asked, holding back her own details.

"Oh yes, quite sure. Sarah and I talked about it more than once. She needed someone to confide in. You know, get it off her chest so to speak," Mrs. Patterson disclosed with nothing else to add.

Regina gave her time to elaborate but only the sparrows kept chirping. "I had a suspicion that might have gone on," Regina explained, seizing the opportunity to breach Loretta's situation. "Mrs. Sheets was beaten something terrible, by her wacko husband."

"How God awful is that!" Beatrice exclaimed as Regina went on to detail Loretta's escape, via the fire stoker. "Christ! Good bloody hell for that woman. It would be a privilege to shake her hand." Beatrice admired the woman's guts.

Regina saw the door opening. "You can meet her. She's under protection right now at my partner's place. With her four year old daughter too. His apartment's on the other side of town." Regina laid it on thick, eager for serious sympathy from her host.

"You're partner's place? Chris? The Colonel?" still bewildered by his rank when Marcus was shot. "That must be crowded?" wincing at how the lady was being treated. "Doesn't your department provide some sort of housing?" Beatrice asked. "Goodness, that poor baby girl."

Regina could feel the elder lady softening. "No budget and she's not a sworn witness yet. It's on us to keep her safe and a roof over Lucy's head. Lucy is her daughter's name," giving Betty a look, loud and clear, stating it's a damn shame! "Plus, we can't verify her husband's whereabouts. We need to hide her someplace." Regina planted the seed, waiting patient, expecting to see her plan sprout and flourish. Beatrice was about to say something then hesitated. Regina stole a peek as she sipped coffee, watching Betty wrinkle her brow, staring into a fall garden and patio landscape. She was contemplating some sort of rescue. Gonzalez could feel it.

"C'mon Betty, let's open the door," Regina said to herself, urging the lady on in silence. Beatrice stayed quiet swinging her foot back and forth like on a hinge, over a crossed over leg. She was about to speak and Regina stayed out of the way.

"You know, I could use some help around this big old house. Plus it's too darn quiet." Mrs. Patterson announced, leaning into her chair, holding a coffee cup steady, sunshine on her face, smiling. "Would it be all right if she moved in here. With me?" Eyes blinking, serious as a long-ball hitter plunked by a fastball. "I mean both of them, naturally." Betty's tongue moved rapidly, pressed against the inside of her cheek. "Oh, to have a little girl running around, laughing in my backyard. It would be wonderful. Loretta's welcome to move in here. She sounds like my kind of girl," Beatrice proclaimed with genuine enthusiasm. "I want a granddaughter, damn it!" Standing to slam her tiny fist on the patio table. Beatrice smiled and shuddered in pleasure.

"Are you sure?" Regina asked, laughing with her, not too loud though. She wouldn't dare dampen any excitement now. "I don't know if we could ask this of you?" Regina struck, set the hook and began playing her catch. "Are you sure?"

"Absolutely! Hell, bring 'em over tonight. Call your bloody partner right now!" Beatrice almost started to yell with anticipation. "You know, I'll tell you the irony of it all. Her screwed up husband, being a cop and all, wouldn't consider looking this close to a crime scene. Uhm, no offense Reggie about the cop thing!"

"None taken," Gonzo responded. "But you're right about the location," which indeed made sense to the detective. "Okay, I'll get back to the office and run it by my boss. This could be perfect. Douglas will never expect his wife living here."

"Never," her host agreed. "It might be a little awkward at first, Sarah having been her husband's lover and all that. It's just the right amount of weird which will give us plenty to talk about. We'll be just fine," Beatrice exclaimed, wringing her hands together tight in a simple display of excitement.

Regina felt obliged to remind Mrs. Patterson about Douglas and her home once again, just to make sure. Beatrice accepted the slight risk. "Just let him come around. The two of us will make it a bloody bad day for Douglas Sheets," Beatrice proclaimed in her finest accent.

•••

"I'm a persuasive little bitch. You know that," Regina bragged. Anderson was impressed with her idea and liked the location change too. "It'll be perfect." he kept muttering, rubbing his right ear.

Chris on the other hand didn't even turn around to face his partner. "Right! Mrs. Patterson, all miss proper and full of Maggy Thatcher offered to take in two total strangers. A child no less. Gimme' a break Gonzo," not buying her story for one second.

"I'll break your head with an elevated fastball if you keep talking to me like that," Regina shot back, sitting in a lump, oozing sticky body sweat. Her queasy stomach pangs urged the detective to vomit soon. Swallowing the urge back down, wondering why it was happening again.

"You're serious?" Chris asked in a subdued tone, recoiling ever so slight. "Are you okay partner? You're face is deep red and that's no racial slur." Walking to Regina's side caressing her damp forehead and offering to fetch a cup of water.

"Water sounds great, thanks. I must be coming down with the flu," Regina exhaled and wiped perspiration from her temple. Chris left the cubicle just as Anderson returned.

"So, no kidding about Mrs. Patterson," Billy asked?

"Why doesn't anybody believe me around here?" Regina snapped back as her flu symptoms subsided. Very fast. Gonzalez caught her breath, downing the cup full of water Chris delivered. She recovered and issued details about Mrs. Patterson's offer. They brainstormed for a while, hashing out some fine points and agreed it should work well. Opting to have the house patrolled as much as possible.

"It's almost poetic," Chris explained, connecting Loretta Sheets with Beatrice Patterson. "Loretta's being helped by a good friend of Sarah Crosby. Sarah was likely killed by Douglas Sheets, Loretta's husband! They should be fighting each other not living together." Chris and Billy issued goofy high fives as Regina rolled her eyes in disgust. "Only our homicide unit could achieve this set-up!" Davis concluded as Regina smiled, nodded, feeling good again. Even hungry.

Gadwalls

Dawn surfaced Tuesday much colder than it had been all season. Fall was finally surrendering to winter furnishing the hen gadwall with a constant feeling to move. To move on, further south. Past Los Banos, past Mendota, past the lower San Joaquin, past Tulare, maybe south to Mexico if Central Valley cold grows deep enough. Both birds sensed the oncoming north wind blowing strong throughout their wintering range. Tomorrow maybe. Each gadwall would take a turn jumping vertically into the air, water spilling from soaked belly feathers, dripping from feet and legs, fine radial spray hurling from powerful wings. Short flights around a quiet pond, most often together, testing the machinery and tempering urges.

Pain eased in the drake's left foot after a stray pellet pierced the scaly webbing. A slight blood trail followed for the next two days, before pink mucous formed over the gash beginning the healing process this morning. Resting full on his right leg, with a wounded left foot tucked into warm folds of side pocket feathers, staying warm and observing fresh flocks of northern waterfowl filling their pond to near crowding. Green wing teal in groups of twenty or more. Pintail flocks chirping the music of a million crickets, divers, cinnamon teal, dark green headed spoonies and mid season mallards called back and forth above escalating winds, frigid in temperature, bitter and indifferent. This change would disperse naive flocks for a few days but the worst to come, would be a bloody carnage taken on the influx of unsuspecting new arrivals. Cold, windy weather forced birds from loafing on open water to seek refuge cover, resulting in effortless decoys, low passes and tired bodies. By tomorrow morning many of the birds surrounding the gadwall pair would be dead.

Gang of Four

"Taking tomorrow off. I need a break," Regina pleaded half serious at best. "Afraid I can't make dinner tomorrow night," handing apologies to a rather pushy Pamela who pleaded for the detective to join their impromptu night out. Gonzalez begged their forgiveness. Nearly a contrition for her refusal.

"Give me a break," Maria chimed in. "You never take days off from work," pressing hard against the cornered detective for more information. All four girls looked at one another, asking in silence, "who's going to spearhead the next attack?"

"Midweek rendezvous? Sounds like serious sex to me," Pam offered judgment knowing first hand any mid week meeting is all about strong desire or parking tickets. Regina savored the attention but never gave in. Not this time. She gave away some deceptive, innocent words here and there, acting like a decoy while a flock of three birds continued to work her location. She loved it!

"Is it about your boyfriend?" Denise asked, wanting to be certain Gonzalez didn't have some minor obligation. "What's his name again? Ted? Tim?" Her intention being obvious and clear, attempting to reveal the mysterious man's hidden name.

"I don't know who you're speaking of, Big D?" Regina answered before taking a healthy scoop from her French onion soup. Gooey mozzarella strings stretched from her lower lip. "You need to bring it harder than that," Regina told herself seeing right through Denise's ploy, no need to respond with cheese threads on her chin and a mouthful of pungent broth. She smiled gracefully wiping her mouth as if sealing shut a secret lover.

"I'll tell you my latest secret if you tell me yours Regina," Pam proposed in a manner catching everyone's attention. Forks and spoons rang out, hitting plates as the younger gal shifted her fish taco to vertical. The gang watched in awe as their coworker ran her extended tongue slowly upward, catching drops of cream sauce and bite size pieces of fish from the open side of a folded tortilla! Her graphic metaphor began to connect, albeit slow at first to all three girls.

"Don't? You didn't? You're not a switch hitter, I know that much!" Maria whispered harsh, leaning over the table eyes wide in disbelief. Their waiter arrived at the table checking for satisfied customers, listening too for bits and pieces of the intimate discussion. "Not now Adam," Maria shooed the young boy away in a wave of her arm, politeness lacking.

"No way," Regina whispered, filled with giggles and excitement. "You tell all anyway, without having to ask!" Gonzalez leaned back into her chair, taken fully by surprise. "You never cease to amaze," smirking with her head twisting slow, in amused wonder.

"You should get help Pam. If I'm following straight, which I think we are, you have beyond a doubt crossed the line," Denise stated in clinical tone, accompanied by a noticeable shake with her still unconfirmed disclosure. Silence ensued as everyone showed open mouths. The silence broke unexpected. "How was it?" the curious married woman asked with a nervous smile, holding her wine glass at an angle to her soft pink cheek. Regina and Maria glanced at one another for some time, faces squinting in unspoken questions. "Are you kidding me? Denise is asking for details? She's interested?" Both wondering the same thing at the same time!

"I have to admit it was kinda cool," the younger girl reported with an air of sensuality and frankness. "She was hot. I was hot. And my man was into it. Big-time!" Rolling the last words out like a circus leader, tossing back a fair size slug of Fat Tire draft.

"Go ahead," Denise implored, finishing her salad in large bites and fast paced. Regina and Maria checked each other again with shrugs, hands near lips and slight head shakes

"I'm not one to kiss and tell D," Pamela stated in a sarcastic tone, just as Regina cleared her throat to question her exaggeration. Responding to a forced cough, the wild one looked straight at Gonzalez. "So, I told you my secret. How about yours?" Pam continued a deep stare, tossing down French fries, expecting information.

"It's time we get back to work. I have to visit someone this afternoon," Regina announced, evading Pam's request the best way she knew how. Maria shot Gonzalez another look of disbelief, wanting very much to hear some details.

"Wait a second," Denise interjected needing to get more information. "Do you think you'll try it again?" the married woman asked in a way combining begging and encouragement. Obvious to all, including their young waiter Adam, the married black woman tingled with curiosity and stimulation.

"We'll talk later," Pam told her workmate, ushering her along back to work. Regina and Maria encouraged a speed up too, unable to stop gawking at the other girls and their new interest!

"We'll talk later too," Maria told Regina, wiping her forehead in a 'too hot' impression.

Beatrice

"Of course you may have more ice cream, sweetheart," Gramma Bee told her brand new granddaughter, just when Regina entered the kitchen. Loretta and a pleased detective connected on the scene as Mrs. Sheets hid her wide grin behind a small fist, enjoying the amusing feature thoroughly. She understood how much her young daughter needed a doting grandmother. Gonzalez knew Beatrice needed a child in her life. Beatrice had her back to the door, unaware of Regina's presence. The detective had left behind a rather gaudy lunch group and walked right into a Norman Rockwell painting. Lucy was all pink smiles while her spider doll Bee-Bee sat limp, watching from an adjacent chair. Chris seated dutiful next in line dripping caramel topping from on his chin. Beatrice sported a red apron while Mrs. Sheets wiped a Kleenex at her moist eyes. Almost dreamlike!

"Reggie my girl. Just in time," Mrs. Patterson heralded her friend like royalty. "Sit down and I'll get you some ice cream too." Lucy cut loose with a heartfelt hello and roundhouse wave with her spoon hand. Reggie was about to decline, changed her mind, deciding to join in next to Davis. She fell into her kitchen chair with a thud acknowledging Chris behind a droll scowl, which gave way to childlike snorts and giggles. She adored the afternoon dessert, reminiscent of childhood days when mama's after school treats appeared opposite her happy brother, laughing and playing on sugar overload. Regina's check-up on Loretta's new digs couldn't be going better with Beatrice and Lucy already gaga for each other. Gonzalez patted herself on the back once again, proud of the arrangements. Mindful however, Douglas was looming somewhere. Probably nearby.

Dry leaves swirled outside forming loose circles with chirping, wavy lines of finches flying low through tree limbs, seeking calm sites behind fences and shrubs. Broken sunlight peeked just underneath fast moving clouds. A loose side door rattled with continuous windblown vibration. An aging woman, a young girl, her mother and new friends all enjoyed a late fall gathering around a worn kitchen table. For now, a murder case, potential violence, ugly memories and tomorrow's hunt, all stashed away and forgotten. Traded for a laughing child, a make-believe grandparent, a calm mom, two relaxed off duty cops, ice cream and winter scarcely held at bay.

Chris' text message from a Captain wondering about his homicide team's location brought the afternoon rendezvous to a close. Detective Davis hugged Loretta goodbye, pleased she would be much better off in her new situation. All said, he would've enjoyed a few more days with mother and daughter. Getting another small taste of family made his apartment feel like home again.

Regina stooped to give Lucy a kiss goodbye as the child held on to grammas' hand with a tight grip and Bee Bee in the other hand. Gonzalez said goodbye turning to leave with her partner. "Reggie," Beatrice called out hurrying to catch up. The detective's heart melted and she turned to face Mrs. Patterson and the two embraced. "I know why you came to visit me yesterday. Thank you." The elder woman choked down tears, holding Regina's warm hands inside her own. The two stayed quiet. Beatrice reached over to caress Regina's cheek. Chris took note and exited in a quiet move leaving the two gals alone. Nothing else need be said.

"I'll call you tomorrow Betty," Regina passed to her friend, first rubbing then pressed her shoulders in a delicate manner before walking fast down a leaf covered driveway. Feeling good about the outcome of her plan, her lover, her upcoming hunt and Lucy. Like flocks of waterfowl Gonzalez would be moving south also.

Regina Gonzalez

Douglas waited patient, like a jaguar for Regina to leave the police station. Three hours plus without a bathroom break before his prey revealed herself. Regina and Chris left work together, pausing to discuss case details in an empty-ing parking lot. Sheets recognized them both without hesitation. Luck was with the big cat when Chris turned right leaving the parking lot and Regina turned left, in the direction Sheets was already aimed.

Having plenty of shadow experience, Douglas kept his object in clear sight. Maintaining a car or two in between for running interference. Not many traffic lights. Only one left turn wait, playing it safe three cars behind. A lone right turn staying well back when Regina pulled into a small parking lot next to her condo. Sheets was able to cruise by slow enough, permitting glimpses of the detective parking in her vacant space. He kept moving in order to stay safe and out of her view. Sheets pulled ahead and ducked to the right side curb, getting a clear line of sight behind. He watched Detective Gonzalez close a dark green door, entering her home. He transformed into a big cat once more, settling in to wait.

"I'll wait 'till dark before making a move inside," the disturbed cop repeated his words a number of times, wide eyed and more than a little jumpy. His left leg remained in a state of constant flexing unaware in any way of his obsessive reflexes. "I need to relocate. Get myself turned around. Face the bitch head on," he told himself bending his intimidation muscles. After starting the truck doug noticed his fuel gauge drooped to an extreme low.

"Shit! Running out of gas on a fast getaway would be kinda stupid don't ya think," Sheets scolded his fried brain. "I'll get some gas, come back and finish what's needed after dark." He pulled away in a hurry making time for Tracy Boulevard. "She'll be here when I get back," Douglas assured his failing, disturbed intellect, intent on finding some cheap gasoline.

•••

"I'm on my way," Regina spoke half out of breath while throwing a haphazard assortment of clothes into a vinyl travel bag. Almost ready to depart. "I'll meet you at the restaurant," Gonzalez said fighting back yet one more light headed feeling. She had to sit down. This episode passed in a few moments as soon as she settled, drawing four or five slow, deep breaths.

"About six-thirty or so," Tom posed on the other end sensing something might be wrong with his hunting partner. "Are you okay Regina? You sound a little out of it? Something I said?"

"No, no. You're cool. It's nothing on your part," Gonzalez said wiping her forehead. Glad she'd made it to her doctor's appointment yesterday yet quietly brooding all the while. "Hope they find out what the fuck is going on here. Soon! I feel like I was hit in the forehead by a low nineties fastball!"

"You're sure?" Tom followed up.

"Positive." Close to a hundred percent again.

"Okay, we'll screw ya later," Tom wisecracked, for the most part serious only to hear Regina respond with a mocking, macho type laugh. Tom decided to leave it at that and said goodbye.

Regina signed off but thought about Ellis and how much she enjoyed his company. Too bad they didn't live closer to each other? Maybe even living together? What it might be like to have a man around the house permanently? Wondering what kind of dad he might, "snap out of it for Christ's sake," shaking herself back to reality. "We're shooting tomorrow. Get your head on straight," Regina joked hearing a sudden gust of wind shake the windows and sweep tree limbs across the roof and gutters. She gathered her last essentials and made for the door. Five o'clock sharp.

•••

Leaving an Arco station on Tracy Boulevard after topping off with high priced gas. "One more turn," Douglas whispered just audible above Verdi's loud, classic concerto pouring from within his truck. He braked before turning right, slowed further, pulling over just beyond a parked red Camry. "I think that's her condo straight ahead," Sheets told himself while checking his GPS.

"That's it. That's her condo," confirming location out loud. Douglas shifted into park holding an engine idle as if he knew Detective Gonzalez was about to appear soon. Sheets felt he parked close enough to recognize his target, at the same time hoping he wasn't close enough to be spotted. A quarter to five, early evening but not yet dark as long murky shadows obscured his dark green truck by means of a low slung solar disk and two nearby sycamores, just about leafless. "Don't think I'm too close?" Sheets wondered to himself, straining his neck and shoulders in a fast circular scan. One advantage lay in Regina's car. Douglas couldn't tell what model type she drove but knew very well where she parked.

He welcomed the oncoming darkness and started what had now become routine. An unconscious squirming, shifting and erratic thinking. "I should be able to force this situation in twenty to thirty minutes," lip speaking the words while checking his watch against the scheduled sunset time. "Not much longer," whispering now little by little to himself, feeling cold air and a steady wind bending trees, blowing twigs, leaves and his faulted intellect. Clutching the driver's side door handle with a taught left hand for nearly ten minutes, Douglas began pulling the lever in even pressure to release a closed door. He was about to start the task at hand. Gun loaded, knife enclosed. He relaxed. Pulled again. Relaxed. This time he pulled and the door popped free just as Regina's front door light blinked on. Douglas froze solid in a full body twitch with substantial panic invading his bloodstream, equipped with no ideas or plans for this. Out walked the detective covered in porch light and hair blown across her face. She locked the door behind but tripped rushing off her two step landing, bent over, left arm flailing trying to stay upright. Douglas laughed out loud, spitting words through gritted teeth begging to see her fall flat. Gonzalez staggered, reversing her steps to regain balance. She stopped dead, stooping to retrieve something from the brick porch. Standing still, holding the item in one hand, examining its face. Her phone had taken a sharp jolt and blinked off. Douglas didn't know what was happening but could see she was pretty upset. He chuckled, very disappointed about the prevented fall!

Gonzalez made it to her car in plain sight, beginning a quick backup before Sheets turned his ignition key. He was still focused on his objective doing the unexpected, watching Regina make a left turn leaving the lot before Douglas reacted and finally starting his truck. Gunning the engine, Sheets pulled out just ahead of an oncoming Prius bearing down fast. A weak horn sounded in front of a raised middle finger. Douglas didn't blink and went back into 'big cat' stalking mode. He decided to follow Regina Gonzalez for as long as it takes. In the sheriff's mind he needed a kill.

Regina moved at a fair pace through town determined to head south as soon as possible, anticipating clear traffic on Interstate-5. Even though commuter traffic was in full swing the big snarls would be tied up along Highway 580 east bound, not southbound. Gonzalez wound her way west through Tracy toward the Corral Hollow Road entrance, punching it down a long on-ramp with a dark green truck trailing distant and unnoticed. Any remaining daylight lingered in the upper atmosphere, highlighted by a fading purplish glow offering no illumination whatsoever. Douglas Sheets was just another blurry set of headlights in her rearview mirror. They moved south. Verdi played loud and clear in the chase vehicle, maybe with a bit too much base. The pace car overflowed with Rachel Yamagata, even louder, but it didn't matter as the leader went oblivious to her music selection. Gonzalez clutched her disabled cell phone waiting, wanting to hear Tom call again. Steady excitement grew about tomorrow's hunt spotting two tumbleweeds roll south along the dirt median separating directional lanes. "Strong winds. Just like Mr. Ellis predicted," Regina murmured out loud, checking her rear view mirror. One set of headlights remained, catching Regina's attention for some reason. Gonzalez flipped her phone open. Not working. No messages. Disappointed. She changed to the outside lane anticipating oncoming cars at the Westley Rest Stop looming ahead. Checking her mirror once again. Two lamps like dragon eyes.

•••

Sheets held his truck at the same distance, regimented, uniform. His temperament was anything but uniform leading to his own lane change delay. He barely noticed the oncoming semi lumbering along a slight downgrade at sixty five mph! Even worse would be the lane merging stripes dead ahead just beyond each vehicles light beams. The large truck anticipated a small truck lane change, therefore keeping his throttle open to maintain speed. A very large truck thought he'd have an open approach soon. Douglas didn't budge, drowning in a seething episode of what he might have to do to get his information. Horns blared, turn lights blinked on and the semi hauling gasoline had no choice but to nudge its way left. Sheets snapped to, swerving his dwarfed truck into the outside lane cussing and waiving a middle finger westerly.

•••

The detective checked her mirror seeing headlamps behind veer in an awkward move, then witnessing the semi trailer swing back and forth also. No contact that she could see, glancing fast, front to rear. Observing. "Sheesh buddy, wake up," Gonzalez spoke as if the rear headlight heard her. She kept checking behind and signaled for a change back to the slow lane and noticed the reckless driver closing daylight between them. "Let him pass," advising herself and switched lanes well out in front. She could see headlights bright and clear in her side mirror, anticipating a steady pass in about ten to fifteen seconds. The lights grew brighter causing Regina to look forward warding off the harsh glare. For some reason the brightness vanished without a passing vehicle on her left side. "Now what?" asking herself in disgust not in the mood to deal with goofy drivers. Checked her side mirror once more, seeing black. Then back to her rear view seeing two headlights slowly cut in behind but safely in front of a steady gasoline semi. "That's odd?" Gonzalez said out loud as if someone occupied the other seat, seeing the vehicle back off a few car lengths. "He doesn't want to lead I guess?" she told herself. "I'll slow down. Maybe then he'll pass?" Cutting five mph off her speedometer when another tumbleweed trotted down the left lane, lit for a brief moment in her high beams

•••

"What the fuck, bitch?" Douglas sounded off recognizing his target cut back on speed. He had no choice but to throttle back too, even as the gas truck behind him signaled and changed to the fast lane, ready to pass. "C'mon bitch, let's go," ridiculing the Tracy cop at every possible chance. Alongside, like a stainless steel warship, sailed the semi hitting seventy five mph and more. Overtaking Douglas with ease and moving on Regina in a steady gain. Chevron passed Regina maintaining the left lane and steady speed until well out in front, before returning to the conservative side. All three vehicles rolled past the Patterson exit and every one of its fast food franchises.

•••

Regina let loose a slight moan, belched a small amount of air wishing she'd taken the last exit. Also wishing her cell phone would start working again. "If I exit and he does likewise, I'm being followed," alerting herself in silence, sliding her right hand to left hip, fingering a sidearm. "God damn phone," she grunted, shook it to generate life, failed and sped up without thinking. In a nervous minute she verified the rear headlights keeping pace. Gonzalez began to wonder how many exits remained between her and Gustine. "I have to get in touch with Tom." Stretching straight she watched her rear view mirror almost as much as her windshield. Serious now and increasing speed another five spot to close in on Chevron's bright yellow tank lights.

They rolled further south, a convoy of three now, escorting each other to the Newman exit. Regina had every intention of taking the turn-off but one more firm knock and an aggressive shake forced her cell phone back to life. Three bars, full connection! Ahead stood a mileage sign. Gustine and Highway 140, two miles. Regina punched in Toms name, hit the green button while her convoy passed the Newman exit at plus seventy five.

•••

"Where the hell are you going bitch?" Douglas grumbled in frustration. "What the fuck are you doing out here in the middle of the valley? It's mid-week.

You have to work tomorrow detective?" Douglas believed he followed along in absolute obscurity. "She's dead ahead and no clue I'm back here! Dead ahead. Sounds perfect to me, right after getting the location I need." Sheets checked his I-Phone. No location finder activated. Loretta's phone was still shut off.

"All right you crazy slut, where the hell are we going?" he let loose with a big laugh. Under a mile to the Gustine exit. Douglas had no clue they would exit there and assumed to drive on by.

•••

"Tom? Oh man, I'm so glad you answered. You're at the restaurant, right?" Regina asked in great relief, scheming an impromptu game plan.

"Awe, you miss me don't you darling," Tom joked sipping a cold draft. "Just got here. What's up?" stretching his legs along a cozy booth, back to the wall.

"That's fine Tom," speaking in a compact nature, taking charge of the conversation. "You're pretty well packed I'm guessing?" she asked direct, checking her mirrors.

"Yep. You bet. Check it out, I got us two bikes for," Tom was caught off sharp by an excited detective.

"Great. Listen up for me. Are the guns in the truck?" Regina came across as dead serious.

"Well, yea. They're locked up in the back," Tom reacted a bit mystified by her anxious tone and nature of the question. "What's wrong?" Ellis went serious now.

"Here's what I need you to do. Very simple," Gonzalez said, fast approaching the exit. She explained her plan to Tom but without thinking hit her right blinker "What the hell am I doing?" She asked herself dumbfounded as a fast moving tanker truck rumbled by in the outside lane. "I just signaled the driver following me!" Regina could only shake her head in frustration, while decelerating at the exit seeing her admirer follow suit with his turn signal flashing. The blinker seemed odd. Out of place to her. "Is that you back there Douglas?" Regina bellowed, looking close but running a stop sign at the bottom of the ramp turning left on a high pitched tire screech. Her follower seemed to proceed in a more casual manner. They headed into town. One seething mad the other beyond nervous. "C'mon Douglas, keep up," Regina mouthed her words seeing rear view headlights fade away.

•••

"Where the fuck am I?" Douglas quizzed himself wondering if he'd ever been on Highway 140 or seen Gustine in his lifetime. "No way," he answered himself as a pair of tumbleweeds crossed the road in line with the right front tire. His truck crushed the trailing weed ball in a crunch, like young hands ripping potato chips from a mylar bag. The road into town was dark with small curves making it difficult at times to see faded lane lines. Plowed dirt fields boarded the road both left and right as wind gusts blew out of the north shaking his small truck every so often. To Douglas Sheets it was all dreary, bleak and depressing. He hated the Central Valley flat lands, preferring mountains, trees and occasional snow. His target in the car up front viewed it all as rather enchanting, even under these strange circumstances. Helped along by the fact her love interest resided in these lowlands and was about to help save her butt.

Sheets blinked twice noticing tail lights getting further away, growing smaller and smaller. "C'mon man, don't let her get away now," urging himself faster when his phone alarm rang out in a chord he waited far too long to hear. Just ahead, the detective made a left turn slipping from view.

■■■

Regina made two turns. One left onto State Route 33, continuing onto South Avenue followed by another left onto Fifth Ave. Straining to see the Pastime Bar's faint sign ahead. She also looked behind expecting two headlights. "C'mon Mr. Sheets, let's go. I'm waiting on you." Douglas was a bit late, a little slow, not pushing anymore. "That's it, keep coming dog," sighting a trace of high beams before his turn onto Fifth Avenue. "Good to go," Regina whispered allowing separation once more from her pursuer. Like a single drake sprig, a few whistles a few chuckles, the bird usually commits. Regina pulled forward seeing Tom, right where she wanted him. Seated comfortably on a dropped tailgate. Regina parked a car length in front of her shooting partner, exiting quick and ran to the tailgate. As planned, Tom reached back pulling out Regina's adopted Citori from a soft gun case, arming Gustine's quiet streets. Just what the pair needed. Gringo rested the weapon on his lap in plain sight with Gonzo standing alongside like a civil war portrait showing off their guns. The truck finalizing this equation moved forward then stopped sharp, short hopped forward again, brakes applied in force. Doug's vehicle rocked and dipped downward, sitting still some ninety feet away, high beams just clicked on, flooding Tom and Regina in brilliant headlight. Everyone froze. Stiff and solid. Quiet, except for the truck engine on a smooth idle. Neither side had a clue as what to do next. They stood silent while a surge of north wind blew Regina's hair across her forehead and chin. Tom decided on full effect by grabbing two shotgun shells from an open box sitting to his left. Regina took one step toward glaring high beams, covering the direct light source with her left palm, determined to get some kind of identification on the vehicle.

Douglas looked at his cell phone and then out over his hood, watching Tom load a rather sinister looking over and under. Regina took another short step into the lights but stopped and shivered as the vehicle began an express retreat, belching smoke and screeching tires. Douglas floored his truck's gas pedal, in no mood to confront the female detective while her brother, boyfriend or fellow cop brandished more firepower than he! Tom and Regina, still as scared children, watched in amazement as the truck or car they couldn't identify, cloaked in high beam glare and drifting smoke moved straight away. Douglas twisted his steering wheel hard to the right which kicked his ass end likewise spinning his truck like a toy. A few well placed trees hindered Regina's vision and her only sight was two red tail lights disappearing into darkness. She thought it very odd when her follower signaled for a right turn just before the vehicle whirled and vanished. "Courteous," she mumbled to herself. Gonzalez couldn't verify Sheets' dark green truck for sure, but knew deep inside who was driving.

Tom just noticed how empty Fifth Avenue was at the moment. Even after all the commotion. Not one vehicle or pedestrian in sight. Not all that unusual considering Gustine's small size. "Where the hell's a cop when you need one?" Ellis blurted out peering up one side of Fifth and down the other. With no clue how his lady friend might umpire the comment.

"Up yours gringo!" Regina shot back pivoting her torso to face the plaintiff knowing Tom was currently oblivious to her career choice. She did find his remark kinda funny and right on time no less.

"What?" Tom's expression made the episode even funnier. "Oh yeah. Hey, sorry about that one darling," apologizing then slid his shotgun back into its carrying case.

Regina wanted to call in the incident but knew she couldn't. A feeling of guilt surfaced into her thoughts. Knowing her and Tom were way too close and he wasn't officially removed from the suspect's list. She mumbled how stupid weird it had all become "Oh hell, they couldn't do much to find him anyway. Unidentified person and an unknown vehicle. Not much to go on, wishing this would all end soon. I'm craving an ordinary love," Gonzalez whispered then looked over to Ellis with a heartache and desire all at the same time. He appeared to be a bit nervous reloading the truck. Regina caved again and sent a short text to Chris and Billy. Few details were submitted, however she emphasized that Douglas Sheets may be on the prowl.

Douglas Sheets

"I have your location Loretta!" Douglas almost shouted, roaring out of town, passing the Quick and Easy convenience store before turning right onto Sullivan Road. "Nothing's Quick and Easy for me damn-it," Sheets muttered in frustration. Highway 140 west this time. Now it was Douglas' turn to check his rear view mirror, almost certain Gonzalez would be in hot pursuit. He expected to see headlights and right on the mark, they appeared. Still pretty far back but Douglas wasn't about to let up now. A hard right curve cut off line of sight between him and an approaching chase car. Keeping his truck's accelerator depressed, Sheets blew around the curve leaning way right and low, as if his own body weight kept the truck on course. Just before tangent he spotted a parking lot ahead to his right, with just enough gap to permit a slam brake entry. He weighed his odds and decided to try hiding, guessing Detective Gonzalez would've called for help by now, opting to see what develops. "If the cop's coming, she might just pass by without noticing," reasoning to himself in low mumbles. "If so, I'll sneak out the back way." Douglas jammed his breaks hard, sliding clumsy but making the turn into a narrow lot between two long warehouses of clucking chickens and a heavy smell of poultry manure. Loose gravel offered poor grip causing his truck to fishtail and skid, tossing stones against a wooden structure. Stopped. Quiet as the surrounding winter almond orchards. Douglas killed the headlights sliding between the two buildings. Turned his truck hard, facing the entrance if needing a quick dash. Rolled his window down, twisting in his seat to glimpse headlights coming his way. "Man that stinks," inhaling his first smell. They appeared different from routine car lamps, moving slower than one expected hearing an engine moaning louder but sounding rough. The vehicle passed. A large moving van trudged along at fifty mph max. Sheets felt relieved but sat tight for ten minutes. No more cars passed coming from Gustine but a few pickups did head into town. No police. Probably duck hunters arriving for Wednesday's shoot, all foreign to Sheets however. He wasn't concerned with unmarked cars going into Gustine, waiting for complete blackness on the road, slipping his truck into gear, rolling to the entrance. Still all clear, Douglas made his way back to I-5 and thought about meeting with Loretta one last time.

Tom and Regina

"You wanna tell me what this is about?" Ellis asked, after settling into 'their' booth at the Past Time. Gonzalez pretended to ignore Tom's demand, signaling 'their' waitress to stop by with a greeting nod and wave. Tom could easily tell she didn't want to explain. He rubbed two finger tips together on one hand thinking over what just happened outside. They were both edgy when he resumed the meeting.

"Are you gonna tell me who that was?" Tom appealed a bit firmer, just as a bored waitress showed, wiping away a few drops of spilled water on the table top.

Regina jumped in fast. "Hello, it's great to see you again," she hailed their waitress, looking at the surprised lady with a wide grin. "I need a beer, very bad." Maintaining her look not wanting to allow Tom a speck of daylight. "How's the fish and chips tonight?" keeping it going her way.

"Looks good as usual. You've been here before I take it?" The waitress asked not recognizing Regina from her first visit. She knew Tom and flashed him a big smile.

"How's it going tonight?" Tom greeted his regular gal.

"It's so dead in here tonight," she responded with a shake of her head. Tom and Regina surveyed the bar seeing only one other occupied table and a couple heavyweights dwarfing two narrow bar stools. It was a Tuesday night after all, plus windy and cold. But music blared, beer was cold, deep fryer was hot, no harm was done tonight.

They ordered food and beer as Regina lingered, inquiring about menu items, hoping to divert Tom's attention away from tonight's events. Gonzalez prepared to lay low about her investigation soon realizing she just dragged Tom inside, asking him to draw the Citori in her defense. As soon as they were alone Tom repeated his questions.

"I shouldn't be talking about this," Regina said with a heavy dose of anxiety, aching for a lengthy drink from a cold beer. Tom stayed silent. "It has to do with the Crosby investigation. Couldn't get firm identification, but I'm almost sure who it was."

"Tell me," Tom demanded. "I'll take care of him for you."

Regina stuttered for a second. She wasn't sure what Tom meant. "What?"

"I'll kick his ass if he threatens you," Tom threatened, looking serious but came up short of convincing the detective. She started to laugh then covered her mouth to keep from being impertinent. Regina hesitated, thinking she might as well give in.

"What the hell. Tom's willing to fight for me," convincing herself, guessing his bravado was probably all talk. Then, just as quick she decided to stand pat. "Nope. Can't say. Won't say," telling her lover with a gentle touch of her hand across Tom's rough chin. "I love your Batman offer however."

"I meant it!" Tom clarified further.

"Your fish will be up in about ten minutes, you two. Relax and give me a wave if you want anything," the hospitable older waitress announced plunking down two cold drafts with a woody thud. "You'll have your own personal server tonight," she added matter of fact as her only other table was ready to leave, promptly departing to bid them thank you and good night.

Regina and Tom sipped from foamy beer glasses each feeling awkward in their lack of words. Tom still hoped for a give-in but Regina wouldn't have any of it. He knew deep inside it was going nowhere. She wasn't about to talk and decided best to back off. "Who knows, maybe tomorrow?" telling himself in secret.

Gonzalez took on a whole new track. "You rescued me tonight. Know what that means?" Regina asked as Tom leaned back, ready to accept any and all honors but no idea what it meant beyond that. "I owe you a life rescue.

We can't divide until I pay up." She had some trouble saying the words and wondered how Tom would react.

"Isn't that from a movie," Tom stated in soft voice. "But I accept." Regina laughed, knowing she'd been exposed. Tom didn't say as much but agreed to with passion. He wanted to seize his affection with both hands, hug her close and kiss her very long and hard. Instead, examining Regina with soft, kind, painfully sad eyes. They both sensed an awkward silence once again.

"Tell me about tomorrow's hunt. Cold? Lots of birds? Limits?" Regina asked in a way to say thanks but I have to keep hush-hush concerning this case. "Where are we shooting tomorrow by the way?"

"Mendota," Tom answered knowing he couldn't break down the detectives perimeter.

"Ugh, hate it," Regina said. "Too close to home. You know what I'm saying?" drinking more beer and delivering a look that spelled slight disappointment.

"We'll be riding bikes in tonight," Tom said in a casual manner, expecting Regina's wince to some extent while asking, 'what's up with that?'

"Okay?" she said very slow not quite understanding. "What the hell does that mean?"

"Yep. I got my bike back from Anthony. He's been waiting on some parts for a while." Knowing Regina didn't quite grasp how a bike would work on the refuge. "He let me take one of his loaners for you to use. You're going to like it."

"What the hell does that mean?" she asked, right on schedule as Tom let loose with a big grin.

"We'll be taking a moonlight ride this morning, my lady." Tom added.

"Holy cow? Bicycles and duck hunting? Are you serious Mr. Ellis?" Regina wondered, joking but clueless how he'd pull this one off.

"Absolutely. You'll love it," Tom went into detail just after their fried fish arrived. "The bike carries everything. Even you!" Speaking animated with just the right amount of amusement. "You can ride a bike, I hope?"

"Of course I can ride a bike dumbass!" Seizing a piece of hot fish, burning her fingers.

Fillets were brought to the table steaming hot. Dark and over-browned on the outside but still moist inside. Perfect for Tom's taste. They ate every morsel, talking loud, content, relaxing with the time they had right now. Ideas on hunting, predictions for tomorrow's shoot, some baseball, shotguns, calling and bicycles. Tom's disposition grew positive to say the least. He didn't care, at the moment, if they hunted or not. It wasn't important right now. Somehow? Sitting here, comfortable, no hurry, playing. Wanting to stroke her passion, rub her brown skin, smell her body close to his.

Soon enough however, they were making their way east through Los Banos, south to Dos Palos, through Firebough, finally reaching Mendota. Dark, quiet, cold and windy. Old newspapers, dead leaves and an empty beer can blew across Highway 180 in town. Regina went quiet not wanting to look at the old, never changing landmarks. A group of hard working Latinos loafed outside one bar's front door as two thirtyish women, most likely unemployed, were leaving a small convenience store carrying a twelve pack of Miller Highlife. Gonzo's eyes went shut avoiding any more of Mendota's heartbreak. Outside of town, after crossing open waters of Fresno Slough they reached a gravel entrance to Mendota State Wildlife Area. Parking in the weekday reservation line was short. Wind gusts rocked the warm camper all night long with no investigation chatter and no sex. Still off limits for the detective.

Sheets

Douglas moved in the opposite direction. Due north. Tracy in his sights. Wanting to see the house Loretta occupied, having her location nailed down. A section of the city which sounded rather vague but for some reason, familiar at the same time. "Is it possible," he posed, talking straight and loud, to himself however. "Are you kidding me? Are you fucking kid-ding me," articulated in staccato verse. Stunned, shocked, set back on his heals! "My wife is now living with Mrs. Patterson. I can't believe it!" Doug's wits began to dull as obsession with Loretta grew louder and more strange. Flawed brainwaves started flickering and circuits blew. His nerves combined with a mounting anxiety to convince him of sordid destiny. "My fate. Fate is the Hunter. One of my favorite flicks," disturbed views echoed in his head. "Fate has brought that old lady and my wife together. It could be a two for one today. Buy one get one free. Double play. Sale days in Tracy, Walmart shoppers! My fate." Douglas eased back, stretched a tight leg muscle and smiled. Content for a moment.

"I'll have to kill you soon Loretta," speaking with a spit filled scowl becoming even more upset considering a wasted trip to Gustine. "Too fucking much could've gone wrong in Gustine," screeching through gritted teeth and tight lips. More spit sprayed around the cab hitting an open dashboard with indiscernible spots.

Sheets stormed past Patterson and Westley fuel and food exits. Past the State Rest Stop, past Chrisman Road to east Tracy. Choosing Corral Hollow Road to make his assault. "I'll quietly sneak in the back way," whispering to himself, as if he might be expected.

Anderson

Chris was home. Alone. Quiet beyond quiet. Dead, bored rigid. Buzzed with an incoming text, knowing it was Regina. Reading aloud, he wondered if his partner was being overly safe or maybe had new information. It seemed odd but Davis was having similar thoughts, all evening long. The wind outside wasn't helping much, causing him to jump a number of times after tree branches scraped along outside walls. Feeling drawn to check on Mrs. Patterson's house but longing to see Loretta and Lucy once again. Davis stood, checked the time at 8:00, staring, fixed in thought at the wall clock when his phone rang. So fixed, he stuttered and gasped, stunned by a shrill ring. It was Captain Anderson's ring tone forcing Chris' instincts to suspect something must be in the works.

"Davis here," answering with an absolute straight manner.

"Hey Chris. Sorry to bother you at home. Did you get Gonzo's text by any chance?" Billy Anderson asked in a tense way, sounding concerned. Davis didn't say a word, reaching for his car keys wishing he'd already left the apartment.

"Hi Captain. Yep, got it just now. Is there something I don't know?" a high strung detective inquired, grabbing jacket and sweatshirt heading for the door. "Is my partner on to something or just playing it super safe." Davis lit his front porch light forgetting to lock the door behind him.

Captain Anderson could hear metal clanking and switches clicking, coming through the phone. He thought about Chris' question for a moment testing his memory, trying to recall if Regina might have told him something. Shaking his head, nothing surfaced. "She didn't say anything to me, that I remember. Hopefully she's just being thorough," Billy responded. "Sounds like you're leaving?" Confirming Chris' movement.

"I'm on my way."

"If you need a hand. Anything at all, I'm available. Gonzo's out of town and won't be working tomorrow," Anderson informed his detective, covering a wineglass with his free hand, signaling Patricia Bailey to forgo a refill of his all but empty Riedel. Billy and Patricia had been at it pretty heavy most of the early evening. In and out of bed twice already, with one 2009 Primitivo bottle bone dry. Anderson was nearing a sexed up, no pain, wine drinking buzz. One moment being tenderly fondled by an undressed redhead, quite younger than he. Then having to refuse more deep red to get semi sober. "I'm thinking this will all be precautionary," Billy told Chris. Trying to convince his detective, as well as himself, it didn't seem serious. Bailey snuggled in close to her companion. Nothing beneath a loose fitting robe but a baggy piece of clothing belonging to the Captain.

Mouthing her question of, "who is it?" The crafty reporter enjoyed their sex but the journalist within her just couldn't let go of obtaining classified information.

"It's Davis," Anderson whispered, covering his phone, choosing to keep Bailey out of the loop.

"What's he want?" the reporter continued digging, all the while pleasing her boyfriend by rubbing one hand over his chest and breast. "Is it something about the Crosby murder?" hand still advancing. Lower.

Billy returned to his phone call imparting a rolled eye expression, silently asking, "what's your problem?" Turning away. "You still there Chris?"

"Still here boss. Making my way to the Patterson house." Stepping on the accelerator all at once. "Look, I'll run by the house, check it out, observe for a while. If I see something out of place you'll be hearing from me." Chris pointed his car in the direction of east Tracy.

"Sounds good." Captain Anderson clicked his phone off. He didn't even notice Patricia's nude body in full exposure behind an open robe. He didn't even notice the sexy touch of her soft hands working lower and lower below his waist. He didn't even notice when Bailey bit his shoulder, whispering, tempting him to come back to bed. Anderson stared outside through a framed window fixing on tree limbs moving back and forth with inconsistent direction.

"Man it's blowing out there tonight," Billy spoke almost lackluster, stepping closer to the cold pane. He touched the glass measuring temperature by touch. It was dry, bitter, no condensation due to a constant stirring atmosphere.

"Come back to bed," Patricia urged her lover, moving in close making sure her upper thighs wrapped his legs. She churned her torso up and down. Slow at first. Then pressing her fold against Billy's padded hips. Getting the message now, leaning into Bailey's arms, feeling her dampness, her touches, her mouth. He accepted but knew he'd be getting a call from Chris. Tonight.

Chris Davis

Chris turned onto Arlington Street, slowed, not quite to a complete stop. He wanted a good look around the intersection of Arlington and Anaheim Drive. Checking parked cars, looking for someone perhaps out of place and to listen. Listening for any noise out of place. Coasting through the intersection, crawling, able to see most of Anaheim Drive without obstruction. Even at night the scene was crystal clear, blown clean by north winds. Early enough this evening with most driveway and porch lights still burning. Including Beatrice Patterson's home. All quiet rolling by Anaheim, continuing along Arlington. Calm and content in the vicinity of Beatrice and Loretta. Chris' thoughts turned back to Marcus Crosby and his early morning murder. "I bet it was just like this. Sneaking through the neighborhood, watching for witnesses, finding the best possible shooting location, waiting." Chris would do the same. Turning his car around and slipping a short way past the Patterson house. Another u-turn set him in place facing his objective, beginning his wait. "I'm always waiting and watching." Thoughts turning one more time back to another icy night alone in the Motherload. Watching for Loretta Sheets. "Here I am again. Where the hell is Gonzalez?" Chris spent a moment pondering his situation. "Guarding her this time," muttering to himself. His ex wife and daughter came to mind. "Doing a worthy deed." Davis felt better to be on guard instead of spying.

Third Hunt
Mendota State Wildlife Area

"This place is kinda weird," Regina told Tom, who was trying hard to wake up, but lost ground to groggy, sleep filled eyes. Gonzalez peaked out the right side camper shell window. Small puffs of dust boiled from a passing truck making its way to a Spartan check station. Sharp gusts of blustery winds rocked their truck with subtle vibration. "C'mon Ellis, shouldn't we be gitten' ready?" shoving Elly's shoulder to get him moving as he cuddled a warm pillow tight to his face and neck. Tom rolled over.

"Ten more minutes," Ellis groaned, unable to shake the sleep. His sleeping bag slipped down below a bare shoulder. Quickly, cold air washed around his exposed arm and neck, sending a shudder and quick pulls on a drooping bag. Tom realized right away how cold it would be today.

"Oh Tom, you feel so good." Gonzalez scooted in close, covering one leg over his waist, letting warm hands roam about his midsection. Tom responded by pressing hard back into Regina's body awakening a little more. "You're so warm baby," Regina cooed into his cold ear permitting her lips to massage an exposed lobe as her tongue explored his neck. Squeezed then ground her hips into his butt, smiling as her hand mistakenly glanced off a budding erection twice, sending sudden shocks through his tingling body. She knew he was heightened and awake now, hearing soft moans when he rolled over to face his sexual pleasure. Regina made fast moves pushing away and sitting upright as groping hands tried following her bulging chest. They dropped helpless however, onto his own sleeping bag.

"Let's go lover. You're awake now!" Snickering at her obvious double meaning. Regina scooted, gathered warm clothes and opened the shell's rear window.

"Hey, I thought we," Tom began a mild protest but was immediately cut off after cold blasts of arctic air roared into their mobile bedroom. Ellis buried his head back inside a warm bag imitating a scared turtle, forgetting fast about morning festivities.

"Holy shit! It's freezing out there," Gonzalez screeched gasping on her own breath, scrambling to put on a fleece sweater and heavy jacket as memories of icy cold, winter mornings rushed into her consciousness. Unhappy thoughts, even colder than the bristling air outside. Searching for extra socks and gloves she swiped from Tom. "Let's go chum. Guys are starting engines, getting ready to roll outa here. C'mon," shoving Ellis once again to get him moving.

"Ugh, okay. You win this one." Rubbing his sore eyes to clear a foggy head. Tom kicked his way out from under warm covers preparing to get ready. Outside, a couple hundred like minded waterfowl hunters made preparations too. Independent from one another, waiting trucks loaded with barking dogs, stored guns, food, outfitted boats, jackets, ammo, waders, cigarettes, hot fires, pissing, grumbling, jokes, anticipation and exhaust fumes. Just another shoot day at Mendota Wildlife.

"It's more like an infantry column assembling for battle," Tom commented, buckling waders, absorbing the commotion surrounding him. "You coming out of there?" In a raised voice making sure his partner heard. Regina had the truck rocking as she squirmed, laying horizontal, fighting to get two pairs of tights slipped on. One, a thin poly. The other, heavy fleece.

"Almost there lover boy. All, most, there." Dropping the tailgate with a clang on her last rhythmic beat. "Jesus Christo it's cold as Satan out here!" Regina hissed, against a biting gust that chilled her entire body. "This reminds me too much of my farm days growing up down here. You either freeze or roast in the lower San Joaquin. Still don't like it." Gonzo's response made Tom notice how Regina sat on the truck tailgate, regal, her brown hair fluttering over olive skin with red cheeks. Childlike. Each leg swayed while zipping a camo jacket snug to the chin. He admired her charm.

"What are you staring at?" aware of Tom's approval but for some reason a tiny bit uncomfortable. "Fetch my boots boy!" he said, handing a stunned Ellis her pokerfaced stare.

"Yeah right," Tom obliged, lifting a canvass wader bag as they stabbed each other with verbal jabs and cutting insults. Guns were laid out, bags filled with items they needed today, decoys checked, flashlights on, bike rack in place. Twenty minutes later found lead vehicles entering through open gates with camo dressed figures surrounding two walk up windows, issuing shoot permits.

"No joking or chit chat this morning. Down here everybody wants a quick check-in, race to the parking lots and a fight for favorite ponds," Tom advised, hoping she wouldn't snarl the routine this morning as a young Fish and Wildlife lady waved them in.

"Don't know what you're talking about," Gonzo responded, exiting the truck, permitting Tom to lead the way.

As they approached the small weathered shack, Tom thought he spotted a sly subtle grin covering Regina's face. "Not today darling, please." Tom held his tongue hoping he read her wrong. "Make sure you have your license and pass ready," planning to get her attention focused on a quick check-in. No use, as his lady glided to a short waiting line of sleep deprived but anxious hunters.

"Well hello boys," the detective announced in a goofball, sexy filled voice. One guy laughed under his breath, three others offered polite good mornings and the young Fish and Wildlife woman just squinted in quiet disbelief. It didn't stop Gonzo to Tom's chagrin. "Where's all the birds today?" Gonzalez looked around detecting little rise from three remaining shooters, who wanted nothing more than to pay fees and get going. "Not too talkative this morning," as an unexpected gust of wind blew through the small group, cutting short Regina's act by sending her hat rolling across a gravel roadway.

"Get your hat Reggie, we're next," Tom assumed, happy the weather gods directed her away from another comedy routine, receiving a pair of raised eyebrows from the young lady leaving the counter. He grabbed his partner's arm and license, getting documents in order, doing his utmost to keep her act at bay. The male agent behind glass checked their license, passes, issued two pink permits and bade them good luck. Tom reasoned they were finished.

"Could you recommend a good place to hunt ducks today?" Regina asked innocent enough, stooping to make eye contact with the Fish and Wildlife agent manning their counter.

Hearing the question made Tom's heart sink. He thought for sure they made it. "The man's pretty busy this morning babe, why don't we," cut off straight away.

"No problem mame," a polite middle aged man replied, snatching a refuge map.

"We have a good north wind today. Should last all day and stay very cold. Perfect weather for fresh northern birds." Rotating the map to face Regina. "Three good areas I can recommend and lightly hunted. Number one. Parking lot five, pond number forty one. Be sure to set your dekes on the north side of the pond. Birds really decoy there on windy days." Tom was taken aback by the cooperative agent as two hunters behind stretched their necks to see the map. DFW continued. "Number two. Parking lot sixteen, pond number twenty four. Set up in a large bay on the northeast corner. You'll see two clumps of tules. Shoot from this side," pointing to a small open area on the map's right side. One more hunter joined in, listening close, patient and thinking.

"I've hunted that pond," the new man verified looking around to other shooters, offering positive nods.

"Me too," another chimed in. "He's right. The birds really work that pond on windy days."

Tom was floored by this point, oberving both the helpful agent and a bizarre politeness from hunters waiting their turns. Never had he seen a display of support and encouragement from the customary, grumpy Mendota crowd. This refuge handles four hundred hunters plus each shoot day and waiting lines must be kept moving. Regina's charms had changed it all this morning.

DFW concluded. "Number three. Parking lot twenty, pond number nineteen." Drawing a small circle on the map to pin point location. Tom was stunned. This is where he planned to shoot! He stood still, looked down shaking his head rubbing a nervous temple. Back to DFW. "Big open water pond. Fat. Kidney shaped. Put your dekes right off the middle point favoring open water a bit. Sprig, gadwall and mallard will work this water all day." He handed Regina a detailed map and confident smile.

"Tom, let's hunt lot twenty. That pond sounds great," Regina spoke out loud. "We have dibs on this pond guys!" She announced, looking around to the building reservation line. Tom was ready to get moving just as two young men yelled out.

"It's all yours lady. Go get 'em!"

"What the fuck is happening here?" Tom asked under his breath. More shooters moved toward the happy check station window shaking hands, high fiving Gonzalez, smiling and wishing each other good luck. It was like the home team just won on a walk off bomb! From inside the booth, DFW sought to offer an epilogue.

"Remember young lady, it's windy and cold," silence enveloped the baker's dozen milling around a windswept hut with small windows. "Don't shoot the first-light birds, without looking close. Spoonies and teal will be flooding into your spread early. Be patient and you can finish with sprig and mallard filling a strap." He gave Gonzo a short nod and she flashed a horizontal peace sign while everyone else stood still and quiet.

Tom remained flabbergasted! "Is this for real?" asking himself. "Sounded like Knute Rockne giving his pep talk. I can't believe it." Mumbling, checking awed faces and rocking his feet to keep warm.

"Let's move Tom," Regina yelled out as a sea of camouflaged parted, opening a path for Mendota's favorite, receiving back slaps and thumbs up.

"Oh Christ," Tom mumbled, following his princess, finally heading back to the truck.

"Today we limit!" Regina scowled. Remaining speechless, Ellis dropped it into drive and pressed on.

■■■

Chris dozed for over an hour. Cars and trucks were in motion around Tracy. Early commuters out to make their way west on the dreaded Highway 580 commute. The most congested corridor, day in and day out, into Bay Area employment centers. In little more than an hour, the usual traffic snarls would develop. Downhill side of the Altamont Pass to Livermore. Highway 680 south of the 580 junction. Highway 880 in any direction, I-80 westbound, further west to Silicon Valley and 'The City'. All within striking distance of Tracy's Central Valley bedrooms. A rather large Dodge Ram rumbled by Chris' window, jarring him from sound sleep as increasing numbers of fortunate to be employed residents passed in each direction.

"Hell, I can't possibly guess who's out to do harm today. I'm going to be short on sleep that's for sure," Davis told himself rubbing one eye with intense soreness.

A few blocks away on Tracy Boulevard settled in comfort, Douglas Sheets opened well rested eyes. Unwilling to venture anywhere close to the Patterson household. Too risky, even for his tainted intellect. Sheets passed the time in quietude, anticipating two double doors swinging open at a nearby Jack In The Box. Lights were on inside the franchise, grease was heating, Hispanic workers prepped various foods, sorted deliveries, but not quite ready for business. "No problem," Sheets said aloud, "I can wait. The Tracy cop on stakeout, he's the one who'll be hungry and sleep deprived in a few hours." Sheets knew he was lucky when he passed Loretta's house. He spotted Detective Davis, eyes closed, head propped on his side window fast asleep, recognizing Chris' face in a heartbeat. "It could've proved disastrous had that detective been awake and spotted me," Sheets reflected to himself. "It's like I'm destined to pull this off," his warping mentality said with a subtle laugh. Douglas needed to formulate plans, unsure on the best tactic, letting a narrow mind wonder between fantasy and rational ideas. "Later today maybe? We'll start something later in the day?" A deputy gone astray was hoping for a good idea. Behind his truck the eastern horizon was exceptionally clear. Bands of pink and orange developed, low over far off Sierra Nevada peaks, giving way to a thin belt of dark magenta. Stars shined bright, deceptive in mass as a dark, clear sky dominated above arctic winds. Douglas could feel icy temperatures absorb his body heat. "My toes are going numb," speaking to himself, wiggling feet to help circulate blood.

But only a few blocks separated two cops. Two cops who couldn't be further apart with intentions, clarity or evil. Both determined in their assignments. Both willing to risk their lives to fulfill their assignments. Both freezing their asses off. Only one can succeed.

Not too far eastward, heavy flocks of waterfowl, shorebirds, raptors and songbirds moved south. Moving with the aid of powerful winds at determined backs. Determined wings on assignment. Douglas had missed his first chance to infiltrate an unprotected Patterson home.

Mendota Wildlife Area

"It's been a while since my last bike ride," Gonzalez admitted, watching Tom bind a six inch bungee cord around the Citori's grip and the bike's cross bar. Her gun fastened just right. Out of the way and off her back. "I like this set-up already," she said in an upbeat voice as Tom continued loading her bike with gear. Regina turned ninety degrees to put the oncoming wind at her back. Feeling far too cold as her right cheek and ear collected blowing arctic air in full force. The detective scanned her bicycle, rolling wide tires back and forth, adjusting its bright headlight, getting a sense for balance and setting a high gear ratio. She grew excited about their upcoming moonlight ride.

"Your saddlebags are full. My saddlebags are full. I'll carry the decoy bag." Tom gave the convoy one last inventory check, noting water bottles, guns, wading staffs, seats, lights on and gloves. He looked at Regina wearing his wool gloves, knowing she didn't bring a pair. "Not good," he told himself.

"Let's go huntin' babe," Regina pleaded, ready for a nocturnal ride and tightening Tom's gloves.

"My hands are going to freeze tonight," Ellis mumbled so Regina wouldn't hear. Nothing he could do about it now. "Let's go," pushing off with heavy loads. Regina wobbled to the end of the parking lot needing more speed to get her momentum established. She giggled, stammered, trembled her handle bars then stood up to pump harder. Tom looked back to see her dig in and get the bike moving faster. "Good job girl," he lauded, low pitched but Regina didn't hear.

Firm dirt and dry wind made for a hard surface. Regina took to the bike like a kid and soon had full control of a worn out red Schwinn. Keeping gears locked at number three she moved along trouble-free, passing carts and walking hunters with ease. Shifting into fourth gear, gaining speed and nearing Tom, hanging close behind. "I like this," Regina yelled ahead to her leading man. Then passed Ellis, by standing and peddling hard, laughing as she took the lead.

"Take the second road to your left just past the canal," Tom shouted making out a long line of willow trees in the distance, marking their pond's eastern border. Hands numb and stinging, Tom knew they still had a decent run down this levee road. "Can't get there soon enough." Lifting each hand intermittently tucking cold fingers under arm pits and flexing for more blood flow. It didn't help much as his movement and cold air combined to make exposed skin miserable. "We'll take your next right at the tree line," directing his partner.

"Look at all the stars. I can't believe it," Regina spoke in awe as a pitch black western sky revealed its secret points of light. "Looks like millions!" The detective kept pace still gazing west, captivated by glowing clusters of jumbled zodiacs. On they rode, crosswise to increasing winds like over-loaded phantoms.

Reaching a narrow gap in the trees lining their levee road, the ride was over. It was back to walking, wading, stumbling and sweating, even in the frosty night air. Tom's hands were numb except for pin like stings, getting the tools reorganized and set to carry. Shotguns were slung, ammo in pouches, a decoy bag stuffed and the wading staffs in hand. Especially the wading staffs.

"Stay close and please don't fall in tonight," Tom warned his somewhat nervous, excited and distracted cohort. Then kissed her warm lips while slipping cold hands around her neck. She recoiled in shock. His fingers were like thin ice cubes.

"Aye aye," Gonzalez pushed Ellis away, drawing her jacket collar tight to chin, motioning him onward.

"Serves you right for taking my gloves," Tom cackled.

They just about reached the tule covered point without incident. Stomping his way across shallow water, taking no chances at losing out on a good location, Tom looked around to check Regina's progress. Not far behind her headlamp shined bright. He however, hit a soft spot of gooey muck in an otherwise firm bottom. His lead foot sinking in as momentum still carried forward. The rear foot advanced, too short, forcing a forward lean with the top heavy weight from a loaded decoy bag adding additional thrust. Forward! One foot stuck tight and down goes Ellis. First to one knee then to his left elbow. Cold water splashed out, away then up under his chin. He waddled in cold water like a camo tinted cape buffalo as pond water found its way inside loose waders. Instant rushes of wet chill swathed his left waist and upper left thigh, thanks to gravity. Worst of all, stinging hands submerged into cold water were then exposed to icy wind, making them burn!

A chuckling Gonzalez cut him even deeper with a strident, "way to go dickhead! Serves you right."

Tom could do nothing but laugh out loud once her gutter talk registered. Standing humble, dripping water. Regina churned muddy water in front of her, reaching Tom's position. Unable to resist a sarcastic issue and without stopping, she struck. "Man up, keep moving!" Ellis could only watch as his partner walked by very casual, a drop of muddy water clinged to the point of his red nose.

Gonzalez achieved the tule point. She rested, breathed hard, reached into a zippered pocket fumbling for her cell phone. "Oops, left it in the truck," It didn't matter. She swiveled for a glimpse of Tom coming in behind but caught sight of two ducks flying low, turning fast then silhouetted against a shooting star plunging vertical. Vanishing! Two birds passed unalarmed, tacking slightly, swerved to open water, caught the wind and vanished too. Luck was all hers, glimpsing a smooth quiet flight almost hidden against a pitch-black backdrop with vivid star show. Regina embraced her good fortune to be out here today. A privilege.

Gadwalls

It had been a rather easy flight out, flying southeasterly from the San Luis Wildlife Area Complex. The gadwall pair joined a large group of mostly widgeon but included a few pintail stragglers too, filling out a medium sum mixed flock. They located another cornfield, generous in uncollected grain adjacent to a fair sized pond. Water supplied by a local Ducks Unlimited chapter working with a large corporate grower through an environmental wetlands easement. Supplying the much needed 'safe rest and feed' habitat for wintering ducks and geese. Feeding heavy and well rested, the hen had a quick urge to begin a long flight south. To continue their southern migration. It would be an easier flight today with robust winds, to refuge areas in the extreme southern San Joaquin Valley. She sensed the other birds weren't ready for a major move. Loafing along the pond's edge, preening, planning a shorter daylight trip seeking large open ponds to the north. Into the wind. They spotted Mendota's vast acreage earlier this morning, skirting the refuges' eastern most flanks during their high flight out. Searching for safe locations in high winds among fairly new settings only made the hen gadwall nervous.

Following a chorus of chirps, whistles and soft quacks, sounding like a prelude to take off, the flock rose. Fast, due to moving air filling wings with lift, they formed a tight V and moved north. Sluggish. It would be an hard effort, forced low into a constant wind stream. Half the calories consumed mere hours before would be spent on a relatively short flight. To make matters worse loud noises could be heard in the distance, just as the sun climbed over snow laden ridges to the east. Sierra Nevada peaks put up an imaginary display in clear air, using a false display of close proximity. Battling headwinds and spotting Mendota's southern most waters, none too soon, navigating a straight course to a chain of large open ponds. The hen positioned herself to the rear of a ragged formation. With a tired partner following suit they enabled a draft situation. allowing them to conserve energy. Increasing numbers of loud noises grew even louder.

Hunting

Decoys skimmed right and left over a wind battered surface. Splashed and twisted by cresting waves heaving into a foaming chop. Wind speeds increased in early morning hours causing two low profile teal decoys to be sucked under water. They emerged in a head first launch, an awkward mimic of diving ducks returning topside. Tom's winduck had wings spinning in a blur, at times lifting itself almost clear from its PVC holder. Regina bet a backrub the mallard silhouette would fly free of its stay before the day ended.

Half past seven in the morning, cold as hell, thirty knot winds, clear skies, ducks everywhere and Tom just returned from gathering his third bird. Another plump mallard to go with his male widgeon. Regina downed her widgeon on the morning's opening attempt. A three year drake. She missed on her next six consecutive swings however!

"That check station guy was right on the mark about this pond," Gonzalez relayed to Tom bending low, blowing a sharp series of chirps on her sprig whistle. Tom squatted lower, reading her motions as a signal to approaching birds. She continued calling, squeezing herself tighter to somehow shrink in size, invisible to decoying waterfowl. Tom fumbled with a dead mallard in one hand, trying to keep his gun postured with the other. Finally strapping the bird, he turned his head, minimizing body movements to get a sideways look at the large flock of widgeon and sprig. He was aligned just right behind a thick clump of cattails, masking his body turn, getting into position to shoot again. Both shooters chirped on whistle calls, guns rested forward, staring, nervous twitching, accelerated heartbeats, waiting on birds to close. Sunshine poured in from their left lighting up the flock. Tom followed three drake pintails on Regina's side and two large, drab birds to his extreme right. Their angled approach would bring two gadwalls right over him as one drake's black rump was clearly on display.

"Drake gadwall, I'll take it," Tom lipped the words, slipping his safety to hazard.

...

"What the hell, I may as well hang around here now." Chris carried on a steady internal debate as bright sunshine lit roof tops, yards, trees and streets. More cars in motion, lights burning inside houses and condos. "Damn, I hate this." A frustrated Davis had to leave the car to stretch his legs, hoping to avoid the growing need for a bathroom break. "I can hold it a little longer," convincing himself but jumping back inside a warm car. "I hope."

All quiet remained around the Patterson home. Chris composed a text, deciding to make contact with his boss and partner. "Still early but nothing else to do," he mumbled checking drivers in two passing trucks. Too big and the wrong color for his suspect. He needed a break, now! His phone rang.

"Captain, I need a break. Is Kennedy available to spell me a couple hours," Chris almost begged his boss.

"I don't have the staff, Chris. Sorry." Anderson expected this. He realized Davis was out there way too long on his own, but no budget, no staff. "I Googled your area and located a park, not even a mile from your location. There's a bathroom there. Go for it. You won't be gone long. What are the odds anyway?" giving Chris permission to leave for a short time. "Kennedy will be free later today. I'll send him out when he's available. Do the best you can and hang tough. I appreciate this one Chris." Giving his detective due credit, hoping to keep him on guard.

"Okay Captain. Let me have those park directions. I have to go pretty bad," Chris relayed, at last able to depart for about ten minutes but never feeling comfortable leaving his position.

...

Widgeon drakes relayed long and short whistles as a leading hen dropped her wings. Not a full sailing dive. More of a controlled glide between wing flutters to continue a forward gain. Her intent was to land however. Birds tracked back and forth, waved up and down, tipping wingtips as individual ducks jockeyed for line of sight and safe collision distance. Lagging behind, a nervous hen gadwall was one bird unsure about the pond's safety. She stayed back wanting to bank away to complete at least one search flight. Loud noises echoed again, too far off to do harm but alarming the hen regarding unseen figures. Her mate stayed joined to the flock, keeping in line and losing height, preparing a fast landing.

Dropping low in unison, beating wings against cold wind, feet spread by some of the wobbling widgeon, maintaining a steady approach. The nervous hen, still wary, scanned dense cover coming closer and closer. A simple glare well inside the weeds caught her eye followed by possible movement. She didn't hesitate. Uttering a faint warning quack, more like a grunt, beginning her express climb to leave the group. The hen gadwall was jarred by a loud explosion, catching sight of a long tail bird crashing to muddy water below. Two more noises rang out chasing her higher and higher. She lost sight of her partner, fearing the worst as panic filled her bloodstream

···

Regina went safety off too, springing from her crouch like a catcher throwing to third and swinging on a low and slow bull sprig. His snowy white breast caught a lot of sunshine as she pulled and fired. Like a lace pillow, the decoying bird exploded in a ball of feathers, wings collapsed, neck slack and down. Head winds pushed his body further down as the hefty bird dropped belly-up into muddy water. Gonzalez, in pure exhilaration, paused to admire her uncomplicated shot but missed an opportunity for another kill. Recognized as 'blowing the double.' Her shot scattered more than a dozen widgeon in all directions as two gadwalls stretched to get elevated. Tom was in perfect shape to cover a large drake detecting its characteristic white wing speculums shining flamboyant. His muzzle adjusted to the drake's bill with little lead required and pulled the trigger.

···

The drake gadwall held both wings steady, committed to the open water pond. Regina's first shot rang out delivering a shock wave and terror as a dark figure rose some twenty yards in front. Stunned, he decided to bore straight ahead beyond the pond in hope of catching wind and speed at the same time. Tom swung on the drake in perfect alignment, pulling the trigger as the large gray bird passed inside of thirty yards. An empty click rang out. By instinct Tom pulled the trigger again, keeping aim. Nothing. Once more, luck would be on the bird's side. Boom! Regina's second shot went off, sounding another ear splitting alarm. An entire flock minus one drake pintail, climbed in separate directions. Then gathered over the pond's center observing two dark figures step clear of hidden vantage points.

"Why didn't you shoot?" Regina asked approaching her bird, spotting two gray webbed feet folded and motionless on a plump belly, stone dead. The sprig bled copiously, covering much of its snowy breast in pink and deep red streaks. Blood drifted from an open bill with his head resting in profile, bobbing over small waves. Regina's excitement was tempered a bit by the marred bird. She lifted her large pintail from tainted water, admired a unique shape then dragged it through unstained water, rinsing blood soaked feathers. Most washed away but trickles of crimson still clingied to thick down on a full breast.

Tom swept his boot through the water a few times, erasing streaks and floating red blobs lingering on muddy water. "I forgot to reload," Ellis answered a bit sheepish. "Too much excitement and commotion, I guess?" Seeing new flocks interested in their pond. "C'mon, we'll get more birds to work in," he said as both shooters hurried back to tule blinds.

"It is more about wind?" Regina asked, strapping her second bird, lifting both to run fingers through colorful feathers, wings and tails. Examining bills and creased webbing. Fascinated by her widgeon's white crown, green eye patch and stubby bill. Continuing to finger its black, curled tip.

"Wind and cold," Tom answered. "Most people connect rain with duck hunting. I'll take wind and cold for good shooting." Wind and cold lasted all morning. Flocks of mallard sailed low into their spread throughout mid morning hours handing Tom plenty of chances to single out the large green headed drakes. He filled his limit by ten o'clock with several easy misses too. Regina used up most of her ammo by nine thirty, emptying her gun on every pass from big to small birds, bugging Tom to give up a few of his shells. By ten thirty all the ammo was spent with Gonzalez knocking down a drake mallard on her last shot. This bird, all alone and wary, decoyed close three times before committing into range. Tom's chuckling kept the elusive bird circling which allowed Regina her chance to dump him into bobbing decoys. Not a clean kill however. Ellis was forced to run down the wounded, swimming bird. After an off balance race, which he won, he dispatched Regina's flapping struggle with a quick broken neck. Easing its thrashing pain in a few seconds. Still hating the chore.

"Sorry about all that," Regina apologized.

"It's okay darlin'. Happens that way sometimes. Nice bird," Tom handed his partner a compliment and a limp drake, watching as Gonzalez ran her thumb and forefinger through an iridescent, green head.

Both shooters sat back in tule covered blinds letting strong gusts whip from behind which eased the severe cold to bearable. Viewing unrelenting flights of waterfowl dropping to their pond. The chilled air, the wind, the cold, the clear sky, even the lack of sleep was all but forgotten. "Seven birds. All before lunch," Regina spoke with a slight dazed look on her red, windblown face. Dealing out a 'way to go' nod and sharp smile to her shooting partner. "Good job."

Tom jumped from his stool unlocking his eyes from Regina rather abrupt. Jammed his 1100 into bent tules and cattails, hoisting the decoy bag and beginning a forced march into open water. Water splashed high and away from each stomping foot. "Let's pick up and get out of here," Tom groused without looking back, sending spray shooting to each side as he pushed his way into steady gales.

"Gees, sorry for complimenting you," Regina muttered under her breath, surprised by Ellis' unusual reaction. "Normally, you enjoy my praise." Gonzalez stood, stretched her arms then moved out to join her riled companion. Braced against her wading staff. "Grumpy," she bawled out, hoping he'd hear. Tom heard just fine, choosing not to respond or look back.

···

It took one more fatal approach and about an hour of close inspection before the gadwalls located harmless water. Following the flock of reckless widgeon into another pond, hiding more dark figures which unleashed many loud noises. Two ducks failed to make it out. One more bull sprig as well as the leading hen widgeon tumbled, wounded mortally into foaming murky water. Two figures materialized, shooting twice on two birds attempting watery escapes. All futile of course with two ducks dispatched while the remaining flock rose to safety. Observing mate and kin annihilated in compelling manner.

The hen gadwall decided on another brake off during final approach, unsure about the green headed ducks bobbing below by means of their stiff movements. Her small brain wasn't capable of perceiving a decoy but instincts said something wasn't right. A tense partner followed close this time staying above kill range. They chose to leave the bold flock this time, beginning a search for calm water on their own. Loud noises below erupted as the flock came under attack yet again. Birds dropped and figures chased. Two gadwalls flew higher, straining into stiff winds for safety.

Loud noises continued into the afternoon as the pair loafed in a small opening surrounded by thick vegetation. Continuous jumbles of cattails, tules and shrubs covered a few acres. Mud hens occupied the downwind side of open water eating disturbed bits of vegetation and insects. Hunters wouldn't set up in a place so dense as most dead birds felled, would be impossible to find. Not letting the splashing mud hens fool them into risky confidence, both gadwalls sailed over the tiny puddle six times before folding and free falling into splashy landings. All was calm. None the less, each far off blast caused slight shudders. Reminding the drake especially how good it was to have his companion nearby.

···

"Not even a twenty minute ride," Regina relayed to Tom stepping away from her borrowed bicycle. "This is the only way to go," breathing heavy words. Nothing close to the usual exhaustion after hiking in waders and carrying gear. Unbuckling boots, set to unload, nap, eat lunch, sex it up. Her and Tom were back to teasing, giggles, stealing grabs on body parts, full bore kissing and heavy breathing.

"As long as it doesn't get too wet. When the roads turn to mud, it's back to walking and slipping and falling," Tom recalled after being forced to walk his bike, to and from, far off parking lots. Powerless to ride over viscous mud. He unloaded his decoy bag, gun, saddle bags and dead birds, sucking a long drink of cold water while sitting on a firm tailgate. He breathed in a dense, wonderful marshy smell emitted by dead waterfowl. Dear to one shooter but a little unsettling to the other. "Let's check out," he added, closing the rear window after securing their bicycles.

"Let's!" Gonzalez replied. The detective forgot all about her murder case. Forgetting all about a dark follower. She forgot all about her cell phone. Perhaps forcing it out, needing a break. The new love in her life snatched all her concentration, focusing on Tom now. Wanting to stay close today, wrapped around with him inside. For some reason she sensed a small amount of impatience rising within. Expecting a change in their relationship like a new closeness. Moving into serious. Then, like usual, as Regina Gonzalez bumped along looking at Tom, satisfied, her detective side began to leak back in. Taking in views from a jumpy passenger seat of bent trees, swaying tule spikes, deep blue water, flocks of low flying geese and swirling pelicans. Thinking back to Los Banos Wildlife Area and her investigative drive through the refuge where she first became interested. Where she first conceded her and Tom would someway, come together. She smiled, warm and cozy in the bouncing truck. Music blared. "It didn't take him long to limit today," popped into Regina's thoughts out of the clear blue. Unaware of any significance it might hold but it seemed odd leaving Mendota so early in the day. "Feels strange," she told herself, still thinking, catching sight of a dozen or so sparrows rush alongside their truck, hopping shrub to shrub. She recalled the Crosby murder scene sitting with Beatrice, talking, songbirds flying low, skittering into gusty winds. Squinting outside, almost like a far off memory now. Her study was cut short as Tom skidded the truck over loose gravel traversing a sharp left turn, bringing the rundown check station into view.

"Let's see if that check-in guy is still here," Tom laughed looking at Regina.

"Yeah. Let's." Gonzalez grinned.

Sheets

"Not too far Douglas, not too far," Sheets spoke in a murmur as if the waiting cop might hear, further down Anaheim Drive. The nose of his truck stopped exactly in line with a tall hedgerow but maintained a clear view down to Chris Davis, on stakeout, trying hard to stay awake. He parked alongside one of many homes for sale in this tract of large houses. Symptomatic of the real estate crash plaguing much of California's inland Valley region. Nothing to worry about from nearby home owners however. Douglas stared like a hunting predator.

Sunshine filled the area, brightening a windy, silent neighborhood. Soon after killing the engine he was rapidly aware of cold air seeping into his warm car. "What's up flatfoot?" Douglas snarled, knowing beyond hesitation the Tracy cop hadn't a clue he was being staked himself. It would take some time before Sheets took his eyes off the target car. "C'mon Mr. Davis. Time for a break. Time to piss. I have a job to do." Sheets sat back, fidgeting in his seat to get comfortable. Continuing his stare down Anaheim Drive. At the same time working on plans, farfetched as always, how he might handle his task inside Beatrice Patterson's home. Consumed by idea and fantasy to a point where he no longer noticed bitter cold or winds whistling like a bottle flute outside. Late morning passed with a Tracy cop lingering in place.

Regina

"Mmm, red panties. I love that Gringo," Gonzalez pointed out rather loud as Tom leaned far forward over a lowered tailgate. Lifting heavy waterfowl on a leather strap.

"Just for you my dear," Ellis declared and waived the birds just below Regina's eye level, blood spattered with floating down feathers leaking away. "I mean the underwear of course," he teased, hanging their kill on a stout metal hook. They continued to empty a packed truck bed, organizing gear, hanging wet waders, storing boots, calls, packs and most of everything else. Regina could tell by now, unloading was part of Tom's ritual. His official close of a day hunting. Everything had its place. Never permitting any valued hunting tools to be thrown in a heap and sorted through days later. Respecting his program she made sure to follow every rule. From here on in however, anything goes. Early afternoon, two tired hunters, hot showers, drinks, maybe more food, followed by clothes being ripped away, sweaty bodies, warm contact and a hardened Tom Ellis.

"Fun day," Regina said taking a seat to rest on a worn sofa, leaning against Ellis' shoulder. Knowing what to expect fairly soon and wanting it to happen. Almost needing it. Sitting back getting comfortable and ready, she sensed that deep swell of nausea growing in her lower stomach, up to the back of her throat. Breathing heavy, becoming warm with small drops of sweat forming on her forehead, under arms, across her stomach and between warm legs. Gonzalez tilted her head to stop the spinning, sure she wouldn't make it to the bathroom soon enough. Rubbing her damp forehead, mouth hanging free, eyes closed and gripping the sofa's fabric needing to hold onto something.

Tom didn't notice. Too tired, his heavy eyes set forward and fixed on the front window view reflecting on hidden secrets. He leaned into Regina's body twirling fingers and rubbing a moist palm against her knees and thighs. "It was fun today," Tom responded after a lengthy delay. Regina squirmed, adjusting her posture as she began to rebound. Just like always, a slow turnaround at first. Followed by an immediate clearing in just a few minutes feeling a hundred percent normal! She snuggled in close to Tom enjoying his soft touches. Growing excited as Elly's touch moved higher yet with no stopping now. Regina moaned in a soft pleasant tone, welcoming each caress and lengthy stroke. Both moved with aggression at one another, finishing loud on the living room floor, partially clothed. Gonzalez on top heaving in deep breaths. Grinding her full body, rising and falling in cadence with panted breathing. Her detective side safely buried away.

Chris

"Nothing. Absolutely nothing," Davis mouthed his words simulating the soul group's lyrics. "It's late." Checking in twice with Anderson and one unanswered text to Gonzalez. "Nothing out of the ordinary," Chris observed, with routine suburbia surrounding the Patterson's home. Beatrice materialized with her newfound granddaughter. Lucy played a quick newspaper fetch, faking runaways down a leaf covered sidewalk, laughed and looked too cute in her pajamas inside an oversized warm jacket. Chris watched close, reminiscent of his own daughter, piercing a wounded heart with another arrow.

"No weirdoes, no threats, no murderers drooling around the house. Absolutely clear," Davis noted, checking in every direction for nothing better to do. "I need a break," he bawled out loud, dialing Anderson to get relief.

...

Sheets was in the same position. Not tired however, knowing he dictated terms in this operation. Able to snooze at will, plenty to eat and mapping out various plans. The only drawback occurred with a growing urge developing in his bladder region. "Let's go Tracy. You've been out here since last night for Christ's sake. One more opening and I can make my move," Douglas stewed in the waiting car as his violent fantasies ballooned into gory details of cruelty. Longing to get even with the wife he hated, rubbing his forehead where she belted him with a blunt stoker. Lucy would surface within his warped plan but Douglas kept stuffing her into the rear of his failing psychological condition.

"Another room will do fine for Lucy. Can't hurt my daughter, wouldn't be prudent." His analysis breaking apart at a rapid pace.

•••

Anderson placed the call. He preferred to keep Davis on watch but knew his detective couldn't stay indefinitely, dialing patrol officer Kennedy to make sure he was available.

"Mr. Kennedy. You're going out to spell Detective Davis for a few hours. Is your schedule open?" Billy asked the young cop, hearing him tell his sergeant, then asking what time.

"Right now," Billy ordered. "Come upstairs. We'll get a vehicle ready and line you out."

"Yes sir," Kennedy responded, excited about his assignment. The patrolman had been patient long enough waiting to be assigned to a homicide investigation. Changing to plain clothes in the nearest bathroom, running three flights of stairs then bursting into Billy's office, Kennedy wasn't about to miss his chance.

Anderson was taken by the cop's zeal, glad to see a display of enthusiasm for a change. "Mr. Kennedy," the Captain addressed him in a formal approach to get his attention. "It's a simple stakeout with a slight possibility of intervention. Very slight." Billy wanted to make clear that Kennedy understood the situation, giving him more details and mapping his location. Already familiar with the Patterson house, as the patrolman was part of the homicide unit securing Marcus Crosby's murder scene. "Remember, stay obscured and keep quiet. Don't try to be a hero. It's a routine watch where nothing is likely to happen." Anderson gave the patrolman a stare and small grin to get his point home. Mark Kennedy understood, growing much calmer. Billy called Chris, relaying the status situation and Kennedy was on the way.

"Great. I have to piss like a racehorse," Chris informed Anderson on the status of his condition. "Tell him to hurry it up." Anderson gave Kennedy the keys running him out of the building now. Thinking how he had Chris on watch way too long. Checking his watch, closing in on three o'clock, giving Kennedy a thumbs up as he sent Chris a confirmation text. "On his way."

Calm once more but ready to go, Kennedy located a white Ford, departing the basement garage among squealing tires and roaring engine. He made good time cutting across town, wanting to arrive early but found traffic clogs up and down Tracy Boulevard. He dodged his way through a few times, changing lanes, always looking for daylight like a small running back cutting up field, out-running slower defenders. Kennedy loved to speed around town managing one good inside move, finding an empty lane and pressing the gas pedal to make sure he made a green or even yellow light dead ahead. All was a go until an older truck exited a MacDonald's on his right, braked hard, stopping fast on a bright yellow light.

Kennedy couldn't believe it, shoving firm on his brake pedal, skidding toward a burley Dodge with a stout metal bumper that screamed aloud, 'I'm very hard!' Ford's front bumper made firm contact causing the Dodge to lurch forward.

"Shit!" Kennedy yelled out, clutching the steering wheel tight with both hands. Not believing his bad luck. "We're going to clear this up fast," commanding himself, exiting swift and striding to a driver's side open window. "Everyone all right?" he asked, giving the impression of safety first.

"I think so," an Hispanic driver said in a low voice carrying a thick accent, checking a young passenger for an okay. "Any serious damage?" attempting to leave the Dodge for a quick assessment.

"No no, stay inside. I'm a cop." Displaying a silver badge to a much more concerned driver. "We're about to settle all this pronto. Pull your truck through the intersection and into that Seven-Eleven, over there," pointing to an open parking lot on the right.

"Yes sir," Vicente spoke with a nod, leaving the crash scene as soon as the light turned green. Kennedy managed to follow close behind on a yellow light of course.

■■■

"I've gotta get to a bathroom," Chris said out loud. He punched a text to Anderson asking how much longer?"

"He should've been there by now!!!!!" Anderson replied with five exclamation marks! Davis checked his contacts list seeing Kennedy's name listed. He pressed the call button, wanting to speak directly with the patrolman. Now!

Sheets had Wagner piped in, keeping attention locked on Davis. "Loretta may get a knife," telling himself with a straight face which imparted an air of absolute breakdown infecting Douglas' ability to reason and act rationally. He sensed an opening soon however, for some reason.

Regina

"Don't look so sad gringo," Regina told Ellis as she gathered her stuff, making ready to leave Gustine. "I'll see you this weekend. Where do we shoot on Saturday?" She asked smiling, feeling well.

Tom hesitated for a moment thinking over his answer. Wondering if he should say? "Mendota again. I have another reservation," Tom said with a rather weak voice laying back into a few worn pillows. He appeared tired, sporting watery sad eyes. "I'd love you to join me in bed Gonzalez," speaking in a serious manner.

Regina pointed to her watch. "It's two thirty and I have to work tomorrow," sitting on the bed next to her love. Close. "I'm going to be dirt tired." Not allowed to finish her words, Tom sat up abrupt and kissed Regina long on her lips. Not too hard with turned up, passionate sex. Soft, with a few repeated short kisses.

"I adore you Regina Gonzalez," he said in a whisper. She felt full inside listening to the words, slipped her arm around him, bending his head lower to her face.

"You okay gringo?" she asked again, taken by surprise, with his serious mood. He rubbed his head against her cheek smelling thick black hair, wishing they could stay together much longer. Spend the night perhaps. "I'll see you Friday night." Regina kissed and licked his nervous lips pushing him down onto waiting pillows. "We'll talk tomorrow lover," Gonzalez reassured her man, leaving the room but holding to an image on Tom's face, Regina had never seen before. Unsure what to make of it. He seemed so serious but Gonzalez adored it.

Chris

"Sorry Detective Davis, but I pulled a real bonehead move on Tracy Boulevard. Be there in about five minutes. I promise," Kennedy told a holding it way too long Chris Davis, with embarrassment filling the patrolman's voice.

"Go ahead and park a few doors down from Mrs. Patterson's home but on the same side of the street," Davis instructed the nervous patrol officer. "I'll meet you back here in a few minutes. Try to hurry things up."

"Will do," Kennedy answered parking his car next to the Dodge. "Sorry about this detective."

"No biggie," Chris replied and hung up. "I gotta go now," he said to himself, turning his ignition key.

Kennedy walked fast around the pick-up to see Vicente checking his rear bumper. "Any damage?" Kennedy asked in a counterfeit, firm voice.

"A small dent in the bumper, right here." The Hispanic laborer pointed right of the license plate, appearing concerned to Kennedy, stroking his chin with slow rubs.

"Let's see your driver's license," the patrolman ordered, maintaining a fake bluster. He lifted his hand to receive Vicente's tag knowing the man wasn't licensed.

A worried Hispanic father looked at his son. "I left it at home. But I can get it." Shuffling his feet on black asphalt while scratching his forehead, trying to invent some sort of alibi. Kennedy gave his son a pleasant look and smiled to ease the boy's tension. "This truck belongs to my brother in law," was the only curve he could deliver. Kennedy felt relieved knowing he could disregard the whole incident and get over to his stakeout. Vicente tried to continue with another pitch. "My son and I are doing a small job. Hauling leaves and grass. Just a side job for some," Vicente didn't get to explain further, as Kennedy raised both hands, signaling all clear.

"What's your name?" the patrol officer asked easing the situation further.

"Vicente Norberto. This is my son Miguel." A worried laborer pointed with pride to his eldest boy. "Senor, I'm just working for some extra cash," cut off one more time. Kennedy was out of time.

"Vicente, I have to be somewhere fast. Let's just forget this whole thing. I won't tell if you won't," Kennedy offered the deal to a pleased immigrant with a dry smile on his face.

■■■

Sheets daydreamed off and on for most of the last hour. His awareness peeked nonetheless on hearing a faint car start, seeing the Tracy detective back up slow, stop and pull forward leaving his observation point. Chris drove to the intersection not far from a large GMC Van parked in front of and screening Sheets' waiting truck. Davis turned right on Arlington Street in a modest hurry, then coasted into another right turn before disappearing.

Douglas sat motionless, a bit wide-eyed and not sure what just happened. Running both hands through his head of thinning hair contemplating what to do next, if anything. He looked all around, staring to see any cars moving on Anaheim Drive. It was quiet.

"Do I?" Sheets challenged himself out loud in a standard tone to his voice. Sitting still, eyes blinking, pondering, surprised. "Let's go," opening his door, not too hasty, to avoid fetching unwanted attention his way. Locked it, embarking on a relaxed walk toward Loretta's hideout.

■■■

Kennedy advised Vicente to get a license. Shook his hand, Miguel's too, then made a polite but fast exit. He needed to get down Tracy Boulevard fast, wishing for a patrol car's flashing lights. Arlington wasn't far ahead but Mark reminded himself, "to make the run in safety!"

Vicente watched the officer drive off with a sense of luck and comedy. His second time in under three months being let off for driving without a license. Miguel entered the truck, waiting to get rolling. His dad stopped, turned back, walking into the Seven-Eleven convenience store, needing a six pack of Modello for later tonight.

Kennedy slowed just in front of Arlington, turned, gliding to Anaheim, turning slower while taking a long look at the Crosby front yard. He remembered Marcus Crosby lying in a heap, his blood staining the concrete driveway. Kennedy failed to notice Mrs. Patterson's front door swinging closed with a loud slam.

■■■

Douglas Sheets didn't hesitate at the walkway, climbed a single step, knocking loud on Beatrice's front door. He heard footsteps approach from inside followed by an older woman's voice.

"Who is it?" Mrs. Patterson shouted out unlocking the door at the same time.

"Police," Douglas said not quite yelling back, calm and affirmed. He checked the street behind him hearing a car driving in from his left, still out of sight. By instinct, Beatrice slid open the security dead bolt, cracking the door a few inches. The sheriff didn't pause as Mrs. Patterson barely issued a 'yes.' He shoved the door back, swinging open very fast, knocking the older woman straight away against a low partition corner. She stood shaking. Shocked yet recognizing the officer right away.

"You?" Beatrice scowled. Eyes wide in disbelief knowing him from Marcus' murder trial. His picture in newspapers once a week.

Douglas slammed the door shut, hearing a very slow car pass by. "You shut up," pointing his Beretta an inch from Beatrice's demure nose, clicking the safety off. She froze, closing eyes as Douglas intended. He gazed out through a narrow side window seeing Kennedy's Ford passing way too slow. "Missed me," he grunted shooting a small drop of saliva from his throat onto clean glass. Reaching out to wipe the pane clean with his pinky finger, knowing another cop had arrived in relief. "Perfect timing," the crazed sheriff let loose a sinister smile considering what was ahead of him now.

"Get out!" Beatrice hissed.

"Shut up you old fossil or I'll blow a pair of eyeballs all over your living room." Breathing hard, frowning, trembling and beginning to sweat.

Loretta heard the loud slam from upfront. Jerking her head sideways as a slight rush of adrenaline flowed into a churning stomach. She slid a plate of sliced fruit from under Lucy's chin, telling her daughter to go to her room. Mrs. Sheets stood up wanting to rush through the kitchen door but halted her stride. "Should I get armed?" asking herself, expecting the worst at all times now. Loretta eyed a wooden knife holder, sliding the wide French knife from its wooden slot. She shoved the blade carefully down inside snug jeans at the small of her back, covered by a loose sweatshirt. The backside blade rested secure along stiff panties and her narrow crack of tight buttocks. Its business edge angled away safe. Hearing Lucy's door close from a narrow hallway, Loretta fingered her cell phone uncertain about sending a text message or not. Moving closer to the living room door, she decided to wait. Not wanting to issue any false alarms.

...

Outside, Kennedy accomplished a rapid three point turn, disappointed Davis wasn't on site. Slight nervousness filled his stomach and legs, ashamed at how his stupid, aggressive driving caused him to be late. "Hope he's not too pissed?" the young cop droned, uncertain of Chris' temper and forgetting his bathroom needs. An edgy patrolman killed the engine. He looked at four or five front doors and glanced at the Patterson front porch, studying its layout. All quiet, as a fair size branch broke away from low hanging sycamore limbs. Dropping straight through a sparse canopy hitting firm and loud on his Ford's rear trunk. Kennedy shook, reaching to feel his sidearm before realizing what triggered the noise. He resettled as Chris drove along side giving Davis the chance to say thanks for his offer of relief. "Feeling better?" Kennedy asked. "Again, sorry I'm late."

"Forget it. Just remember, arrest or shoot anybody trying to get in. Or out, for that matter. Got it?" Chris relayed his instructions quite serious.

"Yes sir," Kennedy responded.

"Call me if you see anything suspicious. I'll be close by," Chris added. "See you in a few hours." Driving down Anaheim following a quick nod. Davis checked his watch at three forty five.

Douglas watched the whole exchange keeping his Beretta leveled on Betty's forehead.

Regina

Gonzalez was sleepy. Early enough in the day to force herself to stay awake, but driving nonetheless with too much risk. She couldn't shake Tom's look from memory, just before leaving Gustine. "He acted so serious," Gonzalez recalled, loaded with uneasy sentiment on one hand but a presumed sense of commitment on the other. "Maybe he's just head over heels in love with me," joking and hoping in quiet as her car sped past the Westley Rest Stop with no plans for stopping. Pressing on, north, trying to get home as soon as possible. "I'm going to need all the sleep I can get," telling herself, yawning and rubbing a burning right eyeball.

Gonzalez took notice of dried out grasses coating small rolling hills to her left, waiving in shudders resembling wild Midwestern prairie. Strong winds continued blowing with high velocity sending her car right and left, punching straight into a powerful airstream. She reached for a forgotten cell phone. Plugging it in to get a fresh charge working. Two text messages waited.

Sheets

Loretta entered the living room just as Douglas shoved Beatrice onto the sofa. She didn't gasp in terror nor scream in fear, somehow knowing by gut instinct, Douglas was present. More important, Mrs. Sheets wanted to convey a strong appearance to her deranged husband. She froze solid however, thighs quivering, almost loosing balance but stood fast.

"Hi babe," Douglas said to his dismayed wife in a ghoulish tone. "I can tell you're happy to see me!" Sheets held a wild eyed look on his wife. Stepping very slow and very close to her.

"Don't touch me Douglas. And if you lay a finger on Lucy or Beatrice, I'll kill you. You might kill me, but we'll die together, I promise you that much," staring back into a dangerous face. After the initial shock diminished, Loretta became less afraid and more aggressive. Feeling the knife handle rubbing skin from the small of her back. Telling herself, "I'll have to use it." She also noticed a small weight drooping in her sweatshirt pocket. Wishing she'd sent that text. Mrs. Sheets moved to a new position keeping her weapons hidden.

"What kind of father do you take me for. I love my daughter. You know that Loretta." Doug acted with an over the top performance, smiling, frowning and back to smiles again. He moved around the room vying for position, well aware of his acting, which only confirmed his lack of sane behavior. Both women schemed in private trying to figure a way to fight this monster. Knowing they needed outside help.

"Walk over here Loretta. Toward me," her husband ordered looking in the direction of Beatrice too. "You stay seated." Pointing at the older woman, directing her to sit still. Loretta knew she must get in close to Beatrice to transfer the cell phone, which may be the last item to save their lives.

"I'm going to take a beating anyway," Loretta admitted to herself. She even managed a tight lipped smile, accepting her life and death challenge. "You kinda enjoy killing woman don't ya sweetheart," permitting the stinging words to settle into her husband's flawed mind. She saw his temper rise, being near him too often when he'd spin out of control. Mrs. Sheets knew her beating would commence at any time and moved to keep a sturdy coffee table between Douglas and herself.

"Don't Loretta. Don't antagonize him," Beatrice pleaded standing in front of the sofa.

"Shut up and sit down lady," Douglas screamed, not permitting Mrs. Patterson to speak. "I decide who gets to speak and who dies," Sheets said in a quiet tone, very calm, lending even more menace to his words.

"You and I know he killed Sarah, don't we Beatrice," Loretta said stepping closer to the older woman and turning slight to the right, away from Doug's view, allowing her to retrieve a dark green cell phone. No one knew the better. Deciding the time was right to get him upset!

"You will never get away with this Douglas. You have to know that. You're a cop for Christ sake." Seeing her words having an impact. "You'll never get away with this. They're on to you right now. Are you willing to kill me? If you do, you'll have to kill Beatrice too. Who's next? Lucy?" Loretta was succeeding in provoking his attack, having one last idea to deal with her deranged husband.

"Shut the fuck up. I know what the hell I'm doing." Douglas realized, even in this state of mind, she was right. He knew it all along but preferred to function inside his make believe world. Moving the pistol toward his head, rubbing its shiny action against his ear then down along the side of a frail jaw. Tapping the barrel on his cheek wondering if his gun would sound an alarm outside. Concluding it would, choosing to use a knife or his hands instead.

"I'll get away with it. You can bank that," Douglas spoke letting his deranged concentration wonder, giving Loretta enough daylight to move another step closer to Mrs. Patterson. "Neither of you will be alive to testify against me. No witnesses to point spiny little fingers at me."

Douglas' rants forced Beatrice to get control of her fears. His repeated threats to kill her and Loretta began to fail. His plans to intimidate and terrorize began to fail. His attempt to take control began to fail. Mrs. Patterson's resolve flipped into confrontation. She stood erect, scowling at the menace occupying her home. "You can't scare me you little twerp!"

"Great job lady," Loretta said quieter. Knowing it helped to get Douglas worked into a frenzy.

"Sit down," he yelled out, striding toward Loretta around the coffee table. Raising his left arm to deliver a backhand on his wife's jaw. She hoped for a quick punch. It came on her right cheek. His swing wasn't square but did catch most of her neck. Loretta added a fake moan, leaned left away from her husband and fell into Betty's arms. Face to face, Mrs. Sheets slid her right hand into Betty's left, passing her phone over. Beatrice accepted the object, figuring out right away what her friend had planned. She leaned back into the falling woman further hiding their exchange.

Douglas moved to grab his wife away from Mrs. Patterson grasp. As he pulled, Loretta pulled back. Staring into Mrs. Patterson's face, Loretta mouthed the word 'text' in one exaggerated movement of her tongue. Beatrice went wide eyed then pressed her jaw tight, signaling Loretta with a look of full understanding what she had to do. Douglas jerked his wife closer, punching her twice with a tight fist. She saw stars but recovered, tasting blood in her mouth. He tried setting up one more slap and punch as Loretta accepted his rough treatment, reaching behind to seize the knife. Touching wood, grabbing tight. In one motion she withdrew the weapon like a sword, thrusting it forward into her husband's side resembling a Roman legionnaire. Loretta could feel the blade glance off sturdy bone. She severed skin and muscle but missed any internal organs.

Beatrice saw the move and gasped in disgust, stepped back, watching blood pour and splatter across her pale tan sofa. "Oh my Lord," Betty choked, covering her mouth with both hands, cupped and shaking as images of Marcus' blood spurting from his open neck came back to haunt. "Why is this happening," she asked herself, feeling light headed.

"Beatrice, go to Lucy. Protect her," Loretta commanded like a battle hardened foot soldier taking control of the battle. She pushed hard into her husband who floundered way off balance. The two combatants waged war between a sturdy oak coffee table and large sofa. His wife's attack took him by complete surprise as shooting pains discharged from the long crooked gash. Douglas was being shoved over sideways, forcing his gun hand to brace himself against the soft couch while covering a bleeding wound with the free hand. He let loose a throaty scream, not so much in pain but frustrated anger, attempting to turn and fire. Loretta anticipated his counter move and shifted as much weight as possible hard into her husband, picking up on smells of blood and familiar body odor. Douglas had most of his weight spread along a gun arm trying in vain to lift himself, rendering his Beretta useless. Loretta saw Beatrice moving away from the living room holding her cell phone open, scurrying to Lucy's room.

"Hurry," Loretta screeched, feeling Douglas reach for her weapon grasping for breath and continuing to push. Hoping Lucy would be safe, Mrs. Sheets launched her second attack. She pulled hard and away on the sharp knife cutting Douglas' thumb, index finger and deep into his palm. He inhaled through gritting teeth unable to protect himself.

In reflex, the cut hand moved to his side, forcing his gun hand immobile due to falling weight. Her assailant's foot was caught under the coffee table as well, preventing any mass to shift over his legs. If so, he might be able to stand and shoot a street fighting wife at close range. "This isn't going like I thought it would," Doug yelled out in obvious disappointment!

Loretta had one knee planted firm into the sofa, gaining in high side leverage. She cocked her knife arm up well behind her head. Her other hand joined in. Together they forced a sharp blade into then through her husband's gun hand and wrist. Blood sprayed out like a lawn sprinkler from a severed artery. Douglas screamed louder, in heavy pain this time just as hand and trigger finger contracted. The 9mm Beretta went off sending a round through two sofa pillows, into a tall grandfather clock face piercing number seven spot on.

···

Lucy clutched Bee-Bee close when her bedroom door swung open, seeing Gramma Bee stumble into the room. Gramma stared into the cell phone panting, pushing buttons with frantic, trembling fingers, composing a short message. Her attempt to call Regina failed with no service available. She hit the send button, seeing her desperate plea was sent successfully. "Oh please God, let her get it," pleading, then rushing to lift Lucy into her arms. She didn't quite know what to do but hugging the child close seemed, in some way, to calm her own jittery nerves.

"My daddy's here, huh Gramma?" Lucy asked the older lady, her head buried into Beatrice's shoulder. "Is he going to hurt mommy?" Whimpering a soft cry as Mrs. Patterson felt the child's tears running down her own neck. Beatrice hugged even tighter.

"The police will come soon to help us," whispering into Lucy's ear, petting the back of her small head, feeling trembles. "Please hurry Reggie," Betty moaned in silence.

Gonzalez

Regina heard the cell phone chime and vibrate. She'd just changed lanes completing a quick pass on two slow moving minivans. Grabbing the phone with an opening flip, setting her turn signal and drifting back to the right lane. Well ahead of one slow moving family behind. She checked the sender, expecting to see Tom's name. Instead, Gonzalez read Loretta Sheets and braked hard, sliding from pavement to gravel and plumes of dust. Never hearing the minivan's horn blare to her rear, passing mad as hell. Regina focused on two words. "Help Us!" She emitted a feeble whimper of combined horror and shame, scrolling fast to Davis' name and pressing the green call button.

"Be there Chris. Please be there," Regina gushed into her phone, threw the transmission into drive, floored it back onto Interstate-5 north, moving into approaching traffic to the outside lanes with more horns screaming. Four rings and no answer. "Pick up, please!"

"Chris here," Davis answered after five rings. His sleepy speech barely audible to a frantic Gonzalez.

"Partner!" Regina let loose with high pitched yell. "Thank the Madonna. Get over to the Patterson house right now." breathing hard and performing a blind lane change to retake the minivan.

"Gonzo. Where are you?" Chris asked confused and quite sleepy. "Kennedy's watching the house ri," Davis was stopped cold when Regina screamed into her phone, also screaming by a silver van.

"Listen. I just got a text from Loretta Sheets. It says 'help us'. Are you close by?" Regina asked, almost crying into her phone while passing a small convoy of Ag trucks lumbering north to feed Bay Area residents.

Chris understood her emotions and started the car. "I'm just down the street. It's gotta be Douglas," pulling out in a long screech of hot rubber. "Get there as soon as you can partner," Davis yelled out speeding toward Anaheim Drive.

"I'll be there in about fifteen minutes. Hurry Chris!" Passing the one mile exit sign for Corral Hollow Road, Gonzalez weaved to a vacant inside lane with the engine close to wide open.

The Patterson Home

The muffled gunshot was heard by Kennedy inside his stakeout car. He jumped, looking toward the Patterson house. Chris drove up fast, jumped the curb, launching a rolling hubcap next to the big sycamore tree and settling into an empty Crosby driveway. "What the hell?" Kennedy mumbled opening his door.

Inside, Loretta and Douglas struggled for the upper hand, so to speak. Blood poured and smeared through much of the living room as well as two combatants. Douglas' gun hand swelled becoming numb and useless but did everything possible to fend off his leopard-like wife from gaining control. His pistol lay flat, static on a blood stained sofa. Loretta reloaded for one final attack, planning to swing for her husband's neck or face, making for an awkward target. They rolled into a clumsy pile, falling off the couch entangled and skirmishing. Douglas couldn't quite regain an upper hand with his loss of blood beginning to have effect.

...

Davis' car still rocked back and forth while he jumped from the front seat, checking his gun and waving Kennedy to move. Deciding against front door entry, remembering Betty's side door being loose with a failing lock. Hearing Kennedy's steps from behind just before reaching a small doorway, Chris formed a plan.

"Go around back. You'll see a window and door into her kitchen," Chris instructed the all ears patrolman trying to catch his breath. "If you see any trouble inside you have to charge in. If not, wait for my order. Got it?" Kennedy made clear eye contact as he withdrew his sidearm. A well worn older .45 caliber. He pulled the action loading a round and nodded in confirmation. Chris was struck how calm the patrolman appeared. Davis waited for Kennedy to move into place before tampering with the defective door. All clear from the patrolman's side. He listened close, hearing muffled sounds coming from inside, rotating the knob a half turn. The lock was set. Applying more pressure, feeling it give slightly, he leaned into and pushed on the frail door adding more weight in gradual increases. Still closed. Davis pressed his foot up against the very bottom sill shoving in concert with his left hip. The failed lock gave way and the door clicked open with little noise. Quiet as possible with his gun drawn, a nervous detective entered an empty kitchen. Checking the room, he saw Kennedy watching every move through the rear window. Acknowledging one another by waiving pistols. Davis heard low groans come from the living room followed by breaking glass.

Douglas rolled onto his back, kicking the oak coffee table, spilling vases and pictures into broken pieces. He saw the shiny Beretta on the sofa with a small streak of blood along the handle, laying motionless just under eye level. Desperate now to reach his weapon, put one into Loretta's eye and end this ridiculous fight. He kept his cut hand pressed on his wife's chin forcing her to breathe through puckered lips and sucking air between clenched teeth. Her husband's blood trickled around tight lips, spitting drops from her mouth. Doug's left arm became wedged under Loretta's right arm, elevating her elbow which kept the dangerous knife hand at bay. She squirmed both feet attempting to stay above her husband thus preventing him from reaching the pistol. They inched along the floor fighting for summit positions. Douglas having to remove his wife to reach the gun as Loretta must stay on top to deliver one more fatal stab.

A beleaguered deputy sensed his strength beginning to wane, little by little, knowing he'd easily get the upper hand if not losing so much blood. No choice now but to put together one last overwhelming effort. Gathering enough resolve to squeeze Loretta as tight as possible with his left arm, which raised her knife hand further, straight up over her head. She stayed on top with her feet pushing against anything that held in place. Like a high school wrestler, Douglas simply rolled himself counterclockwise, forcing his bleeding wife below. The upper hand would be his if he could free his left arm. She kept pushing on her toes now to maintain leverage and weight, over his pinned arm.

"Fuck you my dear," Douglas hissed pulling all he had left in freeing his restrained arm. Loretta was below now, under control, apart from one last possible move. Her husband had to release both hands to reach the pistol granting Loretta use of her knife hand once again. But only temporary.

"I may get in one more stab before he kills me," Loretta planned her attack, scheming with extreme strategy.

Douglas made a mistake by turning as far left as possible, seeking to grab the Beretta. Looking away from a squirming wife, realizing she was about to stab again! Turning in time to raise his wounded right arm and blocking her last possible swing. He reached for her weapon ignoring his badly wounded gun hand still able to seize the knife handle, ripping it clear of her grip. She fought his armed hand. Douglas wrapped both legs around Loretta's torso keeping her immobile. Her husband felt glory was his, raised his hand and knife, prepared to sink the wide blade into her exposed pink neck. Loretta gave a quick scream anticipating his next move. Her weight pinned to the floor, his legs wrapping any escape, unarmed, elbow jammed on her forehead, his hand held high, cocked, holding a knife smeared with blood, in place, to be inserted inside her neck severing cartilage and thick arteries, blackness, death.

Eyes closed, Loretta imagined Lucy in a soft dress, all smiles, safe and delightful. "You're dead, go quietly," Douglas whispered lowering his head a little closer to her face. She could feel his breath cascading across her bruised cheek, tensing to receive the strike. Nothing yet. Anticipating death, panic set in setting off acute trembling. Nothing yet but sensing odd movements.

Regina

Gonzalez blasted one last mile up I-5 to Corral Hollow, blowing right through two stop signs guarding a dusky three way intersection. Getting way beyond reckless, her car was thrown into the opposite lane, pretty much an out of control skid. She was fortunate today no oncoming cars approached. Keeping her speed, running stop lights, passing slower cars, hoping to be spotted by a city cruiser. On cue, she flew by an unseen patrol car waiting a left turn arrow onto Tracy Boulevard.

Stunned by the compact's rate of speed, red and yellow caution lights burst on as patrol woman Michelle Wuertz punched her Dodge, starting a high pitched siren. Regina heard the wail, slowing somewhat to let the patrol car catch and feeling much better.

Wuertz closed fast as lanes cleared of confused drivers stopping to give way. Nearing a curious compact car she noticed the driver holding something outside an open window. It wasn't a gun. Looking more like a wallet as she inched closer. Regina waved the cop forward keeping her badge facing the overtaking patrol car. She spotted her shining star, aware now the small car carried a fellow cop. Michelle dropped her passenger window.

"Where to detective?" Wuertz yelled, as two cars sped along Tracy Boulevard side by side, much too fast.

"Follow me. Keep your lights and siren on," Regina yelled back.

"What's up?" Michelle had to know, head swapping front to side, somehow keeping her patrol car parallel.

"Murder!" Gonzalez shot back.

"Wooooo, let's go!" A petite woman screamed over her blaring siren, signaling 'all in.' Together the two girls screeched and swerved through Tracy, past strip malls, fast food courts, light commercial and a mile of white condos. Hardly a San Francisco style car chase but quite dangerous nonetheless. Regina noticed the following cop enjoying her ride, yelling out roars with an ear to ear grin. Nearing Arlington Street Gonzalez motioned her follower with a sliced throat signal, to cut her siren. The detective lead the way to Anaheim Drive and her friend, Betty.

Before entering Betty's home, Wuertz was instructed to arrange more back up, an ambulance and stay on guard at the front door. "If you see any man leaving that isn't black, shoot him," Regina ordered. Michelle drew her gun changing to severe. Regina hauled her sidearm also running a direct line to Betty's front door. She planned bursting inside, breaking a heavy door jamb, but tried the handle first. In luck again. Unlocked. Entering and expecting gunfire, she kept a high gun and direct aim forward. Her first view inside was of her partner.

Patterson House

"Drop it. Let it go or I'll blow your crazy brains all over the couch." Hearing a voice she recognized, Loretta opened one eye to see Detective Davis pulling back hard on her husband's knife arm. Chris jammed a knee into Doug's back shoving his .45 muzzle hard into his left ear, bending his head way over and pulling harder yet on the knife arm. Douglas wailed in agony this time, as shoulder joints cracked and tendons snapped. His arm went limp and a heavy knife fell meaningless onto bloody sofa pillows. Douglas Sheets went dizzy, wheeling off balance, crashing forehead first to a heavy coffee table then the floor, freeing his trapped wife.

Loretta opened both eyes seeing Detective Davis wrench her husband's hands together, clicking handcuffs tight. Standing over a wounded fellow officer of the law, pulling hard and fast, dragging Douglas away from his sobbing wife. Over at last.

Mrs. Sheets panted hard knowing she just cheated death. Knowing she fought a good fight. Knowing she kept her daughter safe. Rage flooded her core. She kneeled, beginning to swing both arms, hard, wild, out of control. Fists went crashing onto her husband's back, neck and jaw. Repeated over and over. "I'm the mother of your child you fucking bastard!" Crying enraged words between sobs and swings.

Chris enjoyed Loretta's onslaught but knew he had to stop it, and did. He moved slow to pull Loretta into his arms, holding the woman close, feeling her tall upper body heave with heavy breaths. Her arms continued to swing with muted follow through punches over the detective's shoulder. Chris pushed Loretta's head next to his until she finally went limp. She could only sob, held upright by Chris' arms. Davis loved it, saved a life, risked his for her, the detective loved this job! He inspected the uprooted living room imagining her ferocious death struggle.

Regina appeared from the front entry way surprising both the detective and Mrs. Sheets. Gonzalez paused to get her wits about her, glaring at the amount of blood on Betty's sofa. Imagining the most terrible right away. "Where's Beatrice?" Regina asked in a soft way, panting with a sob, expecting bad news and lowering her weapon.

"She's in Lucy's bedroom taking care of my girl," Loretta spoke proudly as Gonzalez rushed down a dark hallway in search of her friend.

"You, are one tough lady," Chris Davis whispered into her ear.

"Your safe houses suck," Loretta responded, unlocking his hold, looking back at Davis, smeared in bloody sweat. Grateful. She gazed at an unconscious assailant, held tight by a black detective. Douglas' right ankle and foot twitched with each comatose impulse, as if struggling to get away.

"Detective Davis, I have to check on my daughter."

"Go," said Chris. She took one awkward stride over a limp husband, turned sharp and delivered a hard kick to Doug's twitching knee with her left foot then ran wild to hold Lucy tight. "Go," Chris chuckled.

•••

Regina moved fast to find Lucy's room aching to make sure Beatrice was all right. Reaching the child's door, shut tight and deciding once more to forgo the quick entrance. "Let's not scare hell out of a young girl and her adopted grandma," Gonzalez warned herself and turned a brass doorknob with a firm twist, swinging the door inward a few inches. "Don't let her be hurt," she begged.

Inside, unaware of what happened to Loretta, Beatrice put herself between Lucy and the creepy door. She kept one hand attached to her granddaughter, wielding a heavy glass candle holder in the other, asserting close contact with Lucy behind. "If that's you Douglas, stay away from here," an armed older woman growled out. Lucy buried her face into Mrs. Patterson's leg.

Swinging in a little more, Regina peeked around the bedroom door, only showing her face, sporting a tight smile. "You two ladies okay in here?" Seeing both girls unharmed was a big relief.

"Oh my, Reggie! Thank goodness it's you." Beatrice relaxed her shoulders, relieved and dropped her weapon with a thud. She turned, knelt down, hugging Lucy tight and letting jittery hands run through her fluffy hair. "It's all over my darling."

Walking inside, Regina only wanted to embrace her friend then heard Loretta's voice and footsteps coming down the hallway. Beatrice stood, seeing Lucy's mom emerge in the doorway. She moved to receive Gonzalez but wouldn't let go of Lucy's tiny hand.

"Hi baby," Loretta whispered to her daughter. Lucy saw the blood smears on her mom's face, upsetting the young gal at first. Mrs. Sheets stooped and Lucy, once again, ran between outstretched arms. They hugged firm, as mother and daughter rolled to the floor cuddling each other in laughs and tears. Regina moved close to Betty, feeling her friend's warm frail body lean into Reggie's strong arms, kissing a wrinkled forehead, relieved.

•••

For the second time inside a month, police arrived in force on Anaheim Drive. Yet another crime scene demanding to be secured. Flashing lights lit the evening suburb, from an idling ambulance in the Patterson driveway. Neighbors arrived once again, each wondering what's happened to their quiet enclave. Identical to Marcus Crosby's murder, Mark Kennedy was in charge of crime scene security. Caution tape was being strung along Anaheim, getting some much needed help from Michelle Wuertz. She, being assigned to lend assistance, chatted up details with Kennedy and Gonzalez regarding those allowed inside their yellow, plastic perimeter. She made general small talk with a rather handsome ambulance driver too. This driver, also present during the Crosby murder, remembered house details and various surroundings. Especially images of blood running down a clean concrete driveway. "Tough neighborhood," telling officer Wuertz with his best, I think you're pretty hot, look in his eyes. Fire department vehicles were a late show, adding to a growing collection of emergency personnel which shaped the location with far too many onlookers

Anderson made an appearance with Chief Yung following close behind, surveying the collection of emergency personnel. Both officers entered the Patterson home looking for positive information. Tracy's Chief of Police hoped this may finally put an end to a baffling Crosby murder.

Patricia Bailey made her entrance. Mulling around outside, not getting much footage, no substantive interviews and unable to slip inside the guarded perimeter. She did manage to saddle up to officer Kennedy demanding to see Captain Anderson.

"He's very busy right now mame." Kennedy tried shielding his boss from a pushy reporter, having no clue whatsoever of her relationship with the high ranking officer.

"He'll listen to me officer Kennedy," Bailey said in a way, that even primed Kennedy to understand what she implied. He did a quick double take, faced the attractive reporter direct then paused to study her expression. She didn't flinch.

Kennedy ran one hand threw his hair contemplating her request. "I'll let him know, Miss Bailey." Mark Kennedy relayed to the pushy redhead.

Inside, a chaotic theater played out in the Patterson living room and kitchen. Douglas Sheets had just been strapped to a metal gurney. Oxygen mask in place and wounds attended. He was alive but nowhere close to reality which meant no questions tonight. The lead emergency tech's opinion was, "leaning toward stable for now but remaining critical." He needed to get the injured man to a hospital fast. Beatrice stood in her kitchen watching a steady river of crime technicians, medical staff, cops, firemen and detectives enter her front door, drift through a blood stained attack site and soon exiting the back door. Mrs. Patterson just wanted it all to end, now.

Anderson, Gonzalez and Yung were doing their best to deliver questions to a spent and weary Loretta Sheets. Getting nowhere. Mrs. Sheets would only speak to Chris Davis even though her first priority remained Lucy. Wanting to hold her daughter, give her comfort and be alone. "I'll talk to the police tomorrow," she told Chris. "Tomorrow will be better." Which ended any additional questions right now.

Regina, Alex, and Billy stood together, side by side, engaged in quiet discussion regarding tomorrow's strategy. Mark Kennedy approached the meeting tentatively, to deliver the reporter's message to his boss. Captain Anderson noticed Kennedy, behaving quite apprehensive.

"What's up Mr. Kennedy?" Billy asked in a comfortable tone. "You look concerned?"

The patrolman hesitated as the group waited for him to say something. "A woman outside. The red headed reporter wants to speak with you. She says you'll understand." Kennedy spoke the words innocent of Anderson's situation. Billy's attention fixed on Kennedy's face with clenched teeth, without responding.

Chief Yung heard the patrolman's words loud and clear, knowing right away his homicide unit's team leader was screwing a reporter. A sexy member of the press. "God knows how much has been leaked to her," Alex Yung told himself, resulting in a dejected face.

Captain Anderson's heart sank realizing he'd just been exposed. Billy couldn't fault Kennedy. The officer was simply doing his job. In a quick moment, Anderson knew how stupid he must appear, staring down at his own brown shoes unable to think of something to say. "What the hell," the Captain thought in silence. "Maybe Yung didn't pick up on it?" Hoping in vain, eyeballing Kennedy once again. "You tell her I'll be out when I can," Billy instructed the helpless cop. Kennedy turned to resume his security duties wondering if he'd just fucked up.

Chief Yung stood erect and stoic rubbing his forehead. Regina's face turned bright red, sympathetic for her boss and reflecting on her own situation, unable to interject. "Let's call it a night here. Leave someone on guard. Inside, all night." Alex Yung ordered his homicide leader, leaving Anderson a stern look, Regina a smile, then departing in a hurry. Words unspoken. No real surprise when Kennedy was ordered to stay the evening! Fire engines left in relative silence. Douglas Sheets went special delivery to a nearby Kaiser Hospital. Neighbors dispersed after polite 'goodnights'. Allowing Chris Davis to give Loretta one last check.

"Will you and Lucy be okay tonight?" Davis asked Mrs. Sheets, pushing her hair to one side and still trying to get cleaned up. "I'll come by tomorrow and check on you, if you don't mind," Davis spoke a bit sheepish.

"I think I'd like that detective," Loretta told the tall detective, for some reason noticing how sensitive Davis behaved, hugging him tight. Feeling secure, finally relaxed, saying, "thank you for saving my life," without voicing a word.

Chief Yung

"No Abbey we haven't questioned Douglas Sheets yet," Chief Yung bemoaned into the phone. "He's still recovering and unconscious most of the time. It's only been a little more than twelve hours for God's sake," raising his voice, intending to let Abbey Crosby know how aggravated he'd become. Abbey paused to give Alex time to calm down.

"That rotten cop has to be involved in my son's murder. Somehow?" Mrs. Crosby told the Chief with her voice breaking into high pitched squeaks. Alex could hear the woman panting hard into the phone. He felt good about her over the top tension.

Speaking very cool, Chief Yung decided to raise her hackles even higher. "Not too long ago you swore the Braden's killed Marcus," quietly letting his statement sink in. "I'm quoting now. You said it had to be them." Alex applied a mocking tone, knowing Abbey was caught singing a different tune.

"Why else would the cop try killing his wife and the old lady. Those two must know something? Have you questioned them?" Mrs. Crosby kept the pressure on.

"Let us handle the investigation. Anything's possible in this case," Yung sighed into his phone. "We have to stay patient. When Sheets recovers, maybe he'll talk." Offering nothing more. The Chief prepared to conclude this conversation now but Abbey wasn't finished.

"Any news coming from the hospital? Is there a chance he's going to die?" Abbey asked settling down somewhat.

"He's stable but unconscious. The doctors say he should recover and perhaps awaken by tonight or tomorrow morning." Yung divulged, knowing he shouldn't hand over any more news. "Douglas Sheets isn't going to die."

"The sheriff's under guard I hope," Abbey stated in continued hot pursuit, much too serious which angered the police chief even more.

"Good grief Crosby," Alex addressed the matriarch in last name only, deliberate and to some extent trying to be rude. "I'll let you know when I hear something." Killing his connection. Abbey repeated Chief Yung's name into a lost call, unaware their talk had ended. The older woman remained stationary, cradling her small phone between a thin waist and the crook of a bent elbow. Thinking, like always, when events happen to go against her. Thinking. Abbey's strongest suit.

"What the hell, I'll try the evening news one last time," whispering Patricia Bailey's name to herself.

"Here she is. Miss big time detective," Maria shouted as Regina approached the round lunch table.

"All this TV stuff is so stressful. Does my hair look right?" Gonzalez joked getting more raised eyebrows than laughs.

Pam did extend a decent high five letting her friend know she handled it well. "Sorry gang but I have another shoot scheduled in about an hour." Regina shook her head giving curls of long hair a chance swing free. She held a glamour pose, playing out her new role way too long before finally sitting to join her lunch crew.

The police station had been a mob scene most of Thursday morning. Reporters moved about the parking lot grabbing everything that moved going into or leaving Station 3009. Most employees and cops stayed inside, hiding out, giving the press time to die down. They did just after lunch hour, as many reporters rushed to Kaiser Hospital on mistaken news of Douglas Sheets undergoing a sudden recovery. The gang, just three as Gonzalez was busy giving opinions on television, saw an opening and took the chance. Successful in making it to Chiles undetected. A text to notify Regina concerning location and once more, another lunch, catching up and added gossip.

Chatting an exciting morning of events, each woman, one by one noticed Denise's new hair style of contrasting color. "Girl, what the hell d-juw do to yo hair?" Regina blared in her best slang impression, staring at a blonde side stripe highlighting her new bituminous black cut. The married woman played it cool and didn't bite. Gonzo looked at her menu but couldn't resist glancing back to the loyal wife. "You've changed since our last meeting," the detective said with her sarcastic tone expecting a response and new information.

"Oh yes detective. She's a changed woman," Pam said, brimming with an overflow of hidden meaning. Denise, unlike her usual self, didn't say a word. Her eyes moved back and forth from menu to Regina's face. Eventually sipping a taste of red wine. Regina's detective side moved forward recalling their last lunch and remembered how they left. Denise being awestruck over Pam's latest encounter. Regina glanced to Maria, squinting a quiet request for breaking news. Maria shot back an affirmative look combined with a slow, positive nod, announcing and confirming the detective's assumption. Gonzo returned to Denise who sat back in her chair wobbling a stemmed wine glass, arm thrown over Pam's shoulder imitating a sex crazed rock star.

"Tell me you didn't. Please Denise, tell me you," stopping to absorb the new data. "This is too weird," Gonzalez spoke without thinking, appearing shaken.

"Hey. Hey, keep your opinions to yourself," Pam shouted, smiling wild, protecting her new found friendship.

"Did you?" Regina stammered. "How could," stopping to check the table. "You're all putting me on. Aren't you?" the detective whispered as she leaned way out over the table. This topic was a little too personal for open discussion. Regina looked close at each associate. Candid faces answered.

"Tell me straight Denise," Regina asked the relaxed and proud woman.

"Tell me about your boyfriend," the newly outed girl said with a soft smile. "And I'll give you all the dirty little details you need," talking in her most sultry, Hollywood voice.

"It's not," pausing for words, "You two? Together? Is it?" Regina had to clarify their standing, pointing at Pam first then back to Denise.

Pam shook her head negative. "She's found her own...partner," emphasizing 'partner' for effect, easing Regina's anxiety a small amount. Giggles around the table added to the lunch group's incredible revelations. "Now, your boyfriend's name?"

Regina froze solid. "I'm short on time ladies. Let's order lunch." Gonzalez hid her red face behind a tall menu unable to handle this anymore.

Estefan

Clay Blevins walked very slow. Hobbling would be more like it, leaning hard on his walking cane. Due to his right shoulder and upper arm being wrapped in heavy bandages. Not sure if what he planned to do today was a smart idea. The aging grower seemed drawn to his idea and simply put, struck him as just a good thing to do. Continuing to put one foot in front of the other, splitting two orchards on a narrow dirt road. Almond trees maturing to his right and a deep, aging walnut grove on the opposite side. Bare almond limbs spread upward, appearing thin and spindly, holding a spattering of leaves. Almost twice as tall, walnut trees sported stout limbs with tangled branches. Clay loved the silence and earthy smells, covering every dormant season the way a wooden warehouse coops unvented air. Every four or five rows, small packs of mourning doves whistled away at low height further back among protective trees. They settle in, comfortable, out of sight and sound. He felt better with each step, spotting a gray farmhouse and barn a couple hundred yards up the dusty road. Clay stopped to rest and look contented on his beloved trees. Sunshine warmed his face, saying thank you to something unseen for all he had and all he had became. "It's the right thing to do," Blevins' spoke aloud, hobbling along on dusty footsteps, flaring speedy birds, quiet growth and orderly trees.

"Senior Blevins. Mother of Jesus be with you. Please come in," greeted in simple awe and silent shame by Louisa, Estefan's mother. Clay stayed near the front door, removing his hat then embracing the frail woman. He patted Louisa's back knowing her pain ran deep with sorrow, feeling a genuine greeting. They stood silent as Blevins slipped his arm around her shoulder, headed toward wooden chairs sitting on the front porch.

"Louisa," Clay started, "we've known each other for a long time. Don't let any of this damage our friendship." The grower tried putting a good lady at ease as tears began to stain her wrinkled brown skin. They both sat looking out over a scrubby grass yard leading to the southern edge of Clay's orchard. Two narrow black and white magpies glided awkward into a corner tree. Their weight bent a feeble branch downward while bobbing for stability. "It was just a lousy accident." Estefan's mother felt slight relief and offered Mr. Blevins something to drink. She asked what brought him out here today.

"I'd love some of your sweet lemonade, if it's not too much trouble," Clay proposed, remembering many hot days working the orchards when Louisa showed, like a dream, carrying jugs of her icy drink. Everyone would drink heavy and be relieved for a moment from their blazing hot labor.

"It will be my pleasure Mr. Clay Blevins," she responded. Before Louisa could leave, Blevins spoke again.

"Is Estefan at home?" he asked, standing in respect for a woman leaving the room, seeing Louisa stopped in the doorway but not turning around.

"He is senior. Should I get him for you?" turning back to look at Mr. Blevins with fear ruling her face and ringing nervous, weathered hands.

"You have nothing to fear Louisa. I just want to talk with your son. With your permission of course. I hope to make sure the boy doesn't," Clay paused, to search for suitable words. "I want to make sure your boy gets through all this." The grower seated himself again in an old wooden chair hoping the boy's mother understood. "There's something he needs to see."

Louisa gave Clay her endearing smile, realizing he was here to help her son. "Senior Blevins, you are the finest man I've met." She left to fetch Estefan and lemonade.

It was a nervous meeting, for both, when Estefan appeared at a squeaking door. He sat uncomfortable for a few minutes, listening to the elder man speak. Clay did his very best to comfort the young boy. Estefan suffered deep guilt at first but the blame changed more and more into shameful stupidity, as Clay continued to talk. He had to convince the boy to learn from his mistake but not to let this mistake ruin his young life. After iced lemonade, warming sunshine and a few jokes, the boy and wounded man grew easy with one another.

"I have something to show you. Come, walk with me," Clay Blevins requested. Two friends left the front porch together while Louisa watched in silence, safe inside, behind a dining room window. They walked slow down a dirt road, trees to each side, hand in hand, one leaning on a thin cane, talking until they reached an intersection. A corner orchard of almond saplings met the face of mature walnuts, as an adjacent field of alfalfa stretched far away to the southwest. Direct sun lingered over the green feed, almost ready to be mowed.

Clay stopped to look over a large rectangular field of fresh planted saplings. Young almond trees, establishing roots, sucking irrigated moisture, ready to bud new branches early next spring. A brand new orchard.

"You and your father worked hard to plant these trees," Clay acknowledged their efforts admiring the healthy young orchard. A large flock of gray doves settled among branches and open dirt on wings whistling like sharp flutes.

"Si Senior Blevins. It's hard work to plant new trees," Estefan spoke with pride.

"Yes. It is hard," Blevins said quietly stepping into soft dirt making up the orchard's survival. "That's why I'm leaving you this orchard, Estefan. When you're older, you will have the trees and you'll understand why I wanted you to have them." Clay looked at the boy, nodding his head in a show of respect then reached out to touch one young frail limb, feeling the tree's life. A planting for many harvest seasons ahead. A planting for a young boy's harvest too.

"Senior Blevins, I will take good care of these trees." Estefan could say nothing more. Choking sobs and weeping large tears over his mistake but comprehending the gift he just received.

An aging grower was thankful too. Estefan's aim had been near perfect. His wound wasn't bad enough to be fatal but perfectly sufficient to halt chemo treatments for his colon cancer. The delayed therapy gave Blevins a brief open window to walk on his own again, to view his cherished trees, see and smell his land he loved so much. He thought of Estefan's uncle, Enrique. Their escape from a fistfight in Mexico, days fly fishing cold rivers with him and his daughter, the way he cared for his trees, a man he grew to love. Knowing it could also be his final walk. Clay Blevins did the right thing, shaking Estefan's sunburned hand and moving away slow, down a dirt road between the trees he loved.

•••

Thursday ended with Douglas Sheets improving but far from ready to interrogate. Friday might offer a modest amount of promise. Two hospital doctors agreed his vital signs demonstrated firm stability. "Maybe tomorrow," issuing positive statements to Tracy's police department, possibly allowing access. But not before their patient had passed beyond critical condition. He also had to be awake!

At Station 3009, most of the press commotion subsided. Anderson scheduled a Friday morning meeting to consider strategy. In reality, Chief Yung ordered Billy to get his staff prepared, knowing they needed to talk. Regina Gonzalez gave a late afternoon interview to Patricia Bailey, curious to see the way her boss's lady friend handled herself. Bailey turned out to be quite clever and dogged in her questioning. Regina was impressed, to say the least, almost slipping twice in revealing confidential information. Davis reviewed police reports one last time but couldn't turn his eyes away from file photos. Scrutinizing, detailing, matching, guessing. He had to leave early, keeping the promise he made to check on Loretta, which was about courtesy tonight. Mrs. Sheets admired the detective's concern and they sat for close to an hour and close to each other, talking of yesterday's near tragedy. Davis enjoyed the way Lucy would interrupt, turn sharp and run off noisily to entertain Gramma. Sparking some of his happier days. Loretta couldn't help but feel good around her closer. "Best day ever," Mrs. Sheets repeated. Davis had slammed the door on Douglas last night. So did Loretta Sheets, hugging Chris goodnight. No questions tonight.

Station 3009

On schedule, Regina arrived twenty minutes late to work. After all, she was recovering from a full week of chases, attempted murder, duck hunting, romance, sexy tales and little sleep. She crashed hard last night, never stirring still in dire need of a few more hours to get even. Gonzalez made it in however, shrugging off her partner's digs and Anderson's dirty looks.

"What's shakin' guys?" Regina shot out with a tight smirk letting them know she didn't care. "Are we headed to the Patterson house or do we get Douglas first?" Regina asked with an evil look on her sleepy face. "Any word on his condition?" hoping for any kind of news.

"Sheets stabilized last night," Anderson informed his homicide detectives, just receiving the update himself. "Hopefully, we'll be going at him later today." Scratching an eyebrow, wondering what Sheets might offer during interrogation. "My office, in about ten minutes," Billy commanded, then checked his watch feeling pressed for time. "We need to talk," sounding serious.

Chris and Regina retreated to messed up cubicles. Gonzalez gathered some documents while Davis opened the Crosby file once again. He checked notes, reports, and findings. Many of which were written by Douglas Sheets investigating Sarah's murder. Scattered among loose papers and printed emails lay a small stack of pictures. Photos of Marcus Crosby, Sarah Crosby, murder scenes and witnesses lay untouched on his desk. Chris began asking himself, "what am I missing here?" He wondered if it might help to put away the crime reports for now. "What else can I do?" Questioning himself, thumbing through file photos. His mind went blank. Clear might be a better description but his attention waned, randomly spreading pictures over paper documents covering his desk top.

Pics of Marcus Crosby with a straight face and a poor resolution profile. Sarah followed. In one large, slight angled pose, she smiled akin to a high school graduation portrait. Another picture caught her staring straight into the camera. Acting, posing, asking, "why are you taking this picture of me?" One more black and white captured her profile with soft shadows, skin detail and subtle bone structure. It struck Chris' attention. He looked closer studying every minute detail. Hair, ears, nose, lips, eyes, cheeks and chin. Sarah's long chin kept stealing Davis' attention. He slid one more picture from the stack. Franny Braden looked back at Chris, almost ashamed, peeking hard at the woman who captivated him for a short time. Chris studied her too. Nose, eyes and lips. Continuing his scrutiny of full lips, fantasizing about feeling her full lips again. Guilty and forced to a stop. Over to Sarah, then back to Franny and to Sarah once more. Comparing features each time. "It's odd," striking him with an unexpected realization. Disregarded. Sarah didn't look closely like her mother. Back and forth between pictures again. "They just don't look like mother and daughter?" Chris said to himself. He laid out the final three photos in a loose row noting the subtle resemblance at best. One contained Henry Braden which forced Davis to mumble aloud, "Henry contains no resemblance at all to his daughter. This is weird?"

"Let's go partner. We need to talk some strategy and schedule. Boss is waiting." Gonzalez shook Chris on his right shoulder. Nowhere close to the way his deep thoughts were shaking him.

■■■

"Sit down you two. Chief Yung called and he'll be joining us, so keep your crummy jokes and baseball metaphors to yourselves," Anderson told his detectives displaying a semi-serious mood. "Got it Gonzo!" Billy demanded, getting settled, checking his cell, making sure silent ring was set before slipping into his shirt pocket.

"What now, Captain?" Gonzalez asked, anticipating her boss's answer.

"It's up to Sheets now. How fast does he recover and how much Douglas will tell us," Anderson remarked, running neutral with his enthusiasm. "I think the asshole just clams up for God knows how long. He's too irrational to confess right away," Billy offered his opinion.

"You never know with these guys," Regina countered including a subtle sigh. She remembered a number of killers throughout her career who felt compelled to talk openly of their crimes. They had to. "Sometimes you couldn't stop 'em if you wanted too. We'll see?" She concluded.

"You sound optimistic Gonzalez," Captain Anderson added, looking at his detective in a curious way. "You know something we don't?" Billy asked, his eyes burning a hole through her casual exterior.

"Just a hunch Captain," she shot back. "Just a hunch." Much softer. Regina had a passing image of her and Tom on his living room floor. She lowered her sight to forgo any type of challenge. Davis remained quiet, listening to their exchange but absorbed by similar images, with somebody else.

"Tell me your hunches," Chief Yung asked with his stern but respectful voice, taking Regina by surprise. He liked to hear a detective's hunches and opinions while conducting investigations. Setting his morning coffee on the corner of Anderson's desk and sliding a chair in close to Gonzalez, taking his seat. "Good morning all," Alex Yung announced, wanting to keep the meeting loose and everyone talking. He took two drinks of hot coffee giving all three cops a chance to speak.

Chris stayed mum. Billy chimed in. "I don't expect to get much from Sheets." Billy reiterated his belief, looking back to his boss to gauge a response. He guessed the Chief as neutral but misread his bosses judgment. Alex Yung was disappointed with Anderson. Fooling around with a sexy reporter wasn't permissible to a person with Billy's rank. Jeopardizing Tracy Police Department's integrity, but Yung would give him a second chance to redeem himself. He always did.

"I'm not so sure Chief," Regina contested her boss looking at Yung then to Davis, wondering if her partner might help out. "We want to get at this nut right away," she added, looking toward Davis again. Chris didn't seem to be paying full attention.

"What are you expecting from our patient," Yung asked, serious in the way he phrased 'our patient'.

"He knows something more about Sarah Crosby's murder. Something we don't know. I'm sure of it," telling her simple hunch to the Chief. "We pegged Douglas to be Marcus Crosby's killer. Possibly." Regina placed firm emphasis on her last word. "If handled right, we might be able to solve our mysteries."

"What about you Chris? You're not saying much," Chief Yung asked the detective, giving Anderson a fast look before sipping more brew, then looked to Davis.

"We have to pressure Douglas. That's a no brainer," Davis finally spoke. He relaxed into his chair feeling confident about his next comment. "A fire must be lit under Loretta Sheets too. We know she's holding back information. Probably about both murders. At a minimum perhaps, leading us to the person who does know." Davis saw Franny Braden unfold in his mind but didn't have the evidence needed to breach her name. "They should be much more willing to talk now."

"Maybe Beatrice too," Davis spoke in low volume but urgent tone. No one else in the room gave much credence to Mrs. Patterson's connection, seeing the older lady as just that. A dear old woman. His comment went all but unnoticed. Davis had one last opinion to offer as a fierce debate raged at light speed in his own mind. "This could be so dumb to bring up now," he said to himself stalling, trying to make a fair judgment.

"You have something on your mind, Mr. Davis. Continue please," Alex said with Regina and Billy assuming the same.

"As far as Marcus Crosby's murder, the true wild card to me, seems to be Franny Braden. I want to put her against the wall and throw rocks!" Chris realized he sounded way too dramatic, hoping he didn't come across too personal also. Davis admitted silently to being way too close with Mrs. Braden and it bothered him now. Gonzalez responded with a slight chuckle. Anderson cringed. Yung agreed half heartedly but in silence. The Chief always held a nagging question in the back of his mind about Henry Braden and the man's guns. To Alex Yung it fit. "She's holding something back," Chris concluded, anxious to find out if he was alone.

Nobody responded right off. They let Davis' comments sink in for a moment. Alex Yung spoke first. "What do you think Billy?" Anxious to hear the Captain's thoughts.

"We don't seem to be getting much from the Braden's. I'm not sure what they could be withholding," Billy said while rubbing his hands in repeated, nervous loops. "I would concede their motive if they carried out the execution. Henry Braden probably makes that shot okay but he doesn't seem the type?" Anderson failed to show much conviction. At this point, Chief Yung grew convinced his Captain was stymied by this case.

Tracy's Police Chief listened for more comments, drinking coffee, standing, peering through the office window. A beautiful morning had developed outside. Further comments failed to arrive. "Love the weather this time of year," the Chief remarked, noticing a clear and calm day developing. Afternoon sunshine would warm the valley for a few hours, following the morning's cold but rain was in the evening forecast. "We're stalled again on this Crosby murder. That seems certain," Alex said, admiring bright sunshine and colorful leaves strewn across his headquarters' green lawn.

"You two go for it," Yung ordered, pointing to Regina and Chris. "Douglas is ready to talk right now," announcing the hospital called an hour ago. "Run his ass through the ringer. Go after his wife too. Don't let up."

"Yes," Davis said out loud with a raised fist. Regina looked at her partner and grinned.

"Billy, get me a report later today. Tomorrow morning at the latest," Chief Yung said leaving the room in a hurry.

Douglas

"Yea, I'll talk to 'em," Douglas told a middle aged nurse after receiving the all-clear from his doctor. Sheets drifted back into reality during Friday's early morning hours. He complained of dry mouth around four thirty in the morning and stayed awake since. Continuing to get stronger as the morning wore on. "Send 'em in. I don't give a shit," Sheets bellowed and squirmed, tearing one cord free from his vital signs monitor. His nurse rushed in reconnecting and resetting the watchful device. "Bring 'em in nurse Ratched, they want to hear my story," Sheets yelled from his murkier than ever world of make believe.

Ratched threw up her hands, more than willing to open the door for Regina and Chris. "So, look who's here," Douglas said, calm and pink and smiling and squirming and waiving his non-tethered arm like a waiter showing diners to their table. "Tracy's finest. Sit down, get comfortable. Would you like anything? My nurse Ratched has been instructed to bring whatever you like." Sheets pointed to a blue clad nurse shaking her head, slow and deliberate, delivering a serious scowl. Two detectives tried ignoring a disillusioned casualty letting the nurse know her patient's shouting meant nothing to them. Ratched couldn't leave the room fast enough.

"Hey nurse! Where you going?" Sheets barked very loud. Heard in the hallway, disrupting patients suffering in adjoining rooms. Detective Davis couldn't stand it anymore, closing the door with a thud.

"Shut up you deranged fuck," Chris grunted the words almost in pain then drew his sidearm. He slid a big black muzzle under Sheets' nose, cocked the hammer and pushed forward which forced Douglas' head back and mouth open. Sheets couldn't yell out now if he had too! Regina, taken by complete surprise, seeing her partner act this way only once before let him run, making sure Douglas noticed her absolute calm.

"No more shouts. No more shit. You got that!" Davis pushed harder on his weapon, opening Doug's mouth and eyes even wider. Sheets tried keeping his right eye on Chris' trigger finger, hoping mistaken pressure or poor movement wouldn't erase his own growing recovery.

"No more Sheets." Regina announced in mocking tone, hands and arms folded across her chest. She stared at Chris' pistol. Slow and deliberate, Gonzalez cradled the weapon in her hands. Covering it like hot bread, elevating the muzzle, moving her partner's intimidation from their patient's face. Douglas kept his head motionless unwilling to risk an unfortunate move.

Everyone calmed themselves. Chris holstered his sidearm after Douglas closed his mouth, lowered both eyes and prepared to talk. Like always, Chris sat back letting his partner commence her verbal attack. This time, it wouldn't be necessary. Douglas was more than ready to tell his story.

"Douglas Sheets. Good to see you again," Regina opened the dialogue. "Sorry about the stern greeting, We were told you wanted to answer some questions. True?" Gonzalez asked in a polite tone.

Doug stared at Regina with a quizzed look on his face. "I suppose I could answer some questions." He looked over to Davis with a frown. "I'm not too fond of having pistols shoved up my nose. What did you have in mind detective?" the deputy asked in an odd but calm disposition.

Regina glanced at Chris who flashed back his, 'I don't know' gesture. She slowly turned her face back to Sheets. "Did you shoot Marcus Crosby?" Regina asked point blank. Douglas didn't move, change expression or take his eyes off Regina. Sitting in silence. Quiet occupied the room. His injured right arm ached inside a new but cracked cast, pushing away too hard from Chris' pistol.

"What?" he asked, serious. Regina didn't know what to say. Standing quiet. "Is this what you two think? Why would I shoot Marcus Crosby? Hell, I was screwing his wife on the side!" Douglas came across like bragging. "Yes, Sarah Crosby and I were having an affair." Gingerly sitting up in his bed while the high strung Detective Davis stacked extra pillows beneath a sore back and behind his head.

"Yeah, we know all about your affair," Regina told him thinking little about his statement.

"Thanks detective. That feels much better," grateful to the man fluffing his pillows who almost blew his head off five minutes previous! "Uh, what do you mean? How did you know about Sarah and me?" Sheets asked in a dumfounded way.

"We know," Chris added in. "It's old news, Douglas. Continue."

"That's news to me," Douglas said and wrinkled his eyebrows, not quite sure if the two cops were lying. "Christ, I'm in hear for no reason. I was trying to shut them both up. None of this mattered?" Sheets was showing signs of mental breakdown, speaking in senseless phrases. Regina had to keep him talking.

"Douglas. Listen. We need to know why you killed Sarah Crosby? You two were having an affair and yet you killed her? Why?" Regina asked with a sense of desperation. She was afraid he'd stop talking. He went quiet for a minute or more. Chris and Regina made eye contact. They waited.

Douglas started. "I didn't murder her. We struggled that night. She wanted to break off our, you know," giving Regina his low life playboy look. "Anyway, we argued for a long time that night. It got overheated and Sarah started swinging her fists at me. I had to hit her. Only once but not too hard. She recoiled, slipped going back, fell and struck her head against the kitchen counter. Square on the corner as she went down. Heavy tile on that counter with little give. Blood went everywhere," Sheets explained his version with simple clarity. "But an accident. A pure and simple accident." Douglas wouldn't add anything more.

"You covered your ass pretty well in the trial didn't you?" Regina intimated. Douglas paused, a bit surprised.

"Good detective work," Sheets complimented her. "Very good work!"

"Why did you take so many fingerprint samples?" Chris asked, walking to Douglas' side, stuffing a loose pillow back in place.

"Making sure my own prints didn't show up. After all, I did hang out there a few times if you know what I mean," finishing his distasteful words with a big crazy smile. Detective Davis hung his head knowing now he'd been onto something, trapped knee deep in crime reports.

"What about Marcus Crosby? Did you murder him?" Chris asked.

"I've said enough. Ask my wife about Marcus. She'll give you some answers." Douglas looked to be clamming up, working hard to roll on his side. He made it with great pain to his hip.

"Do you know who killed Marcus?" Davis asked.

"I assume Henry Braden shot him. I would've, had he killed my daughter." Smiling his crazed grin, looking every bit the part, a lunatic.

"What about your wife?" Regina spoke to Douglas like a daughter. They even stared at one another before Sheets lowered his face.

"She knew what I did," Sheets replied. "I mean, she knew I was screwing Sarah. Loretta assumed I murdered her too. I had to keep my wife," Douglas stopped short on any more details. Chris and Regina knew what he was about to say.

"Jesus Christ. Willing to murder your wife." Gonzalez directed her anger at Douglas, as Chris made sure his small portable recorder was doing its job.

"I was willing to take out a few other people too," Sheets spoke eerily calm then looked Regina right into her gorgeous eyes. Gonzalez had a delightful urge to lift her weapon, aim and pull the trigger.

Franny Braden

"About what time will you be home?" Franny asked Henry with slight pleading in her voice. More of a request than question. "Don't be late. I feel weird right now."

"I'll be there in a few hours, try to relax." Henry detected her anxiety coming through his phone. All the news reports were focusing on Tuolumne County's Sherriff Department and its scandalous deputy. He thought about his daughter's murder and how it would surface all over again. Absurd speculation, new unfounded allegations, badgering reporters, cops wanting to question him and his wife. Henry knew his wife would have trouble coping with another investigation.

Franny's husband tried to get his wife to accept the reality. "You better get yourself prepared. It's most likely to start all over again. You know that my love." His words made her nervous and reassured at the same time. She counted on Henry to be the strong one.

"I know, I know," Franny declared with a high level of stress in her words. "Hurry please. I need you with me." Henry checked his watch realizing he had to finish work soon, to make it home early in the afternoon.

"I'll make it," he told himself. "Be there as soon as I can. Try to relax. Have a stiff drink. We'll leave for Tracy as soon as I get home." Telling her I love you, goodbye and hung up. Henry's interest was piqued, to say the least, by events in Tracy the other night.

Franny Braden expected their phone to begin ringing anytime soon. Images of her with the Tracy detective surfaced. She questioned her actions and self respect. "How stupid was that? To risk my marriage. Again," she chastised herself. "Henry's a good man. I don't deserve him. Strangers at the gate," she thought.

Station 3009

"He wouldn't shut up at first, Captain. But Douglas didn't tell us everything," Regina began a replay of statements to her boss, who sat bug eyed, in modest disbelief. "Sheets admitted to killing Sarah Crosby, by accident."

"Do you believe him," Anderson interrupted, wanting to hear Regina's opinion. "It all seems a little easy. Too fast."

Regina sat down, tired, feeling exhausted. "Yes. I believe him, Captain. Right down to my scared stiff ass!" Gonzalez rubbed her forehead, sweeping a right hand across her head, thick hair and down the back of a sweaty neck. Her upper body shivered and tingled indicating a sudden need to vomit. "I have to get to the bathroom."

"Okay, but what about," Anderson didn't expect Gonzo to move quite so fast. "Gees. We'll talk later. I hope?" Yelling out surprised, as Regina vanished.

Hustling from her chair out of Anderson's office she rushed down a long hallway. Forced to accept the closest bathroom, even if it was the men's room. Just in time. It flowed heavily, gagging her, hard to catch her breath, choking, flowing again, coughing, spitting, finally able to breathe. Regina dropped to one knee, panting, propping herself against a coffee colored partition. Her face almost inserted into the large bowl. Heaving in and out on every breath.

"You okay Detective Gonzalez?" officer Buck asked, finishing off a pee. "Do you need anything detective? You okay Miss Gonzalez?" Buck asked once more concerned for the detective's condition, peeking inside the stall.

Regina turned slowly to face Buck. Head spinning, weak and feeling saliva running from her lower lip to upper chin. "I'll be all right in a few minutes. Thanks Buck. It must be something I ate for lunch. Sorry to disturb you in your bathroom," Regina told the uniformed cop. With his help, Regina got herself seated on the toilet where she rested. A few minutes passed and she sensed the usual turnaround. Completely fine in a few more minutes. She flushed the toilet while Buck, flushed pink, decided to leave her be.

Gonzalez had her cell phone tucked into her jeans front pocket feeling very big right now, pushing hard on her jutting hip bone. She withdrew her smart-phone with trepidation. Two messages still waited on her call list. One from Tom. "Hoping to see you tonight!" Which Regina planned on doing. The second was most impressive, taking her by surprise, in reality, hitting her harder than a Chris Brown fistfight! She thought it over for a minute. "We'll see how it all goes this weekend. Oh shit, this is going to be weird," Gonzalez told herself in front of a large mirror, checking for drips and stains. She fussed a lock of long hair in a casual way, rubbing her stomach, feeling better all over. It was getting close to four o'clock, realizing she was running way too late, in need of getting on the road southbound to see her gringo.

She just started to leave when another guy entered the bathroom. "Oh, excuse me. I'm in the wrong bath. No I'm not," he told Regina riddled with confusion.

"Hi," was all she said, bolting from the boys john.

Regina made it back to Captain Anderson's office just as Chris returned from the Patterson house.

•••

"We can't let this opportunity slip away. Captain, they're ready to talk. Right now." Regina heard Chris' last sentence, just returning, fresh from her latest bout of love making to a toilet bowl.

"Who's ready to talk?" Gonzalez asked somewhat antagonistic, trying to get right after her latest bout of nausea. Sitting in Chris' chair fronting Anderson's desk she asked, "and whom might we be referring to?"

"Thanks for coming back Gonzo," Anderson spoke with a large dose of sarcasm, noticing her slight disheveled appearance. "Your partner wishes to start questioning Loretta Sheets."

"Sounds fine to me. First thing Monday morning?" Regina assumed, thinking more about her weekend.

"No. Try like, right now!" her boss boomed out, thinking about his own weekend.

"It's Friday. Four o'clock. I have plans," Gonzalez shot back looking at Chris across the office, perched on a tall stool. Davis sat motionless, quiet like a panther, eyeballing his boss and partner waiting to pounce. They didn't stand a chance. He knew something.

"It does seem a bit late," Anderson agreed.

"No, right now. Both ladies are in the talking mood." Davis urged. "They're getting ready to have us over for a, a uh," stuttering for appropriate words, "an interrogation gathering!" Chris couldn't think of anything else. "I don't care what time it is," coming across visibly firm. Billy could tell it would be hard to say no. "C'mon partner. Betty said she'd like to see you," lathering it on heavy now. "We'll probably get dinner out of it too." Stepping off his stool to look outside. It was sneaking up on early evening with long shadows and clouds building. "Right now partner."

Gonzalez was torn. She needed her talk with Tom but the detective inside surfaced like a battle submarine. Sleek, sinister, sexy. Wanting to hear everything Loretta Sheets had to say. "I can make it to Gustine, later tonight," she consented to herself, checking the time again. Not a huge problem. "Maybe we can finally bust the Crosby murder," Regina caved, speaking with a smile, looking at Captain Anderson.

"Dinner sounds good." Billy stood, reaching for a dark blue jacket.

"Yes!" Chris fist pumped as if he'd just closed out the bottom ninth.

The Patterson Home

"Hi everybody," Lucy said, greeting three surprised cops standing at the front entrance. "Come in." swinging open two large doors, extending her small arm and dainty hand to signal, "this way please." Each detective passed, impressed, smiling at Lucy's more than just cute display. They entered into Mrs. Patterson's living room, struck by the reality an appalling murder had been prevented right here. Pretty well cleaned with only a few lingering signs of the horrific struggle some forty eight hours previous. Easy rock music played somewhere in the background.

Loretta Sheets climbed from a large padded chair. She dressed rather well tonight, somewhat out of place but it played charismatic at the same time. Tight skirt, loose top, jewelry, make-up and obvious to Gonzalez she spent some time on her hair. Chris examined the goods, seating himself across from her taking notice of Loretta's beauty lines for the first time. He admired how tall she was, very pleased. Regina stroked her long hair and brushed at wrinkled jeans, a bit intimidated by Mrs. Sheets' most recent appearance. Billy stared, growing a crooked grin.

"Hi all," Loretta said, shaking each detective's hand followed by an honest embrace. Her genuine display of expressing thanks once again. All three appreciated the lady's gratitude, relaxed immediately, made themselves comfortable and attempted small talk in front of Lucy. A few minutes passed before Beatrice entered her living room, also dressing upscale. Regina noticed the older woman's haircut, marveling at how much younger she seemed.

Mrs. Patterson carried a tray with two pots of steaming water. Tea was served, among an array of olives, cheese, crackers and cut veggies. Captain Anderson began to wonder if he was here for questioning or invited to a dinner party. Beatrice completed her proper greetings, filling cups with hot tea and spreading plates for each guest.

Regina had to comment. "Tea? First time you've served me tea Betty." Always having coffee with her older friend.

"Change is good sometimes, Reggie." Beatrice claimed and fluffed at her new hair style flashing Reggie a quick smirk. Gonzalez was impressed, lifting her cup, breathing in spicy vapors.

Anderson looked to Chris for any sign of what was happening. Davis sipped tea while giving Billy a sly over the cup wink, sending his boss a silent message to relax and be patient. Anderson surrendered, reached for a few olives, drank tea, leaned back, feeling good.

"Beatrice, your hair is fantastic," Regina complimented. "You look pretty hot." As Betty and Loretta made solid eye contact. They chuckled to each other.

"My new stylist," Mrs. Patterson announced, pointing to Mrs. Sheets. "She goes by L-Babe!" Loretta saluted her tea cup snickering an embarrassed laugh. "I'll see if she can take on any new clients. I might be able to wiggle you an appointment." Lucy nudged close to mom knowing they were paying her compliments.

"Didn't know you were a stylist Loretta?" Chris ventured. "I mean, L-Babe, of course."

"I used to cut and style hair before getting married. Still play around with cuts and do-s on occasion," L-Babe made known, watching as Regina finger combed her long dark hair. "I cut men's hair too, detective. Call for an appointment first." Chris nodded slow, planning to act on her offer. So did Billy. Loretta got to her feet taking Lucy by the hand.

"C'mon baby girl. To your room for a while. The big people have to talk." Mrs. Sheets led her daughter off the sofa. "Say bye," as Lucy gave a shy departing wave and followed mom down the hallway into a bedroom filled with TV and books.

"I'll come back to check on you in a little while punkin-head," Grandma shouted out. Lucy acknowledged Gramma-B before disappearing into her room. Chris hoped it was time for business.

•••

Beatrice moved from her guests to the living room window facing Anaheim Drive. Observing close for any sign of headlights moving down her street. To her left, all black. Waiting. Low level light flickered from somewhere off to her right, projecting radial shadows, rotating across the front lawn and driveway. Beams intensified followed by glaring headlamps pulling into her wide driveway. Spotting light rain falling in diagonal streaks, easterly, through two light beams. "Right on schedule," Beatrice declared, just as Loretta returned to the gathering and the elder woman confirmed arrival with a simple rise of thin eyebrows.

Mrs. Sheets nodded ever so slight, ever so slow, relaying a silent message back to Beatrice. "Told you!" Nobody in the room noticed their exchange as Betty returned to her kitchen. She had to throw back a shot of brandy, right now.

Four firm knocks resonated from a wooden door, stopping everyone cold. Abrupt. "I wonder who?" Loretta fibbed, acting unaware. Three detectives watched as Mrs. Sheets made her way to the front door. They could hear her polite greeting as Davis swore he recognized a voice. He froze. More words were spoken.

"No, not at all. No problem. We hoped you would make it," Loretta spoke with a polite but bold voice.

"It's getting nasty out there." A thick male voice rang out, while Loretta shook two jackets clear of raindrops over the front porch.

"The rain kept getting heavier the further west we drove," Mrs. Braden said. "Hi, my name's Franny. Franny Braden. I don't think we've met?" She introduced herself loud enough for all three cops in the next room to hear. No doubt clear. She knew good and well who it was standing in front of her.

"I'm Loretta Sheets and no, we haven't met." Shaking Mrs. Bradan's offered hand while leading an uneasy couple toward the living room. Henry Braden did a slow double take after hearing Loretta's last name. He was about to joke if she had any connection to a certain police detective in Sonora, until taken by surprise, catching sight of three people standing in a wide eyed group! Franny promptly forgot Loretta's name once she looked upon Chris Davis.

"Oh gosh," Franny gushed into her palm covering a gaping mouth. "What?" was all she could manage next. At this point, Loretta detached herself from the living room discomfort, planning to join Beatrice in her ration of booze!

Henry recognized one of three detectives. "What do we have here," reaching out to shake Chris' hand. "Detective Davies, I believe?" Henry was unable to get Chris' last name right.

"Henry, for God's sake, not Davies! It's Davis." Mrs. Braden allowed a cute laugh at her husband's slip. "And your partner is here too," she spoke with certainty even though the two had never met, formally. Franny leaned forward, reaching out to take Chris' hand but refusing a single step closer.

"Funny seeing you here," Chris let his words fly without thinking. Every bit surprised, as Franny. They both stood awkward, holding each other's hand. Chris retracted first odd enough.

Henry continued to search faces while his wife avoided any direct eye contact. "I don't believe we've met," Henry stated shaking hands with Regina first then Captain Anderson. The two detectives introduced themselves with Henry wondering aloud why he and Franny had never met Chris' partner. "I thought you worked alone?" Mr. Braden added.

Regina didn't know what to think. "Of all people to walk through that door," she repeated to herself more than once. As if it all wasn't weird enough, in comes Beatrice from her kitchen hideout, bringing out another pot of fresh brewed tea, a quart of brandy and an open bottle of Old Vine Zinfandel. Mrs. Patterson went on to greet each Braden with warm hugs and kisses. "This has to be staged?" Regina suspected, watching the older gal work her guests.

"We've come at a bad time," Henry said, preferring to stay disengaged from the detectives. "I didn't know the police would be here investigating?" Finishing his remark with a question. He read Franny's tense body language spotting right away she wasn't up for a social hour combined with police questions. Henry, on the other hand, promptly shifted into curiosity. Intrigued by what may possibly be exposed from this crowd!

"Don't be silly you two," Beatrice interjected right away. "It could be very healthy to talk about things. Therapeutic perhaps," hitting Franny with a huge grin, in a best friend way, hoping she might expose Mrs. Braden for something interesting.

Right there. It all came into focus, the moment Regina knew her older friend had it planned. Rigged and ready. "Betty you conniving, little old son of a gun!" Rushed through Regina's thoughts.

"Beatrice, we came down to see you. To make sure you were all right," Franny pleaded, doing all she could to dance her way out of the homespun visit and impromptu crime inspection. "After reading of what you went through, Henry and I decided to take you up on your invitation. I don't think we'll be much help to the police however," Franny insisted.

"You never know dear. Things may have drastically changed already concerning Sarah's demise," Beatrice insisted. "Sit down. Relax. Enjoy some wine. We can talk." Looking among her guests, making sure they understood.

Henry was already nursing a neat shot of brandy, with his wife knowing perfectly well, he'd be tricky to control and difficult to pry from his chair now. It had all occurred, a magnificent seven, about to produce some honesty?

"Where's my roommate?" Beatrice asked straining her slender neck to scan the kitchen doorway. Loretta returned, biting down soft on the inside of her middle cheek. Tearing micro size bits of mucous membrane from inside her mouth to stifle nerves. She sat with a quick knee bend, between Chris and Beatrice on the sofa, tugged a tight skirt and crossed her legs, making eye contact with Davis. Everyone stayed silent, watching, waiting, enjoying the anticipation, knowing they had something significant to say. The only sound came from one second intervals of clinking rings emitted from a swirling spoon. Beatrice continued stirring tea as well as people, while Chris and Loretta continued staring. "Cling...cling...clinng...." The elder lady preferred to stand behind her sofa, moving back and forth, cradling a teacup, keeping hips loose, pacing. A small tear dripped from Loretta's inside eye, streaking across her nose. Catching it with a slow wipe from her stiff thumb. Loretta Sheets was nowhere close to a full recovery. It would be a while having to cope with poor sleep, agitation, nightmares and fear before turning her corner to getting well.

Regina's heart went out to Loretta. Her mother came to mind for no reason. "You'll be suffering from sudden outbursts of emotion for a long time. Perfectly normal," ran through Regina's thoughts. She crossed her legs to get comfortable.

"Maybe we should leave you alone. This all seems way to personal." Franny rose in another attempt to flee, getting a taste of what could come her way if things got out of hand.

"Deborah, please. Sit down. Try to relax. You seem very high strung tonight," Beatrice ordered with Franny obeying her command.

"I'd like to hear what Mrs. Sheets has to say," Henry added in, drawing a look of contempt from his wife.

"You're ready to tell us something?" Chris encouraged L-Babe. The stirring stopped. Beatrice blew soft on her hot tea, noting how good it tasted. Billy stayed frozen, Regina uncrossed her legs.

"Yep. Ready," Loretta confirmed, nodding her head as Billy removed his small tape recorder, Beatrice drank more tea, Regina crossed her legs.

It began. "First, I have to ask, point blank. Do you know if Douglas killed Marcus Crosby?" Chris asked, wanting to get things rolling. This got the undivided attention of both Braden's.

A simple, "No." Spoken as Mrs. Patterson cleared her throat, sipping, watching every move.

"Go on Loretta," Gonzalez butted in scooting back on the sofa, re-crossing her legs. "How do you know?"

Loretta faced Gonzalez. Paused. "Douglas was with me that morning, in bed. He pretty much raped me the night before. Lousy fuck that he is." Loretta stared down at her feet. Ashamed. Rubbing her cheek a few times with outstretched fingers. Quiet again. No more ringing stirs broadcast from a delicate tea cup.

"I am sorry," Regina said reaching out to touch Loretta's elbow. Rubbing her arm in support. Captain Anderson frowned in pity for Mrs. Sheets but recognized his murder case went wide open again. The Braden's both scooted forward, enamored by Loretta's statements.

"Loretta Sheets has no reason to be lying," Billy assured himself. Loretta answered a few more questions regarding her husband which would demonstrate less connection with Marcus' death.

"You told Detective Davis, your husband and Sarah Crosby were having an affair. Is that true?" Regina asked, looking back to Mrs. Braden, sorry she couldn't be more discreet with the Braden's being present. Loretta confirmed her statement.

Henry was first to speak up. "Sweetheart, did you know anything about this? I had no clue my daughter was carrying on this way. Are you sure about this?" he asked Loretta, staring at his wife in disbelief.

Franny held her tongue for a moment, thinking how to phrase her words. "A daughter rarely confides to her parents about an affair. But knowing Sarah's unhappiness it wouldn't surprise me, considering the way Marcus treated her. Nearly as bad as Douglas treated Loretta." Mrs. Braden decided to answer her husband's question in a round-about way.

"Fricken' rats," Beatrice uttered in a faint snarl heard by all.

"Do you know who killed Sarah?" Chris asked, showing Franny a faint smile as if to say it would be fine.

Loretta glanced at the Braden's with a look of pain on her face, before she answered. "I'm sure Douglas killed that," Mrs. Sheets stopped herself from completing a rough comment. She understood Mrs. Patterson's feelings for Sarah Crosby, let alone Sarah's parents being present. "Douglas killed Sarah Crosby. I'm sure of it," Mrs. Sheets explained, deciding not to insult Sarah's parents.

"How do you know?" Captain Anderson asked, wanting to get a possible corroboration with Douglas' statements. "Did you witness your husband commit murder?"

"I'd love to hear how you know that, too," Franny said standing again, looking down on Loretta, doubting her words. "We still believe Marcus got away with it. He beat her. Marcus killed my daughter, I'm sure." Henry went white and didn't make a sound. His earlier expectation of intrigue was proving to be a good one.

"I hated Sarah for breaking up my marriage," Loretta said in dream-like mood. "Looking back, I should probably be thanking her," she followed, snapping back into the moment. "Douglas was in Sarah's house that night, before Marcus arrived, that much I know." A jumpy Loretta said with a nervous chuckle. "I drove over to her house the night of the murder too, planning to confront her myself." Loretta stopped talking, sighed a deep breath while compressing tight jaw muscles. Everyone waited. "As stupid as it sounds right now, I packed a rather large knife with me. It was meant for affect only but we all know how things can get out of hand, don't we detective?" She turned her head staring straight into Davis' wide open eyes.

"Mrs. Sheets, it's starting to sound like you killed Sarah Crosby?" Regina declared, unsure of what to make of her last words. Franny Braden came to the same conclusion. Henry listened, thinking about his frightened daughter again. His hatred surfacing again. Wishing to get even again.

"No, detective. I didn't kill anyone." Loretta vowed, keeping her blank gaze straight ahead. "That night, I was nearly able to. But, I didn't." Remembering the ordeal like a dream. "Anyway, Douglas took care of it all for me." Loretta's eyes began dripping again.

"How do you know that Loretta?" Chris asked in a soft manner not waiting for her to get composed.

"His car was in the driveway," Loretta testified, "as everyone in Tracy knows by now, their hot sex affair was going strong. Douglas left Sarah's house just before I arrived, speeding from her driveway. He didn't know it was me coming down the road because of my headlights, I guess? Finally getting enough nerve to approach the cabin, I could look right into the kitchen." Loretta paused to sip from her lukewarm tea. "I could see Sarah's face crystal clear. Her eyes wide open looking up at an angle, like she was checking the oven. Bizarre."

"Oh God, please stop," Henry rose, shouting, hands trembling. Franny rushed to his side as did Beatrice. They tried calming him. "I can't stand to relive all this. It drives me insane."

"Henry, sit down," was all Franny could say. She was so ashamed. "Please, sit down my darling." Everyone felt shaken by Henry's outburst. Captain Anderson thought it better to stop things right now. Chris Davis knew otherwise. Billy started sending E-mails, furiously!

"What else?" Davis asked.

"I can't say I witnessed my husband killing Sarah Crosby. Wish I could, believe me," Mrs. Sheets spoke her words with obvious malice. "Douglas left the house ahead of me and before Marcus arrived. This I know for certain. Marcus Crosby was on a bike path, walking back toward the cabin as I drove away. Sarah was already dead." Loretta had little more to offer.

Chris thought about her last words. Consistent with trial testimony and Marcus Crosby's repeated claim, adamant to being away most of that fateful day. Douglas' confession was consistent too.

●●●

"You've been withholding information regarding a murder investigation. I'm sure you know, that's a crime?" Chris asked, perhaps too strong. "That's pretty close to abetting a known criminal. Loretta, why not come forward?" continuing to press a distressed mother.

"Give me a break major. The state wouldn't dare pursue an offense like that, after all that Loretta's been through." Beatrice came to her roommate's aid and continuing to confuse Davis' rank. She put both hands on Loretta's shoulders squeezing with light sympathy

"Major?" Anderson whispered in Regina's ear, sitting straight, puzzled about the rank. Regina delivered her boss a quick wave off letting him know to ignore Chris' assumed status.

Mrs. Sheets reached out to touch the older lady's wrinkled hand. Rubbing bony fingers and wrist. "Douglas swore he'd kill me and Lucy, if I ever went to the police. You can bet the house, I believed him!" Loretta spoke the last three words with strong conviction.

"Didn't you think the police would help? Why wouldn't we protect you?" Regina asked, reading honest fear in Loretta's face.

Loretta just smiled. "Douglas is a cop. I know a thing or two about cops. There was no way any police force in this country could stop my husband," accenting the word husband, "from killing us. Short of solitary confinement without trial." Loretta explained, lifting a white cup. Her tea had cooled but tasted fine, draining what remained, setting the cup down with a loud clink. She wanted coffee. "We would've died," she concluded.

Mr. Braden slumped into his chair draining the final drops of brandy. "My God Franny it looks like we had the wrong man." Henry's words caused everyone in the room to look his way. Squinting! Each person asking themselves if they'd heard him right?

"Henry, please. Sit down and have another drink," Franny said, to stop her husband from senseless talk. Beatrice lifted the brandy bottle refilling Henry's glass. Mrs. Braden knew what her husband was trying to say but his timing was just plain lousy! "It's not what you think," she addressed the detectives, then marching to Henry's side kissing a shiny forehead. Henry appeared to be in a fogged daze.

"A little more liquid confession will do just fine," Mrs. Patterson mumbled quietly.

Three detectives watched the Braden's very close. Henry's words had them baffled but Captain Anderson wanted to finish with Mrs. Sheets first. "If we had known sooner we could've protected you then," Billy pleaded to a tearful Loretta.

"Look how well your protection worked right here," Loretta sniffled through the words. "I almost died in this room just two days ago, Captain." She pointed to the floor in front of Anderson where a faint blood stain endured. Everyone took notice. "Douglas only needed, what, three days to find me? With all due respect Captain, that's some protection." Loretta wasn't trying to insult anyone but it came across that way nonetheless. Three detectives knew enough wasn't done to protect this woman and her child. She was right. They didn't make her safe.

Franny expected to hear tough questions regarding Henry and herself. Nothing came right away. Three detectives had one murder solved. Now they needed to solve their own case.

"I'm going to check on Lucy," Beatrice announced rubbing her roomy's strong shoulders. "Don't go anywhere." Mrs. Patterson ordered, leaving the room. "I'll be right back. My turn next!" Three cops, a couple and one mom didn't quite know what to make of the older woman's last remark.

•••

"How are you punkin?" Want something to eat? Anything to drink?"

Beatrice embraced Lucy, rubbing the hollow of her tiny back.

"Nope. I'm not hungry yet Gramma," Lucy gave Beatrice a rub, cheek to cheek. The young girl studied pictures and flipped pages in an old story book from Betty's early childhood. Vivid black and white images told a dated story of wild animals, mean hunters and children helping to save the beasts.

"You keep reading a little longer. Supper will be ready soon." Mrs. Patterson spoke quietly and pulled the child's loose hair upward letting it cascade between her rubbing fingers.

"Soup again?" Lucy asked with scrunched shoulders and a blushing smile.

"Yes, young lady," Gramma confirmed, pinching her cheeks ever so soft. "I must start cooking with a lot more variety, don't I punkin?" Patting the child's head. "I'll come get you when we're ready," Beatrice cooed before leaving. Lucy grinned, giving Gramma two head nods and a scrunched up nose.

Regina and Chris stood in front of Loretta as if preparing to say good-night. Franny stayed close to her husband, keeping him from talking by rubbing his tense neck muscles. Billy Anderson sat alone checking the recorder, wanting to be sure Loretta's testimony was stored intact. Betty moved through the living room with a swift gate.

"Sit down everyone, supper will be ready in about ten minutes," Beatrice yelled from deep inside her kitchen, clanking soup bowls and silverware.

"Is she serious?" Anderson asked, slipping the recorder inside his shirt pocket. A cell phone vibrated inside his pants pocket. He knew who was calling and chose to ignore her.

"She's dead serious," Regina answered, guessing her older friend had more than food on her mind.

"We'll be staying for dinner," Chris told his boss. "Have your recorder ready just in case." Davis glanced toward Franny Braden making sure they were going nowhere. "You're staying too, I hope?" Asking his dire objective.

Franny had to interject. "We're really not too hungry, after everything that's," she was cut off clean by a yelling Beatrice.

"Henry, I hope you like clam chowder," came Mrs. Patterson's words, yelled from the kitchen loud and clear. "I made garlic bread too." Louder yet!

"Isn't she something," Loretta chimed in. "How often have you been questioned about murder then invited to stay for din, I mean supper?" Mrs. Sheets moved about the room gathering cups, plates, teapots, filling two trays to overloaded. "Relax folks. Have a seat," she said showing a little dry humor. "We'll be ready very soon," carrying tea service and all into the kitchen, intending to help Beatrice keep tonight's supper plans on schedule.

Tracy's homicide unit stood side by side wondering what to do next. "Let's wait for the dinner bell," Franny said, taking a seat and stretching out her long legs, loosening tight muscles. Henry followed suit.

Chris did likewise. "We have Sarah's murder nailed down, without being our case." Davis' words showed the Braden's little consideration for their daughter's death. "If we're lucky, by the time supper is over we'll have a better idea of who killed Marcus." he hoped, keeping his conclusion veiled. Franny scratched nervously at her knuckles.

Chief Yung

His cell phone light blinked before any music played, allowing the device to run its course waiting on three chimes before answering. Chief Yung preferred to let it ring. Working tonight, in wait for his homicide unit to relay their findings. Last heard, they were about to sit down for supper! "Jesus God this case is ludicrous!" Alex groaned. "Chief Yung here."

"Hello Alex. It's Abbey," came Mrs. Crosby's voice, seeming much too tame compared to any of their recent conversations. "Sorry to be a nuisance but you probably know why I'm calling."

"Let me guess. Two to one, you'd like to hear what Douglas Sheets had to say," Alex came across with exactly what the intrusive woman was after.

"Any word? Did he confess?" Abbey asked with way too much civility in her voice. Alex was caught off guard, wondering if she was playing another of her roles, ready to pounce soon.

"I haven't heard from my team just yet. They're at Mrs. Patterson's home right now," Yung answered, making the Chief wonder why he was giving away details to Abbey, of all people. But she sounded much more desperate. "Nothing official. I'll be hanging around my office tonight," expecting a harsh remark at any moment which never came to pass. "Tell you what," Alex spoke in a helpful way, "I'll call you when I hear any news."

"Thanks Alex. I'm grateful and I'll be waiting," Abbey said, actually showing some appreciation. She wasn't in the mood for a fight. Either was Alex.

The Patterson Home

"Let's eat," Beatrice announced, moving from the kitchen, down the hall, into her granddaughter's world. Returning with Lucy hand in hand as six adults prepared seats and arrangements. Beatrice joined the magnificent to make seven as Lucy hopped into a saved chair between Loretta and Franny. Mrs. Braden could hardly remove her eyes from the little girl, just as Beatrice guessed.

Soup was ladled out. A medium thick clam chowder, heavy with carrots, celery and bay shrimp. "I hope you like your soup on the thinner side. So much of today's chowder is way too thick. More like paste," Beatrice preached to her gathering. Ringing a bell in Regina's memory of Tom's cooking and their pre-hunt rendezvous, later this evening.

"Paste? Yuk! I like your soup Gramma," Lucy complimented her new grandmother, turning to Franny for support.

Mrs. Braden laughed and by instinct leaned in, hugging the darling girl. She saw Sarah in her arms, felt her daughter breathing, absorbing the child's tenderness like a drug or fine wine. It was good. "You're absolutely right Lucy girl," the taken woman gushed, keeping a tight hold of the child's frail body. "Gramma's always make the best soup." No one seated confused Franny's affection for what it really was. Sarah was having supper with mom and guests. Which was okay.

Salad passed freely among individual plates and garlic bread filled the dining room with mouth watering perfume. Supper was every bit casual and relaxed, for the first forty five minutes. Courteous chatter and occasional laughs ruled the dinner table.

"Mrs. Patterson," Billy solicited the host with genuine curiosity. "What part of England are you from? I adore your accent." Speaking across Loretta who enjoyed the suppertime conversation.

"Oh thank you," Beatrice replied, leaning toward Mrs. Sheets to address the officer, speaking very soft. "The truth is, I'm not English at all. I've suffered from a rare form of Tourettes Syndrome since my early teens. I can't stop speaking with an English accent. Weird huh?!" Calm, unashamed, normal, going back to her meal as if answering a question about favorite colors. Billy and Loretta were floored but decided to forego any additional queries and kept the disclosure to themselves.

Regina and Henry became engaged in a detailed discussion of high powered rifles and aim compensation with today's scopes. Franny and Regina made glancing eye contact but never stayed long enough to spawn conversation between the two. Chris couldn't stop looking at Mrs. Braden. Often fantasizing of their recent past as she avoided him altogether. Silverware rang out among, "thank you's, I'm full, I'd love some coffee and yes one more piece of garlic bread please." Once again it would be food, the great equalizer which proved time and again, to be the major catalyst for relaxing and possibly talking without restraint. Soon, after a quick dessert of brownies and ice cream, table conversations subsided. Lucy helped Gramma and Aunty clear dishes. The din leveled away, going lower, becoming almost quiet. Lucy would be last to climb into her chair with tender help from her new Aunt Franny. Chris Davis decided it was time to speak.

"Thanks so much for supper," Chris dispensed his adoring praise onto a red faced Mrs. Patterson. Betty nodded in return opening the brandy bottle and setting it center stage. Davis charged ahead, directing his attention straight at Beatrice Patterson. Not so much an aggressive stare but more like a young boy asking his grandmother for cookies. "Do you have some information we could use?" Beatrice pondered her answer as Franny's heart began thumping.

Mrs. Braden was about to gamble again. "Maybe, if I take the lead, the inquisition won't be as severe," telling herself while stealing a few peaks at Chris. She thought he might be chomping at the bit. Franny realized Loretta's story was the truth. She sat back in her chair with a sense of responsibility. With a sense of guilt. "It seems to be my daughter's fault, that's caused your suffering," Franny addressed Mrs. Sheets displaying a slight sense of liability and shame.

Loretta lowered her eyes to a messy table setting of crumpled napkins with lipstick stains, half empty wine glasses and tiny crumbs of sour dough littered about. She didn't quite know how to respond, debating whether to dodge and be courteous or tell Franny just how she felt about Sarah Braden. "Your daughter played a big role in nearly getting me and my daughter killed," Loretta responded, forgetting courtesy. She noticed a sullen look capture Franny's face as her shoulders drooped. Chris examined his faded sexual interest very close, wishing to make Mrs. Braden the center of attention and keep her there. "She had lousy taste in men, that's for sure," Loretta tagged on, admitting an explicit amount of hypocrisy lay attached to her comment. "Can't say my own selection in a husband was much better." Sipping red wine, granting the Braden's a small break concerning their daughter's poor choices. Franny stayed quiet, one hand propped under her chin accenting the lady's long, slender neck. She remained enamored with Lucy's good looks, stroking fingers along the back of her petite head. Beatrice took notice of her admiring behavior as did Chris Davis. Loretta opted to keep any more comments under wraps, deciding it rude, especially the way Mrs. Braden was fawning over her daughter.

Without taking her eyes away from Lucy, Mrs. Braden responded. "Please don't hold it against me. Don't hold it against us," correcting herself, reaching over to touch Henry's hand. It was easy for her to read Henry's embarrassment knowing how uneasy he felt, after listening to Loretta's opinion of his daughter. Like usual her husband would take the high ground, keeping opinions to himself and Franny didn't need an argument to hatch now.

Gonzalez missed very little of the room's supper talk and in due course imparted an unmistakable signal to Chris. With a subtle finger wiggle, they both understood the time was ripe for Gonzo to commence attack. Chris wasn't so sure but like always, in lousy position to stop his partner.

Regina lingered, waiting for that slight lull in conversation. Wishing for some sort of lead in, knowing it wasn't to be. She advanced anyway. "Mrs. Braden, did you kill Marcus Crosby?" Gonzalez asked, a bit reckless but stable.

"What?" Henry bellowed before his wife could respond. "We've been through this already," he addressed the entire dinner table in disgust. His wife stayed quiet giving Lucy a gentle, teasing stab to her pug nose. Acting as though she didn't hear the question. Everyone knew better and waited for Mrs. Braden to comment. At least confirm Henry's remark. Captain Anderson punched an email back to Chief Yung, stabbing at the small keyboard with nimble reflexes. Lucy laughed behind tiny hands covering her face, high pitched giggles became the only sounds in a crowded dining room. Their play went on another round.

"I'm waiting Mrs. Braden," Regina spoke as calm as she could possibly tolerate. Franny continued peek-a-boo with Lucy.

"Answer the detective for God's sake. You're being rude." Betty's attitude came across clear. "I'm interested to hear your answer," Mrs. Patterson rang out. Chris delighted in the way Beatrice provoked Franny, assuming the older woman pressed for information too. He sat patient staring at his fantasy waiting, like a hunter.

"I have nothing to hide detective," speaking to Regina as if they were the only one's present. Blowing a hole through Regina's stare. "I was at a friend's house the night of Marcus' murder. I've told your partner that much." In Chris' judgment, Franny's tension increased with each statement. She realized this wasn't consistent with their initial testimony sparking a shudder in her judgment. The detectives seemed to miss her comment. Chris didn't and hoped her comment wouldn't become a talking point. Secretly, Mrs. Braden wished Henry would say something, detesting her being the focal point right now.

Regina would swing wild again. "Do you know who killed Marcus? Hell, who do you think shot Marcus?" Keeping the pressure on with more useless questions, out of the strike zone.

"That's your job, Detective Gonzalez," turning the question right back on the detective.

"Did Sarah ever confide in you about her affair with Douglas?" Mrs. Patterson queried, for some reason. Davis loved it. Beatrice was taking on some of the interrogation! He could see it having an effect on Mrs. Braden's nerves. She kept mum however. Trying to think over her response while playing cool by teasing Lucy. Franny pointed her finger and poked Lucy's chest. When the child looked down, up came her finger teasing a soft, laughing face.

"Why all the questions?" Franny asked, as the supper table went quiet once more. Betty's stirring spoon, ringing a cadence, heightened the mood. Henry had an open moment to come to his wife's rescue but failed to do so. He waited for the police to reply also. Regina enjoyed the silent tension betting someone would break down.

"Did your baby girl die?" Lucy asked Mrs. Braden, causing Franny and Loretta to look at the young girl with huge surprise. Of all people to break the silence.

"This is better than planned," Davis concluded to himself.

"Lucy, you shouldn't ask questions like that," Loretta corrected her daughter but in the most placid way possible. Any embarrassment faded fast while inside, mom was impressed by her daughter's awareness.

"No. No, don't do that Mrs. Sheets," Franny interrupted. "That's okay. It's good she asks hard questions."

"Is she dead?" Lucy asked again, forcing Loretta to hide her face in both hands. Realizing how difficult it must be on Mrs. Braden. The police kept calm except for Anderson, who kept sending email after email. Henry stared into the fireplace, visions of Sarah running through the house. Betty stirred tea.

"Yes, my daughter died about two years ago." Franny answered direct. simple. Inside, however it hurt. The longer she looked upon Lucy the more it hurt. No words came to mind. Lucy would fix that.

"My daddy tried to hurt my mom," Lucy said, cupping her head under one small hand, fingers wiggling in the air. Lucy's words drew a deep breath from Loretta, trying to keep her face hidden. Everyone knew she was crying, deep in pain, heartbroken in how wrong it was for a young child to know such horrible affairs.

"I know sweetheart." Franny almost failed to say the words, overcome with pity for the poor child.

"Did her daddy want to hurt your baby girl?" Lucy's words stunned each adult with a sense of shock and heartache. Her suffering voice combined with the way she phrased the question made Franny sit up and think quickly about Sarah's father. Chris was caught off guard by Lucy's question, squirming in his chair. He thanked Lucy in silence for her childlike honesty, waiting for an answer. Regina wondered if the questioning had gone too far. Captain Anderson sent another email to Alex.

"Oh no, sweetheart. Her daddy would never have hurt his baby girl." Franny's statement was clearly spoken but confusing to Chris and Regina by her odd choice of words. She came across as if Henry wasn't at the table. Regina peered over to Mr. Braden, holding a stunned face that said, 'I'm right here sweetheart?'

Franny turned bright red knowing her statement was more of careless reaction and needed clarifying. "This is Sarah's father," Mrs. Braden exhaled the words as she raised a hand to cover her pink forehead. She tagged on a soft stroke to Henry's arm, indicating to Lucy and three detectives, just who Sarah's father was. Chris' attention bolted to the file photos sprawled across his desk. He looked at Henry, trying to glimpse some resemblance to Sarah. Davis looked closer.

"I think my daddy wanted to hurt me?" Lucy said with a big lump in her throat. She wiped at small eyes and whimpered. All seven adults choked up, some covering mouths in surprise as eyes watered in sympathy for the poor child's situation.

"C'mon punkin," Loretta rose to shuttle Lucy back to her room. "She's had enough," Loretta said, lifting her love's arm then heading toward the living room. Franny stood also, looking at the child with a forced smile trying to hide deep feelings for Lucy's injured childhood.

"Wait Loretta," the admiring woman asked. "Let me kiss my baby girl goodnight." Kneeling, face to face, hugging Lucy tight. Lucy cuddled in snug, causing Franny to fill with emotion, memories, loss, anger and exquisite joy. Mrs. Braden hugged "Sarah" goodnight this evening and didn't care who knew it. Everyone in the room was touched by her display, extending courtesy by silence. Except Chris Davis. Loretta gave Franny a thank you nod, finally slipping Lucy toward her sheltered bedroom. Henry's wife remained on her knees watching as Lucy left the room. Her broken heart shattered once again seeing young Sarah walk to her bedroom, knowing her husband would be reading another bedtime story. She was coming apart and had to act soon.

"Maybe we should be leaving Henry," summoning her admiring husband. She believed her timing to be perfect if ever to dig herself out of this dangerous situation.

Chris stood up now. Slow and deliberate, leaning on the hard wood supper table, head down. Davis replayed a few scenes in his mind. Vivid images of their few meetings. "Meetings hell," the detective told himself in disgust. "She played me like a fiddle and I fell hard for her erotic charms. She is so charming. She knows something. She's hiding something." Franny made her way to the living room to see if Henry had started to move. She saw Chris instead. Standing, head held low. It shook Mrs. Braden deep to her inner thighs, afraid she was to become the focal point again.

"Franny. I have to ask you something," Detective Davis insisted.

Chief Yung

"Who is it?" Alex Yung spoke without lifting his head but knew somebody occupied the office.

"It's me Chief Yung," knowing right away by her voice, who stood in front of him. "Sorry to interrupt."

"Miss Bailey. What a surprise," Alex said with a delicate slyness radiating from his courteous greeting. Bailey had little trouble identifying the attitude, resembling a poker player displaying a winning hand. "Please sit down."

"I don't want to bother you sir but can you tell me where I might find Captain Anderson?" Patricia spoke in a very soft tone, submissive, almost sorry to be there. "I need to ask him a few questions." Bailey was being up front for the most part as her and Billy were scheduled to meet this evening. More personal than business. "I hate to interrupt you, Chief."

"In search of more Crosby murder details?" Alex asked. "You're not interrupting at all, Miss Bailey. I'll likely be here most of the evening anyway. Sit down," motioning the reporter to take a seat with an extended arm, sitting back to admire the slim reporter's simple beauty. "I'd like the company." Patricia shrugged her shoulders knowing better than to insult or decline an invitation like this. She sat, got comfy, smiled at the Chief and waited to find out what happens next.

"Thanks Chief." Was all she said. Alex paused to consider how best to handle this meeting.

"Billy's questioning a witness at the moment," Alex said, seeing no harm with informing the lady friend of his lead homicide detective just as Billy emailed another detailed message from the dinner party. "Mrs. Sheets, matter of fact," Yung stated openly. "Anderson, Davis and Gonzalez are enjoying a nice dinner, I hope, at Mrs. Patterson's home." He noticed Bailey's face brighten when Beatrice was mentioned. She would love a chat with her. Alex felt at ease to fill in the details of his investigation team's plans, failures and what they've discovered so far. "No, you absolutely may not go to the Patterson house right now." Alex laughed while issuing the order before Patricia Bailey could ask. The reporter sat still, a taut grin on her lips. Yung thought about his Captain, with clear understanding how he got himself involved with this forbidden fruit. Bailey was very sexy and charming as well. "I have an offer for you Miss Bailey," Alex proposed, dealing out another hand of five card stud.

"I'm all ears." Patricia shifted her weight, slithering in her chair like a cobra, anteing up to play her hand.

Chief Yung was about to spell out his terms when a second knock came from his doorway. He stretched to see who else demanded his time.

The Patterson Home

To say Gonzalez and Anderson were caught off guard by Chris' next move, would be an understatement. Regina thought it her job to be on the attack. "I'll follow his lead for a change," cautioning herself, watching Chris's stillness. Davis stayed still except for two fingers on his left hand, flexing up and down, playing dull drumbeats on the wood table. Staring at a stain on the carpet.

"What the hell," Davis mumbled to himself under an exhaled breath. "Here goes."

"What is it Mr. Davis?" Franny asked, appearing more than a little inconvenienced. She shied away from direct eye contact with Chris. Looking to Henry, back to her detective relationship, back to Henry, biting her lower lip.

"You're not telling us everything," Detective Davis released his words before raising his head. Resembling a judge taking control of an unruly courtroom. Regina squinted, resting her chin in a thumb-forefinger cleft, smirking as she wondered what knowledge her partner had stashed away.

Franny's initial thoughts centered on images of her and Chris in his bar, in his car, in his apartment. Panic invaded better judgment and her lower stomach began to tingle. "I have nothing else to say," she submitted giving Chris a direct stare, trying to appear in firm control but her voice cracked just before ending the final word. Franny's mouth quivered for a brief moment behind compressed lips. Regina noticed, following every move now without removing her watch. Shifting eyes right to left, Chris to Franny then left to right. Mrs. Braden gave Henry a glance, seeing him sitting still, not preparing to leave.

"I believe," Davis hesitated by choice. "I believe you have," stopping again to observe her reaction. He swore his target was growing beyond nervous, watching as she scratched forearms, running one hand non-stop, through her dark hair. Regina couldn't stay quiet any longer.

"Mrs. Braden, please. If you know something." Regina launched her attack to keep the pressure on. "If there's something you should be telling us. Now's the time. Do you know who killed Marcus Crosby?" Gonzalez left the dining room to chase Mrs. Braden into Betty's living room. Chris followed.

"Franny, there's something or someone else," as Chris' volume rose and his manner became much less cordial, breathing hard, knowing he had to begin intimidating while the woman appeared vulnerable for once.

"Neither of you have any hard evidence on me," Franny fought back with louder words and a long sweep of her left arm. "You're chasing shadows," she added. But her biggest fear rose within her. Anxiety deepened. Giving in, truly materialized for the first time.

"Franny Braden. Sit down dear. You look flushed, please sit down," Beatrice urged her friend to relax but irritating her guest that much more. She paced in front of the fireplace. In reality, she wanted to escape the room and return to Henry's side, who stood confused at the dinner table. Chris controlled one escape route to her right and Beatrice plugged the other. A large sofa contained the middle. Franny Braden was now a caged leopard silhouetted by fire.

"Damn it Franny, tell me. Tell me what you're hiding," Chris shouted, no longer bluffing, more of frustration. He startled everyone now, to a point of shock, except for Captain Anderson who listened close and continued to email in short bursts. Beatrice thought the detective went too far but stayed quiet.

Henry entered the room. "Detective, your tone is way out of line. Please," Mr. Braden was promptly cut off by Chris' continued pursuit.

"C'mon Franny, tell me. Tell me right now!" Chris maintained his high-balling volume, ignoring Henry's plea, generating his target to shudder and recoil in fear like a small girl. Like Lucy. One hand shook in small vibrations, like Sarah. Even Regina second guessed her partner for going too far but she understood, Davis was attempting to shock a potential criminal into submission. "Right now Franny Braden. You and I have been way too close," Davis shouted even louder, walking a fine line along their aborted romance.

Franny stepped away, losing balance and stumbling from emotion. "I have nothing to say!" She yelled back, tears started to flow.

"Tell me. Now," Davis cried out, panting deep with a heaving chest stepping toward her in an aggressive way.

"What do you want from me?" Mrs. Braden screamed, wiping tears from each reddened cheek. Her emotions flying in all directions. "I don't know anything," she groaned in a crying voice, head lowered, sobbing now, hands covering her face. Covering her pain. Davis decided on one last try, screaming out his own pain, perhaps in vain.

"You're lying Franny," Chris snarled his words this time, lower in volume but more sinister, forcing Beatrice to step back in fear. Alex stopped an email making sure his detective was still under control. Loretta sat down, reminded of her husband's anger. Regina froze, except for a quivering hand. Franny turned her back to Chris, cupping both hands over an open mouth. Her head moved from side to side, trying to kill the whole episode.

"Tell me what you know. You're not leaving here until you do!" Chris pressed on, ignoring Henry's continued demands to stop.

"Chris, please," Beatrice begged him to quit. Regina was quiet, too scared to speak.

"Mrs. Braden tell me your secret, God Damn it. Tell me what you fucking know. Now!" Chris was breaking apart now himself, as Henry moved to assist his wife but was caught by Regina and Beatrice stopping a possible fist fight. Franny sobbed, her shoulders racked by uncontrolled shudders, face buried in red hands, ready to explode or pass out.

"Stop it," Franny screamed in shrill panic, with one last try. "Stop it right now you fucking nigger, you're going to ruin my life!" Groaning each word in a harsh counter attack, amounting to Franny's last attempt to decoy Chris from his focus. Davis stopped, standing in place, each breath audible in the abrupt stillness. All five onlookers stopped on one unmistakable word. Henry was taken aback by his wife's slur. Anderson managed an email laced with exclamation marks. Davis knew, he just succeeded.

"Franny?" Henry called out, approaching his shattered wife but stopping at Chris' side. "Mr. Davis, I want to apologize for my wife," stumbling for any words to express regret. "I am so sorry." Mrs. Braden was breaking apart, leaning against the brick fireplace mantle, sobbing like a child nearly out of control. Embarrassed but crying in fear.

"Deborah Braden, never say that word in my home, ever again. Is that clear?" Beatrice ordered. Regina and Captain Anderson made eye contact, each one shrugging shoulders waiting for Chris' next move.

Chris held his ground, watching Mrs. Braden with a face of calm anger. Staring at his suspect no longer holding his desire. Loretta sat in silence. Little expression on her face curling into a tight ball of interlocked arms and legs, clueless to what could happen next. A few seconds of quiet passed before she made eye contact with Davis, delivering a quick smile as if to say go ahead and finish the kill. Davis relaxed but continued breathing in and out very deep. It gave Franny time to recover ever so slight, before he launched his second attack.

"No. Oh no," Davis said in a calm way, his voice almost fatherly now shaking his head negative. "Nope. Not this time Franny," slipping extended fingers inside loose pant pockets. Very cool. Very sure of himself now. Chris knew he'd won this war. "I'm not buying anymore," he told a recovering lady, stepping next to her. "I know you don't need a lover. I know you're not a lesbian. I sure as hell know, you're no racist." Chris reached out and touched Franny's soft shoulder. By reflex she turned, rushing into Chris' grasp burrowing her face deep into his chest. She held tight, sliding an arm over his neck, kissing his temple and dripping tears across his cheek. They held together for a while as her husband watched. Henry never suspected his wife's attraction to Davis, even now, viewing their embrace as Franny's way of saying, "I didn't mean it." Her apology. Mr. Braden was only half right!

"Lesbian? Of course she isn't a lesbian," Henry said, engulfed with confusion. "A lover?" Asking in disbelief. Beatrice thought she understood.

"C'mon girl. Tell me a secret," Chris whispered into the wounded lady's ear, caressing her cheek, reveling in her wonderful smell as strands of loose hair caught his mouth and eyelashes. "It's okay."

"Oh my God you think I'm horrible," Franny Braden shed tears. Choking words as she wept. "Please forgive me Chris," she said, hugging the man she was now drawn to, once more. Regina Gonzalez was blown away by what had just occurred. Unable to stop from jumping in one more time. She placed her hand on the woman's shoulder, pressing soft in a display of sympathy.

"Mrs. Braden," she spoke to her like a child. Gentle. "If you know who killed Marcus, you must tell us." Trying her best to force the situation that one final step. Chris inched toward the sofa as Franny remained knotted to Detective Davis. An arm over one shoulder, both hands clasped behind his upper back, inching along. Mrs. Braden turned her head to face Regina, clearing her nose and forcing a child like simper. She wanted to keep her secret hidden, trying hard one last time, but failed. Mrs. Braden surrendered.

"It was Sarah's father who killed Marcus, my dearest," Franny spoke her words like a southern belle. A strange accent captured her voice, continuing to clutch the detective. "Sarah's father. Your current boyfriend, darling. Tom!" The entire group eyeballed Henry Braden in depth except Regina. She stared, fixed into Franny's eyes waiting for her correction. It didn't come as the weakened lady turned her head ever so slight, slowly shifting a smirk into a sympathetic frown. Regina maintained her target, peering straight through her face knowing the correction wasn't coming.

"Franny, sweetheart?" Henry began his plead. "What the hell are you saying? You know perfectly well I didn't shoot Marcus." He beseeched his wife to tell the honest truth, looking at Chris and Captain Anderson too. "She's not herself right now. She knows I didn't shoot anyone. Franny you have to tell them the truth," he begged, moving in close to his beloved wife, rubbed her back up and down tenderly with open palms. "She isn't making sense," Henry addressed the group, his voice shaking and cracking but wouldn't look away from his only love. Billy resumed thumping emails knowing Chief Yung would have a hard time making sense of this message.

Mrs. Braden began to uncoil from Chris' arms. She still leaned into his chest, wiping tears and a runny nose. Attempting to compose herself, knowing what lay ahead was going to be most difficult. Beatrice handed Franny a napkin from the dining room but looked to Regina, seeing her friend in need of support.

"You know for a fact, this Tom Ellis shot Marcus?" Chris asked, wanting another confirmation. "Did he tell you he did it?"

"I always assumed he committed the murder," Mrs. Braden answered with confidence. "He certainly had the motive. We met a few days ago. I had to be sure." She could see Beatrice returning a look of thanks for not revealing the shotgun shell she'd given up. They could both be accused of withholding evidence but Franny Braden decided to keep it their secret. "Tom told me he shot Marcus Wednesday evening." Playing their final meeting deep within her memory. It hurt to recall Tom's stare of final despair.

Regina's memory dialed in the woman in front of Tom's house. "That was you waiting in the truck," she said, shoulders slumped in despair. Gonzalez began subsiding very fast, into a stupor. She urinated a small amount into her jeans leaving a wet stain between her legs. She only thought of Tom and their reckless relationship which she wanted and needed, more than anything else. Tom Ellis had to be in her life, more than anyone could imagine but knew it wouldn't happen. Grief and fear were running wild. Everyone else in the room went from surprise to confusion to, 'what did she mean by Regina's boyfriend?' Mulling over Franny's words simultaneously. Captain Anderson punched even faster on his phone. Deborah Braden had to return order to her courtroom. She had to explain.

"Henry!" His wife scolded his name with stern temperament, as if about to issue orders.

"What do you need my dar," his wife cut him off, clean.

"Henry, save it and sit down. Please." Again ordering her husband like a young boyfriend. Loretta and Beatrice scurried to open a seat next to Mrs. Braden but wanted to be front and center for Franny's story. Henry sat, bending slow like a child being scolded, in fear of what his wife had to say next. Anderson kept the communication line singing. Loretta kept asking Beatrice who Regina was seeing? Chris remained loose, embedded in the soft couch glowing over his assumed victory. Regina sat still, in a daze but coherent, almost terrorized however by Franny's next revelations.

"Henry?" Franny asked. "Do you love me?" Rubbing her husband's cold hand. She was tender.

Henry lowered his head, raising his wife's hand to his lips, feeling the worst was yet to happen. "You know I do," her husband whispered with devotion.

"Tell me."

Henry paused to give his beautiful wife a long, serious look.

"Tell me. Please." Franny spoke her words with the mildest of voice. Asking. Begging him to tell her.

"I've always loved you. Always will." Henry leaned in to kiss his wife's lips.

Franny cried a bit more. Softly. "Then we'll get through this my love," telling her husband with a tender order. "I don't deserve you, Henry Braden." She scooted close to her husband, patting his chest, caressing his face. "I have something to tell you."

Chief Yung

Alex Yung rose from his chair. Bending over his desk he saw Abigail standing patient in the small doorway. "Mrs. Crosby. Do come in please," Alex requested, waived his hand to direct the gray clad woman to a seat flanking Patricia Bailey. The reporter's high back chair concealed her presence until Abbey reached the open side. Her look of surprise was too good to miss when she realized who occupied the office with Chief Yung. Alex grinned with deep satisfaction while beginning a worthless introduction.

"Abigail Crosby, this is Patri," cut off clean when Abbey interrupted in obvious disgust.

"Yeah, yeah. We know each other Alex." Mrs. Crosby exposed her feelings with a quick, "Bailey." Followed by a slight nod before taking her seat.

"Hi Abbey," Bailey responded without looking at the older woman, hardly acknowledging her presence.

Alex understood right away these gals were well acquainted and hated one another. "Don't get between these two," Yung warned himself.

The Chief took plenty of time to retreat behind the safety of his desk. Checking his laptop for another email from Captain Anderson, gave Alex time to consider the situation at hand. What should be said and what couldn't be told for now anyway, glanced at two nervous ladies. "You're here for information too, I assume," Yung addressed Abbey.

"You can guarantee that much," Bailey quipped before Abbey could say a word, adjusting posture, squirming to angle as far away from past bondage as possible.

Alex was thrown off at first with no insight into her sarcasm. "Were these two working together in some way?" Contemplating in silence.

"Try being civil for once," Abbey scolded the reporter, getting Chief Yung's full attention.

Abbey was about the least civil person Alex ever met. He continued observing the two while their body language spoke volumes. He saw a rich, powerful woman and a reporter. One needing information to further her career while the other wanted to know who murdered her son. It occurred to the Chief in a sudden burst how well connected Abbey was to further a working girl's career. The long legged reporter would have first hand info from a homicide Captain. How convenient! His computer soft chimed with another incoming communication from, who else, Billy Anderson. Chief Yung locked onto his monitor, leaned back then clapped his hands. Abbey and Patricia figured something went down at the Patterson house, each leaning forward toward the Chief's desk hoping for scraps. Alex looked up to see two vultures with outstretched necks. "Maybe I can cut 'em off?" he joked to himself.

"Let me guess, if you will. A wild guess," Alex announced to his evening guests. Pausing. "You two have been mining my people for case information," Chief Yung accused, then hesitated to study their reactions. It only took Bailey a few seconds to flush like a surprised quail.

"She's been digging me for news since the murder went down," the reporter disclosed, indicating a culpable Abbey Crosby with a sweeping left hand and extended thumb. Bailey didn't think before talking.

"You idiot. What the hell's wrong with you? He won't give us anything now!" Abbey revealed her hand too. Bailey knew her reckless statement probably cost her any chance of commanding an exclusive story. Abbey rose from her chair to stretch a tight back muscle, deliberating whether to prolong or end their meeting.

"Abigail, sit down please. Sit down," Yung pleaded in a polite way for the older woman to stay put. He decided to give in and make a deal. Alex reached way under his desk to access a lower shelf, retrieving his bottle of twelve year old Oban, Scotch whiskey. "You two will get the news as soon as it comes in to me," entrusting both ladies with his verdict. Abbey took her seat, whirling her face away from Bailey in a show of faux Hollywood loathing. She also eyed the liquor bottle feeling she could use a drink.

"It's going to be a long night," Chief Yung reported, uncorking a long neck bottle and setting out three small cocktail cups made of clear plastic. "Who needs a drink?" the Chief offered, eyeing his watch. Nearing nine o'clock already. Bailey declined, even though she needed a drink. Abbey accepted without flinching, even clicking Alex's small cup in thanks.

"I don't feel like eating alone tonight. How about Chinese. Ever notice how cops always order Chinese in the movies?" Alex tried a little charm to convince his lady friends to stay as another email posted from the Patterson home.

Tom Ellis

Rain continued falling, soaking Gustine along with most of the lower San Joaquin. Typical of early winter rains however, were the southern storms, California's Pineapple Express. Sweeping in from the lower Pacific with warm temperatures, usually a lot of wind, sometimes a lot of rain, always melting a lot of early Sierra snowpack. Rarely bringing in a lot of northern ducks. Tom understood these conditions, sitting alone by a warm fire in his spacious living room.

No messages had arrived from Gonzalez for more than two hours. Ellis waited, uneasy but staying faux positive Regina might just show up, reading her last text one more time. "Supper with Beatrice. The Braden's just arrived. Interesting now! Will be late tonight, sorry. Kiss Kiss—Lick Lick! R." Holding his cell phone Tom moved to stoke the fire, lingering to enjoy its feel, sounds and shifting flames. Gazing around the room to examine pictures, artwork, knick knacks, furniture, tokens of his years.

He told Regina they'd be shooting Mendota again tomorrow. "I think I'll switch." Tom thought Los Banos could shoot well at first light, even in a warm storm. "Besides, I have a reservation at Los Banos!" Telling himself while flashing a sly grin. "It might just give me enough time?" Stoking the fire set free a dense shower of sparks and embers. Peering into swirling flames with heat waves rubbing a worried face. Concentrating on a plan. He shuddered hard when his cell phone chimed, knowing exactly from where it came. "I'll see you later. Wait for me. Love you too much. R." Tom read Regina's message a few times, unwilling to budge from the hospitable fire. Ellis wondered what it could've been like had they met a few weeks earlier. "Good God, what am I going to do?" Speaking aloud in a trembling voice.

He moved through the house. Logging inventory of his life's collection. Belongings he cherished and stuff that meant nothing. Favorite sauté pan, French knife, stereo and hidden pictures of Sarah Braden, his daughter. Mostly long range snapshots of her walking home from school. Playing at an unknown park.

One photograph clipped from a newspaper article. Her high school graduation picture, sent in secret from Sarah's mother. Hand delivered in the mailbox one day with a simple note attached. 'Your daughter.' Tom appreciated the gift.

Nearing midnight, Ellis arranged a light breakfast and simple lunch of leftover chicken with fruit. After packing, he asked himself if lunch would be necessary. "Who knows, something might change," whispering very low. It didn't matter. Getting lunch and breakfast together was part of the event. His pre-hunt ritual repeated a couple hundred times or more must be completed.

Hunting gear loaded, decoys, sleeping bag, over and under, wood seat and thermos of coffee. Before leaving Tom sealed an envelope addressed to Regina Gonzalez. He stoked the fire again scattering small chunks of charred wood. Faint embers pulsed bright, then weak in crimson radiance. One final glance around, one final check of his phone, one final thought of his mistake. On the fireplace mantle Tom left the envelope, cell phone and sprig whistle. On the way out he locked the front door, took two strides, stopped, turned and walked back to unlock the door. "No need for a forced entry." Slipped inside his truck never once looking behind. It rained steady but this drive to Los Banos Wildlife Refuge was uneventful.

Patterson House

Supper had long ended and getting late. Outside the storm intensified with wind and steady rain pushing in from the south. No heavy downpours, warm temperatures and high snow elevations. The group inside could care less, waiting for the final act as Franny Braden began her confession.

"Henry, I'm sorry," explaining how Tom Ellis became involved in her life. "We knew each other from our high school days in Los Banos. Tom was two years younger but we dated here and there, before I graduated. We met a few times in the next couple years." Franny continued, telling Henry how Tom drifted away, "right before you and I met. I had all but forgotten about Tom Ellis."

She went on to remind Henry of their early years. "We didn't see eye to eye too often in those days," rubbing her husband's arm, feeling sorry for him and knowing how much it must hurt. "You wanted a child so bad. Remember?" Franny's soft words poured tears from Henry's eyes as she petted her husband's pale cheeks. "How many times did you recite the different ways you'd spoil our first child," staring at Henry with her searing eyes. "But, we had a rough time getting me pregnant, didn't we? I still recall all the scheduled sessions, monthly timing, doctors, diets and exotic foods. Nothing worked," she said, bowing her head low and rubbing her bloodshot eyes. "You seemed to withdraw from me. It hurt something awful to drift apart in a loveless marriage. All your thoughts were centered on children," Franny informed her husband. "I needed some of your attention, Henry. You know how self centered I am." The couple laughed very soft at their inside joke.

Franny had a hard time saying her next words. Tears and sobs got the best of her. "It was about this time when, out of nowhere, Tom showed up. We began a very stupid affair," managing to finally reveal her dishonesty. She looked past Henry now, seeing Regina Gonzales sitting taught on a gray chair, rocking back and forth with both arms wrapped to her waist. Listening but tense, nerves wearing thin. Franny commiserated with the detective's suffering. "I got pregnant." Mrs. Braden spoke the words and went silent. She didn't know what to say next. Regina's head went down, slowing her rocking motion.

"You were so excited," Franny told her husband. "In the blink of an eye you came running back to me. It felt so good again." Holding a tight fist to her mouth as if to cover the words of shame and guilt. "I let you believe my baby was yours, forced to let things take their course. I'm very weak you know." Mrs. Braden admitted, leaning to press her face into Henry's chest. She cried with a loud moan. Her husband sobbed too. The room was quiet but tense, like a theater, when the villain is exposed.

Henry understandably, was the most surprised wearing a look of disbelief, then shame, then anger, then just a long blank stare. "I had occasional thoughts about Sarah not being my daughter. They would surface now and then but never stayed with me. By no means giving it much attention." The poor man spoke in shock.

"We'll get through this Henry," Franny whispered. It took a while but Henry nodded, still in a faint daze.

"Sarah looked more like you," Henry told his wife. "I would never had known," trying to make sense of his new, bizarre situation. "I still love her. I spoiled her. She's my daughter." Henry said while looking at faces in the living room. They all nodded in agreement, understanding his pain.

"Your daughter loved you very much. She still does, I'm sure." Franny was proud of her husband's words. She married a good man.

Chief Yung

Chinese food arrived and consumed too fast. Both female combatants were a little more polite during dinner while Chief Yung, starved for food and details, engulfed his meal with reckless manners. At one point, Patricia and Abbey looked at each other with raised eyebrows and expressions of disgust. Abbey even mouthed the words, "Holy Shit!" Following one of Alex's most poignant belches. Two more emails arrived, the last of which obliged Chief Yung to make a phone call.

"Where's Judge Rosales?" Alex asked in a calm voice, clearing his soggy throat while speaking. He glimpsed both ladies with raised eyebrows, listening and hoping he would finish dinner. Alex smiled before intentionally looking down. "I need an arrest warrant right away. When do you expect to reach him?" Pausing to receive a response. Bailey eyeballed Abbey one more time, issuing a scowl and a hopeful sign with crossed fingers. "Call me on this line as soon as you reach the judge. Understand?" A police officer on the other end understood completely. Abbey and her reporter wanted details.

"What's up?" Bailey asked, always first to jump in.

"We need an arrest warrant and our one judge is somewhere up to his ears in Stockton's nightlife. Like every Friday night, I'm told." Alex knew the ladies wanted to hear whose name is on the warrant. "Judge Rosales is famous for chasing girls and late hours at his favorite watering holes. We'll get him sooner or later," the Chief revealed, keeping his stall tactics alive.

"Are you going to tell us?" Abbey asked in a serious voice with sad eyes, suggesting mild begging. "It's Henry Braden isn't it? It's not that crazy cop?" Abbey almost shouted her speculation now, mouth sagging, waiting for an answer. Bailey knew it couldn't be either man, with Henry most likely at the Patterson house tonight and the crazy cop already in custody.

"Tom Ellis," Chief Young answered in a somber voice, reading from his computer screen avoiding a face to face with Abbey.

"Come again?" Mrs. Crosby requested.

"The shooters name. It's Tom Ellis. He lives in Gustine," Alex answered over again.

"Who the fuck is that?" Abbey shot out, sitting rigid on the edge of her chair. She began to cry. Abbey wanted it to be the Braden's. She was never close to Sarah, didn't like her. Marcus had married way downward, in her greedy opinion. Henry came off as socially inept and Franny Braden's raw beauty intimated her. "What the hell. Why did this Ellis guy murder my son?" Abbey felt exhausted and cried openly. Bailey, for some reason rose to offer the poor woman some genuine pity. Rubbing Mrs. Crosby's shoulders, generous to provide her rival some sort of relief.

"You two are going to love this story," Alex said, with rude timing, disregarding Abigail's condition. "My people are on their way back to the Station." Patricia Bailey couldn't wait to hear about Tom Ellis.

Patterson Home

"No arrests will be made tonight," Captain Anderson informed the Braden's. "But, be warned." Anderson shifted his gaze from Henry to Franny and Loretta. "If the DA sees it different and decides you've committed a crime, we'll be coming back to arrest you both." Anderson delivered his warning very crisp, very clear. "I'd notify a lawyer soon," finishing with serious attitude making everything that much worse for the upset couple. Mr. Braden nodded positive with Franny's face buried into her husband's arms, never considering she might be headed to jail soon. Henry patted his wife's head, doubting it would ever get that far. "We didn't murder anyone," he told himself.

"You okay partner?" Chris asked Regina, running her hand over reddened eyes. "We have to get back to the station. Can you handle making an arrest?" Gonzalez took a paper towel from Loretta Sheets. Dried her eyes and wiped a runny nose.

"She'll be fine," Beatrice said to Chris as her supper party was concluding.

"I can't believe I didn't see it," Regina said, coming back slow from her dazed confusion. For a few seconds she sensed another nauseas assault coming on. "Not now," commanding herself, swallowing hard, drinking water and pushed the upwelling down. "Let's go," she ordered clear and firm. "Can't keep Chief Yung waiting."

The evening ended with whimpers and hugs instead of fist fights and bloody screams. Beatrice heard a remarkable story leading to the death of her Sarah Crosby. She also inherited two roommates, whom she imagined could offer great comfort in her golden years. Especially Lucy. Mrs. Patterson said goodnight, excusing herself to tuck the child into bed after hugging her tight.

Three detectives made for the door but Regina turned to look back. She saw Mrs. Braden alone on the sofa. Gonzalez forced herself back to the older woman. They gave each other a sympathetic look, face to face, knowing the same man intimately. Deborah stood.

"You're in love with Tom?" Franny asked with a benign tone.

"You were too," Regina pointed out, dodging her question. "At one time?"

Mrs. Braden frowned. "How couldn't I?" she admitted to the detective. "Tell him I understand."

"I wish I understood." Regina shook Franny's hand, blinking away tears as she studied a decoying face, turned and left the house. "Don't know if I really care for that woman," the detective said to herself.

Chief Yung

After midnight found Alex, Patricia and Abbey still occupying the Chief's office. They waited, impatient, anticipating the homicide unit's return. Yung and Bailey made small talk while Abbey dozed, hand under cheek in her chair. Both gals were permitted an exclusive audience within Tracy's Police Department and neither was about to blow this chance. They waited on. Bored. Tired. Stubborn. Fervent. Committed.

Abbey's eyes opened wide without moving a muscle. A split second later, rumblings, voices and commotion heralded from the hallway. Mrs. Crosby and Patricia swiveled to see Yung's staff coming through the door. Chris dragged two chairs from another office and perched himself atop a wooden stool. Above and behind Regina. Alex could see Gonzalez had been crying and wondered about her emotional condition. Chris rubbed his partner's shoulders aggressively, hoping Regina would snap too!

"So children," the Chief started. "What do you have for us?" Opening the forum to any of his three detectives as usual. Captain Anderson, sitting next to Mrs. Crosby, as far as possible away from his girlfriend, began dictation.

"We have our killer," Billy said, stuffed with confidence, turning slightly to face Patricia Bailey. "Tom Ellis of Gustine pulled the trigger on Marcus." Looking now to Mrs. Crosby, asking to pardon his poor word selection. Billy relayed the details of Franny's story. The hot love affair, bearing Tom's daughter, hiding her secret from Henry until this evening. Even through Sarah's murder trial.

"Henry had no clue? Don't you find that hard to believe?" Abbey interjected. "Is there any chance she fabricated the entire story, as a decoy, to cover her husband's ass?" A doubtful Mrs. Crosby proposed, with little conviction. "I was convinced Henry shot my son."

"No way Mrs. Crosby. I don't see it that way at all," Chris intervened. "Henry Braden doesn't have the makeup for murder. Not a chance."

Abbey turned to see Detective Davis, bearing a look of frustration on her face. "Everyone's capable of murder detective," Abbey stated the obvious. By this time Mrs. Crosby didn't have much left to say. Everyone in the room began to feel for the older woman. Her son long dead. Abigail Crosby was alone and hurting.

"Do you plan to arrest him tonight?" Abbey asked, slowly pressing into her chair. Alex could see Mrs. Crosby suffering from the long night as views of Marcus' murder were probably playing out again in her mind. "What do you know about him?" Asking the very words Regina didn't want to hear.

Three detectives went silent after Abbey raised her question. No one wanted to breach the tender subject of Regina's relationship with Tom Ellis. Gonzalez understood the awkward silence and felt obligated to begin explaining. Just before she initiated her admission, Yung jumped in.

"Good question," Alex said leaning forward on his desk. "We've had Detective Gonzalez tailing Mr. Ellis very close for a few weeks now. Ellis has been a suspect since day one. I would call her assignment undercover work." Running a smoke screen for his staff in a clever way. Regina turned to face Alex, flashing her smallest, most endearing smile. Without uttering a word she said thanks. Thank you to Chief Yung in a huge way. Alex nodded back to Regina. Better to help his staff than burn down an entire department.

Hearing of Ellis for the first time, Patricia Bailey eyeballed her about to be ex-boyfriend. She relayed a simple head dip lowering thin eyebrows, which silently asked Billy, "why didn't I know about Tom Ellis?" Billy shrugged his shoulders trying to convey his own lack of information. She flashed Anderson a lip song, quietly singing her disappointment. Chief Yung noticed Bailey and Anderson still attempting their relays of information. He read Billy's last email, which turned out to be a good way to break this pair. For good!

"It's late. Regina," the Chief hailed and stopped. "Do we have," stopping again, wanting to select the right words. "What intelligence do we have on our man Ellis tonight?" Alex's question sounded more like an army general but getting it by Bailey and Abbey. Almost ordering Regina to turn and play her part.

"My last contact with Ellis has him in Mendota tonight. Bird hunting again, I assume." Regina update as Billy and Chris played along with hidden grins.

Alex leaned hard into his desk chair, pondering moves like a manager with two on and one out. "I'd sure like to bring him in tonight, if possible." Bailey and Abigail hung on every word. "What's your opinion. Can we arrest him out there tonight or tomorrow morning?" In reality Yung was asking all three detectives for opinions.

"It would be perfect," Regina said without pause, thinking how ideal his arrest on the refuge would be. "Poetic," she told herself. "He may not expect us coming out there," she added. "We'll have the surprise factor in our favor." Coming across confident but knew Tom would certainly be aware of what went down tonight.

Chris didn't know what to expect on the refuge but grew excited about finishing off the investigation. "I'll go along with my partner. Let's get after him." Anderson was all aboard too, clueless to Mendota Wildlife whereabouts!

"Let's do it then," Chief Yung gave his go ahead. "All of you will be lacking sleep. Is that a problem?" Alex asked seeing how late it was getting to be.

"We're fine Chief," Regina answered for all three.

"Good," said Yung. "Billy, we've finally located Judge Rosales. Here's the address and directions," handing Anderson a Google Map printout. "Hump it up to Stockton and get our arrest warrant signed. Use discretion when seeing the judge. Hell, it could be a cathouse for all I know." His boss directed as the reporter gave Anderson a long stare. "You can rendezvous with Chris and Regina in Mendota. Take Kennedy with you. He needs the experience." Alex stopped to think for a moment, making sure everyone was accounted for and lined out. "I want Buck to go along with Davis. He's knows something about duck hunting!" Getting a round of laughs from his team.

"Will do." Billy accepted an envelope with printed directions and arrest warrant then made a quick exit, locked on Bailey's stare the whole way out. She was about to say something but Alex cut her short.

"Hold that thought Miss Bailey, I have something for you too. Just a second," the Chief alerted Patricia. He seemed to have the situation well planned. In reality, opportunities appeared from nowhere and Alex took advantage. Very lucky.

"My boy's not answering his phone," Regina told Chris. "We'll contact the refuge on our way down. They may be able to hold him at the check station?" Gonzalez instructed, leaving Chris in a haze and nowhere close to understanding what she was talking about. Regina thought how Tom could be spooked from the sweat line, should Fish and Wildlife get too aggressive. "Tom would put two and two together pretty fast," Regina told herself, preferring to avoid a wild chase through Mendota. Chris and Regina would need backup and to assemble gear before heading south. Two detectives scurried to gas up an SUV then grab a couple uniformed cops. That left Chief Yung alone with the two ladies again, unable to plan it any better.

"This sounds like a wild goose chase to me," Abbey hissed to Alex. "I need some sleep. Can I call you in the morning to see where this hunt ends?" asking Yung for permission.

"I can do better than that. I'll call you, first thing, when I get any news." Chief Yung told Abbey, catching her off guard by his suggestion. "Can I show you out," continuing overly polite to his one time friend.

"I'll let myself out," Abigail snorted. "Good luck Patricia." Bailey watched Mrs. Crosby leave, looking drained. The reporter nodded her head and without a clue, took charge.

"So Chief, all of a sudden it's just you and me. I get the exclusive?" Patricia began pushing her situation. "This Ellis character, a real lunatic?" allowing her reporter instincts to surface. Bailey was already locating directions and mileage to Mendota, California. "Where in Mendota did your detective say Ellis would be?" unaware of a connection between duck hunting and Mendota SWA.

Chief Yung stayed still, holding dear to his blank impression, making Bailey more nervous with each passing second. He knew she didn't have a solid location, enabling a play on the reporter for as long as he cared! "You and I?" Chief of Police flirted with her English correction.

"I give you that one," Bailey chuckled, enjoying the spar.

Alex sipped a little whiskey. Checked his computer and cell phone. He could tell the reporter in front of him knew the hand he was playing. Chief showed his cards. "Detective Gonzalez didn't specify Ellis' location. I'd like to think she did it on purpose?" Yung stopped cold, enjoying Patricia's twitches, pursed lips and hair tugs. Bailey was at a loss for words again knowing her good looks wouldn't soften the Chief's stand. Alex permitted it all to linger, enjoying the composed reporter's waning self-assurance.

Bailey had to break the silence in the worst way, however she still didn't quite have the words. "Can you tell me anything about this Ellis guy?" she asked, gambling on a subject change. "I was at the crime scene, you know. He almost blew Marcus' head off," unable to invent something more.

"He deserved it. A lousy, brutal, wife beating bastard. The wealthy scum bag," Alex said in a relaxed, knowing what the hell I'm talking about, tone in his older voice. "Revenge," he continued. "I should say flawed revenge," raising an index finger for quiet, reading two emails from Captain Anderson. Billy was nearing Stockton and closing in on the judge. "That's good," Yung mumbled under his breath.

"I'm sorry," Bailey responded to Alex's last comment, with no need now to worry about breaking silence. Chief Yung did that for her!

"It was all a big fuck up on Ellis' part. He killed Marcus, sure in his own mind Mr. Crosby murdered his daughter. Simple revenge." Chief Yung stated his position with an obvious amount of sympathy in his voice, for Tom Ellis. Bailey was just short of flabbergasted!

"You seem to have an understanding for Ellis' crime? Tracy Police condones the public taking law into their own hands these days," Bailey reacted, wanting to keep the Chief talking.

"Don't be ridiculous. On a one on one basis, I can understand how it happens." The Chief began to question if this conversation had become way too personal. "Maybe too much booze?" he thought. It was also getting late and the cop needed sleep, which always tilted his fences.

"You understand how Ellis became judge, jury and executioner," Patricia let loose with her perspective. "C'mon, for crying out loud you're the Chief of Police. You're sworn to protect, aren't you?" Patricia pushed hard now, second guessing her own attack. "How will he react?" She asked herself. Alex covered his mouth over a deep yawn. A combination of sleep deprivation plus a bit of anxiety. He leaned back in his chair resting elbows atop each armrest, raised his right hand and pointed a wobbly finger at Bailey. Smirking, which gave the reporter a chance to calm down. She smiled. Charming him.

"You don't have kids, am I right," Yung asked.

"Nope." Patty answered.

"Neither do I," Alex said nodding to the reporter. "I was blessed with a nephew, however. My sister's boy, Josh. The cutest damn kid you would ever want to meet." Which started the Chief's tale. "A great looking boy, on his way to Berkeley to study biology and play baseball. He could throw ripe strawberries through a battleship. Tremendous arm. Left hander!" Narrating and reminiscing at the same time. "Josh loved wildlife and had barely turned eighteen." Alex sipped his scotch. Bailey didn't know where all this was headed.

"Josh stopped in Manteca for gas one evening, on his way home from trout fishing." Chief Yung had taught the boy how to fly fish. "He loved it, learning the nuances of casting flies, right away. Josh and I loved fishing California's trout streams. Some of the greatest days I've ever known."

The Chief recounted his nephew, standing near a gas pump filling his tank. Alex stopped again, having a rough time telling his tale.

"Inside the station store, unknown to Josh, a robbery was taking place." Alex narrated the incident. "Shots were fired. The owner opened up on two armed rednecks from Stockton. He dropped one but missed the other. The surviving criminal returned fire, shooting wild of course, shaking like a cornered coyote." Bailey had an idea where his story was headed next.

"That last round barely clipped a display stand, shattered the store window, striking Josh in the forehead. My boy died instantly." Alex stared at his blank desktop, watching the dramatic scene replay in his mind like he did almost every day.

Bailey recalled the incident, being a new reporter at the time. "Chief I am so sorry," she told an emotional cop, soft as possible, giving him all the time he wanted. Yung kept a heartbreaking face locked to his desktop.

"It gets interesting now," he said. "The day of the puke's arraignment," Chief Yung made a point to be in the courtroom, bypassing the security screen. "I had it all planned," Alex delivered his words like a confession, talking very low and deep in shame. Bailey thought she knew where he was going.

"I had my sidearm, loaded, ready," Yung confirmed, stopping to keep himself under control. "The gang banger appeared in court showing no regret. Acting the part of hit man telling the court to get fucked." Alex's better judgment won out after witnessing this kid's reckless actions. "I even made a subconscious move with my right hand to draw the gun. Rubbing its wood handle and oily metal." Chief Yung stared at Bailey without expression and very serious. "I wanted to kill that scum bastard dead, myself. So bad."

Bailey felt uncomfortable by this time. Yung had gone too far, she thought. "I don't know you that well," telling herself. "I'll take that drink now Chief, if you're still pouring," the reporter yearned, in need of a liquid jolt, deciding to intrude. "But you didn't pull the trigger. You let a judge and jury pass sentence on the lowlife."

"That's right. I also recognize how a person loses that control, then takes matters into their own hands." Alex responded, deliberating his position again and again, in silence. "If that jury somehow found Josh's murderer innocent, I'm not sure I would've maintained control." Alex spoke the words, believing in his own prediction but none too proud of his conviction.

Bailey could never buy into the Chief's scenario, seeing firsthand how grotesque the carnage can be when guns are used to settle issues. "I'm sick of guns. This Ellis guy is a hunter, from what I heard tonight?" Patricia wanted to get her side stated.

"He is," Yung answered.

"Hunting bothers me more and more. It seems like murder too. Sometimes." Scratching her head and neck to relieve apprehension. "Maybe I should stop?" Patricia asked herself, then ran through her own stop sign. "The jury got it right in Marcus' case, Chief. This time they got it right," Bailey said with conviction, holding her outstretched arms in place for impact. "Your position in particular can never permit murder to be sloughed off or understood. What Tom Ellis did can never be justified. No matter the circumstances."

"Don't get me wrong Miss Bailey, as police we know where to draw the line. Hell, I had to step back from that fucking line myself!" Yung admitted and frowned, thinking about his day in court. "Murder is never tolerated." Shuffling his tired legs in the chair and sitting straight to get his blood flow going. "Maybe it's my own warped comprehension now, the way revenge can lead a person over that line." Observing the reporter biting her finger nail. "Murder is never justified. That's what makes all this so tragic. A desperate father kills the wrong person." Alex spoke staring into the past.

"No," Bailey chose to correct. "A desperate father kills an innocent person. Greek tragedy this time." Patricia said no more.

Alex would go quiet too. Standing, stretching, pouring out two small drinks then sliding the bottle back into its resting place. "Are the birds Ellis shoots innocent victims too?" the Chief asked for some reason.

"Maybe. I don't know." Bailey's response was half hearted. "Are the birds you and I eat innocent victims too?"

Chief Yung didn't comment but he would propose a bargain. "You're a smart gal, Miss News Reporter. I have a deal to offer you."

"Let's hear it," responding fast, glad to be leaving the murder subject. Patricia shifted in her seat with no idea of what the Tracy Chief of Police was about to offer.

"You can have the exclusive. I'll give you and a cameraman complete access to Ellis' arrest," Yung dealt part of his hand.

"I certainly accept Chief. Thanks." Bailey said with a big smile. "What must I give up?" she countered.

"Very simple," Alex stated. "My Captain. You have to stop," Yung paused, went silent, choosing to pass on using the sexual word. "Seeing. You must agree to stop seeing Captain Anderson." Emphasis on 'seeing!' "Right now. There's no room for his rank and your press credentials in my department. What say you Miss Bailey?" asking straight and direct. He printed directions and signed a press pass, showing his sincerity.

"Mmm. I like Billy," Patricia said in a whisper. She thought for a moment getting the Chief's attention. "Done." The reporter leaned forward to shake hands and grab her pass. Transaction complete.

"Good," Alex said, knowing she'd accept. "Here's the location in Mendota, directions and you have the pass. It'll take about an hour and a half from here," outlining the route south. "Get your crew, some boots and raingear. Looks like you're gonna be needing it." Alex stood. "Billy has the signed Arrest Warrant," checking his last email. "My crew will be leaving soon. Good luck to you Miss Bailey." Patricia left in a hurry, I-phone to ear planning her mission south and didn't even say thanks.

Gadwalls

With the hen flying point, both gadwalls moved along the western border of Los Banos SWR, aware of occasional loud noises erupting in the distance which kept them flying very high for security. Another shoot day. Favoring open water for food and safety but searching cover this morning to wait out the rain. Surging instincts pulled them south, knowing it was their time to move further along the flyway. Today, maybe. Tomorrow for certain, letting the bold southern air mass pass through.

Making a long wide turn easterly to commence their search. Wings feeling light and well fed as rain drops streamed from oiled feathers, inspecting small ponds and large open water. They drew fire from frustrated, sky busting hunters well concealed below in mist, rain and dark tules. Never close enough to cause real danger.

In the distance off to her right, the hen gadwall spotted open water, studded with clusters of tule islands. Appearing calm so far with no loud noises, plenty of coots, a few stiff ducks but no movements. She lead them higher still, preparing for a slow, controlled descent. Prepared to scrutinize every patch of tules with discerning eyes more than once. Along the south shore a group of green headed birds glided into view. Not as high but setting out to inspect the same water. Four birds turned in unison, bunched tight, flashing blue wing feathers and short tails. Legs raised for a quick retreat, wings taut and spilling air. So far, all clear.

Tom was high balling four mallards with minimal success. They appeared interested in his decoys but wouldn't commit. The small flock circled Ellis' pond four times sensing danger near his blind then flared upward on approach, for no apparent reason. They veered toward the field to his left, covered with large growths of tules and cattails flanked by small ponds. Very thick. Tom's calling was having a rough time keeping the mallards interested, watching in frustration as all four locked up and dropped without fear to a small narrow pool a few hundred yards away. He failed to notice two gadwalls following at a higher distance. Likewise, they failed to notice Tom, growing very interested in his calls. The hen grunted an all clear and began a steep descent rolling hard left and flying behind Ellis over the secluded water. Her drake close to one side. Lower and lower with wind cutting a loud hiss. Tom heard the air whistling, squatting ass deep to remain hidden, checking right, seeing nothing but grey clouds and waving tules. No birds but a louder swoosh. "They gotta be right over," whispering, rising to look behind. Sure enough the hen gadwall was directly overhead but going away fast. Tom saw the drake coming on quick and raised his shotgun to swing a hefty lead. "Drake gadwall," he grunted, touching a loaded trigger. Voicing "bang!" Out loud, postponing the blast, issuing silence instead. The startled drake saw the dark figure and launched a straight rise. His hen close to one side. Tom chose to pass on the close in bird. "I love drake gadwalls," he justified.

This lucky pair of gadwalls looked for the resting mallards among shallow water with heavy cover, landing safe along two calling hens. Tom watched in approval, this time with a tight frown. Each gadwall moved to seek shelter.

Final Hunt

Kelly Crisp had her Department truck fueled and idling just outside the check station door. No more hunters would be permitted to enter the refuge. Los Banos State Wildlife Refuge was in a state of lockdown. Accounting for the dozen or so pissed off shooters milling about in frustration next to her warming truck. Caution lights blazing.

"Look guys, I'm sorry but we have a criminal situation in progress right now. Nobody goes in. Nobody gets out." Kelly shouted to camo laden groups waiting out a sweat line since shooting time. "Hunting today is out of the question," Kelly assured them. "Sorry."

"This sucks," one dog tired hunter shouted.

"It does at that and my hands are tied." The refuge manager relayed to the group of disgruntled waterfowlers. Crisp noticed three SUV's rumble in from Henry Miller Road. All three parked in a hurry with Gonzalez leaving a spacious cab from the lead vehicle. She jogged over to Kelly offering a handshake and greeting.

"Kelly Crisp, we meet again," Gonzalez said, clad in waders and bright yellow rain jacket. "Sorry we couldn't be here earlier, but we spent the morning decoyed to Mendota Wildlife by our suspect. He got us this time." Holding a thin smile and appearing a little dumb.

"I got your call just before leaving for the day. Your suspect, Tom Ellis," checking a printout for location, "is hunting out of lot number four." Kelly informed the Tracy Police detective. "Just like that fateful day a few weeks past," as the manager lifted a hood over her head. Rain was on the increase again, followed by a series of wind gusts from the southwest, spraying moisture on her cheek and chin.

"Are you ready to get going?" asked Gonzalez

"You bet."

"I'd like to ride with you and have my crew follow in," Regina proposed.

Kelly nodded positive. "Fine by me. Let's get rolling before this damn weather gets any worse." Gonzalez and Crisp jogged to an idling department truck.

Regina yelled out, "follow us." Getting thumbs up from each police vehicle.

Miss Crisp made way, aiming her wheel hard left, arcing through the parking lot. She swerved around a small group of rejected hunters discussing dismal options, blowing by with a short wave and thin smile, gunning the engine and moving east bound onto Henry Miller Road.

After a quarter mile Regina had to ask an obtuse question. "Why are we going this way Kelly?"

Kelly seemed surprised by her question. "Parking lot four. The entrance is out this way," Crisp answered with polite but obvious logic in her tone. "Ellis is hunting out of lot four. We've confirmed his truck parked there."

"I thought you used the check station road to access all parking lots?" the confused detective asked.

"All except parking lot four. Hunters have to leave the check station on this road. The entrance gate is just ahead," pointing out two gate posts on the left side. "Didn't we go over this when you first investigated the refuge?" Crisp asked, then recalled missing the detective when she left the check station on her field trip. Kelly knew she blew it and felt to blame. Noticing Gonzalez nodding her head, confused, deep in thought.

"You probably did but I was in a big hurry that day. My bad," Regina answered. It hit her now. Realizing how Tom got away with it. She could only scoff, shaking her head, visualizing Ellis leaving the check station parking lot on Henry Miller Road. "Probably flew past lot four's entrance in total darkness," speaking to herself. My lover continued east then doubled back somewhere making his way north to Tracy, shooting Marcus and ditching the rifle. Nobody would suspect anything wrong. "As long as he returned to Los Banos refuge unnoticed, making check out time." A limit of ducks lay cover for his perfect alibi. "Nice job gringo. Well done." Gonzalez replayed it over to herself, rather obvious now. She marveled at it all, in a disturbed sort of way.

"I hope you're good to drive out here Buck?" Anderson asked, waking from an early morning nap.

"No problem Captain. A little mud never stops me," Buck answered moving fast, gunning the four wheel drive.

"Just stay with Fish and Wildlife," Davis chimed in from a roomy shotgun seat. "No need to get crazy now." Chris looked out over the open country of bending vegetation and cold rain which further unraveled his jumbled nerves. Detective Davis didn't function well away from firm pavement, buildings and plenty of traffic. Both cars and people. Muddy roads, marsh foliage, scattered ponds and wildlife seemed alien to him. It wasn't his element to say the least. Chris Davis was pure city boy. The wide open spaces, deniably of course, intimidated him. One very large red-tailed hawk glided very slow, ten yards ahead of the truck. Davis watched as the raptor's wide wings fluttered in strong crosswinds, sweeping back and forth, hunting prey. Chris wondered if wild birds like that ever attacked people but was too embarrassed to ask.

They reached lot four as a refuge patrol truck waited to join the convoy. Kelly instructed her patrol and one Tracy Police vehicle to loop around north, approaching ponds eighteen and nineteen from road 2-B. "I'll drive in on the main road, from the south." Crisp directed. Her idea was to stop any chance of Ellis biking out, fleeing on any of the major roads. Five trucks left lot four; two Fish and Wildlife pick-ups, two Tracy Police vehicles and one black SUV carrying Patricia Bailey, her cameraman and a press pass. Caution lights flashing.

■■■

Tom pulled on a dripping hood, shaking it in and out, spraying water drops left and right. It wasn't raining hard but fell steady since shooting time. No need for a heavy jacket on his ride out to the pond thankfully, as warm air filled the Valley behind the southern storm front. Ellis hoped for a break in the rain, allowing him to shed the heavy coat and a chance to dry out. Warm air plus his accumulated sweat was enough to feel as though he'd been standing unprotected in constant rain. He left his blind of tules to look around, dwelling on the law's arrival. Almost eight thirty with no sign of the expected assault.

"Maybe they still don't know?" Tom whispered, sitting low, spotting a lone cinnamon teal gliding just off center above his open pond. He whistled a few shrill beeps as the fiery brown bird made a quick roll, intending to inspect his bobbing spread. At one point dipping low to the pond's surface then rising fast, clipping beyond his outermost decoy. Ellis kept chirping, standing slow to keep sight of the small duck, betting an odd chance typical of teal, it might return fast and low. Tom stood erect, stretching to see over waving tules watching the cinnamon traverse his pond's edge. Turning and still low, turning harder, but like an infield fly the drake lifted almost vertical.

"That's sort of weird," Ellis mumbled, following the bird's path as it flared higher and away. Tom spotted three clear reasons for the unexpected flare. Yellow caution lights became visible through falling rain, bumping along the gravel road bordering his pond leading away from lot four. Tom's heart sank, without a doubt whom the trucks were seeking. Turning away, only to spot two more vehicles making a slow crawl over a muddy, secondary road bounding the pond's opposite levee, closer to his blind.

"Maybe they've found me?" Tom spoke his words with little anguish, even able to brandish a fateful smile. "I wonder if Regina will make an appearance?"

...

"That's his bike. No doubt," Regina shrieked, excited, short of breath. Kelly stopped the truck, using her radio to inform the other convoy of their discovery. "Mallard and sprig decoys separated to form a wide landing zone and one wind decoy, spinning like a room fan." She continued scanning two clusters of thick tules, looming off center from the pond's middle. Both patches lay roughly two hundred yards out with one bunch a little closer. "He's inside one of those tule stands but I'm not seeing anyone."

Gonzalez twisted Crisp's binoculars straining to focus close on each suspected blind. At one point imagining herself the hen widgeon, scanning for movements, desperate to spot any hidden figures, perceiving danger, in terror of loud noises erupting. "C'mon gringo, even you can't stay still forever," Regina whispered, continuing her scan as Chris, Buck, Captain Anderson and two uniforms approached from behind.

"You think he's still there partner? Maybe we flushed him out," Davis supposed, very aware of the constant rain, bulky chest waders, and uncomfortable clamminess.

"He's out there. I'd bet on it," Regina answered, oozing confidence as her boots squished into oozing, refuge mud. Unwilling to lower her binoculars, needing a glimpse of the man she had passionate sex with a few days earlier. The man she loved. "I suspect the left side tule patch. It's closer to open water. That's where he always," Regina stopped to stare closer. "Yep. Yes! There he is. I can see the top of his hat. He's looking back at us." Giggling, making out a dark green hat moving ever so slight, from side to side. "He's barely moving," Gonzalez said with a more somber voice feeling for Tom's situation. Imagining his fear.

"You're sure Gonzo? It's him?" Chris asked, slipping in sticky mud almost falling into murky pond water.

Gonzalez lowered the binoculars. "Tom Ellis!" She screamed his name as loud as possible. Three mud hens flushed fifty yards down the road, scooting over open water. All wings and green feet churning both spray and panic. "I know you're out there damn it," yelling even louder, pushing more coots away from her position. "Give yourself up Tom!" Raising the bino's to see his hat slowly disappear inside dense tules. "It's him. If it wasn't, that poor bastard would be coming out to see what all this shit was about." Lowering glasses, appearing grim. "It's him."

"Couldn't agree more, Detective Gonzalez," Buck said, staring over open water looking for movement too.

"So, what now?" Anderson asked, pulling his hood strings tighter. Water fell from the Captains nose, not at all in favor of confronting an armed criminal. Especially under these conditions. He was at a loss in unfamiliar surroundings, growing wet, feeling stupid.

"Captain Anderson," Davis already had the location lined out. "Let's get him surrounded. We have two trucks on the opposite road. Tell Kennedy what's going on," Chris instructed.

"That's the problem," Anderson whispered. "I don't know what's going on." Trying to force a smile and shaking his jacket of soaking rain.

"We should spread some of our uniforms and Wildlife agents to get our suspect surrounded." Davis recommended, pointing to possible locations on three roads while Crisp directed her agents into place by radio.

"Look people," Regina snapped orders to her group now. "He's not dangerous. I promise, Tom Ellis will not try shooting his way out. He would never hurt me," mumbling her last words so no one would hear. Regina believed in her assumptions, however Tom was surrounded with no sign of giving up.

"Chris," Regina shouted.

"Right here," her partner answered in a calm voice then swallowed hard.

"You and I are going out there to bring him in. Alive." Gonzalez demanded, checked her handgun like a good cop, zipping snug a heavy yellow jacket, ready to wade. Regina Gonzalez was in command now.

•••

Tom flashed back to one of his happier moments, years ago at The Sixth Street Diner in a small but cozy, downtown area of Los Banos. Sarah was in her junior year of high school. A lengthy survey contract kept Tom near Los Banos for a few months. Construction staking and topo surveys gave him the chance to keep an eye out for his daughter, soon learning a few of her hangouts. He discovered Sarah and a few friends would have ice cream floats at the Diner, almost every Wednesday after school, when the weather grew hot. Which it often did in Los Banos.

Sarah's father grabbed a booth one such hot Wednesday afternoon, ordered a late lunch and waited. Sure enough to Tom's enjoyment, Sarah and three friends bounded inside filling the vacant booth behind her unknown father. Taking pleasure in his daughter's laughs, boy talk, classes and college aspirations captured him. A memory he visited on a regular schedule. Every day. This would be the closest he ever got to Sarah, listening and hanging on each charming word. One of the best days of his entire life. Spending an afternoon with his daughter.

He had the waitress put their treats on his bill. All four girls giggled in delight once learning the day's ice cream would be free of charge. Sarah happened to pause and thank the stranger personally. He and his daughter, for one time only, made direct eye contact and exchanged a few marvelous words. She was fabulous!

Head down in pure delight, Tom's dream ended with loud voices from the levee road. Peering through thick tules, crouching, making out a group of figures across the pond. "Is that Gonzalez?" Ellis posed aloud.

...

"Chris. Come over here," Regina ordered her partner, wanting to laugh but didn't. "Your wader straps are tangled." Davis was busy trying to get his chest high boots to stop pulling down so hard. Gonzo approached like a mom about to fix her son's diaper. Unbuckling each snap, uncrossing two straps, untangling the harness. "You had both straps on one shoulder, looking like a South Carolina catfish farmer." Needing a joke to relieve building tension from the two of them. Regina couldn't avoid looking Chris in the eye, indicating a genuine concern. Davis understood her unease.

"You ready partner? I need you now more than ever," Gonzalez implored, barely able to get the last words out, her voice cracking with emotion like the sharp clicks emitted from wader buckles snapping through nervous fingers.

"I'm out of my element," a jumpy Davis said, surveying the watery surroundings. "Better keep an eye on me."

"I will. Guaranteed," Regina spoke with a solemn tone, raising both hands to her friend's shoulders. "Promise me you won't shoot Ellis. Nobody gets killed today. Promise me." Gonzalez spoke very soft but Chris read her serious tenor without question.

"You got it," Davis lowered his forehead to gently butt Regina's. "I'm still carrying my sidearm," Chris admitted. Regina nodded and displayed a nervous grin which relayed her silent confirmation. They both walked to Captain Anderson briefing him of their simple plan. Regina noticed a young patrolman removing his sniper rifle from a hard plastic case. The weapon shined of gun oil, in turn delivering an ominous shape of dark wood and cold metal.

"Hey, hey!" Regina shouted out to the marksman. "Let me tell you something. If I'm not gut shot and floating belly down on this pond or dead by drowning, you sure as fuck better not shoot my suspect!" Regina grew much louder and walked toward the rifleman. "If you do," stepping close to an opened mouth patrolman, poking his rigid chest, looking up the entire time, "I'll shoot your ass. Clear!" Gonzalez concluded with a small drop of spit on her chin.

"I think so," an intimidated marksman responded glancing at Captain Anderson for confirmation.

"Do not shoot until me or my partner gives the order." Regina ended her tirade with Billy Anderson relaying a silent okay to the flustered sniper. Gonzalez wouldn't stand for anyone dying today.

"Let's go Chris," Regina ordered.

"Watch it out there detective Gonzalez, he might be armed," Buck warned, absent minded and two hundred percent sober. Everyone within talking distance froze solid. Regina and Chris in knee deep water, turned around to face patrolman Buck who looked back with an air of true grit on his pale face.

"He's duck hunting, Buck. We know he's carrying a shotgun!" Regina exclaimed, sending Buck a brain dead leer and shaking her head. As did Chris, Alex, two uniforms and Kelly Crisp.

"Uh yeah, right. My bad," red faced Buck responded.

Giving Davis a big smile. "Let's get going partner." Two detectives continued wading into clear pond water stirring mud and vegetation, splashing, clouding each step toward Tom's blind. Chris wavered for a moment, close to falling again but caught his balance. Sticky mud. "I wish I had a wading staff," Regina whispered stepping closer to Chris.

...

Keeping low and motionless, Ellis knew very well he'd been located. On the levee his bike was being examined from every possible angle, trucks moved in, people pointed, shouted and what looked to be a video camera, was carried by one individual. Not quite understanding how the press was already present. "I might make the news tonight?" Tom muttered under his breath

"I won't make it easy for them," assuring himself, forcing his way further back into thick tules and cattails. Looking through dense growth across a small open area containing his wood seat, decoy bag, resting gun and two dead birds. A pair of widgeon, drake and hen, taken from separate flocks. Scattered on the water encircling his wood seat floated five spent cases. Yellow, bobbing up and down in tiny ripples. His day so far, totaled three clean misses and two hits, had come to an end.

"It's never that good in this God damn south wind," talking out loud in frustration, keeping low but stretching his neck to get another view. Back down after seeing two trucks flanking each side of his pond and shapes moving along two levees. All four sides covered. Rain wasn't getting lighter but a faint blue streak emerged to the southeast. Ellis could see police officers had him surrounded. Gazing at both widgeon, focusing the drake's emerald green eye patch above its short pointed bill. Tom realized how much he loved their stubby shapes in flight and shrill whistles. Three in cadence leading to an extended final note. How many times had small flocks of widgeon responded to loud whistles, circling, ready to commit.

"Tom Ellis," came Regina's booming voice, loud and clear, causing a vigorous stir in his mid section. He uncoiled, rising slightly for a clear look wishing he could just disappear. Melt away into muddy refuge water and thick vegetation. Gonzalez continued yelling, knowing he would face her now. Tom watched the commotion then went back to admiring the widgeon's superb marks.

•••

"Watch for a drop-off," Regina warned her struggling partner. Chris almost fell twice already, swearing loud each time. "You'll get your balance soon, keep at it," Regina urged him on, noticing the rainfall getting lighter but each gust of wind seemed stronger however. Keeping a slow, steady advance with no sign of Ellis hidden deep inside his clump of green cover. Closer and closer. Individual points of tule reeds became visible but even partial vision failed to penetrate inside the outer hedge. Knee deep, hiking through open water Chris became aware how vulnerable he and Regina had become. Davis drifted off to his left, right in line with Ellis' wind decoy. Wings rolling.

"What the fuck is that thing?" Chris mumbled, getting closer for a clear inspection, catching sight of faint black and white blinking. A fake sort of flicker emitted from spinning wings. He stopped wading to verify the subtle clank from worn bearings in the decoy's rig. Regina noticed Chris drawn to the flashing wings similar to decoying waterfowl.

"It works on people too," Gonzalez thought to herself. "Don't get too far away partner," she called out. "It's just a decoy." Letting herself focus on the beating wings. Nearing Tom's outermost decoys, two loud noises erupted from the tules. Spray exploded in front of Davis first, followed by a salvo across Regina's bow. Chris let loose a chilling scream as Gonzalez spun around. Screeching to the snipers on the levee road.

"It's okay. Don't shoot," Gonzalez shrieked, hands held high and waving overhead. "Don't shoot," she yelled, facing Crisp and Anderson. "Don't shoot!" Yelling once again, expecting to hear rifle shots returning fire at any moment. Chris went to one knee in shallow water and firm bottom, drawing his gun. Pintail decoys bobbed to his right while the spinning wing contraption clanked away, straight ahead. Gonzalez exhaled in relief as neither marksman opened fire, assuming her threat must've worked. She thought how stupid Ellis was to let loose two volleys of gunfire.

"You going to shoot me Gringo?" Regina yelled out, hands cupped to her mouth. "I don thin so," yelling even louder, mocking her own slight accent the way Tom often teased her. She breathed hard not sure what would happen next. Chris tried to keep low, hyperventilating, bent over his left knee. "You going to shoot me Tom?" She yelled out once more.

"If I have to, I will," came an unexposed response. Regina knew his voice loud and clear. She couldn't see him but knew it was Tom, her lover, her man, her suspect. Gonzalez glanced to her partner maintaining his stiff crouch, vulnerable and wide eyed alert. Trembling.

"Don't worry Chris, he won't shoot us," Regina declared in support, beginning her advance again in very short strides. Rain increased at the moment. Blown diagonally by a sudden burst of wind. Sheets of water sliced in wavy curtains across the pond, soaking two cops.

"No closer Regina. Stay put right next to that hen decoy," Tom shouted as he stepped clear of his tule blind into open water. 'Her' Citori rested on his right shoulder. "Don't come any closer. I'm coming out." Elly's voice sounded solemn but not yet defeated. Regina's heart went out to him. Sorry for his lousy situation.

Tom walked toward her very slow, watching Chris close as he stepped. His heavy boots didn't splash but moved through muddy water like a serpent. Wading staff in one hand shotgun in the other getting closer and closer until she saw his wonderful full face again. He smiled to her.

•••

From the levee two marksmen held crosshairs on Tom's chest as he approached Gonzalez. Billy had just finished reading another email. Chief Yung received verification on the .222 recovered from the Merced River. Registered to one Jonathon Ellis from a 1970 purchase in Medina, Ohio. Billy chuckled, watching his detectives returning to the job at hand. With a composed tone of voice, "hold your fire," Anderson ordered. "You heard the lady, nobody dies today." Needing to ease some building tension cloaking those covering from shore. "Jonathon Ellis. Must be his father," Captain Anderson said to himself.

"Is she a little crazy or what?" Miss Crisp asked Billy, displaying concern as she bit down on her upper lip, watching close through steady binoculars. Kelly couldn't help fixating on flashing wings too but never bought into the decoy's reputation as an effective draw.

"Gonzalez knows what she's doing," Anderson said propping his detective. "Keep your rifles fixed on him just in case. I'm never one hundred percent certain in circumstances like these." Billy heard commotion coming from behind and soon recognized Patricia Bailey's voice. She ordered the cameraman to begin recording, right now.

Occupying the foreground, Bailey concocted a rather lengthy prelude to the scene developing behind her. "Held at bay. A cop and a killer. Bravery. Reckless. Dangerous encounter." Were phrases Patricia weaved into her report. All alone, taking control and advantage of every morsel of drama. A professional in action, reestablishing her sinking career. Billy glanced back to check out his lady friend. She never noticed him.

•••

"Told ya I'd meet you at the refuge gringo," Regina quipped, holding back a powerful urge to charge and embrace him unyielding, covering his dejected mouth with her warm breath and benevolent lips. Tom stood next to a teal decoy closest to his blind. Regina stayed near a hen sprig marking the extreme edge of his decoy rig. Scattered dekes rocked and twisted in wind and waves, separating two lovers now, originally helping two lonesome hearts come together.

"You didn't mention bringing along the entire Tracy P.D. with you." Tom tried his best at forcing a casual smile. "Mr. Davis. Good morning to you sir," finishing his greeting with a distant hand wave.

"Good morning Tom. We finally meet. Too bad it's under these lousy conditions." Chris offered his best hello feeling safe to stand again. Regina's head turned to look at each man as tears began flooding her eyes. Davis felt the weight of his handgun pressing against his damp ribs. A reminder, Tom Ellis is a murderer.

"Just a little rain today, Mr. Davis. Not too cold. Welcome to my escape," Ellis joked, making light of his trapped position.

"Yeah, just light rain." Davis surveyed the pond, decoys, tules, his partner and their suspect standing about fifty feet in front of Regina, holding a loaded over and under. "What do we do now?" Chris' thoughts ran wild. Gunshots in the distance added to a budding strange scene, increasing his worried edge. All parties went quiet for too long, tightening jumpy nerves.

"Regina speaks very high of you detective," Tom complimented, breaking silence. Davis nodded his appreciation.

"So, you wanna follow us back to the levee Tom?" Regina asked in her tender manner, with great difficulty however, choking back tears to get the words out. A piercing lump in her throat took over. Rain swelled again, spilling from a soaked hood to her red cheeks.

"I don't think so Gina. Not this time," Tom answered. Gonzalez didn't like the way he replied, suspecting he had some sort of plan in mind. She rubbed at drops of water trickling and clinging to her dark hair, saturating small curls pressed to her forehead. The detective in her came up empty regarding what to do next. Regina started to worry deep inside.

"Good job on the Mendota set-up," Gonzalez said in desperation, hoping continued dialogue might soften his hard-ass attitude. "I thought for sure we'd be chasing you around the Valley today or tomorrow."

"No, not my style. I just wanted to get a few hours out here alone. Waiting for you to show of course," Tom rejoined as a flock of pintails passed over very high, chirping, causing him and the detective to look upward. The flock bunched together tight, seeking security after spotting caution lights flashing bright. Once Regina lowered her eyes, she grasped why Tom was out here. His gaze lingered on graceful sprig until the group disappeared into mist and murky air. It would be a long time before Tom would enjoy his cherished hunts again. For a brief moment she even sympathized with his decision. Holding back deep secrets, hiding out, revenge for his daughter's murder, allowing her to fall in love with him, letting himself become trapped. She was sorry Tom Ellis was trapped.

"You understand," Tom said in a grateful way.

"I wish I could understood it all Tom." Her emotions scattering, boiling to the surface along with her nausea. "You really had me decoyed on this one. Is that all it was?" asking Tom as tears blended with rain drops blown in her face. Chris stayed silent, listening close, hearing Regina's pain. He thought about Sarah. Franny. Marcus. His stupid decision. His cold wet feet.

Tom returned to his love with heavy eyes and a bit insulted. "At first, yes. It seemed like a good idea being close to the investigation. Everything changed after our Thanksgiving dinner. You've had me hooked since then." Tom lowered his Citori breaking the receiver, slinging it over a sore shoulder. Regina knew he carried the gun this way only when it was time for serious talk. Chris spotted two brass shell bases raised in the chambers. "I love you Gina. I gave up on ever finding bona fide love long ago. But I sure as hell found it with you." Shifting the over and under to his other shoulder. Coots scattered from open water far off to their left, spooked by Fish and Wildlife agents moving along the levee road. "Sorry for fucking all this up for you. For us. I just hoped to hide what I did to," Regina waved her right hand, interrupting Tom's plea.

"How could you pull the trigger?" Regina's voice raised with emotion, causing Davis to take a step in her direction. "Maybe Marcus Crosby was a flaming asshole. He did beat your daughter after all. There's little pity for him but you just don't shoot someone down like that." Gonzalez cried harder now and in an odd way needed to be close to her affection, more than ever. "Tom, you killed an innocent man. Douglas Sheets is responsible for Sarah's death. You can't play God."

"Regina, you and I played God out here a few times. Shooting ducks together, never thinking much about killing," Tom spoke his words without conviction. Believing it wasn't the same. Realizing now how bad his mistake would be in a court of law. He couldn't bear the outcome.

"You and I both know it's not the same," Gonzalez reacted.

"Sarah was my daughter. Fathers protect their daughters. With more passion sometimes." Tom's own words rang hollow to himself as he repositioned his shotgun yet again. "I knew it was stupid as soon as I pulled that trigger. Regret the whole fucking thing." Turning away, scanning the levee, marsh, decoys, swaying tules and back to Regina. "I love you too much."

"Then you seduced me," Gonzalez said with a frail voice. Chris could see his partner beginning to crumble. "I love you gringo," her serious gaze and sobs confirmed Regina's honesty. Ellis began breathing harder. A physical reaction to his lover's marvelous words, her fragile appearance and realizing his own fate.

Her partner watched the exchange as it progressed from bad to tragic, in his opinion. Davis decided to act. "Tom, let's go back now. We'll collect your gear. You're under arrest. Come with us. Right now," Chris bluffed, aware he had no control whatsoever outside of pulling his own weapon. He knew a bloodbath would probably ensue.

"Regina, I hope you find some way to forgive me." Tom forced the words as his voice cracked. "Chris, I'm going back to my blind," Tom said, lowering the Citori cocking it closed to make a statement. Ellis gave Regina one last absolute look. Eyes fixed, then turning in the squishy mud and splashing by rocking decoys.

"Tom, you can't run. We have you surrounded," Regina yelled, wiping eyes and cheeks with palms of both hands.

Tom stopped, facing Chris this time. "Mr. Davis, you keep her away from the blind please." Ellis stated firm. Chris didn't understand at present, watching their suspect stride away, wobbling in soft mud. Neither detective moved. Observing, too dumfounded to take action.

"Was he getting something from the blind?" Davis asked himself in silence.

Strong gusts pelted rain against low hanging hoods and waders. A small brown chop developed on water unshielded by tall tules. The wind duck spun in a blur. Reaching the outer edge of tules Tom turned one last time, issuing a muffled yell downwind. "Tell Franny, I'll say hello to Sarah for her." Elly vanished into thick vegetation. Chris understood his request now.

"Tom Ellis," Detective Davis issued a feeble plea. "Come back with us, please." Striding next to Regina, getting close.

"What?" Regina asked with a comic look on her face. Squinting hard. "What did he say?" asking louder, leaning into Davis grabbing his tight wader straps. Chris was knocked off balance, shifting hard to one side and tripping over a stuck left foot. Regina never released her grip. "He said something about hello to Sarah?" Regina squealed. "Chris. What does that mean?"

Davis looked toward the blind. No sign of Tom. "Jesus God," Gonzalez screeched, realizing what was about to happen next. Rocked with adrenaline she flailed and screamed. "We have to stop him," Gonzalez bawled as Chris stepped in to embrace and capture his partner.

"It's too late partner," Davis told her, his pity for her running wild. Chris expected a gunshot at any second.

Regina exploded into rampant screaming and flailing arms. She broke free of Davis, moving toward the green tule patch. Toward Ellis.

"Regina. Stay here. You can't," Chris reached out, fighting his way through swinging limbs, elbows and fists. Underneath a building surge, Regina pushed hard with all she had. Chris' grip slipped away stumbling with both feet tangled in a hen mallard decoy line. The soft plastic cord stretched but wouldn't part. Bad for Davis as he sprawled into muddy water. His right hand inserted into soft refuge mud. The hen decoy slipped up next to Davis' face as an orange bill barely poked his ear with its bobbing motion, scarring him to lunge from the plastic intruder by crawling through pond water on all fours. The hen stayed with him due to tangled lines, staring with a slight upturned smile on the decoy's bill, eye to eye. Portraying this watery nightmare even more surreal.

Regina fell over too. Sticky mud and weighted momentum drew her far to one side, splashing into shallow water. Her filling waders went unnoticed as she reached a stage of absolute fear and panic. Images of Tom's intention drove her into whimpering grunts, violent breathing and blurred vision. Just managing to stand but leaning to one side, Gonzalez began a wet run toward the tules. She only covered half the open water space before falling again.

■■■

From Captain Anderson's viewpoint not much made sense concerning his homicide staff. Too far away for a good look, he couldn't possibly comprehend the circumstances. "Chris and Gonzo should've been issued radios. Fuck, damnit!" Knowing he blew it on this one.

"What's going on out there?" Crisp asked the Captain, concentrating hard, getting a better view with her binoculars than Anderson could hope for.

"I wish I knew," Billy responded in a tone of evenness but grave distress.

Down the levee, Patricia Bailey reported the same item. Pointing toward the tule patch and two stumbling detectives. Her narrative grew louder, almost shouting, losing touch with professional quality while the drama played.

Anderson chose to vacate dry ground, being the last cop wearing chest waders and waded into pond water to help his staff. "No shooting, you got that," Anderson pointed to the sniper looking through a large black scope, promptly finding a large hole and splashing a slow fall into cold water.

"Yes sir," came the reply without looking away.

"I'll see to it," Miss Crisp yelled out, pressing binoculars tight to her face, keeping the scene close.

Anderson didn't know what to make of her words, returning upright with difficulty, dripping mud and pond, second guessing his support plan.

■■■

Way off, from the edge of the adjoining field four mallards jumped. Getting altitude very fast. Gunshots pounded in the distance keeping the flock alarmed. Both gadwalls had joined the group, hen right drake left, filling the rear of a compact 'V' formation. They pushed hard across prevailing winds in direction of the blinking lights, almost appearing as beacons in heavy rain and limited visibility. The flock began a slow descent above open water. Four mallards turned left rising to safe height. But each gadwall stayed on course beginning a slow, cautious descent toward Ellis and his pond. The hen was drawn to blinking lights and her mate as usual, followed.

■■■

Inside a spider web of thick tules, Tom stepped past his wood seat eyeballing various hunting gear. Decoy bag, a strap of widgeon, shell holder, calls, wading staff. The odd simple items of his life which provided his real pleasures. Nothing fancy, some homemade, inexpensive and reliable. Similar in value to his past few weeks getting close to Regina, granting a taste of genuine love and pleasure. Reliable. "My revenge," he said out loud. "So fucking dumb." Faint chuckles drew his attention upward. Passing over was a high flock of mallards as two smaller ducks broke from the rear formation, circling with a slow but safe glide. No whistles, chirps or grunted quacks. Just nervous wings emitting a faint swoosh.

"Gadwalls I bet. Love drake gadwalls." Tom followed the pair's glide, nearly overhead now. His gun's muzzle came up under his chin, feeling two cold barrels poking wet skin just above his throat. He swallowed, raindrops forcing eyes shut, smiled. A thumb acted separate from his brain and pulled the trigger. Only a faint burning sensation in his mouth was detected, before blackness.

■■■

Gonzalez stumbled ghastly through thick mud and knee deep water trying her best to scream out. She had to make him stop, hold him tight, forgive him, say I love you gringo, slap his cheek. Words wouldn't surface between heavy breathing, choking, tears and panic. Chris closed in fast from behind.

"I can stop her," Davis thought. Rain poured again as storm clouds billowed higher and temperatures rose. A large wind gust was followed by abrupt stillness. Both detectives were rocked by the gun blast. No doubt what just occurred. Chris stopped fast and looked to his partner, watching her body flail in one limping stride. She covered her face in both hands.

Regina screamed. "Tom!" Fell to her knees face down, head shaking, yelling in a low pitched growl, "No!" Gonzalez stayed frozen in place weeping deep, wailing Tom's name while submerged to her waist in muddy water, soaked in rain. "I'm going to have your baby," whimpering her final words in agony. She drooped even lower into Los Banos mud and refuge water. Silence followed. Regina was spent. The only audible sounds above gusty winds, 'Click, Click, Click,' from spinning wings on Elly's wind decoy. Even the warm rain went quiet.

Chris moved with a slow gait to Regina's side. Standing close, being sure to touch her shoulders with his hips. Afraid to speak but fortunate to be at her side again when she needed him. Gonzalez shook her head violently. Water sprayed from her drenched hair plus splashing hands into cold water to clear mud and stood up. She leaned into Davis, cradled to his chest. Reaching up to caress his face and offering silent thanks.

"I want his shotgun," she told her partner, taking two short steps toward the blind. "And the wading staff."

"I'll get 'em Gonzo. Stay here." Chris directed, then grabbed her jacket and pulled. Forcing a stop. "I'll get the fucking gun for you." Davis waded and pushed his way into thick, bloody vegetation, bloody water and mangled corpse. He spotted the Citori angled muzzle down a few feet from Tom's body. Lifted the weapon and shook his head. "Good God," muttering in disgust. Regina took one more step seeing the wading staff floating a few feet to her left. Two more steps with a long reach revealed a clear view of bloody water and Tom's right hand, quivering with intermittent spasms. Nerve signals firing, impulses to keep moving, final movements. Regina thought of the ducks they killed, belly up with feet twitching. Trying, even in death.

■■■

Above open water the gadwalls heard a muffled, loud noise. They banked hard into a stiff wind, rising easy to safety. The hen began a long, slow circle, peering down on flashing lights, dark figures moving, dark figures standing in open water. Open water the gadwalls avoided today. With a sharp quack the hen changed course for safe water and heavy cover, finding a quiet bay. They spent the day close. Sleeping in touch on a small, tree covered island. Secure. Tomorrow, after the storm front passed they would migrate south, leaving the San Joaquin Valley.

Readers Guide

Part I

1. What kind of bird is a Gadwall? How are the Gadwalls used by the author?

2. Why do Refuge Personnel check hunter's killed bird numbers and species?

3. The Central Valley town of Tracy lies at the extreme south end of what waterway formation?

4. Who partially witnessed the early morning murder and what was identified?

5. What was Chris Davis' best asset when questioning a suspect?

6. Who raised Regina Gonzalez as a child?

7. Who found the murder weapon and how was it located?

8. Did Beatrice withhold crime evidence from the Tracy police? What is it if any?

9. What happened to Sarah Crosby? What did Beatrice believe happened to Sarah and why?

10. Where was Tom Ellis on the morning of the Crosby murder?

11. What was reporter Patricia Bailey's plan to get inside crime evidence? Why does she approach Billy Anderson? How does Captain Anderson handle his detectives?

12. Why does the author write about the 'Gang of Four'? Who makes up the group?

13. How do Abbey Crosby and Chief Yung know each other and why does it impact the investigation? How did Abbey impact Marcus' trial and who are the Braden's?

14. What makes Regina fixate on Tom Ellis and why is he a suspect?

15. Why does the author give details of Central Valley agriculture, geography and drought?

16. Where does Regina interview Tom and what significance does it have on her past? What is Tom's occupation? What are Regina's feelings during her first drive south?

17. What connection do Chris Davis and Franny Braden reach? What evidence do the Braden's give up? How does Sarah meet Marcus?

18. Why does Regina visit the Los Banos Wildlife Refuge? How does Buck help her? What does she learn on her follow up visit?

19. What makes Douglas Sheets and his wife important to the Crosby murder case?

Part II

20. Does Patricia Bailey achieve her goals after meeting with Anderson? Who else is she forced to deal with?

21. Why does Regina meet Tom in Gustine? What plans were made at the meeting?

22. Estefan needs the Jackal. Why?

23. How do Chris and Regina conduct their meeting with Douglas Sheets? What do they learn? What does Sheets learn?

24. What excuse does Franny offer Chris in their private meeting? What is Plan A? What is Plan B?

25. What was Thanksgiving like for Regina? Why is food important to the Gang of Four?

26. Mrs. Patterson and Regina establish a personal relationship and what is learned? Who shows up at one of their meetings? What impact do children have on Regina?

27. How does Sheets plan to deal with Beatrice?

28. What significance do the hunting trips realize? Why? How does Regina react?

29. How do Estefan and Clay Blevins engage one another? What impact does it have on the Crosby murder case?

30. Where do Chris Davis and Loretta first meet? Why? What is learned?

31. What information do the Gang of Four lunches uncover about the investigation?

32. How does Chris get info on Douglas Sheets? What is learned? How does the homicide unit react? What does Loretta present in the way of case information?

33. The Crosby murder case becomes extremely muddled. How many suspects are involved?

34. What does Beatrice offer to give Franny? What is Regina's connection to Clay Blevins? What occurs on Franny Braden's third meeting with Chris Davis? What's wrong with all these characters?

35. What finally develops between Loretta and Douglas in their home? Who prevails and how?

36. Who moves into Chris' home? Who moves in with Beatrice?

37. What affect does winter cold have on the Gadwalls and Pacific Flyway waterfowl?

38. Who trails Regina Gonzalez on her trip to Gustine? Who helps her?

39. What plot does Captain Anderson assume? Who does he prepare to guard and why? Where is Regina and why? What happens on the watch?

40. What is revealed of Pam at the final Gang of Four luncheon? Is it case related and why?

41. What is given to Estefan and from whom?

42. How does Chief Yung handle his homicide detectives as the case develops? What secrets does he reveal?

43. Who is the first to confess? What convenes at the who's household? Is the truth ever revealed? Where does the final curtain call take place?

44. What fundamental moral commands the ending?

www.ingramcontent.com/pod-product-compliance
Lightning Source LLC
Chambersburg PA
CBHW022016050726
47499CB00004BA/996